THE
COURSE OF
EMPIRE

THE
COURSE OF
EMPIRE

ERIC FLINT AND
K.D. WENTWORTH

For Algis Budrys,
friend, mentor, and terrific writer;
and for Christopher Anvil, who once
told this story his own way.

THE COURSE OF EMPIRE

A Baen Books Original

Baen Publishing Enterprises
P.O. Box 1403
Riverdale, NY 10471
www.baen.com

ISBN: 0-7434-7154-7

Cover art by Bob Eggleton

First printing, September 2003

Library of Congress Cataloging-in-Publication Data

Flint, Eric.
  Course of empire / Eric Flint & K.D. Wentworth.
      p. cm.
  ISBN 0-7434-7154-7 (hardcover)
  1. Human-alien encounters—Fiction. I. Wentworth, K. D. II. Title.

  PS3556.L548C68 2003
  813'.54—dc22

                                                      2003014258

Distributed by Simon & Schuster
1230 Avenue of the Americas
New York, NY 10020

Production by Windhaven Press, Auburn, NH
Printed in the United States of America

CAST OF CHARACTERS

Human characters

Rafe (Raphael) Aguilera: Former tank commander, employed at the refit facility in Pascagoula.

Willard Belk: Human tech at the refit facility.

Jonathan Kinsey: Professor of history, specialist on the Jao.

Ed Kralik: Jinau commander.

Ben Stockwell: President of the Jao's native government of North America; Caitlin's father.

Caitlin Alana Stockwell: Daughter of Ben, student at the University of New Chicago; Jao hostage.

Gabe Tully: Resistance agent; forcibly drafted into Aille's service.

Rob Wiley: Former U.S. Army lt. colonel, now military commander of the Resistance in the Rocky Mountains.

Jao characters

Aille krinnu ava Pluthrak: Subcommandant newly arrived on Terra; commander of all ground forces.

Ammet krinnu ava Binnat: Female veteran of the conquest.

Banle krinnu nao Narvo: Bodyguard/jailer assigned to Caitlin Stockwell

Chul krinnu ava Monat: A terniary-adjunct working in the refit facility in Pascagoula.

Dau krinnu ava Pluthrak: Pluthrak elder

Drinn krinnu Sant vau Narvo: A member of Oppuk's service.

Hami krinnu Nullu vau Dree: Pleniary-superior stationed in England.

Jita krinnu ava Hariv: Commander of the Jao forces in the initial phase of the Terran Conquest, replaced by Oppuk.

Jutre krinnu Kio vau Dano: Fraghta to Kaul.

Kaul krinnu ava Dano: Commandant of all Jao military forces in the Terran solar system.

Llo krinnu Gava vau Narvo: Pilot.

Meku krinnu ava Pluthrak: Current Pluthrak kochanau.

Mrat krinnu nao Krumat: Officer stationed at Pascagoula.

Nath krinnu Tashnat vau Nimmat: Supervisor at the Pascagoula refit facility.

Nikau krinnu ava Narvo: Narvo elder; one of Oppuk's pool-mothers.

Oppuk krinnu ava Narvo: Jao Governor of Terra

Pinb krinnu ava Hariv: Elderly Jao Subcommandant whom Aille replaces, no longer on Earth.

Ronz: Preceptor of the Bond of Ebezon Harriers; a member of the Strategy Circle.

Shia krinnu ava Narvo: Oppuk's former fraghta.

Tamt krinnu Kannu vau Hij: Aille's female bodyguard, part of his personal service; later Caitlin Stockwell's bodyguard.

Tura: Pleniary-superior of the Bond of Ebezon Harriers.

Ullwa krinnu Sao vau Binnat: member of Oppuk's service

Vamre krinnu Vallt vau Kannu: Production director at Pascagoula refit facility.

Wrot krinnu Hemm vau Wathnak: Retired veteran of the conquest, now residing on Earth

Yaut krinnu Jithra vau Pluthrak: Aille's fraghta.

A note on Jao naming conventions:

The Jao do not use surnames in the human manner. The designation *krinnu* indicates the kochan, or clan, to which the individual is affiliated. It can be translated by the English term "of the."

If the individual is directly a member of one of the great root clans, *krinnu* will be followed by either *ava* or *nao,* indicating whether the individual was born in one of the primary or secondary marriage-groups of the clan.

If the individual is directly a member of one of the lesser kochan, his or her kochan will be indicated by the *krinnu* designation, followed by the term *vau,* which then indicates the root clan to which his or her kochan is affiliated.

Thus, *Yaut krinnu Jithra vau Pluthrak* can be translated as: "Yaut, of the Jithra kochan, affiliated to the Pluthrak."

PROLOGUE

"The Pluthrak scion has left Marit An, Preceptor. He should be arriving on Terra soon."

The Bond of Ebezon's strategist did not look away from the holo tank which, at the moment, was depicting the latest known activities of the Ekhat in Markau sector. "Send a courier to Terra then, Tura. Inform our agents that it is beginning."

"Finally," she said.

He turned and studied her. The young pleniary-superior's posture was excellent, the gestures and stance subtle and subdued in the manner that the Bond preferred in its private discourse. In public, of course, Harriers were expected to maintain a completely neutral posture at all times. Tura had risen quickly in the ranks of the Bond. The Preceptor had great hopes for her; indeed, had selected her for this assignment with the specific aim of furthering her training. Not the least of the responsibilities of the Strategy Circle was training its own replacements for the time when its existing members grew too old to serve.

"Do I detect a trace of amusement in the lay of your ears?" He waggled his own whiskers with understated humor.

"Not amusement, exactly. Call it . . . exasperated *rueful-patience*."

The Preceptor tried to summon up an image of that combination. It could be done, by a master movement stylist, but it would be an exceedingly difficult tripartite posture. The Preceptor's old bones almost ached at the thought.

"Finally, indeed," he murmured. "Twenty years, it has taken us."

The pleniary-superior seemed a bit confused, and the Preceptor realized he had lapsed into a humanism again. He did that often,

1

of late. Not surprising, of course, as long as he had studied the species.

"A 'year,' Tura, refers to a Terran orbital cycle."

"Ah." She did the calculation in her mind. It was not easy. Translating the particulate human notions of time into Jao concepts was always difficult. "A very long time."

The pleniary-superior's eyes moved to the holo tank. It was still showing the reported Ekhat movements, but, not long since, she had seen the image of a young Pluthrak there. The same scion who was even now on his way to Terra. The Preceptor had spent much time, studying that face.

"Do you think he can do it?" she asked.

The Preceptor shifted into a very subtle version of the tripartite posture *best-attempt* coupled with *uncertainty*. It was very elegantly done, as always.

"There is no way to know. We can only create the situation, which we have done. There is always the chance he will shrink from the task—and, if he doesn't, the impossibility of knowing in advance what, exactly, he will create as well as destroy. Such is the nature of strategy, Tura. The element of unpredictability is inherent to its working."

"Yes, Preceptor," she said respectfully, and left.

Just before entering the doorfield, Tura paused for a moment and looked back at the Preceptor. He was turned away from her now, back to studying the holo tank.

There was fondness in her eyes, as well as deep respect. The old Preceptor was a splendid commander, and in all respects. The greatest of the Bond's strategists, even if, officially, only one of five members of the Strategy Circle. But, also, someone who invariably treated his subordinates with courtesy and dignity.

Tura had no doubt at all he would order her death in a moment, if he thought it necessary. The Preceptor was perhaps the most ruthless Jao in existence. But that knowledge only brought further admiration. If he found it necessary to do so, she was quite sure he would be right.

As she passed through the doorfield, she sternly corrected herself, remembering one of the Preceptor's maxims.

He would *probably* be right. Strategy did not deal in absolutes.

PART I:
Firsts

CHAPTER
1

Aille krinnu ava Pluthrak found Terra a world of unharmonious contrasts. His ears, set low and back on his skull, swiveled to take in the nearby murmur of the sea, along with the unnerving screeches of an avian lifeform native to his new posting.

Windward, water of a startling blue lapped at a pale expanse of sand, while, heartward, unbridled green plant growth vied with the graceless piles of stone and glass that guarded the periphery of the great Jao military base. In front of one building, several rectangles of red and gold fabric had been secured to the top of a pole. Even from here, he could hear the cloth snapping in the breeze. Bizarre, but he supposed they must serve some purpose.

The compact, elegant ship behind him radiated heat from its descent through the atmosphere, its engines ticking as they cooled. His favorite kochan-mother, Trit, had thought the vessel too showy for one as newly emerged as Aille. But Meku, the current kochanau, had said Pluthrak must maintain its status for all to see. The more so since the Governor of Terra was Oppuk krinnu ava Narvo—a scion of Narvo kochan, with whom Pluthrak kochan's relations were very strained.

Exhilarated at finally having the opportunity to be of use, Aille attenuated his perception of the moment's flow in order to better take in his new surroundings. The wind-tossed waves slowed to languid, enticing swells and reminded him that he'd had no opportunity to swim since leaving Marit An. His ship was equipped with adequate sanitary facilities, but not the luxury of an actual pool. After the long trip, his skin felt desiccated, his nap stiff, and his whiskers reduced to lifeless strings. He longed to immerse himself in this new sea, despite its alien scent, and sluice the accumulated dregs of travel away.

First, however, he must officially accept his new command. Later, when the flow of arrival was complete, he would indulge himself.

The yellow sun of this solar system beat down, brighter than Nir, his homeworld's star, which was farther along in the main sequence. He gazed out past the base's buildings, whiskers quivering. The land before him was so unrelentingly—flat.

He thought wistfully of the cliffs back at his kochan-house. There, the tide pounded against massive black rocks both early and late, and the breeze was always filled with the refreshing cool tang of spray. Here, the sultry air was thick with indigenous salts and more than a hint of decay. Well, his time on Marit An had completed itself. It was the duty of all Jao scions to cast themselves into time's river in the ongoing struggle against the Ekhat, and that he would do.

The voyage from his birthworld, Marit An, to Terra had been long but fruitful, filled with discourse with his fraghta and study for the responsibilities which awaited him. It was his last opportunity to take advantage of the older Jao's accumulated wisdom before assuming his new post as Subcommandant and he did his best to absorb as much as possible. By the end, he believed he knew the indigenous species as well as anyone could without ever having come nose to nose with one.

Farther away, in the distance, Aille could see several ruined buildings. Those were apparently a legacy of the Jao conquest over twenty orbital cycles ago. He had detected more signs of unamended damage as he'd swept in for landing: fractured, overgrown roads, cast-off machinery, abandoned dwellings now inundated by wilderness. By all reports, this political moiety had resisted long after the rest of this stubborn world and therefore had suffered proportionally greater damage.

They were an odd breed, these "humans," frustrating in their reluctance to be civilized and unique in many respects from any other species ever conquered by the Jao. Recorded reports detailed their long resistance to Jao rule and it seemed they were not completely subdued even now, so many orbital cycles later.

Pockets of discontent and unrest apparently still persisted across the globe.

It would take a few solar cycles for his timesense to synchronize with local circadian rhythms, but for now Aille allowed normal flow to reassert itself. Then he drew in a deep breath as his stolid fraghta, Yaut krinnu Jithra vau Pluthrak, emerged from the ship. The older Jao's *vai camiti*, or facial pattern, was plain yet pleasing, strong and highly visible, unmistakably Jithra to anyone experienced at reading faces. Yaut hesitated halfway down the ramp and his nostrils flared at the unfamiliar scents.

The Jao, ever practical, used filters to sanitize their atmosphere wherever they constructed their kochan-houses so that unpleasant scents did not intrude. But, according to reports, Terrans rarely concerned themselves with such matters, although they were generally more sensitive than Jao to environmental conditions.

According to his briefings, this particular base was one of the first built after the Jao's initial invasion of this world, and still the largest. Constructed on the site of an already extant shipyard, it had been intended to impress on the local political entity just how pointless resistance was by then. Nevertheless, almost another orbital cycle had been required to effect full control. Several major population centers, including the ones known as "Chicago" and "New Orleans," had been destroyed in the process, allegedly still sore points with the quarrelsome natives after all this time.

Aille locked his hands behind his back, cocked his head at the precise long-practiced angle of *measured-anticipation*, and waited as a detail of jinau soldiers in crisp dark-blue uniforms emerged from between buildings. They marched across the hard surface, their legs matched in stride, providing his first look at the conquered species outside vids and stills.

They were shorter than most Jao, slender of build where Jao tended to be square and solid. The outlines of bones were clearly visible through their mostly naked skin, wherever they neglected to cover themselves with fabric. Their features were not quite balanced, the eyes too far apart, the faces too flat, giving them a comic exaggerated look. The ears were the most disturbingly alien, little more than stationary rounded flaps on the sides of their heads which never suggested the slightest hint of what they were thinking.

Of course, the most surprising thing he'd learned about this species was that they were timeblind, having to rely on mechanical devices to know when something would happen, or when it was time to act.

He gauged their approach with a critical eye. Their upper garments bore the red jinau slash, signifying Terran troops trained and overseen by the Jao. A single figure in the place of honor at the rear wore a traditional weapons harness and trousers, marking himself as Jao, but even if he had been dressed otherwise, Aille would have known by his height and breadth of shoulder that he must be one of his own kind.

He descended the ramp, Yaut following hastily at his heels. "This is a first meeting," the fraghta said in a low voice. "Firsts are always crucial. You must begin as you mean to go on."

Yaut was ugly, his facial pattern marred with scars earned over a lifetime of combat on assorted worlds, and proud of his hard-won skepticism. A head shorter than Aille, he had to lengthen his stride to keep up. "Let me precede you, as is proper, or they will think you have no status!"

"Humans do not reason like that," Aille said without slowing. "According to the records, they do not deem it honorable to be always last. The psych studies indicate they are actually intrigued by novelty. They like to be first."

"Only because they are reckless." Yaut's whiskers twitched in disapproval. "Since they breed like vermin, they can afford to expose themselves. If one falls, twenty more will take its place."

Aille let the remark pass, as none of the natives were close. By all reports Terrans were very sensitive about the matter of "face," as several Jao studies termed it. Had they overheard Yaut's caustic comment, it would have been a most inauspicious beginning.

From what Aille had seen so far, the older Jao, assigned by Aille's kochan upon the recent completion of his qualifying studies, was consistently and unrelentingly skeptical of Terra's worth. There was a definite possibility the current Pluthrak kochanau had even selected Yaut for that very trait, hoping to inculcate prudence in a scion more than one of his kochan-parents considered to be somewhat rash and impulsive.

But whatever else might be said of this rogue world, its inhabitants had held off the Jao for an astonishingly long time. The conquest of Terra had proven far more difficult than any other the Jao had undertaken, except when they directly confronted the Ekhat themselves. Some of that was simply due to Terra's enormous population. With their profligate breeding habits, humans on this one planet alone probably had almost a fourth of the entire population of the Jao, who were scattered across hundreds of star systems. Terra's human population, even after the massive casualties they suffered during the conquest, simply dwarfed that of any other species ever conquered by the Jao.

But that was not the only explanation, nor even the principal one. Human technology was also far above anything ever encountered among the many other races the Jao had conquered. Reading what was hinted at but not stated directly in the reports, Aille suspected, in many respects, human technology was more advanced than that of the Jao. The conquered species seemed to possess an intrinsic cleverness which, if properly harnessed, might be wielded effectively against the Ekhat.

And that would bring status to all.

The leader halted at the foot of the ramp and waited for Aille's acknowledgment. The pale-gold nap of his cheek bore a single incised bar and he had the characteristically skimpy *vai camiti* banding of Krumat, a provincial kochan much inferior in status to his own Pluthrak.

The Terrans lined themselves up behind him like bombs in a crate. Patterns, Aille thought, with a dismissive twitch of his nose. This species was said to be obsessed with sharp corners and meticulous spacing, seeking to impose artificial order everywhere possible.

He met the Krumat's flickering green-black eyes. "Subcommandant Aille krinnu ava Pluthrak," he said, speaking first, as was his right, and giving his own identifying designations. He extended his hand, showing the bau given him by his kochan at his departure. The bau was a short, somewhat stubby rod. Most kochan made their bau from various woods, but Pluthrak used the shell of one of Marit An's sea-beasts. The material, with its glossy near-white color, was almost as much a symbol of Pluthrak as the traditional carvings on it.

There were not many carvings, and those simply generic to the kochan, indicating that the scion who carried the bau was young and inexperienced. But it mattered little. It was a Pluthrak bau, and it showed that the great kochan had bestowed its blessing on the scion who carried it: *here is one fit to command.*

The officer inhaled sharply as though someone had struck him, though at the last he managed to turn the sound into a muffled cough. Aille was more or less accustomed to such reactions. Pluthrak status had that effect on many.

"Vaish," the officer said. The traditional greeting of inferior to superior signified recognition of background and ties, far more than their disparity in military rank. His voice sounded somewhat strained. "I was told to expect a new Subcommandant, to command the jinau troops, but not that so illustrious a scion had been appointed."

"Your designation?" Aille asked, his tone casual.

The other flinched, most likely not prepared to be recognized at this point on such an intimate level. It was an honor to be known by one's superiors and not always accorded. "Pleniary-Adjunct Mrat krinnu nao Krumat, at your disposal." His posture indicated *respectful-attention* as they took one another's measure, but just for an instant the Jao's eyes shimmered a bright glimmering green, a sign of unease.

Aille was not surprised at the unease; indeed, he'd been expecting it. Terra had been Narvo territory since the conquest, and normally the great kochan moved delicately around each other. For Pluthrak to send one of its scions to Terra in order to assume a major post was a subtle statement that it no longer considered Narvo's influence on the planet untouchable. Needless to say, the prospect of being caught in the middle between the two greatest of Jao kochan was going to make those who belonged to small and poorly affiliated ones more than a bit nervous.

But Mrat recovered his poise quickly. He stepped aside, his body retaining the lines and angles of *respectful-attention*. "I turn command of these jinau troops over as the foundation of your personal guard. May you enlighten them many times over."

Aille studied the naked Terran faces. Without whiskers to give them expression, or velvety nap to cover the skin, or even facial banding to indicate their background, they seemed curiously immature, like Jao juveniles before their *vai camiti* came through. He walked closer, a nonchalant slant to his ears, tapping his new bau against his palm.

"I understood my command was to be of mixed troops, Pleniary-Adjunct. By all appearances, these are native to the last individual."

Mrat glanced up and his eyes flashed bright-green again before he returned his gaze to the sunstruck pavement. "True integration has proven difficult, Subcommandant. Units composed of both species tend to be—" His ears wavered and Aille caught a hint of *shameful-failure*. "—unstable."

"I saw none of this in the reports."

The Krumat stiffened while Yaut adopted the aspect of *indifferent-waiting*, his deceptively casual ears drinking in every phoneme. "Commandant Kaul krinnu ava Dano deems such mention unnecessary. He believes . . ."

The officer's golden face creased in concentration as he searched for a properly prudent explanation. "He believes that younger and less experienced officers, such as myself, have exaggerated the problem." The Krumat's eyes wandered to the restless, untidy sea as white-capped breakers rolled in and deposited slimy green streamers of vegetation in their wake upon the sand. His ears were canted bleakly. "I am quite sure he is correct and I therefore wish to make restitution for my error. Shall you require my life?"

"No!" Aille responded instantly, very startled. His pulse raced as he fought to contain his surprise and maintain his calm posture. Flow threatened to slip from his grasp so that time raced past. With a slow, deep breath, he tightened his timesense, making perception occur at his bidding, not whizz by out of control.

One heard of lives being surrendered for crucial mistakes made during battle, or other such major failures. But he'd never expected to be offered such here in this setting, in front of a squad of jinau, for nothing more that what seemed a minor lapse. The kochanata experts had told him that they sensed Narvo was losing control of the situation on Terra. Was this a sign of it?

Yaut threw him an approving look, quickly suppressed, then locked his hands behind his back and waited with an air of *intense-concentration*.

"As you wish, Subcommandant," the Krumat said. He stepped before Aille, his shoulders straight, his arms angled to indicate *resignation-to-duty*. "Shall I show you to your quarters?"

"I wish to go first, Pleniary-Adjunct," Aille said. "Is that not how the natives accord one another honor?"

The poor Krumat looked as though he might faint at this impropriety. "But we are Jao!"

Aille glanced over at his troops. Several were watching the whole scene as though they spoke fluent Jao, or at least enough to piece things together. "And they are not," he said pointedly. "Which way?"

"Straight ahead," the Krumat said, and gestured toward the third building to the right, which was stiff with straight lines and in full sight of the wrack-littered shore.

Aille set off and the troop of Terrans fell in behind. Yaut edged up until he was almost even with his charge. "This feels strange," he said under his breath. "Keep your wits about you, youngster. The Commandant of military forces on Terra is Kaul krinnu ava Dano, and Dano is traditionally aligned with Narvo."

Aille made no reply. But his fingers tightened around his new bau, as he wondered indeed how long he would be able to keep it.

After Mrat krinnu nao Krumat saw the new Subcommandant safely installed in his quarters, he retreated to his office and sank onto his pile of dehabia to stare at the map-walls. That brute Kaul had withheld the Subcommandant's identity, reserving it, no doubt, so that Mrat might experience the shock of this moment and reflect on his own unworthiness to hold even this unexalted post. Kaul went out of his way to make Mrat feel most keenly the lowly position of his Krumat kochan.

The new Subcommandant Aille's kochan, on the other hand— *Pluthrak!*—extended over many worlds and enjoyed widespread favor, developing associations wherever it turned and producing countless illustrious scions down through the generations. Mrat's own Krumat was nothing in comparison, just a backworld moiety formed less than a hundred orbital cycles ago by the union of two very junior taifs. Their resources were few and they had only two kochan-houses completed even now. When he'd finished his training, certainly no wily old fraghta had been available to guard him from serious errors.

The com buzzed, bringing word of yet another fight in the comestibles dispensary. He stood and stared blindly out the window at the evil-smelling sea, vast and glittering beneath this overbearing alien sun, then went to inspect the damage.

Voices stilled as he entered the ugly box-shaped room. Food lay strewn everywhere and the humans had already been driven into a line along the far wall. He knew the species well enough now to recognize the expressions on their bruised and bloody faces as defiance and resentment. One Jao was seriously hurt and had already been removed for treatment. Two humans lay dead on the floor, along with two more who were badly injured.

His shoulders tightened. Waste. It was all a stupid, pointless waste. One of the Jao soldiers had evidently made a comment that offended the natives and once again chaos was the result.

Humans put their barbaric pride above all else. They simply had no idea how to cooperate like decent civilized beings, how to build association so that the strength of others reinforced your own, rather than strove against it. How they'd survived their own naked aggression this long without exterminating each other was a mystery.

Someone had to make them understand, before the Ekhat swept this way. Staring at the shattered crockery, the gaudy crimson of human blood spattered across floor and wall, with here and there a few spots of orange-colored Jao blood, he realized it was not going to be him. Though he had tried repeatedly down through the five orbital cycles he'd been stationed here, he simply did not have the skill and never would.

On his way back to his office, he considered how best to restore discipline. But by the time he arrived, he discovered it was a moot point. Kaul resided on the base himself, and he had already moved quickly. The Commandant had given orders to have the most prominent of the involved humans put down. By now, it would already have been done. Jao punishment was always swift.

No fewer than five, it seemed. Mrat was surprised at the severity of Kaul's actions. Doubtless, the Commandant thought he could not afford to appear weak, with a new high-status officer taking command of the jinau troops.

Perhaps this Pluthrak, fresh from training and with his grizzled fraghta, would be able to make the humans see what was at stake. Mrat thought it unlikely. But it had better be someone, and soon. The most recent reports on Ekhat activities in this galactic region were ominous. No one on this world, Jao or human, had time for this kind of divisive nonsense.

Aille's new quarters were disappointing, two painted squares with flat walls and tight angles where they fit together. The air felt dead inside, as though flow itself couldn't penetrate. And, worst of all, there was no pool, only a cramped bathing facility that could hold but a dollop of water at a time, barely enough to dampen one's nap.

Sighing, he changed into his new harness, which was of a high-quality dark-green augmented by colorful yellow and green Pluthrak banding about the buckles. For some reason, the air in their quarters was artificially chill, a waste of energy, and he directed Yaut to find the temperature controls.

"Terrans have a narrower comfort range than Jao," Yaut said a moment later. "They're much more susceptible to extremes." He resumed unpacking Aille's kit and stowing the items away, fingering the ceremonial halfcape he had tailored on the voyage to this world. The fabric was very fine, the traditional Pluthrak insignia ornate. Yaut had sewn it himself that his charge might show to his best advantage on this first critical assignment.

Aille was just contemplating a walk to inspect the base when someone knocked with a summons from Commandant Kaul krinnu ava Dano.

Yaut deactivated the doorfield, accepted the flimsy from an unblinking Terran soldier, then keyed the field back on in his face. He held the order out as though it were contaminated. "Not one to waste time, is he?" Yaut's own face was fierce beneath its scars.

"Would you be, if you were in his position?" Aille ran a brush back over his head, smoothing the golden nap. "I would certainly want the measure of a new subordinate."

"You are Pluthrak," Yaut said. "By that alone, he has your measure."

"Pluthrak's measure, not mine." Aille thought of his six pool-parents, stern individuals who had impressed upon their charges day after day that *the honor of one was the honor of all*—and had them repeat it nightly before surrendering to dormancy.

"Do not be the first to let down Pluthrak," they had said at the start of every day, and then again at the end. "And above all, die well."

Dying was easy, he thought. Anyone could achieve that. Dying well was another matter altogether.

Yaut inspected him, green-black eyes narrowed. "The harness is a fair fit, though I can make it even better. The halfcape does not drape correctly, though. I did request that you try it on before we arrived."

Aille moved his shoulder, raised his arm. "It is fine. Stop fussing."

"It is my function to fuss," Yaut said. He smoothed a wrinkle and stepped back, trying unsuccessfully to smother *prideful-approval*. "Are you going to keep him waiting?"

They could hear the motor of the vehicle sent for them just outside. "That is tempting, but I think not," Aille said. He picked up the carved bau and tucked it beneath his arm.

Yaut opened the door and they stepped out into the fierce yellow sunshine again. A human escort waited beside a vehicle. The vehicle was of Terran origin but had been refitted with Jao maglev suspension. The driver's brown face dripped with moisture as he opened the door for them, though they could easily have worked the mechanism themselves.

"How are you called?" The Terran words felt strange on his tongue, as Aille settled in a seat both too short and narrow for his powerful legs.

Yaut gave him a startled look, but Aille had learned from the reports that humans routinely presented their names upon first meetings. It was actually considered the baseline of politeness.

"PFC Masterton, sir!" The Terran slammed the door and ran back around to the control seat with an air of great efficiency. "I hope you had a pleasant trip."

"Space travel is rarely pleasant," Aille said, "but then one does not traverse space in order to experience pleasure. One travels to make one's self of use."

"Uh, yes, sir." The soldier glanced at the two of them over his shoulder, then devoted himself to operating the vehicle.

They passed several large groups of Terrans walking in that peculiar regimented order again, their legs pumping like cogs in a machine, before they pulled up in front of a sleek black building all curves and quantum crystal. Unlike Aille's quarters, Commandant Kaul krinnu ava Dano's command center was obviously Jao-designed, the first bit of "home" Aille had seen since arriving on this world.

Inside, the light was comfortably low, the dimness scented with familiar astringent herbs. Their escort led them to a black crystalline wall that shimmered into transparency at their approach. "In here, sir," Masterton said. He waved the doorfield off, then stepped aside, his alien posture stiff and unreadable.

Yaut slid in front of him and this time Aille allowed it. This was Jao business and the fraghta, with his greater experience, knew better than he how to proceed.

"Keep your ears down, lad," Yaut whispered, then strode ahead, shoulders and arms falling easily into *dutiful-respect*, as though he'd done this thousands of times.

Commandant Kaul was standing before a permanent map of Terra on the far wall, so that they could see his profile. He was a brawny individual, as thick-bodied as any Aille had ever seen, and well marked with a striking facial pattern that accentuated his strong bone structure. He wore his harness as though it were the richest of robes. That was to be expected, of course. Dano was one of the great kochan, even if it did not have quite the status of Narvo or Pluthrak.

"I find it strange," Kaul said, without turning around.

Aille waited a respectful distance back, his head high. "Yes, Commandant?"

"That Pluthrak would accept an assignment on Terra to command jinau."

Aille decided to let pass, for the moment, the question of whether he commanded all ground forces on Terra or simply the native troops. Now, he sensed, was not the time to seek confrontation on the issue; since, clearly enough, the Dano's remark was a probe to create such discordance.

So, he said nothing. The Commandant was thus forced to turn and face him, instead of maintaining what was almost a deliberately impolite stance. His eyes blazed as bright as a warning buoy, and the dark banding along both his cheeks and chin was all the more impressive.

"Of course, we are delighted to be the recipient of such a favor. Rarely are conquered worlds blessed with such an illustrious scion."

There was a faintly sarcastic tinge to his tone of voice. Aille reminded himself that Dano was linked to Narvo by many long associations. He was not in friendly territory here.

But he let none of that show. "I am honored to have been accepted for this post. Pluthrak desires only that I be of use here and serve well."

"As if anything ever goes well on this misbegotten world!" With a wave, Kaul darkened the wall again. "How honest were your trainers about the nature of this assignment?"

Aille glanced at his fraghta, but Yaut gave no clue as to how he should respond. "As honest as was possible, I believe, Commandant."

"No doubt they told you almost nothing, then." Kaul sank into his chair and stared broodingly at a glittering holomap projected in the image tank above his desk.

Aille realized suddenly it represented the Markau sector, contested for some time between several of the Ekhat factions.

The holomap rotated slowly, gleaming green and gold in the dimness. The Dano's eyes caught and reflected the lights. "This world is a wretched place, literally overrun with the dominant lifeform to the point of ecological disaster. Rife with chaos. Despite their cleverness, it is a marvel the natives did not exterminate themselves with their own technology long before we arrived."

"They are said to be extraordinary fighters." Aille studied the map. "Are there not a few areas still outside Jao control?"

"That is false!" Kaul turned on him with lowered ears. "We control every scrap of land worth the effort."

"I see." Aille schooled shoulders and face to express only *mild-interest*. Dive shallowly, he told himself. This individual was overprickly, even leaving aside his Dano attitudes toward Pluthrak. "I look forward to being enlightened."

"Make no mistake, humans are not intelligent in the same manner as you and I," Kaul said. "Their minds are constructed in the fashion of a cunning predator who is first and foremost an individual, unable to put the greater good of anything or anyone ahead of its own momentary needs."

Aille found a point on the wall above the Commandant's head, then let his eyes unfocus, so that he seemed to be watching, and waited.

"And they are frivolous beyond belief!" Kaul spread his hands on the gleaming black desk and stared down at them. "The ways they can avoid meaningful labor outnumber the stars themselves— 'art,' 'pets,' 'gardening,' 'movies,' 'music'! The list goes on and on. They are so obsessed with *ollnat*, things-that-might-be, that a significant portion of the population devotes itself to inventing lies, then recording them on every media possible and circulating them planetwide."

Aille had undergone language imprinting during every dormancy period on the journey out, but his vocabulary acquisition was not yet complete. The Terran terms were unfamiliar and he made a note to have Yaut look them up. "It sounds like an interesting challenge. I am honored to be allowed to assist."

"You will have to 'get your hands dirty,' as the Terrans put it."
Kaul balled his fists. "The natives must be constantly disciplined.
They say one thing to your face, then conduct themselves in the
most devious fashion possible the rest of the time. We cannot
afford Pluthrak subtleties here. If you do not think you can do
all that has to be done, you might as well request a less challenging
assignment."

Yaut seemed suddenly restless, changing his weight from foot
to foot, moving his hands as though unsure what to do with them,
never quite falling into a posture that could be interpreted. Aille
glanced sideways, trying to glean what little he could from the old
soldier's expression, but found he could not decipher the message.
He steadied his ears, on his own for the moment. "I can do
whatever needs to be done, Commandant," he said. "The Governor has only to command."

Kaul fell silent, so that only the whisper of filtered air was
audible. The holomap rotated like a planet on its axis, its lights
hypnotic. The three of them watched and Aille tightened his
timesense so that the moment's flow stretched out and all seemed
to stand still. What was Kaul trying to say, he wondered, but
nothing came to mind. In the background, Yaut exhaled softly and
he let his perception return to normal.

"Markau is no longer being contested," the Dano said abruptly.
"Reports have just come that the Complete Harmony faction of
the Ekhat appears to have routed True Harmony and the Melody.
There are early indications they will now sweep this way. Flow is
inconclusive, but it feels as though it will be sooner rather than
later to most of the experts."

Aille's eyes flickered back to the holomap and he stepped closer,
trying to make sense out of the tiny rose, green, and amber lights
which were even now in motion. "Why would they, so soon after
a major contest?"

"Who can say?" Kaul said. "No one has ever decrypted what the
Ekhat want, except to be alone in the universe."

CHAPTER
2

"I just found out the new Subcommandant's clan is very highly ranked," Professor Kinsey told Caitlin Stockwell, the moment he came into her study cubicle. "*Pluthrak*, no less! Do you think he would grant me an interview for my book?"

Startled, she looked up from the computer terminal where she sat surrounded by piles of musty books she'd carted over from the library. Professor Kinsey was a perpetually rumpled man of middle height with a broad brow, his skin color coffee-and-cream, his silver hair tightly curled.

Caitlin had been attending the University of New Chicago in central Michigan for almost five years now. Having gotten a bachelor's degree the previous winter, she was currently working toward her doctorate in history and serving as a research assistant for her graduate adviser, Dr. Jonathan Kinsey.

Kinsey was a specialist in American history, but two years ago he'd gotten it into his head to do a book on the history of the Jao. He'd even managed, somehow, to secure permission from Earth's Governor, along with a vague promise of cooperation. Caitlin suspected the authorization originated more from inattention and misunderstanding than actual approval, since Jao seemed to lack the cultural concept of "history" as humans understood the term. Not that they didn't have a sense of their own past— quite a keen one, in fact—but it seemed to have more in common with clan oral traditions than a modern human concept of

19

history as a specialized intellectual craft. As a rule, Governor Oppuk, even more than most Jao, gave short shrift to what he considered frivolous human intellectual pursuits.

She'd grown very fond of Kinsey in the months since she'd met him. But, not for the first time, Caitlin found herself wishing that the man's impressive scholarly acumen was not accompanied by all the other stereotypical features of an absentminded professor.

"I really don't advise it," she said, as forcefully as she could while keeping her voice low. Caitlin's Jao guard, Banle, was lurking in the corridor just outside the cubicle.

"Are you sure?" he persisted. "Your knowledge of Jao customs is far better than mine—I'll be the first to admit—but . . . the opportunity! He's *Pluthrak,* Caitlin. Probably the most prestigious kochan there is, among the Jao."

Caitlin glanced at the door, wishing that Kinsey's voice was as low as his common sense. Unfortunately, Banle was fluent in English—and her full name was Banle krinnu nao Narvo.

"Perhaps." Then, almost hissing: "Except—quite possibly, Professor Kinsey—for *Narvo.*"

That finally jolted Kinsey. Caitlin saw him glance nervously at the door himself. Her terse comment had reminded him that Narvo, the kochan which had overseen the conquest and been given Terra to rule, was Pluthrak's long-standing and most bitter rival in the complex world of Jao politics. And that Narvo considered itself to be every bit the equal of fabled Pluthrak.

So it seemed, at least, insofar as humans had been able to figure out how the Jao managed their internal affairs. The human term "politics" was only a rough approximation of the way the Jao looked at the matter. Kinsey had told her once—in private, of course, when Banle wasn't around to overhear—that for all their technological mastery, what he could see of Jao society reminded him more of ancient human barbarian tribes than civilized societies. The complex and convoluted interactions between their clans—what they called "kochan"—carried as much if not more weight than what modern humans would consider politics.

There were times that Caitlin herself thought Jao notions had more in common with her now-dead grandmother's amused descriptions of the clan bickerings and dickerings of her family's back country Appalachian ancestors than they did with anything modern humans generally meant by the term "government."

*Your great-great-uncle swiped one of our pigs but I'll let it pass
on account of your great-great-aunt married my great-grandfather's
second cousin and seeing as how their third oldest son helped my
great-grandfather put up the fence on what used to be great-
grandpa's uncle's land until the uncle's wife died and he married
the Widder Jones and after he died that no-account daughter of
the Widder's by her first husband Tom Hobbs got it. So I'll give
you a fair price on this moonshine, seeing as how you ain't properly responsible for the fact that them Hobbs is all a bunch of no-
account . . .*

The stories had amused Caitlin, as a little girl. Now, at the age
of twenty-four, the amusement had faded. Like some of her
mountain-country ancestors, the Jao could be instantly murderous. And from what Caitlin could tell, the longstanding rivalry
between the great Pluthrak and Narvo kochan was equivalent to
a Hatfield-McCoy feud about to erupt—on an interstellar scale,
with humans likely to be caught in the crossfire.

What made the situation all the worse was that, for reasons
Caitlin couldn't begin to fathom, the Narvo had chosen to put one
of their most savage scions in charge of ruling Terra. The Governor of Terra was Oppuk krinnu ava Narvo. Even by Jao standards, Oppuk was given to brutal methods; and, quite unlike most
Jao, was also given to sudden and frightening rages. Caitlin was
not sure Oppuk was entirely sane, although it was not easy to
determine that with an alien species. But, sane or not, having him
in charge of Terra was like being under the control of Devil Anse
Hatfield.

The huge figure of Banle loomed in the doorway. It was time
to end this discussion. She bit her lip, trying to think how to phrase
it diplomatically.

Caitlin had been largely raised among the Jao and, unlike most
humans, knew how to interpret formal Jao postures. Banle's stance,
no doubt casual to uneducated human eyes, actually communicated *promise-of-threat* at the moment. Caitlin knew any blatant
disrespect on her part would come at a price. She still had a small
scar on her shoulder to prove that, not to mention the memory
of more than one set of bruises.

"It's better not to seek the notice of power," she said. "If the
Subcommandant wishes to meet you, an invitation will come.
Otherwise, you should not trouble him."

And if you're lucky, it will never happen, she thought. She wished most fervently herself never to meet this new Subcommandant. Caitlin's life was enough of a tightrope-walking act as it was, without getting herself involved in Jao clan feuds.

Fortunately, Banle seemed satisfied. Even more fortunately, Professor Kinsey had a rare moment of common sense and, muttering a polite phrase, left the cubicle. Within a minute, Caitlin was able to go back to her work, suppressing a sigh of relief, since Banle was also adept at deciphering human expressions—and doing her best to execute a posture of *concentration-on-immediate-task.*

The posture was well done, she thought, even with the handicap of being seated. It ought to be. From a very early age, Caitlin had applied herself to learning the complex Jao system of body language. As the years passed, she did so partly from growing interest. But she'd begun the work, with a discipline unusual in a young girl, for simple reasons of survival. Much as an infant, finding herself being raised among wolves, might learn how to bay at the moon.

Caitlin stopped by the New Chicago University student union for a break, after working on Dr. Kinsey's files all morning. Reluctantly, because it was the only space available in the crowded cafeteria, she took a seat at a table occupied by Miranda Silvey and several of her friends. She normally avoided that little circle, because she considered them all nitwits, at best.

Not to her surprise, she discovered they were all speculating about the new Jao officer, Aille krinnu ava Pluthrak.

"They say he's just like a Jao prince!" Miranda Silvey said. She was a tall, golden-haired girl with the healthy good looks of one who had never gone hungry. "That's why he's starting out at the top, instead of coming up through the ranks. I wonder if they'll have a reception for him." She turned to Caitlin, who had slid into the orange plastic seat next to her in the busy dining hall. Silverware clinked and the smell of today's special, spaghetti, filled the air. "You're a bigwig, Caitlin. Will you get an invitation, if they do?"

Caitlin dumped her knapsack on the floor, then squeezed a slice of lemon into the cup of tea she'd carried with the other hand. Her Jao guard, Banle, lingered a few feet away, having taken up position in front of a brick pillar.

"My father doesn't send me to official functions," she said in a low voice, though Banle had ears like a fox and no doubt heard everything. "He keeps his political and family life separate as much as possible." She glanced back at Banle whose angled body was communicating *suspicion*. "Can we talk about something else?"

"But your parents are close to Governor Narvo, aren't they?" Miranda persisted, picking up her fork. "I bet you get to meet him all the time."

"Jao do not 'get close' to humans," Caitlin said. "I'm not sure they have friends, the way you mean it, even among their own kind." She was irritated enough to add, a bit pedantically: "Besides, it's not 'Governor Narvo.' Narvo is his clan designation, not his surname. It's either Governor Oppuk or the Narvo Governor. One or the other, but not both."

"Well, I'd love to meet the Subcommandant." Tracy Guin's round face grinned. "They say he's really young and dashing. And—"

Caitlin blocked out the rest of the chatter and concentrated on eating her meal, trying to control her temper.

Idiots.

Worse than that, really. One of the many negative side effects of the Jao conquest had been a sharp differentiation between human nations, and, within each nation, its various classes. Those nations that had resisted the Jao conquest militarily—the United States being foremost among them, because it had had by far the most powerful military—had been subjected to ferocious direct rule thereafter. Those that had surrendered quickly, like Japan and most of Europe except for England and France, had been allowed far more in the way of local autonomy.

The same, within each nation. Those people who collaborated quickly and readily were granted more privileges. In a war-devastated area like North America, which still hadn't recovered from the destruction of the conquest, that could mean the difference between eating well—and enjoying a higher education—or just barely scraping by.

Miranda and her friends were the inevitable byproducts, some twenty years later—a group of college students who'd been born and raised since the Jao conquest, and had the screwiest ideas about the universe and their true place in it.

She gave Miranda, still prattling cheerfully about the "Jao prince," a sidelong glance. The girl had no idea what a Jao really was. First and foremost, the Jao were *conquerors*. They used humans, and the resources of Terra, entirely for their own purposes. Whatever Miranda's delusions were, the fact was that the Jao neither required nor wanted anything emotional from humans. Not affection, not friendship—and certainly not a bunch of silly college girls mooning over them!

Fortunately for Miranda, and all the brainless twits like her, the Jao were not interested in the sexual favors of human females. So they were ignored completely, instead of becoming the concubines of their conquerors.

Too bad, really, Caitlin thought savagely. She would have been delighted if someone like Miranda or Tracey could assume her hostage duties even for a few days. She could use a break from the constant surveillance and they needed their eyes opened.

Why they couldn't just travel to the Chicago or New Orleans craters and get educated that way, she didn't know. The thought of all that devastation sobered her every time. The Jao had destroyed Chicago and New Orleans during the conquest without even having the excuse of retaliating against human use of nuclear weapons. Caitlin knew from her father, who'd then been the Vice-President of the United States, that the U.S. government had considered the use of nuclear weapons and finally decided against it.

The Jao invasion had come as a complete surprise to everyone, since Jao technology enabled them to circumvent Terra's electronic early warning systems. They'd struck hardest in North America. Clearly, they'd already been able to determine that continent contained the most powerful human military forces. Their troop landings had taken place in several areas in North America, and rapidly expanded outward from there. By the time the U.S. government could react coherently—which had taken days, since the Jao had used their advanced technology to suppress or at least disrupt human electronic communication—Jao troops were too closely mixed up with human armies and civilian populations for the use of nuclear weapons to be a viable option. Not unless the U.S. government was prepared to kill tens of millions of its own citizens in the process, and radioactively contaminate most of the continent.

They hadn't been. But, in the end—for Chicago and New Orleans, at least—it hadn't mattered. The American armed forces had put up their most ferocious fighting to defend those two cities. After days, even though they were killing ten human soldiers for every one they lost, the Jao casualties had mounted significantly and they hadn't made much headway. So, they lost patience.

Not even that, really. "Patience," like every other human characteristic, was something that could only be fitted onto Jao psychology in a loose way. It might be better to say that the ever-practical Jao simply decided they could afford to lose the resources of those areas in order to end the thing. And, given their technology and control of space, they hadn't had to worry about radioactive contamination. Two chunks of rock taken from the asteroid belt and accelerated to 50,000 miles per hour had done just fine, thank you.

And the fact that, in so doing, they'd butchered millions of people hadn't bothered them in the least. Nor did it still, twenty years later, so far as Caitlin could tell.

She finished her meal, and decided the rest of the tea wasn't worth listening to the imbecilic chatter around her. Caitlin snatched up her knapsack, scraped back the chair, and headed for the door. Booted steps across the tile told her that Banle wasn't far behind. But then, Caitlin thought resignedly as she pushed open the outer doors, she never was.

The Jao "bodyguard" accompanied her everywhere, night and day. Banle krinnu nao Narvo had been her constant companion since she was four years old. Banle had been given that assignment shortly after the Jao had dragged her father, Benjamin Stockwell, out of hiding. He'd been the highest-ranked surviving member of the U.S. government and they'd appointed him head of their North American regional government—which now included both Canada and Mexico, since the Jao were unconcerned over the nuances of human national relations.

Caitlin's father had not tried to resist, once captured, despite his reluctance to take on the task. He'd hoped he might be able to use the position to alleviate conditions for the human population of America. And, whether he could or not, by then he'd learned that the Jao had a very short way with protests. His choice had been simple: obey or be "put down."

Caitlin had learned as much herself, and done so at a very early age. In truth, Banle krinnu nao Narvo was as much Caitlin's jailer as guard—and, someday, might very well be her executioner. Caitlin was a lifelong hostage to her father's cooperation. As long as he did what Earth's conquerors wanted, rubber-stamped their decisions, put a familiar and trusted face on the puppet human government of North America, she would be safe. The moment he or she got out of line, she would pay the price.

She'd had two older brothers, both dead now. Her oldest brother had died fighting the Jao in the initial invasion, the other at Governor Oppuk's hands some years later. Caitlin was well aware the enigmatic Banle would have no trouble breaking her charge's neck, should she ever think it necessary or be given orders to do so. She, and her parents, had exactly what few freedoms the Jao permitted them, and those only as long as they served well.

That was why, when she heard tales of a highly ranked new Jao officer arriving on Earth, she was intrigued but not in the least bit interested in making his acquaintance. Many of the pampered students at the university were Jao-crazy. They pursued all things Jao either from simple mimicry of their rulers, or in the vain belief it would someday procure them privilege. Many of them painted their faces in imitation of Jao *vai camiti*, and a few had even gone so far as to make the grotesque decorations permanent tattoos.

For them, no doubt, the arrival of a scion from the legendary Pluthrak kochan was a matter for great excitement. But Caitlin knew one more Jao, however exalted, would make no difference. He was bound to think just like all the others who had come before him. His kind were a single-minded species, intent on molding humans into something useful—as they defined the term "useful." They cared about nothing else; certainly not what humans thought.

Blessedly, when Caitlin got back to her study cubicle, Banle decided to take one of the naps that the Jao were prone to. Some time ago, Banle had set up a cot in the next room for that purpose.

They were like cats, that way, more than humans. Instead of sleeping heavily for many hours at a stretch, Jao would simply "catnap" occasionally through the course of the day. The short, light sleeping periods were concentrated during the nighttime, as a rule, but so far as Caitlin had ever been able to tell the Jao could nap at any time—and could function as well at night as during the day. In some ways they preferred to function at night, since they found Terra's sunlight rather harsh.

Not that they looked in the least bit feline, except for the "tigerish" way in which their powerful bodies moved. To a human, a Jao resembled a walking sea lion more than anything else—and even that resemblance was only a vague one. Their snouts were much shorter and blunter, for one thing, and they had rather massive jaws and chins, which sea lions lacked completely. Their long and mobile ears were certainly quite unlike those of any terrestrial marine mammal.

There were some obvious vestigial traits of their marine ancestry—there were still webs between their toes, though not their fingers—and they were superb swimmers. Still, regardless of their origins, they were now clearly land animals, not marine ones. Although their torsos were longer in proportion to their legs than those of humans, their legs were real legs, not awkward semi-flippers. In fact, they could easily outrun humans, in a sprint if not over long distances.

But the vague resemblance to sea lions was not one that any human really thought of, any more. To humans, sea lions and seals—even great walruses—basically looked "cute." And there was nothing at all cute about a Jao. Fearsome, yes; impressive, yes—even, sometimes, "handsome." But never cute.

Not more than five minutes after Banle left, Dr. Kinsey entered the cubicle again. He gave a quick glance at the door to Banle's room, to assure himself that it was closed, and then spoke in something of a hurried half-whisper.

"I know you don't think it's a wise idea, Caitlin, but would you please intercede for me if at all possible? It's *Pluthrak*. We know almost nothing about that kochan, beyond the fact that they enjoy enormous prestige and seem—from what I've been able to tell, anyway—to be famous for their subtlety. Quite unlike Narvo! Which—alas, poor Earth—is famous for its direct effectiveness. If I can use an analogy—yes, yes, I know analogies between humans and Jao are dangerous, but this one seems good to me—the two kochan seem to serve a different function for the Jao. The Pluthrak rapier to the Narvo cutlass, if you will. Or maybe it's the difference between the nobility of the pen and the nobility of the sword."

Caitlin grimaced. Kinsey responded with a half-smile.

"Just try, will you? It might be important, Caitlin, leaving aside my professorial manias. If we could ever figure out how to get a little wedge in somewhere . . ."

She sighed. "Don't even think it, Professor. Talk about dangerous analogies! A wedge is just a piece of metal, or wood. Humans trying to wedge themselves between Narvo and Pluthrak . . ."

She'd brought a cookie back from the cafeteria. She picked it up and applied sudden pressure. The cookie broke into pieces, scattering crumbs across the desk.

CHAPTER
3

Yaut studied Aille surreptitiously. The two of them had not been together long. The young officer was still an enigma to him, and it was difficult to serve enigmas well. Word back in the halls of Pluthrak had been that this particular youth was dynamic and forward thinking, perhaps the most promising scion the great kochan had produced in several generations. Those same qualities, however, made him too restless by far to remain docilely at the kochanata among his learned elders and benefit from further instruction. They felt he needed *wrem-fa*, body learning, where the student was required to act first, then process the experience intellectually later.

So far in their short association, though Aille could sometimes be impulsive, Yaut had found his charge thoughtful in a way rare for the young. Rare for any Jao, truth be told, not simply young ones. This tendency spilled over into brooding occasionally, but still boded well for the future. It was Yaut's mission, as fraghta, to see that the full measure of his potential was realized.

Physically, for a certainty, the young officer represented the best the kochan had to offer—from the classic Pluthrak black band across the eyes, which lent him an authoritative air, to his powerful, fit frame and exceptional height. The marriage-group that had produced him was known for its fine, strong progeny and Aille was no exception. He radiated a restless energy combined with curiosity that Yaut found promising.

Aille was pensive now, as they were conveyed back to their quarters in a native groundcar. Yaut's charge gazed out the window at the sprawling, hodgepodge base with its mingled Jao and Terran architecture. He seemed to be studying the native jinau soldiers and the peculiar way they traveled, legs striding out together as though they were parts of a machine, rather than sentient creatures.

Then he leaned forward suddenly. "Stop," he ordered the native driver. "I wish to walk the rest of the way."

Aille spoke in quite good Terran, which he'd studied extensively in preparation for this assignment. Or "English," rather. If Yaut remembered correctly, that was the name of the dominant tongue on this continent. One of the many ways in which humans were bizarre was their insistence on retaining a multitude of different languages. Jao, sensible beings, had only one language.

"Sir?" The driver glanced back over his shoulder and the vehicle slowed. "It's one hundred degrees in the shade out there, and that doesn't even take into account the heat index. Our Mississippi sun isn't a force to be taken lightly."

"You—" Aille hesitated, searching his still limited vocabulary, then switched to Jao. "You underestimate Jao resilience." His ears were decidedly eager. "Stop."

"Yes, sir," the Terran replied, speaking now in Jao also. He got out of the vehicle, as soon as he had brought it to a stop. "Do you want me to wait here, or perhaps down the road? In case you need me later?"

"That will not be necessary," Aille said, fumbling with the unfamiliar door mechanism. After a moment, it yielded with a click.

The driver seemed startled, Yaut noticed. Had he intended to open the door for Aille himself?

And if so, why? Aille was obviously not crippled. It was a mystery, as most things about these humans seemed to be.

Yaut rose from his seat and followed Aille out into the blaring yellow sunlight. It was not the heat, Yaut thought, involuntarily squinting, but the strong light which distressed. Most Jao kochanhouses were located on worlds birthed by less insistent stars.

"Yes, sir." The Terran raised his hand to his brow in a sharp gesture that seemed freighted with enough meaning to be a minor posture. He then returned to his seat and reached for the vehicle's controls.

Aille cocked his head. "Wait," he said, putting a restraining hand on the vehicle's door. "Can you explain what 'pets' are?"

"That's a human custom," the Terran said. His eyes, a startling blue, looked away, as though he were ashamed. "'Pets' are animals with which humans have a close emotional relationship. They are very common among us, as civilians. But standing orders say we are not to waste resources on them in the military."

"I see," Aille said. He lifted his hand. "Proceed."

"Thank you, sir. Have a pleasant evening!" A moment later, the vehicle turned back, then whirred off across the base.

"Let me look into the matter further," Yaut said. "I will see what I can find out."

Aille's eyes, black as volcanic obsidian, blinked. Not even a hint of telltale green glimmered in their depths. "I wish to be expert on the character of these Terrans." He set off walking, then turned to his fraghta. "Do you think they are as bad as Kaul krinnu ava Dano intimated? I had a different impression of them, after my studies."

Yaut shielded his eyes from the bright sunlight with one hand and grunted. "In my experience, deciphering reports is one thing, fieldwork something else altogether." He hesitated. "I have heard, however, that they are much like quarrelsome children, newly emerged, but never mature."

Aille set off. Once again, Yaut had to yield the lead, since the youth charged ahead. The two of them walked along an avenue of dreary box-shaped buildings, each sharp with corners and colored a dull, unrelenting green. The pavement radiated a pleasant heat beneath their boots and the air bore the imprint of the nearby sea. Aille turned down first one row, seemingly at random, then another, running splayed fingers over the local building materials, checking doors and windows, trim, and even what appeared to be actual stone wrested straight from the depths of the local earth.

"These are constructed, not poured like Jao structures," he said finally. "See the joints and fasteners? Very inefficient. You can already see evidence of deterioration."

"Wastes a lot of space, too," Yaut grunted.

"Yes. But, on the other hand, consider the advantages on a world as heavily populated as this one. This boxy configuration allows them to stack rooms one on top of the other. As many as a hundred rooms tall, in some instances, according to the reports I read. No Jao edifice I've ever heard of uses vertical space that extensively." He pondered for a moment. "There is a lesson here, Yaut. Perhaps we should not presume, so quickly, that what the natives do is simply capricious."

An answer did not seem to be required, so Yaut waited for him to walk on. Flow was slow for now, slipping past like a meandering stream. Nothing official was required of them at the moment. They could afford to take their time.

They rounded another corner just as the breeze shifted, bringing a chorus of excited Terran voices. Aille's ears twitched and his head turned to pinpoint the source.

"Come on, lucky eight!" someone out of sight was saying in the native language. "Come to Papa!"

Aille doubled back down the street and darted between two of the crude buildings. Yaut followed, muttering.

Three human males of varying sizes, all clad in dark-blue jinau uniforms, were kneeling in a half-circle formed by three smaller buildings, staring intently at a pair of diminutive white cubes on the pavement. Perhaps they were some sort of training device, Yaut thought, coming closer.

"Are you 'Papa'?" Aille asked the nearest male. He spoke in English, evidently determined to improve his grasp of the language.

The man looked up, then lurched backwards onto his rump. His mouth hung open and his eyes, dark brown with this one, widened. "Wha—?"

He recovered quickly. A moment later, he was on his feet, standing rigidly and making that peculiar motion of touching his forehead with his hand held rigid and flat.

Aille cocked his head, his gaze bright with curiosity. "If you are not 'Papa,' then which of you is, and why do you want eight? Eight of what?"

"There is no—Papa," another said, also now on his feet and making the same curious hand-to-forehead gesture. "It's just an expression, sir." This human was slighter than the other, topped with the reddish overgrown nap the locals called "hair." His skin was very pale and his bland unmarked face was shiny with moisture.

"I see." Aille locked his hands behind his back. "Are you practicing some sort of skill set?"

The third male, rising last, stooped to pick up the cubes and long rectangles of green paper. The latter he stowed in a pocket. His face, a pale tan, went paler beneath its thatch of yellow hair.

From their uneasy stance, Yaut suddenly deduced the situation. "I believe, Subcommandant Aille, this must be one of the activities forbidden by Commandant Kaul." He glanced at the humans for affirmation. "Is that not so?"

The red-haired one started to look away, then squared his shoulders. "Yes, sir."

Aille stepped closer, his ears raised. "Is this 'art,' then?"

The first, broad-shouldered for a human, and with a much darker skin than the other two, made a curious sound. Almost as if he were choking. The third man, the one who'd picked up the green papers, gave him a sharp glance which Yaut suspected was one of reproof.

"Meaning no disrespect, sir," he said. "This is called 'gambling.'"

Aille held out his hand and the human surrendered the tiny cubes. "Really?" he said, turning them over so Yaut could see enigmatic black circles pressed into their surface. "If it is proscribed in the military, as I have been told, then you would expect to be punished for it. Yes?"

The three dipped their heads in what Yaut had learned from indoctrination tapes was a crude, but universally understood, affirmative posture.

Aille rolled the cubes in his hand so they clicked. "Interesting. Yet still insist you on violating the rules. Since they are—contraband, I think the word is—I shall keeping them for further study. In the meantime—" He fixed them with his aristocratic gaze. "You will putting yourselves on report for this infraction. Fraghta Yaut will receive your names and ranks, and we shall speaking further of this when I am better informed."

Yaut pulled out his personal board, thumbed the record function on, and looked inquiringly at the humans.

The red-haired one made a noise deep in his throat. "PFC Curtis Ray Berry, sir."

"Allen Rogers, Spec Four," the dark-eyed human with the dark skin said.

The third was only of middle height but had more presence than the other two. Thin, but very fit-looking, he met Yaut's gaze as squarely as a Jao. Indeed, there was a hint of almost Jao fierceness in his stance, which was accentuated by his bright green eyes. "Gabe Tully, PFC."

Yaut deactivated his board. "Done."

Aille turned and strolled off, the matter finished. Yaut ducked his head and followed. Just as they rounded the corner, he heard one of the humans say, "Who in the hell was that?"

"I dunno," one of the others said, "but did you see his face? I never saw a Jao marked like that before. He looked like the Lone Ranger, with that black mask across his eyes."

"Idiots!" the third said, his voice growing fainter as the two Jao walked. "Didn't you hear what the other one called him? Subcommandant. We've just met our new CO, old Pinb's replacement. Of all the luck. He . . . not . . ."

And then Yaut couldn't make out anything but a faint murmur. Lost in thought, Aille retraced their path, his nose to the briny sea wind, the blinding sun in his eyes. Yaut, as was becoming all too usual on this world, was obliged to follow.

Since they had eaten already that day, Aille did not partake of the meal delivered to their quarters that evening, preferring instead to sit outside on a bench and study the stars. He tried to pick out known systems from this unfamiliar vantage point. This world was much closer to Ekhat-held territory than his home system of Nir and there were no other Jao outposts in the intervening reaches. If the Ekhat did sweep this way, he mused, Terra would be ill-equipped to put up any meaningful resistance. Once the conquest was finished, the great Jao fleets had gone elsewhere. What was left behind was simply a small flotilla, and enough ground troops to maintain order.

Windward, the lights of the converted shipyard gleamed in the darkness and he could see sparks flying as work went on through the night. On the other side of the base, vehicles hummed up and down the access roads and several companies of jinau soldiers were training down on the sand with night-sight equipment. The base seemed much busier than it had under the full light of day and he was tempted to get a closer look.

He'd left his quarters' doorfield off and could see Yaut seated before the datacom, researching a number of questions in the base archives.

Flow eased by until the fraghta came outside and stood behind him, companionably silent.

"Well?" Aille said finally.

"I found references on 'gambling' as well as 'games of chance.'" He turned his scarred face upward, also studying the stars. "There has been a great deal of trouble on the issue. Of the many things labeled a waste of productive time and initially banned, it seems to have been one dear to human sensibilities. Eventually, it was decided to remove the proscription against it, since enforcement was essentially impossible. The one place it was retained—no logic to this, that I can see—was in the military. Typical Dano," he sniffed. "Always so concerned to look more forceful than even Narvo."

A troop of jinau jogged by, their stride timed in that curious unison. "But what *is* 'gambling'?" Aille asked.

"Now, that is still a bit of a mystery to me. Perhaps there is a religious component to it that I have not detected. If so, it makes Dano's prohibition even more absurd. It never pays to meddle with the customs and superstitions of a subject people, so long as they are obedient."

The fraghta looked discomfited. "It is apparently a ritual which involves the surrender of valuable goods in varying amounts, but I could not figure out exactly what was provided in return. Most of the time, it seems to be nothing at all, beyond the vagaries of chance. "

"Yet they obviously enjoy it, enough to take considerable risks." Aille turned his gaze to the black expanse of the sea that glittered out on the horizon under the starlight. The night breeze, rich with spray, surged against his face. "Strange."

"They are indeed a strange species," Yaut said. "We may never understand them. It is probably more practical merely to teach them to understand us."

"No, that is not good enough." Aille stood, his ears drinking in the night sounds. "That is the Narvo way. Very effective, often. But it has been tried for twenty years on this planet—and, according to what I was told by the kochanata experts before I left, to no great effect. Terra is unlike any other world we have conquered. The population is immense, and its industry and technology impressive. It has a much deeper past than any previous subject species, all of whom were primitives barely able to form metals. A complex and elaborate culture, far more so than ours in many ways."

He paused, trying to find the best words to express concepts with which he was still wrestling himself. The kochanata experts had been able to point to Narvo weaknesses, easily enough, but that was a far cry from being able to advance solutions—as they had been the first to admit. So, in the end, they had opted for the time-honored method of the great Jao kochan. Take the most promising scion and send him or her to make the test.

"The conquest of this planet was far more difficult than any we faced before," he continued, "and took far longer. By all reports, the humans fought like cornered beasts, often very well and always very savagely. If I am going to be an effective commander, I want to use their energy and cunning. Pluthrak has always worked differently than Narvo, in seeking association. But to do that, I have to know more. I need to understand them, as much as possible."

Yaut's homely face was impassive. "Then I will see what I can arrange."

"What do you mean?"

"I would rather not say for now, "Yaut said. "But a proper fraghta always rises to the occasion. I will find a way."

Though Yaut hadn't been with him long, Aille knew that look already. It would do no good to press him. The get of Jithra, his kochan, were notoriously close-mouthed. Yaut would reveal nothing until he was ready. Which was proper, of course. The relationship between a fraghta and his charge was not one of simple subordination. It could not be, or the fraghta could not function effectively.

Aille stood and stretched until his joints popped. "What is our schedule tomorrow?"

"The orders on my board say we are to report to the remanufacturing facility," Yaut said. "There, you will begin to acquaint yourself with the defensive resources of this world. Governor Oppuk wishes you to be thoroughly familiar with this area of operations before you take up specific command responsibilities."

"Very well."

Yaut hesitated. "One thing more."

"Yes?"

"According to the last postings, there was trouble on the base today, not too long after we touched down. Some sort of fight between Jao and human soldiers. Two humans died outright, one

Jao was badly hurt. Commandant Kaul ordered five of the humans involved put down afterward."

"Did the notation say what the fight was about?"

"An insult of some sort. The report was not specific."

Troubling, Aille thought. The penalty, more than the incident itself. Jao officers should be smarter than that. Why put down so many? Clashes between Jao occupying troops and natives were common enough, after all. They had happened on many planets. If extreme penalties were needed, singling out one who had been prominent in the fracas—two, at the most—would surely have been sufficient to restore discipline. Dead natives produced nothing of value, nor fought off any Ekhat. And Aille had learned enough from his studies to know that humans in particular were quick to resent punishment, even when it was properly authorized.

Another vehicle pulled up and disgorged a company of soldiers burdened with full loads of unfamiliar equipment. "I am going down to the shore and observe the training," he said.

Yaut keyed the doorfield on, then edged into the lead as any good fraghta would, given the opportunity.

CHAPTER
4

Gabe Tully slipped through the hot, sticky Mississippi night, trailing the new Subcommandant as he left his quarters. This one was a conundrum. Jao just didn't mix with natives or ask about local customs. Above all, they didn't go for unattended, seemingly purposeless strolls. Leisure was not a part of their psychological vocabulary. Unless he was going for a swim, something was definitely up.

He'd bet a hundred new-bucks that encounter earlier today wasn't a fluke either. The Jao had probably set it up, perhaps even suspected Tully had Resistance ties. For his part, the craps game had been all about gathering intel. Soldiers were much more likely to spill interesting information when their minds were otherwise occupied, and now his own mind was buzzing with what he'd learned since about this particular Jao.

To begin with, Aille krinnu ava Pluthrak was young, far more so than most Jao officers assigned to the base. And he'd been assigned a plush, high ranking job, even though he'd apparently just completed his training. The "ava" prefix in his name indicated he was a member of the inner circles of one of the root clans, as Tully understood Jao customs. Root clans were serious business in some way the Resistance hadn't quite managed to work out. At any rate, local Jao management had fallen all over themselves, trying to see that everything was perfect: his quarters, his driver, even his first meal. Very strange, since they liked to pretend they

38

were egalitarian, that one Jao was much the same as another and cooperation was their byword.

That must be why Commandant Kaul had come down so hard after the mess room fracas this afternoon—nervousness about this new Subcommandant. Five men executed for nothing more than a brawl! A bad brawl, sure, but no human commander would have meted out such instant and savage punishment. Even for the Jao, it was extreme.

Tully hesitated, his back flattened to the wall. Footsteps scraped on the concrete, then several Jao officers walked past just around the corner, neither of them this Pluthrak. He held his breath. Jao had ears like cats, though there was certainly nothing else catlike about them.

When he dared look again, Pluthrak had disappeared. He decided to keep looking and see if he could pick up the trail. Much as he would have liked to rearrange the Dano's face, doing so would ensure an even higher human death toll in the coming days. Jao discipline was invariably swift, often fatal, and not at all above falling upon civilians, when they couldn't find a guilty party easily at hand. Jao psychology made little provision for anyone learning from his or her mistakes. Their attitude was simple and brutal: kill the one who made the mistake, and let everyone else learn the lesson.

Tully's mind wandered into speculation. If a Jao had a fatal accident, however, one that couldn't be traced back to a human hand . . . Kaul was too smart to put himself at risk, but this new Subcommandant was apparently not so cautious. Once Tully caught up with him, something fatal might be arranged. It'd be tricky, of course. For a human to use physical force against a Jao—especially a Jao as big and young and obviously in superb condition as this new one—was a lot easier said than done.

Tully considered the thought for a moment longer, then shook it off. Leaving aside the difficulties involved, he'd been sent here to gather intelligence, not to risk himself by trying to carry out the assassination of a single Jao officer. He'd had some success in his assignment, and needed to continue before deserting and making his way back to the mountains with his report. The level of anger among human workers and soldiers on this particular Jao base was high, because of the harshness of the local commanders. They were more willing to cooperate with the Resistance than sepoy troops or workers on Jao military projects usually were.

The Resistance needed that cooperation, as reluctant as many of its members were to work with collaborators. Twenty years after the conquest, Tully knew the situation was grim. The Resistance needed to deepen its roots in the population here in the occupied territories, while people still remembered what it was like to be their own masters. With every passing year, that memory was fading. If they didn't turn the situation around before many more years had passed, their conquerors would be too firmly entrenched and humanity would never take back its own world.

In the darkness, Tully grimaced. It didn't help that the Resistance was badly factionalized, with groups often falling out and fighting among themselves. Tully had spent most of his life since the conquest holed up in the Rockies with Resistance units under the command of Rob Wiley. Wiley's people were well organized, disciplined, and had the support of the local population. But since Tully had volunteered for the sepoy troops in order to gather intelligence for Riley, he'd been shocked to discover the hostile attitude that many humans in the occupied territories had toward the Resistance. Some of that was because Jao retaliation for Resistance actions often fell on bystanders. But, for the most part, it was because many people had had unpleasant experiences with the Resistance.

"Unpleasant" was putting it mildly, in some cases. Not all Resistance groups were as motivated and disciplined as the one Tully belonged to. Being honest, Tully admitted that many of them weren't really much more than bandits, who spent far more time and energy extorting and abusing human civilians than they ever did fighting the Jao.

Tully's mind went back to the young Subcommandant. Why had he bothered to confiscate the dice? And why hadn't the three of them already been punished? Put themselves "on report"? Kaul would never have bothered with that. In the Commandant's current mood, he might well have ordered all three of them immediately executed even for a petty infraction like gambling on the base.

The issue wasn't really the gambling, anyway, it was the rigid Jao attitude toward obedience. Granted, the Jao had no use for gambling, since it produced nothing beneficial, nor taught or honed any useful military skill. From their viewpoint, it was a worthless and distracting enterprise—like mountain climbing, horse racing, ornamental gardening, fine art painting—the list went on and on. Civilian humans could still do these things, although even they were no longer allowed to allocate major amounts of time and resources to them. Everything of value now belonged to the Jao.

Tully remembered how effectively the Jao had made their attitude clear. Fifteen years ago, the last expedition to Mount Everest went forward as planned, despite an edict by the Jao Governor of Earth that the expedition was a pointless waste of manpower and resources and therefore banned.

Thirty minutes after the climbers had begun their final ascent, the top few thousand feet of Everest had been vaporized by a Jao-guided rock from space, the same type of weapon they'd used to obliterate Chicago and New Orleans. The poor devils up on the mountain probably had never known what hit them. But the rest of Earth had, and the Jao had made their point as they always did: very bluntly.

Tully skirted the last of the Jao living quarters. Still no sight of the Pluthrak, but he could see the sweep of the landing field not far from the shore. The small ship that had come in earlier was still there. That was unusual, because few vessels docked here permanently. This one had evidently arrived with Aille krinnu ava Pluthrak. Was it perhaps still here because it was reserved for his personal use?

The ship, bathed in beams of blue light, was slim as a needle and looked highly maneuverable, more than any other Jao spacecraft he'd seen. The hair rose on the nape of Tully's neck. If the Jao had many more of these, it could be bad news for the Resistance. Part of their protection now lay in the fact it was too much trouble for the Jao to transport troops back into the Rocky Mountains where they had dug in.

But, again, Tully shook off the thought. Another thing that had become clear to him since he'd joined the sepoy army—much to his disgruntlement—was that the Jao really didn't take the Resistance too seriously. They would retaliate instantly and savagely against any Resistance actions, true. But they rarely bothered to send expeditions into the mountains to ferret them out so long as the Resistance was quiescent. So it was not likely, all things considered, that the Jao were starting to bring in special ships designed for anti-insurgency warfare. The design of the ship in front of him was probably due to other needs.

Their mysterious war against the Ekhat, perhaps. The Jao hinted at terrible things lying in wait out there in the universe that justified their harsh rule. The worst was said to be the Ekhat, a species that reportedly made the fiercest Jao look like kindly nannies. They were always predicting destruction that would rain upon everyone, human and Jao alike, if they didn't prepare and prepare and prepare. Most humans, even most collaborators, just thought it was an excuse—self-serving Jao propaganda to justify their conquest and their outrages.

Tully had thought the same himself, once. Now, he was no longer so sure. In the past few months, he'd gotten to know the Jao much better than he had observing them from a distance. As far as Tully had been able to determine, Jao felt no guilt at all over their brutal excesses. Shame just wasn't part of their psychological makeup. They did whatever they deemed necessary to keep control and made no excuses of any kind. So why would they bother developing elaborate propaganda schemes to keep humans pacified? Their standard "propaganda" method was uncomplicated and straightforward: *do as we say or we will kill you.*

Tempted, Tully wondered if he could get close enough to the ship to gather any useful information. He edged across the open tarmac, calculating. Those light beams were security devices, no doubt. Break one and you were probably toast. Still—

"Being well crafted, is it not?"

The voice, Jao by its inflection, stopped Tully in his tracks. Windborne sand ticked against his face. He spun around, heart thudding in his chest.

The Jao facing him had that startling band covering his eyes much as a human bandit wore a mask. It was Aille krinnu ava Pluthrak.

Aille watched the Terran soldier, trying to gauge its reaction. Short and fragile though it was, compared to a Jao, it did seem to be male. Was it uneasy, perhaps even worried? He was coming to realize that their faces were much more mobile than he'd thought they would be, from the reports he'd read before arriving, once he mentally adjusted for the lack of whiskers and those tiny, immobile ears. Alien emotions fleeted across its face like waves before the wind.

Staunch and alert, Yaut moved up to Aille's side, hand on his weapon. "Area of restrict!" he said in crude English. "What doing you here?"

The human glanced over its shoulder at the landing field. A sweep of red lights outlined the boundaries in all directions while the blue stasis beams protected the Pluthrak courier. The Terran shook its head. "Just what the Subcommandant here said, sir. Admiring that ship."

"Are you a pilot?" Aille asked, ears twitching.

"No, sir," the human said, "but I hope to be certified to work on Jao engines one of these days." It exhaled softly. "I'd sure like to know how that technology works."

Curiosity was understandable, Aille thought, but still the presence of this one alone out here in the darkness seemed suspicious. Did the species often wander about like this, regardless of regulations?

"You are male?"

"Yes, sir," the soldier said and flicked his gaze toward Yaut, who stood between them like a shield.

"Jao techs are generally female. They having—" Aille searched his newly acquired vocabulary for the right word. "—more affinity for the work." He peered at the man's shirt, trying to decode the unfamiliar glyphs etched on the small plate across the breast, by only the glimmer of starlight. "Were you not one of the gamblingers we apprehending earlier today?"

The man stiffened. "You must be mistaken, sir."

But that build, slender yet very strong-looking for a native, seemed familiar. So did the shape of the face and the subtleties of the stance, and the Terran symbols seemed to spell out the same name. And the hair, hadn't it been that same yellowish shade? He turned to Yaut. "Check your board," he said in Jao. "See if this is one of the three."

"Don't bothering," the Terran said in Jao. "I submitting self for censure."

"Gabe—Tully," Yaut read out anyway. "PFC."

"You interest me, PFC Gabe Tully," Aille replied, also in Jao. "Are you not aware of the punishment for intruding into restricted areas of this base?"

Tully inhaled deeply and locked his arms behind his back. "Yes, sir. It . . . can being very severe."

"You could be put down for it, if I chose—or if the Commandant chose. And yet you risk coming here, nonetheless. Why?"

"I wanting to see the ship better, sir."

"That is irrational." Aille considered. "Are all Terrans this stupid?"

The Terran made no response. Aille walked around the stiffly braced human, studying him from all angles. The sea breeze rifled the curiously colored hair. "You possess valuable military training?"

Again, as earlier in the day, the Terran exhibited that curious head dip which signified assent.

"And, if you force me to punish you for a serious infraction of regulations, you thereby deprive the Jao of your talents? Perhaps permanently."

Head dip.

Something tickled the back of Aille's mind, something that would not step forward and make itself known. Was the species perhaps prone to acts of self-extermination? What explained this bizarre stubbornness?

He came to a sudden decision. An odd one, perhaps, but it was an odd situation.

"Therefore, I shall not let you force me into unstudied action," Aille said. "You are attached to my personal service as of now."

Yaut glanced at him with *alarm* in the cant of his ears.

The Terran's head whipped around. If Aille was interpreting his expression correctly, he was confused and puzzled—as well as afraid, of course.

"My fraghta will accompany you back to your quarters to collect your gear. Then you will return with him and await further instruction. His name is Yaut krinnu Jithra vau Pluthrak, but, of course, you will only address him by name with his permission—which will not come quickly or easily, if at all. He is a stringent trainer, you will find."

"I don't understand!" the man blurted.

Aille could see in Yaut's eyes that the fraghta did not understand either. Actually, Aille himself did not fully grasp the implications of this action. But he sensed that something important was at stake here, something which would forever elude him, if he merely had this Terran punished without further investigation. And what better way to understand the species than to take one into his personal service?

He would study Gabe Tully and see if the idea lurking just below the conscious level of thought would surface and make itself known. Gambling . . . the Jao courier ship . . . Terran deaths . . . Jao insults . . . unwarranted risk taking . . .

It all hinted at something potentially useful if he could just pull it together. He would keep this Terran at his side until he knew what it was.

Tully wound up bunking on the carpet. The Jao's quarters were well appointed and he could have used the couch in the corner, but the crusty one called Yaut didn't offer its use and he wasn't about to ask.

First, he wasn't about to ask because he was completely confused by the situation and a little amazed that he was still alive. Mainly, though—speaking plainly and simply—because Yaut scared him. He wasn't big, as Jao went, and Tully was pretty sure he was fairly old. But the way he moved was frightening, with its little hints of controlled savagery. And while Tully didn't really understand all that the Jao word "fraghta" implied, he knew a little.

Only the most prestigious Jao had fraghtas. They seemed to be a weird combination of advisers, protocol experts—and killers. Rob Wiley had once told him that a fraghta was something like a medieval-style Japanese shogun's chief samurai. Tully didn't know much history, beyond American, but he had watched some old Toshirô Mifune movies. And that was what Yaut make him think of. Yojimbo—on a bad day, in a really grumpy mood.

Zzzzzt. Plop goes the head.

So, he stretched out on the floor, keeping very still, while Yaut fed information into a datacom. Finally, the fraghta rose, gave him a disapproving look, and disappeared into the next room. His arms behind his head, Tully stared up at the ceiling, which was dimly visible in reflected starlight from the single small window.

The newly arrived Subcommandant must suspect his connections to the Resistance. That was the only thing that could explain his strange behavior. Twice today, this Jao had passed up opportunities to have Tully punished—or possibly executed, the second time. Going into restricted areas was a lot more serious offense than gambling.

That made no sense. Jao didn't give humans a second chance when they broke rules, in Tully's experience. The Subcommandant must have a reason for doing otherwise. Tully had to get off the base before the Jao went to work on him for names and specifics.

But even leaving Yaut aside, that formidable looking front door was sealed with a field and the telltale red light gleaming beside the sill indicated the presence of an alarm. Tully might be able to pick the lock, given enough time, but he had no way of circumventing the alarm with nothing more than the current contents of his pockets. He would have to wait until tomorrow, then find an opportunity to make tracks.

In the meantime . . . He listened to the sounds coming from the other room. The door stood open, but he heard only the faintest breathing. Though Jao did not sleep the way humans did, they did experience a sort of dormancy phase, though he'd never seen one in that state himself. The Resistance knew very little about the species beyond what battlefield autopsies had revealed. They were stronger than humans, and showed signs of being evolved from water-adapted ancestors. Their bones were denser, their reflexes a bit slower than that of humans. But even though they weren't quite as fast, once they got started, hand to hand combat with a Jao was like trying to fight a gorilla.

But all that was external. What lay between those large and twitching ears was what mattered. How did they think? What motivated their decisions beyond the obvious desire for resources and power? What was reasonable to a Jao? And, most important, what would convince them that humans were too much trouble and they should abandon the effort to hold this world? Terrans had spent twenty years trying to learn those basic facts about their conquerors and had so far failed miserably.

Tully decided that Yaut must be in dormancy. He eased up off the floor and padded quietly over to the sleek datacom embedded in the wall. Colors flowed across its screen like currents in a river. Yaut had left it on, or perhaps they weren't designed to be turned off. Information lay locked behind those colors, if he could figure them out, but Jao never allowed jinau like him access to this technology. He had about as much chance to hack his way in as a monkey would setting up a homepage on the Internet.

Tully lay back down and closed his eyes, weighing his options. His very limited and bad options. On the one hand, he was tempted to remain where he was, in the hope that he might be able to gather more information. On the other hand . . .

No. The risk was too great that the Subcommandant would start torturing him to get information on the Resistance. Or . . . use some method to do so. There were actually no reliable reports of Jao using torture. The creatures were terrifyingly savage in the way they dealt out instant death, but they didn't seem to linger on it. Still, Tully resolved to escape, the first time he got a chance.

CHAPTER
5

The creature was still dormant when Aille rose the next morning. He studied the supine body sprawled across the middle of the floor, head lolling so that it looked dead. His own head was abuzz with new words and syntax and grammatical structures from the language imprinting program he and Yaut now underwent every dormancy period. Half of what he'd absorbed this time skittered through his brain like dry leaves blown in the wind. Much made no sense at all, and the remainder was often puzzling. Still, being familiar with at least one of the planet's languages could only make him more effective on this assignment. A small amount of disorientation was acceptable.

Dawn came in shades of intense red here, the rising sun a great crimson orb low on the horizon, the clouds orange streaks. Aille stepped over Tully, wondering that the normally competent Yaut hadn't provided it a proper nest, and then neutralized the alarm and keyed the doorfield off. Warm humid air rushed against his face and he inhaled the welcoming tang of the ocean.

There were predators in these waters, he remembered from his briefings, but none as large as the ones on his birthworld. The ones here were said to be rare. No real danger even to humans, as inept as they were in water compared to Jao. Aille trotted off toward the shore, leaving Yaut to watch over his new acquisition.

The water had slightly less viscosity than the sea on Marit An, but it was cool and the waves rolled over him with pleasant familiarity. He ducked and swam until he had worked the kinks out of his muscles, then walked back, when the sun had climbed a bit higher, his nap sleek and wet.

He found Yaut standing over the human just outside their new quarters, the fraghta's hands clenched, ears quivering in obvious fury. "It attempted to get away!" he said in Jao. His whiskers were bristling.

"'He,'" Aille corrected. "It admitted to being male last night."

"It will not be male or female or anything else, if it attempts to run again," Yaut said, "because I will grind its bones to powder!"

The human sat on the concrete, arms resting on bent knees, green eyes staring straight ahead as though Aille and Yaut were not even present. Although it had manifested a rudimentary command of Jao last night, it didn't even twitch at the death threat. A large purple blotch now discolored its face on one side and Aille found himself very curious. He shook the rest of the water out of his nap, then walked inside. "Bring it—him," he said without looking back.

A blink later, the human landed with a thump in the middle of the room, and Aille bit back a sigh. His new fraghta was very short of patience when something outraged him. He would have to remember that.

"Attempting to escape from service!" Yaut keyed the doorfield on, then stalked about the room, eyes blazing with green fury. On the floor, the human pulled itself together and resumed its previous position, though its eyes looked a bit dazed. "I would have put it down already and saved you the trouble, but it is technically a member of your service, which requires your permission."

Aille turned and gazed at Yaut impassively, then picked up a brush and worked on his damp nap. "Perhaps he is just badly trained. Surely you could do better."

Yaut's ears swiveled warily. "You wish it trained, rather than put down?"

"He wished to escape," he said and put aside the brush. He studied the human from the corner of his eye. "Does that not suggest he has something to hide? I find my desire to know what weighs larger than violations of custom or practical concerns. Remember that the dead always keep their secrets."

"Then I will, of course, train it, if that is your wish." Yaut's neck was stiff with *disapproval*.

"And check on its background," Aille said. "I wish to know where it came from and what contacts it has."

Yaut picked up his comboard. "I will put a search of the records in motion. In the meantime, I advise you to have it housed elsewhere. It is not fit to share quarters with civilized beings. Trying to escape from service!"

The human glanced up at the fraghta surreptitiously, then looked away again. Aille reached for his weapons harness, where Yaut had left it waiting, and shook it out. At his feet, the human flinched at the unexpected snap.

Aille dressed while considering Yaut's advice. "No," he said finally. "Bind it, if necessary for our safety, but keep it close at hand. These apparently puny creatures held off our forces for longer than any sentients we've ever encountered. It was not simply a matter of their enormous population, nor even of their sophisticated technology. I want to know how they did that, and I think this one might be able to give me the answers. Some of them, at least."

Yaut glared at the human.

"And work on your Terran," Aille added, donning the rest of his uniform. "To speak another species' language is to have an insight into their psychology. I will strive to improve my command of Terran as well."

The human looked up, with that almost Jao-like direct gaze that had struck Aille the first time he met him.

"It's called 'English.'"

Aille directed Yaut to offer the human a tray of food from the dispenser, but the creature waved it away. Either it wasn't hungry, or Jao food did not appeal to his new acquisition. Aille decided he would worry about the logistics of feeding it later.

For now, he was due at the refurbishing facility. He passed up nourishment himself and let his fraghta finish dressing him, taking care with the cloth trousers, the ribbons, the drape of his ceremonial halfcape off his windward shoulder. Firsts were important, as Yaut had noted yesterday. Between them, they would do Pluthrak proud.

A vehicle arrived. It was similar to the one from the day before, a human device refitted with Jao maglev technology. The human jumped out and knocked at the open door, even though Yaut was waiting beside it.

He then raised his hand to his forehead in that sharp, practiced motion which was becoming very familiar. "PFC Andrew Danvers reporting as ordered, sir."

"And-rew Danv-ers." Aille had trouble stringing the human syllables together. The skill would require additional practice. "Do you speak Jao?"

The human soldier hesitated, then answered in English. "A bit, sir, if you do not mind hearing it mangled."

Tully rose and came to the door. "I can translate a little," he said in Jao, "if need be."

Unlike yesterday, the human's grammatical phrasing was good, and even his accent had improved. All in the space of one night, Aille thought. His suspicion that there was more to this human than was immediately evident was strengthened.

Yaut gave Tully another fierce look and Aille realized it would take little provocation for the fraghta to simply put him down him and secure permission retroactively. Attempting to escape from personal service was a grotesque violation of custom, and, like any fraghta would, Yaut felt it keenly.

"Yes," Aille said in English. "Translate where necessary."

The soldier named Danvers glanced at Tully and his eyes widened. Aille supposed it was in reaction to the dark purple blotch on his face where Yaut had struck him.

Aille gestured Tully into the vehicle, as Yaut followed. The human sat in the front with the driver. Yaut rode in silence next to Aille in the rear, his ears clearly displeased with the situation. Aille could almost read his mind: A fraghta's whole *vithrik* was bound up in providing advice along with the voice of experience, and, already, Aille was not heeding him.

The wind was warm and Aille heard the tantalizing sound of waves breaking on the shore as they turned inland and drove along the coast. After a short ride, the vehicle pulled up to a cavernous building open almost its entire length on one side. Cylindrical black ships were cradled in immense frameworks within, as humans swarmed over them like worker insects. Sparks flew behind jumbles of cable and Aille could hear the screech of metal being cut.

Danvers and Tully hopped out immediately. Danvers opened the door to the vehicle and rattled off some words in English, which Tully then translated into quite good Jao. "This is the Refit Facility, sir," he said. "Your personal work area is up on the second floor. Danvers wishes to know if you want him to guide you there."

"Not yet. First, I wish to learn what exactly is done here."

There was another quick exchange between Tully and Danvers. "He will find you a different guide, then, sir," said Tully. "He's not familiar with the facility itself."

Before Tully had finished translating, PFC Danvers had already disappeared into the building without waiting for Aille's assent. That was interesting. Aille had read in the reports that humans in hierarchical systems were normally compulsive about getting permission for everything, even once their duties were clear. Apparently, this jinau had been associating with Jao long enough to have absorbed some elements of Jao rationality.

Yaut stood in the open entrance and stared at the long sleek black ships. "Very big," he grunted, "but oddly proportioned. Perhaps they are intended for fast assault or landing ground troops."

"They are submersibles," Tully said, his gaze riveted to the cradles, "meant for undersea travel. 'Submarines,' we call them, or 'subs' for short. These are the finest in the world. Attack subs and boomers that used to belong to the United States Navy."

"Undersea travel?" Yaut's eyes narrowed. "Why expend resources on that?"

"Because three quarters of our world lies under ocean," Tully said.

Submersing must be difficult for this species, Aille realized, so that they needed artificial aids to achieve it for any length of time. He doubted Jao would ever have conceived of such craft. His kind could travel underwater with very little effort and were born craving the stars instead.

Still, he thought there was something slightly evasive about Tully's response. Aille could understand why humans would have developed seagoing vessels to such an extent. But why travel *under* the water, simply to transport cargo and personnel? The storms on this planet were simply not that severe. There must be some other, or additional reason, for them to have developed a submersible capability.

He broke off the rumination. The Jao supervisor was approaching. She was female, bowlegged and stocky. Her nap was lustrous with health, colored the russet of an exotic far-off kochan like Kaht or Mashdau. Her voice was deep and throaty as her calm black eyes took his measure. "Vaish, Subcommandant. I hope all meets with your approval."

"As do I." He regarded her calmly. Some kochan had done well here. She was bold and forthcoming, alert, a credit to all who'd bred and trained her. "May I have the honor of your name?"

Her eyes crinkled with pleasure. Since Aille's status was vastly greater than hers, he had been perfectly free to dispense with her name, if he so desired. "Nath krinnu Tashnat vau Nimmat. I am one of the supervisors here."

Not a root sept then, but still a related offshoot. Like Yaut's Jithra, very honorable. "I wish to tour the facility," he said, "so I may be more efficient carrying out my duties."

"Yes, Subcommandant." Nath turned and he caught sight of her heartward cheek. No bars of office were incised into the skin, but a shiny patch indicated where one must have been until sometime in the recent past. For some reason, Nath had been demoted.

She headed into the facility, letting Yaut come after her and leaving Aille the place of honor at the back. Aille glanced down at Tully, then followed, trusting the fraghta to restore propriety.

Yaut glanced over his shoulder, then with muffled exclamation, darted back to seize Tully's arm and jerk him ahead of Aille.

"For a jinau, you are very stupid!" the fraghta snarled in Jao. "Show proper respect!"

Yaut's grip was crushing. Jao were much stronger than humans. Had Tully resisted, his arm would have been broken. True, he seemed to smolder resentfully at being manhandled in front of everyone. But he came at once, and kept his gaze straight ahead until Yaut released him. Clearly, although some of his actions would indicate otherwise, he was not stupid. Indeed, he even seemed quick-witted.

What could Tully know—or think he knew—that was so valuable he would risk death or a beating to conceal it? Aille found himself wondering. He could see no other explanation for Tully's attempt to escape from service. And how could he be so certain Aille would get it out of him, if he did not escape? Perhaps he would learn all the answers eventually, if the creature survived.

Yaut was employing *wrem-fa*, body-learning, where physical responses were used to instruct rather than verbal explanations. The ancient method was quite effective with Jao, but it might not be with Terrans, he realized. Tully at any rate certainly did not seem to be responding well so far.

Ahead, a pungent, not unpleasant, smell filled the air. It was an oddly familiar smell, too, though still distinctive. Nath saw his nostrils twitching and said, "Yes, that's the odor of fresh cut wood for the cradles. Native varieties, of course. It's a primitive material, but effective and easily to hand. Humans use wood in their construction far more extensively than we ever do."

"I see." Aille walked past presses and saws, cranes and winches, drills and bank after bank of diagnostic equipment, some of which he recognized from his just completed training. He would not be required to operate any of it, of course, but he'd had it drilled into him that a good officer understands what his staff are doing at all times. To be ignorant of such matters was to court sloth and inefficiency.

Up close, the ships were impressive. The black hulls swept overhead, much bigger than they looked at a distance. They had a massive appearance, even more so than Narvo ships. He could see what appeared to be weapon ports, now closed, on some of the vessels.

He turned to their guide. "What are the workers trying to accomplish, Supervisor Nath?"

"These Terran ships, originally constructed to travel underwater, will make very suitable hulls for spacecraft once their technology is updated," she said. "So we're currently installing Jao drives and sensing systems, as well as replacing all controls pertaining to operation in a liquid environment, rather than the vacuum of space. Later we will refit the weaponry."

He reached out and rubbed the metal with his fingertips. It was surprisingly warm to the touch.

"I will show you the interior," Nath said.

Aille and his little entourage followed the supervisor. Drill bits squealed as they passed. Welding arcs flashed. Cables snaked across the concrete floor and up into the sleek ships as the race to refit Earth's fleet of submarines went on.

Following Supervisor Nath, Aille climbed the scaffolding that bracketed one of the curiously oblong ships and descended a ladder into its interior. It was much closer inside than anything a Jao would have designed. Not only were these Terrans smaller in frame, but they must also must be relentlessly social, he reflected, to be able to live on top of one another for extended periods of time. He couldn't even imagine a marriage-group being able to take these conditions for more than a few solar cycles at a time without losing cohesion, much less a gathering of unrelated individuals who lacked the common bond of kochan or taif.

Nath, showing the quick mind he had already suspected she possessed, seemed to have divined his thoughts.

"The plan is for jinau troops to staff the vessels, after the refit, with only a few Jao in command. There should be enough room for the Jao officers, after the unnecessary equipment for operating underwater is removed and replaced with our own spacegoing systems. As a rule—though not always—Jao technology is more compact than human."

She continued to explain as they moved through the cramped ship. Very quickly, Aille came to realize that the reports he'd read had drastically understated the sophistication of human technology. Where the reports tended to use terms like "convoluted" and "excessively intricate"—often enough, "bizarre"—Nath's explanations showed an appreciation for the subtlety involved. Many areas on the submarine served double and triple duty, depending on what was needed at any particular moment. He was particularly intrigued by a table in the "wardroom" used as a surgical bay in times of need.

Tully had waited topside with Yaut, who wasn't about to let the human out of his sight, but he wished Yaut were here so he could see what the wily old fraghta would have made of all this. He turned to Supervisor Nath. "Have you ever ridden in one of these under the water?"

She grimaced. "Once. It was a dreadful experience, being closed in with that many humans. These ships can dive quite deep, much deeper than any Jao could possibly swim."

"I wonder why they expended so much ingenuity and resources on such travel?" He ran a hand over the gleaming fittings. "Have they constructed cities beneath their seas, or discovered resources that can only be extracted this way?"

"They did utilize some underwater resources," she said, "and humans seem to set great store on the concept of 'exploration.' They're like crechelings, that way, always wanting to climb and dig and wedge themselves into the most inaccessible places. They think nothing of scampering up cliffs and mountains, and even crawling through caves. In fact, it is impossible to keep them from it, even when they are quite likely to die in the attempt. But these particular vessels were warships, not exploratory ones."

Aille was surprised. "Why would they fight each other under the water? They can't live there."

Nath fell into a quite elegant rendition of *rueful-puzzlement.* "Hard to say. I get along with them rather well, but they still sometimes seem like lunatics to me."

"How large a crew did this one carry?" He ducked his head, but still grazed his ears as he stepped through another hatch into a forward chamber filled with equipment.

"Over a hundred," she said. "I gather the number varied, according to the type of submersible and the nature of the mission. Records are spotty. They destroyed much of their armaments, once defeat became inevitable. A number of these ships were taken out into the ocean and 'scuttled,' as they term it. Deliberately sunk."

He turned and met her eyes. "And their crews?"

"Most of them left the ships beforehand, leaving a few officers to do the 'scuttling.' Those officers mostly died. Humans are unfathomable, in some ways. Courage is of course admirable, and a virtue for any sentient species. But they seem to think nothing of throwing away their lives for the most trivial reasons. We had already defeated them, so what was the point of destroying the ships?"

He rubbed his head with one hand, thinking. Such a strange species. He wasn't sure he was ever going to get his mind around their alien way of thinking.

Nath led him then to the rear of the ship, where the propellant system was being replaced with a Jao drive appropriate for space. Only Jao techs worked back here. Such advanced knowledge was forbidden to humans.

The techs, all female and all bred from hearty if not high-status stock, were pleased to have their work admired. In fact, they expended far more time explaining it to him than he had intended. Clearly, they were deeply impressed to be visited personally by a scion of Pluthrak.

It was all very bewildering to Aille. Jao technology was being spliced into Terran, often, it seemed, with uneasy results. When, at length, he was able to free himself, he'd had enough of technical details for the moment.

"I'll take you to your office then," said Nath.

"What is an 'office'?"

Nath looked momentarily abashed. "Sorry, I meant your personal work area. 'Office' is the Terran term for it—English term, I should say. Like a lot of Jao who have been here for a while, I have picked up some native expressions. That one is particularly handy."

He returned topside to Yaut and Tully. The supervisor conducted them to the second floor and promised to return later to take him through the ground assault vehicles.

The room was cool and quiet, though composed of those ubiquitous Terran straight lines and angles. Conditioned air was being pumped in through vents at a steady rate. Aille sank into a black chair upholstered with what the supervisor had told him was Terran "leather," a local product evidently very durable. It was soft and supple, yielding to his weight. Very pleasing in a tactile way, he decided.

Was the substance rare? Nath did not seem to think it was. If so, it was odd that this "leather" had not already become an item for export. Like the many signs of ruin and decay he'd seen in the short time since his arrival, Aille found that disturbing. What was the Narvo Governor doing with this planet?

Yaut took up a post in the corner of the office, consulting his comboard, while keeping an eye on his new human trainee. Tully remained standing. His restless green eyes roved the walls, the doors, and Aille could almost see his escape plans forming.

But that was a minor problem, which he had already arranged to forestall. He'd had a brief, quiet discussion with Nath, in which the supervisor had proved as efficient and helpful as she had with everything else.

A knock sounded on the door. Yaut keyed the security field off. A human stood there, wearing civilian clothing instead of a uniform. He held up a gleaming black band. "You requested a locator, sir?"

"That is correct," Yaut said.

"Come forward," Aille said, motioning at the man.

The human, gray-haired, shorter and more squat than Tully, came into the room. Yaut took the locator and turned it over to key in Aille's personal code.

Aille leaned back in the chair. "Your name is Willard Belk, yes?" The human nodded.

"Supervisor Nath recommended you to me," Aille said. "You are now attached to my personal service. Henceforth, you will report only to me. Your other duties are secondary."

"Yes, sir. Will you require a locator for me as well?"

Aille stared at him, nonplussed for an instant. "No, of course not. Why? You have done nothing to require it."

Tully's head jerked up. He glanced sharply at the black band and Aille could see understanding dawn in his eyes. The human lurched to his feet, his gaze riveted to the device in Yaut's hand.

"You should see which hand he prefers before you place it, sir," Belk said. "He has less chance of tampering if you place it on his more dextrous hand."

Tully whirled upon him. "Collaborator!" His heartward hand curled into a fist. For a moment, Aille thought he intended to launch himself across the room and strike the other Terran.

Whether he would or not immediately became a moot point, as Yaut pinned him easily to the wall with one hand while holding up the locator with the other.

"Preferred hand?" Yaut was clearly mystified. "Humans have affection for one limb over another?"

Belk eyed Tully's still-clenched fist. "I'd say he's right-handed, sir. Most humans are."

"I do not understand," Yaut said.

"This one." Belk stepped forward to point at the Terran's heartward hand—the one he had made into a fist. "Put it on this one."

With a heave of his powerful shoulders, Yaut grappled Tully and held him still, then clicked the black locator band around his heartward wrist. As the contacts closed, a bank of tiny amber lights sprang into life. When he was released, Tully sagged back against the wall, staring wildly at his wrist, his gaze that of a cornered animal.

His eyes fell on Belk and grew narrow. "Stinking bootlicker," he hissed.

Belk's eyes were equally slitted. He rattled off a number of words in his own language, too quickly for Aille to follow all of it.

"—uck you too, weasel. Tell it to my wife and kids. The ones you murdered twenty years ago, you—" Incomprehensible terms followed, which Aille suspected were pure invective. "—ance on your grave, weasel, and any weasel I find."

Aille was puzzled by the exchange. Tully seemed much too young to have slain anyone twenty orbital cycles before. He suspected what was involved here was a human clan quarrel of some kind, rather than a personal one.

By then, Belk had regained his composure. He turned away from Tully and faced Aille, shaking his head. "What do you require from me now, sir?"

"Inform your supervisor that you have been taken into my personal service."

"Yes, sir!" A moment later, the man was gone.

CHAPTER
6

Tully pried surreptitiously at the sleek black band around his right wrist. But, even as his fingers pulled and wrenched, he knew it was pointless. The device wasn't going to come off. He'd seen these before—on corpses. Fueled by the electrical energy of his own body, it would never come off until it lost power, and that wouldn't happen until he died.

And, until then, the Jao would always know where he was. His days as an effective spy were over, unless he could figure out a way to get rid of it, and now even escape would be impossible. He glared at Aille, who was staring into the console built into the desktop, one hand propped under his broad chin in a curiously human gesture.

Tully's head suddenly rocked back and hit the wall. A moment later, dazed, he slid to the floor. He blinked up through a red fog and realized Yaut had cuffed him with the back of one hand.

"You are in his service," the fraghta said roughly. "All who see you will know this, therefore you can no longer behave without manners. All you do reflects on Pluthrak!"

"Why?" he said in Jao around a split lip. "What possible use could I be to the likes of him?"

Aille turned to look down at him with an expression Tully could not name. Green patterns glittered in those black eyes, changing from second to second like a kaleidoscope. "You will make yourself of use by telling me your secrets," he said.

"I don't have any secrets." Tully tried to rise, but his legs buckled and he sagged back against the wall. The room seemed to swell and shrink, as though it were breathing. "None of us do. You stripped away all of Earth's secrets twenty years ago."

"Not all." Aille turned back to his console. His ears were relaxed, unconcerned. "Yaut has been checking your background and the results are interesting. You never stay anywhere very long and your records are for a younger individual than your appearance indicates. Very scanty records, too. I think you have still a few secrets and, soon enough, I will know them all."

In the afternoon, after familiarizing himself with the electronic data retrieval systems in his work area, Aille again sallied forth into his new realm, this time to inspect the ground assault vehicles undergoing refit with Jao technology in an adjacent series of buildings. There was an astonishing variety of forms filling bay after bay, tools and parts scattered everywhere in what could only be called controlled confusion.

Most of the vehicles were painted the same bewildering patterns of light green and tan splotches on a background of darker green. Did this color scheme have some cultural significance? he wondered. He had read that Terrans were very superstitious. Perhaps these colors were intended to appease their gods.

There wasn't as much refitting to do here, since these vehicles were already meant for surface travel. But their primitive mechanical propulsion systems were all now being changed out with Jao maglev components able to handle any terrain.

One entire section of the refitting floor was devoted to replacing kinetic energy weapons with Jao lasers. Tully gazed at them with what seemed to be a mixture of glumness and disapproval, but was otherwise docile enough.

Aille stopped beside a massive vehicle topped with a rotating gun turret. "Did they develop all these vehicles for their struggle against the Jao?" he said, raising his voice to carry over the omnipresent screech of power tools.

Nath snorted. "I think you will find these creatures the most quarrelsome beings ever evolved! From their earliest recorded history, they have fought one another as vigorously as they ever resisted us. All of these armored vehicles and mobile assault weapons were in service long before we made landfall on this world."

"Interesting." Aille walked around the large vehicle, noting the thick armor plating, the open hatch above and the bristling array of communications antennae. The metal was cool and grainy beneath his hand. "Perhaps that was why they were so effective in their initial resistance—they had a great deal of practice."

"Perhaps." Nath sounded unconvinced. "It boggles the mind, though, to think of kochan fighting kochan, pitting strength against strength, rather than creating associations and binding assets in a common cause. Think of what they might have accomplished, had they molded themselves into one massive unified power, rather than a squabbling cluster of minor political states. It would have taken us twice as long to conquer them, if we could have done it at all without obliterating life from the planet."

She stepped aside as a pair of human techs wheeled a Jao laser generator on a cart toward a gutted vehicle. "In the long view, our conquest benefits them as well. They might have annihilated themselves altogether before very much longer and the Ekhat would have encountered no resistance at all in this sector. Now, perhaps they will have time to mature as a species and create a new cooperative social order."

Voices rose suddenly above the clamor of metal against metal and the whir of saws. Aille rotated until he located their source, then threaded his way through techs and machinery, finally emerging near the end of the refit bays where a grizzled dark-haired human male was facing off with a larger Jao official.

"You can't just slag these guns!" the human was saying. "In fact, it's stupid to replace them with lasers in the first place!" His face was reddening, a hue which Aille was coming to associate with overstimulation in humans. He cocked his head, trying to read the creature's posture. Was that fear? Anger? Greed?

A handful of humans crowded around, their faces showing a similar response. Two Jao guards pushed them back, then exhorted them in low voices to return to their stations.

"I fought at the battle of Chicago," the man continued in an insistent tone of voice, ignoring the guards. "We took your tanks out right and left. If you Jao hadn't had air supremacy, things would have turned out very different. Don't think they wouldn't."

With the flick of an ear, the Jao official seized the human's shirt and lifted him into the air. "Your only function here is to make yourself useful to the Jao. Either you do the work assigned without further comment or you go to the stockade. We are not interested in preserving inferior human gadgets."

Aille glanced at Nath. The supervisor was obviously striving for *indifferent-patience*, but he could detect underlying unease, perhaps even anger. She did not seem happy with the official and the way he was conducting himself, he thought.

Aille stepped out of the shadows and the Jao official seemed to see him for the first time. He released the human he was clutching and swatted him away with a cuff to the side of his head.

"They are idiots," he said. "They persist in believing their primitive toys have value. Too bad we cannot shove them forward to face the Ekhat on their own. Then they would have some idea of what was coming and stop prattling about the merits of their technology! If their hardware was so superior, why does Terra belong to the Jao now?"

"Indeed." Aille glanced at the human who'd been arguing. He looked dazed from the cuffing he'd received. It hadn't been a severe blow, but humans were less sturdy than Jao. "Just exactly what is it this one wishes to preserve?"

The Jao glanced at a discarded gun mount and scowled. "One of their primitive kinetic weapons. We will melt it down and make something useful out of it."

"Perhaps he has a point," Aille said. "It is true, after all, that our ground vehicles suffered tremendous casualties during the conquest. Inflicted, as I recall, by these same perhaps-not-so-obsolete kinetic weapons."

"And who are you, to have opinions? I see no command bars on your cheeks!" The Jao official seemed to suffer from a short temper. He braced his shoulders, then gestured at the human he'd cuffed and bellowed at the guards. "Take this human to the stockade! I do not want him on the work floor stirring up the rest of them."

"No, I do not think that would be wise." Aille stepped forward. "Leave him where he is."

The guards looked to Nath who waved them back. "Do as he says," she commanded. Seeing the cant of her ears, they obeyed immediately and took up a formal *waiting-for-instruction* stance.

Jowls quivering, the official turned on Aille. "I do not know who you are, smoothface, but you have no idea how to handle these creatures! They are worse than crechelings, because they are incapable of learning from their mistakes."

Yaut stiffened at his tone, and even Tully, skulking in the background, looked as surprised as his alien physique would allow.

What would have old Brem said, Aille wondered, and then knew. Despite the aggressive tenor of the moment, kochan-father Brem would have seen this as an opportunity to widen association. "This individual expressed a difference of opinion," he said carefully. "It was not given in the most respectful of manners, perhaps, but disagreement on how best to be of use is not a punishable offense." He regarded the official in the attitude of *mild-expectation*. "If I am in error, I will amend my behavior."

"Ignorant upstart!" The official was quivering with rage. "You should return to your birthing compound and learn to listen to your betters!"

"I am striving to instruct myself here," Aille said. He curved his arms in the classic *wishing-to-be-of-use* posture favored by Pluthrak body-stylists. "The disagreement is clearly over how to make these machines—these 'tanks,' as I am told they are called—function more effectively. This human may be right, or he may be wrong; but, either way, holding an erroneous opinion is not a crime."

The Jao took the human worker by the arm and shoved him toward the two guards. "I want this troublemaker punished!"

"Director Vamre," Nath said, assuming a stance of *most-urgent-need*. "Will you join me outside for a consultation?"

"I will not!" Vamre glanced at the guards. "Well?"

The two pairs of green-black eyes were steady as they looked to Aille. Clearly, they now realized who he was. "Do not obey him," Aille said to them. "No one need be punished here. Even if there were such a need, Director Vamre lacks the authority to have it carried out against my wishes."

"We will see about that!" Vamre shoved the argumentative human back against the side of the tank and strode off, every line of his body a crude rendition of *not-to-be-thwarted*.

The man put a hand to his head and then turned to Aille, limping a bit. "Thank you," he said, speaking now in Jao. "I did not mean to make trouble. I was only trying to do my job properly."

Aille ran a hand over the tank, studying the gaping undercarriage where the massive treads had already been replaced with much more compact magnetic suspension drives. The smooth ice-blue metal of Jao origin glittered, contrasting against the dull, mottled human colors. "Do you truly believe your kinetic energy weapons superior to Jao lasers?"

"If you want to fight in an atmosphere anything like this one," the man said. "Your ordnance was designed for fighting in a vacuum, not terrestrial combat. We were able to get around Jao lasers any number of ways, from steam clouds to throwing up chaff."

Yaut's scowl caught his eye. Aille turned away so the fraghta wouldn't distract him from this line of investigation. "And Jao technology has nothing to offer?"

The man spread his hands. Aille noticed his skin pigmentation was browner than Tully's, his face more lined, his thick black hair shot through with gray. "I didn't say that. The maglev drive is a pure joy. And Jao targeting systems are superior to our own, not to mention your countermeasure electronics. I have no problem with them."

"Have any of those systems been installed yet?"

"Yes, they have, sir." The man glanced up at the top of the tank where a dull-green hatch stood open. "Would you like to take a look?"

"I would," Aille said. He watched the other climb laboriously up onto the lower deck, favoring his heartward leg, then followed.

The human pulled himself onto the turret and then lowered his body feet-first into the interior. A moment later, his head popped back up. "This is a grand old lady," he said in Terran. "She deserves to fight again."

"It has gender?" Aille stepped up to the tank's lower deck, then eyed the narrow hatch, wondering if he would fit. It looked too tight for Jao shoulders. "Jao machines are not equipped with gender. In what regard do Terran machines possess it?"

"Only in our minds," the man said. "Humans like to personalize things." He pointed to a notation in human script along the side of the vehicle, and then to a similar notation on the tank next to it. "We call this one *Iron Mistress.* Over there's *Horny Horse.* That one's, ah, not female."

It was all quite mystifying. But Aille put the matter aside for the moment. The human had just thrust out his hand, the fingers extended and the palm open. "My name is Rafe Aguilera."

Naming oneself without invitation was a grave social error

among Jao, but he doubted this human was being intentionally rude. Aguilera stared at him, hand outstretched. Ritual touching was important to this species, Aille remembered suddenly. He had read of that. With only the slightest hesitation, he grasped the proffered hand.

Aguilera's skin was warm, the palm hardened by work, the fingers strong, though the underlying bones were frail. The human tightened his grip, then released Aille's hand and dropped back down into the vehicle. "You can't see the new electronics unless you come inside." His voice echoed tinnily.

With a sigh, Aille thrust his feet into the open hatch, then wedged himself through, sticking at the shoulders until he squirmed. The dimensions definitely had not been designed with Jao in mind, he told himself as his bones creaked.

It was dark inside, until Aguilera flipped several switches. Then a bank of controls came to life, gleaming red and amber in the dimness with occasional spots of green. Aille blinked in surprise. The interior was well crafted, every *az* of space utilized with nothing wasted, an unexpectedly elegant arrangement. Again, as he'd found earlier with the submarine, human technology could be dazzlingly subtle.

Aguilera had settled into a seat at the front of the vehicle and was gazing at the controls and periscope with the satisfaction of a successful predator. "Those were the days," he said softly in Terran. "My last assignment was as tank commander, right before I took the hit on my leg that put me out of action for good. We thought we couldn't lose, once we finally had a chance to mix it up with you on the ground."

"But you did lose," Aille said, calculating the approximate age of this individual. "And, by all accounts, your species does not taking loss lightly, which makes me curious. Why do you agree to share your—" He searched for the right word. "—expertise with your conquerors?"

Aguilera sat back in the seat, hands laced across his middle. In that position, he almost looked as though he'd assumed *careful-contemplation*. But humans were not Jao, Aille cautioned himself. They did not reason like Jao. He must never fall into the trap of believing they did.

"I was a good soldier," the human said at last. His skin gleamed red under the indicators' light. He reached out and brushed dust off a glowing dial. "A damn good soldier, in fact. I tried my hand at other work after the war, whatever I could find, but soldiering is really what I'm good at. And I couldn't do it anymore, not even for the Jao, with this bad leg." He grimaced at the limb stretched out stiffly before him. "But then this refit was mandated. When the call went out for skilled workers, I realized I could at least use what I knew to put these babies back into service. I got married a few years ago, and now I have kids—and my family needs to eat. This outfit pays better wages than you'll find anywhere else in this part of the world these days. So here I am."

Interesting. Aille wondered what Yaut would make of that explanation. Beneath the alien idiom, it was surprisingly Jao-like, for creatures deemed semi-incomprehensible in the reports. Aille was beginning to think that "semi-incomprehensible" was an evasion, of sorts, almost a dereliction of duty. Just a sloppy way of saying: *understanding them is too much work.*

Aille leaned over, wedging himself into a tight space never meant for the breadth of Jao shoulders. The new electronics were grafted underneath the console, their housing ice-blue against the duller Terran shades. If the submarine had been cramped, it was roomy next to this. He had to exhale to extricate himself. These machines would have to be staffed by jinau troops. No Jao would ever be able to function effectively down here.

"Activate the laser sight," he said.

Aguilera nodded and flipped several more switches. The hum of the Jao targeting mechanism sprang to life and throbbed through him, comforting in its familiarity. He had trained on these. Like Aguilera, here was something he knew how to do.

He squeezed between the front chair and the console, eyeing the spliced interface. "The systems are compatible?" he asked in Jao.

"To a point," Aguilera said. "It has taken a great deal of creative engineering and we won't really know how successful we've been until we field test."

Aguilera's command of the Jao language was genuinely excellent. Even his accent was not very pronounced. Aille took one last look around the interior, then climbed back out, painfully squeezing himself through again. Yaut glared up at him from the floor, while Tully stood against a dismantled tank nearby.

Aguilera followed him as Aille hopped down. He motioned to Yaut, who, by the angle of head and spine, looked to be fully in the throes of *impatient-disapproval.* "This matter warrants further investigation," he said. "Arrange some interviews with Jao veterans of human battles as soon as possible. I am curious to know the validity of this one's claims."

His eyes surveyed the massive battle machine with its scorch marks and dents. "If he is right, then we are making a grave error in allocation of resources. With the Ekhat nearly at hand, we have no room for errors."

Yaut grunted his assent and motioned to Tully.

"And leave Tully with me," Aille said, holding out his hand for the locator control. "I am not sure he can survive any more training today."

Yaut passed over the small black rectangle, then disappeared into the maze of maintenance and refit bays. Aille turned to the supervisor, Nath krinnu Tashnat vau Nimmat, who was pacing with more than a hint of discomposure in her manner. "Shall we proceed?" he said.

"The director has been too busy to heed base bulletins," she said. "He did not realize who you were."

"I took no offense," Aille said. "I am newly assigned, with no command bars. He committed no error, beyond believing he had the authority to punish workers under my command." He paused. "Have there been punishments meted out for similar expressions of opinion?"

She reached out and rubbed at a deep scratch on the side of the tank. "Yes," she said. "Director Vamre considers humans to be only 'clever, semi-trainable vermin.' If it were not for the urgency of the refit schedule and the shortage of experienced Jao technicians—who couldn't fit themselves into many of these work spaces, anyway—he would not allow them on the floor at all."

"Interesting." He trailed as she led him toward the far end where mobile artillery were also being altered according to Jao specifications. Tully did not immediately follow, then Aille heard his muffled exclamation of pain as the distance exceeded the device's set range and it dispensed a substantial shock through the wristband.

Such was *wrem-fa.* Feet shuffled as Tully hurried to catch up.

CHAPTER
7

Yaut retraced his steps back through the huge building, then stood blinking out in the torrid yellow alien sunlight, trying to decide how best to carry out his current responsibility. His charge was becoming independent far too fast for Yaut's tastes. Youths like Aille always thought they were ready for action much sooner than reality dictated. They thought what they'd read and heard and reasoned out was just as useful as anything their assigned fraghta had experienced.

Nothing substituted for experience though. The senses taught wisdoms the conscious mind only partially comprehended. *Wremfa*, body-learning, it was called, laid down lessons in the brain too deep for conscious understanding.

Fortunately, his own body-learning was telling him that Aille's instincts were good. Veterans would know the right of this. If human kinetic weapons had any value, veterans of the local conquest would certainly say so—to him, in private.

He found their Terran driver using a cloth to polish the outside of the vehicle in which they'd arrived. "I wish talking with Jao soldiers," he said in the slippery local tongue. "Where this doing best?"

The spindly creature brushed pale overgrown nap back out of his eyes. His skin gleamed with moisture. "I can take you to Jao Country," he said in Terran. "There are a number of clubs back on the base."

Yaut waved a hand, signifying *tentative-acceptance*, then reminded himself to nod, as these creatures most likely did not understand Jao postures. "Being acceptable. Take."

The driver opened the door for him and Yaut slid in, wondering at the reasons for this peculiar behavior. He made no objection, though he certainly would have, had the action been done by another Jao. That would have been a deliberate insult, an unspoken insinuation that Yaut was too feeble to open a door for himself. But here, he was quite sure, was simply another of those peculiar native customs.

Yaut's nose crinkled at the human odors that still clung to the upholstery. The odor was not unpleasant, simply unfamiliar. The door clicked shut as he was moving over and then the safety field winked on.

The vehicle lifted on its magnetic repulsars and glided across the steaming concrete roadway. Outside, Yaut noticed a few clouds had formed and already their undersides were dark-gray and ominous. He checked his board for a local weather report: Rain, it said, followed by more rain in the evening. The temperature, though hot, was within the comfort range for Jao, but commanders were cautioned to remember that humans had much less tolerance. Experience had proven the creatures tended to die when overworked in this level of heat.

Strange, he thought. Why had they ever inhabited this latitude, if their physiology was not suited for these conditions?

The Jao, of course, had been crafted, not left to the messy randomness of evolutionary chance. The Ekhat had come across them when they were only low level sentients, then redesigned them to be hearty, able to withstand any number of climatic extremes, and highly intelligent. Slaves were too valuable to be allowed to die at the slightest environmental provocation.

The driver increased the vehicle's speed so that buildings flicked by, little more than blurs. He had the impression of human faces, Jao faces, other vehicles, sleek structures poured and molded in the Jao fashion, rather than heaped up, then bolted together as humans did. The car swerved to one side and stopped suddenly in the shadow of a looming portal, but the safety field pinned him safely in its grip.

The driver turned and looked over the seat, his face a pale oval. "This is as far as I can take you, sir. Humans aren't allowed past this gate."

Yaut peered out into the garish yellow sunshine. A heavily fortified guard post blocked the way. Two uniformed Jao gazed back at him without curiosity. "What being beyond?"

"Jao Country," he said. The safety field faded. "They'll let you in." He scrambled out, then opened the door for Yaut again. "But I'll have to wait, unless you want me to go back for the Subcommandant."

Yaut pondered. "No," he said, still struggling with the native language, "he will seeing to his transport. Waiting, you."

The driver nodded and climbed back into the vehicle.

Yaut straightened his halfcape, then approached the gate with its two Jao guards. The nearer, a female, was obviously low-kochan, though sturdy enough. Her shoulders slumped in *jaded-indifference*. The other, also female and even more indolent, had no visible *vai camiti* and only one small service bar branded into her heartward cheek. She affected a credible, though graceless, *lack-of-perception*, gazing out over his head as though he weren't there.

The gate was made of a sliding metal grill that could be retracted to admit traffic. The guards stood behind a window inside a small building, barely large enough to hold the two of them. He stepped up to the windows, whiskers bristling. The effrontery of these two! They should be soundly beaten! He wondered if Aille would be displeased if he took a few moments to do it here and now on his own initiative.

The first guard's eyes flicked toward him as he reached out for the bar blocking his way. "What do you want, short-legs?"

It had been a long time since Yaut had heard that particular insult. These days, most Jao would take one look at the array of service brands on his cheeks, not to mention his scars, and know better than to make careless personal remarks. Discipline had slipped here—good sense, even more so.

"What difference does it make what I want?" he said, holding fast on to his temper. "As I understand it, this portion of the base is restricted to Jao only. I am Jao. I wish to come in."

"Not so fast," the shorter of the two said. "We have a log to fill out. State your purpose."

"I am on the business of Subcommandant Aille krinnu ava Pluthrak," he said, holding himself in *stern-admonishment*.

The guard glanced over at her workmate. "Pluthrak?" she said. "Here?" Her posture subtly shifted to imply *rude-disbelief*.

The other's ears flattened in amusement. "Hey, short-legs, I have Pluthrak business to conduct too. Perhaps I should accompany you."

"How interesting," Yaut said. "I was not aware, as the Subcommandant's fraghta, that he had requested your assistance, but by all means, come with me. In fact, I insist upon it."

She was, he noted, a rangy, raw-boned creature, who bore but a single service bar on her own cheek. Her *vai camiti* was a scattering of haphazard stripes of no discernible pattern, as though two widely divergent kochan had produced in her an unsuccessful mixture of genes. Homely as well as ill-mannered, such as she would never be called back to her birthworld to breed.

He pulled out his personal board, noted her badge number, then dispatched a command to reassign her to Aille's personal service. Two blinks later, it was approved. He repressed a sigh. Aille's retinue was growing more quickly than Yaut would have preferred. But that was to be expected in a posting like this, he supposed.

He turned back, pleased to see *startlement* overtake the guard's— no, former guard's—entire body. "I hope you have experience as a personal bodyguard," he said. "Or, if not, can learn quickly. Subcommandant Aille dislikes incompetence. I detest it."

"I—do not understand." In her confusion, she had abandoned any attempt at more sophisticated postures and fell into the arms-akimbo childishness of *open-bafflement*.

Turning the board around, he held it up. The small screen displayed the notation that her file had been transferred to Aille's direct command. She turned to the other female. "I have been reassigned," she said. "Just like that!"

"Oh, not 'just like that,'" he said testily. "You had to work at it. Most guards would just have admitted me, after ascertaining my identity. You had to go out of your way to bring yourself so thoroughly to my notice. Now *vithrik* forbids that I should leave the rest of the base prey to your ineptness."

Her ears sagged. "You cannot mean this! You have not even asked for my qualifications."

"Beyond being an idiot in need of reeducation?" He snorted. "I am doing this facility a kindness. With you at the gate, humans will overrun us in no time!"

She looked as though she would continue protesting, then lowered her head and subsided. He let his body settle into the lines of *gruff-approval*. This one would not require as much training as the dull-witted Tully. And Yaut had sensed some potential in her, beneath the coarse exterior.

"Precede me," he said, as the gate slid open.

The artillery was much more impressive than Aille had anticipated. Kinetic missile weapons were normally the most primitive of tech. Nath showed him row after row waiting out on the refit floor, pieces with bafflingly intricate designations: "howitzer" was the only one he remembered. For creatures who had been formed by haphazard evolution, rather than by the deliberate craft of a more advanced species, humans had certainly invested a great deal of ingenuity on their weaponry.

That, along with their vast population, had been a potent factor in their able defense of Terra. Humans reproduced at an amazing rate. They had, in fact, overbred this world, forcing many of their fellows to extend their habitat into marginally habitable areas. In a few hundred more orbital cycles, they might well have poisoned their environment irrevocably. It was actually fortunate for them, as Nath had remarked earlier, that the Jao had arrived when they did. This species needed a firm hand in curbing its excesses.

A certain percentage of the artillery had already been refitted as Jao lasers. Aille wondered if these workers felt as strongly about Terran tech as had those converting the tanks.

Ears down, he turned to Nath. "Summon the human called Rafe Aguilera to my office to wait for my return."

Her stance altered to the rigid bow of *reluctant-aquiescence*. "If you have changed your mind and wish him punished, I can see to it immediately and save you the bother."

"For disagreeing with policy?" Aille's whiskers twitched as he glanced out over industrious humans busily removing barrels and electronics from their defeated artillery. Several, who had been surreptitiously watching the two of them, hastily ducked down and reapplied themselves to their jobs. "If that has become a crime, then are we not all guilty of it from time to time? Shall we punish ourselves at the first hint of divergent thought?"

Her body was difficult to read. Aille thought she was both uncertain and . . . trying to conceal something.

"Whatever you wish, Subcommandant," she said.

"Forget I am Pluthrak, for the moment." He saw blatant, unalloyed *incredulity* overtake her. "I am Jao first, and Jao want only what is best for the coming battles. If we keep an open mind when these Terrans have ideas, we might gain an edge. As far as we know, the Ekhat have no Terrans under their control."

"They have more than a thousand other races, including some isolated pockets of Jao," Nath pointed out. "I find it hard to believe Terrans could change the balance in our favor."

His gaze turned inward. He saw again the visual records of the Terran Conquest, the casualty lists longer than any in Jao history except when battling the Ekhat themselves. "They fought long past the point of reason," he said softly. "When you examine the history of our engagements, these creatures were cunning, utterly undaunted. They sacrificed their own people, their own lands, to gain the least advantage. It took so much more to make them surrender than we had ever anticipated. We can use those same qualities to our advantage, if we are wise enough to understand them."

"All that may just indicate how foolish they were. So says Governor Oppuk. I have heard him point out myself that those inhabiting this political moiety lost huge amounts of breeding stock and arable land through their stubborn resistance. A more intelligent race, he says, would have understood they were defeated long before and preserved what still remained to them."

Aille found the way she worded her statements revealing. Now he knew what she was trying to conceal. She had faithfully reported the Governor's words, without actually stating she agreed with them.

For someone in her position, caution was not surprising. But Aille was Pluthrak. He would not offend Narvo unnecessarily, but he had no fear of them either.

"I think he is wrong," he said bluntly. "With planning, we can turn these same Terrans into a great asset—but only if we accept that a weapon must be used according to its own nature. Trying to hammer with a spear is simply stupid."

Her whiskers twitched and she lowered her voice, moving in closer so only he could hear. "You are Pluthrak, so you can afford to take chances, but the rest of us cannot. Do not get sentimental about these humans. They did indeed fight very well, and, to be frank, I think Aguilera is right in his dispute with Vamre. But they do not think the way we do, and you cannot depend upon them. They have much courage and intelligence, but no honor."

He fell silent, realizing it was unseemly to argue with her larger acquaintance and experience with this world. But he'd viewed the records over and over until he knew them like the markings of his own face. The histories of the invasion told a different tale, to him. A tale of a species whose sense of honor was very different from Jao, but there nonetheless. That, he was sure—not capriciousness and perversity—was what explained their behavior.

He considered Nath closely for a moment. She had taken a considerable risk, speaking so frankly to him on such short acquaintance. There was that to admire about her, along with much else. And, certainly, it would be pleasant to have her in close proximity. Her *vai camiti* was truly quite splendid.

"I will take your viewpoint under advisement," he said finally. "It may be I am in error, and I will want your counsel. As for the other, I am taking you into my service. You need no longer be wary of such as Vamre." He thought it would be needlessly undiplomatic to add the rest: *or even Narvo.*

For a moment, Nath's composure was lost in a childish stance of *open-surprise.* But she recovered quickly, and assumed *delight* combined with a hasty *determination-to-serve-well.* "You do me great honor. What duties will you require of me?"

"For the foreseeable future, simply continue with what you are doing. Of course, now you will be able to oversee the work without interference from such as Vamre. Immediately, I wish to speak to the Rafe Aguilera person, to probe his logic."

"As you wish," she said, and then led him down the gleaming rows of Terran weapons.

Yaut stopped at a corner and gazed down the various streets. "I wish to speak to veterans of the Terran Conquest," he said. "Advise me where they might be found." He purposely avoided using the guard's name since he had no intention of acknowledging her for some time yet. In order to be of use to the Subcommandant, she needed first to learn humility.

The female hesitated, her shoulders slumped in *downhearted-indecision.* "There is a Binnat association hall around the bend," she said finally. "It was built some time ago, so a number of the older ones congregate there."

"Lead me," he said gruffly, then followed her, turning heartward twice, then windward, coming at last to a Jao structure of dark-blue laced with gold that gleamed beneath the relentless sun.

"It was constructed for all the associated kochan and taifs of Binnat," she said. "So many have been assigned on this world that the kochan provided funds for this to be poured over fifteen orbital cycles ago."

It was a sturdy building, the material well crafted, though a bit showy, useful in allowing planetside Jao to maintain their kochan associations far away from home. He approved. Pluthrak had done the same for its own on a number of worlds.

There was no doorfield in use. "Wait," he said, then stepped inside. The interior of the single large room was dim, the lights recessed into its sinuous walls mellow in contrast with the local star's brash radiation.

A few individuals lolled on heaped dehabia, traditional soft thick blankets that, by the look of them, must have been imported all the way from some kochan's homebase. None of the loungers looked up at his entrance, though he could feel the shift of their attention like a quaver in the air. The subtle woody scent of tak threaded through the room, reminding him incongruously of childhood and long-ago companions. His kochan-house, Jithra, had smelled like this, but only at special times in the orbital cycle, when social observations were to be kept. Had he happened onto one such locally?

A small pool occupied the far end of the room and several Jao were swimming. A broad-chested male suddenly loomed before him, his dark eyes gleaming, his whiskers stiff. No less than seven service bars had been incised into his cheek. "This is the Binnat kochan-house," he said, his body prickly with *perceived-infraction.* "I have not seen your likeness on the recorded roles."

"And you will not," Yaut said, assuming the rather aggressive posture of *rightful-inquiry.* "I make myself of use as fraghta to the new Subcommandant, Aille krinnu ava Pluthrak, who wishes to consult with veterans of the local conquest that he might have the benefit of their hard-won wisdom."

"Pluthrak? Here?" The male's face contorted. "Since when?"

"Last-sun," Yaut said patiently. "Have you any veterans available?"

A doorfield dissolved at the opposite end of the large room, admitting a female, along with a veritable haze of tak, so rich it brought visions of ceremonial food and clothing to mind. He blinked hard, remembering. . . .

The walls at Jithra had been done in dark-blue and silver, the floors in gold. He and his agemates had hunted in the sea for tasty mirrat, small finned swimmers which only migrated through the area at that time of the orbital cycle. He could still taste their salty freshness.

But there was something odd here, as well. A strange noise of some sort, coming from the chamber from which the female had emerged. A series of noises, rather, strung together in a complex and oddly mesmerizing fashion. It was an alien sound.

"Ammet," the male said. "The new Subcommandant is Pluthrak!"

She sauntered forward, *disbelief* written in the lines of her massive neck and shoulders. One of her ears was damaged and drooped toward her cheek. "Not here," she said. "Pluthrak would never—"

She cut off her words, as if with a blade. Obviously enough, she had suddenly seen the chasm of great kochan rivalry gaping wide before her. Binnat was a respected kochan, to be sure, but too small and weakly associated to want to be caught between Narvo and Pluthrak.

All these Binnat were off-duty, of course, and this was meant as a place of repose, but Yaut sensed a vein of something deeper at work, indolence and disregard, even discontent. Alarm prickled up his back. He had thought the Narvo Governor's discipline sadly lacking, but this went beyond simple lack of discipline.

"I seek veterans," he said sternly, "to be interviewed this late-sun."

"We two could go." The male glanced around. "Do you require more than that?"

"Two will suffice for now, though the Subcommandant may ask for more later," Yaut said and turned to go. "Present yourselves at the Refit Facility." He would let Aille handle their attitude and see how the youngster acquitted himself. It would make for an interesting learning experience at the very least.

Still puzzled by the sound, he glanced through the still-open door to the chamber. From the new angle, he could peer within. To his astonishment, he saw a human working at some sort of large machine, while several Jao sat nearby watching the creature. A moment later, he realized that the machine was producing the noise.

His surprise was great enough to override politeness. "What is *that*? And I thought humans were not allowed here."

The two veterans glanced back. When their eyes returned to Yaut, he saw that their postures were a sloppy rendition of *uneasy-defiance*.

"It is called a 'piano,'" the female named Ammet said.

"What he is doing is called 'music,'" added the male veteran. Now, the *defiance* in his posture shaded toward something close to *outright-challenge*. "We like it."

It was not until he'd emerged from the association hall that Yaut realized neither of them had explained the violation of rules regarding the presence of the human. But he was not surprised. It was indeed as Aille had told him the kochanata experts had foreseen. Narvo was losing its grip on this world. Everything was askew. An official posture of Jao supremacy—in the familiar unrelenting Narvo manner—combined with discordant admixtures everywhere. Threads unraveling instead of coming together.

Yaut had never seen anything like it, on any conquered planet he had visited or served upon. This was not association. This was madness, growing.

CHAPTER
8

Caitlin Stockwell generally avoided people, as she went about her business on campus. They were really just acquaintances, anyway, with a few exceptions, people who wanted to know her because of who her father was and her family's prominence. They just wanted to use her, basically.

Of course, she thought, walking along the winding river path on her way back to the dorm, the Jao wanted to use her too. They were just more open about it. Everyone and everything should be of use, according to their philosophy.

She glanced over her shoulder, but Banle was giving her space for now, hanging back in the shade about twenty feet, probably to spare her eyes from the bright light. Fortunately, the campus was mostly deserted in August, with only a handful of graduate students and professors in residence, either finishing up summer work or preparing for the fall. Everyone who had a decent home had already left.

For her, though, leaving would have meant returning to her father's mansion in St. Louis, the city that was now the human capital of North America—more precisely, the human administrative center. The real "capital," in the sense of the seat of power, was of course Oppuk's palace in Oklahoma City. Caitlin's father had deliberately placed the human administrative center as far away as he could from Oppuk's glowering presence, without moving it so far away as to give obvious insult.

Here, on a campus in central Michigan, she only had to deal with her bodyguard/jailer, Banle. There, in St. Louis, the entire Stockwell household would be under Jao scrutiny night and day. Oppuk had allowed Caitlin's father to establish himself outside of Oklahoma City—if for no other reason, because Oppuk disliked dealing with humans anyway, except as menial servants— but he had also made sure to keep a strong Jao presence in St. Louis.

True, compared to humans, the Jao were quite unsophisticated when it came to espionage and internal security surveillance. They had nothing equivalent to the FBI—much less such all-pervasive secret police as the old KGB or the still-older Tsarist *Okhrana*— and they used human informers in a desultory manner. But with their military power and their much-superior electronic capabilities, it hardly mattered. Jao clumsiness enabled the Resistance to survive in their little nooks and crannies all over North America. But they would have quickly spotted any attempt by human officials in the highly visible center at St. Louis to organize anything on a broader scale than the localized efforts of the various groups in the Resistance.

"Hey, Caitlin!" a male voice called.

She turned to see Alex Breck jogging across the grass toward her. He was tall and lean, with badly cut black hair that kept falling in his eyes. For the past week, Alex had been trying to get her to go out on a date, with her doing her best to evade the problem. A problem, in his case, because she would have enjoyed it. Alex was one of the few people on campus who liked her for herself. Of that, she was quite sure.

"Caitlin, wait up!"

She stopped, and clutched her briefcase to her chest as though it could protect her.

"I've been calling you for days!" He stopped, breathing hard, his brown eyes trained on her face.

"I—haven't been checking my messages," she said, which was a lie and she could see he knew it. "I have a lot of work to do for Professor Kinsey before classes start again." She raised her chin. "He's writing a book about the history of the Jao."

"Yeah, I know," he said. "I just can't figure out why. Don't we all hear enough about the Jao day in, day out, as it is, without writing books about them too?"

Privately, she agreed. "It's important to Professor Kinsey," she said for Banle's ears, "and I'm getting paid for it."

"Right," he said and reached for her hand.

She tried to take it, then lost her grip on the briefcase and everything tumbled into the grass. In a second, they were both on their knees, picking up books and papers and pens. He laughed and she sat back on her heels, the wind in her face, laughing with him.

"Come on," he said, then tucked a stray lock of hair behind her ear. "Quit avoiding me. Let's go out to dinner tonight."

She gazed up at his honest expression, then sighed. "I'd like to," she said, "but you don't know what you're asking for. I—don't have a private life. I never have." She looked back at Banle's tall golden figure, standing at the edge of the shade, nap dappled with sunlight. "That Jao over there has been my jailer since I was four years old. As far as I know, she'll be with me until the day I die. She may even be my scheduled executioner. If the Jao ever decide they have a good reason for me to die, I can promise you I'll be dead before anyone can blink twice."

His brow furrowed. She could tell he didn't really believe her about this either.

She stuffed the last of her papers back into the battered briefcase. "I can't date anyone. It just isn't fair to them, and I certainly wouldn't enjoy trying to have a relationship with Banle looming over my shoulder. Maybe someday things will change, but for now I'm not holding my breath."

She closed her eyes, remembering her dead older brother, Brent. "If I let myself care about someone, he'll just make another hostage. I have enough to handle already being a hostage myself."

"I see." He stood and then, after hesitating a moment, stalked back down the path, giving Banle a wide berth.

And so much for that. Too bad. I liked him.

Actually, he didn't see, she thought, as she resumed walking. He didn't have the faintest idea of what her life was really like, but that was okay. She didn't *want* him to see. Things were bad enough as it was, without adding another player.

Banle closed up the distance between them. "Were you in danger?" Her body was angled in *perception-of-threat.*

"No," Caitlin said hastily. "We just had a minor disagreement."

"Your parents are too permissive. You should be educated in your

own kochanata where your elders can impart the important values," Banle said, "not here among strangers."

"Leaving home to go to a university is the human way," Caitlin
said. "I want to be here."

Banle only wrinkled her snout in disapproval.

Rafe Aguilera was waiting when Aille returned to his office,
Tully in tow. Big for a human, though still smaller than a Jao,
Aguilera was pacing the corridor with his limping gait, plainly
nervous.

Aille keyed off the doorfield and went inside. Tully followed,
edging toward a corner once they got into the room, his green
eyes fixed on the two of them like a caged animal.

"You are not here for punishment," Aille said to Aguilera in Jao.
"Although most would say you deserve it." He met the human's
strange dark-brown eyes in their eerie nests of white. "You do
understand that?"

Aguilera glanced at Tully, then lowered his gaze. His jaw muscles
were tight. "I let myself get carried away," he said finally. "But I
didn't mean any disrespect. I just wanted to do the job right, to
be of use. Isn't that what you Jao want, for us to be of use?"

"'The ripples of being of use spread ever outward,'" Aille said,
quoting one of his earliest lessons. "'One who is not of use might
as well be dead.'"

"So I've heard." Aguilera threw back his bony shoulders, arti-
culated differently in some way from Jao anatomy so that what
might have been *forthright-acceptance* was distorted into mean-
inglessness.

"I wish to know more about your ideas concerning these Terran tanks," Aille said, sinking into his chair. He leaned back. "I
think your ideas may have merit. So does Supervisor Nath."

The thin lines of hair over Aguilera's eyes raised. "Nath? She
never—" He bit off whatever he had intended to say.

"She has been properly reticent about expressing her opinions,
in the past time. But now that I have taken her into my service,
she is freed of other obligations and—" It was his turn to bite off
the end of the phrase. *And worries*, he'd been about to say. But
there was no reason—indeed, it would be quite improper—to
indicate such concerns to a human.

Aguilera's body relaxed. The rangy human rubbed his hands

together. "You don't have to take my word for it. A number of the men down on the refit floor fought at Chicago, like I did. Why not ask them how they coped with Jao weapons?"

"Very well," Aille said. "Arrange a meeting." He paused, his body automatically falling into the shape of *absorbed-reflection*.

Aguilera stared out through the door to the glass wall in the corridor that overlooked the refit floor, his eyes on the work below. "Is it really true there's another race out there, even stronger than the Jao?" he said. "One ready to kill us all?"

"You mean the Ekhat," Aille said. "Yes, they are 'out there,' as you put it. The reason they have not swept Terra and its inhabitants aside like so much refuse before now is that this world is not near any of their framepoints currently in use, and so has not come to their notice."

Aguilera turned to him. "But what do they want?"

"No one has ever been able to establish that, no matter how carefully they study past encounters," Aille said. "As nearly as we Jao can tell, the Ekhat simply want to be alone in the universe with their own perfection."

The human seemed to ponder that statement. "Then how have the Jao survived?" he said finally. "Did you chase them off your homeworld?"

Aille was puzzled. "How could a human—especially one with responsibilities such as yours which bring you into close contact with Jao—still be ignorant of such basic facts, so long after the conquest?"

Aguilera's shoulders made a lifting-and-falling motion which, if Aille remembered correctly, was roughly the human equivalent of *puzzled-uncertainty*. "You Jao never tell us anything about yourselves."

Now, Aille was more puzzled than ever. The methods of forging association with conquered species were well known, tried and tested. It was much like raising crechelings. Of course, one maintained authority and, when necessary, punished disobedience or disrespect. But one never lied or dissembled to them, either, any more than kochan parents were untruthful to the crechelings in their charge. Association required trust, and trust required forthrightness.

Again, the question forced itself forward: *What has Narvo been doing here?*

But Aille saw no reason to raise that issue before Aguilera, much less Tully. Being forthright with subject species was not the same thing as kochan back-biting gossip, after all.

"Actually," he said, "we Jao have no idea of what particular world birthed our race. All our histories begin when a sizable population escaped the slave compounds of the Ekhat."

"They captured your whole race?"

"No, they crafted us, from a semi-sentient species swimming in an ocean somewhere so that eventually we could work and fight for them as slaves."

"Slaves?" Aguilera ran a hand back over his unruly black hair.

"Yes, and we were the fortunate ones," Aille aid. "Apparently, for whatever reason, they must have seen some promise in us. Most intelligent or semi-intelligent species they encounter are exterminated immediately."

"So if we don't help prepare for their coming," Aguilera said, "we'll fall too."

"Most likely," Aille said. "Now, return to the refit floor and arrange the meeting."

Aguilera gave the human nodding gesture, then slipped back out the door.

"I don't really believe that," Tully said, speaking for the first time since they'd returned to the office. "I think you Jao just make all that stuff up so we'll stay in line."

The phrase "stay in line" sounded peculiar, especially coming from someone whose Jao was obviously quite good. How instantly, Aille thought, these humans thought in terms of order and regimentation. Their minds seem to run in straight lines everywhere. Perhaps that was why they encountered so many obstacles to proper association. Straight lines made for corners.

But there was a more pressing matter at hand. "You are in my service now," Aille said. "On the one hand, that gives you the right to question me, but I suggest you refrain from insinuations that I am being untruthful. If Yaut were present, you would already be bleeding again. He is a forceful trainer."

Tully drew back a little, but did not cringe. He was courageous, whatever else, that much was clear. Aille decided he had made the point sufficiently well and moved on. "Beyond that, while you may think what you wish, it does not matter what you believe as long as you make yourself of use."

"And how exactly do you expect me to be of use?" Tully held up his wrist with its locator.

"I do not know yet," Aille said. "It may happen that you cannot be, after all."

"Then what?" Tully raised his chin. His eyes glittered with that stubbornness Aille was coming to know.

"Then I will decide what else to do. But that flow may never complete itself, so why concern ourselves with it?"

Tully started to say something else, but broke off. Yaut had returned.

The fraghta had a raw-boned scruffy female drifting in front of him. The scion of Pluthrak studied her for a moment. Blunt-eared, as well as blunt-faced, she seemed to lack the intelligence Aille preferred in his subordinates. His hands formed *bemused-surprise* as he gazed at his fraghta.

"Vaish," Yaut said, as though nothing were untoward. The doorfield activated with a faint crackle.

Aille's nose twitched.

"This one is in need of training," the fraghta said. "I brought her along so it may be accomplished with greater ease."

"I assume then, she has also joined my service?" Aille's ears quirked at an ironic angle.

Yaut swiveled his windward hand to indicate *diffident-assent*. "The bau-holding scion of a great kochan should have a large service, and wide-flung. You need a nose in every pertinent area."

"True, but have you considered that perhaps we are accumulating too many too quickly for effective training?" Aille's gaze flicked to Tully, who was now standing against the wall. His stance was rigid, exuding unease. "You are, however efficient, only one."

Yaut followed his gaze. "Apparently training proceeds," he said, eyeing Tully, "whether I am here or not."

"Apparently."

"I have uncovered two Binnat who may meet your needs," Yaut said. "They—"

A rap sounded on the door. Yaut keyed the doorfield off.

A group of humans stood outside, led by Rafe Aguilera. "Subcommandant?" He glanced within to Aille. "Here are the men you requested. I served with some of them myself, and the rest I know by reputation."

"Do they speak Jao?" Aille asked.

"Not all of them."

"Then send those who do not away for now," Aille said. "But retain a list of their names. I will interview them later, when my English has improved."

Aguilera spoke in low tones. Three of the seven nodded, then bowed their heads and left.

"Now," Aille said. "Explain your methods of disabling Jao ground combat vehicles."

A male with very little of what Terrans called "hair" on his head stepped forward. He looked patchy and unfinished, as though he had molted improperly. "They were hard to defend against in rough terrain," he said, without meeting Aille's eyes. "Those maglev drives go over anything, but we could sometimes disperse your lasers with steam. A man could hide and wait until a Jao vehicle passed, then disrupt the laser from the side with a steam bomb. It worked more often than not, although it was always very dangerous for the man doing it." He stood a little straighter. "I did it twice. Got—ah, the human word for it is 'decorated'—the second time."

The man proceeded to give a description of the "steam bomb." Then, the rest began participating, depicting other methods the humans had found to thwart, at least partially, the Jao lasers. Very soon, Aille found himself being convinced. He had never thought upon the matter before, but he realized now that the Jao methods of warfare were the ones they had inherited from the Ekhat.

But the Ekhat were not conquerors. They were exterminators, usually. Or, when they did capture sentient species to make them slaves, simply captured enough for a breeding pool and exterminated the rest. They did not fight very often on the surface of a planet occupied by an intelligent species. After grabbing a few of its inhabitants, if any, they simply obliterated the planet. Their weaponry and tactics were designed for battle in the vacuum of space.

At one point, Yaut tried to interject an opposing view. "Our weapons and methods have served us well on many occasions," he said gruffly. "How do you explain that?"

The humans fell silent, not knowing how to respond since obviously they had been told very little about the Jao and their past. But Aille already knew the answer.

"No other species we conquered was technologically advanced.

Most were simply barbarians, barely able to forge metal. Even inefficient weapons will serve, against a weak enough opponent. Against humans, the weakness was exposed. That is clear to me now. It should have been clear to everyone long ago, had anyone thought to study the matter and listen to the vanquished."

And why didn't we? he wondered. For a moment, he was tempted to fault Narvo. But that was a superficial answer, at best. He thought the true reason was the same: humans were unique, in Jao experience. The Jao had never consulted with other conquered species on proper methods of war and weaponry, after all. Why should they, when every opponent they had faced before the humans fought them with nothing more than muscle-powered weapons. Except the Ekhat, of course, but the Ekhat used the same weapons as Jao.

Aille paced a few steps, in deep thought. "I wonder, though, what the records of our battles with the Lleix would show? I have never studied them."

"I have," said the fraghta. "They do not tell much, and nothing very specific. Those 'records' are really nothing of the sort. They read more like kochan ceremonial chants than anything else."

Aille was not surprised. The battles against the Lleix were more a matter of Jao legend, than factual accounts. Those battles had happened long ago, before the Jao had managed to break free of the Ekhat. The Jao had still been slave warriors when they exterminated the Lleix at their masters' bidding.

Aille returned to his probing. Most fascinating of all to him, as the flow of time passed and the humans continued with their accounts, was seeing something begin to emerge for the first time since he'd set foot on the planet. Association, finally. The first shoots of it, at least.

CHAPTER
9

It was early-dark before Supervisor Nath krinnu Tashnat vau Nimmat tracked Director Vamre to a dark alcove in his association hall. He glimpsed her muscled form as she passed through the door, then looked around the shadowy room. He grimaced and settled deeper into his pile of rugs. The aromatic scent of tak filtered through the hall, reminiscent of home, and he had been feeling distinctly better. He'd already half-forgotten the clash with the young upstart officer, although he still had every intention of filing a sharp protest with Commandant Kaul.

No doubt Nath just wanted to inform him of some quota not met, or several native workers who had once again absconded with insignificant bits of Jao technology. She was ever scrupulous, that one, but he was off duty and interested in none of it.

After a moment, Nath spotted him and approached, the well-bred *vai camiti* on her face very much out of place in this unassuming setting. Though she was subordinate to him in assignment, she was of Nimmat, making her kochan ties vastly more auspicious than lowly Kannu, hardly surprising. Most were.

She settled on a pile of worn dehabia beside him, lightly, as though she weighed no more than a crecheling. Ignoring murmurs and stares of others in the hall, she took the oblique angle of *regretful-revelation.* "The officer you argued with today was the new Subcommandant, Aille krinnu ava Pluthrak."

His whiskers went numb and he struggled upright in the pile of blankets. *"Pluthrak?"*

"None other." Her eyes gazed at him impassively, green blooming here and there, and her posture betraying nothing. He could see her classical training in the least flick of an ear. It took the exquisite training only given to those associated with a great kochan to move with such unconscious grace.

"As you recall," she said, "I requested that you accompany me outside so I could tell you."

Vamre felt ill, a sensation which deepened as Nath continued. "I am told this one is of the clearest water, *namth camiti*, the highest ranked youth of his generation. I was greatly honored a short time ago when he took me into his personal service."

Then, obviously having satisfied *vithrik*, she abandoned him to his dark nook, while all around him others talked on and a stick of aromatic imported tak smoldered in a nearby brazier.

Took her into his personal service? It was all Vamre could do not to groan aloud. He and Nath had never gotten along well under the best of circumstances. Now, she would be impossible to control. With the prestige of Pluthrak swelling behind her, for all practical purposes it would henceforth be she and not he who dominated the situation in the facility.

But Vamre had far more pressing worries than his relationship with Nath. He tried to remember what he'd said out on the refit floor, and how the young Pluthrak had responded. Though he had no service bars incised on his cheek, his *vai camiti* had indeed been distinctive—why hadn't he recognized it? And there had been a fraghta in the background, too, he realized, quite stiff and proper with duty. That alone should have been a clue that all was not what it seemed. No new officer from a minor kochan, much less a taif, would have a fraghta accompanying him. How could Vamre have been so stupid?

It was clear he must apologize, if it weren't already too late. Vallt, his own kochan, was meager, its proffered links to other kochan seldom even acknowledged, much less accepted. Kannu, his root clan, was hardly any more recognized. Through his heedlessness, he had put his entire generation of crechekin at a disadvantage, both now and in the future. Whenever their name came up, this particular Pluthrak would think only of him, and his advice no doubt would inevitably be to turn aside. Nor would it be simply this one Pluthrak. The same would be true for all others with whom he would form association—and there would be a multitude. No kochan was more adept than Pluthrak at creating a web of associations. "Subtle as a Pluthrak." Mighty Narvo could think itself Pluthrak's equal, but no other Jao shared that opinion except their affiliates and close allies.

He lurched onto his feet, his trousers redolent with tak, and headed for the door. It was not yet full-dark. Perhaps he could speak with this Pluthrak before dormancy overtook him.

The eyes of his distantkin watched as he left, but, though at least a few must have overheard, no one offered to come with him and attempt to mend what was probably irretrievably broken.

Aille received the two Binnat gravely, his arms at *quiet-attention* for their benefit. The newly acquired nameless female guard skulked in the background, but had realized at some point earlier that the even lower status Tully was in his service too, so had recovered a bit of her equilibrium. Yaut stood at the room's perimeter, whiskers writhing as though seeking prey.

The Binnat, a male and a female, settled in the chairs before the desk. Aille thought of switching off the three dimensional internal diagram of a submarine he had been studying, but they seemed intrigued, so he left it on. It rotated slowly in the air above the desk's gleaming black surface, light playing over its outline.

The shorter Binnat, a stubby male with several shiny scars on his windward side, leaned forward, his joints set in unmitigated *frankness*. "Your fraghta said you wanted to know of the Battle of Chicago, Subcommandant."

Not a sophisticated or subtle fellow, Aille surmised, just an old soldier, direct to a fault and unwilling to play complicated games of *vithrik*, no doubt unable to rise in rank because of it. "Yes," he said, his own body shifting into unmodified *attention*. "How would you say the Terran troops fought?"

"Like wild beasts, but very cunning ones." The Jao's eyes flared green at the memory. "Beasts not smart enough, though, to understand when they were already defeated. We gave them every opportunity to surrender, but they kept coming at our lines, hundreds and hundreds of them, trained, untrained, old and young, fighting long past the point of sanity. We had to crush them in every way possible, destroy their infrastructure down to the last bridge and road, even kill their young, before they accepted defeat."

The other Jao squirmed, as if the memory made her uncomfortable. "They were very difficult to deal with, because they were so impractical," she said in a low voice. "They even have words for it in their own language: 'fanatic,' 'zealot,' and there are others. Sometimes, if we locked them up, they refused to eat and died of starvation. Other times—not many, but some—they killed themselves and each other, sometimes even their own offspring, rather than submit."

Green glinted off the long lines of the sub. Red winked here and there to indicate command posts. "What about the jinau troops?" Aille asked.

"Very capable, sir," the first said, "but it is always difficult to know if you can trust them. They're inherently unstable, I sometimes think, because they are too clever."

"And yet they seem honorable," Aille mused. "I found several arguing with the director today merely because they wished to do 'a good job.'"

"It is difficult to fathom," the first Binnat said, "due to their quirky natures. They tell many untruths."

"They will say anything," the other added, "if it will obtain what they want. They will swear to it, then act later as they please. In the beginning, many Jao died before we understood this."

"And what of the lasers on our assault vehicles?" Aille asked. "These humans insist they were easily thwarted by very low-tech solutions, steam, thrown chaff, and the like."

"After the initial assault, our lasers performed poorly," the first said. "That is true. And it is also true that their own weapons were often terrifyingly effective."

"Was any study ever carried out afterward?"

"Not that I know of." He glanced at his fellow veteran and she flicked an ear in agreement. "We had won, after all."

"I see." Aille's whiskers drooped in an unguarded moment of *contemplated-folly* until he caught himself and amended the gesture to the more tactful *contemplated-action*. Yaut caught his eye and Aille read *repressed-interest* in his stance.

"You have a question, fraghta?"

"Yes," said Yaut, stepping forward. "How often did Jao troops abandon their own weapons and use Terran ones instead?"

An excellent question, thought Aille, and one he would not have thought to ask himself.

The two Binnat glanced at each other. Then the female said, reluctantly, "It was known to happen. Now and then."

Her male companion, in his blunt manner, bolted onto his feet to display *amused-derision*. "'Now and then!' Say rather: as often as we could manage it. Which was not often enough, so far as I was concerned. The big problem was that we could not fit into their tanks. But we employed every piece of their artillery we could get our hands on, once we learned how to use it."

The fraghta stared at him. Aille was certain that Yaut had more questions he wanted to ask, but, after a moment, the fraghta stepped back. Clearly enough, there were some further matters which Yaut intended to discuss with these Binnat—but not here and now, in front of Pluthrak.

Aille was not disgruntled. A good fraghta would often handle things privately and in his own manner. Not the least of the reasons for Pluthrak's eminence was its habit of trusting its affiliated kochan and taifs.

The doorfield flared and another Jao entered. Aille squinted at the newcomer's *vai camiti* for a moment, until he remembered where he'd seen that particular facial pattern. "Director Vamre," he said, falling into a carefully neutral stance.

"I—" The director was radiating unsophisticated *misery*. "I have been so busy, I did not listen to the day's updates. I did not know!"

The two startled Binnat retreated to the shadows at the back of the room. Yaut's ears twitched and even Tully seemed to catch a whiff of the Jao's distress.

"'Did not know?'" Aille repeated unhelpfully.

"That you were of Pluthrak!"

"Many are of Pluthrak," Aille said. "Certainly you cannot be expected to know all of them."

"I did not know a Pluthrak had been assigned here!" Vamre krinnu Vallt vau Kannu paced toward the two astonished Binnat, then appeared to notice their lower-ranked presence for the first time. He stiffened. "On Terra, I mean, and I should have."

"There are many interesting tales told about this world, despite its isolation," Aille said. "Pluthrak wished to have firsthand experience of Terra, hence my posting."

"I would not have spoken so bluntly," Vamre said, "had I known."

"Does the situation alter itself, when explained to different ears?" Aille took up *cold-indignation*. "Why should your words be different to Pluthrak than any other? Truth is truth."

"I judged without listening, thinking you brash," Vamre said, his eyes turned away. "But so great a kochan as Pluthrak is never brash. You must have had your reasons for siding with the Terran."

"Pluthrak is composed of individuals," Aille said, "and therefore capable of a great many things, not all of them fortuitous. In this instance, however, I do not think it brash to suggest we might at least consider what these Terrans have to say about the ongoing refit. They accomplished a great deal on their own, before ever we came here, and they must surely know the limitations and possibilities of their own technology much better than we can."

Vamre bowed his head, seeking with visible effort to control himself. "Young Pluthrak, I fear you will know these creatures better after some passage of time. They are devious and resentful, ever mindful of their defeat and quite capable of giving the worst of misinformation to exact revenge."

Over in the corner, Tully snorted and crossed his arms. Yaut's nostrils flared, but he said nothing.

Aille settled back in his chair and stared thoughtfully at the agitated Jao. "I shall take your advice under consideration, Director. Thank you for being so kind as to offer it this late in the solar cycle." His body assumed the lines of *weary-attention*, a subtle posture that had taken much practice to perform gracefully. He thanked his instructors now that they had drummed it into him so he could assume it between one breath and the next.

Vamre gazed at him bleakly, whiskers limp with resignation. "May others always heed your words," he said in a rather parochial leavetaking. "May all seek your attention." He turned and left.

Yaut stared after him thoughtfully. "That," he said flatly, "was interesting."

The two Binnat emerged from the shadows, the cant of their ears betraying *embarrassment*. Combined, in the case of the male, with more than a hint of *contempt*. Aille suspected the two Binnat were acquainted with Vamre, and had little regard for him.

"We also shall leave now," the tall female said, "if the Subcommandant has no more need of us."

"Your viewpoint has been useful," Aille said. "I trust I may call upon Binnat, should I require further education. Or have my fraghta do so."

"It would please us mightily to be of use at any time," the Binnat said. "With your permission?"

Aille wrinkled his nose in affirmation and the two left the room.

Once outside, the two Binnat stared at each other.

"These are treacherous waters," muttered Ammet. "Any time Narvo and Pluthrak currents come together, lesser kochan are caught in the whirlpool."

The stubby male was more sanguine. "True enough. But this world needs a cleansing. You know it as well as I do. Narvo has lost—"

He broke off. Not even one as blunt as he was prepared to finish that sentence.

Tully had studied Jao assiduously in preparation for this assignment, trained by two of Wiley's people who were fluent in the tongue. But his command of the language was not yet good enough to follow every nuance of the argument between the director and Aille. The problem was compounded by the fact that so much of Jao communication with each other depended on that freakish body language of theirs, of which Tully had only the roughest grasp.

Still, this much was now clear to him: There were deeper dissensions and hidden quarrels among the Jao themselves than either he or Rob Wiley had ever realized. And this young Pluthrak appeared to be shaking things up. Perhaps his plan to escape had been hasty. He might be of more use where he was, for the moment. So far, Aille had shown no inclination to question Tully about his Resistance contacts. Tully was beginning to realize, for reasons he still couldn't make clear, even to himself, that the Pluthrak had no intention of torturing him. "Training" him, yes— whatever that might mean to a Jao—but not subjecting him to what humans would call the "third degree."

I'll stay a spy, then. Truth is, this is all way more interesting than anything I've seen yet.

Aille rose. Immediately, his new female Jao bodyguard rose also and headed for the door.

Yaut beckoned at Tully peremptorily. "Come!"

Tully started to bristle, but suppressed the reaction almost instantly. *You're a spy, dammit! Be a good little boy.*

He hurried to precede the three Jao out through the building to their waiting transport below. He sat in front with the driver, but the Jao female was left behind to walk. She also was in Aille's "service" now, whatever exactly that meant. At any rate, she didn't seem any happier about it than he was.

The sun was setting, the horizon turning red with dusk. Cicadas buzzed in the trees and he could hear the boom of the surf to the south. A storm must be blowing in from the Gulf. The day was still sweltering, but the car was fairly new and so had no air conditioning. Jao did not feel extremes of heat or cold, and had no use for air conditioning. That could be tough on the humans who had to spend time with them. He settled back, letting the hot heavy air run over his face and cool him as much as possible.

The driver pulled up at Aille's quarters and leaped out to open the door. The two Jao emerged. "Shall you be needing me anymore this evening, sir?" he asked.

Aille waved a careless hand. "Perhaps," he said. "Remain until further orders."

He nodded, then climbed back in the car and settled down to wait.

Tully watched them dissolve the doorfield and enter the typical Jao structure which had no corners, nor indeed any straight lines. For the moment, they didn't seem to notice he was lagging behind. He turned to the driver. "I need you to get word to my unit, Danvers. I don't want them to think I just disappeared."

Danvers blinked at him, then yawned. "If the Subcommandant wishes them to know, he'll tell them."

"They might list me as a deserter, dammit!" He gripped the hot metal of the open window with angry fingers. Any second now, the locator device around his wrist would deliver another punishing jolt. The last one had nearly scrambled his brain. He couldn't delay much longer.

"Tully, you are an idiot. Don't you get it? He's Pluthrak, and he's taken you into his *personal service*. That's never happened before, as far as I know—and you're worried about piddly regs? God, what I'd give to be in your shoes."

"Service!" he said contemptuously, then flinched at a warning tingle in his wrist. He held up his arm with the sleek black band. "Seems more like slavery to me!"

"You're supposed to be jinau," Danvers said, squinting suspiciously. "Don't you know anything? And why did you sign up in the first place, with an attitude like that?"

Pain raced up his arm, exploding into a white-hot nova behind his eyes. Tully cried out and dropped to his knees, unable to see or hear. Then it retreated just long enough for him to get to his feet and stagger toward the door.

Inside, he slumped against the wall, sweat drenching his face. He wasn't sure how long he could go on like this, leashed like a damn poodle.

Kaul krinnu ava Dano listened to his pleniary-adjunct's recorded report on the new Subcommandant's movements throughout the day, then stumped around his spacious quarters. His posture exuded crude, but satisfying, unmitigated *suspicion*.

The Dano bodystylists who had instructed him in his youth would have been appalled, but he'd always found the more vulgar postures relieved his tension as nothing else did. In public, with other Jao, he behaved in accordance with the highest standards, but in private these days he often found himself indulging his baser impulses.

Perhaps it was being forced to associate with these misbegotten natives for so long. They had only the dimmest understanding of how to bodyspeak and few of their postures had ever been standardized. Certainly, as far as he could tell, none were ever taught or properly refined. Each child was left on its own to pick up what little it could. No wonder it was so difficult to instruct them how to behave in a civilized manner.

He dropped into his chair and stared moodily at the holomap's latest revelation of Ekhat movements. It spun slowly above his desk, gleaming red for contested systems, blue for threatened ones, amber for those yet uninvolved. Bad news there, nothing but bad for some time. The Bond of Ebezon would have to send help soon or see this system lost. He had little hope they would do so in time to make a difference. The initial hopes for Terra, with its potentially vast resources, had long since faded because of the intractability of the natives. With the war against the Ekhat flaring up in many places, the Jao fleets were kept busy elsewhere.

He pushed those concerns aside, since he had no control over them, and went back to his ruminations. This newly arrived Pluthrak was conducting himself very strangely. For a youth so supposedly promising—*namth camiti*, it was said—he had spent far more of his time consorting with Terrans than his own kind, not at all what Kaul had anticipated. That Pluthrak had sent him here to undermine Narvo was obvious. But how did Aille krinnu ava Pluthrak expect to expand Pluthrak associations without using his time to seek out other Jao?

To be sure, his fraghta seemed proper enough. Maybe they hadn't sent this newly released youth here to embarrass Narvo. Maybe— he found himself gripping his hands in unabashed *anticipation- of-another's-misfortune*—they had sent this particular individual to Terra because he was disappointing, either unwilling or unable to conduct himself according to Pluthrak's high standards. Perhaps his elders believed that here on turbulent Terra he would be ground up by Narvo, thereby finally becoming of use to the kochan by hardening the antagonism with their great rival.

There was something . . . not quite right about that possibility, however. That would be a blunt tactic, quite unlike Pluthrak. Narvo, certainly—even more, Dano. Kaul's own kochan shared Narvo's belief in the efficacy of direct action, which was the reason that Narvo and Dano were so often allied.

Kaul continued his pacing and thinking. How could he work the new situation to Dano's advantage? No other members of Pluthrak were stationed here at the moment, though undoubtedly there were some affiliate kochan dotted in various assignments about the planet. Pluthrak was both too numerous and successful for it to be otherwise.

If this Aille behaved unfortunately, and Pluthrak were informed privately, they might come to trust Kaul's judgement and seek association with Dano where previously none had been desired. That would be a great advantage to the kochan. Dano's alliance with Narvo was long-standing, and certainly not something to be toyed with lightly. But it was an unequal alliance, since not even Dano's great numbers could offset Narvo's military power, and Narvo was always overbearing. True, Dano had managed to retain its status as a great kochan, but as things now stood the flow of time could eventually reduce it to nothing more than an affiliate of Narvo.

He urged caution upon himself, mired for the moment in the crude posture of *extreme-wariness*. Narvo's power on Terra was wielded by Oppuk, who was even quicker to exercise power than most of his kochan. There could be no hint—not a visible sign!—that Kaul was in any way seeking to form association with Pluthrak. As unnaturally as it came to one of Dano, Kaul must be subtle here. "Subtle as a Pluthrak." He must attempt to associate with Pluthrak by undermining Pluthrak's own scion. Then, if Oppuk noticed, he could only be pleased.

Kaul came to his decision. Flow had swept this Pluthrak youth within reach of Narvo's grasp, and to a lesser degree, Dano's. Perhaps he could be seized and put to use, fashioned into a tool to fit Dano's hand.

He stopped and took stock of his body, the sloppy lines, the ungainly angle of shoulder compared to arms, the unsightly twist of torso. If he were to take advantage of this opportunity, then it would be wise to become more restrained.

He visualized long ago lessons, instructors who had embodied the most graceful of postures, those for which Dano had been most famous, then subtly altered his limbs, gradually managing the precise beauty of *determined-anticipation*.

CHAPTER
10

Over the next few solar cycles, Aille immersed himself in the routine of this vast, noisy facility, which apparently never shut down. Terrans, he discovered, could work efficiently enough during any part of the solar cycle. Unlike Jao, they were naturally diurnal. But, relatively frail though they were, their bodies were able to adapt to varying cycles. And they were able to work for much longer intervals than Jao, who needed shorter but more frequent periods of dormancy. Matching the needs of the two species put considerable stress on the Jao supervisors, but it also kept the refit far ahead of any schedule it might have achieved with an entirely Jao work force.

Unfortunately, more often than not, supervisors with the same disdainful attitude as Vamre krinnu Vallt vau Kannu were in charge. Reflecting the attitudes of the Dano Commandant, they drove their native workers mercilessly, never listening when it came to a difference of opinion with humans on how the refit should proceed. As a result, worker disaffection was rampant.

That problem would begin to ease, now that Nath's prestige had risen so greatly through induction into Aille's service. Aille had chosen her somewhat impulsively, but he'd had Yaut check her records thereafter. To his pleasure, though not to his surprise, Nath had the best production record of any of the Jao supervisors— and the lowest incidence of reported clashes with human workers.

Nath's official rank still remained relatively low, true. But, as always with Jao, rank was one thing; kochan prestige and influence, another. The other supervisors would begin looking to her for guidance, and taking her behavior as the example they should follow. Partly they would do so from ingrained custom and habit, but also from their desire to increase association with Pluthrak.

A worse problem, and much harder to solve, was the unhealthy state of kochan relations. To a point, rivalry between kochan and kochan, taif and taif, was inevitable and beneficial. But on this military base—and all across the planet, Aille suspected—the rivalry had become much too harsh and discordant. Rivalry for the sake of rivalry, it often seemed.

Aille found himself summoned repeatedly to unsnarl some disagreement between different clans and get work restarted. Hij and Binnat seemed especially at odds and unwilling to seek accommodation between them. Commandant Kaul krinnu ava Dano apparently turned his head, when faced with such problems, and expected the individuals involved to solve their differences without his input. Aille could not see how the ensuing chaos benefited anyone and worked subtly to lay the foundations of association. Such was always Pluthrak's approach, as he had been taught since he was a crecheling. Pluthrak did not share Narvo's belief in the efficacy of simple command, much less the cruder Dano version of it.

Nath had told him she thought the discordance among kochan was partly caused by the influence of the humans, among whom many of the Jao had been immersed for a very long time. Human behavior was often characterized by such pointless antagonisms.

Yaut confirmed her assessment, when Aille raised the matter with him.

"She's right. If anything, she's understating it. The Binnat veterans told me that, even during the conquest, the humans fighting them seemed obsessed with what they called 'interservice rivalry.' Apparently—bizarre creatures—they made a sharp distinction between those of their soldiers who fought on land as opposed to those who fought on water or in the air. Not a temporary, practical distinction, as we do, but a permanent and rigid one— as if these artificially separated units of soldiers were kochan of some sort, except kochan who had no conception of how to associate."

Aille stared at him.

"It's true!" Yaut insisted. "Can you imagine anything more superstitious? You might as well divide your troops according to . . ." He groped for an analogy, then laughed abruptly. "According to 'gambling'!—which I think I'm now coming to understand better. One of their commanders was even reputed to have said: 'The Jao are the opponent. The *enemy* is the Navy.' "

Aille was more dumbfounded than ever.

" 'Navy' is the term they used to refer to their soldiers—their grotesque kochan-that-wasn't—which fought on the water," Yaut clarified.

The fraghta thought for a moment, then continued. "She's right about the rest, too. I'm amazed at how thoroughly Jao who have been here for some time become influenced by humans. Many of the veterans—even more so, the ones who have retired here—have taken up human customs and habits. Go into the Binnat association hall—many of the other kochan halls, too—and you're likely to find them listening to what humans call 'music.' That's something which reminds me a bit of ceremonial chanting, but vastly more intricate. And, as often as not, you'll find human decorative work— what they call 'art,' or 'painting,' or 'sculpture'—ranged alongside proper kochan insignia. About the only thing you will not find are Jao engaged in 'gambling,' which even the oldest veterans consider ridiculous."

The fraghta fell into *bemused-bewilderment.* "I don't understand it, not at all."

Aille rose and went to the window, staring out at the flat terrain beyond. After a moment, he spoke softly.

"I think I do understand it, Yaut. I am beginning to, at least. This is a new experience for us, and one whose ramifications we have still not accepted. Terra is a planet whose species is as advanced as our own. More so, to be honest, in many ways." He heard Yaut make a little choking noise and flattened his ears with amusement. "Heresy, you think? Yet does any Jao think the Ekhat are inferior to us?"

He turned around, facing Yaut squarely. "No? I thought not. Unfathomable, yes—but certainly not inferior. It would be hard to make that claim, after all, when the Ekhat not only created us but have destroyed parts of us since many times over. The problem is that we have come—all of us—to think too much in the Narvo way, or the Dano way. Superiority is measured too much by success in conflict. But is that not just as much superstition as the humans measuring soldiers by the terrain on which they fight?"

The fraghta pondered his words for moment. Then, grunted something that was not so much agreement as acknowledgement. His lines indicated *willingness-to-consider.*

"Since we defeated the humans—not easily, to be sure—we quickly relegated them to the status of our inferiors and tried to rule them accordingly. All the more so, since rule was given to Narvo."

Yaut was listening, now, instead of simply reacting with indignation. Aille knew he would, once he put the matter in kochan terms. Like any fraghta, Yaut thought automatically in terms of kochan influence. But since he was Jithra, long affiliated to Pluthrak, he just as automatically translated influence into association.

"I . . . begin to see, I think. Try to drive under a kochan, or a taif, instead of associating properly, and it will simply spring up shoots elsewhere. It is inevitable. Instead of order, you will create discordance yourself."

"Exactly. Narvo can claim as it will that humans are simply a subject species, and hammer them every solar cycle with the intent of making them such. But reality is what it is, not what you wish it to be. The end result is . . . among other things, veterans with many service bars adopting alien habits and customs. Which, in itself, is simply association. But association which is unguided, haphazard, often not productive—and sometimes downright dangerous."

Yaut stared out the window also. "I have never thought of humans as if they were a kochan."

"Of course not. Neither do they. And perhaps that is the problem. Or the entrance to a solution."

Yaut brought his eyes back to Aille. "Do not advance too fast, young one. Narvo rules here, not Pluthrak. And, to be honest, most Pluthrak would think you mad as well. I would myself, except . . ."

Again, he made that little choking sound. "Me, as well! It is impossible not to pick up human quirks. They have a saying, you know—one of the Binnat veterans told me. 'There is a method to the madness.'"

Aille was reminded sharply of the gulf he was trying to bridge.

Trying to find a way to even think of a bridge, it would be better to say.

"'Method to madness,'" he repeated. "Only humans would think in such a manner." He laughed softly. "I would call it 'insane,' except I am beginning to sense there is a method to it."

The next day, Aille noticed Yaut staring thoughtfully at another Jao supervisor, an older Nak male this time, who was proving himself unusually efficient, and put a hasty stop to further additions to his personal service until he'd dealt successfully with those already acquired. The Terran, Tully, remained recalcitrant and incommunicative. If the human survived Yaut's intense version of *wrem-fa*, he might provide interesting insights into the Terran character. For now, Aille would wait.

On the morning beginning the second artificial time segment known as a "week" of his Terran assignment, Aille drove out to meet Rafe Aguilera, at the human's request, on a nearby testing range, to observe a demonstration of laser-mounted tanks compared with kinetic projectile equipped vehicles.

On the way, he reviewed all the technical terms Terrans employed to designate the passage of time. He found the term "week" especially puzzling—how had they ever decided to allocate exactly that much of an orbital period to this temporal designation? He could think of no astronomical or biological pattern that corresponded to seven solar cycles.

It was such an odd quirk of their species. Terrans were as fond of chopping up time into artificial units as they were of constructing sharp corners on buildings and lining themselves up into neat rows.

Yaut accompanied him to the range, as was proper, and brought Tully, since it was prudent to keep him under close surveillance. The nameless Jao female Yaut had acquired for his bodyguard had been left back at his office. She was rough and untaught, Aille reflected, but apparently more intelligent than he had at first surmised. With a little polish, so that she moved and spoke better, she might become quite acceptable. Yaut actually did have an aptitude for sniffing out good raw material.

The two of them had continued to submit themselves to a language imprinter every night since arriving to improve their command of the dialect called "English." The phonemes formed more easily on their tongues now and their command of syntax had improved, but both of them still struggled with vocabulary. Terrans had so very many words that appeared to mean the same thing, but did not. The species was endlessly obsessed with subtle shades of meaning.

They drove out from the base past the workers' quaint boxlike quarters, using the opportunity to practice English with their driver, then entered an area that had not been reconstructed after the conquest. The cracked road, filled with craters, had been left in disrepair, since maglev vehicles did not require level pavement. Discarded groundcars lay on their sides, pitted and rusting while clouds of insects filled the steamy air. An entire scruffy, black-haired family of children seemed to be living in one wreck. Their heads popped out as his transport passed and they stared after them with vacant blue eyes.

The driver, Andrew Danvers, shook his head. "Squatters," he said. "Security cleans out this area regularly, but they always creep back."

At one point, a pack of small brown-furred animals burst out of the trees and chased them, uttering excited cries every few strides. Danvers glanced at him in the rearview mirror. "I'll report them, when we get back. They don't like wild dogs this close to the base."

Ears canted in *surprise*, Yaut watched the beasts fall behind and finally give up, panting. "Wild dogs?"

"They used to be domesticated," Danvers said with a shrug, "but after the conquest, hardly anyone had food for pets. Many of the dogs had to fend for themselves, and eventually went wild. We have to exterminate them every so often now or they can be dangerous."

They drove in silence until they reached the testing range, a broad sweep of sandy flats about twenty *azet* from the shore. Aille climbed out of the car, then examined the sky. It was a hot day, and very humid, with low hanging clouds that threatened rain. It rained here frequently during this season, though usually not for long. The air was always heavy with moisture and the variety of small crawling or flying lifeforms was astonishing.

One alighted now and crept across his breast. He regarded its orange and green shape dispassionately. Since Jao body chemistry apparently was not to the tiny predators' taste, sooner or later, this one would abandon him for more promising prey. Humans, he'd observed, sometimes suffered greatly from the attentions of such pests.

Aguilera climbed down from a waiting tan and green tank, then limped across the sandy ground to give him what Aille now understood was called a "salute," a unit of formal human body-speech which signified *respectful-submission*.

Tully emerged from the front seat and stood beside Yaut, somehow managing to suggest truculence without engaging in anything so formal as a posture.

Aguilera gestured at two opposing lines of tanks waiting out on the firing range. "If you would take your place up on the observation deck, we'll commence the tests."

A metal tower had been constructed on the far side of the field. By its linear design, it was Terran in origin, boxy and regimented without a single curve. Aille angled toward it across the broad sandy flat, startling several mottled-brown avians into flight. So limited these Terrans were, in many ways, as if to offset their complexities in other. As far as he could tell, they never experienced flow in any of its forms.

Perhaps it was because their species had evolved on land, instead of the water. They had no ancestral, instinctive memories of the movement of the waves and the currents. Yet why didn't they open their eyes and simply look? The universe had no corners, no orderly lines of this and that. Time was obviously a whole-in-motion, a flow, not a bundle of chopped up bits to be experienced one after the other.

He found the tests themselves quite interesting. First, three tanks outfitted with Jao lasers drifted into position and took aim. They were precise in their firing patterns and devastating to both small stationary targets far down at the end of the range as well as moving targets set up on maglev drones. Human soldiers directed by Aguilera were able, though, to creep up from the sides and disrupt their effectiveness with steam, tiny aluminum strips, and even handfuls of chaff, just as predicted.

Then three tanks still equipped with old fashioned human kinetic armaments surged forward, humming on their new maglev drives. Their firing patterns were not quite as effective as the laser-mounted tanks. It sometimes took several shots for them to find their range, and they produced quite a bit of recoil, which had their maglev drives fighting to maintain position. Targets were not vaporized, but blasted into untidy bits with large sections sometimes remaining.

At the end of the test runs, all six tanks pulled up and faced the observation deck. The hatches popped open with a clank and the sweating crews climbed out, watching him expectantly. Aille leaned on the rail, thinking. He and Yaut would have to correlate results, but there was a great deal to consider here, much interesting data. Aguilera did have a point about the vulnerability of Jao weaponry in an atmosphere.

But, no matter what their final conclusions, he suspected the Governor of Terra was not going to be easily convinced to change policy. Not when his name was Oppuk krinnu ava Narvo, who had, a generation earlier, been the most promising scion of that kochan—*namth camiti*, as Jao called it, "the clearest water."

Tully hovered at the rear of the lofty observation deck, feeling dizzy because of the heat. He thought he was coming down with the flu as well. His head ached, and he felt nauseated. After the tests were concluded, Aille and his driver headed down the stairs, and Yaut threw him a look that meant "come along or get your brains rattled."

His dizziness was worse, and now mosquitoes were whining around his ears. He swatted, but the hum grew louder. Yaut's rigid, disapproving back receded before him and he hurried after the fraghta before he exceeded the sensor's range and earned another round of punitive shocks. Sweat plastered his shirt to his chest. Jao didn't seem to feel the heat. Word was, back in the Resistance camps in the Rockies, they didn't feel cold either, finding themselves equally comfortable in either extreme.

They'd been bioengineered by another species, which gave them advantages humans didn't possess, but that origin must have its weaknesses too. If only he could figure out what they were, this misery might be worth it.

The dizziness got worse. He must be sicker than he thought. His vision was a little blurry, too. He gripped the metal handrail, which was already hot from the morning sun, and fought to make his eyes track. Then his foot slipped and he sat down hard, blinking up at the relentless sun. It blazed down and speared through his eyes, deep into his brain where it seemed to be melting a hole.

"Tully?" someone was saying. "Get up before—"

The by now familiar shock convulsed his body. He curled around it, as though he could contain it somehow, so maybe it wouldn't be as bad as the last time.

"Tully, goddamit, get up!" Someone pounded back up the steps, then a hand grasped his arm, yanked him to his feet.

He blinked hard and thought he could make out Aguilera's lined dark face somewhere in the middle of all that static. Fingers bit into his flesh. "Do you want your brain fried? Move it!"

His feet didn't seem to be working though, as lightning ricocheted through bone and marrow, neuron and skull. He seemed to become part of it, as though the lightning could transform him so that he might finally understand some essential truth which had always eluded him before.

"Turn it off!" Aguilera called down over the railing, then hastily threw Tully over a sweaty shoulder and thundered down the metal steps. Each step made the pain worse, as though nails were being driven into his skull. He could feel how his would-be rescuer shared the shocks, wherever their damp flesh met, could feel him stagger with each new bolt of pain. "Turn it off before you fry his goddamned brain!"

Time fritzed out so that he was aware of nothing but the white agony throbbing along every nerve. Then somehow he was on his back, the sun beating down on his face. He tried to pull an arm up to shield his eyes and couldn't. "He's no good to you dead!"

"It is not your concern," Yaut's stiff voice answered. "The man is in Pluthrak service, and must accept proper training."

"Damn your training," Tully heard Aguilera say. He was vaguely surprised to hear the collaborator speak so sharply to the fraghta. "This is wrong, treating a man like a caged beast. Kill him, if you must, but don't torture him. The Jao are better than that."

"Are we?" Yaut said, and Tully thought he heard something deadly in those words, like an adder about to strike, unexpected, out of innocent looking shade.

"Shut—up," he said weakly and flailed at Aguilera without finding a target. "When I want someone to—to plead for me, I'll—" His vision grayed out again and he was alone with the pain. "I'll damn well do it myself. Which I won't. Not to these bastards."

The lightning ebbed, though he could feel echoes of it all through his body, as though it had blazed a trail that remained after it had gone. His arms and legs trembled and jerked and his mouth tasted of blood. He'd bitten his tongue at some point.

"It never learns," Yaut said in Jao. "Indeed, I believe it is not capable of learning. It is mired in its early experiences and cannot be retrained to any other purpose."

"I am not interested so much in training," Aille answered, "as in why it makes the choices it does. If I can learn to understand it, then I may understand them all."

Tully laughed weakly, rolling his head in the dirt.

"Why is he doing that?" demanded Yaut.

"He doesn't know what he's doing," Aguilera said. "He's only half-conscious."

I know exactly what I'm doing, Tully wanted to say. *I'm laughing because it's all so damned funny, you, a collaborator, of all people, trying to stand between me and these furballs.*

But his mouth wouldn't work and his bitten tongue, swollen now, was no better. His eyelids fluttered and then he was falling into somewhere else, dark and cool and quiet.

"I had no idea they could get ill so quickly," Aille told Yaut later, when they had returned to their quarters with the unconscious Tully.

"Neither did I. But they're sturdier than they look, in other ways—or, at least, this one is. A Jao who had been jolted that thoroughly by a locator would barely be alive."

Aguilera had come with them. Aille and Yaut watched him tending the injured man with a devotion neither Jao could understand.

"Is he of your kochan?" Aille asked, as Aguilera bathed Tully's face with cool water. "Is that why you are caring for him?"

"Kochan—that means clan, doesn't it?" Aguilera rinsed the cloth in a basin of water he had filled and looked up. The centers of his eyes were a shade of brown so dark that, in the room's dimness, they seemed almost as black as a Jao's.

"Something like your word 'clan,'" Aille said, "as I understand the concept."

"Most humans in this country aren't part of a clan," Aguilera said. "Americans did have what we called 'extended families' who often lived far apart, but after the conquest, when our infrastructure was destroyed and transport systems were mostly down, contact between separated family members mostly fell apart." He put the cloth down and rose. "I have no idea what happened to any of my cousins or aunts and uncles after the fall of Chicago."

"Then, if he is not of your kochan," Yaut said, "why do you care whether he lives or dies?"

The muscles in Aguilera's face tightened and he sat back staring at his clenched hands. "I can't explain that," he said. "I don't think Jao brains are wired for the concepts."

Aille moved closer, the velvet nap on the back of his head prickling. "Try," he said. "I wish to understand."

Aguilera's eyes narrowed and he looked up at the ceiling, as though seeking to perceive something just out of sight. "It's like all humans are of the same clan—you would say the same kochan—like we are all related and have to look out for each other, even when we don't like each other or agree with what the other is doing. We have to preserve life wherever we can. Not to do so would make us immoral."

"I do not know this word 'immoral,'" Aille said.

Aguilera dipped the cloth back into the water and then wrung it out. "I don't think there is any way to translate it that would make sense to a Jao."

"Continue!" Aille felt his body shift into the planes of *determined-seeking*. "You will keep trying until I understand."

Tully stirred on his pallet on the floor, mumbled something, then was still again. Aguilera dragged a hand back over his gray-threaded hair, suddenly radiating weariness. "Perhaps it's best if I just go now, sir," he said and stood.

"No," Aille said. "Explain this word 'immoral'."

Aguilera stood, his body ramrod straight, staring off into the distance. "It comes from the root word 'morality,' which means right conduct. Immoral means something wrong, something no one who is decent would ever do. Humans think it is immoral to kill unless defending one's self, family, or country. It doesn't mean some individuals don't do it, but they are considered criminals. As a people we abhor it. We therefore also consider it our duty to aid those in distress. I don't much like Tully, to be honest, with his damn self-righteous attitudes, but he is human and therefore my responsibility; my brother, as it were."

He saluted. "With your permission, I will go home now. I haven't seen much of my family, this past week."

"Yes," Aille said. "You have given me much to think about."

Yaut watched the human leave, then turned to Aille with a scowl, his ears tight with *aggravation*. "So," he said, "now you know. They believe in an association which cannot exist, and confuse honor between kochan with this vapor they call 'morality.' Everything is turned inside out. By our standards, they are all quite insane."

"So it would seem," Aille said.

"Do you really think you can form association with such?"

"I do not know. But I can try."

Aille decided to say no more, at the moment. What was finally coming into focus for him was still too blurred. For all his skills, Yaut was a fraghta, not inclined or trained to welcome new concepts. It was important that Aille not push him too quickly, not force a clash.

Because Yaut was wrong. Or, at least, only half-right. True, by Jao reckoning humans were indeed insane. But what Yaut never considered was that other standards might exist—and that what mattered, in the end, was simply that there *were* standards. Of any kind.

Aille, looking back from the discussion just now completed with Aguilera, understood more fully the association he had felt with the human veterans earlier. Even Tully had been affected by that association, he thought. True, Tully had spent most of his time glaring at the other humans. Apparently, he considered them all to be exhibiting that form of improper behavior he called "collaboration."

But that, too, was significant. As significant, in its own way, as Aguilera's compulsion to give aid and comfort to Tully when there was no logical reason he should.

Yaut would have been simply outraged, if Aille tried to explain it now. The time for that was not yet here. To think of association as a form of improper behavior was tantamount to thinking as an outlaw for a Jao. Anathema for a fraghta. But for humans . . .

It was more complicated. Aille did not think for a moment that he understood it clearly yet. Perhaps he never would, not fully. But one thing was now plain to him. Much had divided Tully and the other humans in that room; much divided Aguilera and Tully in this one. Such divisions were inevitable, he supposed, for any species that thought in straight lines. Yet all of them, according to their own angle of approach, were behaving according to honor.

That was the beginning, always. The lesson had been drummed into him by the kochanata instructors from his earliest memories. *Honor is the base upon which association is poured. Without it, there can be no edifice at all. Everything will spill askew.*

He was on a world full of honor, then. Alien honor, yes; so spiny and angular to a Jao that it seemed a haphazard pile of sticks. But that was a problem to be solved, not a jumble to be declared meaningless.

Where there was honor, Aille could pour an edifice.

The next solar cycle, however, Aille discovered that he would have to postpone his further efforts with the humans.

Governor Oppuk krinnu ava Narvo had scheduled a reception for the recently arrived scion of Pluthrak, to be held at the Governor's palace in the capital. Oklahoma City, it was called.

That was a great honor, of course. It also ushered in a time of peril. Like a great sea beast rising from the deep, showing its spine before its maw, kochan rivalry was coming to the surface.

PART II:
Honors

When the Bond of Ebezon's most important agent on Terra received word of the Governor's reception for Aille, he felt a moment's deep regret. He would have liked to be present at the occasion. "Like a fly on the wall," as humans put it, in one of their charming little saws.

But, it was impossible. First, because he had not been invited, and would not be. Second, because it was not yet time for him to move toward the center of the flow.

An observer he had been, simply advising the Strategy Circle; an observer he would remain. For a time, at least.

Still, it was a pity. The agent was sure he would have much enjoyed himself. The first reports coming to him from Pascagoula were very promising. The agent had, among other things, carefully studied Oppuk krinnu ava Narvo for twenty years. Long ago, that study had led him to despise the Governor. Finally, after twenty years, he thought Oppuk was about to find himself . . .

Challenged? That was not strong enough.

The agent searched his mind for a suitable human expression. Yes, of course. *Catch a tiger by the tail.*

CHAPTER
11

Caitlin Stockwell alighted from the Jao transport and stood on the sweltering tarmac, gazing west at the Oklahoma horizon that stretched out in the dusty distance beyond the airfield. The "invitation" had come two days ago. Although her parents were apprehensive, she had been commanded to attend and they had not. With any luck, she could keep her head down at the reception for the Pluthrak and return to college none the worse tomorrow. If she were very careful, Oppuk might not even notice she was here.

Professor Kinsey had been "invited" to accompany her also. Caitlin wasn't sure why. Kinsey himself swore to her that he had made no request for it—not that he wasn't practically hopping up and down with eagerness to go—and she believed him.

She suspected that was Banle's doing. Her Jao bodyguard seemed to have gotten it into her head that Kinsey was the equivalent of a fraghta for the young woman—a particularly incapable fraghta, to be sure, but the best humans could come up with.

For all their smugness regarding Jao "straightforwardness" in contrast to human "dissimilitude," the Jao were just as capable as any Borgia or Machiavelli of maneuvering under false colors. The coming reception for the new Pluthrak was anything but straightforward. A great honor on the surface, it was actually an arena for clan conflict.

Unfortunately, Governor Oppuk had decided that Caitlin would make a nice decoration for the arena. Even more unfortunately, he'd decided to add Kinsey for an extra little bit of bunting. This was going to be dangerous enough for her, without Kinsey. With him . . .

Caitlin practically cringed. Kinsey was a kindly and well-meaning man, to be sure, as well as a good historian. He was also famous, even among his own human academic colleagues, for being a social bumbler. The sort of person—this was a true story, apparently—who would attend a funeral for a colleague's wife, and then ask him after the conclusion of the service how his research was going.

The land here was as flat as she remembered, from her few visits, as well as hot. The late August air was humid, almost too thick to breathe, after the comparative coolness of Michigan.

Oklahoma City was not the site humans would have selected when deciding upon a new capital for what had once been the United States. Neither would Jao, Caitlin would have thought, with their love of the ocean. But perhaps the Narvo Governor had been motivated by uncomplicated power considerations. The capital was about as centrally located as possible, in North America.

She turned back to Dr. Kinsey. His dark eyes sparkled as he looked over the scene. He'd had no misgivings about accepting this invitation. He was acting like a kid on the eve of Christmas.

Her guard Banle emerged behind them, preceded by a human steward portering their luggage. The sturdy Jao, in her dark-blue harness and trousers, looked characteristically unruffled despite the heat. Her facial markings were distinctive. Dark bands striped both cheeks, but left clear the simmering green-black eyes in that golden face. In an unguarded moment, Banle had once revealed that many of her kochan were so marked. It was the most in twenty years the Jao had ever let slip about her origins.

"Transport to the Governor's palace should be waiting," she said, her body carefully devoid of expression.

Caitlin had learned to read many formal postures, so the big bodyguard had grown adept at concealing her emotions. It was a constant struggle between them, almost as old as she was.

With Banle following, the small party proceeded into the bustling terminal. Caitlin ignored the staring locals who were clearly startled to see humans accompanied by a Jao. That Banle was more than a mere bodyguard should have been apparent to anyone with half a brain, since high status Jao always claimed the rear of any procession as the place of respect. Banle had always made a point of not allowing Caitlin to do so.

The transport was indeed waiting, a black groundcar with maglev fittings that would render the sure-to-be dreadful roads moot. She settled inside, sliding to the middle of the leather seat, and noted gratefully that it was outfitted with air conditioning against the late summer heat. So, she told herself, they were treating her more as guest than hostage this time around. Perhaps the reception was not going to be as tense as she'd feared.

Their driver was human, but locked away on the other side of a thick panel of opaque glass. She leaned back against the upholstery and watched the city slip past. The section near the airport was fairly prosperous, small shops mingled with single family dwellings. Most of those were in good repair, but farther out they encountered a section littered with rusted automobiles and prowled by feral looking potbellied children with arms and legs like match sticks.

The children played listlessly in the dust, looking up as the massive black vehicle swept silently by. One of them picked up a chunk of displaced concrete, but didn't throw it, though Caitlin could see how tightly his fingers curled around the jagged shape.

Did they go to school? Caitlin wondered. Did their parents have any kind of employment beyond scratching in the ground to make the defeated-looking kitchen gardens she saw in almost every yard? Was any kind of medical care available? What would become of them? Her father tried to negotiate services for such as these, but the Jao had no concern for what they termed the "useless" of humanity. Anyone, or anything, that could make itself of solid, practical use was good. Anything that could not, such as those pathetic starving children back there, was beneath their notice.

Most bridges were still out in this part of the city, as well as highway overpasses, which lay in huge fallen sections like the bones of some extinct animal. She'd seen video records of life before the Jao, the cars, the entertainment options, the bookstores and movie houses, the amazing variety of sports and electronic games.

"—conduct a series of interviews," Professor Kinsey was saying. She realized, with a start, that he had been talking for some time without her really listening. She wrenched her attention away from the devastation outside.

"Do you think the Jao officials at the reception will speak freely about themselves?" she asked.

"If I frame my request properly." His brown eyes blinked and he pulled off his glasses to clean them. "I must make them see the end results will be useful to the Jao, as well as us. They love practicality."

"They will not prattle idly about themselves and events that happened so long ago," Banle said suddenly. The sleek golden head turned to regard them. "What is happening now is of interest. What happened in that struggle so long ago is not. We came to make Terra of use in the coming fight and that is all anyone needs to know."

The tiny fine hairs prickled on the back of Caitlin's neck. "You mean the fight against the Ekhat."

Kinsey leaned forward eagerly. "What can you tell us about them? There's so little information available in the open records."

"Such as you will never see an Ekhat," Banle said. "When they come, as they surely will, the battle will be fought in space. You will most likely be dead before it is over, along with most humans on this planet. It is not necessary to concern yourself with their appearance."

"Nevertheless," Kinsey said, obviously taken aback, "I am curious." He glanced aside at Caitlin.

"I am not authorized to provide such information." Banle's green-black eyes turned back to the window. One of her shoulders tightened into what Caitlin read as *unease*. "You will have to seek access at a higher level."

Like the Governor of Earth, Caitlin thought. She did not relish meeting this particular Jao again. Her father, Ben Stockwell, hated working under him and in the end had accepted the role of President only to protect his family and ameliorate the worst aspects of Jao rule. He had, to this date, been able to get them to allocate at least some small portion of resources toward rebuilding war-devastated areas like Illinois, Texas, Louisiana, and Virginia. He'd also argued effectively, so far, against plastering the continent's mountainous and more remote areas with bolides to eliminate the last of the Resistance.

The vehicle turned abruptly, stopped at a massive security gate manned by Jao guards, then was waved through to a tree-lined boulevard full of deep green shadows and lined by a veritable sea of begonias so that red and pink and white filled the eyes. That was a surprise. Jao didn't usually think of flowers, or indeed of any sort of ornamental foliage, at all. They did have an aesthetic sense, but it was bound up closely with either behavior—such as their elaborate body language—or practical arts such as architecture. She wondered who'd decided to authorize the impressive display.

Surrounding human habitations had long since been removed from this area and the green grounds swept to either side as far as she could see. The palace itself lay at the end of the boulevard, all sleek black curves of quantum crystal against the bright sky, with no right angles, unmistakably Jao.

Banle blinked at the unexpected beds of flowers and her body shifted into *shocked-disapproval*.

Caitlin suppressed a smile and stared over the Jao's shoulder. Waste of resources, was what Banle was thinking, she was quite sure. Waste of labor and space, fulfilling no useful function. Was the Narvo Governor becoming decadent?

The car pulled up before the black palace and a liveried human attendant, who had been waiting back by the wall, hurried forward to open the door. Again, Caitlin found that odd and out of place. Jao considered the human custom of opening doors for others as a gesture of respect to be grotesque. An insult, even.

It was possible, she supposed, that the attendant had been acquired simply for this reception, as a courtesy to the human guests. But Caitlin thought that was unlikely. First, because Governor Oppuk was, to put it mildly, not given to being considerate toward humans. Second, because he certainly wouldn't do so directly—and this attendant was wearing Narvo colors.

Could Oppuk be adapting to human customs himself?

Caitlin emerged from the car, blinking at the torrid sunshine. No pointless flowers here, just black crystal steps and the stark lines of a protective overhang, almost like a portico. Ah, well. She turned as Banle gestured imperiously. Only time would tell, but this visit might well be more interesting than she had anticipated.

When the invitation had surfaced in Yaut's electronic queue, he'd immediately realized its importance and taken it to Aille. He'd found the young Pluthrak in his office in the refit facility, going over the latest figures.

The younger Jao looked up as Yaut entered. He had been

swimming down at the cordoned-off Jao area at the beach earlier and his nap was dark-gold with damp. "Kaul still insists we proceed with the replacement of all kinetic weapons, despite the results of the tests."

"Then you will replace them." Yaut had served too long to entertain any illusions of sense winning out over duty. "If the lasers serve poorly, we will switch them back, and then, if you are fortunate, Oppuk will not hold it against you for being right."

"But it wastes resources!" Aille stalked across the dim room. "As well as time. And, according to reports, time may be what we have the least of!"

"It is your job to accomplish this foolish task quickly and without further protest." Yaut keyed his personal board on and laid it on the desk before Aille. "Then, if it does not work out, your task will be to cover it up as best as possible."

"And the Terran work force will be disgruntled," Aille said. His ears were aslant with *foreboding*. "The workers will see it as yet another affront to their expertise in these matters, and they do have a point. The tanks will be much less effective for combat in an atmosphere, refitted as Kaul would have them."

"Forget about the refit for now," Yaut said and indicated his board with its message. "We have been summoned to a reception in the population center known as Oklahoma City to be held in your honor by Governor Oppuk krinnu ava Narvo. I had hoped such a meeting between the two of you could be put off, but it seems you have already come to his notice."

Aille's eyes flashed as he realized the implications. Historically, associations between Narvo and Pluthrak had been few, opposition nearly constant. It was not in Narvo's interests for a Pluthrak to do well here, or anywhere else, for that matter.

"Why did he accept my appointment in the first place?" Aille asked. "I still do not understand that. Granted, it would have been rude to refuse, but Narvo has never hesitated to be rude."

"You are young," Yaut said, his body stiff with *blunt-truth*. "The young often make mistakes because that is the nature of learning. Such mistakes could be employed to cast Pluthrak in a bad light, harming future associations which then might never come to pass."

"So I cannot afford to make any mistakes," Aille said.

"No," Yaut said, "not even those which are sure to be forced upon you."

"Like this pointless refit." Aille sat back in his chair and stared out over the work floor, which was visible through the glass wall beyond.

"I was thinking more of Tully." Yaut exhaled, fighting the exasperation he felt over this matter. Guidance must be firm, he told himself, but ever subtle. "That is one burden I would have counseled you not to take up. However, we could put him down before we leave."

"No, the Terrans are watching what I do now," Aille said. "They know about Tully. Even Aguilera, who disapproves of him, does not want him dead."

Yaut could not help gesturing in *stymied-frustration*. "Once we leave," he said, "despite the locator, he will find a way to escape. Only my constant vigilance has restrained him this long."

"Then bring him with us."

Yaut circled the desk so he could study the invitation again. "Quarters for five have been set aside, which is an insult, although a sly one. The Governor's staff must know you have already begun to assemble your own service, now that you are in place."

"So, after Tully, we can take along only two more." Aille composed his hands in the classic form of *careful-contemplation*. "The female bodyguard, I suppose, then?"

"Tamt," Yaut said. "She has progressed to the point that I have granted her right to be named."

"And Aguilera," Aille said, eyes still focused on his hands. "I will add him to my service. He can assist you in keeping an eye on Tully."

"Two Terrans out of four you are to be allowed?" Yaut cocked his head, very dubiously. "Might it not be better to select another Jao?"

"We are on Terra," Aille said. "I have been given charge of all jinau troops. If I do not demonstrate the ability to form associations with the natives, then I will look ineffective."

"True." All the same, Yaut shuddered. "Which makes it all the more important not to be embarrassed by Tully. Let me arrange an unfortunate 'accident.' Perhaps he could drown while accompanying you on a morning swim. Terrans are notoriously poor swimmers, and his fellow natives would deem it noble if he perished while attempting to provide companionship."

Aille's ears flattened. "They would never believe it. Tully has done nothing so far without being forced. He will go with us and he will behave, or we will make him wish he had."

That, Yaut thought, was much easier desired than accomplished, but for now, he held silent.

When the order came through, Tully had been assigned for the morning to Rafe Aguilera, who therefore had the damned locator control on his belt. Aguilera had stationed him down in the next refit bay, working to remove the engines and tracks from old Bradleys. No one would trust him to install the new maglev drives, of course, but he could hardly damage anything crucial while stripping outmoded equipment.

One bay over, he saw a Jao floor-supervisor stop and hand Aguilera a board to sign off. Aguilera read it, then looked up. Tully sat back on his heels to wipe sweat from his brow, surreptitiously gauging the older man's reaction.

"Goddammit!" Aguilera narrowed his eyes, obviously angry. "Are you sure about this?"

The Jao's ears shifted into an angle that made Tully uneasy. He realized he was becoming all too conversant with Jao body language.

"You question orders?" the Jao said in heavily accented English.

"No," Aguilera said, "but I thought we'd proved our artillery worked better in an atmosphere—" His gaze strayed to the upper floor, where Aille's office was located. "Never mind. I'll check with the Subcommandant, when I get the chance, just to be sure."

"These—orders!" The Jao loomed over Aguilera and the difference in their body masses was all too evident. As always, the human looked fragile in comparison. "You follow—without question!" He cuffed Aguilera, knocking him to the floor.

"Hey, wait a minute!" Tully was on his feet before he'd realized he'd spoken. "He didn't deserve that!"

The Jao turned with all the grace of a bulldozer. He was not angry, Tully realized with a start, reading the lines of his body. The big alien was just confused. The cuffing he'd given Aguilera would not have done more than jar another Jao. It certainly wouldn't have felled them.

Probably new to Terran service, Tully thought. He could almost see the wheels turning inside the Jao's head. Humans were supposed to serve, he'd been told. They did not argue about decisions any more than a refrigerator had an opinion on whether it should be plugged in. After a very short time, Aguilera had grown accustomed to having Aille krinnu ava Pluthrak's ear and had forgotten how few Jao were interested in hearing what humans had to say.

He dropped his gaze. "Forgive him," he said in Jao, as humbly as gritted teeth would allow. "He is tired from working all night and forgets himself. Orders will be followed, of course."

Other men had stopped and were watching, their faces grimy, their hands full of tools that could become weapons on a moment's notice. They bunched together, muttering. Tully pulled Aguilera to his feet. "Tell him!" he whispered forcefully.

"Forgive me," Aguilera said, weaving and unable to focus. "I meant no disrespect."

The Jao sniffed, then strode off. Tully stared after him for a moment, his face tight with anger. "That was stupid," he said finally.

"Yeah." Aguilera passed a hand over his pale face. "Get back to work," he said finally to the watching men. "This isn't doing any good."

"But the tanks—" Ed Patterson began.

"They want them with lasers," Aguilera said, "so they'll get them with lasers. Then, maybe, if these Ekhat do ever show up, they'll kick their fuzzy butts and they'll all have to go somewhere else to have their war."

Tully eyed the locator control box on Aguilera's belt. He should have plucked it off when the other man was half out on his feet. Then he could have been off the base in fifteen minutes.

Aguilera caught his eye. "Want it?"

He flushed and looked away.

"What's it like, back there in Rockies?" Aguilera's voice was low. "Plenty of medical supplies, enough to eat, warm clothes? Can the kids go to good schools? Is there fuel for cars? Munitions for guns?"

There was damned little of any of that, Tully thought, but whose fault was it? Certainly not the Resistance's!

He was not surprised that Aguilera had figured it out. Collaborator or not, the middle-aged ex-soldier was no dummy.

"Just let me go, Rafe," he said in a low voice. "Sooner or later, this Subcommandant and his goddamned fraghta are going to crack me like a nut, and then I'll spill everything." He hooked his thumbs in his belt. "You're human. You can't want that."

"What I want," Aguilera said, "is what's best for humanity. We've lost this battle, but we don't have to lose the war. If you keep your head down and stop making trouble, you might just learn enough to help down the line when things are different." He glanced around the refit floor where most of the workers had resumed the morning's tasks. "Right now, there's no chance of getting rid of the Jao. We have to survive and learn as much as we can."

"You mean collaborate!"

"I mean, as Patton once said, 'no one ever served his country by dying. You serve by making the other dumb bastard die for his country.' The first rule here is to survive and get as much out of the Jao as we can in the process."

Tully glanced over his shoulder, but the Jao guard had wandered to the far end of the row. "Then you think the day will come when we boot the Jao off Earth?"

"I do." Aguilera straightened, then grimaced at a kink in his back. "Maybe not in my lifetime, or yours, but at some point; history has proved that empires always fall. Hell, when you get right down to it, we Americans thought we were on top of the world—and then the Jao came."

"But all those empires, Rome and England and even America, were human," Tully said. "You can't count on the Jao being the same."

"No," Aguilera said, "but it's all we've got left to hope for. Until then, we have to survive."

CHAPTER

12

"Miss Stockwell," a gravelly Jao voice said as a pair of immense oak doors swung open and Caitlin's party entered the palace.

How strange, she thought, glancing back over her shoulder at the surprising wooden panels. Jao ordinarily preferred doorfields to crude physical barriers such as these.

"I am pleased," the voice continued, "that you and Dr. Kinsey accepted my invitation."

The "invitation," of course, had been a command. She ran fingers back through her short wind-blown hair as an excuse to hide her expression. The entrance hall, constructed of cool gray stone and a ceiling that loomed far overhead, was dim, as Jao quarters so often were, but also unexpectedly primitive. It had actual corners and huge pillars framing the doorway carved in the likeness of ceremonial bau. Like the flowers outside, they were a form of human decoration, adapted to Jao sensibilities. Jao just didn't do that, in her experience.

"Governor Oppuk," she said with a feeling of dread as she waited for her eyes to adjust.

Kinsey stepped forward, a smile on his face. "This is an extraordinary opportunity, being allowed to put together a history of the Jao! I can't thank you enough for giving me permission to do so!"

Oppuk krinnu ava Narvo, the Governor of Terra, was dressed in customary Jao dark-blue trousers with the halfcape draped over one shoulder so many of the conquerors affected. Its insignia, meaningless squiggles to human eyes, had been worked in a bright, fierce scarlet.

"It is perhaps time Terrans knew more of the Jao," he said in accented English. One of his ears swiveled lazily. "They are like ignorant children, understanding nothing of the dangers awaiting them beyond this solar system, dangers which require us, your protectors, to expend great amounts of resources and energy."

"To be sure," Kinsey said, "but my book should remedy that. I'm eager to get started."

Narvo turned to Caitlin. "It has been long since flow brought us together," he said. "Are you now considered emerged?"

Her father had struggled to keep his family sequestered from his job as much as possible, not wanting them to come to the attention of their powerful overlords. This one, in particular.

"Yes," she said, though she had no idea what "emerged" actually meant. Jao were notoriously close-mouthed on the subject of their biology and development.

The Governor was massive, even for a Jao, the velvety nap covering his skin a rich red-gold. His *vai camiti* was composed of three uneven stripes slanted at forty-five-degree angles across nose and eyes, rather like a zebra. He occupied the middle of the spacious foyer as though he were an ornamental statue and regarded them in a perfect attitude of *amused-disdain*.

Caitlin had known Jao as far back as she could remember. There had even been times—thankfully long past—when Banle had remained in her bedroom when she slept. She'd begun learning bodyspeech at the age of four, almost as soon as she'd started to learn English. The Governor apparently wished to appear magnanimous and accepting, coming to meet them personally like this, but his body betrayed his inner thoughts: he was far from respecting humans and their ways.

She glanced at Dr. Kinsey who was radiating pleasure. Without thinking, she curved her arms and let her fingers fall into *amused-acceptance*. "It was kind of you to invite us," she said, knowing full well no Jao in Oppuk's position would ever wish to appear "kind." The Jao understood kindness, in their own way— they had several terms for it, in fact—but it was closely associated with their complicated clan relations and bound up with their notions of proper relations between individuals of different status.

Applied to subject people, the closest equivalent in their language connoted "weak" or "foolish."

It was a stupidly imprudent thing to say, of course, but she was finding it harder than she'd expected to contain her hatred for the creature who had murdered her brother. Her remark was a petty way to strike back, but she felt better for it. And, in any event, she'd spoken in English, where the same insult was not implied.

He blinked at her posture, then shifted into a rather stiff version of standard *welcome*, apparently startled into an uncustomarily coarse singleness of expression. "My castellan will see you to your quarters," he continued in English. "You should find them adequate."

Dr. Kinsey turned and threw his arms wide. His face beamed. "I am certain we will find them nothing less than splendid!"

The burly Narvo canted his head, his ears hovering on the edge of *insult*.

Caitlin sighed. The Governor, it seemed, was not a subtle individual, and Kinsey had so little experience with Jao, he was confounding him with his exuberance. Humans were not supposed to be happy in the presence of Jao; impressed, yes, perhaps even awed, but not wild with delight. It was not the business of Jao to please humans.

"Jao taste in design is noted across the world as being eminently preferable," she said, her bearing now shaped to *quiet-reverence*. "My father has sought to emulate it in our own residence, though never so perfectly as it deserved."

"As well he might," Kinsey said. "I hope to see the President's official residence at some point too."

At that moment, mercifully, a human woman dressed in black palace livery padded forward out of the shadows. "Shall you go to your rooms now, Miss Stockwell, Dr. Kinsey?"

"Yes," Caitlin said hastily before Kinsey could speak again and worsen the situation. "Please."

Governor Narvo held his ground and watched as they were forced to detour around him as though he were a pillar. Caitlin could feel the weight of his green gaze even after he was out of sight.

Aille piloted his own Pluthrak courier to the Governor's private field at his residence, having been assured that berthing facilities capable of servicing it were available. Tamt krinnu Kannu vau Hij, his newly acknowledged bodyguard, went along in the second seat. Though there was room for all of them, Yaut remained behind to shepherd the rest of his party via less elegant transport. Let Oppuk meet him accompanied by only his Jao bodyguard, rather than a fraghta or several humans, he had counseled. It would make a better impression.

It was the first time the two had been separated, since his current assignment, and Aille was understandably nervous about being without Yaut's sage advice.

The green and tan landscape, as the ship descended, was startling in its aridity. A few small ponds shimmered in the metropolitan area below, along with some thready rivers, more sand than water in this season, it seemed. But there was no ocean and only a few insignificant lakes, not even good-sized by Jao standards. Why was the Governor's residence located here, of all places, when this continent possessed so much inviting seacoast?

As in Mississippi, evidence of past devastation still lay everywhere, even after twenty orbital cycles. Collapsed buildings sprawled like decaying bodies, rusted girders exposed and shattered glass bright beneath the sky. Smashed vehicles were scattered like broken toys and few of the bridges had been restored. Aille was surprised that so few repairs seemed to have been done since the conquest.

When he and Tamt popped the hatch and emerged from the ship, the air that met them was hot, though not nearly as moist as that of Mississippi. His ears waggled as a small vehicle rushed toward them and stopped just short of the ramp.

A pair of Jao stepped out. "Vaish, honored guest," the foremost, a sturdy male, said. His body was all *respectful-attention* with just the hint of implied *awe*. "Governor Oppuk sends greetings."

The other, also male, actually mirrored his fellow servitor's stance, to Aille's surprise. Tripartite postures were extremely difficult. He himself had mastered only a few very formal ones. These two had been well trained, Aille thought, feeling strangely naked without Yaut at his side. Tamt hastily took her place in front, ceding him what little honor there was to be had in this situation.

"I am delighted to be present," Aille said, holding himself in a safe rendition of *appreciation-of-service*, a posture learned very early by all Jao crechelings and one he was confident he could perform perfectly. How he comported himself here would reflect upon Pluthrak and would be reported to the Governor. He must be aware of that at all times.

Aille realized with a start the two were identical, matched down to the pale-russet of their nap and the slant of their *vai camiti*. Clutch-brothers, certainly, but also genetically identical, a rarity among his species. They gestured at the cart, which had four seats, two in front, two behind, unfortunately all seemingly fabricated for human proportions. "We shall escort you to the official residence."

Aille allowed Tamt, her whiskers bristling and looking suitably efficient, to precede him down the ramp. *Pride* was apparent in her bearing, as well as *respect*—but the two were not properly combined so that, at points, they clashed and cancelled each other out. He must have Yaut coach her further upon their return to Mississippi.

The drier heat was pleasant as he walked, playing across his back and shoulders like a deep massage. This climate, he supposed, might have its compensations despite the dearth of decent bodies of water.

He did not ask the names of his escort, nor did they offer such. It was not their place, as underlings, nor had they performed any unusual service worthy of his notice. Still, he found himself thinking of his human workers, how they freely offered and inquired after names, almost as though no worthwhile exchange of information were possible without first knowing to whom you were speaking.

The seats were indeed small, human-sized at best, and most likely intended for smaller specimens of the species at that. Tamt looked unhappy, despite her efforts to disguise it, but wedged herself into the back. He sat next to her and affected not to notice the disparity in the seat's meager proportions compared to his own. The vehicle, like most of those at the base in Mississippi, was of human manufacture and refitted with Jao maglev drive. But, by now, Aille was perfectly aware that a more spacious vehicle could have been found for this purpose. Here was a small, sly, studied insult—and not, he was sure, the last one he was going to encounter.

The Governor's palace, though traditionally constructed of poured quantum crystal, lay at the end of a long avenue of tall native trees and was surrounded by various other kinds of native vegetation. These, although obviously tended and regulated, performed no useful function he could discern. Beds of colorful foliage spread out in every direction, dominated by a strange washed-out shade of red, along with true reds and whites. In the name of good manners, he stifled his bewilderment at the display and assumed instead an air of *overall-approval.*

As they drove, the pair of servitors observed him from time to time over their shoulders, and he thought he detected, even in the well trained cant of their ears, a trace of hostility.

He forced his mind to focus on representing Pluthrak honorably. The Governor might have some valid reason for this garish spectacle, after all.

The cart stopped before massive doors in the center of the palace. The doors had been constructed in the human fashion out of a solid opaque substance, rather than an energy field. Beside him, Tamt squeezed out of the too-small seat, her eyes vigilant, and took up a protective stance. He followed, his whiskers aquiver with an intense rush of curiosity he could not quite subdue.

"Governor Oppuk awaits you within," the first servitor said. Then, to Aille's barely suppressed astonishment, a human servitor in Narvo colors appeared and opened one of the doors.

Tamt stalked through, and then Aille. The two servitors followed, so that they all stood in a cavernous, cool dimness made of rectangular gray stones piled one atop another. Despite the traditional Jao-styled exterior of the palace, the interior was distressingly human. "Look at these corners," Tamt said and reached out to touch them with the ends of her fingers. "They are so—abrupt."

The servitors glanced at one another and their eyes flashed bright-green before they took command of themselves. "Governor Narvo has adopted aspects of the native style of building," one said. "Local materials and craftsmen are readily available and thereby less costly, and it impresses the natives, who need to constantly be reminded of their place."

"Of course," Aille said, but it all rang false to him. He knew enough about humans, by now, to be sure that they would not be impressed by seeing their conquerors adopt native styles. Pleased, perhaps—if the adoption was accompanied by other forms of association. But otherwise it meant nothing. What "impressed" them, taken by itself, was simply Jao superiority in battle.

"Governor Oppuk is in the solarium," the second servitor said.

The last word was an English term, spoken somewhat awkwardly. "Will you come this way?"

He cocked his head in assent and then allowed Tamt to again precede him, this time through a series of hallways and large echoing rooms, none of which possessed flow, in the classic Jao sense. Instead, the building had an odd cut-up feeling to it, as though it started and stopped in fits and no one ever quite got to where he was going. How did the Narvo live like this?

The "solarium" turned out to be a vast room with glass panels set into the ceiling, so that the sun cascaded through and made the walls vibrate with light. Trees in tubs lined its straight edges, their branches filled with the small colorful avians called "birds." Aille blinked and realized most of the room had been dug out for a deep pool. It was most natural looking, outlined with slabs of black rock and a steady pattern of artificially generated waves lapping its sides.

Out in the middle, someone was swimming. Aille stopped as a dark, wet head popped up out of the water and regarded him with glittering eyes that had gone mostly green. The face's *vai camiti* was very bold, but a trifle unbalanced, three black stripes slashed at varying angles. "Ah, Aille krinnu ava Pluthrak."

Aille stood at the water's edge, the briny scent of this microcosm sea washing over him, and let *intense-interest* wash through him. "I am honored to answer your summons, Governor."

"Of course you are." Oppuk swam over in one sinuous motion and heaved out onto the rocks. "And I am honored by the generosity of Pluthrak—to waste one of its illustrious progeny on this chaotic world."

For far too long, Narvo had refused to ally itself with Pluthrak in even the smallest of matters. Such association would have been powerful, and mingling their potent bloodlines through a marriage-group would have spawned offspring who would make their mark on the galaxy. But Narvo had spurned all Pluthrak advances, and now the two were at odds almost at every turn. Aille had heard much of this rivalry, since he was a crecheling, but had never before been in the presence of a Narvo. His whiskers tingled with warning, though he held his body to *intense-interest* through fierce concentration.

Oppuk krinnu ava Narvo shook himself, then gestured at a silent human servant, who appeared out of the shadows, eyes downcast.

"What do you think of this room?" he asked nonchalantly, though his shoulders hinted at *outright-challenge.*

"It is quite bright," Aille said, trying not to blink, "but otherwise reminiscent of my birthworld." Whatever he thought of the light level, the room had an exquisite scent. "Marit An's seas smell very much like this."

"I had an odor expert brought in from Narvo's Pratus." Oppuk thrust his arms out as though he were a child, and the servant hastily slipped a standard weapons harness over his shoulders. "Expensive, of course, but as ruler of these creatures, I have to maintain a standard they will respect. And then, such a room makes living in this landlocked region more bearable."

The sweep of the waves, modest as they were, touched that part of him that ached for home. Aille longed to leap into the water and swim until the grime of his trip was gone. *Intense-interest,* he told himself, not *intense-longing,* and though his whiskers twitched, his body held form. "I was wondering why you located the palace here, when this continent possesses so much seacoast."

"Convenience. It is centrally located in this continent, which is where we met the greatest resistance." Oppuk stepped into a pair of flowing trousers. "And ready access to resources. We were forced to destroy much of this polity's infrastructure before they would yield. Lackluster as it is, this was the best location, though I often travel to one of the coasts for respite."

He was an impressive specimen, Aille thought, mature and fit, though his nap looked a bit patchy with age.

"Perhaps you will have the opportunity to swim in here," Oppuk said, "before you return to duty."

"That would be most welcome," Aille said, his jaw tight with the effort of retaining a posture that did not arise from his thoughts.

"Yes," Oppuk said, "I am sure it would." The human servant cinched the trousers around his waist, taking care not to actually touch him. "Feel free now to examine your quarters. All guests will attend your reception later in the current solar cycle."

Aille lowered his eyes, then turned to the two servitors who had conducted him, *question* now seeping into his bearing.

"There will be a number of natives present," Oppuk said offhandedly, before either could speak. "That, however, will most likely not trouble you, since you have actually taken several into your personal service." *Refined-distaste* flattened his ears, wrinkled his nose, made his brow rise.

"I command jinau troops," Aille said. "I seek to understand the way their minds work so they may be made of more use."

"Humans, when properly trained, make barely adequate servants," Oppuk said. "They breed in such quantities that we may secure some benefit out of them on the battlefield through sheer numbers. But I assure you that little of what you and I would recognize as true 'thought' occurs in their savage little minds. They are, according to one of their deceased elders by the name of Kipling, 'half-devil and half-child.'"

Flow surged and Aille's heart raced. What would Yaut counsel, if the fraghta were present this very moment? However he responded, he must not bring shame upon Pluthrak.

He took a deep breath and assumed an air of *chastened-enlightenment*. "Thank you, Governor," he said. "I look forward to being further instructed through your observations."

"Perhaps," Oppuk said. "If I am in the mood." He glanced at the two Jao servitors and they hastened to the far exit, one fitted this time with an ordinary doorfield. "This way," said the nearest.

Upon arriving in landlocked Oklahoma City, Yaut found Aille had been relegated to an insufferably primitive annex, one full of angles and lines, with no sense of flow, while light was allowed to flood in through a veritable wall of windows. He directed Tully and Aguilera to stow their small parcels, then surveyed the site. "Unacceptable!"

Tully retreated to a corner—his favorite move, predictable as the sunrise—and watched warily. Rafe Aguilera scratched his head, which probably indicated some sort of emotional state, but communicated nothing to a Jao.

Yaut prowled the rest of the space, finding a sanitary facility, two small storage bays, and five sleeping platforms. But no pool, not even a small one. "Intolerable!" he said, coming back into the common area. "I do not understand! Is this Narvo deliberately trying to convey offense? A few petty insults are to be expected, naturally. That idiot tiny vehicle they sent to fetch me!—and Aille too, I am sure—but this is excessive."

The doorfield shimmered off, admitting Tamt and Aille. Yaut

glared at his charge as though these miserable quarters were all his fault.

Aille wrinkled his nose, though his posture was carefully neutral. "I see you have become acquainted with our accommodations."

"Did you insult the Governor even before you arrived?" Yaut felt *righteous-indignation* sweep over him. "It must have taken a great deal of preparation to craft something this unsuitable!"

"It does not matter," Aille said. "Soldiers on the battlefield endure whatever conditions present themselves. We have far more important things to concern us at this point."

"He is testing you," Yaut said.

Aille's gaze flickered around the appallingly crude surroundings. "This sort of thing is beneath my notice. I do not choose to see these corners."

"How can you miss them in this flood of light!" Yaut glared at the windows. "Can we not do something?"

Tamt stepped forward, her shoulders all *eager-to-serve*. "Let me," she said. "I can go to the staff and secure coverings."

"Coverings?" Yaut regarded her blankly.

"Human dwellings have such things," the bodyguard said. "I have seen them. They call them 'curtains,' or sometimes 'drapes.'"

"When were you ever in a human habitation?" Yaut said.

Tamt hesitated, her posture dissolving into meaningless unassociated elements. She did not speak for a moment. When she did, her voice was low. "Now and then," was all she said.

Yaut's ears lay flat with *disapproval*. "You too? What is this fascination with the natives? You will be ruined, if you are not careful, by the time you return to your kochan for reassignment."

"That will not happen," she said, her voice even lower. Just for an instant, her eyes flashed the shocking bright green of *intense-shame*. "Some time ago, I sent in my request to stay permanently. I have not heard the answer yet, but I am sure it will be granted."

"Why did you make the request?" Yaut stepped closer, studying every angle of her body, the tilt of her ears, the twitch of whisker, the angle of shoulder and arm, leg and torso. In his experience, admittedly brief, this particular female was not able to think one thing while performing another. She should be able to keep nothing back.

Tamt gazed out the intolerably glaring windows, as though she could perceive something after all in that annoying blaze of light.

"I am low status," she said finally, "little wanted in the kochan-house, or anywhere else, for that matter. But, here, on Terra, humans will always speak to you, despite all unworthiness. I . . . am comfortable among them."

"But they are uncouth!" Yaut could not contain his outrage. "You prefer such to your own kochan?"

She flinched, but did not meet his eyes. "You are valued," she said. "Or else you would not be fraghta to our young Subcommandant. You do not know what it is like to be never seen, never called, never selected or even noticed." She flattened her ears. "They dispatched me to Terra, to this subjugation which has no end, and never inquired after my successful placement or continued survival. In all the time I have been here, I have heard nothing from them. So, in the end, I decided to stay." She turned away from the light, blinking. "I am sure they will not object."

She must have been most unpromising when newly emerged, Yaut thought, to have been distanced so thoroughly from her kochan. Perhaps they had planned for her to die in struggle here, bringing honor to her own in at least that small measure, and she had even failed to achieve that.

"I will bring honor to the Subcommandant," she said suddenly, as though he'd spoken his thoughts aloud. "I will make them all see him, in every way possible! No one shall overlook him, I promise!" She hastened to the door, keyed the field off, then on again behind her.

Aille stared after her, thoughtfulness written across his youthful face. "Interesting," he said. "You seem to have grazed a nerve."

" 'Interesting,' " Yaut said dourly, "hardly covers it."

"I do not understand."

"If this one has found a reason to stay, so must have many others." He turned his back on the garish spill of light and considered. "There is a thing which happens sometimes to Jao under extreme stress who have been too long from home, especially those of low status. They lose their sense of identity and lapse into slovenliness. When that happens, their kochan is shamed before all."

"Really," Aille said, "such a thing can hardly be common?"

"More common than anyone would like to admit," Yaut said, "and you have already taken three humans into your service. Make certain no one has further reason to suspect it of you."

CHAPTER
13

Dr. Kinsey burst into Caitlin's room as soon as she answered his knock with a distracted "Come in." She'd left the doorfield deactivated in any case until Banle returned.

The professor's lined face was beaming. "You look lovely, my dear! What an elegant dress!"

She smoothed the skirt of her long gown, newly tailored by one of the best dressmakers in Oklahoma City. The material was woven of what appeared to be almost a molten silver. "It's wasted on the Jao, of course. They don't understand fashion, but the humans in attendance will notice. For my father's sake, I have to uphold the family image."

He sank into the closest chair. "My first Jao dinner! I suppose it would be impolite to actually take notes."

Caitlin shook her head, then crossed the room to straighten his old-fashioned blue and red tie. Blue and red, jinau colors. Could he have been more obvious? She repressed a sigh.

"It certainly would. And keep in mind that Jao don't use meals as sit-down social functions, the way humans do. They—well—graze might be the best term for it. They normally eat only one meal a day, and they're quite capable of going several days without food and still functioning at near-peak efficiency. Tonight, food will probably be provided at various stations around the room, a great deal of which will almost certainly not be to human taste. Nibble before accepting a full portion. And don't be shocked if they disrobe without warning. They don't have the same body taboos we do and there will likely be a pool provided for spontaneous swimming."

"Will I be expected to swim?" He looked both intrigued and alarmed.

"Heavens, no!" She fought not to laugh in his face. "Jao can hold their breath for a quarter of hour or more. They're practically like seals in the water. Compared to them, even the best human swimmer is just dog-paddling. If you tried to join in, you'd probably drown in the first minute."

"Oh," he said as she released his tie and stepped back to study the results. "Well, I've got a lot to learn, but that is what I'm here for. I still can't wait to get started!"

She sighed. "Dr. Kinsey, this so-called 'reception' won't be fun, and they wouldn't like it, if we did find it obviously so. They're not here to provide entertainment for humans. You should be subdued in your conversation, respectful, but not openly pleased about the things you see and hear tonight. They find that kind of enthusiasm irritating, or even offensive."

"Really?" He smoothed his hair, then dropped his hand. "I'm glad you told me." He hesitated. "Are there any other subjects I should avoid, perhaps religion, for instance?"

She shook her head, then picked up a small silver earring in the shape of a sand dollar and cocked her head to one side to put it on. "The Jao were deliberately crafted by the Ekhat, Doctor, not evolved through natural selection and accident."

"I know that," he protested.

"Then consider the consequences. They know exactly who made them and why, which makes them singularly indifferent to what they term 'superstition.' They have their own quirks, of course. But those all seem bound up with matters of custom and proper conduct, not what we'd consider religion or even ideology in general."

He made a rueful face. "You should write this book instead of me. You've certainly had more interaction with the Jao than anyone I can name."

"Of all the people on Earth, it can't come from me," she said. "They watch me all the time. If you put my name anywhere on that book and then they found some error or unacceptable attitude—as, I must warn you, they most likely will—my father would pay the price. Or I would. What they might be willing to let pass as a misunderstanding on your part, they'd see as a deliberate insult coming from me."

She closed her eyes and reached for calm. "Don't forget what happened to my brother. I am willing to help all I can, as long as you keep my name out of it."

"Very well," he said. "Perhaps you'll at least get a paper for your graduate studies out of this."

"Not even that," she said. "I took a degree in history, then continued in that area for my doctorate because Jao can hardly object to or concern themselves with any views I have on what took place before they brought us the, ah, benefit of their rule."

She glanced at her watch. Seven o'clock, probably time to go, though Jao did not assign meaning to bits of time and hold themselves hostage to them. They understood "now" and "imme-diately," "soon" and "later," and even "in a little while." Anything beyond that could be interpreted as the individual felt or needed. Their legendary timesense allowed them to feel when to do things in some fashion humans were never going to understand, a sort of internal clock that far out-rivaled her kind's rudimentary sense of time.

Banle appeared as they exited the room and then fell in behind, another of her on-going subtle insults. Caitlin made small talk with Kinsey, affecting not to notice the snub until they reached the reception.

"Oh," she said, dropping to one knee. "It's my shoe. Go on and I'll be along in a minute."

As Banle was already halfway through the door, the Jao could hardly retreat without looking indecisive. Caitlin lingered, adjusting her shoe strap for another few seconds, then followed the two inside. Banle's shoulders were clearly set into *angry-frustration.* Caitlin turned away, determined not to notice. Kinsey charged into the crowd, glowing face surveying the Jao.

They might well have been outdoors in some vast park. The floor had been planted in soft green grass with trees in tubs scattered throughout. A huge pool in the shape of a natural lake dominated a room as spacious as an exhibition hall, though there were sev-eral others as well. The air was redolent of the sea, but subtly alien.

Her gaze swept upward to a startling series of skylights set into the ceiling. Jao eyes were more sensitive than humans' so they normally preferred rooms without extraneous light sources, especially windows. Since the month was August, days were currently long at this latitude and, outside, the summer sun, though slowly setting in the west, was still vigorous even at this hour.

She saw several Jao clad in ornate halfcapes glance up at the skylights, then move away, ears and whiskers expressing *discomfort* briefly before they tamed them into more tactful postures. What was Governor Oppuk trying to say with this oddly human display, she wondered.

Locating his palace here in the center of war-torn North America was a carefully calculated insult—meant to remind Americans that those among Earth's nations who had submitted to the inevitable had survived with their infrastructure intact, and others had not. Twenty years later, most of the destruction had still not been repaired. This glowering palace was Narvo's metaphorical bootheel in America's face.

Banle moved off into the crowd, eyeing the luxurious pool in this vast echoing space. The Jao were mad for water, whenever they could indulge themselves. Her guard was no exception, having to make do with the river next to her campus most of the time. Caitlin drifted in the opposite direction, hoping to lose herself in the crowd for at least a short time and so gain some measure of privacy.

A number of humans were in attendance, though none made any attempt to speak to her as she passed. Several, she noted with distaste, had actually gone so far as to paint false *vai camiti* across their faces, giving them all the charm of oversized raccoons. She wondered if they realized *vai camiti* were hereditary patterns that denoted bloodline affiliations. It was possible they were insulting some of the Jao here tonight.

"Has the young Pluthrak arrived?" she heard one Jao ask another on her right. She hesitated, catching a flash of pale-gold nap and turned her head just enough to get a look at the pair. Most Jao spoke freely around humans, never expecting them to speak enough of their language to comprehend.

"I have not yet seen him," another replied. "If he were here, I think we would know. It is said he is extremely well marked."

"All Pluthrak are well marked," the other said dryly. "It is their fortune, as being plain is ours."

Caitlin edged further around, enough to see the two speakers in question. One was a broad-shouldered female with the tan and green insignia on her cape that denoted assignment in France.

"Well-marked is one thing, well-spoken quite another," the female said. Her arms and a luxurious set of whiskers performed a rather sketchy version of *amused-interest* before settling into the more socially neutral posture of *polite-reserve*. "He is so newly emerged, he is bound to be still dripping, and the young always make the most interesting mistakes. I have no doubt Oppuk will strip him clean of all *vithrik* and send him diving back into his birth-pool."

The female's conversational companion was a scarred older male missing much of his nap and wearing no halfcape, which meant he was probably a military commander stationed somewhere on the planet. "Never underestimate Pluthrak," the male said. "They are capable of thinking six different things behind the same posture with never a whisker out of place, not unlike these wily humans. If he is true to his line, he might do very well here."

Hmmm. When she'd heard about the new officer entering the scene, she'd been so preoccupied with her own personal situation that she hadn't really thought through all the political implications. She still thought Kinsey's reverie of using Pluthrak as a wedge against Narvo was just that—a reverie, and one likely to be dangerous to the dreamer. But she should observe this individual for herself so she could report back to her father. Each new kochan that sent representation to Earth complicated a situation already complex beyond the comprehension of most humans. Competition between Jao factions had never improved humanity's condition so far, but . . .

Things could change, maybe. The truth was, she admitted, she knew very little about Pluthrak. No human did, so far as she knew. The most legendary of the Jao kochan, it was also the most mysterious.

"You're Caitlin Stockwell, aren't you?" a human voice said behind her.

Startled, she turned to meet the eyes of a human clad in a trim dark-blue jinau uniform, the red stripe across his chest bright as a cardinal. "Yes," she said. "I'm afraid I don't recognize you, Mr.—?"

"Ed Kralik," he said, holding out his hand. The man was of medium height with a muscular frame. He was somewhere in his early forties, she estimated. His obviously fit and vigorous body made him seem younger, but that was offset by some prematurely graying hair. Quite a handsome man, in fact, in an understated sort of way.

"Major General Kralik, actually, at your service."

She recognized the name, now. Kralik was one of the highest-ranked human officers in the jinau forces. There were three major generals, each in command of a division. Her father, if she remembered correctly, thought well of this one.

"Hardly at *my* service," she said, allowing him to take her hand in his callused one for only a brief second, then releasing it. She brushed at an imaginary speck on her silver gown. "Not when you're wearing that uniform."

His salt-and-pepper hair was cut almost as close as the velvety nap on a Jao's skin, so that he seemed more like one of them than not. He straightened his shoulders and one corner of his mouth quirked upward. "Strange comment coming from a member of the First Family."

"We don't consider ourselves that," she said, feeling her face warm. This was why she usually avoided parties—she never knew what to say to people. Either they wished to cultivate her good opinion because of her political connections, or they ran the other way as soon as they realized she was a notorious collaborator's daughter. The situation with men was even worse, since sexual interest often complicated the situation further.

She lifted her chin. "Servitude under the Jao was forced upon my father. He never sought it out, and it's certainly no honor."

She regretted saying it, as soon as the words came out. Kralik was being pleasant, and she had no reason to sneer at him. She realized she was more tense than she'd even thought.

"And it's supposed to be different for me? Or any of us?" His eyes were gray, like clouds sweeping inland over a stormy sea. But he seemed more relaxed than offended. "We all do what we must, Miss Stockwell, whether we like it or not."

"Yes," she said, reminding herself to govern her tongue. She had obligations to her father, if nothing else. It would not do to offend the Governor's guests for no purpose beyond relieving her own stress. "Is this your first visit to the palace?"

"No," he said. "I was here in December, the last time Oppuk needed a tame human for display."

Her eyebrows arched. "Display?"

"You know." He didn't smile, exactly. But his lips curved a bit and she caught a glint of steely humor in his eyes. "One that can be expected to converse pleasantly about respect and duty and making oneself of use, who won't pester the other guests or soil the pool, and who'll demonstrate how civilized humans are capable of becoming if only someone will take the time to train them properly."

The corners of her own mouth curved. "Oh, yes," she said. "I've been on display in that sense a few times myself, though my father tries to keep it to a minimum."

"I thought perhaps you had."

She caught the word "Pluthrak" again, this time from a trio of Jao who were shedding their uniforms on the grass as they headed for the room's most elaborate pool. "Do you know the one they're all talking about, this new Pluthrak?"

"Aille krinnu ava Pluthrak, to use the full name. I don't think he's here yet. They're flying him in from the big military base at Pascagoula, Mississippi. My new boss, as it happens."

"Have you met him yet?"

"No," Kralik said, his gray eyes searching the multitude. Voices were growing louder, more boisterous. The pool was becoming more crowded. He stepped closer so he didn't have to raise his voice. "I've been away, recruiting jinau in the Calvada area, down around Stockton, mostly. But I assume meeting him is why I was summoned here tonight." He rocked back on his heels. "And on very short notice, I might add."

"If he's as bad as Oppuk," she said under her breath, "you won't enjoy the experience."

"Miss Stockwell, I never enjoy interaction with the Jao. But he won't be as bad as Oppuk, I don't think. Or Commandant Kaul. And I certainly won't miss Pinb, whom he's replacing." He gave her a level look. "The Jao don't intend for us to enjoy their company, so I'm never disappointed when I don't."

He knew, she thought. This Kralik was canny, and had no illusions about the Jao. They weren't devils, but they didn't reason like humans and they certainly did not have Earth's best interests at heart. So many collaborators had convinced themselves that the Jao would uplift humanity, give them advanced technology and take them to the stars, if only they could behave well enough to deserve it.

Well, they might eventually make it to the stars, all right, she thought, but most likely as cannon fodder, servants, or mechanics, certainly not as equals.

Kralik held out his arm. "Would you like to sample some of the 'treats' of the evening, Miss Stockwell?" he said with a twinkle in his gray eyes. "I saw some smoked eel over there and that usually isn't too objectionable."

Oh, yes, he knew the Jao, she thought, even down to what passed for their cuisine. And it was a relief for once not to be the only human present who wasn't thrilled with the invitation. She accepted his arm. "On one condition," she said. "You have to taste it first!"

Aille had intended to leave Tully safe under Tamt's watchful eye, but the female never returned from her foray for window coverings. Obviously, they were not as easy to come by as she'd thought. He didn't want to trust Rafe Aguilera here in the Governor's palace with the locator. When all was said and done, the two were both human. Deep down, it just might be too much temptation for Aguilera to resist.

"Tully will have to go with us," he told Yaut, as he adjusted his halfcape.

Tully's eyes widened and he jerked to his feet, nostrils flaring with what Aille read as alarm.

"Unacceptable!" Yaut favored the human with a glare. "All in your service must behave impeccably at the reception. Your early selections reflect upon your ability to form proper associations. It would be bad enough to take any human, but this one?"

"We cannot leave him here," he said, forcing his ears and shoulders to reflect *sober-reason*, "so he will have to go. At least, that way you will be able to supervise him properly."

"If you had let me put him down," Yaut said, "no one would have to supervise him!"

Tully straightened, tucking his long-fingered hands underneath his arms. Aille had noticed him assuming that posture before, and decided it was Tully's way of expressing *contained-distress*. Aille thought it must be an individual posture, since he'd never seen it duplicated on another human.

"I think he will behave," he said, turning to the yellow-haired human. "If he does not, he will have your displeasure to deal with, and he understands that very well, do you not?" He made eye contact with the human.

Tully looked away almost immediately, his jaw muscles working.

"The Subcommandant asked you a question!" Yaut raised his hand to strike.

Aille restrained him gently. "It is a simple question," he said to Tully, straightening the human's jinau uniform, brushing off specks of dust with the absorption of a kochan-father grooming one of his own get. "Will you give me honor in the Jao way, as I am sure you very well know how, or shall I heed Yaut and let him deal with you in his fashion? You must decide. Flow quickens and I must admit I am more than a bit tempted to let Yaut do as he wants. He is my fraghta, after all, and knows better than a humble young officer what is most efficacious in such situations."

"You're just going to kill me anyway. So why not go ahead and do it now?"

Again, that tantalizing hint of secrets so important. And, again, that almost Jao-like directness in the face of death. Tully would gladly make himself of use to his species by dying to put his secrets forever out of reach. Impressive, looked at the right way. Aille found himself all the more determined to bend this one to his will and not allow him to escape, even through death.

"He will come," he said to Yaut. "He will advise me on proper behavior toward the human guests and keep a respectful demeanor at all times, or you will take him outside and rip appendages off his body until he repents. The small ones from the feet, 'toes,' I believe they are called. Then the ears."

"Good idea," Yaut said, his face crinkling into *agreeable-mollification.* "Those knobby ears are their ugliest feature."

Tully's hands strayed toward his head and the mentioned ears, which had turned an unsettling bright red.

"Do you understand, Tully?" Aille brushed a last bit of lint off the shoulder of the dark-blue jinau uniform. "At the first hint of insubordination or disrespect, you will leave with Yaut and then return after being disciplined."

Tully nodded stiffly. After taking the locator from Aguilera, Yaut disabled the doorfield and the three of them set off toward the reception. They questioned a human servitor at the first opportunity and were directed from there through a series of convoluted corridors into a huge light-filled room dominated by no less than three pools. Many of the Jao attendees were already swimming and Aille felt immediately drawn to the water.

The air bore the pleasant scent of seawater and wet rocks, with just the ozone hint of an approaching storm, well done, indeed, he thought. A number of humans, most of them jinau, were watching from the periphery, conversing with one another and sampling Jao tidbits, which had been arranged in traditional fashion on thin slabs of rock at various stations.

Oppuk krinnu ava Narvo saw them from across the largest pool and motioned for them to approach. Aille fell back to allow Yaut and Tully to lead as he threaded through the crowd. Tully glanced around, as though to see if anyone were watching, then fell into place, thereby saving his toes and ears, just barely.

Oppuk's service was thoroughly insinuated throughout the attendees. Many of them were Narvo themselves, by their distinctive *vai camiti*, similar to the Governor's, but Aille picked out a number of other familiar facial patterns too. Mostly those were of subordinate kochan, such as Sant, allied to Narvo as Yaut's Jithra had been long allied to Pluthrak. The matched pair of males who had escorted him from the landing field were there as well, conspicuously armed and waiting only a few steps away.

Aille's ears swiveled in confusion. Did the Governor expect trouble even here in his own residence? Was this world held as loosely as that?

The Governor was speaking to a sturdy human female, as Aille approached, and, though he had signaled to him a moment earlier, he did not acknowledge him until the female, looking up into Aille's level gaze, blushed and broke off herself.

"Subcommandant," she said in heavily accented Jao, "welcome to Earth."

She did not offer her name, a sign of her close acquaintance with Jao customs. "It is a most intriguing assignment thus far," he said, moving closer, holding his entire body safely shaped into *appreciative-interest*. "I am honored to serve the Governor."

"Why has Pluthrak sent you here?" Narvo said, his body crying out *rude-suspicion*. "I must know before I can work out how to use you. Why would illustrious Pluthrak, who never attempts anything at which it might fail, send a well-regarded scion to this grubby ball of dirt and rock?"

Aille could see Yaut and Tully off to the side, and to their credit, neither flinched or flicked so much as an ear or whisker. "To learn," Aille said. "Pluthrak and Narvo have stayed apart too much. It is perhaps time to pool our strengths and see where that might lead."

Suspicion glimmered greenly in the Governor's eyes, bright as a circuit about to overload, then was mirrored in the lines of his arms. "To learn, yes, I had thought as much, to learn Narvo's weaknesses, to bring accusation before the Naukra Krith Ludh that we have not subdued this mangy, vermin-ridden world properly!"

"Have you not?" Aille dug deeply into his memory and recalled his lessons with the Pluthrak movement-master, how to cock the head, splay the fingers, shift his weight, place the heartward leg just—so, until he had melted without apparent intent or effort into *forthright-admiration*, adding the difficult-to-hold angle of ears that specified *longing*. A tripartite posture, and a particularly ambitious one at that. "I thought quite otherwise, in my admittedly limited travels so far, but perhaps I was mistaken."

A wave of excitement ran through the crowd. Even those Jao not close enough to overhear the conversation could read enough of their postures to glean a great deal. There were a few murmurs of admiration for Aille's obvious classical movement training. After all, just presenting postures to the young did not guarantee they would be learned, then used to proper advantage when the time came. Despite his youth, Aille had obviously learned, and, as they could see, quite, quite well.

Narvo glared, but there was no arguing with Aille's stance and he finally backed down. "You might be of some use after all," he said grudgingly, "but being relegated to an assignment this lowly means they will never call you back to breed."

Aille stared at him, fighting to hold onto at least the elements that comprised *admiration*, even if he lost the rest. Breeding was an intensely private matter, for the great kochan, rarely mentioned outside the kochan-house. He had never thought to hear it bruited about here, where even aliens were present, in such a casual fashion.

"They have posted you to a dungheap of a world," Narvo said. "Would they have done that to a truly promising scion? You are obviously expendable, whatever your accomplishments. Whom did you manage to anger, despite your youth?"

Aille knew that wasn't true—and so did Oppuk. Pluthrak valued him appropriately, considering his inexperience, and he would have an equal chance to breed when the time was right, along with the rest of his clutch. The insult was nothing more than a provocation, and for what purpose? Could a Narvo with Oppuk's experience truly be that rash? The great kochan did not insult each other lightly.

But the Governor said nothing further. An instant later, he turned away and dove into the pool.

A moment later, a willowy human female with short dark-gold hair stepped forward, her shoulders and arms gracefully shaped into *bemused-commiseration*. She wore a sleek draping of silver fabric that swirled around her legs and obscured several of her lines, so that the posture was truncated. "Well," she said in flawless Jao, "that made an interesting beginning."

CHAPTER
14

From a few feet away, Caitlin had watched Governor Narvo interact with the newcomer, a tall Jao with a regal bearing and velvety nap the color of newly minted gold. The two Jao danced. No other word could describe it, however much Jao were mystified by the human notion of dancing, along with most other human forms of art and recreation. Black eyes flickering green with emotion riveted one another as their bodies flowed from one shape to the next; all carefully stylized, each finger, whisker, and ear placed just so.

In human terms, she mused, watching the exchange, one might have labeled Oppuk krinnu ava Narvo a bully, trying to use his authority on this world to cow his new subordinate. And not succeeding, she thought. But these were not humans, and thinking one could understand them according to human interpretations inevitably led to trouble. That the Narvo did not like this new Pluthrak was apparent, though, and Caitlin was sure that the animosity went beyond simple kochan rivalry between Narvo and Pluthrak.

When Oppuk turned away, she stepped forward, driven by a sudden impulse and spoke in Jao. "Well, that made an interesting beginning."

The Subcommandant turned and favored her with his full attention. His *vai camiti* was the most striking and unusual she'd ever seen, a solid mask of black over his eyes, like the that of a raccoon or a thief.

"You speak Jao very well," he said in English, "better than any human I have encountered."

"I have had the boon of a Jao bodyguard since I was very young," she said. "I grew up knowing Jao as well as English."

He gestured at her arms. "Were you formally trained?"

She realized she was still holding the shape of *bemused-commiseration* and shook her arms out, letting the form go. "No," she said, rubbing her shoulder, which ached with the effort of holding the position, "I just picked up a few postures here and there by keeping my eyes open."

"Then you observe closely," the Jao said. "It would take a Jao youth many sessions to perform equally as well, although . . ." He stepped back and narrowed his eyes.

"What?" The weight of that green gaze lay heavy upon her and she realized a number of people, human and Jao, were staring. "Did I do it wrong?"

"It is the fingers," he said. "Humans have one too many for the strictest classical purity of the form, but you could de-emphasize the defect by holding two of them together." He reached for her hand and demonstrated, pressing her ring and little fingers together into the arch that indicated *commiseration*.

His touch was cool, his palms corded steel beneath the velvety nap. She held the pose for several seconds, letting him study the effect, then dropped her hand self-consciously. "I see," she said. "Thank you for the instruction, Subcommandant. I shall endeavor to be worthy of the lesson."

"Yes," he said. "We all strive to be worthy, every light and dark, every cycle. It is a constant struggle."

He was still studying her when a stubby dark-russet Jao spoke quietly into his ear. Caitlin took advantage of the distraction to slip back into the crowd. Kralik, who had been standing nearby, came alongside her.

"Not so fast," he said in a low voice, when she finally paused beside one of the rock ledges where a rainbow of food samples was displayed. "What was that all about?"

"I'm not sure." Her cheeks were hot and she knew how flustered she appeared to the human eye. How unfair, she thought, that with her species, such signs were involuntary and all too obvious for anyone who happened to be looking. Jao were able to select which emotions they wished to present to the world. Humans were always at the mercy of theirs.

"You did something, and said something. But I couldn't tell what because your voices were too low. And he was commenting on it, right? I understood that much."

"What I did, I think, was make a fool of myself!" She selected a gray-pink bit of flesh, bit into it and tried to ignore the gamey taste. "I tried to imitate one of their formal postures, the ones they use when they talk among themselves, but I didn't do it very well and he was instructing me."

"Formal postures?" Kralik looked baffled. "I know they use a lot of so-called body language—way more than we do, that's for sure—but I wasn't aware it had any formal structure to it. Subcommandant Pinb never told me very much, and Kaul even less."

"Body language with the Jao is rigidly codified," she said, shaking her head. "Except that it's far more elaborate and taught by highly accomplished movement masters. No well brought up young Jao—not from a great kochan, for sure—is complete without his carefully acquired vocabulary of formal postures. And there are a multitude of them. It's a bit like trying to learn Chinese ideograms, except in body language."

She gazed at Subcommandant Aille across the room where he was now in serious conversation with the Jao who had approached him. "I should have left well enough alone. It probably looked like a poodle trying to do a curtsy!"

"Interesting," Kralik said. "I hadn't realized it was that codified. I've learned to interpret their mood through their body language, after a fashion. But I'm not always right, so I don't depend on it."

"That's for the best," she said. "Some of their values and emotions have no analogs in human psychology and culture. You can never count on understanding what they mean."

"What did this one want?" Kralik said.

"I'm not sure," she said, "but I've a feeling I made myself look like an idiot."

"Well," he said. "At least you got his attention. That was more than I've managed to do. I want to meet him, since he's my new commander, but they don't like it when you introduce yourself without invitation. And, so far, he's showing no signs of being interested in the matter himself."

"From what I gather, Governor Oppuk was giving him a hard time," she said. "This is probably not the most auspicious moment."

"Then I'll wait," he said, his expression hard. He gripped his hands behind his back. "I've become good at that."

She made a face. "Haven't we all? What exactly does his rank signify, by the way? I'm familiar—to an extent—with Jao social customs, but not the way that translates into official military position."

"Well . . . It's more fluid, among the Jao, than it would be for us. Kaul krinnu ava Dano, as the Commandant, is theoretically in charge of all military forces in the Terran solar system. He'll have two Subcommandants, one in charge of space forces and one—that'll be the new Pluthrak—in charge of ground forces."

Kralik's lips quirked again into that not-quite-a-smile. "That's the theory. In practice, leaving aside the fact that they don't make the same distinctions we do—used to do, I should say—between the army and the navy, it's a lot fuzzier. They also don't make the same distinctions we do between civilians and military personnel as such. I've heard there was already a minor clash between the Subcommandant and the production director in the big refit facility at Pascagoula, in which the director got slapped down quick and hard. And if I'm reading the tea leaves properly, I think there's something of a tug-of-war going on between Kaul and Aille over whether his authority extends to all ground forces or just the jinau troops."

The crowd parted and Banle appeared, nap still dripping from her swim, uniform over her arm, eyes dark and expressionless.

Caitlin glanced at Kralik, then smiled. "This is Major General Ed Kralik, Banle. He will report to the new Subcommandant."

Banle's ears flashed *irritation*. She knew that Caitlin was needling her subtly, proffering such an unwanted and un-Jao-like introduction. "Indeed? I thought I saw you conversing with the Pluthrak Subcommandant." *Question* was implicit in the narrowing of her eyes, the tilt of her head.

Yes, of course, Banle would want to know what the two of them had said. It was part of her function as jailor/spy. The Jao had been derelict in her duties, allowing herself to be lured by the magnificent pools and leaving Caitlin to run about unsupervised.

Caitlin gazed out over the sea of heads, both human and Jao, and spotted the Subcommandant, now standing beside the largest pool and watching Narvo swim. "Yes, we spoke," she said. "He is a fascinating individual, most observant. He wanted to know where I had received my education in formal movement. I told him you had been most instructive."

Banle's whole body reacted, framing a posture Caitlin did not recognize. "I have never given you instruction!"

"But you have, Banle," Caitlin said with all the innocence she could muster. At her side, she could feel Kralik growing tense. Struggling to contain his humor, too, she thought. Caitlin was playing a dangerous game, here, but she couldn't resist the chance to jab at the overbearing Banle. "Every day, every hour, since I was too small to remember, I have had your shining example before me. How could I do other than learn?"

Banle did not answer, merely struggled back into her harness with short, sharp motions, then the trousers, and then took up her customary glowering post behind Caitlin's shoulder, forcing the human to take the lesser place. Caitlin sighed. What little freedom she could expect from the evening was now over. She might as well locate Professor Kinsey and make sure he stayed out of trouble.

Aille realized he did not know the human female's designation. Jao-like, she had not presented it before Yaut had interrupted him with a few sharp observations on certain of the kochan represented here. Then, when he'd turned back to the puzzling woman, she had disappeared into the crowd.

She'd said she knew Jao as well as English. By her fluency of speech and almost complete lack of accent, he felt certain that was indeed no idle boast. And she was the first human he'd encountered who had acquired even a minimum of the Jao movement vocabulary. He was highly intrigued. Despite Yaut's warning, what an addition to his personal service that one would be! If he could arrange it, though, he cautioned himself. With her unique qualifications, she was most likely already assigned elsewhere, perhaps even to Oppuk's own service.

Tully was gazing after her with an unreadable expression, his hands and arms rigid at his sides.

"I heard what the Governor said." Yaut was holding himself to the strictest of neutral postures. "Shocking, to display the antagonism of one kochan against another for all to hear and comment upon."

"I did not interpret his words that way," Aille said. "I heard insecurity and worry, lack of faith and fear of incohesion. Narvo seems much in need of highly placed associations."

"Do not make the mistake of thinking you will be the source!" Yaut bristled with *admonition*, then remembered where he was and resumed his neutral stance. "If you can refrain from giving actionable offense here, that is as much as anyone has a right to expect."

Most of the Jao were either swimming, or had just finished. Aille began to shed his harness, including the halfcape. It would be an insult not to sample Narvo's hospitality, and Aille would counter Narvo ill-grace with Pluthrak courtesy. Yaut accepted each article as Aille pulled it off with an air of long suffering.

"There is always trouble between our kochan," Aille said softly, just before he plunged into the inviting green water. "But this Narvo apparently feels matters have gone too far to be amended. As his subordinate, it is my duty to restore possibility."

"And if you cannot?" Yaut stood aside as Aille dove straight and clean into the choppy pool.

Aille considered as the water, cool and delicious, closed over him. If he could not bring about change, then he would fail and bring shame to Pluthrak. Therefore, he could not fail. He must succeed, whatever the cost.

He swam with long, joyous strokes, feeling the water cleanse his body and invigorate his nerves. The alien ocean at Pascagoula had been acceptable, but these salts had been specially formulated to soothe Jao sensibilities. Narvo was clever, indeed, to fabricate such a marvel to entice and impress his guests.

Finally, he surfaced and shook the water from his eyes. Yaut was still waiting where he had left him, more or less patiently, with Tully nearby. But he saw the human female watching him too, from over by the wall, along with the man who had accompanied her. Aille headed for the simulated shore with powerful strokes.

Jao everywhere, so many, it made Gabe Tully's teeth ache. He wanted to leave the noisy, crowded reception hall with its ostentatious pools, but Yaut had a constant eye upon him, even though the Subcommandant was busy attending to whatever social amenities Jao recognized and thought necessary.

The woman who had approached Aille, though, had looked familiar, the cropped blond hair, the large blue-gray eyes. She wore a long, shimmering silver dress that must have cost a bundle. He sorted through his memory, seeking until he had it. She was Caitlin Stockwell, daughter of the ultimate collaborator, so-called "President" Stockwell!

Ice flooded through him. She was allowed access to this kind of luxury, while, outside, America deteriorated just that much more every day. Only the Jao and those who played ball with them were allowed to be civilized now. The rest of America could go to hell for the crime of having fought the hardest for their freedom.

Over in the pool, the Subcommandant broke the surface, gazed about, then made eye contact with him. He stepped back, unnerved, feeling almost as though Aille could read his thoughts. As surreptitiously as he could manage, he eased back into the tapestry of milling bodies, gold, brown, and russet naps of the Jao threaded with the more flamboyant colors of human clothing. He couldn't get far, he knew, not with the damned locator on his wrist, but he needed a bit of privacy to collect his thoughts.

Why had Caitlin Stockwell sought out the Subcommandant? Was she looking for some way to betray her country even more thoroughly than her family already had? He thought of the children back in the refugee camps in the Rockies, the shabby blankets, the few stained books available for their education, and their wide eyes at night when one of the older men or women would tell stories of the glory America had once been—before the conquest.

What did prissy Miss Caitlin Stockwell, with her silver dress, clean hair, and manicured nails know about any of that? His hands clenched.

"Here I am," a low voice said in his ear.

He jerked around and met the Subcommandant's green-black eyes.

"I did not mean to avoid your notice," the Jao said, looming over him so that he was inundated in the wet-carpet smell of the other's nap. "Eagerness simply overcame me and I slipped into the water when your attention was elsewhere."

Yaut thrust the Subcommandant's harness, trousers, and cape into Tully's arms. Numbly, he shook out the dark-blue trousers as though he performed duties of batman every day. The Subcommandant accepted them matter-of-factly and put them on.

He would never get used to casual Jao attitudes about nudity, Tully thought. The situation was all the more grotesque because Jao sexual organs were not much different from human. When clothed, the females were hard to distinguish from the males, because of the absence of breasts and the fact they were just as large and muscular. Naked, however, the difference between the two Jao sexes was obvious. But the Jao seemed completely oblivious to the matter.

He glanced at Stockwell again, who was now talking to a man in a jinau uniform. He was in early middle-age, not particularly tall, but had a powerful-looking physique.

Aille followed his line of sight. "Are you acquainted with that female?"

His eyes turned back to the Jao, widening a little. "Everyone in America knows who she is."

"Then enlighten me," Aille said, forcing a wet leg into his trousers.

"That's Caitlin Stockwell, the only child of Ben Stockwell." Forcing himself to be honest, he added: "The only surviving child, I should say. Her older brother was killed fighting Jao during the conquest. Nobody quite knows what happened to the other one, but he's dead too."

That still didn't seem to register on the Subcommandant. Tully added: "Ben Stockwell was the former Vice-President of the United States, before the conquest. He's now the appointed President of your puppet—uh, your native government of this continent." He watched the girl tuck dark-gold hair behind her ears then and smile, a solemn Jao bodyguard keeping watch at her shoulder. The gray-haired man linked arms with her, and the two moved off, speaking to a number of the humans present as they walked.

"The scion of a prestigious kochan, then," Aille said, settling his halfcape back into place across one shoulder.

Tully started to protest that humans didn't have kochan, then stopped. He didn't precisely know what the Jao term "kochan" meant, but it seemed to approximate the human notion of "clan." Now that Tully thought about it, the Stockwells were probably as close to a true kochan as you could find in North America. Old Eastern money, on the father's side, with a long tradition of public service.

"Yes," he said, a bit sourly. "Very prestigious."

The ornate halfcape with its green and gold insignia was crooked in the back. Tully's fingers straightened it before he thought, then he saw Yaut blink at him with surprised approval.

Play the part, he told himself. *Sooner or later, they'll make a mistake, then you can either escape or die trying and none of this will matter.*

Aille moved off into the crowd, regal in his bearing compared to most of the Jao present. Even Tully could tell that much. If Aille had been human, he would have been like a well-brought-up young prince at a provincial reception. Behaving graciously, to be sure— but still a prince, and exuding that fact with his every word and movement.

Yaut glided easily before him. How did the fraghta do that, Tully wondered, hurrying to keep up. It was as though he knew where the Subcommandant was going before he knew himself. Did those two have some sort of mental contact which allowed him to actually predict the other's wishes? He rubbed the gleaming black locator band beneath his sleeve and tried not to brush against any of Earth's alien conquerors as they crossed the floor.

Oppuk krinnu ava Narvo practiced the subtle art of watching without being obvious as the new Subcommandant prowled the reception, speaking here and there, spreading his influence like oil over water. Why had Pluthrak sent him this burden? The question burned through him, but he was no nearer to answering it now than when he had first learned of the assignment.

Aille krinnu ava Pluthrak was too young to be a real threat to his authority, too inexperienced to be of any genuine use, and yet far too appealing for comfort. The Jao in the crowd seemed invariably drawn to the youthful officer. Oppuk needed to keep him close, so he would know the instant he was up to something, and yet bury him under inconsequential duties so he would never accomplish anything of worth or attract favorable notice. How to achieve these contradictory aims was a puzzle, and unfortunately Oppuk had never been good at solving puzzles. His talents lay in other directions, and his normal method with puzzles was to smash them.

His nose wrinkled in a sour grimace and his two identical guards, born of allied Sant, a kochan long dedicated to service to Narvo, trained their enigmatic gaze upon him.

"Can we be of use, Governor?" they said, in that unnerving unison they often achieved.

He could not tell them apart, which bothered him. His fraghta long ago had come across the pair when they first emerged from the creche-pool and had them trained especially for his personal service. They were a novelty. Genetic duplicates were much more rare among the Jao than among the humans. He'd heard it said that humans often whelped their get in pairs and occasionally even in threes and fours.

"No," he said, "I do not need you at present. Remain on guard."

He noticed the jinau officer, Kralik, monitoring the Sub-commandant, as a subordinate should, quietly, without putting himself forward or interfering. A rare moment of approval washed through Oppuk. Humans so rarely knew their place without a great deal of instruction and reinforcement. It was good to see one who could control himself in the absence of external cues.

"Governor?" a human voice said from his side.

He looked down. A short man with a disgusting bare patch on his crown gazed up at him, looking vaguely familiar. Oppuk had seen many male humans so afflicted since he arrived on this world, long ago. At first, he had assumed such hair loss was a sign of disease, until he learned it was just a common degenerative process associated with aging. He almost shuddered. For a Jao, that would have been a major affliction.

Two dark-haired human females flanked him, both clad in long clumsy garments of heavily brocaded fabric that impeded their steps. Wary, his personal guards moved in, but Oppuk waved them back. "You wish my attention?" he said.

"I am Ambassador Matasu," the man said, bowing from the waist until Oppuk could not see his eyes. The two women bowed as well. "From the land of the rising sun, your most loyal province, Japan."

"Yes." Oppuk gazed down at the creature in disgust. Not only had it forced its barbaric name upon him, it smelled of floral aromatics, which the denizens of this world often applied to themselves in the mistaken belief that the natural scents of their bodies were noisome, while blatant artificial odors were somehow more acceptable. Their preoccupation with such matters was almost as intense as the classical study of movement was for his own species.

Nevertheless, despite the creature's reek, he preferred not to give offense here. Japan provided many manufactured goods to the Occupation, since its resistance had been sensibly short-lived and the Jao had not been motivated to lay waste to it as they had North

America and parts of Europe and the Asian mainland. Japan's infrastructure was thus in good shape and their people had prospered under Jao rule, paying their taxes and providing much in the way of material support, sometimes even more than the required levy.

They produced few jinau, on the other hand. Most of the human troops came from North America and those parts of Europe and Asia which had seen the most fighting. That was not unusual, of course. In fact, it was one of the few ways in which humans were like most conquered species. Those moieties that had a martial spirit naturally produced most of the jinau after their conquest.

"There is rumor of an entertainment being planned," Matasu said, dark eyes gleaming like bits of bright glass in his wrinkled face. The creature was very old, Oppuk realized. "In honor of the new Subcommandant."

Oppuk had not scheduled any such "entertainment," as the human meant the term. Activity merely for diversion was not a Jao practice. In addition, he was quite put out already at being forced to officially receive a Pluthrak scion on this level. But the Terran creature was right. His staff should have arranged some sort of expedition or tour, he now realized belatedly, and it irritated him that a human should be aware of his duties better than his own service.

He felt his ears descending into *chagrin* and took hold of himself, lest he betray his innermost thoughts. "My staff has considered many venues," he said, schooling his posture to mere *mild-interest*, "but has not yet decided upon which would be most suitable."

"I was hoping for one of North America's famous hunts," the Terran said, his eyes turning in the direction of Aille krinnu ava Pluthrak and then back. "Wildcats in your Calvada area, or perhaps eagles nesting on the shore of one of the Great Lakes, or even—" He licked his lips and moved closer. "A whale hunt along your northwest coast."

"A whale hunt?" Oppuk was perplexed. He did not recognize the name of that particular beast. "What exactly is a 'whale'?"

"It is a marine animal, quite large, which lives all its life in the sea." Matasu's eyes blinked, so dark-brown they almost seemed black. "Of course, Earth has many species of whales, but the natives of that coast used to have a ritual for hunting one particular variety that was quite beautiful."

Oppuk snorted. "Jao are not interested in frivolous human 'rituals.'"

"Of course not!" Matasu fluttered his fingers. "I quite understand. In this instance, however, I believe you will find the whale is making itself of use, which is of course what we all strive for."

Drinn, his castellan, stepped forward. *Concern* was written in the lines of his body that this Terran was dominating the Governor's attention. Oppuk ignored him. "And how exactly does a nonsentient animal make itself of use to anyone?"

"By requiring expertise to be brought down so skills can be practiced." Matasu's face stretched into that nauseating native expression meant to denote pleasure. "And by being eaten. Their flesh is most delectable."

"It does sound intriguing," Oppuk said. He motioned Drinn closer. "Furnish the pertinent information to my service and—"

"Governor, please!" Caitlin Stockwell slid to the front through the murmuring crowd. Evidently she'd been listening. Her face was rather pinker than before, an unhealthy and unappealing shade. "Many whales are still endangered species. If you authorize a hunt even this once, then it will become the fashion all over the world. At the very least, there may be trouble with environmentalists."

Oppuk looked at her coldly. The young female was getting above herself, a trait her father had all too often displayed. "I think I shall attend this so-called whale hunt," he said, "as will Subcommandant Aille, since it is to be conducted in his honor." He motioned to Drinn. "See that it is set up," he said, "and soon."

CHAPTER
15

Her father would be horrified. That thought kept rattling around inside Caitlin's head. Benjamin Wilson Stockwell would hear of this travesty, even before she could tell him herself. Although he would disapprove, he would be powerless to prevent it. And all the while, he and everyone else would know she had opened her big fat mouth at a delicate moment and made things worse. Caitlin was so tense—anger and frustration that had been building for so many years—that she'd been taken completely off-balance and blundered badly.

If she'd just kept quiet, Oppuk perhaps would not have been interested in such a purely human pursuit or forgotten about the whole affair before it could be organized, but now—

She stared dumbly at the Governor's twitching nose until Kralik took her arm and tactfully guided her away. "A whale hunt!" he said, grimacing. "I don't think there's been one for years."

She felt cold, even though the room was stifling.

"Be practical, Caitlin," he said in a low voice. "It's no worse than most of what goes on under Jao rule, and not nearly as irreversible as when the mountain climbers provoked them into plastering Everest. It's only one whale. The ecology will survive that."

She nodded, managing to keep walking until they reached a bench next to a rushing artificial waterfall that fed into the main pool. Kralik settled her where she was bathed in the music of water flowing over rock. Kinsey joined them there. After Caitlin introduced

162

him to Kralik, the professor disappeared back into the murmuring crowd in search of "punch," though she well knew he would find no such thing at a Jao function.

"Tell me of these 'whales,'" a deep Jao voice said.

She glanced up from clenched hands into the distinctive *vai camiti* of the guest of honor. "I—" Her voice failed her.

"That is a posture of distress, is it not?" Aille indicated her hands. "I have sometimes noted it among those in my service, as well as a number of the human workers engaged in the refit operation. Why does this 'whale hunt' distress you?"

Caitlin took a deep breath. "It does not matter," she said shakily. "The Governor requires a whale hunt, so one will take place."

He was big and broad, the nap on his skin a rich gold and still dark with damp from his swim. Inside the broad stripe on his face, his eyes crawled with iridescent green like lightning playing across some distant alien sky. Even to human eyes, he was a handsome figure.

Two members of his personal service stood before him, as was proper. One was Jao, short but powerful-looking. The other, strangely enough, was human. Like Caitlin herself, he was blond, but his hair was straw-colored rather than dark-gold. And though his body was whip-thin, he looked very fit. She tried to catch the man's eye, but he quite pointedly would not look at her.

"Tell me of your Pluthrak homeworld," she said, in an effort to change the subject. "I don't recall a member of your kochan being assigned to Earth before."

"There is no one homeworld for us. Pluthrak is spread across twenty-nine planets," Aille said. The lines of his body flowed from *polite-inquisition* into what she thought was *wistful-remembrance*, without the slightest awkwardness or any indication of conscious attention. "The kochan-house that spawned my birth-group was located on Marit An, a green and gold world whose oceans possess almost the same fragrance as this room."

Personally, she thought the room reeked of decaying seaweed and fermented fish, but kept the observation to herself. "Twenty-nine worlds," she said. "Isn't that a lot, even for a great kochan?"

"It must seem so to a species that has never possessed more than this one world," he said, his ears dancing through a multitude of expressions too rapidly for her to decipher any of them, "but we do not maintain a high population on any one world, which would make it an attractive target for the Ekhat. Jao breed for ability rather than numbers, in any event."

Unlike humans, Caitlin thought—who according to Jao opinion, bred like rabbits, yielding to sentiment and lust where practicality should have been employed.

Banle appeared at her shoulder and took up her post, rigid with *disapproval*. "You approached the Governor without invitation," she said. "That was badly done."

"I regret my clumsiness," Caitlin said in Jao. "I have been too long among humans at the university and forgotten my manners."

"True," Banle said, turning her back on the Subcommandant so that he was excluded from her field of vision, effectively in Jao terms making him simply not-there. "I have often counseled your father against indulging you so. He should assign you a strict fraghta."

Aille gave the guard a penetrating look and moved off, a tasteful exit in Jao terms, though rude in human context. Caitlin repressed a smile. She suspected this new Pluthrak, though young, was going to be a thorn in Narvo's side. She certainly hoped so.

"Here," Dr. Kinsey said, pressing a tepid glass of water into her hand. "That's the best I could do, I'm afraid."

"Thank you." She sipped gratefully, then gazed out over the crowd with a tight face. No doubt, that sniveling rat Matasu had only brought it up because he knew how Americans felt about such things. It was a childish display of one-upsmanship. Japan had fared far better beneath the Occupation than her former enemy turned ally. The archipelago's native government now didn't hesitate to rub it in, whenever the opportunity presented itself.

The entire hall was abuzz about the expedition to be held in Aille krinnu ava Pluthrak's honor. Most of the Jao were uninterested in a quaint native hunt, but Tully found the attending humans' reactions varied from eagerness to utter disbelief.

Aille turned to him after leaving the Stockwell girl in the care of her escort. "The idea of a 'whale hunt' distresses some of your fellow Terrans," he said. "Why should this be so? Is it not one of your ancient rituals?"

"For some people," Tully said. "Certainly not all. I don't know about Jao, but humans do not necessarily share the same customs and values."

Yaut was watching him with glittering black eyes. Green burst across them, then faded to ebony, revealing nothing.

"It is but one whale," Aille said, "one unthinking animal. Why should it not make itself of use?"

"Why indeed?" Tully kept his face blank, his hands locked behind his back, his shoulders braced. His eyes were trained on the pool, the frolicking Jao, the uneasy, milling humans, some of whom wanted nothing more than to be Jao, and others, to be a million miles away from here. The air was filled with spray, as the Jao dove, and more than a few of the humans were soaking wet.

The death of a single whale was of little consequence, as Aille had said. But the principle involved did matter, as well as the predictable reaction of many humans. The Resistance had a stronghold in the Pacific Northwest, which had largely originated out of old environmentalist groups—some of which had been fanatics even before the conquest. They would be almost sure to try to strike back.

Which would be stupid, in Tully's opinion, given the inevitable Jao retaliation that would follow. The Jao committed crimes against humanity every single day—hell, twice a day on Sundays, as the old geezers in the refugee camps liked to say—big crimes like the destruction of Chicago, events from which the human race would never recover, even if the Jao were to pack up and leave tomorrow.

Aille threw an uninterpretable look at Yaut who seemed to understand. "I wish to know more about this situation," he said in Jao.

The stolid fraghta did not answer, but his ears indicated *assent*. At least, Tully thought they did.

The huge hall of humans and Jao seethed as Aille passed among them, speaking when necessary, but trying mostly to observe. The light streaming down from the holes in the ceiling made his eyes ache, but Oppuk did not appear to suffer.

There were odd currents here, he told himself, watching the lines of bodies. Intentions ran like a subterranean river beneath the meaning of the words. One political moiety's contingent had come forward to propose the hunt, another obviously opposed it, much like kochan maneuvering for position and influence in the far-off Naukra Krith Ludh.

Did Narvo understand what discord he apparently sowed here

this evening by agreeing to this hunt? Watching the Governor, whose shoulders and spine were set in an indifferently executed *amused-observance*, he thought most likely he did.

And perhaps Narvo was right. His logic was easy to understand, after all. The Terrans were a conquered race. With their brash psychological makeup, they needed to be reminded of their place from time to time. Or, remembering they far outnumbered the Jao on the planet, they might be tempted to rise in revolt despite the technological disparity between their weapons. If they did so in unison, the revolt would be difficult to suppress. Allowing the rivalries between conquered moieties to wear out their energies was a time-honored way of avoiding that possibility.

Still, Aille was not satisfied. "Be not too clever," his kochan-parents had often instructed him, "lest you outwit yourself." Yes, the tactic was time-honored, but it was always necessary to be careful with it. Push the thing too far, and you could drive a conquered moiety into rebellion by adding native humiliation to alien conquest. What was the use of that?

At any rate, Tully was behaving himself rather well. And Aille was now almost certain that the human, despite what appeared to be a lack of education, was far more intelligent than he tried to portray himself as being. Aille studied Tully, the lines of his arms, the cant of his head, the set of those restless little eyes, the furtive glances his way. The creature had learned something here, which Aille should also know. He could tell that much, just not what exactly.

Tully's gaze, he noticed, returned quite often to Caitlin Stockwell, who was conversing quietly by a tumble of rocks where the water bubbled up and then raced down into the main pool. The dark gold of her hair caught the late sun streaming down through the skylights so that she seemed an anchor of light and the rest of the room merely dancing about her.

Aille was uncertain, but he thought the female would be considered extremely attractive in human terms. Since humans, unlike Jao, were subject to sexual arousal at all times, perhaps that explained Tully's interest. Yet he did not think that explained all of it, or perhaps even any of it.

He decided to probe further. He motioned to Yaut with one ear and then allowed the fraghta to precede him across the room. An instant later, Tully picked up on the cue and moved off, only a step behind Yaut. Aille noted a glimmer of *approval* in the fraghta's demeanor. Really, Tully was becoming almost well trained.

The same Jao female still loomed over Stockwell's shoulder, her body stiff with unmitigated disapproval. Her *vai camiti* was reminiscent of Oppuk himself. Was she perhaps of Narvo, too? And, if so, why had one with that birthright been assigned to such dull duty as trailing around after a native?

Water splashed behind him. Spray soaked his back and he turned to see a group of Jao plunging, clothed this time, into the alluring pool. They were forgetting themselves before this mixed company, obviously letting the water go to their heads. Amidst all this, though, Oppuk watched—not them, but Aille, his gaze pointedly fixed.

Aille relaxed his body into *unconcerned-interest* and settled on a bench beside the human female. He gestured at the wild swimmers. "Your species does not enjoy the water?"

Her eyes were blue-gray within their nests of white, the color of the Terran sky just before early-dark, he thought.

"We swim," she said, "after a fashion, but nothing to compare with Jao."

Aille watched the bodies knifing through the green water, the gleaming wet heads, the excitement each and every swimmer exhibited. "Perhaps you could learn."

"Some things cannot be learned," she said, staring past him. "They can only be lived by those who possess the inherent capacity. I fear this is one of them."

Aille glanced at the looming female Jao. "Is she in your service?"

Savage-hatred erupted in the female's body and for an instant, Aille thought she would strike—at the human female, not him. "I am in Oppuk krinnu ava Narvo's service, no one else's!"

Caitlin Stockwell paled as Yaut stepped between Aille and the female, baring his chest to the implied assault.

"My mistake," Aille said smoothly. "I am a newcomer here, as I am sure you know, and only wish to understand the situation so I will not give offense."

"Humans are not allowed to accumulate a personal service, as is customary for Jao." Stockwell closed her eyes, seeming to struggle for control. "Banle has been my lifelong guard, assigned to watch me since I was very small, for my—my safety." The last word came out in a strangled whisper.

Tully seemed to understand far better than Aille did at the moment. His lips thinned.

"You are in danger?" Aille leaned closer, his ears twitching with interest. "From whom?"

"My father heads the human government on this continent for the Jao," she said. "There are many who resent him. They might strike at him through me, had they the chance."

"Indeed?" Aille glanced up at the Jao female. "Your name?"

Rather than being pleased at being asked, her body was all *reluctance.* "Banle krinnu nao Narvo."

Of the root kochan itself, then, though "nao" instead of "ava." She'd been birthed and reared in one of the secondary marriage-groups.

Banle turned her face away, blanking her body so it conveyed no meaning at all. "I am on duty and not available for personal conversation."

"Very sensible," he said.

They sat then in silence, Jao and humans walking past, occasionally greeting him, but ignoring Caitlin for the most part. The air shimmered with late-day light and spray from the diving swimmers hung in the air. He relaxed, savoring the sea-smells, wet rocks, salts, and water, all far more ancient than his species.

"Whales swim," Caitlin Stockwell said finally. "They spend their entire lives in the sea."

"Are they fierce?" He studied her face, but without mobile nose or ears, without even whiskers, it was hard to discern her mood.

She laughed, but it was a harsh sound, not merry at all. "No, they have very little idea of how to protect themselves, much less attack! They are so huge, they have no natural enemies except man—and now, it seems, Jao also."

"Then they provide you with a food source?"

"Some think so," she said. "In the past our species hunted them for their oil, bone, and flesh, but thankfully we found substitutes before we drove them into extinction."

"Are they in danger of becoming extinct now?"

She stared down at her intertwined fingers, which were so much smaller than a Jao's. "No one knows. There's been no money or resources for a study to find out since—" She broke off, her lips compressed.

"Since the conquest," he said.

"Yes." She breathed deeply, her eyes gazing past him. "We have redirected our resources, as ordered, to more important matters, such as preparing the planet against the expected attack."

"Quite right," he said, pleased to reach a point in the conversation where both species agreed. Tracking a few animals to see how many of them lived in a habitat made very little sense when one thought of the ferocity of the Ekhat. The Ekhat, who exterminated entire systems in accordance with their mad philosophy, down to the bacteria.

The human male who was standing nearby, Aille now realized, was the same one who had been at this female's side earlier. She lifted her face up to him, then, a moment later, turned to face Aille.

"Subcommandant, may I introduce Major General Ed Kralik, the human officer who commands one of your major jinau forces on this continent?"

A rough snort escaped Yaut at the ill-mannered proffering of a name, but Aille was intrigued enough to ignore the breach of courtesy. Caitlin, after all, despite her knowledge of Jao language and postures, was only human and couldn't be expected to behave with exact propriety all the time. But he suspected she was well aware that she was violating custom, and did so deliberately.

"Indeed?" he said, letting *amiable-interest* shape his limbs.

"Yes, sir." Interestingly, Kralik did not make that sharp gesture-of-respect humans called a "salute." Apparently, he was more familiar with Jao customs than most humans Aille had encountered in the military. "I'm commander of the Pacific Division. I would have flown down to Pascagoula to report in, but I've been on assignment out west, recruiting jinau."

"Are the ranks depleted then?" Aille asked.

"A bit." Kralik's eyes glanced at Oppuk. "Jao discipline is very exacting, sometimes fatal. That makes it difficult to get as many re-enlistments as I'd like."

Aille made a mental note to investigate further, in private. The lines of Kralik's body were very hard to analyze, even more so than with most humans. But something in his stance suggested to him that the human officer was not saying all he felt on this matter.

"You must tell me more later," he said. "There is much for me to learn so I may be efficient in my new post."

"I look forward to it, sir."

"You have heard of the upcoming whale hunt?"

"Yes, sir." Kralik's face was unrevealing, likewise his tone of voice. But, again, some subtlety in his stance suggested disapproval.

"I will want to take some jinau along as a personal guard, I think," Aille said. He glanced at the girl at his side. "Miss Stockwell believes there may be opposition from the natives."

"Possibly," Caitlin said. "Depending on where it takes place. If you could persuade the Governor to arrange it over in Japan, I think there would be no problem at all. Or Norway, or Iceland. They have a long cultural tradition in those countries of hunting whales. If it happens here, on one of our coasts, though, there may be trouble."

"I see. Can you handle such problems if they arise, General Kralik?" Aille was not certain—another thing he would have to check—but he thought a simple "general" was the proper form of address. He did not understand, anyway, the purpose of the seemingly meaningless "major" added as a prefix. If he understand the term "general" correctly, a general was a major figure by definition. Could there be such a thing as a minor or unimportant general?

Kralik answered immediately, without needing to think the matter over. "Yes, sir. I've got a good company stationed here. We can use them."

"Perfect, then." Aille studied Caitlin. "You should come too," he said. "Your presence would indicate approval of the activity, which would alleviate local rumblings, and you could supply advice to keep us from committing inadvertent cultural errors."

The female Banle glanced sharply at him, ears and whiskers quivering with *perceived-slight*.

"I would be glad to do whatever is needed," Caitlin Stockwell said, "although I must warn you that Governor Oppuk is not overly concerned with the good opinion of natives." Two splotches of red had bloomed in her cheeks.

"It is not necessary that the natives approve of Jao actions!" Banle loomed over her human charge. "It is only necessary that they obey all orders!"

"As they shall," Kralik said smoothly.

"Then it is decided," Aille said, "and we can look forward to the hunt."

The two humans exchanged an enigmatic glance. "Yes, indeed," Caitlin said and her eyes seemed to burn brighter. "My father will be pleased."

CHAPTER
16

The morning after the reception, word was conveyed to Aille via a human servant in black livery—the whale hunt had been scheduled for two solar cycles hence in a remote area on the one of the continental coasts. "The Pacific Northwest," as the human termed it. The political moiety of Japan was providing a vessel from its own water fleet already in that area to serve the purpose.

Kralik appeared at his door soon after, inquiring if Aille wished to review such troops as he had available to provide an escort.

"Are they all jinau?" Aille asked as Yaut fussed with the lay of his halfcape.

"Yes, sir. Experiments with mixed squads have not been successful."

"I do not understand that," Aille said, signaling Yaut to cease his endless realignment of seam with seam, a subtlety of appearance he doubted most natives would appreciate. "We have successfully integrated Jao and native troops on many planets. And humans are ferocious fighters. That much is obvious by what has already passed. Jao respect such. Why then have our two kinds made poor companions in arms?"

"If I knew that, I wouldn't be a jinau," Kralik said, then sighed as Yaut glared at him, *perceived-disrespect* written in the fraghta's stance. "Sorry, sir. I shouldn't be flip. It's an important question."

"Yes, it is," Aille said. "Does your species recognize the importance of association? I was not sure, after reviewing the available

171

records. It seemed, in the past, before Jao arrived, there had been much dissension amongst your political entities over issues I could not interpret."

Kralik braced his legs and settled into what seemed to be a waiting stance. "I'm not sure I follow your meaning, sir."

"To accomplish anything of worth always requires more than one individual," Aille said. "The most important endeavors are always achieved in concert."

Kralik appeared to consider, his gaze drifting up and heartward, as though someone just out of sight stood there. "We do work together, when the situation requires it," he said. "Especially in the military. But we also have a long tradition of valuing individual worth, 'role models' and 'heroes,' we call them."

Aille was not familiar with the concepts. "I do not think Jao have these. Perhaps that is the problem."

"Perhaps." Kralik's body was very proper, almost forming the lines of *willingness-to-be-instructed*, were it not for those horribly immobile ears that detracted from every sensible conversation.

Aille turned to Yaut. "Fetch Tully and I will review my new command."

Yaut disappeared into the spacious back room with its sanitary accommodations and returned a moment later with a damp Tully in tow, struggling to put his arm through his uniform sleeve.

Aille cocked his head in *amused-bewilderment*. "Have you taken up swimming after all?"

Tully stared down at the floor, but said nothing, while Kralik made only a muffled sound.

"Perhaps he seeks to become more Jao in his personal habits," Yaut said, pocketing the sleek black locator control. "That is appropriate."

Kralik keyed off the doorfield and stepped through, taking his proper position, at the forefront. "This way, sir."

Caitlin sat at the breakfast table, toying with her toast as Dr. Kinsey wolfed down a pecan waffle across from her. At least Oppuk's kitchen knew how to feed humans. "I can't do this," she said. "It's bad enough they're following through with the blasted whale hunt. If I go along, it will send the wrong message."

"What can't be cured, and all that." Kinsey's dark eyes blinked at her myopically through his glasses, then focused on his fork and the morsel of waffle dripping with syrup. "It seems to me that the more you protest, the more our Jao masters will be determined to carry out this pointless exercise. You should go, smile benignly, as though they're a bunch of four-year-olds discovering the joys of mud pies, and behave as if the whole affair is quite beneath you. I predict they'll get bored and go on to something else after a few days, maybe even before they actually find a poor whale to slaughter."

"If it were anything but a hunt, I'd say you were right," she said. "But the Jao seem to have an infinite capacity for anything humans don't like. There are bound to be protesters, at the very least, once the word gets out, in that part of the country. And that will just egg the Jao on. That's how they *always* react to open opposition, Professor. The Jao didn't drop a bolide on Mount Everest because they really cared that much about the 'frivolity of mountain-climbing.' They did it because a specific expedition went ahead after it had been specifically ordered not to—and so they made their point as brutally as possible. Disobey us and we will even destroy your tallest mountain."

She shuddered and set her toast aside. "I don't want to be there."

"You really have no choice, I'm afraid." Kinsey chewed for a moment. "Look on the bright side, Caitlin. The new Subcommandant seems to have taken a shine to you. It's all quite interesting, from my perspective. The addition of a new clan in the mix is going to change things."

"Yes, but not necessarily in a good way." She massaged the base of her neck, feeling tension coiling there like a snake. "The last thing I want to do is get between two high-powered kochan like Narvo and Pluthrak. *Especially* between those two. Did you see the way the Governor looked at this Aille? It chilled my blood."

Kinsey held up the shiny aluminum case of his mini-recorder, then placed it on the table between them. "I must confess I was too busy talking to some of the Governor's other guests to observe their interaction. Did I tell you? I learned some simply fascinating things about the Jao homeworld last night."

"Homeworlds," she said and stood. "Nobody knows how many there are. Nobody human, at least—and I don't think even the Jao do. That knowledge is lost in their prehistory. Aille told me that Pluthrak alone has twenty-nine and that's the most specific information on the subject I've ever heard."

"Oh, my." Kinsey blinked. "Twenty-nine? For one kochan alone?"

"They are so powerful, we'll never get rid of them until they want to go. And when—or if—they do, how much of this world will be left in their wake? They've already converted many of our factories and resources to their exclusive military use. The rest . . . many of then, especially here in America, stand in ruins."

"For the war they're always talking about," he said.

"For the war against the mysterious Ekhat, who may be mythical, for all we know." She leaned over the back of her chair. "Maybe they exterminated the Ekhat long ago and now just use them as an excuse for whatever they want to do."

"I freely admit I do not know as much about the Jao as you, my dear," Kinsey said, "but it's always been my impression the Jao make no excuses for their actions. Speaking as an historian, they remind me of the ancient Romans, in the way they combine practicality with ruthlessness against any opposition from their conquered territories. Or the way the Mongols ruled Asia and parts of Europe. The point being, Caitlin, that they would not waste their time developing elaborate reasons to do what they wanted, simply to dupe a conquered people. They'd just do it."

The doorfield to her room faded and Banle entered. As always, the Jao guard did not ask permission.

"Governor Oppuk requires your presence," Banle said, eyes ignoring Kinsey.

Caitlin released the chair. "Let me finish dressing," she said. "And I still need to brush my hair."

"Oppuk does not care about the state of your grooming." Banle's body was tight with *disapproval*, and Caitlin thought she saw just a hint of overlying *fear*. "You will come now."

"Shall I come too?" Kinsey asked.

"No," Caitlin said before Banle could speak. "I doubt I'll be long."

"Very well," he said, standing. "Call me when you're back."

She nodded and, carrying her shoes in one hand, trailed Banle out the door into unairconditioned corridors already torrid with the region's wretched rising heat.

Kralik led his little party through the twists and turns of the Governor's palace out into the sunshine, keeping his eyes front and his mouth firmly, and prudently, shut.

In his experience, one Jao was pretty much the same as another—

only some were a lot more so. Down through the years, he had found them by turns indifferent and pugnacious, not to mention single-minded and exacting, with no way to tell which it would be on any given day. Many things, which had obsessed humanity down through the ages, they cared nothing about. Religion was one example, philosophy another. Other concepts, such as *correct-association* and *polite-movement*, which most humans couldn't even comprehend, occupied a great deal of their attention.

In other words, they were mostly the classical "riddle wrapped in a mystery inside an enigma." Kralik had advanced through the jinau ranks by saying as little as possible and keeping his head down, dealing fairly with his human troops, but taking care to enforce Jao discipline as instructed. He told himself he didn't have to understand their reasoning. He just had to obey. That was always the bottom line.

This Aille krinnu ava Pluthrak, though, seemed different. He had never seen a Jao appear to listen to humans so closely. Was this Pluthrak kochan really something special, as the Jao seemed to believe? The fellow actually had taken several humans into his personal service. As far as Kralik knew, that was unknown among Jao. Strange behavior, indeed. Very strange.

He stopped, then motioned the trio over to the groundcar he'd obtained, stood by as Aille and his uncommunicative fraghta climbed in the back, then motioned Aille's human, Tully, into the front, and took the driver's seat himself.

Normally, as a general, he wouldn't do so. But Kralik liked to drive, and since the situation was unusual anyway he saw no reason not to indulge himself. The Jao wouldn't know the difference, or care if they did. Whatever their faults, they suffered from very few of the human foibles concerning prestige and protocol. Kralik had long since learned to let a Jao, no matter how prestigious or powerful, open his or her own doors. And the only time he saluted them was to maintain the example in front of human troops, for whom the gesture did matter.

The day was already sweltering and the car, of course, had no air conditioning. Jao ignored extremes of heat and cold, so such amenities as climate control were reserved for high ranking human collaborators. Kralik was just a jinau, a dime a dozen, a human might have said. Air conditioning was unavailable for the likes of him, general or not.

If the Stockwell woman had been along, matters most likely would have been different. Kralik smiled, half-ruefully. He'd been drawn to her initially by nothing more complicated than her leggy good looks. But, very quickly, he had found himself far more impressed by her poise and intelligence. One look in those blue-gray eyes and it was obvious she had seen and experienced things far beyond what one would expect for a woman of her years.

She was a piece of work, half Jao herself, some people said. Because of her father's position in the government, she'd spent more time with aliens than humans as a child until she was old enough for a tutor. He'd watched her last night, trading bodyspeech beat for beat with Governor Oppuk and the Subcommandant as though she'd been born to it.

Her family had prospered under Jao rule, when so many had not. But she hadn't painted a *vai camiti* across her face, as did many high-placed collaborators. Some even went so far as to have a *vai camiti* tattooed on them. Nor were all such simply toadies trying to curry favor. Some, motivated by various reasons, had gone over to the conquerors in both body and spirit.

Kralik had been tempted to do so himself, at one point, when he was younger. He'd fought the Jao during the conquest, as a young Army lieutenant fresh out of ROTC. Then, when he'd finally returned home to Los Angeles after the defeat at New Orleans, he'd discovered his family had been destroyed.

His mother had died from one of the diseases that ravaged so many large cities after the infrastructure collapsed. For that, he could blame the Jao. But it had been humans, bandits claiming to be "Resistance" who were "requisitioning needed supplies" who had smashed their way into his father's hardware store and shot down his father and older brother—and his sister-in-law in the bargain—when they tried to stop them from rifling the till.

It had been chaos in many places, in the weeks after the surrender, and the police had often stood by unless paid to do otherwise. Paid in something other than money, since U.S. currency was no longer worth anything. Kralik had had nothing, beyond a field commission as captain and some decorations given by a government that no longer existed. The local police had shrugged their shoulders.

A brutal crime, and a stupid one—since the money the robbers had murdered three people for was worthless anyway. The sheer stupidity of it had outraged Kralik almost as much as the crime itself. In his anger, and—being honest—because he had no idea what else to do, he'd volunteered for the jinau once the Jao established it shortly thereafter. For a time, he'd been bitter enough to contemplate adopting a *vai camiti* himself. But, soon enough, his service had made him realize the Jao would never see humans as their equals. No matter what they did, humans would remain simply servants, industrial serfs, and sepoy troops. Clever with their hands and fierce enough to fill out the front lines of a good fight, but not acceptable in polite company.

In the end, it was the business of humans to survive this occupation, and he was busy trying to do just that. All he and the rest of the people on this conquered planet had was now. Humanity's tomorrow would have to take care of itself.

He pulled up at the barracks and realized Tully, seated next to him, had not said a single word. Kralik could sense a deep sullenness in the man, but Tully was apparently being very careful to keep his emotions hidden. As soon as he set the brake, the other man hopped out and waited silently as Aille and his fraghta opened their own doors and stood blinking in the bright Oklahoma sun.

The buildings before them had, at one time, been part of Tinker Air Force Base, back when the United States had possessed its own air force. These days, the Jao didn't distinguish between different branches of service, except as immediate practical arrangements. Fighting, whether on land, sea, air or space, were all of a piece to them. A Jao soldier might move from one to the next, in a matter of a few days, if he or she had a suitable skill.

These barracks, rundown as they were, had been delegated to the jinau. Kralik ducked through the door and was met by a young woman in sweat-soaked jinau blues, sitting behind a battered desk. Her hair was buzz-cut blond, her eyes framed in sun-wrinkles. She rose and saluted.

"At ease, Lieutenant Hawkins," he said, returning the salute. "I've brought the new Subcommandant to review the company. Are they ready?"

"Yes, sir!" She dragged a hand back over her sweat-sheened forehead and picked up the phone.

Five short minutes later, Aille and his entourage went to inspect the company. The unit stood outside under the sweltering August sun, formed into precise rows, their captain at the very front.

Despite being furred, for all intents and purposes, the Jao looked cool and unflappable.

Aille tapped his ceremonial stick, what the Jao called a "bau," against the heel of his free hand as he walked along the rows. His eyes flickered green and then went black and unfathomable. His right ear twitched. "Have these troops seen combat?"

"Some of them, sir. Less than a fourth, though, at a guess. Most are too young."

Sweat rolled down the assembled jinau faces, and Kralik could almost see the wheels turning inside their heads. What did the Subcommandant want? Was he already displeased? Jao could be notoriously fey, by human standards. There were even a few unsubstantiated tales of entire companies being "put down," as Jao termed it, after failing to meet some esoteric standard humans could not comprehend.

His own uniform was already plastered to his back with sweat, but he was determined not to show his discomfort. "Would you like to see them drill, sir?" he asked, hoping to break the tension.

"'Drill'?" Aille said. "That means 'march about in patterns,' does it not?"

"Yes, sir." Kralik took care to keep his hands down, his chin up, his voice neutral.

"I do not see how execution of meaningless patterns translates into fighting skill," Aille said. "Though perhaps there is some purpose to it which you could explain to me later. For the moment, however, I am not interested in such demonstrations."

"Yes, sir."

Aille raised his voice. "However, I do wish to speak to those who fought when the Jao first arrived on this planet. Especially any who had experience with human tanks or artillery, or successfully defended against Jao laser technology."

Kralik nodded to the captain, who immediately bellowed out the order. "You heard the Subcommandant! Those of you with combat experience during the conquest, form a line to the right. The rest, return to quarters."

Without fuss or discussion, the unit split into two contingents. The much larger portion moved toward the barracks again, eyes front, mouths tightly shut, obviously pleased to escape further notice. The smaller contingent, trying to hide their uneasiness, stepped forward and hastily assembled new ranks.

The Subcommandant glanced up at the cloudless sky, his eyes dark inside the unique black mask of his *vai camiti*. The sun blazed down out of a sky as hard and reflective as diamond. Kralik knew that although the heat did not cause distress, Jao found the brightness of midday uncomfortable. Still, they rarely gave in and wore filtering goggles. He suspected that was the Jao equivalent of "saving face," not that they would ever admit it to a human.

But Kralik had no grudge against this new Jao officer—not yet, at any rate—and saw no reason to discomfit him. "Would you like to conduct the interviews in an office, sir?" Kralik nodded at the barracks. "We find the sun very hot at this time of day."

"Yes," Aille said. His body, taller than most Jao, shone under the relentless light so that he seemed poured from molten-gold. "That would be best."

Inside, Kralik seated the Subcommandant behind Hawkins' scratched metal desk. Tully and the silent fraghta assumed identical stances on either side. Outside, the combat vets lined up to come in one by one.

The first, a grizzled sergeant from Montana named Joe Cold Bear, took up parade rest before the desk, his body carefully stiff so as not to commit some accidental posture that would translate to the Jao as disrespect.

"You fought against the Jao?" Aille asked without preamble.

Cold Bear's teak-colored eyes studied a water stain on the wall above the Subcommandant's head. "Yes, sir. At the Battle of Chicago."

"What was your function?"

"Infantry, sir."

"I have been told," Aille said, rising and walking around the desk, "that human kinetic-energy weapons were unexpectedly effective against our version of what you call 'tanks.' Furthermore, that the effectiveness of Jao lasers was occasionally hampered by various low-tech methods such as steam and chaff." His ears were forward.

An unwary chuckle escaped Cold Bear at the memory, then his mouth compressed. "Yes, sir. A man with a steam bomb—sometimes, in a real jam, just a jury-rigged sack of tin foil confetti—could sneak up on one of your tanks from the side and blow the targeting all to hell. Just for a very short time, of course, but that was often all we needed. Your armor sucks. Uh, sir."

The fraghta's ears rose. " 'All to hell?' 'Sucks'?"

"Colloquial varieties of technical terms, sir," Kralik said, giving Cold Bear a warning glance. "Roughly translated, the first means 'very much' and the other, ah, means 'not good.' You will hear the expressions from time to time among the ranks."

"Begging your pardon, sir," the Montanan said, his seamed face grim. "I meant no disrespect."

"I am still acquiring Terran vocabulary," the Subcommandant said, with a glance at Tully, "or English, as I am told it is called, though I have absorbed most of your syntax and grammar. Those terms will no doubt prove useful."

Tully's green eyes flickered toward Kralik, and he seemed to be choking a little, but he said nothing. Kralik wasn't sure what Tully's position with the Subcommandant was, but his initial assumption that he was an informer of some kind had faded. If anything, the sullenness the man exuded was aimed at the Jao, not his fellow humans.

Even if he had been an informer, Kralik would have covered for Cold Bear. Kralik wasn't going to stand here and let one of his men be disciplined for disrespect if he could help it. But he was now sure that Tully wouldn't let the Subcommandant know about the slight deception.

Aille questioned Cold Bear for a few more minutes, then dismissed him and summoned the next. The interviews proceeded slowly, always the same questions and mostly the same answers. How did Jao technology perform during the conquest, especially at the famous battles of Chicago and New Orleans? Was it true human kinetic-energy weapons performed better than the Subcommandant had been led to believe?

The human soldiers were clearly surprised to be asked about their experiences and opinions. Jao normally did not care about such things, nor appreciate being apprised of them. The human troops' eyes were wary, their postures carefully neutral. One by one, they came in through the squeaky screen door and reported to the Subcommandant far into the morning.

Tully's left leg was cramping, but he would not give in and ask for a chair. Yaut would like that, he thought, glancing at the fraghta, for Tully to show weakness or ask for favor. It'd be just another excuse for "correction." He'd show them. He could last as long as two frigging Jao!

But it was so hot. He'd had nothing to eat and little to drink since yesterday, and he still wasn't completely over his illness. Dehydration was becoming a real possibility, and passing out cold on the floor would not prove anything but his utter worthlessness.

The slick black band on his right arm itched as sweat pooled beneath it. He had to make himself leave it alone, stand silent as a Jao, as though he weren't sweltering in the goddamned August heat.

CHAPTER
17

Despite Banle's assertion that Oppuk couldn't even wait a minute for Caitlin to brush her hair, the two of them stood out in the hall for three hours before she was admitted into an audience she had not sought. Jao rarely misjudged temporal flow to that degree, and Caitlin suspected Banle had known they would not be needed until then. It was just one more not-so-subtle display of power on the Jao governor's part.

It was petty, too, in that respect quite atypical for Jao. Caitlin would give Terra's rulers that much: as a rule, they were less prone than humans to the bureaucratic mindset that enjoyed rubbing inferior status into subordinates through trivial measures like keeping someone waiting. Oppuk, unfortunately, seemed to combine the worst traits of both species.

At length, a human servant emerged through the doorfield's blue shimmer, eyes downcast, and indicated with a small motion of his hand that they should go in now. Relieved to finally be doing something, Caitlin stepped forward. But even before she touched the field, she could tell it was still set at a fairly high frequency, almost too solid to pass through. She laid her palms against its scintillating surface and felt the resonance in her bones.

"Go!" Banle said, hanging back, determined to have the place of honor this go-round.

"Just a minute," Caitlin said, then turned to the servant, who was waiting, silent as a shadow, by the wall. There was a bruise on the man's face, she suddenly realized. "Can you turn it down—"

Banle seized Caitlin's shirt at the nape of her neck and shoved her through. It was like being forced through concrete that had almost solidified. Caitlin struggled to breathe, caught for a second in the middle, then staggered on through as Banle's superior strength prevailed. They both emerged into a small room, comfortably dim and cool. Evidently, she thought, trying to control her ragged breathing, Oppuk wasn't showing off his ability to tolerate sun today for the locals as he had been yesterday at the reception.

The humid air was thick with a bitter smell akin to the stench of rotting seaweed, causing her eyes to burn. She eased out of Banle's fingers and took up a strictly neutral stance, which she hoped would not give Oppuk the opportunity to find offense. He was very fond of being offended, was Oppuk krinnu ava Narvo.

She'd had an older brother once, lanky, flaxen-haired Brent, who had told her jokes and taken her riding on his horse, but no more. Four years after the Occupation began, Narvo had requisitioned him from her father to be trained as a translator, then hadn't approved of his accent, after having him instructed in Jao. "Simply barbarous," the Governor had been reported to say, before swinging a massive fist and crushing her brother's cervical vertebrae. She'd been six that year, but she still remembered the terrible emptiness of her house, along with her parents' grief. The body was never returned. Governor Oppuk had disposed of it for them, as a "courtesy."

The big Jao was seated before another one of their pools, watching the water trickle in from an overflow channel. He was quite naked, though she knew no Jao ever took notice of such things.

"They are all connected," he said in the complex tones of his own language.

She composed her limbs into an uncomplicated neutral stance, one just short of outright *indifference*, and prepared to wait. Either Oppuk would make sense, or he would not, but trying to hurry him would not be wise.

"The pools," he said finally. "I thought it would be amusing, to create an entire indoor waterway. We do not have anything that ambitious even in the biggest kochan-house back on Pratus."

She abandoned neutrality for *polite-interest*, but dared nothing stronger. "The pools run from room to room throughout the palace?"

He rose and prowled the length of the artificial stream, then stared at the wall through which it disappeared. "If you threw a dead body in at the beginning," he said, "it would float unencumbered to the opposite end, before meeting the pumps and filters. I had it designed that way, less trouble for the servants."

"I see." Cold dread prickled along her spine. The one thing she could be certain about was that Jao cared nothing about what made more work for servants. Especially not a Jao like Oppuk, who used mainly human servants. So, what did he want? His own posture was intricate, and she was not good enough at reading formal movement to depend on her own interpretation.

He turned back to her and, in the lay of his ears, she thought she caught a flash of . . . *jealousy*?

"What did you think of him?" he said, as though they'd been having some other conversation altogether. His body assumed the sharp lines of *bold-insistence*.

She flinched. "I regret I do not know who you mean."

Banle, who had taken up a stance of *readiness* back by the wall, glanced at her. Caitlin could read her unease.

"The Subcommandant," Oppuk said. "Young Pluthrak."

"He was very . . ." She wracked her brain for something innocuous, yet complimentary. "Very gregarious. We had an interesting exchange of words."

"So," he said, and his eyes danced with ominous green, "even a human can see that much. I should have known."

She longed to look away, but dared not take her attention off him.

"Your clutch-mate, Brent," he said. "Do you remember him?"

"Brent was my brother," she said, her throat aching with tension, "and I do remember him, but humans are born singly most of the time, not in clutches as are Jao. We were not clutch-mates."

Oppuk's head canted and his eyes were again the black of onyx, unreadable. "I was told that," he said, "when I first came to this wretched world, but never credited such foolishness."

She waited, fingers trembling.

"Jao offspring are whelped in clutches for convenience, but each is born of a single female." He lumbered forward to loom over her. "If humans reproduce only one child at a time, how did their numbers reach such incredible proportions?"

"I cannot say," she said in a strangled whisper. "I only know what I am told."

"Of course, since you have not been permitted to breed yet," he said, "you do not possess all the facts about the act and its consequences. I will interview you again after your kochan has selected your marriage-group and you have produced your first progeny."

"Yes," she said, her eyes trained on his muzzle. The fierce whiskers gave him the aspect of a walrus; and, although he was not as large as one, Oppuk was far more dangerous. Her cheeks heated, but she took solace in the fact he would not understand the reaction indicated embarrassment in a human. "I—I would find such a conversation instructive."

Without another word, Oppuk slipped into the small pool with only a faint splash and dove to the bottom. There, he settled on his back, watching his visitor up through the rippling water as though she were prey.

Banle motioned at the door and then stalked through, without waiting to see if Caitlin would, or even could, follow. She launched herself at the field, arms outstretched, and managed to struggle through on her own. Though, for a minute, blood pounding in her ears, she thought she might not make it.

Just beyond, Banle was standing still, facing the long hallway before her, arms akimbo, ears pinned back in a posture Caitlin had never encountered before. The Jao must have been in a hurry indeed to have gone first.

"Did you understand what that was all about?" she asked.

"You do not want to know," Banle said in English and shook herself. "Hope you never have occasion to find out."

Aille counted the morning at the base well spent. The jinau unit Kralik had selected to be his escort—a "company," as the humans termed it—was rich in experience, and most of those he interviewed agreed with Rafe Aguilera. He'd deliberately left Aguilera back at the palace with Tamt, not wanting him to influence the unit's testimony in any way, but it seemed his advice had been accurate.

Humans had indeed devised a number of low-tech methods for

neutralizing Jao lasers, which, though not always effective, had worked often enough to make considerable trouble for the invading troops. With more time on their side, or the strength of a united planet behind them instead of one riddled with quarreling factions, they might have influenced the invasion's outcome in a very different direction.

His ears flattened as he worked out the implications. His trainers had certainly never broached such possibilities, when preparing him for this assignment. He doubted if they had any idea how close humans had come to presenting the Jao with a sound and humiliating defeat. Narvo had overseen the conquest, as it had the rule afterward, and they had obviously shaded their reports to the Bond of Ebezon to understate the problems they had encountered.

Shaded them badly. To a degree, it was expected that kochan reports to the Bond would be shaped to their advantage. But this went beyond anything acceptable. This verged on dishonor. It was puzzling, too, from the standpoint of Narvo's influence. Aille was quite certain that many of Narvo's affiliated kochan and taifs— those who had suffered most of the casualties—were still quietly resentful of the way Narvo had made light of their sacrifice.

An insane method for deepening association! What could they be thinking?

"We will stay here on the base until we leave for the whale hunt," he told Yaut, after dismissing the last of the interviewees. "I wish to familiarize myself with the workings of this unit."

The air hung hot and heavy in the little room and Kralik seemed to be moving more slowly than before. Tully remained in the corner, watching them all with that enigmatic green gaze.

A glimmer of approval flickered in the fraghta's eyes, then subsided. "I will send a driver back for Tamt and Aguilera and our few possessions," he said, "and send thanks to Oppuk krinnu ava Narvo for the boon of his notice."

Narvo's notice . . .

Aille considered that "boon," in light of the upcoming hunt. The two were obviously intertwined and Narvo was notorious for its ability to infuse apparent gifts with subtle aggression. Caitlin Stockwell had expressed apprehension about the proposal, even though the hunting of such creatures was an activity humans themselves had suggested and apparently developed long ago in their history. Was Oppuk maneuvering Aille into a situation that would cause his nascent association with humans to fall apart?

He pried himself out of the too-small chair and motioned to Tully. "I am concerned."

The human glanced at Yaut and stood a bit straighter. "Sir?"

"What do you think it means, this hunt?" Aille asked.

"I—don't understand." Tully was fidgeting, which, in a Jao, would have the same meaning as the phrase "chattering nonsense" would for a human.

"I asked you at the reception, but you did not provide a satisfactory answer. Will humans find this whale hunt a good thing or bad?" Aille persisted, studying his servitor for clues. "Will they protest, as has been suggested?"

Tully ran spread fingers back through his short yellow hair. "There's a few who won't like it," he said. "Well, maybe more than that, especially if some Jao goes out there gunning for whales."

Yaut stiffened, but Aille motioned him back with a lift of his shoulder. " 'Some Jao,' like me?"

"Exactly like you." With a start, Tully seemed to remember his place and even adopted a fairly respectful posture. Neutral, at least. "People used to care about those whales, contributed money to save them, put bumper-stickers on their cars, made movies and wrote books about them. Nowhere more so, probably, than in the area you're doing the hunt."

"Your species does have a strange affinity for associating with lower lifeforms," Aille said. "This has been noted many times in the records, though there is no analog in the Jao personality."

"Well, we certainly didn't keep whales as pets," Tully said. "It wasn't that, but folks thought they were more intelligent than most other mammals, perhaps close to sentient. Some scientists even speculated whalesong was a sort of language."

"Interesting," Aille said. "Yet the hunting persisted?"

"In some countries. Japan, for one. Some of the Scandinavian countries too, I think. " Tully shrugged. "And that's who brought up the whole idea, wasn't it? The Japanese. I figure they just want another chance to stick it to the United States. I don't think they ever did forgive us for beating the crap out of them back in World War II."

Old political rivalries in play, then, Aille thought, rival out-of-date factions. Such considerations had no place in this new order.

"Humans have much more important things to worry about now," he said, "than the outcome of some ancient war. The Ekhat—"

"Yeah, yeah." Tully raised a hand. "I've heard it before. Hell, we all have. 'The Ekhat are coming and we have to get ready.'"

Yaut bristled at Tully's dismissive tone, but Aille stepped between the two, preferring to handle the incident himself. "The Ekhat are indeed coming," he said softly, his whiskers quivering with restraint. "If you had seen them, experienced firsthand what they do to alien lifeforms, you would not say their name so casually."

"So they'll attack us, will they?" Tully seemed unaware of Yaut's rising anger. "Kill our families, bomb our cities, take away our freedom. How is that any different from you Jao? And who knows? Maybe these Ekhat will help us if we help them. They say 'The enemy of my enemy is my friend.'"

The phrase had the ring of antiquity, as though it had been much used down through the generations. No wonder Terrans did so poorly when it came to fostering alliances. "The Jao have a different saying." He paused, seeking to translate it accurately. "'Do not come between two enemies, for they will surely crush you in their eagerness to annihilate one another.'"

Tully's face reddened in that peculiar way Aille was coming to associate with distress. Baffled, he studied the human's angles for clues, wondering if he would be forced to put the man down after all. Tully was affiliated with this disruptive outlaw clan called the "Resistance," that much was clear. But if he could bend him to Jao rule, make him see that association was his only viable option, then Aille might be able to deal with all the rest on this world who remained intractable and know how to bind them to the Jao cause before it was too late.

Silence hung in the stuffy room until Kralik cleared his throat. "As Tully said, there may be a few protesters, sir," he said, "but when you know us better, you'll understand that humans never agree about anything a hundred percent. Even if the Jao decided to leave tomorrow, someone somewhere would protest. It's just our nature."

"Such divisiveness and devotion to self interest is why your kind have been conquered," Yaut said. "If you had stood together, you might have held this world against us. Do not ever forget that."

Kralik glanced at Tully, then nodded, and for a moment, Aille read utter fury in the lines of Tully's body, as though he were on the edge of losing control and attacking the other man. Yaut's ears flattened as he too picked up the insinuation and readied himself for response. Kralik, on the other hand, seemed almost relaxed, as if he had nothing to fear from Tully. Aille suspected the older man was a much more capable hand-to-hand combatant than Tully—and knew it.

Apparently Tully had the same assessment, for he turned away abruptly and moved as far away as he could while staying in the room. He stared out a window, one fist clenched. His heartward fist, Aille noted, the one whose wrist was banded by the locator. Tully's other hand rubbed over the device under his sleeve.

Kralik shook his head, slightly. It seemed to be a subtle indication of disapproval, but Aille could not determine if the disapproval was of Tully himself or something involving his training.

By now, Aille was quite impressed with the human general's capability. Yaut, too, it seemed.

"His training is not yet complete," the fraghta said. "He will either improve his manners or die. I do not care which."

"Yes, sir," Kralik said, "I can see that."

PART III:
Leviathan

When the Bond of Ebezon's agent learned of the whale hunt, he moved to the window in his human-designed residence and stared out over the ocean.

On one level, he was not surprised. Oppuk's hatred of humans had, years earlier, passed into the realm of unsanity. Still, even for Oppuk, this action was egregious.

Stupid, as well. The reports coming from Pascagoula had made clear already that the young scion of Pluthrak was, indeed, *namth camiti*. Foolish to leave one's guard open against such a one, regardless of his youth and inexperience.

Oppuk, of all people, should know that. He had been *namth camiti* himself once, Narvo's pride. And, within a short time after arriving on Terra, had proved himself by displacing the Hariv who had been possessed *oudh* before his arrival. Jita krinnu ava Hariv had not been as arrogant as Oppuk was now, but, secure in the shrewdness and sagacity of his age, had not taken the challenge of the Narvo *namth camiti* seriously enough—until it was too late, and he was forced to offer his life.

The agent had been there himself, at the assembly of the Naukra where Oppuk had taken the old Hariv's life. Oppuk had driven the ceremonial dagger into the neck vertebrae as surely and as forcefully as he had outmaneuvered Jita from the moment of his arrival on the planet. It had been a superbly delivered deathstroke—quick, clean, as custom demanded—even if the agent himself thought Oppuk had been a bit excessive in the use of his massive muscles. But then, that was always Oppuk's way. In that, if nothing else, he was truly *namth camiti* of Narvo.

For a moment, the agent considered whether there was any way he could be present himself, at the whale hunt. He would like to observe the dance more closely, in order to gain a better sense for the young Pluthrak.

But, leaving aside the obvious difficulties—no one had invited him, after all—it was probably still too early. And besides, he thought with some amusement, the center of the flow was coming toward him, in any event. Perhaps he would not have to do anything, beyond wait.

He was good at that, after all. The agent had now waited for twenty years.

CHAPTER
18

Oppuk went down to the Great Room, where he had received his guests the day before, and swam. The staff had cleared away the last of the detritus from the gathering and he had the space to himself. The vastness soothed his nerves and helped him think. Eyes open, he dove into cool waves tinted the precise green of Pratus' largest sea, the Cornat Ma.

He'd known the truth for a long time. Narvo would probably never let him return to Pratus. His chance to get off this hateful ball of earth and rock had faded as the orbital cycles passed. Now, at his age, it was not likely to ever happen. He would never be brought back to breed, simply left here to rot away and take Narvo's deepening shame into oblivion with his eventual death.

Terra had been conquered, but the natives had resisted so fiercely, the victory had come at such a terrible cost and taken so much longer than initial flow had seemed to indicate, that someone had to accept the fault. As the young *namth camiti* from mighty Narvo assigned to the conquest, Oppuk had maneuvered skillfully to force the existing commander of the Jao forces to do so, associating deftly as he convinced everyone the failure was due to the commander's excessive caution and hesitancy.

Jita krinnu ava Hariv, that had been. The old Jao's eyes had glared hatred at Oppuk even as he offered up his life for the failure, before the assembled elders of his kochan and Narvo's and many others, as well as representatives of the Bond.

Narvo had accepted the offer, of course, and thereby elevated their scion Oppuk to the paramount position and transferred *oudh* from Hariv to Narvo. It had been a pinnacle of triumph and success for both his kochan and him, confirming once again that Narvo was supreme in the field of battle.

But what neither Narvo nor Oppuk had understood, at the time—though Jita had tried to warn them—was that the conquest of Terra was far from over. Oppuk, once in command, had ordered an all-out massive assault on the most powerful of the human moieties, what they called the United States. The result had been the Battle of Chicago, a brutal and vast conflict covering much of the area south of the great lakes of North America.

The savagery of the humans had been incredible. They, too, had poured everything into the battle. Oppuk had not really believed the reports he was getting—from Narvo and affiliated commanders, now, not Hariv—until he finally descended from orbit to observe from a close distance. What he had seen in the days that followed horrified him, as it would have any civilized being. The natives combined insensate fury with a gruesome penchant for self-immolation. They thought nothing of surrendering their lives, as long as it meant taking Jao with them. They set ambushes everywhere, even baiting traps with the bodies of their dead comrades, mates and offspring. And their weaponry had been far more effective than Oppuk had assumed, having dismissed Hariv's reports as self-serving twaddle.

The experience had come as a complete shock to the young Oppuk, the proud *namth camiti*—as he had been then, so long ago—of great Narvo. The hatred he had developed for the natives had settled into his bones, and never left. They were altogether vile creatures: naked and uncouth, hideous beyond belief with their flat, expressionless faces, without sophistication or merit or *vithrik* of any description. Yet, in the end, he had barely defeated them—and then only by giving up the battle and ordering the outright destruction of the area. And again, shortly after, when another great battle began to take shape along the southern coast of the continent.

He'd thought, at the time, that the worst was past. But the many solar cycles that followed had been no better. The vicious beasts were no easier to rule than they had been to conquer.

Even still, pockets of resistance smoldered back in those

misbegotten mountains. And elsewhere, in other mountains and other forests on other continents. He could reduce the camps of the vermin to slag, with enough bolides, but that would render much of this continent and other parts of the planet uninhabitable. Then everyone would know he had missed enough of the stragglers to allow them to breed replacements for those he had killed. And such action would expend many resources at a time when quickening flow suggested the Ekhat might be headed this way, as long predicted.

More troops and materiel had already been lost here than in conquering all the other worlds under Jao hegemony put together. Even now, a huge garrison was required just to hold it, without the potentially vast resources of the planet being released for the war against the Ekhat. Few in the Naukra Krith Ludh would overlook that once it became obvious, and Oppuk was sure the Bond's suspicions were mounting all the time.

The situation was maddening, and there was no end in sight. None, at least, that would come quickly enough to salvage his once-promising life. Maddening, and for much too long. Oppuk knew, in some part of his mind, that his own grasp on sanity was weakening. Indeed, was already badly frayed.

And this was a time when he needed to think clearly. Pluthrak, obviously, had concluded that Narvo's hold on Terra was weakening. So, much as Narvo itself had done with Oppuk, they had sent a *namth camiti* to begin the challenge.

But he did not allow himself to think about his mental state very often. It was not the Narvo way to dwell on such inner subtleties. That road led to paralysis. The Narvo stance toward the universe was direct, shaping it rather than being shaped. Oppuk had defeated Jita, but Aille would not do the same to him. Narvo, after all, was not Hariv. He would crush this Pluthrak upstart.

Finally, he let himself rise to the pool's surface and blinked up into the carefully expressionless face of Drinn, his castellan. "The transport is ready, Governor," the servitor said, "at your convenience."

Oppuk heaved himself out onto the broad black rocks, then shook the water out of his nap. "And the female?"

Drinn did not even flick a whisker. "Which female, Governor?"

"The Stockwell progeny," he said. "Is she still in residence?"

"You have not yet given her leave to depart, Governor."

He had not, had he? The thought pleased him. He had suppressed his awareness of her to the point he had forgotten about her for the moment. He was pleased, too, that his ploy, put into action so long ago, had apparently been successful. After his dispatch of her brother, this little female had applied herself quite diligently in the learning of Jao. Her diction was flawless, and she even moved well—for a human. He would employ her skills in the approaching days, when the Ekhat arrived and her fellow humans would need to be exhorted to both fight and die well.

As for the father, his lifespan was approaching its end. Oppuk was weary of Ben Stockwell's many small subterfuges on the behalf of his species, and the wretch was getting old as well. Humans aged faster than Jao, it seemed. With the Stockwell girl ready to be trained at last, he could put the father down and install her in his place as figurehead President. Who better than a daughter from Stockwell's own kochan educated in many things Jao?

"Tell her she is to accompany me on the whale hunt," he said, remembering her evident distress over the whole idea. "Have her brought out to my personal transport immediately."

Drinn's black eyes flashed green with amusement, then the castellan resumed a classic rendition of *respectful-appreciation* colored by just a hint of *anticipation* in the lay of his ears.

Oppuk enjoyed the elegance of tripartite postures, though he was far too busy to engage in them himself. "So," he murmured, "all that training was not wasted."

The castellan disappeared through the blue sparkle of the doorfield as Oppuk gazed around the vast echoing hall regretfully. His whiskers twitched. He would miss the palace pools, with their carefully crafted scent mixtures, but he understood this hunt was to take place out on an ocean. It would not be Pratus, of course, and he would most likely never see the magnificent green spray of the Cornat Ma again. But, vile as it was, this world was his— so he would dredge from it what scant diversions it could provide.

And the President's progeny would make herself useful while he did.

Kralik arranged transport up to the Oregon coast via the resources of his Pacific Division. That allowed the Subcommandant to take, not only his personal service, but the entire jinau company as an honor guard. The general had watched the young Jao question the company's veterans yesterday with growing surprise. All morning long, Aille krinnu ava Pluthrak had studied the face of each man or woman in turn, asked intelligent questions, then listened to the answers. He'd made notes himself or directed his fraghta to do so, and requested additional details whenever he felt the information was not clear.

Aille was still Jao, of course, with the air of inherent superiority and entitlement that seemed bred into their very bones. Nothing would alter that. But he had really listened, and Kralik had never before encountered a highly placed Jao who did.

Then there was the fact that the Subcommandant had taken not one, but three, humans into his personal service. Everyone knew that was just not done. Of course, the selection of Rafe Aguilera, Kralik could understand. Aguilera had served as a tank commander during the invasion—and a damned good one at that, by all reports. The Subcommandant was in charge of the refit of tanks, among other weapons, down in Pascagoula. Aguilera clearly offered a great deal of experience and knowledge in a critical area.

But Gabe Tully was another matter. For one thing, the man clearly had Resistance sympathies at the very least. Kralik suspected he was actually a full-fledged member. Although Tully tried to hide it, his every move subtly radiated defiance. Once, during the interviews, his sleeve had slipped up his arm and Kralik had caught sight of a black locator band, the kind Jao used when they wanted to make sure a prisoner didn't escape. Whatever else he was, Tully did not have the Subcommandant's trust.

Kralik decided to keep a close eye on Tully while the unit was on the coast. After that, well, the Subcommandant would just have to make up his own mind. If he wasn't worried about Tully, then Kralik wouldn't let the man's attitude bother him either.

Several years ago, the Pacific Division had been allotted several refitted Jao transports that were too damaged for deep space, but adequate for suborbital boosting. They allowed for quick travel anywhere on the planet, and Kralik had ordered one of them placed at the disposal of the Subcommandant and his jinau escort and his personal service.

The members of the Subcommandant's personal service who would accompany him, it turned out, numbered only four, counting the fraghta. Apparently there were two others, a Jao female production supervisor and a human factotum, but they were being left behind in Pascagoula to continue their duties there.

The previous Subcommandant, Pinb krinnu ava Hariv, had been a leftover from the conquest—old and absentminded, long past needing a fraghta and often ignoring his responsibilities for days at a time. Pinb's service, though it numbered more than fifty, had been as slothful as he was.

Aille krinnu ava Pluthrak's service was tiny in comparison, but Kralik was sure the new Subcommandant already knew more about the jinau forces he commanded than Pinb had learned in fifteen years. It would be interesting to see where this all led.

From one viewpoint, Pinb had been a blessing. He was disdainful of humans, true, but had seemed equally disdainful of the Governor—indeed, all things Narvo. His neglect and indolence had allowed Kralik to pretty much run the Division as he chose. But it had also kept the Division in a sorry state, and Kralik was first and foremost a good professional soldier. If he could get along well enough with the Pluthrak scion—and so far the signs looked promising—he would be much relieved to have a firm and capable hand in overall charge. Even if that hand was covered in golden Jao fuzz.

The Subcommandant had risen early and taken advantage of the base's pool, which had been built in the human style, back before the Occupation. No humans were permitted to use it now. It was reserved for Jao officers, when they did not have access to more esthetically pleasing facilities.

Kralik found Aille krinnu ava Pluthrak in the borrowed office, going over unit records. The fraghta, Tully, and the raw-boned Jao female who was also in his personal service were lined up behind his back. The air already hung hot and thick and a fly was buzzing around the ceiling. The Subcommandant looked up as Kralik closed the old-fashioned door behind him with a click.

He did not bother to salute, since it meant nothing to Jao and there were no human soldiers around—leaving aside Tully, whose status was unclear. "The transport is ready to leave for the coast at your convenience, sir."

"I wish to take several of the guests from the Governor's palace along with us," Aille said. His nap was still damp from his swim. As far as Kralik knew, Jao never bothered with towels.

"Give me a list, sir," Kralik said, "and I'll send a car."

"The female you were accompanying yesterday. If I remember correctly, her name is Caitlin Stockwell," the Subcommandant said. "She may have a servant or two she wishes to take along as well. You will have to inquire."

"The President's daughter?"

"And inquire if she is available for assignment," Aille said suddenly. "With her knowledge of Jao and formal-movement, she would be a valuable addition to my service."

Kralik's eyes narrowed, but he was able to suppress any other reaction. The Subcommandant did not seem to realize other Jao did not want humans on their personal staff, that the idea would no more occur to them than it would occur to a human to hire a chicken as an accountant. These Pluthrak were indeed horses of a different color. "Yes, sir, I'll see to it immediately."

Caitlin Stockwell would probably have to take that overbearing Jao bodyguard along with her, he thought, mentally calculating the number of seats he needed to reserve. And maybe the professor who had appeared to be her traveling companion, perhaps even a chaperone of sorts. He wrote out an official order, then summoned Hawkins to drive over to the palace and fetch the Stockwell woman and her entourage. With any luck, they could lift in less than two hours.

Aille had just settled into a private compartment aboard the suborbital transport when Kralik looked in.

"Subcommandant?" he said, then fell silent.

Aille read hesitation in the human's downward gaze, underlain by . . . dread? "What is it?" he asked patiently.

"Miss Stockwell won't be joining us."

Tully dropped into an oversized seat meant for Jao, dwarfed by its proportions like a child. Aguilera sat in the one next to him.

Aille let *question* seep into the lay of his ears. Kralik's manner hinted he had more information to impart.

"She—" Kralik entered, his steps seeming reluctant. "It seems Miss Stockwell has gone on ahead to Oregon with Governor Oppuk. I imagine we'll be seeing her when we reach the coast, unless the Governor has other plans."

"Has the Governor added her to his service then?" If so, Aille thought, he could hardly be surprised.

"I don't know, sir," Kralik said.

"It does not matter," Aille said, reaching for his personal board in order to make a few notes. "Either she will be there or she will not."

"Yes, sir." Kralik straightened. "Entirely right."

The human was clearly reading some subtext into this situation that Aille could not perceive. He debated whether he should quiz Kralik on it, then decided against it. Not in front of Tully, who had been so disrespectful this morning that another incident might induce Yaut to put him down, then seek permission retroactively.

And, if he hadn't suspected that was exactly what Tully wanted, he might have been tempted to render approval beforehand. Tully could be . . . wearisome.

The door opened again and a black-haired human female glanced in. "We'll be taking off in five minutes, sir," she said. "I just wanted to be sure everyone was buckled in."

Sturdy and broad-shouldered, she reminded him a bit of his Pluthrak dam, who served on faraway reconnaissance so that he had only seen her thrice so far in his entire life. "You are the pilot?" he said.

"Yes, sir." She met his gaze without flinching, as many humans did. "Is there anything you want before we lift?"

"I wish to come forward and observe," Aille said. "I have worked hard to develop my own piloting skills, but have never had an opportunity to fly this sort of a ship."

"I'm afraid there's no room forward for observers," she said, the muscles in her face tightening. "If you could sit second, though, I . . . well, I could maybe give you the copilot's seat."

He noted the sudden whiteness of her knuckles as she gripped the doorframe, her thinned lips. Most likely, she thought it would endanger the ship to have an inexperienced backup, but for some reason was reluctant to say so.

"Not this time, then," he said, "But I would like to sit second on a training flight at some point. An experienced officer should know the strengths and limitations of all the vehicles under his command."

"Yes, sir. I'll let you know the next time a training flight is scheduled." She closed the door and Aille could hear the clank of the outer hatch.

He looked at Tully and Aguilera. "I did not fully understand that exchange. She clearly did not want me to sit second, so why then did she hesitate to express her true opinion?"

Aguilera looked uncomfortable. "You put her on the spot, sir. She was afraid to say no."

"It was her duty to refuse, then," Yaut said. "By hesitating, she endangered the ship."

Tully punched the back of the seat in front of him. "Don't you get it? No one on this world tells a Jao he can't have or do something. It's not good for your health!"

Yaut raised his hand, about to cuff him. But Aille, moving still more quickly, restrained him.

There was something...

Could it be that this was *not* simply sullenness and disrespect?

He looked at Aguilera. The older human was stalwart, he thought, and not given to pointless resentments. "Is this true, what he says?

Aguilera glanced at Tully, his lips twisted in what Aille thought was a human way of indicating sourness. But, after a moment, he nodded.

"Pretty much, sir. Tully's exaggerating, like he always does. Nath's always been straight with us. A couple of the other supervisors. Chul krinnu ava Monat. A number of the guards on the base in Pascagoula, too. But..., yes. That's usually how it is. When a human deals with most Jao, it's always risky to tell them what they don't want to hear."

Aille and Yaut stared at each other. The fraghta's ears were now flat with *indignation-at-others*, rather than *direct-anger*.

"Sixty seconds until we lift," came a male voice over the intercom. A warning rumble of engines vibrated through the walls. "Please be sure seat harnesses are locked and all personal items have been stowed for the duration of the flight."

Aille and Yaut took their seats, in front of Tully and Aguilera. The Subcommandant stared out the window.

"You were right."

Yaut grunted. "Not right enough. This is much worse than I thought. The humans even have an expression for it, like they do for so many madnesses. They call it 'killing the messenger.'"

Aille swiveled his head to look at him. "Explain."

"It means exactly what it says. Apparently it is human custom—

often enough, at least—to punish the one who conveys unpleasant information. Sometimes even put them down for it."

The transport began lifting from the ground. Gazing down at the land, as it receded, Aille could think of nothing but a vast, pustulent disease. Even the few traces of water seemed like nothing more than open sores.

"Narvo has gone native here," Yaut said softly. "I could see it in many of the lowest, but now I see it in the highest also."

Aille began to nod, until he realized what he was about to do. Adopting a human custom as well, going native himself.

But then, after considering the matter, he allowed the nod to proceed. And, to his great relief—and satisfaction—saw Yaut return it with one of his own.

For this, a fraghta could always be trusted. Aille was not violating custom, but following it. So spoke the wisdom of Pluthrak. Association was never to be feared, so long as it was done well and properly.

Narvo had not done so. Narvo had failed in its duty—as miserably, Aille now thought, as any kochan ever had. And, worse yet, had compounded the error by trying to conceal it, leaving error to fester unseen.

The result was inevitable. Association was happening, naturally, as it always did. But it was a disease, here, not a source of strength. Human failings, adopted by their conquerors while they thrust aside everything else. Like shoots, springing up everywhere. The revenge of a race that had been beaten—beaten and beaten again—but never conquered.

How could they be? Association was the only true conquest. That, too, had been one of the earliest lessons Aille could remember. He could still remember the expression on Brem's face when he first spoke that truth to the attentive crechelings.

It had immediately been so blindingly obvious to Aille, even as a crecheling. Had he not already, by then, risen to preeminence among his clutch-kin? By exceeding them, to be sure—but *never* by pushing them aside, much less driving them under. He rose with them, never against them. Helping them up, as he rose, so that they would support him.

How could it have happened? he wondered.

By the end of the flight, he thought he knew. Narvo was a blessing to the Jao, in so many ways. The mightiest of the kochan, always the fiercest in battle, always the strongest in victory, always the most stalwart in defeat.

Pluthrak appreciated that, and was regretful that Narvo had always refused their many approaches. But Pluthrak was Pluthrak because it never forgot that strength had its own dangers.

When the aircraft landed, Aille arose. "Subtle as a Pluthrak," he murmured, as much to himself as Yaut.

"Yes," said the fraghta. "There will be no association until Narvo is brought down here. That is now clear. The battle must be joined."

Aille began the battle, in the small way immediately available.

He stopped Tully and Aguilera with a gesture, as they rose to precede him.

"I will punish you for disrespect, dishonor, or disloyalty. For speaking truth as you see it, never."

The humans stared at him. Aguilera nodded at once. Tully, after a moment, looked aside.

Two victories, then. Small ones, to be sure. Victories, still.

CHAPTER
19

Caitlin found the Oregon coast refreshing after the stultifying heat of Oklahoma in August. She stood on the edge of a cliff and gazed down at the white-capped waves whipping themselves to froth on the black rocks below. At her feet, a rickety wooden stairway zig-zagged down to the postage-stamp of a beach. The wind battered her face with cool spray and tousled her cropped hair.

She'd been told, upon landing, this was near the Makah Indian Reservation, which was home to humans who had trod this land long before anyone had known aliens inhabited the stars. Perhaps the Indians had conceived of gods and demons, or some other sort of beings who came from somewhere else and imposed their own goals and desires on men. That was close enough to the reality humanity lived with these days.

Upon request, the Makah had already provided several hunt-ing guides who had advised that this was not the best time of the year for whale hunting. They should all come back in the fall when the magnificent gray whales were migrating. The meat and blubber would be tender then, they had said. The Makah would be glad to lead the hunt and then later share their best recipes.

Of course, Oppuk would not wait two or three months. The hunt would go on as scheduled, even if the Jao had to send another ship to drive whales into the bay. She shuddered. It was barbaric, as though the Jao were determined to nourish the worst in her species, not its best.

But there was nothing she could do. At this point, any effort she made to stop the hunt would only make the situation worse. Since Oppuk had insisted she come, she must play the game; look attentive, but bored, and hope the hunt would at least be mercifully short.

A temporary building, called a hant, was going up in the background. It was a sort of a field tent, if you could compare something as big as a small villa to a tent. Jao-fashion, it was being poured from materials preconfigured to shape themselves to this pattern, rather than constructed, and would house the Governor and his guests until the whale hunt was over.

Most likely it wouldn't have a pool, but she supposed the Jao would be able to make do with the Pacific Ocean as their playground. The water looked almost green today, choppy and white-topped out under the growing cloud cover. That wouldn't bother them, she thought sourly. Less sun was always welcome among Jao.

"You are wanted," Banle said from just behind her shoulder. As always, Banle avoided Caitlin's name, as though using it would elevate her above the status of a performing monkey.

She turned and looked up into the striped face. "Yes?"

"The Governor summons you." There was a muted air of *disapproval* about the Jao's shoulders and in the line of her spine.

"Then I suppose I should go," Caitlin said, irritated at losing her freedom so soon.

The Jao's hand flashed out and cuffed her cheek, making her stagger back dangerously near the cliff's edge. She clapped a hand to her face, aching, but not surprised. Her words—her stance even more so—had not been properly respectful. Banle had lived with Caitlin enough years to interpret the subtleties.

"You have come to his notice," the Jao said, a fierce edge to her voice. "There are many who would be grateful!"

Like you, Caitlin thought. Her cheek throbbed and she knew she would have a bruise.

Curtly, Banle motioned her ahead. "Be quick."

The hant, as they approached, was nearly complete, all curves and sleek lines. It probably had a great deal of "flow," Caitlin thought, if you were a Jao. Try as she might, she had never been able to perceive the elusive quality herself. Sometimes she suspected Earth's conquerors just made it up to baffle humans.

She presented herself at the entrance, was scanned by a pair of matched guards, then allowed through the doorfield, which was set at a level that rattled her teeth. Inside, she found herself in a broad open space surrounded by corridors. The air was filled with the acrid scent of smoldering tak, which, to the human nose, had all the charm of burning tires.

"Miss Stockwell." Drinn, a principal member of the Governor's service, motioned to her through the haze. "The Governor wishes to speak with you."

Following his direction, she threaded a maze of fabric corridors to a back room, even larger than the reception area. Oppuk krinnu ava Narvo looked up from a holo of a Terran ship sailing on an ocean somewhere. "Move for me," he said without preamble.

Startled, she stopped. "What?"

"I saw you at the reception," he said. "You have mastered formal movement, at least at a rudimentary level. Move for me. I wish to see how proficient you truly are."

Heart pounding, she found *modest-surprise* shaping her hands, her arms, setting the cant of her head. The ears were supposed to be involved in this posture, so it wasn't an optimal choice, she suddenly realized. But Jao ears figured into so many postures, one couldn't avoid movements that required them, or you would have no vocabulary at all.

"Interesting," Oppuk said, gazing at her as if she were a prize heifer. "Let me see something more difficult, *bemused-reverence*, perhaps, or *benign-indifference*."

Her cheeks heated. "Might I ask what this is all about, Governor?"

"No." His red-gold face was quite bland. "If I ask you to show off your movement skills, then you will do so."

Remember Brent, she told herself. Then, as now, the Governor didn't need a good reason for the things he did. The Jao had absolute power here and Oppuk was the embodiment of that power. If he said "move," then she would indeed move and hope it was good enough.

She performed *bemused-reverence*, as he had demanded, then *benign-indifference*, *awed-respect*, *eagerness-to-be-instructed*, changing every thirty seconds, then every twenty, every ten, her heart hammering, her body drenched in perspiration. As soon as she settled into one posture, she was considering the next, how best to make a graceful transition, how to economize, so that the curved fingers of one posture could move but slightly into the cupped hands of the next. Change and change and change. She was no longer thinking, just becoming, over and over again. For poor lost Brent, she thought. For her family. For all of Earth. She would be good enough. She would not fail—

"Enough!"

Startled, she looked up and met Oppuk's glittering green-black eyes.

"Who instructed you?"

"No one—formally," she said, out of breath, muscles jumping from the strain. "I watched Banle and the other Jao who came and went in our household."

"You do mirror the Narvo style," the Governor said, "though crudely." He stared over her head, seeming to see something that wasn't there. "It will not do. If you must move like a Narvo, then you will learn properly and do us credit."

She waited, not knowing what was required of her.

"From now on, you are attached to my household. I will acquire a movement master for your instruction. There must be one or two on this benighted planet." He glared at her. "You will learn and learn well, so that in the end you may be of the most use."

"In the end?" she echoed hopelessly, knowing a Jao would never deign to explain himself.

"I have plans," Oppuk said. "You will learn how you fit into them when the flow is right for you to be of use. Until then—" He glared at her, *fierce-warning* written into every line of his massive frame. "You will apply yourself diligently!"

Or it would be Brent all over again. She understood perfectly. She would refine her skills until she could serve the Governor's plans.

Either that, or she would die.

But for the color of the sky, blue instead of ice-green, and the brightness of the sun, Aille might have thought himself back on Marit An. The briny scent of the sea here was very close to that of his homeworld, the sound of waves breaking on the rocks so reminiscent of those below his natal compound, he could close his eyes and see every detail again in his mind.

If he had been Governor, this was where he would have made his palace, not on that dusty, landlocked patch of ground in the center of the continent. Why had Oppuk felt it necessary to deny himself the sensual pleasures of such a coastline?

Yaut wandered up beside him, then gazed out over the restless white-topped sea. "Enticing," was all he said, but the twitch of his ears, the dance of his whiskers expressed *longing* much more clearly than mere words.

"Indeed," Aille said. His own body was eager to experience that wild surf, but he didn't delude himself that Oppuk had brought them all this way merely to enjoy themselves. Though this trip was supposedly in his honor, they had come to prove something—to him, perhaps, to the rest of the Jao stationed on Terra, highly likely, and to the indigenous population, most certainly.

The Governor was under great stress and his increasingly unsane reactions made the stress worse. It was now obvious that Oppuk krinnu ava Narvo felt trapped, here on Terra. And well he might, Aille thought, at this stage of life when he might reasonably have expected to be called home. For a scion of his age and status to remain unmated, far from his kochan's marriage-groups—such would be hurtful to any, much less one who had once been the *namth camiti* of great Narvo.

The vessel that would take them out on the whale hunt would not be here until next-light, Aille had already been told by a member of Oppuk's service. With experienced eyes, he examined the horizon now, seeing dark-blue clouds lying low and faraway, then gauging the height of the waves assaulting the jagged black rocks below. His nose wrinkled, sampling the wind. "Storm," he said to Yaut. "We may not be going out tomorrow, even if the vessel does arrive."

"Indeed," Yaut said, raising his own nose into the wind-borne spray. "It would be wise, however, to allow some other voice to convey that probability. 'Killing the messenger' is an unsanity which seeps down from above."

It certainly didn't take the wiliness of an old fraghta to see that, Aille told himself. Everything about him irritated Oppuk. "Pluthrak and Narvo have no history of association," he said. "I begin to understand why."

"Remove yourself from his notice at the first opportunity," Yaut said. "I do not think he will summon you again. You can use that time in the darkness, to shape the battle."

"Why does Narvo oppose Pluthrak so vehemently?" Aille turned to meet Yaut's eyes, which were pulsing bright green in an unreadable mood. "I have never heard an explanation."

"Some of it, of course, is the clash of kochan style. But much of it is ancient, going back to the Before Time. A disagreement about which genetic line was first to fight free of Ekhat control. We believe it was Pluthrak, which most Jao believe also, but Narvo has always insisted they were first. They could be right. It is not an issue that means as much to Pluthrak as it does to Narvo. There is even a possibility it was neither kochan, but some other; one which did not survive and so has no voice left to speak their name. There is no way to prove either the positive or negative, and neither kochan will relinquish its claim."

"How can it matter?" Aille asked. His ears flicked restlessly and his body suddenly ached for the freedom of the foaming waves below. "It was all long ago and the struggle against the Ekhat grows always more savage. We have more important concerns that should bind us together, not drive us apart."

"True," Yaut said, "but Oppuk no longer sees beyond this world. He has lost all sense of flow."

Aille stiffened. "Are you sure?"

"Look at that dreadful habitation he built, half-Jao without, half-human within, and, even worse, where he built it," Yaut said. "Consider the quality of his personal service, his manners, even the way he moves. Everything is stilted and hybrid, not wholly one thing or the other. He cultivates useless ornamental vegetation and opens the interior of his dwelling to this star's overblown radiation. He is lost, infected by this world's culture because he refused to acknowledge it, unable to find his way. Such is always the price the victor pays, if he does not restrain fury and hatred when the flow of time requires it. Conquest is not battle."

To lose flow was to never know where you were in time, or when approaching events would take place. Everything one did would be out of step. Aille considered as the wind strengthened, carrying the scent of rain.

That would make it easier to defeat Oppuk, of course. But Aille allowed himself a moment to grieve for the once-great scion. No Jao, not the lowest, should suffer that fate.

"I am going down to swim," he said. "Will you come?"

Yaut turned toward the cliff, considered, then stepped back, his body taut with *resignation*. "I left Tully, along with Aguilera and Tamt, back at the hant to help Oppuk's people pour the last few forms. I am confident in Aguilera, but there is still no telling what Tully will do, if not supervised properly. As we have brought him along, we are responsible."

Yaut lowered his head and turned his back to the wind, heading toward the gleaming black hant. Then in the distance, Aille saw a ramshackle group of vehicles pull up and humans pile out. They seemed to be waving their arms and shouting, though the wind swept their voices inland.

This had the shape of wrongness, Aille thought. Regretfully, he gave up the thought of swimming, and followed the fraghta.

Tully heard the shouts before he saw the cars. He and the rest of the conscripted work crew had just poured the last form. His back ached with the effort of keeping the applicator in place so the preprogrammed building slurry poured out at the proper angle.

He straightened, put one hand to his head and squinted over the gleaming black surface, which was already half-set. Much as he detested the Jao, he had to admit that this way of erecting a dwelling was a lot faster and smoother than the human way.

People were shouting and waving . . . something . . . over their heads. He couldn't tell exactly what. Placards, he supposed, except that something over there seemed to be metal, catching the last of the afternoon sun and reflecting it back into his eyes.

Caitlin Stockwell emerged from the hant just ahead of Governor Narvo, her face pale and pinched. The Governor's sleek red-gold head surveyed the approaching mob and his movements had that stilted dance-like motion. "What is this?" he said to one of his guards in Jao.

"A group of natives from a nearby population center," the closest one said. "They seem to be angry. Shall we disperse them?"

Tully sucked in a sharp breath. Whoever these idiots were, they didn't have any understanding of what they faced. Jao "dispersal" was quite likely to be of the lethal sort. Jao took disrespect very seriously, and made no distinction between police and military tactics. "Disperse" and "put down" were practically synonyms for them.

He dropped the slurry duct, after making sure the flow was cut off. Then, pulled off his protective gloves, wondering if he could get close enough to warn the approaching crowd back before the damned locator brought him up short.

Aille krinnu ava Pluthrak came jogging up, closely followed by Yaut. For once, Tully was glad to see a Jao coming instead of going. The Subcommandant's ears were pricked as far forward as possible and he looked curious, rather than angry. "What do they want?" he asked Tully in a low voice.

Tully listened. The words were growing clearer with each passing second, and some of the demonstrators carried signs. "It's the hunt," he said. "They want us to go home and leave the whales alone."

Aille's eyes flickered so green, Tully could see no black in them at all. "Find the leader," he said. "Ask him to come forward and express his concerns. I will listen to what he has to say in Governor Oppuk's name."

"And if I do not wish to listen?" Oppuk said in Jao, his body strangely twisted.

"Of course you do not wish to listen," Aille said. "This is far too insignificant a matter for your attention. I will listen for you, as a good subordinate should, then either correct them as you would yourself, or dismiss them in your name."

Oppuk held the Subcommandant's gaze, then glanced aside at the approaching mob. His whiskers flattened. "They distort the flow. It is ugliness."

Aguilera hurried up from the supply dump a few meters away, where he and Tamt had been helping to mix the slurry. His salt-and-pepper hair was plastered to his skull by sweat. "They don't mean any harm, sir," he said to Aille.

"Then why are they here?" Aille said.

"It does not matter why they are here," Oppuk said. "I want them dispersed!"

Aguilera looked distressed. "Let me talk to them, sir. I'm sure I can make them understand how misguided this is."

"Pah!" Oppuk said. "Talking will do no good, young Pluthrak. These creatures understand only force. The sooner you realize that, the more effective you will be." His ears swiveled. "Or is it Pluthrak policy to shun force, when possible?"

Tully saw Yaut stiffen. That had the ring of an insult, he thought.

"I have brought one of the units newly under my command," Aille said, "as well as my personal service. I would be honored to handle this, if you will allow me."

Put that way, from the Jao assigned to command jinau troops, Oppuk could not refuse without making the implied insult an open one. That was Tully's guess, at any rate. Tully didn't understand the ins-and-outs of the thing, but he knew the Jao—especially the big shots—were constantly engaged in an intricate dance involving their honor and status, however they saw it.

Apparently he was right. The Governor turned his back and reentered the hant on its completed side, without saying another word.

Caitlin Stockwell took a step after him, then stopped, her hands knotted together. "Please don't hurt them," she said to Aille in a strangled voice. "There isn't a base near here. I imagine many of these people have never even seen a Jao. They have no idea what they're doing!"

She was probably right. Tully stepped forward. "I'll talk to them," he said with a sideways glance at Aguilera, "if you'll unleash me and turn the locator off. Otherwise, I won't be able to get close enough."

Yaut wrinkled his muzzle. "I will give it to Aguilera. If they both go, there will not be a problem." He turned to Tully. "Unless you think to overpower him, and leave with the human mob."

Tully realized with a start that the possibility of escape had not occurred to him. His jaw tightened. He must be losing his grip. "This isn't about me. It's about those poor miserable idiots over there who are about to get their fool heads blown off!"

Aguilera ran a hand back over his disordered hair. "Well, come on, then. We'd better get started. I can't move too fast with this bum leg."

Together, they waded through the grass, Tully painfully aware of his blue jinau uniform. Collaborator, he thought angrily. That was exactly what he looked like in this get up.

A hefty fellow with a face of fish-belly white glared as they approached. "A pair of Jao lapdogs!" he said and spat into the sand. "Go back to your masters!"

Aguilera clasped his hands behind his back. "Where are you from?"

"What the hell difference does that make?" The man tightened his grip on a sign that read "Stop the Slaughter on Earth's Seas!"

"Wherever it is, you probably have homes there," Tully said, "and families waiting." With a sudden pang, he thought of the refugee camps back in the Rockies, the only home he had ever known, and a piss-poor one at that. "If you ever want to see them again, you need to hop back in those cars before things get out of control."

"Or what?" A starved-looking woman with flyaway white hair, who had to be at least sixty, stepped up to the big man's side. Her sign, carried in arthritic hands, read "Jao Bastards, Go Home!"

Jesus. In spite of the cool sea breeze whipping up over the cliffs, Tully felt as though he'd stood too long in the sun. "Lady, do you want to die for this?" His voice was urgent. "Jao don't have a sense of humor, and they hate disrespect worse than about anything you can name. They'd just as soon kill you as look at you."

"You can crawl for them, if you want!" Another woman pushed through the crowd. Her curly red hair hung down over her cheek, partially obscuring her face. "We're not going to! This is our world!"

He looked at their faces. They were well meaning patriots, just like the people he'd grown up with back in the Rockies, but they didn't have a clue. Like many humans, living in small out-of-the-way towns, they'd had little if any direct contact with the Jao. This was not a fight they could possibly win.

"Look," he said, "we all do what we have to in order to survive these days. These stupid signs aren't going to change anything. You're just taking a bad situation and making it a hell of a lot worse." He glanced over his shoulder at Oppuk's Jao guards, who were prowling back and forth like thwarted sentry dogs, their flickering eyes trained on the crowd of humans. "Believe me, you don't want to draw the Governor's attention like this. If you're going to resist, there are a thousand better ways. Don't be stupid!"

"You heard what the man said." Aguilera jerked his head, pointing toward the parked vehicles. "Load back up in those cars and hit the road. It's just one whale."

"One whale today!" The woman brushed her red hair out of her face. "And then they'll get to liking the sport and pretty soon there won't be any whales at all."

"You don't understand the way they think," Tully said. "Make a big deal about it, and I guarantee they'll get rid of the whales just to make a point about who's in control. Remember Mount Everest? Don't make this worth their trouble!"

News didn't always travel fast these days, with many rural areas isolated. But almost everyone had heard of Everest and seen pictures of the truncated cauldron of rock where the world's most famous peak had once stood.

"From the Jao's viewpoint, you're just a handful of native peons who are getting above themselves," Tully said. "Peons are cheap at the price. It wouldn't take Oppuk ten minutes to order a ship from orbit to target the entire Tillamook Bay area and after that you simply wouldn't be a problem any more."

A stunned silence fell over the crowd.

"Ever see the crater where Chicago used to be?" Aguilera asked conversationally. "I saw it happen. Fortunately, I was just far enough away from the blast radius."

The old woman turned away, her eyes bright with unshed tears. Her male companion put an arm around her and led her back toward the cars. After a moment, the red-haired woman followed. Tully watched them go, feeling the black band around his wrist like a lead weight. He wanted to go with them. Goddammit, he belonged with them, not here. He had become a Jao lapdog, just like they said.

"You did a good thing," Aguilera said in a low voice at his shoulder. "Probably saved more than a few lives here today."

"Yeah, I'm a real prince," Tully muttered as he watched the townspeople straggle away in twos and threes. "Guess that's why I feel so dirty."

Vermin! Oppuk thought, pacing the perfect curves of his new receiving chamber. This entire world was infested with vermin! Clever vermin, yes, with a great deal of fight in them, but useless in the end. They couldn't be trained to anything practical, never behaved as manners and protocol required, and their breeding habits were simply appalling. No wonder the genotype varied so wildly. If the Jao could establish a eugenics program, then in a thousand generations they might make something useful of them. Contemplating it, he felt a rare sympathy for the difficulties the Ekhat must have faced back when they had first crafted the Jao from primitive semi-sentient stock.

He dropped into the newly installed pool, which had been filled with local ocean water, then floated on his back, staring at the whorls across the black ceiling. The Naukra Krith Ludh did not understand what this world was really like. If they had, they would have just incinerated it, despite its resources, to keep it out of the hands of the Ehkat, and moved on to something with more promise.

Twenty orbital cycles ago, he had arrived full of enthusiasm, proud at having been chosen by Narvo for the much-prized Terran posting. Today . . .

His greatest hope left was simply that, if the Naukra grew wise and commanded the destruction of the planet, they would permit Oppuk to supervise the ending of what he had begun. Everest was still a moment he remembered with pleasure. With so much more pleasure, would he do the same to Terra itself.

"The crowd has been dispersed," Drinn's dispassionate voice said from behind.

"How many were put down?" he asked, hoping the answer was "all."

"None," Drinn said. "Several members of the Subcommandant's service persuaded them to leave."

He splashed upright. "The female bodyguard?"

"No, the two human males. They spoke briefly and then the natives stuffed themselves back into their vehicles and departed."

Oppuk ducked under the water to clear his head, and calm his sudden fury. He'd thought this predilection of Aille's to take humans into his service the foolish fancy of one newly released from the kochanata, but perhaps not. The Pluthrak might be bold enough, even so young, to plan an open contest with Narvo. If so, his humans might indeed have their uses.

Still, it would have been wiser to kill all who had dared to protest. Such soft-headedness, common when you allowed humans to deal with their own species, was always a mistake and sent the wrong message. The Subcommandant had avoided trouble now only at the cost of more recalcitrant discord later. Humans were incorrigible. Oppuk knew that like he had once known the currents of his own birthpool.

Oppuk felt the rage drain away, and the lines of *pleased-anticipation* overtaking him. There was a trap here, waiting for the Subcommandant. Oppuk would give him the space to stumble into it.

CHAPTER
20

The next day dawned cool, gray, and wet, though fortunately the main storm had not reached the shore, as Aille had thought likely. Rain slanted out of the direction humans called "west," blowing across the sea in great glittering sheets. Obviously, he was not familiar enough yet with weather patterns on this world to make accurate judgements.

Outside the hant, both Tully and Aguilera, awaiting ground transport to the docks, managed to project *aggrieved-discomfort* without a fragment of Jao body-speech between the two of them. Hands shoved deep in his pockets, Tully muttered something about "drowned rats," a phrase for which Aille had no reference. Aguilera was his usual reticent self, but hunched his shoulders against the driving rain and futilely kept wiping his face as though to emphasize his condition.

Tamt, being Jao, gloried in the wet, and for the first time since Yaut had called her into Aille's service, looked actually *pleased*. Her stance was unrefined, but genuine, and Aille had to admit the fraghta had done well with her. Of course, instruction was a fraghta's specialty. He supposed he should not be surprised Yaut had been effective. It did make him wonder how well the fraghta would do with him in the end.

Caitlin Stockwell emerged from the hant to stand at Oppuk's side. Her stance was subdued, as neutral as Aille had ever seen it. "Miss Stockwell," he said, and she glanced at him, seeming startled before she damped that out as well.

"Is 'Miss' the correct honorific?" he said. "I have undergone English imprinting during every dormancy period since I arrived on this world, but my usage is not always accurate."

"Yes," she said, crossing to his side with a backwards glance at Oppuk. "It's quite correct. I'm sorry if I gave any impression it was otherwise."

"I assumed, after my invitation, you would be using my transport to this area," Aille said, "but I see you came with the Governor instead."

"I had hoped to travel with you and General Kralik," she said, "but the Governor requested otherwise."

"An honor," Aille said, though he thought by the slope of her shoulders perhaps she did not find it so.

"He has officially attached me to his household," she said. "I am to be tutored in formal movement by a Jao master, as soon as one can be found."

She was to be a mere servitor, then, not a member of the Narvo's personal service. Aille thought that was a mistake on Oppuk's part. But, of course, Narvo did not see things as Pluthrak did. He cocked his head, trying to read her lines, but they were ambiguous at best. "This does not please you?"

"It—" She gripped her hands together, twining her fingers in a quintessentially human gesture he couldn't decipher. "I had hoped to continue my education at the university. This—development—will disrupt my plans."

She was wearing a slick outer covering with a hood that shed the rain and did not seem to be suffering as were his own two humans. He touched the yellow material with his fingertips, finding it pliable and cool. "Your species is not fond of rain?"

"Not—generally." She managed a wan smile. "Especially not when it's chilly, like today."

"Ah, yes," he said, "Our bodies do not regard such things very much, a small legacy of the Ekhat. We were designed to be comfortable in a wide variety of circumstances."

At that moment, the ground transport arrived to take them down to the docks at Tillamook Bay, where the Japanese trawler awaited them.

The groundcars were of human design, though converted to maglevs, and showed signs of deterioration, including rusted patches on the vehicle bodies. The roads betrayed a lack of maintenance as well, and what habitations they passed were in very poor condition, with refuse strewn about and a number of starved looking small beasts skulking in the brush, including one lithe white-furred creature Aille had never encountered before. Humans appeared to watch the groundcars pass, despite the species' apparent distaste for getting wet.

The pelting rain eased off as they pulled up to the docks and, in accordance with Jao etiquette, he emerged last from the car. Voices rose and Aille looked up to see a crowd of natives forming on the parking area above the docks.

Caitlin stepped out of the car, then narrowed her eyes. "More protesters," she said to Aille in a low voice. "They're not going to let this drop. Since the Governor is doing this in your honor, can't you just request some other activity instead, one less controversial? We could tell them we were just going out for a cruise, or perhaps we could fish for shark."

"I cannot refuse the Governor's attention," Aille said. "There is long-standing strain between Narvo and Pluthrak. I would only add to it by questioning his judgement over such an inconsequential matter. Pluthrak depends on me to behave in an honorable manner here. I can do nothing else."

Her blue-gray eyes seemed very large in her small oval face. "Don't you see?" she said. "He's deliberately provoking them. They feel very strongly about this. There is going to be trouble, and, whenever there is, humans always pay the price."

He could see her hands trembling, an element of human body-speech he'd never before observed. Did it indicate dread, perhaps, or eagerness? He was uncertain how to respond.

Without acknowledging the crowd, Oppuk strode down to the end of the rickety wooden dock, which was slick with rain, then used a temporary walkway to access the vessel. It was smaller than Aille had expected, but trim and gleaming, bristling with equipment and what seemed to be a huge projectile weapon of some sort at the far end. Along the side of the hull was marked the name *Samsumaru,* apparently another example of the human quirk for personalizing material objects.

One of the Governor's service beckoned to Aille, *haste* implicit in the set of his ears. Aille started to comply, then stepped aside as several humans trotted down the weathered wooden planks, carrying the slim shaft of a portable Jao laser. He glanced back at Yaut, *question* in his eyes.

Yaut flicked a whisker. "There has been much complaining in this area," he said. "The Governor would like a chance to flex his muscles. According to his staff, things get very boring in that dusty palace in the center of the continent. He likes a good row now and then."

Then Oppuk did indeed expect trouble. Aille glanced at Caitlin, who was studying the crowd. She knew, he thought. They all knew. The natives were being deliberately provoked here, just as she said. Although he did not understand why the life of one sea animal should matter so much, he could see, if they did nothing to prevent its death, they would have lost in some important regard involving their sense of honor. And if they did indeed resist, Oppuk would ensure they lost even more.

He motioned to Kralik. "Have the unit stand by here on the docks," he said. "I think there will be some expression of local dissatisfaction before the hunt is over."

Kralik nodded. His sodden hair clung to his skull, but his eyes were sharp now with anticipation. "Do you want me to stay behind with them?"

Aille considered. "No," he said finally, as the wind buffeted him, "if there is trouble out on the water, I will need my most experienced advisors at my side."

Kralik pulled out a pocketcom and disseminated a quick order to the unit's commander.

Someone shouted up in the parking lot, then several fist-sized rocks arched down, falling far short of the docks. Oppuk's guard emerged from the water vessel, weapons ready. The Jao guards fired immediately, their lasers raking the distant crowd. Screams broke out, and then the crowd scattered as most fled inland.

Caitlin turned her head away and hurried toward the fishing trawler. Aille delayed to evaluate the altercation, minor as it was, until all the participants had either been put down or routed.

"Ineffective," Yaut commented, rain dripping down his snout. "That cannot be how they defended this planet, with shards of rock and loud, disagreeable sounds."

"No, indeed," Aille said, "it cannot."

Then they turned and walked down to the ship together, Tully and Aguilera automatically taking the lead as though they had been born to serve in this capacity.

*   *   *

Oppuk watched the Subcommandant for signs of weakness, after
he arrived at the docks. But the young Pluthrak merely observed
the situation with an infuriating air of *calm-interest*, neither taking the offensive, nor trying to hinder the guards' response.

The Stockwell scion had fled below deck. He leaned on the metal
rail, as the trawler cast off, savoring the cool spray on his whiskers. He considered having her summoned, but let the matter go
for the moment. Flow was not urgent here. Nothing was going to
complete itself for a while. She was no doubt afraid to face him
after the way her species had behaved back there on the docks.
Foolish, but there it was. As though he would discipline such a
valuable hostage for that bit of unproductive nonsense. As long
as she was in hand, her father would remain amenable.

Too bad the Stockwells had never replaced the son he'd killed.
For such a fecund species, the natives were surprisingly sentimental
about their progeny, and he had found children made effective
hostages. When he did eventually allow himself the pleasure of
killing Caitlin Stockwell, it would be a long time from now, when
he had made much use of her, and for a far greater return than
disciplining a few unruly savages.

Still, the outright disrespect rankled. He would have to do
something about the locals' brazenness. It had been quite a while
since he'd carried out a salutary object lesson. With this species,
Mount Everests were required, every few orbital cycles.

He savored the memory of Everest, for a moment. The issue itself
had been trivial, and his fraghta had urged him to simply ignore
the expedition. In truth, Oppuk had followed her advice, in the
time which came after, quietly allowing the ban on mountain
climbing to be rescinded, along with most of the other bans on
frivolous human behavior. But he'd been unwilling to ignore the
defiance and had taken great satisfaction in Everest's destruction.
By then, the humans had already driven Oppuk into a rage by their
obstinate behavior.

His fraghta had left his service, thereafter, pleading age as the
reason for her return to Pratus, even though both of them knew
the real cause was her frustration at his unwillingness to listen to
her. He'd known, even at the time, that her quiet disapproval would
harm his reputation in the kochan. But he'd been beyond caring,
by then, sure—as he still was—that his forthright methods were

the only ones that would ever prevail over humans. And, truth be told, he was relieved to be rid of the jabbering old wretch.

In retrospect, in a coldly rational sense, it had been a mistake. For a fraghta to become so estranged from her charge to abandon his service reflected much less on her than it did on him. The kochan elders would have taken note, and gauged him accordingly. But he'd do it all over again. By the end, he had detested the creature. She had plagued him incessantly, becoming increasingly more critical of his decisions until he could bear it no more.

On the forward deck, Aille krinnu ava Pluthrak was watching a pair of human techs mount the Jao laser cannon on the bow of the trawler. He turned as Oppuk approached. "You expect trouble, Governor?"

"Not expect," Oppuk said. "Anticipate. I hope to rattle their teeth a bit. I am weary of the unreasonable creatures."

A trio of white avians swooped low over the boat, uttering shrill cries. Oppuk drew his side arm and fired at several. It never did to allow one's skills to deteriorate. One smoking body fluttered to the deck, while the others veered off, squawking in protest at their close brush with death.

Actually, the one he'd hit was not quite dead, but lay jerking and issuing weak peeps. Oppuk nudged it with his foot. "This world is fecund, literally teeming. The variety of species is astonishing."

Aille picked the avian up, examined its anatomy, then wrung its neck, so that its thrashings were stilled. He studied it calmly, his stance so neutral, Oppuk could glean nothing of his thoughts. "I look forward to being further educated," he said finally, offering the feathered carcass to Oppuk.

"Throw it into the water."

Aille did as he was bid, then turned back to the harpoon mount. Oppuk watched, deeply envious. This youngster had it all before him, having not yet made mistakes that would derail his career and strand him with no prospect of further advancement or mating.

It would be pleasant, very pleasant indeed, to destroy this one. His prospects, if not his life itself. Something to look forward to.

Caitlin made herself climb the metal steps back up onto the deck finally. It was close below, almost claustrophobic, and she decided she would rather know what was going on than hide down there, tossed about the small cabin like a salad.

Banle was making herself scarce for the moment. Caitlin was grateful at least for that.

The trawler cut across the waves toward the cape that separated the bay from the open sea. Out past its protection, the sky was a dark-gray and she thought she could see a veil of heavier rain in the distance. This was not a day for pleasure boating, she thought, but then there was nothing pleasurable about this trip. You only had to catch a glimpse of their aerial escort to know that, three tiny Jao scout ships that skimmed in and out of the low-hanging clouds, like flat stones skipping across water.

The two Makah guides stood on the prow of the *Samsumaru*, their long black hair tied back, their dark eyes intent on the horizon. They came from a whale-hunting tribe and saw nothing wrong with this venture, whether it involved humans or Jao. According to tribal tradition, whales were their rightful prey and had been as long as anyone could remember.

There was no use appealing to them, so she didn't even try. The sheer weight of her own helplessness, of humanity's helplessness, was crushing. If only there were something she could do!

"You are distressed," Aille said over her shoulder.

She turned, surprised. She had not heard him come up behind her. "Yes," she said, her shoulders assuming *obedient-acquiescence*. This close, she could smell his wet nap, an alien scent, subtly different from Banle's, but not unpleasing. "But matters will progress as you Jao wish. That is the nature of conquest, is it not?"

He said nothing in response, simply leaned over the rail and watched with her as the cape's narrow spit of land grew ever larger. His profile was dark today, his nap turned dark-gold by the rain, but his black eyes crawled with green.

She wondered, as she had many times before, what biochemistry explained the way Jao eyes changed color so constantly and vividly. It was the most frightening thing about the beings, even more than their size and brute strength. When their eyes flickered so, they seemed like sorcerers—or demons. She could almost see the thoughts moving through his mind as the trawler headed for the gap on the north leading to the open sea. See them, not make them out. They were alien thoughts, whatever they were.

An hour later, they were plowing through larger waves that broke across the bow and drenched them repeatedly in cold spray. Despite her raincoat, Caitlin was soaked, but still she remained on deck. She had to stay, she told herself, so she could bear witness later. The whale's passing should not go unremarked.

One of the Makah guides suddenly cried out, lowered his binoculars and pointed to the north. After a moment, the ship heeled over obediently, then wallowed in the troughs between waves and lost speed. Caitlin grabbed for the rail, slipped and went to her hands and knees, scraping them raw as she fought to keep from being dashed against the rail. Arms seized her waist from behind and hauled her back.

"Why aren't you wearing a life vest?" a male voice said in her ear.

Gasping, she twisted just enough to look up. "General Kralik! I didn't know you were aboard."

A thin smile flashed across his normally serious face. "You'd best get below, ma'am," he said. "Else you might be swept overboard and we'd have to waste time hunting you instead of that dangerous whale." He held her a moment longer, his arms solid and reassuring, then released her and stepped back.

"Yes," she said, her cheeks suddenly warm despite the chill. For a moment, she had been acutely aware of Kralik as a man, rather than an officer.

The *Samsumaru* lurched and she fought to keep her balance on the wet deck. "I—would hate to be the cause of that." She rose, using his arm to steady herself, then stopped as his words had a chance to sink in. "Have they spotted a whale then?"

"Sonar has," he said. "It's supposed to be early for whales to come through here. According to the literature, gray whales migrate in the fall, so I was rather in hopes we wouldn't find anything today, but sonar has come up with two promising hits. It looks like we won't go back empty-handed after all."

"I see." She didn't want to see, didn't want to know any more, but ignorance had never been an acceptable excuse with her father. See it through, he would have told her. Stockwells may be many things, not all of them admirable, but they're never cowards. You have to keep trying until the day is done.

She wished this day were done, but wishing in her experience never improved the situation, and longing for what you couldn't have only made life seem harder.

"I'll stay on deck, then," she said. "I don't want to miss the Governor's hunt, but you're right. I will put on a life vest."

He opened a metal locker and dug out a bright orange flotation vest. The bulky shape was stained and frayed, obviously made before the conquest and having seen better days. She held out her arms as he settled it over her head. Her nose wrinkled. The slick plastic stank of fish—long dead fish, at that.

She buckled the straps herself, then, up by the harpoon mount, one of the Makah guides, John Bowechop, shouted. "Over there!" he kept saying, gazing intently through a pair of battered binoculars. "Hard left! Hard left!"

Caitlin squinted and thought she could make out two large glistening circles on the waves through the rain. The Subcommandant crossed to the Makah's side with the sure-footedness of a cat. Emerging from the shadows, several Jao from Oppuk's staff jerked the canvas cover off the harpoon mount as the Governor looked on, his form a study in anticipation.

Banle appeared from the other side of the trawler, wet as a seal and oblivious to Caitlin for the moment.

"We'll have to get closer," Kralik said, his face grim. "A lot closer."

And maybe they wouldn't be able to, she thought with a glimmer of hope. *After all, why would a whale just hang around and wait to be harpooned when it could dive and escape? They were supposed to be fairly intelligent—*

The *Samsumaru* veered to the left as directed and an immense wave inundated the bow, soaking Caitlin and Kralik. She shook the water out of her eyes as he pulled her away from the rail. "You should go below!" he said over the shrill of the wind. "You don't really want to see this."

"If I don't watch," she said, glancing at the Governor, "who will tell about this day?" Oppuk motioned to Aille to take a position at his side, his own stance *triumphant-expectation.*

"There are other humans on board," Kralik said.

"No one who cares," Caitlin said. "No one but me."

"Oh, I care," Kralik said, "for all the good it will do." He turned back to the sea, staring out across the waves, his gray eyes hard as steel.

He was doing what he had to do, she realized, as were they all.

Twin spumes of spray rose from the ocean's heaving surface five hundred yards off the bow, still further to the left. One of the

Makah shouted and the Governor's staff readied the harpoon. Hydraulics whined, tiny green indicators flashed. It was really going to happen, she thought, her heart beating wildly.

One of the Jao escort ships swooped low over the trawler, then swept back up into the clouds. Another faceful of spray left her gasping, half-blinded by the stinging salt. Oppuk bent over the harpoon and gazed through its sight.

Caitlin crammed a knuckle into her mouth, then made herself lower the hand. *Calm-acceptance*, she told herself and tried to let the soothing form flow over her. She'd had a lot of practice with that one. It seemed her whole life called for it.

The whale breached, bigger than she'd expected, gray and magnificent, free, the symbol of everything Earth had lost to the Jao all those years ago. *I'm sorry*, she told it. *You have to submit, just as we all do, but someday—*

The harpoon boomed and even as it was racing toward its target, Oppuk's staff members were readying a second shaft. The harpoon struck just as the whale hit the water, sending a sheet of spray twenty feet into the air. The line sang as it played out from the immense reel. Caitlin blinked hard, strained to see through the fine, driving rain. Had the whale escaped?

The line went taut with a crack. The trawler lurched and sea was stained dark red as their quarry struggled to submerge. With grim efficiency, the second harpoon shaft was loaded. Oppuk put his eye to the sight, then turned to Caitlin, seeming to notice her for the first time in hours.

His eyes flashed an intense actinic green, like sheet lightning heralding an approaching storm. His stance shifted into what she thought was *cruel-enjoyment*. She wasn't sure. It was a rare posture, for Jao.

"Miss Stockwell," he said, "perhaps you would be so good as to fire the next shot?"

CHAPTER
21
<hr/>

Aille stepped between Oppuk and the Stockwell female, who obviously shrank from taking part in the hunt. Certainty beat through him—if he did not act, she was sure to invoke offense, which was precisely what the Governor intended. Oppuk's unsanity was obvious, now, especially with that obscene posture.

Aille knew the Pluthrak variant on *cruel-enjoyment*, of course. His kochan-parents had taught it to their crechelings, so that they would know how to avoid it at all costs. That stance made one vulnerable to folly—and open to enemies.

"Although it is only proper for the Governor to have the honor of the first shot," he said, "I must confess I wish to claim the second for myself."

Oppuk's eyes met his and flashed an intense molten-green. For an instant his body displayed *savage-hatred*, startling in its purity. Even the normally unflappable Yaut, a few steps away, hissed in a breath at such a revelation before dampening his response.

But the Governor recovered quickly. "Of course," Oppuk said, abandoning the weapons mount with an air of condescension. "This hunt is after all in honor of Pluthrak deigning to waste one of its celebrated scions on this undeserving world."

"Alas, I am so newly emerged, I have never had the opportunity to become 'celebrated,'" Aille said. He touched the tender new service bar on his cheek, etched there a mere two nights ago by Yaut. "Although I hope to at least serve well."

He saw Kralik tow Caitlin Stockwell along the deck until the two humans stood well back. Her hood had dropped onto her shoulders and soaked hair clung to her head almost like golden nap. Aille knew the pair should go below where they would not tempt the Governor to notice them any further, but they seemed unaware of the risk they were courting. They looked small and fragile and dangerously exposed, like offspring released too soon from the creche.

The whale surfaced again, then disappeared with a flick of its massive tail flukes. Up on the trawler's forward deck, Aille put his eye to the harpoon's sight and waited, holding on with both hands as the ship lurched. He had been told that whales were air-breathers, not properly fish, so this one would have to resurface again before too long.

The creature was mighty, there was no doubt of that, and he could see why humans had found them fascinating and why some of them objected to the hunt. Now that Aille had seen one, he had grave doubts about the enterprise himself. The whale's narrow, almost triangular head possessed a strangely intelligent, self-aware gaze. It had never been the custom of Jao to make sport of hunting sentient beings.

But, they were here to hunt this particular beast and hunt it they would. The Governor had so commanded, and for Aille to oppose him directly would be a serious error. Combat between kochan was a delicate thing, with victories more often measured by subtle nuances than direct triumphs. The point, after all, was not to *defeat* Narvo, but to force them to associate properly.

The whale would have to make itself of use, thus, as did all reasoning beings. Sometimes that required the laying down of one's life. Aille readied his hands on the controls and waited for the wounded whale to break the surface again.

The first harpoon's rope creaked and then the whale's immense back parted the waves like a gray boulder. He angled the harpoon's sight as the trawler pitched, depressed the trigger—and missed as the whale once more dove, almost as though it were trifling with him.

The human crew unshipped another harpoon and handed it off to the Jao for reloading. Then the trawler jerked as the whale suddenly ran heartward beneath the choppy waves, sawing the rope against the metal railing. Beneath his feet, Aille could feel the thrum of the trawler's laboring engines. Wait, he told himself. It would have to surface again.

Oppuk stalked back and forth at the rail, trying—not very successfully—to conceal his anger. "I lack your eye for shooting this device," Aille said. "Have you any advice?"

"Try not to miss this time," the Governor said curtly, then fell against the cabin as the whale surfaced again, this time beneath the trawler so that the boat lurched sideways. Aille gripped the harpoon, fighting the tilt, and waited as his pulse raced. This creature was indeed clever. Might one ever be converted into an ally? he wondered. Imagine swimming with such a massive, cunning being. What a partnership that would be!

Its huge gray head broke the waves, but not as high this time, as though the whale were growing tired. *You weary, great one*, Aille thought. *It is time to submit.* He put his eye to the sight, acquired his target, and fired.

This time the harpoon struck the leviathan midbody before it could submerge. The attached rope sang through the air, then went taut with a snap that jerked the trawler forward. Several of the watching humans went to their knees, Tully and the Japanese ambassador among them.

"A true shot," Yaut said, suddenly at his side, though he had not been close before.

Oppuk gripped the rail and watched the floundering whale as the sailors again reloaded the harpoon mount, then looked to the Jao for who might take the next shot. He motioned impatiently for Caitlin to come forward. "Come," he said, "I think even a human could not miss now."

She closed her eyes, then let *humble-refusal* shape her body. "I fear it is too great an honor," she said. "I have never trained as a warrior or served in the military. My father would be quite angry if I put myself forward in such a way."

The Japanese ambassador glanced quickly at Stockwell and then came forward, stopping in front of Aille. "There is danger of the carcass sinking, once the whale dies," he said, bending low in an obvious posture of submission. "The crew says it would be best to secure it with several more harpoons until it can be winched onboard for flensing. May I recommend that his Excellency's skill is needed here."

Interesting, thought Aille. He realized at once what was

happening. Whatever the nature of the conflict between the two human moieties, the Japanese were clearly attempting to avoid unnecessary further humiliation of their opponent, now that they had won the initial sally. It was well done, quickly and smoothly— and boldly, too, given Oppuk's obvious ill-temper.

Very Jao-like, in fact. Just so did kochan properly battle with each other.

Oppuk's hand began to rise, as if he were tempted to strike the old Japanese ambassador. But he lowered it, his stance stiff, and then pointed at Aille. "It is the Pluthrak's hunt. Let him see it to the conclusion." Thereupon, he stalked off.

Aille moved at once, since it was now time to end this little contest with the Narvo with a small but clear victory. He solicited the crew's suggestions on their placement, via the ambassador's translation, then fired two final harpoons.

When it was done, he followed Yaut and the rest of his service below decks. The Stockwell scion, after glancing at the Governor, attached herself to them. The area below decks was another of those spaces, Aille found, never intended for the breadth of Jao shoulders. But he knew Yaut had his good reasons for taking them there. Oppuk and most of his personal service were remaining on deck, enjoying the wind and rain while the crew went about the business of winching the whale up onto a processing deck where it could be butchered. Given the situation, it would be best to put some separation between them now.

Caitlin sat hunched at the little table in the galley, her hands over her ears as the gears squealed. Kralik and Tully were carrying on a conversation that seemed intended to distract her, while Aguilera drummed his fingers on the table's gleaming surface, his face intent, apparently lost in thought.

A hollow boom sounded outside and something struck the water. The trawler, which had been idling, pitched hard to the right.

Aille looked past Yaut up the steps. "Are there predators in this area?"

"Nothing big enough to bother a ship this size," Kralik said. He rose from the table and bounded up the stairs, two at a time.

Again, something whumped and the ship quivered.

A moment later, Kralik stuck his head in the doorway. "We're under attack!"

*   *   *

Tully's first impulse was to grin. The local Resistance was taking action, it seemed. Real action, not stupid rock-throwing and sign-waving. Good for them!

Then he caught Aguilera's dark eyes on him. "Get a grip," the older man said. "Even the densest Jao knows what a smile is and our Subcommandant is not exactly dense."

Yaut had already dashed topside, followed by Aille. The *Samsumaru*'s engines roared back into life and the ship surged forward. Aguilera listened for a moment, then broke out his sidearm. "Damnation," he said, "they'll only get themselves killed, and half the folks back home too!"

That sobered Tully. It was indeed the custom of the Jao to retaliate against civilians who aided rebels—and they were none too discriminating about it. Down through the years, he had seen it happen over and over again. It made the rebels wary concerning sabotage or assassination, selecting only those targets that couldn't be traced back to a particular town.

Aguilera started up the steps, then stopped and glared back at Tully. "Get your ass up on deck before anyone notices you're not there!"

Yeah, that wouldn't look good, Tully had to admit. And, besides, he couldn't let Yaut and the locator control get too far away without suffering the consequences. With a sigh, he heaved to his feet, and, bracing himself with hands on the walls on either side of the narrow passageway, he followed Aguilera up into a confusing maelstrom of noise, wind, and rain.

The three Jao escort ships swung low out of the clouds, taking shots at four fiberglass powerboats fighting the waves. But these were just about the worst conditions possible for effective use of lasers. The wind had risen, driving the rain sideways, and it was hard enough just to stand on deck. Except at point-blank range, most of the energy of the lasers just went to vaporize raindrops.

Tully gripped the chill, wet rail and watched. The boats were fragile and undersized, laughable even. A handgun or rifle would do no good at this range and the craft were too tiny to carry anything much bigger. "Idiots!" he muttered and wiped the salt spray out of his eyes. "What do they think they're going to do? Throw rocks at us until they manage to scratch the paint?"

Then he caught a glimpse of two men in the bow of the closest boat struggling to load something long, white, and slender into what he suddenly recognized was a rocket launcher. He leaned over the rail and squinted. Red stripes circled one end and he could make out a row of numbers. . . .

His grip tightened painfully. They weren't so foolish, after all. "Oh, man!" He closed his eyes. With a weapon like that, they actually had a chance to do some real damage to this tub. Not smart. Not smart at all.

Normally, he would be all for retribution exacted against the Jao, but so many would pay for this—and after the demonstrations on shore this morning, Oppuk was already enraged.

Three Jao had switched on the newly mounted laser cannon and were taking methodical calibrations, conferring in low, unhurried voices. The Subcommandant and Yaut had drawn hand weapons and were both taking a bead on the lead ship, waiting for the jouncing boats to sweep closer.

One of the Jao escorts banked and fired at the little powerboat, which swerved aside and disappeared behind the immense swell of gray waves to the south. Underneath their feet, the trawler rumbled, accelerating with all the speed of a lumbering elephant as the crew navigated toward land.

The laser cannon operators fired at the third boat just as it emerged into an area relatively clear of rain. The speedboat disintegrated in a spectacular explosion. Water sizzled into steam as the beam continued for several seconds before being switched off. The chill, wet air was filled with stench of incinerated fiberglass.

Dumb bastards! Tully saluted them silently for their courage, while wishing they'd had the wisdom to select their targets more carefully.

Aguilera and Kralik joined Aille and Yaut at the rail, both armed. Tully hovered behind their backs, impotent and cursing under his breath. Even if the boats called off their ill-advised attack at this point, affront had already been given. Oppuk would do what he always did, when confronted with human intransigence. He'd make the price so high in terms of the lives of the innocent, that the occupied lands would think long and hard about harboring and giving aid to rebels in the future.

Tully watched with growing dread as the closest escort fired, narrowly missing one of the remaining attackers. A roar indicated the laboring of its engines, then it too turned and headed out toward the open sea. The escort followed. Within two seconds, they'd both disappeared from view.

Aguilera scanned the low-hanging clouds, his face wet with rain and spray. "Is that it?"

"I doubt it," Tully said. Rebels would not give up so easily, he thought. They had inflicted no real damage yet and would be loathe to have risked so many civilians back on shore for the little they had accomplished out here so far.

"I do not understand how they could have fired upon us at all," Aille said, his eyes flickering green. "Our scout ships possess highly effective electronic countermeasures against targeting mechanisms. And they should never have been able to get so close without being detected."

Kralik's eyes swept the gray-green waves. "The missiles they're using are low-tech, line-of-sight and wire-guided, so electronic countermeasures wouldn't work well if at all. And the boats have fiberglass hulls, not metal ones. They planned this out carefully, and came well prepared for the situation. The weather favors them entirely. That was one of the first things we learned, during the conquest. We always fought you Jao in bad weather, if we could, best of all in a heavy rain. Your lasers may be great in space, or under ideal conditions on land. But they're piss-poor otherwise."

Yaut's ears flicked and Tully thought he detected a measure of respect in the fraghta's stance.

A muffled *thwump* sounded, then bits of smoldering fiberglass and metal were falling with the rain to litter the *Samsumaru*'s deck. Kralik ducked under cover and Tully hurried after him.

Kralik's gray eyes narrowed. "That's two," he said bleakly. "Maybe the remaining boats will take the hint and sod off."

But they wouldn't, Tully thought. They had worked up the nerve to do this and by all that was holy, they would see it done or die trying, most likely the latter. A grim smile twisted his lips so that he had to turn away. He almost wouldn't mind dying on this bucket of bolts at that, if these poor misguided bastards could send Governor Oppuk to the bottom with him.

Then he had to shake his head—drown a Jao? Like that was going to happen.

The three manning the laser mount were craning their stubby Jao necks, trying to spot the remaining powerboats while the trawler heeled across the waves and began to pick up speed. Below, on the flensing deck, the whale had been opened, then abandoned only partially butchered, as the crew had to tend to the business of getting under way. The hot reek of blood and entrails filled the air.

An escort came across their bow and disappeared into the clouds again. Tully wiped his face off with the back of his hand, hoping the action was over for now.

Caitlin Stockwell peered up from the stairwell. "What was it?" she asked, her face white as marble.

"Rebels, most likely," he told her, "but I think—"

"Caitlin, get below!" Kralik said. "There's still two left somewhere out there! They could come back any second!"

Her eyes were huge and blue-gray, mirroring the angry storm. Kralik reached for her arm to urge her to safety, and then something struck the bow with a great crack. The *Samsumaru* shuddered and shards of metal exploded outward.

Oppuk fell forward at the impact, flinging his arms out so that he sprawled across the metal deck in a most undignified fashion. Hands were pulling him back onto his feet even before his head stopped ringing. He blinked hard, trying to make the scene before him come together.

The laser mount was gone, along with its crew of three. A human missile had made a direct hit. He realized with a start that Drinn was speaking to him, but he couldn't make the words out over the white-noise in his ears. He shook the helping hands off and took up *baffled-incomprehension* so that Drinn left off the useless talking.

Another explosion came, somewhere out of sight, shuddering the ship again. The immediate impact seemed smaller, but the part of Oppuk's brain that was still functioning knew the damage was worse. That missile had struck at or near the trawler's waterline.

With a groan that even he could make out, the trawler settled over windward. The deck pitched and he had to flail for balance. His gaze fell upon his arm and he realized a piece of metal shrapnel had sliced the flesh. Orange blood dripped down his forearm and then was diluted by the rain. He had been injured, yet had not even felt it.

Drinn was already trying to dress the wound, but he was in no mood to be fussed over. "Where are they?" he shouted over the noise inside his head. "I want them exterminated! Down to the last one!"

Aille krinnu ava Pluthrak ran past, sidearm drawn, headed for what was left of the bow rail, his attention trained on something in the water below. Oppuk shook his head and suddenly could hear a little better. It was a motor, he realized, a small one and close.

All three of the escorts swooped low over the listing trawler, but didn't fire this time. What was wrong with them, he raged. Was everyone under his command incompetent these days? Didn't they realize he held their lives, as well as their honor, in his hand? Had they lost all sense of *vithrik*?

The escorts banked and swung back again, still holding their fire. He turned to Drinn. "Establish a link!" he said. "Order them to fire!"

Drinn's body went rigid, executing the most neutral of stances. "They cannot!" he shouted over the wind and the rain and the ringing in Oppuk's head.

"They most certainly can!" He drew his own sidearm and glared up at the banking scout ships. "If they do not, I will shoot them down myself!"

"But, Governor," Drinn said, eyes ablaze with strong emotion, "the attacker has come alongside. They cannot fire without hitting us too!"

CHAPTER
22

Aille fired down at the humans in the fragile craft bobbing in the water below, but the wind spoiled his aim. Then something exploded down in the engine room and the trawler heeled over into a severe list. He lost his balance and tumbled backwards, sliding into Yaut, and then together with him into the forecastle wall.

Before he could regain his feet, the attackers were firing up the side of the trawler in preparation for boarding. He recognized the distinctive chattering sound of the weapons, having observing his jinau use similar weapons in training. What humans called "automatic weapons" or "machine guns." Commandant Kaul had made disparaging remarks about the primitive devices, but Aille did not share his opinion. Under these conditions, the human weapons were at least as effective as those of the Jao.

Flattening his ears, he motioned to Kralik, who was on his hands and knees, trying to scramble upright. "Contact our unit back on shore," he said. "Order them to pick us up. This ship is going down."

Kralik's brow creased. "They didn't bring sea transport," he said even as he reached for his com. "But I'll see what I can do."

He began firing off rapid instructions. They were only half intelligible to Aille, leaving aside the unfamiliar human military jargon, above the rising roar of the wind and waves. In addition, the crew was shouting and weapons-fire continued in sporadic bursts.

When Kralik was finished, he said, "There were some other ships at the dock, and I'm having my soldiers requisition one of them. But they're not sailors. By the time they find someone who can operate the vessel and get out here, it'll probably be too late."

Tamt, Aille's bodyguard, came barreling around the far end of the deck, ears swiveling and shoulder singed. She supported Oppuk with one arm, settling him against the forecastle beside Kralik. The Governor's arm was badly gashed, one ear was dangling, and he seemed dazed.

"Most of the Governor's service are dead!" Tamt said, schooling herself with a visible effort to display *calm-observation*. "And the rest are injured. You must all take cover."

"We cannot," Yaut said with a glance toward the heaving gray-green sea. "The attackers are preparing to board. After that, it is anyone's guess as to whether they will be able to kill us before this ship sinks."

Fortunately, Aille thought, the chance of uninjured Jao drowning was so low as to be negligible. Oppuk, on the other hand, and the other wounded, were in no shape to swim to shore from their present position. If forced into the sea, they would most likely die.

"Are there survival craft available on this vessel?" he asked Kralik.

Kralik lurched to his feet, bracing against the trawler's worsening list. "Should be." He motioned to Aguilera. "We'll see what we can find."

Aguilera glanced at Tully, then handed the human his sidearm. "Make yourself of use, old son," he said in English, "and don't get stupid on me." Then he rose and left, limping after Kralik.

Tully hefted the weapon with a strange look on his face. His body seemed uncertain, but Aille cautioned himself not to put a Jao interpretation on human gestures. That stance might just as easily translate into pleasure at being trusted, or excitement in anticipation of the coming firefight. It was difficult to say exactly what anything a human did actually meant.

With a shout, a small green ovoid came flying over the trawler's side, then rolled unevenly down the slanted deck toward them. Aille narrowed his eyes, trying to make it out.

"Jesus Christ!" Tully scrambled forward and frantically swatted the ball-like object back over the side. Then he fell to the deck, arms locked over his head, eyes screwed shut. A moment later, a muffled explosion sprayed water and mist everywhere. Aille realized the object had been a delayed-fuse bomblet of some sort, and had erupted after plunging into the sea. Tully had saved their lives by knocking it off the deck, but unfortunately the bomblet had not exploded soon enough to kill the humans who had tossed the thing from their boat. Aille could hear the sound of their angry and startled voices, though he could not make out the words themselves.

Yaut flinched, then took aim and fired at the head that appeared above the side of the deck. Its owner ducked, then popped up again and fired a long burst of projectiles that punched a row of neat holes in the trawler's metal housing. Imitating Tully, Aille flattened himself against the deck.

"Subcommandant?" Caitlin Stockwell's frightened face peered around the stairs. "What's happening?"

"Go below!" Kralik shouted at her from above. His forehead was bleeding an unsettling shade of red from a scratch over one eye. "We have armed boarders! You have to stay out of sight!"

"How many are there?" Aille asked in Jao, his eyes on the spot where the would-be boarders had last appeared.

"Four, I think," Kralik replied in the same language. "They are working their way down toward your position. Their next assault should come straight at you."

Then they would have to move. Aille eased Oppuk's unsteady weight into the top of the stairwell, then motioned Yaut, Tully, and Tamt to follow him. Tully glanced back, clearly concerned about the Stockwell scion. Aille waved him on, putting all the force of his will in the gesture. The young female would either obey orders or die. They did not have time to coddle her.

However small scale, this was war.

Oppuk blinked up through mist that was half rain blown into the stairwell and half fogged vision. His ears rang as though his battered head were made of metal and someone had struck him with a stick. Just beyond the open door, he heard shouting and weapons-fire. The air stank of chemical accelerants. He could not remember what had happened. Had the boat malfunctioned in some manner? Putting a hand to his spinning head, he rebuked himself. He should have known better than to trust human technology. Their primitive devices often failed at the most inopportune times.

He tried to stand, then someone grasped his face. "Governor!"

He flailed at the hand, trying to free himself, but his eyes wouldn't focus and his throat seemed frozen.

"Governor, you must keep your head down," a voice said in heavily accented Jao. "The attackers have boarded."

Attackers? With a shudder, it came back to him, the small boats, the low tech weapons, the explosion that had collapsed a portion of the deck, killing Drinn and—how many more?

His mouth tasted of blood. "Who—?"

"Rafe Aguilera," the voice said. "I serve the Subcommandant."

One of Pluthrak's nasty little humans, then. His hand itched to reach out and throttle this creature in retribution for the attack. "Get away from me!" He lashed out weakly, but failed to find a target.

"As you wish, Governor," Aguilera said. "Since you do not require my help, I will rejoin the Subcommandant and see what I can do there."

Footsteps receded across the metal deck, and then he was alone with his anger and the pain in his arm and ear. More shots were fired, ones with the especially loud reports that indicated projectiles. Rebels often used such archaic guns, which were crude but surprisingly effective.

His sight was beginning to clear now. Oppuk pulled himself up with his uninjured arm on the metal door frame, willing his shaky legs to hold him.

"Are you all right?" a soft voice asked in Jao from behind.

He whirled around to find Caitlin Stockwell gazing up at him from several steps down. "We are being attacked by humans!" he said angrily.

She bent her head in a graceful rendition of *abject-misery*. "Yes," she said. "I am sorry."

"Sorry?" Oppuk glared down at her. "I will make you 'sorry.' Indeed, I will make your entire species 'sorry' for this!"

She climbed the last few steps and eased past him to gaze out on the tilted deck. "Governor, these few rebels do not speak for my people."

"Do they not?" He seized her ridiculously slender wrist. The bones gave as he tightened his grip and he had to snort. No Jao female would ever be invited into a marriage-group to pass on such a woefully lacking genotype. He knew humans came in sturdier variations because he employed a number of them at the palace. This one was obviously inferior. Stockwell should have discarded her early on.

"Your people are inherently treacherous!" He shook her. "Did your father plan this?"

She fought to free herself. "No, of course not!"

"I do not believe you!" He grasped her throat with his other hand. The ache in his head resurged, bringing a momentary fuzzing of his vision. She twisted in his grip, then something hard and cold struck him on the side of the head. Then again, and again, and again. He staggered back, gasping at the pain.

When he could see again, he was alone.

After Kralik located the lifeboats hanging just below the bridge, he worked his way back around the increasingly sloped deck looking for Aille and the rest, while dodging stray shots from the other side. From the list, the *Samsumaru* was definitely foundering, as the Subcommandant had predicted. It would go down—and sooner, probably, rather than later. At this point, no one could use the lifeboats because, even if they got them into the water, the attackers would just pick their occupants off. The boarders had to be eliminated first.

Cold and wet, he climbed the steps to the small bridge to get a vantage point, then crept along the rail. Where was the Subcommandant?

"Ed!" Caitlin Stockwell waved up at him from where she crouched behind a winch housing. "Governor Oppuk has gone crazy!" Her face was bruised and her rain jacket torn. Even though she had a good-sized wrench in one hand, she still looked like a drowned puppy.

Several bullets whined overhead and the air reeked of burned powder. Thunder cracked and lightning illuminated the underside of the clouds. He swore under his breath, then lay on his stomach and scooted forward to reach down under the rail for her. Another shot ricocheted off the bridge. "Goddammit, Caitlin, why didn't you stay below?"

"Oppuk was going to kill me," she said and stretched up on tiptoe. Though tall for a woman, she couldn't quite reach his fingertips. "He's blaming me for the attack!"

He scooted closer to the edge of the small elevated deck just below the bridge, then another burst of automatic weapons-fire made him cover his head. A flake of metal scored his cheek and he could feel the warmth of his blood mixing with the hard, pelting rain.

"Maybe you should come down here instead." She glanced over his shoulder and retreated behind the winch housing.

"I think you're right." He scrambled to his feet, then plunged down the ladder three rungs at a time. "Now—" He slid into her crevice and examined her purpling cheek. She was trembling beneath his fingers. "What's this about Gov—?"

A human came into sight, firing with what looked to be an old Uzi. Kralik dove for cover, pushing Caitlin ahead of him. He heard the air whoosh out of her lungs as he fell on top of her, then struggled to bring his gun up.

Fragments of deck flew as the Uzi continued to fire. He moved again, pulling her along with him. They crouched side by side, breathing hard, and at this angle he could just glimpse their attacker's face. It was painted, to match the camouflage outfit he was wearing. Fortunately, the rain obscured his vision worse than it did theirs.

Kralik edged back, then waited, gun at the ready. Caitlin got to her feet, going the opposite direction before he could stop her and presenting herself as a target. Though she hadn't dropped the wrench, he noted.

"You there, you're making a mistake!" she called out above the wind. "We're human, just like you!"

With an incoherent snarl, the attacker spun and moved toward the sound of her voice, squinting to find her in the rain. Caitlin threw back her head and waited, never once looking at Kralik beyond and giving him away.

My god, she has guts, he thought, as the attacker moved into full view. He would only get one good shot and she had to know he could easily miss. His stomach contracted as he squeezed the trigger.

The man in camouflage jerked as though someone had cut his strings, then tumbled head over heels and fell twitching and bloody at Caitlin's feet. She stared down at him, her body angled so precisely, hands extended, she might have been striking a classical ballet position.

But that pose wasn't anything born of human culture, he realized numbly. It was one of those damn Jao postures, though he couldn't tell which particular one. How strange to think that, under stress, she would fall back to that. She looked up at him and her blue-gray eyes seemed portals into another world altogether from the one he'd been born into. Was this what Earth's children would all become someday, well-trained little Jaolings?

He took her arm and pulled her away from the corpse. "Are you all right?"

She blinked and the otherness fell away. She was just Caitlin again, all human, bruised, and very, very scared. He pulled her into his arms and clutched her trembling body.

When the other boatful of attackers reappeared, plowing through the immense gray-green waves, Aille knew they couldn't wait any longer. If more attackers managed to board, they would be outnumbered and no one would be left alive to be rescued when his troops arrived. A very poor showing for only a few days into his first command! Pluthrak would be shamed.

He ordered Tully and Aguilera to cover them, then motioned Yaut and Tamt forward as he skulked toward the rail, employing what little shelter he could find. The trawler tilted skyward on this side and rolled with every wave, so that they had to struggle to climb, making themselves targets.

Tully fired two spaced shots, to distract the attackers as Aille crossed the last bit of open deck. A surprising exultation ran through him as he fought his way through the wind. This was what he had been trained to do for cycles now. He was finally getting a chance to be of use, in a refreshingly clear and direct way.

He pulled himself up to the rail, tucked his weapon into the harness, and then dove into the wild waves below. The water closed over his head with a silken hiss and then he was swimming joyfully as Yaut and then Tamt joined him. In the chill, dim greenness, he motioned them to follow, then swam around the bow of trawler to the other side where the second boat was powering down to maneuver for boarding.

Beneath the water, the wind was no longer a factor and he made easier progress than he had on deck. His head popped above the surface and he pulled himself up on the motorboat as it tossed about. The five humans who had been aboard it were already on the side of the trawler, clambering up the hull using ropes, obviously better climbers than Jao would have been in similar circumstances.

He heaved into the boat with a single smooth motion, drew his laser and killed the nearest assailant, a stout female beginning to climb the hull almost directly in front of him. She fell back against him and cracked Aille's skull against the gunwale. His head spinning, he fought to free himself as Yaut landed beside him, pulled the female's corpse off and cast it into the sea.

The boat rocked hard, then Tamt joined them and she and Yaut, working in unison, quickly burned down three more humans who were already halfway up the hull. The fifth, however, made it all the way, then turned and aimed down at them with his automatic weapon.

Yaut dove back into the sea. Tamt hesitated, staring upward, and Aille pushed her back in. A shot cracked and he tensed, waiting for the telltale bite of injury. Then the human toppled over the railing and sprawled across the bow of the little boat, glassy-eyed and broken.

Tully's head appeared above the rail, wet yellow hair plastered to his skull, green eyes glaring. He nodded down at them, then withdrew, his footsteps running across the slanted deck.

Yaut heaved back into the boat, his ears set at an unfamiliar angle. It took Aille a moment to read the posture as *astonished-respect*.

Aille was pleased that, by the time the company finally arrived, the other three attackers were dead, one by Tully's hand, the other two at Kralik's. Even Caitlin Stockwell had accounted for herself well, especially for someone with no training. She still carried the sturdy wrench she had appropriated for a weapon.

Oppuk's injuries were not life-threatening, but the Governor's reason was impaired. Apparently, at some point in the fighting, he had received a blow on the head along with the earlier injury to his arm. Aille assigned Tamt to tend him until help arrived.

The jinau company had commandeered a fishing vessel and found them, using Kralik's pocketcom as a beacon, after the *Samsumaru* capsized. Three of the human crew and Matasu, the Japanese ambassador, had also survived. The small lifeboats were filled to capacity. Overcapacity, in fact; but Aille had ordered the uninjured Jao to wait in the water, himself included, holding on to the side of the lifeboat.

There was no sign of Banle, the bodyguard assigned to the Stockwell scion. Aille presumed she had also perished in the attack. Caitlin Stockwell sat next to Kralik, huddled and silent. Her face, beneath its bruises, was paler than Aille had ever seen it. She looked up as the fishing boat neared and a human waved at them from the bow.

Kralik waved back. "Sergeant Cold Bear!"

The Montanan cupped his hands around his mouth. "Hold on, sir! We'll have you all aboard in a minute!"

One of the little silver scout ships hovered above, as though to make sure the trawler was indeed filled with allies, then swooped away. Aille watched them go. They had not been very effective, just as his jinau had warned him.

A short time later, they stood on the deck of the tiny trawler, the humans blue-lipped with reaction to the rain and the cold. Dr. Kinsey, who had come with them, was wrapping Caitlin Stockwell in a dry blanket. "I'm so sorry!" he exclaimed, then blinked at the wrench Caitlin was still clutching in her hand.

Oppuk glared at the human female, but she met his anger and didn't turn away.

"She knew this would happen!" the Governor said, his body shifting from posture to posture without ever fully realizing any of them, as though he were babbling. "She must feed information to the Resistance! That is why we have been so disgracefully attacked!"

Kinsey carefully pried loose the wrench and laid it aside. "Her family has never been anything but loyal."

Aille considered Oppuk's charge, then discarded it. "I do not think she was at fault," he said. "The attackers nearly killed her too at several points. I believe she was just as much a target as any of us."

Sergeant Cold Bear came up to Kralik and saluted. "We have all the survivors on board now, sir. Do you wish us to make an attempt to retrieve the bodies?"

The Governor snarled. "Of what use is dead meat? Get us back to shore! I am going to destroy this nest of rebels before they have another chance to attack!"

"What do you mean, 'nest of rebels'?" Caitlin asked. With her golden hair plastered to her small head by rain, she looked almost as sleek as a Jao.

Oppuk rounded on her savagely, his body now completely overwritten with crude, unalloyed *fury*. "I intend to scour this entire area of humans," he said, "starting with the nearest large population center!"

Two spots of red bloomed in Caitlin's pale cheeks as she glanced first at Aille, then Kralik. "You have no cause to do that!" she said. "Most of the people will be innocent. If you're so determined to assign blame, look to yourself! You were being deliberately provocative! I warned you that this whale hunt would cause trouble and you got it! Attacking a town will accomplish noth—"

Oppuk seized her by the heartward arm and dashed her against the nearest winch. Something cracked and she cried out, then slumped to the deck, her arm at an unnatural angle and her mouth open in a rictus of soundless agony.

Oppuk motioned to the nearest armed jinau. "Put down this animal immediately!"

The soldier, a young male, looked nervously at Kralik. His grip tightened on his rifle. "Sir?"

Oppuk's hands twitched. "I require her life! Put her down!"

Kinsey threw his body over the fallen female. "Governor, no! You can't do that! Her father is the leader of your own government!"

Kralik's hand went to his own sidearm, but Yaut shouldered him back and stood between them, stolidly neutral.

Tully's green eyes went from Aille to Yaut, glimmering with some unreadable sentiment. He still had his weapon, however, and Aille knew that Tully was quite capable of turning it on Oppuk. Would probably do so, in fact. Something indefinable in his stance made clear that, whatever animosity he might bear toward Stockwell, he—like Kralik—would not accept her being put down at Oppuk's command. The Governor's unsane fury was driving the humans here to the point of killing him, whatever the consequences might be.

That same fury had also disarmed the Narvo against a more subtle form of defeat. Quickly, Aille stepped forward.

"This hunt was staged in my honor and the female is present at my invitation," he said, his bearing shifted into a flawless rendition of the difficult tripartite *righteous-honorable-anger*. He surprised even himself with the heat of his emotions. Such complexity had never come easily to him. "Since you have dismissed her from your household, she is under the protection of Pluthrak, not Narvo! Pluthrak's honor is at stake here and you will not impugn it for a petty, self-indulgent display of personal anger!"

"Crecheling!" Oppuk spat. He glanced around, but his entire service had perished in the attack on the *Samsumaru*. He was quite obviously without immediate support—and, even in his rage, was still sensible enough to understand that he was teetering on the brink of a chasm that would engulf him. The lines of kochan honor were clear here.

Oppuk pulled himself together, assuming the posture of *regretful-recognition*. It was impolite, to be sure, but acceptable.

"Very well, since you invoke Pluthrak's honor, the matter is closed." His ears wavered, then took on a crafty angle. "I will, however, expect you to conduct my reprisal." He glared down at Caitlin, who was hunched in wordless misery at his feet. "It will be your first major combat command, a good chance to earn that honor you seem to be so eager to achieve."

PART IV:
To Burn in Salem

It was time, now, for him to swim into the center of the flow. The agent of the Bond understood that the moment he received the report. Battle was about to be openly joined.

He wondered, for a moment, how the young Pluthrak would proceed. But he did not wonder for long. This one was truly *namth camiti*—perhaps even, as the Bond's preceptor hoped, something greater. *Namth camiti,* not of Pluthrak alone, but of all Jao. Perhaps, even—the agent's own great hope—what he himself had awaited for twenty years. *Namth camiti* of humans as well as Jao.

That, it was still too early to determine. But the agent had no doubt at all what tactic the young Pluthrak would use, to bring down the Narvo brute. With one so young and bold and self-confident, it could only be advance-by-oscillation.

To be sure, it was the most dangerous tactic as well as the most adventurous. Oppuk himself had not dared to use it, when he brought down the Hariv. But Jita had been a cautious and canny clan leader, against whom advance-by-oscillation was ill-suited. Against the Narvo as he had become, swollen and gross with twenty years of arrogant rule, the agent thought it would work splendidly.

A whale hunt. It was a fitting way, the agent thought, for a leviathan to drive himself onto the rocks.

CHAPTER
23

The population center Oppuk chose for destruction was called Salem, a small city not far inland that was also the administrative center for the local district. What humans called "the capital of Oregon."

Despite Oppuk krinnu ava Narvo's desire for haste, Aille delayed as long as he could. Time flowed and he let it slip past him, using the excuse of assembling the needed troops and requisitioning materiel from the most proximate Jao base, a major population center in the same district known as Portland. Through a visual feed, he watched humans on the other side of the town from the positions his forces had taken creeping away in the still-driving rain, some carrying bundles in their arms, others, children. His troops had orders not to interfere with anyone trying to evacuate.

Aille wanted to delay the assault as long as possible, without directly defying the Governor, in order to minimize the casualties. Noncombatants were wont to run, while soldiers would stay and fight. The rebels obviously wanted confrontation, judging by their earlier actions, so he had no fear of the real enemy getting away. It was not worth Jao time and effort to pursue those who posed no threat, and ran the risk of stirring up the native population still further.

Oppuk krinnu ava Narvo felt otherwise, of course. Perhaps that was Oppuk's own personal idiosyncrasy, or perhaps that was

Narvo method—but Aille had been shaped by Pluthrak, not Narvo. He had been taught that subject populations should be ruled, certainly—with a strong hand, if need be—but never pointlessly brutalized.

By nightfall, light artillery and tanks, both those of Jao origin and a smattering of human equipment refitted with Jao augments, had arrived. They were being readied by a regiment of Jao troops aided by a few human techs.

Oppuk had flown into a fury, when he'd seen the first of the Terran tanks arrive. Aille had instructed Kralik to mobilize the Pacific Division as well. The Governor tried to insist that they be sent back, but Aille had politely refused.

In doing so, he was on firm ground. The line of authority was clear, here as well, and on two counts: Pluthrak had been given the honor; and, in any event, Aille was Subcommandant of all ground forces. Which, now that the Governor's position was weakened, Aille had enforced in its full measure. There would be no more attempts by the Dano Commandant to claim that Aille only commanded the jinau troops. Kaul, clearly enough, had gotten a report on what had happened in the whale hunt, and was maneuvering accordingly. So, needlessly to say, were the officers from all the lesser kochan. For the moment, Pluthrak had the advantage.

Oppuk's wounds had proved superficial and easily treated, and he now waited inside an enormous hant he had erected inside Aille's new temporary military base. Oppuk had poured the thing immediately, even diverting military resources to do so. He intended, apparently, to personally observe the destruction of Salem.

That was another small mistake, again driven by the Governor's inability to control his temper. Yaut was pleased. Oppuk would have been wiser to accept his defeat—which was still but a small one, after all—and return to his palace in Oklahoma City to begin repairing the damage.

Banle, Caitlin's guard, had appeared at the docks, sometime after the trawler had transported the rest of them back, having apparently abandoned the fight early on to swim to safety on her own. She'd been skulking about ever since, sullen and silent.

Kralik had disappeared briefly, after they docked, but was also back now. Aille suspected he had personally transported Caitlin

Stockwell to a human medical facility, a gross misuse of his time under current circumstances.

He suspected he knew the reason, though. Humans did not mate as Jao did, through marriage-groups and careful consideration by their kochan of where the best possibilities for association lay. Instead, they paired off, sometimes serially, often failing to form lasting relationships since their liaisons were motivated by sudden fancy. Most likely, Kralik had taken one of these inexplicable human fancies to the Stockwell female. Under other circumstances, such would have been interesting and Aille would have liked to study their behavior. Coming in the midst of this particular flow, however, it was an unwarranted distraction.

"Do not leave again without informing me," Aille said, studying a refitted green-and-brown-splotched human tank drifting past on its new maglevs. His posture was *grim-displeasure.*

"Yes, sir," Kralik still bore long clotted cuts on both forehead and cheek. Evidently he had not sought medical attention for himself, whatever else he had been up to. "It won't happen again."

The rain finally desisted into a mere spattering of isolated drops, but the air was still delightfully damp. Aille tapped the bau against his leg. "Is the Pacific Division standing by?"

"The First Brigade is, sir," Kralik said. "I won't be able to get the rest of the division here for another two days, at least. More likely three."

Yaut reappeared, preceded by Tully and Aguilera. The two human members of Aille's service seemed to be mastering the technique of leading without knowing where they were going, using subtle hints of the fraghta's position to guide them.

A Jao ground combat vehicle drifted to a stop before him. The pleniary of the Portland unit, Hinn krinnu Vatu vau Waf, a seasoned veteran of the conquest, climbed out and sat on the edge of the hatch. He was a solidly built Jao with a well-shaped *vai camiti* that covered eyes and muzzle as well as cheeks so that most of his face was shrouded in black. "The unit is ready to attack," he said, and allowed *annoyed-boredom* to creep into his lines.

Aille's snout wrinkled in irritation, but he quickly submerged it in the most neutral of postures. With that *vai camiti*, Hinn was bound to appear forceful, whatever else his body might indicate. Perhaps that had gotten him a bit further in his career than he deserved and he had become careless of proper movement.

"Yes," Aille said. "Proceed."

Without another word, Hinn slid back into his vehicle and closed the hatch. The vehicle rotated noiselessly and headed toward the town, quickly followed by the rest of the unit. As with most Jao ground force regiments, this one consisted of thirty fighting vehicles and enough others, more lightly armed, to carry the infantry. Some six hundred soldiers, in all.

Aille donned a headset so he could monitor communications as the regiment advanced. On the screens in his command center, he could also observe the town itself from satellite imagery. Most of the city was dark, probably an indication of how many inhabitants had already fled.

Tamt stood before Aille's shoulder, ready, but not obtrusive. Her training at Yaut's hands was continuing to go well.

Rafe Aguilera was pacing back and forth in the rear of the command center with what Aille interpreted as suppressed nerves. "That's the same type of tanks we met at the Battle of Chicago," he muttered.

Kralik narrowed his eyes as he watched the Jao combat vehicles gliding toward the city on the screen, pale blue in the deepening darkness. "They haven't changed a bit since then, have they?" He turned to Yaut. "Does it just take a long time for upgrades to reach us because we're so far from your homeworlds?"

"Upgrades?" Yaut allowed *puzzled-misunderstanding* to pervade his shoulders. He had not encountered this English word before. Neither had Aille.

"Improvements," Kralik said. "New technology, the latest advancements."

"Why would we change anything?" Yaut said, his eyes trained on the advancing line. "This equipment works well and we know how to operate it. Replacement parts are already manufactured. What more is needed?"

"How long ago did you develop this line of technology?" Aguilera asked, as the lead Jao vehicle began firing at the first structure it encountered.

"It came down to us from the Ekhat," Aille said.

"So it's not really yours," Tully said. "Someone else invented all this stuff. You just maintain and use it."

The vehicle's laser fired a second time, a third, and then the structure burst apart with a muffled explosion. Shards of burning wood flew through the air. The tank glided on to the next building, an ice-blue presence in the night.

Tully could not sit still, but Aguilera was already pacing, for all the good it would do anyone in the doomed town, so he tucked his twitching hands under his arms and shuffled his feet to dissipate his nerves. How could the rebels have been so stupid—going after the Governor, himself, for God's sake? Tully had heard that the Resistance groups in the Northwest tended to be reckless, but this was worse than he'd expected.

He wanted to pound someone's face, beat sense into them, but it was far too late. He ached to slip off into the darkness and see if he could help protect the town against this one-sided attack, but that was impossible as long as he was shackled with the locator band. Yaut had evidently disarmed it on the ship, once they were under attack, but the damned thing was certainly working now. He'd had a good-sized shock out of it just fifteen minutes ago, when he'd gotten careless and wandered too far looking for a place to urinate.

He watched gloomily on the screen as, one by one, the buildings along the street being used to enter the town were blasted into burning splinters by Jao tanks. But no one flung open the doors and ran as they approached, or popped up behind an open window and got off a few well-placed shots. None of the buildings had lights on, either.

Tully edged around Yaut, peering closer. It was almost as though . . . no one was home. His heart raced with sudden hope. Had Salem perhaps been evacuated? Maybe this wasn't quite going to be the slaughter Oppuk had envisioned.

He studied Aille, for a moment. There was something about his posture . . . Tully couldn't tell exactly what it was, but suddenly he knew. The Pluthrak Subcommandant was looking pleased with himself. And Tully suddenly realized that when he'd caught a glimpse of Oppuk earlier that day, the Governor had seemed more furious than ever.

I will be good God-damned. The sly Jao bastard planned *it this way.*

He reviewed everything he'd seen since the whale hunt in his mind. Looking at it, this time, not from the angle of a bitter rebel but from that of a soldier who'd had enough time in the service to know how to goldbrick.

Yup, he did. Dragged everything out as long as he could. Hurry up and wait. Had Jao aircraft buzzing the town constantly, making sure everybody knew all hell was about to break loose—but carefully kept routes of evacuation open. He could have easily positioned troops around the entire town. Salem's not that really that big. Maybe . . . what? A hundred thousand people? Can't be much more than that.

Kralik had been consulting with Aille, most of that time, providing him with the expertise of a human general who knew the lay of the land. As commander of the Pacific Division, the western part of the continent was his turf.

Tully now studied Kralik. The general's face was calm, impassive, unreadable. For a moment, his gray eyes met Tully's, then looked away.

Him too!

Tully had to suppress a laugh. When Kralik had disappeared for a while, Tully had simply assumed it was because he had the hots for the Stockwell girl and insisted on personally taking her to the hospital. *Cradle robber,* he'd thought at the time. The general was almost old enough to be her father.

That didn't really make sense, now that Tully thought about it. True, Kralik obviously had the hots for Stockwell, even if he wasn't being uncouth about it. But he was a *general,* fer chrissake, in a combat situation. And, from everything Tully had seen, a particularly coolheaded one. However concerned he might have been for Caitlin Stockwell, delegation of authority came automatically to him. Kralik would have just ordered one of his junior officers to see the girl got to a hospital safely. He wouldn't have left his post to do it personally.

There was only one reason Tully could think of, for Kralik to have done that. Because he needed to get in contact with someone and couldn't afford to be discovered doing it. That meant finding a human telephone, instead of using his regular communicator.

Tully was still staring at the general. Again, Kralik's eyes met his. This time, though, something seemed to flicker in them before he looked away.

For the first and only time since Tully had joined the jinau to ferret out what intelligence he could, he actually felt like saluting an officer.

You're okay, General Ed Kralik, even if you are a damn collaborator.

Tully wondered if Kralik had passed along any specific knowledge, regarding which routes and tactics Aille would be using in the attack. Probably not. Kralik was a decent guy, sure enough, but he was still a jinau officer. He wouldn't have gone that far. And it didn't really matter anyway. Between Aille's stalling and Kralik's warning, the human authorities in Salem would have had enough time to evacuate anyone who was willing to go.

The Resistance units would stay behind, of course, since the city's authorities had no control over them. But that meant it was going to be a straight-up fight, not a slaughter.

As he continued to watch, Tully realized something else. The young Pluthrak Subcommandant was still dragging his feet—only, this time, as flamboyantly as possible. The Jao forces invading Salem were making slow progress because they were destroying *everything* as they went. Every building, every shack—hell, they were blasting away street signs!

Even with the lightning-quick Jao targeting mechanisms and dead-sure aim, and the sheer destructiveness of lasers designed for space battle used at point-blank range, it was taking time. More time for the civilians to get out of the way.

Tully was sure that Kralik had recommended this avenue of approach for exactly the same reason. The Jao forces were advancing into Salem from the southeast, taking one of the commercial boulevards that branched off from I-5. Tully wasn't familiar with Salem, but this boulevard was generic to almost any small city in North America: just an endless row of fast food joints, gas stations and car dealerships, most of which were long-abandoned and half in ruins, anyway. For twenty years, Oppuk's rule had oscillated between savagery and negligence. Salem was in no better shape than most of America's small cities, even ones that hadn't been directly damaged during the conquest.

Almost gleefully, Tully watched another car dealership explode into ruins on the screen. An old Hyundai dealership, this one. Glass flying everywhere, of course, flames pouring out—but there weren't even any cars being wrecked. From the looks of it, that dealership had gone out of business at least a decade earlier. A lot of the windows had already been broken even before the Jao lasers hit them.

And my daddy swore by Fords, anyway. Buy American, he'd always say.

The invaders finally met resistance when they started entering the residential districts. On the screen, yellow bursts of automatic weapons-fire split the night, distinctly different from the Jao laser beams.

Aille tapped that carved stick of his against the heel of his hand. The thing the Jao called a *bau*, which had some significance to them that Tully had never really understood. It had something to do with kochan status, was all he knew, not military rank as such.

"I am getting disturbing reports," the Pluthrak Subcommandant said. "I must go closer and observe in person. Come with me, General Kralik."

Knowing what was expected by now, Tully hurried to precede Aille out of the command center, with Aguilera alongside and Tamt on their heels. Once they got outside, he saw that the rain had started up again. In fact, it was coming down hard. Yaut motioned to a Jao vehicle standing by and it pulled up before them. The vehicle was a Jao equivalent of an armored personnel carrier, with the curved and rounded lines that characterized all their vehicles.

Clambering into it, Tully discovered the interior was designed something like a large van; except, here too, Jao rounded lines prevailed instead of human boxy ones. It was all very artistic, he thought sourly—like "art deco," if he remembered the right term—but a pain in the ass to sit up straight in. Jao, with their long torsos and relatively short legs, were comfortable riding in a half-crouched position. Humans weren't.

The fraghta and Aille got in the front, next to the driver, while Tamt, Kralik, Aguilera, and Tully piled into the rear.

Tully's fingers turned the locator band round and round his arm. He felt like a tagged pet monkey. True, he could console himself with the thought that Aille was using a major general as if he were just an aide. But that wasn't much consolation, since Tully didn't really have anything against Kralik; and, in any event, the general never seemed like the type of officer who fretted much over his status.

Moving as quickly as Jao ground vehicles could, it wasn't long before they had overtaken the Jao column fighting its way into Salem. "Fighting" was the word, too. The vehicle they were riding in had audio equipment as good as the screens that substituted for windows on all sides. Automatic weapons-fire was a constant rattle now. The Jao had obviously found the combatants. At one point, the vehicle had to maneuver around a Jao combat vehicle resting crazily on its side, smoke rising from its turret and its maglevs failed.

"It takes an armor piercing shell to do that kind of damage," Kralik observed. "They must have some more handheld missiles, or some antitank guns."

With an emphasis on "some," Tully thought, holding on as the vehicle swerved to avoid Jao foot troops in the middle of the road. He knew just how hard it was for the Resistance to get its hands on that kind of ordnance. Even old-style human weaponry was scarce, this many years after the conquest.

But, wherever and however they'd gotten the weapons, Tully knew that Aguilera was right—and he also knew that the Resistance in the Pacific Northwest was going to be pulling out all the stops in this battle. In fact, they must have been planning and organizing this operation for some time. They wouldn't be committing their precious heavy weaponry otherwise.

An orange-red explosion filled the night and sparks lit up the sky like fireworks. At a low-voiced command from Aille, the vehicle stopped. A moment later, to Tully's surprise, the Subcommandant and Yaut were piling out.

The vehicle's doors flew open and Tully hurried to follow. Yaut had the locator control and he didn't dare let him get too far away. Better to be shot than have your brains fried.

Despite the heavy rain, he could smell something burning, acrid and strong. Another damaged Jao vehicle was nearby. Not one of their tank equivalent, but the kind they used as personnel carriers. Several figures lay on the wet ground beside it, Jao by the shape and size. No one was tending them. Dead? he thought with rising hope. The rebels had actually drawn blood!

A *lot* of Jao blood, in fact, more than Tully had ever seen. There were small pools of the orange stuff on the street, not just the few drops you normally saw.

The Jao didn't usually bleed much. As with almost everything else, their bodies were tougher than human ones that way also.

Tully even knew the reason, because Rob Wiley had explained it to him once.

"They stop bleeding so much faster than us because instead of thrombocytes they have micro-threads. Think of it being like superfine glass-fiber in their veins, only it's an organic compound with silica and aluminum in it. That's why their blood is that weird orange color."

Aille bent over one of the corpses, studying it for a moment. "Come," he said. "I have to observe more closely. This is not right."

Something in the distance erupted, staggering Yaut and causing him to fall to one knee.

"What was that?" Yaut looked back at Aille. His ears sagged and his head buzzed from the force of the explosion.

The Pluthrak was still standing, although he too had obviously been rattled. Aille shook himself until his whiskers flapped, and his eyes were luminous with emotion in the darkness. "It came from underground, I think," he said. "A storage tank of some sort, perhaps?"

"A volatile fuel depot," Yaut said. "That would make sense."

"Fraghta, are you all right?" A hand pulled him onto his feet.

Yaut turned and saw the dark-haired human male, Aguilera. "I am undamaged," he said, letting his body fall into the sternness of *perceived-error*. He heartily disliked being touched without invitation.

"I don't think that was a fuel depot blowing up, sir," said Kralik. "They probably filled some of the water mains with gasoline and now they're blowing them to create steam. Not that it's really needed, in this rain, but they must have been preparing for days. No way to predict the weather that far ahead."

Aille stood. "You are saying that this is a well-planned ambush, not a hastily organized resistance."

"Yes, sir," Kralik replied. "Meaning no disrespect—to the Jao—but your Governor's temper is notorious. I'm willing to bet this whole thing was designed to draw an attack on Salem, starting with the assault on the whaling ship. This is the logical place for someone who thinks like Oppuk to retaliate. Nearest big town and it's the capital, to boot."

"But . . . the casualties they would produce, among humans."

Aguilera gave Tully a glance that seemed hostile, then shrugged.

"The Resistance thinks that way. Kill some Jao—collaborators, too—and be damned to the rest. You're back to fighting in a city, which is where humans have the best advantage."

Tully opened his mouth, as if to protest, but Aguilera silenced him with a sharp hand gesture.

"Hush!" His head was turned, as if he were listening intently. So was Kralik.

Yaut heard the noise himself, now that the two human soldiers had brought it to his attention.

"Oh, Christ," hissed Aguilera. "Where in the hell did they get *tanks*?"

Kralik turned to Aille, his posture full of obvious *cautious-anxiety*.

"We've got to get under cover, now. They'll have infantrymen with them, too."

Aille and Yaut started to turn back to their vehicle, which was quite some distance away.

"No, not there! There isn't time." Kralik pointed to a nearby building, a dwelling set back from the street with a small grove of trees before it. "That vehicle is a death trap, as close as the tank sounds. Over there, quick, where we'll be out of sight. And get the driver out! Tell him to take cover somewhere."

Yaut looked to Aille. "Do as he says," the young Pluthrak commanded. "He may be right—and I want to observe this, anyway."

Yaut spoke into his communicator. A moment later, the Jao driver emerged from the vehicle and disappeared behind another building. The roaring sound of the approaching tank was very loud, even above the din of the battle.

But they were all hidden in the grove, now. Suddenly, in addition to the roar of the engine, there was the added sound of a great squeal, very painful to the ears.

"That's the track, braking so they can make the turn," Aguilera whispered. He raised his head a little. "Yeah, they're coming around the corner. Looks like they've got . . . call it maybe a dozen foot soldiers in support. Raggedy bunch. If we're lucky, they won't spot us here."

Aille saw a tank running on primitive human-style metal tracks looming into view through the rain. The tank's engine was incredibly loud, but he was surprised at the relative lack of noise coming from the tracks themselves. They must have some sort of padding between the metal blocks. Not for the first time, he was struck by the sophistication of human technology. Like the submarines or the interior of the tanks he had seen, what appeared at first glance to be crude and simple could be extremely well designed.

There were also, as Aguilera had said, some foot soldiers accompanying the tanks, following behind it with weapons ready. Why? he wondered. This was obviously part of human military doctrine, not a fluke, because Kralik had predicted it.

Then, watching the way the human foot soldiers studied the area, weapons ready, Aille thought he understood. Humans were not arrogant in battles on difficult terrain, as the Jao had come to be after their long string of easy conquests. The tanks sheltered the infantrymen while they, in turn, protected the vehicle from surprise attack from the flanks and the rear. He could see where it would be an effective combination, fighting in the narrow and cramped quarters of a city.

The tank had now advanced far enough into the street to come into line-of-sight of their abandoned Jao vehicle. It halted immediately, its gun mount swiveling as though seeking prey, then fired.

It was a direct hit. The vehicle seemed to erupt from inside, hatches and other pieces flying everywhere, the noise incredible. Flame and smoke poured out. Aille had no doubt at all that if there had been anyone in that vehicle they would have been instantly killed.

He flattened his ears in pain at the loudness, breathing hard. White lines shivered through his vision. Laser weapons were almost inaudible. Jao ears found extreme noise disorienting.

The tank began backing away, to his surprise. His relief also, because if it had advanced much further it would have been difficult to stay hidden from the foot soldiers.

Kralik seemed to understand his puzzlement. "I don't think they expected an encounter here, sir," Kralik murmured. "They were probably just changing their position to set up an ambush. These are insurgents, not regulars. They won't want to face off with Jao troops on the open streets. They can't have many tanks, since they must have been hoarding them for years, hidden somewhere."

The explanation made sense. To Aguilera also, apparently, because the experienced human veteran now stood erect. The sound of the tank's engine had faded away considerably.

"We'd all have been toast, if we'd been in that vehicle," he said forcefully. "Not even that. Don't ask me where they got 'em, but the rebels are using DU sabot rounds. Silly to use 'em, though, when HE would have done just fine. Your Jao vehicles have armor designed to reflect lasers. They'll stand up to a coaxial machine gun, but otherwise they're even more vulnerable than our tanks—uh, their tanks—are."

"What is a 'DU sabot round'?" Aille asked.

"It's just a shaped piece of depleted uranium, with a casing," Kralik explained. "The casing—that's the 'sabot' part—peels off after the projectile leaves the barrel. What hits the target is the shaped penetrator: fifteen kilos of solid uranium, moving about two thousand meters a second. It'll punch through damn near anything—even reactive armor, which you don't have—and once it penetrates . . ."

He grimaced. "The uranium vaporizes, basically. It's like a fuel-air bomb going off in a contained space. The resulting heat incinerates anything organic or flammable—and, at that temperature, most substances are flammable. If we'd been inside, there'd be nothing left of us but molecules."

"Interesting," Aille said again. "I can now see why the veterans found the weapons so terrifying."

Although the tank was gone, the sound of the battle was intensifying. Aguilera moved out of the grove by the dwelling. A shot cracked suddenly, and he crumpled.

Aille flung himself down, along with the rest.

"Come on out!" a human voice cried from the darkness. "Or I'll fill the rest of you bastards full of holes too!"

CHAPTER
24

A stream of cursing came from the ground as Aguilera tried to rise. Aille recognized some of the vernacular, but not all.

"Stay down, you jinau son of a bitch!" The voice sounded within the male vocal range to Aille, and, if he was not mistaken, quite elderly.

His guess was confirmed. "You old idiot!" Aguilera rolled over, face contorted, clutching his windward shoulder. "They'll flatten this egg-sucking town and kill everyone in it, and for what? A goddam whale!"

"That whale just brought things to a head!" A bandy-legged man moved into sight, a rifle in his hands. His head was almost absent of hair altogether, usually a sign of great age for humans, and he did not move easily. "Now drop the weapons, or I'll drill you for sure!"

"If he were going to fire," Yaut observed to Aille in quiet Jao, "he would already have done so. He hesitates for some reason."

"He's not a member of the Resistance," whispered Tully in English. "Just a cranky codger too stubborn to leave his home. And he just shot the only wad he's got left."

He rose and knelt beside Aguilera, opening his shirt to inspect the wound. "Put the gun down, old-timer, there's no point to this. They'll wreck the whole city before they're done, and there's nothing you can do about it."

Seizing Aguilera by the shoulders, Tully dragged the taller man

266

into a pool of light cast from a lamp in the entrance to the small dwelling. Then sat back on his heels, laughing softly. "I'll say this, old man. You may have lost your hair, but you sure didn't lose your balls."

Aille's whiskers drooped. Sometimes he thought he would never understand humans—for a certainty. He examined the old one's posture and decided that there was no immediate danger. He'd become familiar enough with humans to understand that the old one now exuded *abashed-indecision* rather than *fierce-determination*.

He rose and approached. Aguilera's entrance wound, he could see, looked very small. It was certainly non-lethal, even for a fragile human. Just below the collarbone; bleeding, but not badly.

"What's so funny?" hissed Aguilera.

Tully was still making soft sounds of amusement. What the humans called "chuckling," now, not outright laughter.

"That hole's damn near invisible. Rafe, old son, you've been laid out by a .22!" He glanced at the weapon gripped by the old human. "A single-shot, to boot. Looks just like the first gun my daddy bought me."

Aguilera punched at him weakly with his good hand, but missed and sucked in his breath at the pain the movement cost him. Even Aguilera's grimace, though, seemed to have some amusement in it.

"I can't believe it," Aille heard Aguilera mutter. "How humiliating."

Their assailant stepped closer, staring at Aille. His rifle was still clutched in his hands but not aimed at anyone. If Aille understood Tully's vernacular properly, the weapon was no longer armed in any event.

"Are you the Governor?"

Tully stood so that he loomed over their captor.

"Not hardly," he said. "Jesus, don't you ever watch the news?"

"The news?" The man snorted. "What for? All them fuzzheads look ali—"

Moving quickly and easily, Tully snatched the gun out of the old human's hands. The human's squawk of protest was driven from his lungs as Yaut brought him down. The fraghta's hands moved to break the man's neck.

"Stop, Yaut!" commanded Aille.

Yaut obeyed, but when he looked back his eyes glittered green in the night.

"He is harmless now."

"He raised his weapon to you!" Yaut was seized by anger which bent his body into sharp angles. "He has no respect!"

"He does not know me," Aille said.

"He knows you are Jao. He should respect that, whatever else!"

"Yes," Aille said, his posture *sober-reflection*, "and yet . . ."

He studied Tully and Aguilera. Both of them returned his gaze with dark, unfathomable expressions. Then, he looked at Kralik. The general's face, too, had that same expression.

There was something critical involved here, Aille realized. He did not understand what it was, but that it was critical he was quite certain. This was one of those rare moments in which association hung in the balance.

"Release him, Yaut," he commanded. Gesturing at Aguilera: "He was the one injured, not me. Let him decide the proper punishment."

Aguilera stared at him, then at Tully. A moment later, they exhaled deeply. Even with the difficulty of assessing their alien postures, Aille did not mistake the sentiment that infused both of them. What a Jao would call *relieved-appreciation*. Kralik's reaction was more contained, but clearly the same.

It had been the right decision, then. For the first time, ever, he could feel the bonds of association. No tentative shoots, these, but strong lines.

"Oh, hell," Aguilera said. "Just slap the old coot upside the head and—*wait!*"

Yaut's hand had already begun to swing when the last word brought it to an abrupt halt. He peered quizzically at Aguilera.

"Uh . . . it's just a figure of speech." Aguilera winced. "If *you* do it, you'll tear his head off." He looked up at Tully. "Do us the honors, would you?"

"Sure," said Tully, smiling crookedly. He rose easily, took two strides over to the old human, and gave him a little swat with the fingers on the top of his bald head.

To Aille's surprise, the old one's eyes filled instantly with water. "Tears," humans called it, normally a sign of great pain or anguish. Yet Tully's blow would hardly have sufficed to crush an insect.

"I've lived in this house my whole life," the old one said, the words coming in short, gasping sobs, "since Marge and me got married. She died, just two years ago—but she died in our bedroom."

"Yeah, I know, old-timer," replied Tully softly. "And by tomorrow, it'll be nothing but cinders. But it's just a house, when all's said and done. And Marge is safely out of it. You better come with us."

He lifted the oldster to his feet, all but shoving Yaut aside to do it. Then, helped Aguilera to his feet also. The wounded man's face glistened in the dimness, bathed in a thin sheen of water, though the rain had not started again. "Even if it was only a lousy popgun, he needs medical attention."

"Take him back, then." Aille said. "I will remain and observe further. Tell the medician I authorize treatment." He glanced at the oldster, understanding that Tully would not relinquish him now. "Both of them, if the other needs attention also."

"I can't." Tully held up his wrist with the gleaming black locator band. "Not unless Yaut goes too."

Yaut fished in his carrying pouch, then threw him the control box. "Go."

Tully's face changed as he stared down at the smooth black rectangle. "But—"

"Either you comprehend *vithrik*, or you do not," Yaut said. "I have trained you as well as I can. The rest is up to you."

Tully's pale face looked from Aille to Yaut. "I'll be back as soon as I see to Aguilera and the old fellow," he said, almost as though he didn't believe it himself. "I will."

"You are of my personal service," Aille said. "Whatever your beginnings, among Jao, to be so trusted is counted of great honor." Their eyes met in the darkness, the green of Tully's reflecting the light from above.

A long burst of automatic weapon fire came from the next street over. Kralik turned, obviously trying to pinpoint the source.

Aille took Aguilera's hand, trying to imitate the same grip he had often seen one human use with another, though it seemed awkward. The bare skin felt strangely hot against his own palm. Their body temperature was higher than a Jao's. He had not realized that until this moment. "We will continue to observe," he said. "Now I want to see how effectively my Jao equipment operates."

"Watch when they fire," Aguilera said faintly. His blood gleamed black-red under the light from above. "See how they—" He swayed and Tully took more of his weight. "—how they deal with the lasers."

His chin drooped to his chest and Tully swore. "Later!" he said, and then slipped off into the darkness, half-carrying Aguilera and the old human.

Aille's party skirted two more brief firefights to reach the center of the fighting. Now that the Jao forces were in the town itself, they'd encountered fierce patches of resistance in many places. Much of the battle raged from structure to structure. Finally, they came to a main boulevard down which some Jao fighting vehicles were advancing. They stopped to observe, crouched behind the rubble of a destroyed building.

"There!" Kralik pointed, into the inadequate light shed by the few remaining street lamps on the street ahead. "That's what Aguilera was talking about!"

Aille squinted and could just make out thousands of tiny metallic strips floating down through the laser cannons' angle of fire. Whenever a beam hit a strip, portions of it were reflected at odd angles and the beam lost coherence.

He rose higher, heedless of stray projectiles, every line of his body shaped into *startled-interest*. "What are those?"

"Bits of aluminum foil," Kralik said. "The same thing we used during the conquest. Ours were manufactured for the purpose. These are probably improvised, cut up from common household supplies."

From the next street over, a rebel tank fired through the aluminum strips without problem, but the Jao beams continued to be sporadically disrupted. Suddenly, one of the Jao vehicles was badly damaged by some sort of missile. Immediately, humans firing burst-weapons broke out of a nearby house and swarmed over it.

"I advise you strongly to order your troops to fall back, sir," Kralik said. "Or this is going to get very ugly. You don't have a large enough force, and they are neither trained nor equipped for this kind of street fighting. Not against an opponent as obviously well-prepared and numerous as you're facing here. If you keep pushing ahead, your soldiers are just going to—the human expression is 'bleed out.'"

An explosion lit up the night as one of the Jao vehicles took a direct hit. Aille stared at what was left. All the soldiers in it were obviously dead, the vehicle itself nothing but a gutted, burning shell.

Bleed out. It was a savage expression. The sort of thing a certain predator might think up. The kind of predator that is not strong enough or powerful enough to kill its prey outright; so, instead, tears at the flanks until the prey dies of blood-loss.

Such predators were often pack animals, Aille remembered.

"Yes, you are right. Yaut, give the order."

The fraghta brought up his communicator, but hesitated. "The Narvo will be enraged. He will try to use this to discredit you."

"Yes, I know. I also do not care." He gazed at Kralik. "Partly because *vithrik* is what it is. Partly because the withdrawal will only be temporary. Am I not correct, General Kralik?"

"Yes, sir." The human officer's face was creased with a very thin smile. "This is jinau business."

CHAPTER
25

Once Tully got far enough away from the fighting, he started looking for a car. He figured he had enough authority derived from Aille to commandeer a vehicle. "Commandeer," under the circumstances, being a euphemism for "hot-wire and steal it," since he didn't have any intention of returning whichever vehicle he swiped back to its rightful owner.

It hardly mattered. The Subcommandant was willing to fudge with the Governor's order to destroy Salem enough to allow the population to evacuate. But Tully was quite sure he would see to the physical destruction of the city. Once the dust and ashes settled, nobody was going to miss an old human automobile.

And it would be old, too. Most of the cars humans still owned in North America were antiques, kept running until the bodies just rusted out. The relatively few new cars still being made were expensive, and Tully was unlikely to find any here.

Eventually, he came across an old pickup that still had half a tank of gas in it. A Ford, ironically. He didn't bother trying to jimmy the lock. Tully and both men with him were already soaked by the rain, so he just smashed in the window on the driver's side. Between his father's training—he'd been a mechanic—and his own misspent youth, Tully had the engine running within seconds.

There was room in the cab for all three of them. Fortunately, there was also a map of Salem in the glove compartment. Tully didn't know the city, neither did Aguilera—and the old man was now sunk in a complete depression, barely reacting to anything around him.

Eventually, they found their way back to I-5 and headed south toward the military encampment Aille had set up as the base for the operation. Traffic was nonexistent, southbound. Leaving aside the rain, the old interstate, once in pristine condition, was as ragged as most things were these days in North America. So Tully had to drive slowly, despite his worries about Aguilera. From a .22 or not, a bullet wound was still a bullet wound.

But when he made a comment about it, Aguilera shook his head. "I'm not worried about that. What I'm worried about are trigger-happy Jao."

As if that had been a cue, a Jao aircraft swept by overhead, not more than five hundred feet above the road. Tully stuck his head out of the window and saw that the scout car was beginning to circle around. The Jao had spotted the pickup and were coming to investigate.

"Bad news," he muttered, hauling his head back in and gripping the steering wheel more tightly. "Mood they're in, they'll likely shoot first and ask questions later."

"Stop the truck," hissed Aguilera. "Let me get into the bed. Maybe when they see the jinau uniform they'll let it go."

They did, and they didn't. True, the scout car didn't just blast them. On the other hand, it continued to pace the pickup for a minute or so, as Tully continued south, and apparently got in touch with the military base. They hadn't gotten more than a few miles further before two Jao combat vehicles coming northbound on I-5—on their side of the divided interstate, human traffic laws be damned—had intercepted them.

The first minute or so was tense. The Jao suspected them of being deserters, and Tully knew that the normal Jao method for dealing with desertion was summary execution. The aliens considered "court martial" another frivolous human pastime.

Fortunately, however, the Jao were not as prone as humans to assume that everyone lied at the drop of a hat. Rather to his surprise, they accepted Tully's explanation without question—and the mention of Aille's name worked like a charm. By now, it seemed, all Jao troops on Terra knew that the new Subcommandant had taken humans into his personal service. Discovering that Tully and Aguilera were the fabled creatures in question, their suspicion and hostility vanished, replaced by something akin to country rubes gawking at exotic animals in a zoo.

There had been a time, and not so long ago, when Tully would have been angered by that. Another example of Jao arrogance and xenophobia. But his experiences over the past period had taught him to see the shades and colors in Terra's conquerors. They were no longer simply a monochromatic oppressor—as the lumpy shape of the locator tucked out of sight in his pocket reminded him, all the way back to the base.

That didn't take but a few minutes, since exotic animals have their privileges. The Jao officer had summoned the scout car and the three humans were flown the rest of the distance. With, of course, the two pilots of the scout car gawking at them the whole time.

After Tully saw Aguilera and the old man into the medical compound, he wandered through the darker areas of the base until he found shelter from the rain under a tree. The base had been set up hurriedly in an agricultural sector of Willamette Valley, and sprawled all over. Tully decided he could run the risk of staying there until sunrise, before anyone noticed him or thought to ask what he was doing.

By sunrise, Aille would be back. Whatever decision Tully was going to make, he didn't have much time to do it.

For the first time in his life, Tully was suffering from divided loyalties. He had been Resistance from the time he was a boy. This was the first real chance he'd had to escape since he'd been dragooned into Aille's service, and he'd learned a great deal that might be valuable to the Resistance. It was his plain and simple duty to escape and rejoin Wiley's forces in the Rockies. Try to, at least.

On the other hand . . .

He had told Aille and Yaut he would return; had given them his promise, his word. And he could no longer deny to himself that the young Jao scion of Pluthrak—even the crusty old fraghta— had had a genuine impact on him. The vow he had made was not something he could simply dismiss as a necessary lie given to conquerors. Things had gone beyond that. How much farther beyond, and in exactly what way, still confused Tully.

Maybe there was a third alternative, he thought. His fingers closed around the smooth cool box in his pocket. Maybe the fraghta wouldn't ask for it back now, and he would retain control over his own movements. He could stay a bit longer—maybe more than a bit—and learn more about how the Jao top levels of command operated. In the long run, he was starting to think, that might be more important than anything else he could do.

His command of Jao, good to begin with, was improving every day. And leaving aside language, he was coming to understand much better—sort of—the way that the Jao thought. Jao were constantly jockeying for influence, and it was now obvious to him that relations between Aille and the Governor were coming to a breaking point. The rebels in the Resistance could find a way to use that to their advantage, if they understood how to play one Jao off against another. And he could be the one to crack the social code. The rebels might just have a chance to drive the Jao from this world yet. Or, at least—

He sighed. Finally, he'd actually let himself think the words. *Or, at least . . .*

What?

He didn't know. But he was no longer as certain as he had been that humanity faced only two options: get rid of the Jao or die trying. He pulled the locator out of his pocket and stared down at it. In the darkness, he could barely see the device, even held in his hand.

Everything was dark, nothing more so than the "third way" he was groping for. But he decided he could live with that, at least for a while.

He found the Subcommandant along with Yaut and Kralik just outside the Governor's command center, which Oppuk had set up on the military base. It was one of those poured edifices the Jao could erect with incredible speed. The structures seemed odd to humans, on the inside even more than the outside, but they had the advantage of being quick and easy to produce without expending much time and labor.

Tully was sure about one thing, though: Oppuk would have commandeered enough labor to make sure that, within the hant, there would be another one of those damned pools. You'd think that right here next to a battle, the Governor could do without it for once. But Oppuk, Tully was coming to realize, had all the Jao vices and precious few of the conquerors' virtues.

Yes, they did have virtues. That much, if nothing else, he'd learned from Aille and Yaut.

Kralik looked a bit done in, sitting on a log, forehead resting on bent knees with an ominous rip in his uniform. There were some small bloodstains on the ripped material, too. Apparently, the general had gotten wounded after Tully left, although it didn't look serious.

The Subcommandant and Yaut seemed unruffled, however. The awkward Jao bodyguard, Tamt, was haunting the edges of the little group with an air of being very much put upon, and they'd apparently acquired yet another new member for Aille's personal service, a Jao built like a fireplug. None of them were beauty queens in Tully's estimation, but this fellow was ugly enough to strike fear in the heart of a rabid bear.

Jesus, he'd only been gone a few hours. How many members did a Jao bigshot have in his personal service anyway—fifty? Two hundred?

Inside the innermost recesses of the hant, Oppuk's ears swiveled. The sounds of the battle had faded away, he suddenly realized. Could the young Pluthrak possibly have prevailed so quickly? For all of the Governor's public derision of humans, he knew full well how savagely and effectively the creatures normally fought on their own chosen terrain. He had expected it would take at least three solar cycles for the inexperienced Pluthrak to crush the insurgents, probably longer—and then, not without suffering severe casualties.

Now uneasy, he emerged from the pool where he had been floating. Water sluiced from his body. Parm, one of his new service, stepped forward with an ornate harness and pair of loose trousers. Arms extended, he let her dress him, moving automatically to step into the garment, his mind on other, more important matters.

A bowlful of woody tak had been set to smolder at his feet. But it had not been tended properly and now smelled burnt, rather than aromatic. He whirled and kicked it across the floor. Parm gazed down at the glowing embers silently, a hint of *resentment* blurring the shape of *abashed-regret* more appropriate to her failure in duty.

"Clean it up and get out!" He felt angry enough to demand her life. But . . . then he would just have to elevate another incompetent in her place, who would certainly be no better and quite possibly worse.

She bent over the mess, picking up the coals with bare fingers and returning them to the metal bowl. He straightened his harness, while she worked, adjusted the trousers, considering.

If Aille succeeded quickly in Salem, having taken full responsibility for the campaign in such a dramatic public fashion, it would redound to Pluthrak's credit and not Narvo's. It was for that very reason that Oppuk had insisted on a hastily planned and organized attack, overriding the young Pluthrak's sensible caution.

But perhaps he was being unduly concerned, Oppuk reminded himself. The quiet that had fallen over the battlefield might have an even simpler explanation: the Pluthrak's assault had been driven back from the human city. Perhaps Aille would be so shamed by this very public failure, he would offer his life as recompense.

If so, Oppuk would accept it.

Tully approached Kralik. "Do you want me to get you some medical attention, sir? Or take you to the medical compound?"

Kralik looked up at him wearily. Obviously, the general hadn't gotten any sleep either, and he was a good fifteen years older than Tully.

"I've already sent for a medic, but thanks. It's just a scratch." Kralik's lips quirked. "You look a little done in yourself. How's Aguilera and the old guy? And did you ever find out his name?"

"Jesse James, probably," Tully snorted. "No, sir. But I didn't ask. That way—uh—"

The general's smile widened. "That way, if the Jao change their minds, you can claim you don't know who the masked stranger was and he musta hobbled off thataway."

"Uh. Yes, sir."

The general patted the log next to him. "Have a seat, Tully."

Tully was already regretting the impulse that had led him to ask Kralik if he needed medical attention. The general was a good enough guy, sure, but he was still a jinau general. But, there was no way to refuse.

Gingerly, he took a seat. Kralik studied him for a moment with those disconcertingly calm gray eyes. Then said softly:

"Give me a name, Tully. And don't try to lie."

"Excuse me, sir?"

"And don't act stupid. You're not 'sympathetic' to the Resistance, you're part of it. I want to know which part."

Tully glanced at Aille and Yaut, who were some distance away.

"No, I haven't told him," said Kralik. "I'm sure Aguilera hasn't either, just like I'm sure Aguilera's figured it out too. For that matter, I doubt if Belk told, even though Belk knows and he hates your guts."

Belk was the one who'd called him a "weasel," which was the term diehard collaborators used for members of the Resistance. Tully hadn't seen much of Belk since the day he'd had the locator fastened to his wrist. Whatever Aille was doing with that member of his personal service, Belk's duties kept him elsewhere.

"Why does he hate my guts, sir?" He rubbed his wrist. "I never even met the guy before he showed up with this damn thing."

"Well, look at it from his point of view, Tully. He came back from the fighting twenty years ago—he'd been in the Navy—to discover that a crowd of 'patriots' in his home town had gone on a rampage, looking for 'alien-loving collaborators.' For some reason or another, they picked his family as a target. He thinks it was because of an old grudge between his wife and another woman. Whatever the reason, they were all hung. His two kids along with his wife. The girl was seven years old, his son was nine."

Tully winced. "Jesus. Where did that happen?"

"Texas. Amarillo, to be precise."

"*Those* assholes. North Texas is the territory of—well, never mind names. But I think that so-called Resistance group there is working for the fuzzies. The shit they pull couldn't be designed better to piss people off. That's what Wiley thinks too."

"Wiley? *Rob* Wiley?"

Tully scowled. "No names. Uh, sir."

Kralik looked away. "I knew Wiley was in the Resistance. High up, of course, with his experience and training. And he's somewhere in the Rockies, which fits your background. Yes, I checked." His eyes came back to Tully. "Just so you know, Lieutenant Colonel Rob Wiley was my battalion commander during the conquest. One hell of a fine officer. Give him my regards, will you, if and when you see him again."

For a few seconds, Tully studied the general's gray eyes. Just as calm as they always seemed. Kralik was pretty unflappable.

"What's this all about, sir?"

"I don't know, to be honest. But things are starting to change, I think. The day might come when I need to get in touch with somebody who pulls some weight in the Resistance. If so, I could trust Rob Wiley."

He chuckled, seeing the expression on Tully's face. "No, I'm not likely to defect, no matters what happens. My own grudge against you bastards is pretty well faded away, by now, since I know damn well the guys who killed my father and brother and sister-in-law were just common crooks. But what you're doing has no point anymore. You don't have a cold chance in hell, Tully. Leaving aside Jao control of space, you don't have any of the other prerequisites for a successful guerrilla movement. Just start with the fact that you've got no secure base area to work from, not even any neutral territory. That's why you're still such a political mess, twenty years after the conquest. How many Resistance groups are there, anyway? With nothing uniting them— neither program nor structure—beyond 'Jao Go Home.' That's because you can't even hold an authoritative congress anywhere to bring sensible order to yourselves. Where would you assemble it, and be secure? It'd take you years just to organize the thing, as scattered and divided as you are."

Tully's eyes moved away from the general's. He'd heard Wiley complain about exactly the same things.

"Face it, Tully. I did, long ago. There's no getting rid of the Jao. Give the Resistance twenty more years, and they'll be nothing left of any of them but outright bandits. Somehow or other, we're going to have to make an accommodation with the Jao, whether we like it or not."

Tully stared stubbornly at nothing in particular. He heard Kralik chuckle softly.

"Never mind. I'm really not in the political conversion business. And I've rested enough. I'd better go over there and see what the Subcommandant's up to."

The general rose and Tully looked up at him. Now, Kralik's eyes had the look of winter seas.

"Just give my regards to Colonel Wiley, if and when you see him. And tell him that I'd really just as soon never have to do to him what I'm going to do to these trigger-happy idiots in Salem tomorrow. But I will, if I have to. And if I'm running it instead of some Jao appointed by Oppuk, I'll dig Rob out of his hole in the mountains. They don't know how to do it, but I do."

He turned and walked away, heading for Aille. After a moment, Tully rose and followed him.

"I have been consulting with Wrot krinnu Hemm vau Wathnak, who is a veteran of the original conquest of this world," the Subcommandant said to Kralik, when he and Tully came up. "He agrees fully with your assessment of the current military action. We Jao are ill equipped for this engagement."

Wrot's ears waggled. "The natives have a saying for it, like they do for so many things. 'Bitten off more than you can chew.'" He said it with an air of almost human cheer. "Before I retired, we found ourselves in similar situations many times. In my experience, it is always a mistake to fight humans in the midst of their cities, if it can possibly be avoided. They are infernally clever about ambush and sabotage, and their weapons are ideally suited for such terrain and tactics."

Tully stared, wondering where they'd dug this one up.

Aille's stance changed subtly, so that he looked somehow more confident, more in charge. "Yes, I have come to the same conclusion. I will therefore hand the campaign over to you, General Kralik, and your Pacific Division. Launch the attack as soon as you are ready."

Kralik's eyes glittered. "Yes, sir." He began to turn away.

"One moment, General," said Aille. He was looking toward his command center. The structure Aille had had poured for himself was much smaller than the one nearby erected by Governor Oppuk. Yaut was emerging from it, holding something in his hand. One of those short, sticklike things the Jao called a "bau," Tully thought. Except this one, like the one Aille carried, looked to be made out of some kind of bone or shell instead of wood.

Yaut came up and gave the thing to Aille. The Subcommandant immediately turned and extended it to Kralik.

"I give you the bau, Ed Kralik. Bring it back with honor."

CHAPTER
26

Kralik stared down at the bau in his hand, unable to think what to say, while his fingers traced the unfamiliar carvings. There were few, and those simple, which indicated a fledgling commander. It fact, he thought the simple carvings were identical to those on the one Aille himself carried. Given Kralik's experience, that was a bit ironic—he actually had more combat experience than most Jao officers on Terra. He certainly had more than Aille, for whom Terra was his first assignment.

A bau was not the same thing as a rank, or even a badge of office. It was more personal, more in the way of a record of individual achievement. The Jao equivalent, Kralik had sometimes thought, of the "I love me" wall many human officers used to display various military achievement records and awards. But he knew it was a far more formal thing, for the Jao. And it was connected to a kochan, somehow, in a way Kralik did not really comprehend. He'd ask Caitlin. Maybe she or Dr. Kinsey understood the subtleties involved.

But, whatever the fine points might be, the substance was clear enough. For the first time—ever, so far as Kralik knew—a jinau officer had been given a bau. With further accomplishments, the rod would have carvings added to it. What was more important— far more—was that the mere giving of the bau indicated a profound change in his status. Not "social equality," exactly. With their complex hierarchical view of things, the Jao did not share that human concept.

Call it . . . *acceptance.* A barrier removed.

"Return it once you have your victory," Aille said. "A carving for Salem will be added."

"Yes, sir!" Kralik transferred the bau to his left hand and saluted, then motioned a waiting command vehicle forward. This was a human-designed vehicle, essentially a Humvee with Jao maglev drive and communication equipment. Like almost all jinau equipment, it had seen better days.

Once he was in the vehicle, sitting in the front, he saw the driver was staring at the bau in his hand. The young male driver then looked at him, freckle-faced and eager. A bit awed, too, Kralik thought. The driver also understood something of its significance.

"Well, hurry up!" Kralik snapped. "What are you waiting for, a damned engraved invitation?"

Aille monitored the progress of the Pacific Division's brigade from within his command center. Between satellite observation, Jao scout cars in the air, and the various visual and audio links that had been hurriedly made to key elements in the brigade itself, he had a good sense of what was happening.

With Kralik in command and using human tanks and other kinetic weapons, it soon became obvious that the rebels' tactics were not as effective as they had been against the Jao. The jinau troops wasted little time and effort simply destroying buildings, but concentrated their attacks on the pockets of resistance they encountered. By midday, especially with the experienced Wrot by his side commenting on the situation, Aille had come to grasp the key tactic Kralik was following. The jinau general used his infantry like delicate fingers, probing for resistance. Then, when resistance was found, drew the fingers aside slightly and brought in the tanks and artillery to deliver the actual blows. And the blows, when they came, were brutally powerful. If Kralik did not waste effort destroying buildings for the sake of destruction, he was instantly prepared to level them in order to kill the insurgents within. His tactics were subtle, but ruthless.

Wrot supplied snippets of commentary and observations throughout. The principal one being that Kralik's tactics would be even more effective if Jao combat aircraft were coordinating their actions with him.

"Better still," the gruff old veteran pronounced, "if you let the jinau have their own aircraft. Before we swept them from the skies, their aircraft gave us grief during the conquest. Not against our own aircraft, of course, with our much superior electronic countermeasures, but our ground troops. But make sure you don't let any of that lunatic human rivalry infect the thing. If you decide to let them have their own aircraft, make sure you keep an eye on the pilots. Before you know it, the maniacs will be pestering you for their own uniforms, insignia— even a separate command structure. Humans are charming creatures, all in all, but they can find a way to dissociate anything."

Yaut had found Wrot—or rather, Wrot had found him, shortly after they returned from Salem. Wrot and Yaut were old comrades, who'd served together long ago in the conquest of Hos Tir. "When we were both young and reckless," as Yaut had put it, his posture one of *amused-affection-remembered.*

Aille had studied the old veteran, after Yaut presented him. He still seemed sturdy and clear-eyed, though his *vai camiti* was so scarred, Aille had difficulty discerning its original pattern.

The Jao, with a total lack of self-consciousness, was staring back in *rapt-attention.* "Subcommandant," he said. "We heard Pluthrak had granted us a scion, but I came up to see for myself." He blinked. "There's no mistaking that *vai camiti.*"

"Came from where?" Aille asked.

"The population cluster of Portland," the veteran said. "I have been living there since my retirement. I rode up with the troops assigned to this exercise. There are still more than a few who know my face."

Several small explosions lit up in the distance, and he turned to gaze at them, his body shifting into a rough rendition of *grim-disapproval.* "You will lose a lot of people before this is over," he said, "many more than necessary. Humans excel in this sort of fight."

"You have seen this type of battle before, then?"

"Too many times," the fellow said and gestured at his scarred face. "Took my share of wounds too; more than my share, some would say."

Yaut was gazing at the two of them and there was something in his stance, an element Aille couldn't quite interpret. He wanted something, expected something of him . . . Yaut's eyes glittered bright green in the darkness, like a signal about to illuminate.

Then Aille realized the opportunity this fellow's experience on this world represented. "Your name?" he asked.

Lines of pure *pleasure* suffused the old veteran's body. "Wrot krinnu Hemm vau Wathnak."

Hemm was an outlying junior kochan allied with larger Wathnak, reportedly rustic and uncultured. Reliable, but too blunt to forge new associations easily. He'd never heard they were otherwise than sturdily honest, though. "I could make good use of an additional seasoned voice, especially one familiar with this world."

It was an invitation, only, since it could be nothing else. Alongside his many bars of service, Wrot had the mark of retirement carved on his cheek also—the *bauta,* as it was called. The term derived from *bau,* and indicated a life completed to the satisfaction of both kochan and Naukra.

For Jao, the status and the cheek mark was voluntary. Most chose never to take it, even when so entitled—Yaut had not, for instance, though he certainly could—because it removed all automatic associations, even kochan. An individual who chose the *bauta* thereby chose to spend what remained of his life however he wished. Great freedom, yes, because no one could any longer command him. But also, for most Jao, a life too lonely and dissociated to be enjoyable.

Wrot glanced aside at Kralik, who was bleeding from the small wound he'd received earlier with almost Jao stoicism. "I heard you have taken more than one human into your service," he said.

Was that *disapproval* canting those bedraggled ears? "I have," Aille said. "How else am I to understand this world and make myself of use?"

"Quite right," Wrot said, "and very sensible for one of your youth. More sensible than that arrogant imbecile Narvo sent here to be Governor, for a certainty. It would be an honor to serve Pluthrak."

"Welcome to my service, then," Aille said, his angles set in *respectful-welcome.* "You do me and Pluthrak honor."

Which was true, of course. Rarely did a bauta accept personal service. But Aille made a mental note not to use Wrot for delicate negotiations. Whatever the old bauta's skills and abilities—

which must be great, or Yaut would not be looking so pleased—
tact was clearly not one of them.

"You enjoy the company of humans?" Aille asked

"Oh, yes," Wrot replied. "Not that they don't often aggravate me.
But they are a more clever people than we, and I enjoy cleverness. And at my age—especially being Hemm, which humans would
call 'stick-in-the-muds'—and having spent a life on campaign, I
find my current existence on Terra endlessly interesting. Humans
have more ways to divert and entertain themselves than you can
imagine, and I enjoy many of them. They have a saying for that
too, of course. I think they have a saying for everything. 'How are
you going to keep them down on the farm, once they've been to
Gay Paree'?"

The saying meant absolutely nothing to Aille, but it seemed to
amuse the veteran.

"Surely you cannot spend all your time engaged in human
diversions?"

"Of course not. Most of them are sheer silliness. What they call
team sports, I can understand—I actually enjoy 'football,' although
they won't let me play—but why would anyone not insane choose
to climb a rock cliff? And most of what they call 'music' and 'art'
is awful stuff. Sheer cacophony, painful to the ears, or witless daubs
of pigments scattered across a surface to no conceivable purpose.
Mind you, many humans share my opinion also."

His ears flattened with amusement. "No, I mainly occupy myself
by teaching. And studying."

"Teaching?" Aille was puzzled. Retired members of a kochan were
often used as instructors, of course, the best of them elevated to
fraghta. But, in the nature of things, a bauta had no further
obligations to their kochan. "Teach who? And what?"

For a moment, there was a trace of *abashed-awkwardness* in
Wrot's posture. "I teach humans. There is an institute of instruction
in Portland—what humans call a 'university.' Since they have no
proper kochan, humans substitute these institutes for the purpose
of educating their most promising crechelings. This one is small,
but very old and prestigious. They call it 'Reed College.' Not long
after I set up residence in Portland, some of their elders approached
me—very diffidently, ha!—and asked me if I would be willing to
instruct their crechelings in our language."

Aille and Yaut stared at each other, both dumbfounded. Aille himself, *namth camiti* of great Pluthrak, had only invited Wrot to join his personal service with considerable diffidence. That a kochan-less gaggle of humans would have the audacity to so approach a bauta . . .

Wrot stroked the *bauta* on his cheek. "Crude and coarse Hemm may be, young Pluthrak, but I was taught even as a crecheling that to begin by assuming disrespect is a grave offense against association."

Aille had been taught the same thing. But he realized now, more fully than he ever had before, the difference between formal instruction and body-learning. This old bauta was wise with *wrem-fa*, because he had not wasted his life.

"Instruct me," he murmured.

Wrot was still stroking the mark. "They intended no offense, nor disrespect. By their customs, it was an honor. I took it so, and was intrigued by the idea. So, I accepted—and have not regretted doing so, since. Human crechelings can be quite charming, some of them, and all of them are at least interesting from time to time. They are even more adept than Jao crechelings at getting themselves into complicated little troubles. What humans call 'a pickle.'"

Aille began to pursue the matter, but had to break off the discussion for a later time. The battle in Salem seemed to be reaching a climax, and he turned his attention back to the screens and monitors.

The climax was brief and violently destructive. Kralik, he now realized, had deftly maneuvered the remaining defenders into a stronghold near the center of the city. It was a large, ornate-looking edifice, apparently the administrative center for the region. What the humans called "the state capitol," which seemed to have some symbolic significance to them. Perhaps the rebels thought Kralik would hesitate to destroy it.

But, he didn't. The edifice was isolated from the rest of the city by one of those large expanses of open terrain called "parks" that humans enjoyed—though this one, for no reason Aille could see, was apparently called a "mall." Kralik was therefore able to attack it ruthlessly, without fear that the destruction might engulf some of the human civilians who were still straggling out of Salem. He did not use his vulnerable infantrymen at all, except at the very end. He simply used his tanks and artillery to pulverize the structure, only sending in the infantry to look for survivors.

There were none, not there. Kralik had turned the building into nothing more than a pile of burning rubble.

By dawn of the next day, the fighting was all over. The jinau brigade had captured thirty-seven resistance fighters, most injured to some degree, and five more humans who were noncombatants but whom Kralik considered part of the rebellion.

"Probably support staff for the Resistance in this area," Wrot said. They watched the monitors, which showed the small band of dirty and demoralized prisoners being herded into vehicles by jinau foot soldiers. "Most of the real civilians had left before you got your act together."

"What act?" Aille turned to him with *baffled-inquiry*.

"It's a human colloquialism, endlessly adaptive," Wrot said. "Applied here, it means 'before you organized your troops into an effective unit.'"

"Interesting," Aille said. "I will remember that expression. At any rate—" He turned to examine what was left of the city. "—I intended the innocent to leave. There is no *vithrik* in killing those who do not wish to fight."

Kralik came on the monitors, seeking further instruction.

"Most of the city is still intact, I believe," said Aille.

"Yes, sir." Kralik's face bore no expression Aille could see beyond respectful attention. "Do you wish me to order the brigade to start razing Salem?"

Aille hesitated, but only for an instant. His sense of how *vithrik* worked with humans was becoming a strong and sure flow. "No, General. Your brigade has done its duty, and done it very well. I will have the Jao units carry out the city's destruction. They will begin as soon as you report your last soldiers have left."

Aille though he detected a trace of *relieved-appreciation* in Kralik's expression and posture. It was difficult to tell. The jinau general was superb at concealing his sentiments, almost like a human version of the Bond of Ebezon's Harriers.

"As you wish, sir." Kralik hesitated, for an instant. "It will take me some time to extricate all my troops."

Aille concealed his own amusement. *No doubt it will. Kralik, like me, will give the civilians remaining as much time as possible to flee.*

"That is understood and acceptable, General."

Kralik saluted and his image vanished from the monitor.

Aille rose from his seat. "And now, I must inform the Governor of our success."

He and Yaut exchanged a look. This, too, would be a battle. But Aille now felt confident in this arena of struggle also—and so, judging from his stance, did Yaut feel confident in him.

Confident in him, perhaps, but not necessarily in Aille's sense of flow.

"Wait," Yaut suggested. "Wait until Kralik has returned."

"Why?"

"I'm not sure, yet. But I think it will help to have the jinau present himself when you—" He gave a glance at Wrot, but obviously decided that the old bauta was in their full confidence. "—trap the Narvo. Again."

Subtle, Wathnak was not—its junior affiliate Hemm, even less so. Old Wrot's posture was one of pure and unalloyed *anticipation-of-another's-misfortune.*

"To witness that alone," he growled, "would make my personal service a great honor."

CHAPTER
27

Oppuk lounged in his hant and watched the visual link, fuming, his shoulders and the line of his spine stiff with *outrage*. The fighting had progressed far better than he had expected, once the campaign had been turned over to the jinau troops. It was affront enough that Pluthrak had assigned someone with no experience, as though this world were so easy to handle even a crecheling could do it. Now the young upstart and his natives had increased the insult by seeming to prove it so.

He would grind their bones into powder before he was finished here, would hack their young to pieces and sear this land with cleansing flame. He—

Forcefully, he broke off the moment of reverie. The situation was growing perilous, with the Pluthrak challenging him ever more openly. This was no time for Oppuk to be wallowing in fury, much as he wanted to.

What he wanted even more was to be back at his palace, swimming in his specially formulated pool instead of the miserable little substitute he had available in this hant. The wild water on this planet was subtly off, the salts too high in mineral content, too full of impurities. He longed to immerse himself in the scents and tactile sensations of his kochan-world, even if they were only simulated, so that he could regain his equilibrium.

A Jao servitor approached. "Kaul krinnu ava Dano has arrived, and wishes to speak with you."

No doubt he does, Oppuk thought sourly. The Commandant, ever watchful of Dano's interests, would be probing to find advantage.

"Send him to me." Oppuk rose, doing his best to squelch the smoldering anger. It was very difficult. He could remember a time, long gone, when he had enjoyed the endless maneuvers and tactics of kochan rivalry—and been very good at it. But his time on Terra had caused that pleasure to fade, along with so many others. Now, he simply found it tedious and irksome at best.

Dano, as always, was blunt. "Pluthrak swells. This victory, coming so quickly and by using his methods, will swell him further. Do not compound the situation by confronting him immediately. Allow him the time to stumble. He is talented, but very young and impulsive. Such is my advice."

Oppuk felt his temper rising again, and struggled to restrain it. He could not afford to offend Dano. Pluthrak and Narvo might be preeminent among them, but Dano was still one of the great kochan. Since his arrival, several orbital cycles earlier, Kaul had generally allied himself with Oppuk. With the Subcommandant grown so large, in such a short time, Oppuk needed to retain the confidence of the system's top military officer.

But, try as he might, he could not force himself to do more than issue a grunt. It might have been agreement . . . or might not.

Dano studied him for a moment, then assumed the posture of *duty-fulfilled*—with a trace of *skepticism* in the slant of his ears—and withdrew.

Testily, Oppuk summoned his servitor and began putting on his harness. He would follow the Dano's advice, at least to the extent of receiving the young Pluthrak's formal announcement of victory.

"And?" asked Kaul's fraghta, Jutre krinnu Kio vau Dano.

Kaul, now that he was out of the Governor's sight, allowed his posture to lapse into a harsh and crude version of *folly-observed*. "He may have once been *namth camiti,* but it is hard to imagine. The flow of time carries Oppuk further and further into folly. He reacts to everything now like a maddened lurret."

Jutre glanced at the entrance to the Governor's hant. A lurret was one of the great herbivores that roamed the Dano world of Hadiru. An old rogue male, to be precise, notorious for their insane furies. They had been known to charge headlong against combat vehicles.

"If the Pluthrak has taken his measure—which he will, by now, with *that* fraghta to advise him—he will advance-by-oscillation. I think he is doing so already."

"Risky," Kaul murmured. "Very risky. Admittedly, a dazzling tactic that would appeal to a youngster, especially one full of himself. He too, it is said, is *namth camiti*. But . . . would he be that incautious?"

Kaul considered his fraghta's assessment further. Advance-by-oscillation was a tactic often mentioned in kochan rivalry, but rarely used in actual practice—precisely because of the risk involved. One attempted to force another kochan into association by steadily increasing the dissociation, matching move to move by swinging ever outward. Each measure, ever more extreme, forcing extreme measures from the other—until one or the other violated custom irreparably.

Dazzling, indeed, if it succeeded. But the chances were far greater that the aggressor, being the one required to initiate each stage of the dance, would misstep first and plunge into the abyss.

"And we should do what?"

"For the moment, nothing but observe." The sound of an approaching vehicle could be heard. Jutre's ears rose, his whiskers twitched. "The Pluthrak is arriving."

When the vehicle came into view, Kaul could see it was a jinau vehicle. Not just any such, either, but the vehicle that bore the insignia of the Pacific Division's commander. Indeed, he could see Kralik riding alongside Aille.

The significance was obvious, and Jutre put it into words.

"I was right," he said. "Advance-by-oscillation, it is. He is deliberately provoking the Narvo."

A movement from the Governor's hant drew Kaul's attention. Oppuk was emerging. One glance at the Narvo's posture was enough.

"He will succeed," said the Dano gloomily.

It did not take him long, either. Kaul and Jutre observed it all from the side. Before Aille could do more than begin his report, Oppuk interrupted him brusquely.

"You may submit those inconsequential items later, in a written report. For now, I wish only to know the extent of the punishment."

"The city is being razed, Governor, and—"

"How many of the creatures are *dead*?" The Governor practically snarled the words.

His stance mild, Aille looked to the jinau general standing by his side.

Kralik cleared his throat. "We counted one hundred and seventy-two of the rebels dead. There are undoubtedly more who perished in some of the demolished buildings, whose bodies will not be recovered. I estimate a total of perhaps three hundred. Along with another forty or so captured, most of them wounded."

"*Three hundred?* In a population center of this size?"

Kralik stared straight ahead, not meeting Oppuk's furious green-filled gaze. "Yes, Governor."

"Why were there not more? There should have been thousands—no, tens of thousands!"

"I believe most of the townspeople evacuated soon after it became apparent our forces would attack," Kralik said. His posture was rigid and formal. The bau tucked under his arm was absolutely still.

Oppuk whirled on Aille, whiskers stiff with outrage. "And you did not prevent it?"

"You ordered the town destroyed," Aille said. "You said nothing about its population."

"You had your orders!"

"And I followed them," Aille said. The young Pluthrak's posture was a superb rendition of *calm-assurance,* perfect for the situation. His tone of voice, also, was appropriate. Mild, but firm. "I admired your wisdom in punishing the locals through destruction of their property while not agitating them any more than necessary through excessive loss of life."

"You mock me!" Oppuk loomed in his face, every line of his body screaming *challenge.* The Narvo was older, and not as tall, but massively built. Watching, Kaul thought Jutre's analogy to an enraged lurret more appropriate than ever.

The Pluthrak seemed completely unfazed, his *calm-assurance* never wavering, his voice steady. "How so? I wish only to serve, Governor, as do all here, Jao and jinau alike. We have all learned a great deal today."

"Yes," Oppuk said, "we have, and do not make the mistake of thinking I will forget it!" He turned away, ready to stalk off.

Kaul began to exhale with relief. This had been bad, but not as bad as it could have been. Then, seeing that his fraghta's posture was still tense, he grew tense himself.

What more could the Pluthrak do?

The jinau general stepped forward. The human's face and posture were unreadable, as Kralik generally was, but there was something tense in the set of his shoulders. Before he even reached for the bau under his arm and drew it out, Kaul knew exactly what Pluthrak had planned.

"One moment, Governor," said Aille, still in that mild-but-firm voice. "A carving for Salem needs to be added to Kralik's bau. Pluthrak can do it, of course, but the honor is properly Narvo's."

The Governor froze in mid-turn, staring down at the bau extended toward him in Kralik's hand. With an exclamation of fury, Oppuk seized the bau from Kralik, broke it in two and cast the pieces at Aille's feet. Then, lunged back toward his hant, scattering humans and Jao alike from his path.

Aille gazed down at the broken bau at his feet, then lifted his eyes to stare at Dano.

There was no way for Kaul to pretend he had not observed. Nor would Jutre have allowed him to, in any event. Dano was traditionally allied with Narvo, yes. But Dano was a great kochan because it had its own honor. The *vithrik* of a fraghta, more than anything, was bound up with protecting that honor.

"Yes, I saw. I will so report the incident to the Naukra." He decided that honor allowed him a bit of leeway. "If this matter reaches their ears at all."

"It will," said the Pluthrak's fraghta. "Be sure of it." Grimly, Yaut said aloud what was now obvious to all: "Battle is joined, between Pluthrak and Narvo. It is in the open now, and can have but one end."

Kaul and Jutre did not speak further until they had entered their own aircraft and were heading back to Pascagoula.

"In the open, indeed," said Kaul. "We must look to Dano, now. Dano alone."

"Yes," agreed Jutre.

✶   ✶   ✶

Once Oppuk and the Dano were gone, Aille allowed his posture to reflect *justified-wrath*. The posture deepened as he contemplated the broken bau on the ground.

"That was dangerous," said Yaut, though his tone had no reproof in it. "He could have demanded your life."

"He would need a better reason than this," Aille said softly. "I would have refused, and, if Oppuk was foolish enough to take the matter before the Naukra, they would sustain me. If the Naukra hesitated, the Bond of Ebezon would intervene on their own. Breaking a bau!"

He made a small gesture toward the pieces on the ground. Oppuk's action had been a gross offense against custom. The giving of bau was a kochan matter. Oppuk could have refused the carving, to be sure. But he had no right to question Pluthrak's giving of the bau, much less proffer outright insult. It was precisely to keep kochan antagonism from crossing such bounds that the Naukra existed in the first place—and had its fearsome military arm, the Bond of Ebezon, to enforce their authority. A military arm that had wide powers, moreover, which it was not reluctant to use. More than once in the past, the Bond's Harriers had enforced custom directly, not even waiting for the Naukra to assemble and deliberate. And this was a clearcut issue, not ambiguous in the least. Narvo's intemperate arrogance was obvious to all. Not even Dano would try to argue the matter.

Aille gazed toward the town. Even in the rain, the glow of burning Salem could be easily seen. "If I am to be of use, truly of use, then I must do as I feel necessary and deal with the consequences of my actions. Whatever else, I am Pluthrak—and Pluthrak is not to be bullied by Narvo. Certainly not such a specimen as Oppuk. It is a mystery to me, now that I have assessed the Governor, why Narvo ever sent him here."

Kralik bent to pick up the pieces of the bau. "I'm sorry, sir."

Aille stared at him. The jinau officer had done as Aille had directed, but Aille had given him no reasons. The human would have only the vaguest sense, if any at all, of what was involved.

"There is no reason to be," Aille said. "You have done nothing dishonorable, Ed Kralik. The dishonor was Oppuk's. I will have another bau made for you, one whose carvings reflect your victory at Salem. The Governor had no right to break this one. This is an old posture between Pluthrak and Narvo, begun long before any of us here today were born. In the end, it will play itself out."

"Yes, sir," Kralik said, but Aille could read worry in the human's eyes.

Worry was appropriate, he thought. Oppuk was quite right, of course. Aille had defied him by subtly reinterpreting his orders, but he could not have acted otherwise. The needs of *vithrik* even more than the logic of advance-by-oscillation guided him here. The governing of humans required a light hand, if association was to proceed. Exactly how and in what way that was to be done, remained unclear. But to continue on in the old way would be against *vithrik*. Pluthrak's understanding of *vithrik*, if not Narvo's.

Looking back over the events that had occurred recently, much was now clear to Aille. Whether or not to hunt the whale was a minor issue; in and of itself, simply a flap about local custom and religious practice. Even humans could not agree about its propriety. Oppuk could easily have sought a different activity, or simply changed the locale, avoiding the entire confrontation altogether.

Instead the Governor had let himself be drawn into the squabble and made them all a target in the process. Punishing this entire town had only compounded the mistake. It would have been enough to demand the surrender of the rebels who had taken refuge there.

Instead, now they had a number of Jao casualties in addition to the human loss of life. Kralik was right—this had been a well-laid ambush. Those who prepared it had obviously done so with Oppuk's not-sane temper in mind, knowing that he would strike here. Had Aille not withdrawn the Jao troops and let the jinau handle the matter, the Jao casualties would have been much worse. In the end, of course, they would have crushed the enemy—but Aille was quite sure the Resistance would have used their ferocious battle and the casualties they inflicted to rally further support among the native populace.

He studied the broken bau, and came to a deep resolve. That was Narvo's method, which was clearly failing. Pluthrak would follow its own course.

As Yaut had truly said, battle was openly joined. And could have but one end.

PART V:
Interdict

The Preceptor studied the message from his agent on Terra. More from amusement than anything else. There was not much to study, really, once he'd read past the brief account of the arrival of an Interdict vessel at the Terra framepoint. He'd already passed the gist of that on to Pleniary-Superior Tura, but hadn't told her of the message's ending. She'd have been too outraged.

Just three words:

Position yourself now.

Not the least of the reasons that agent was the best the Preceptor had was that he was the only one who would ever dare send such a message. The Preceptor glanced at Tura, standing not far away waiting for his orders. The pleniary-superior herself, despite her rank and capability and self-assurance, would not have had the nerve to so instruct the Preceptor.

Not yet, at least. He had great hopes for her in the future.

"Our agent—ah—recommends that we position the fleet. I agree with his recommendation. See to it, Tura."

"Yes, Preceptor. The entire fleet?"

"Only the harriers, for the moment. If we need support vessels and lighter craft, we can add them later. Immediately, I will want to be able to overawe any resistance. For that, sixty-three harriers will do perfectly."

"And we will need them anyway," Tura observed, "if the arrival of the Interdict presages an assault by the Complete Harmony."

"Yes, that too."

She cocked her head slightly, tilting her ears. "But you do not want to intervene yet? The fleet is to remain here, at the framepoint connecting to Terra? That might be dangerous, Preceptor, if the Complete Harmony is on its way."

"Yes, it might. But I, too, in a different way, have no choice but to advance-by-oscillation. The Pluthrak must retain the lead here, not the Bond, or twenty years of work will go for nothing."

He deleted the message from his private holo tank. "And if Terra does not survive, so be it. Strategy is always a matter of weighing one risk against another."

CHAPTER
28

Aille and his service, along with Kralik, boarded the first suborbital shuttle back to Pascagoula. He waited only long enough to send Tamt to fetch Caitlin Stockwell from the medicians. Aille wanted to make sure she was among the passengers. In Oppuk's enraged mood, he might conceivably try to harm the young human.

Tamt showed up with her after the rest had already embarked. Aille spotted Stockwell as soon as she appeared in the hatch. Kralik spotted her at the same time, and immediately rose to greet her.

Her skin was very pale, almost translucent. That was a sign of physical distress in humans, he was coming to understand. The bruise on her face was dark purple in contrast, her heartward arm splinted and supported by a sling. She glanced inside, then made her way between the rows of seats with halting, weary steps, flanked by Kralik, who appeared concerned.

"Broken," she said in Jao, with a hint of *apologetic-regret* in the line of her shoulders, then sank into the seat next to Aille, leaned her head back against the cushion and closed her eyes. Tamt sat next to her, on the other side.

Jao bones were very strong, breakage occurring mostly when other accompanying injuries were life-threatening. Humans, he was reminded yet again, were much more fragile. He would have to keep that in mind when ordering his jinau troops into combat situations. As effective as they'd proven themselves to be in ground

301

fighting, Jao troops would still far surpass them in direct hand-to-hand combat. If he remembered correctly, humans even had a special name for that type of service: *commando units.*

Aille determined to have some Jao units added to his jinau forces to serve in cases where such duty was required. That would have the added advantage of increasing association between Jao and humans in a harmonious manner.

Oppuk would be hostile to the idea, of course, but this was a purely military matter. No doubt, Dano would be hostile also. But at this point, Aille was quite sure, Commandant Kaul would not try to oppose him directly over such an issue. After Oppuk's violation of custom, Dano would be retreating into neutrality.

The shuttle's engines roared to life and the vessel quivered with power. Aille noticed that Tamt seemed more than a bit uneasy, giving him frequent glances. And, once he studied her more carefully, saw that she bore the subtle signs of having been involved recently in a fracas of some sort.

He twitched his whiskers, inviting an explanation.

"Someone who said she was Banle krinnu nao Narvo appeared at the medicians' compound. She said the Stockwell human was attached to the Governor's household. She tried to take her away."

Perception-of-difficulty swept over Aille and he shifted in his seat to accommodate its shape. His ears flattened. "Indeed? How did you prevail?"

Tamt was very nervous, now, her seated form shifting awkwardly from one half-assumed posture to another. "I—ah. Ah. It proved necessary to subdue her physically. Which I did."

Kralik grinned fiercely as he buckled Caitlin's slender form into the safety harness, then settled in the row facing them and reached for his own harness. The sound of the engines deepened as the shuttle lifted from the ground.

Looking still more uneasy, Tamt now glanced at Yaut. The fraghta's expression was ferocious. "Did I do the right thing?"

"Most certainly!" exploded Yaut. "How could you do otherwise? Does Narvo's arrogance have no limits?"

Seeing the sudden *relief* flooding Tamt's posture, Yaut controlled his anger. He had just realized, Aille thought, what a great risk Tamt had taken—or thought she had, at least. For one of her lowly status to physically attack a Narvo, even one of *nao* status, had taken courage and devotion.

"You did well, Tamt," the fraghta said gruffly. "Very well indeed! You are credit to yourself and to Pluthrak. Ha! Would that I had been there to see it!"

Had Yaut been there, of course, the fracas would never have occurred. Leaving aside his status, no Jao not crazed with reckless fury would be so brash as to seek physical confrontation with such as Yaut. The fraghta of the great kochan were not chosen for their sagacity alone.

Aille decided to elaborate, for the sake of quieting Tamt's nerves. Poorly trained as she had been before Yaut took her into service, the female obviously did not understand all that was at stake. That was not surprising. Low-status minor kochan such as the one that had produced her participated diffidently, if at all, in the rivalries among the great root clans. She would not understand the subtleties and permutations.

"The fact that Caitlin Stockwell had once been attached to the Narvo's household was irrelevant," he said, "a flow that was completed. His assault upon her indicated dissatisfaction with her performance. To administer physical punishment upon a member of one's household in public is an extreme measure, and is equivalent to formal dismissal. It has always been thus, among the great kochan. Therefore she was free of obligation and I added her to my service. In doing so, I was quite within custom. She was thus a member of my personal service and under Pluthrak's aegis when the Banle creature made that most improper demand on behalf of Narvo. Your actions against her were quite correct, Tamt—dishonorable to do otherwise—and Pluthrak will see that no harm comes to you because of it."

The taut lines of Tamt's body eased and she sat back in her seat, finally relaxed.

Aille now studied Kralik, since the human was preoccupied with gazing intently at Stockwell. The human was doing his best to conceal it, but not even the alienness of his posture could disguise the truth. The jinau officer was very tense. Anger, most of it—clearly Aille was correct in gauging that the general had formed a personal attachment to the Stockwell female. But there was more than simple anger. There was also . . . something very close to exhilaration.

That was inevitable, Aille thought grimly. Dangerous also, but the danger was another product of Narvo's misconduct. Firmness with subject species was a necessity, true enough. All Jao knew that, certainly the scions of great kochan. But Oppuk's rule on Terra had gone far beyond anything that could be called "firmness." Aille could only imagine how much hatred and resentment the Narvo had stirred up in twenty solar cycles—even among such as these, the scion of a prestigious human clan and one of its top jinau officers.

Madness!

On the other hand . . . madness that could be turned to good effect, if association was done properly. Properly, and delicately. The links between Narvo and humans must be exchanged for links with Pluthrak—but without undermining the necessities of Jao rule. Raw exhilaration at the abasement of Narvo was inevitable, yes— even a potentially valuable weapon—but it could easily become a blade that cut indiscriminately.

He and Yaut exchanged meaningful glances. How good it was— how splendid—to be finally working in tandem with his fraghta. It was as if they were two hands guided by the same mind.

Yaut cleared his throat. "Given the Narvo's unstable temper, I think it would be wise if we appointed Tamt as Stockwell's body-guard. At least for the moment."

"I agree," said Aille immediately. "I have no further need for one, in any event. After the latest Narvo outrage, Oppuk will be care-ful to avoid even a hint of Narvo threat. Direct threat, for a cer-tainty."

The same was now just as true for Stockwell, of course, but Aille was sure the humans would not understand that. And one look at the expressions on the faces of Stockwell and Kralik made clear that the meaningless gesture was much appreciated.

By Tamt also, it seemed, oddly enough. Most Jao would have been at least quietly offended to be appointed the bodyguard to a native. But the expression on Tamt's face—her posture even more so—indicated nothing but *satisfaction.*

Aille saw Stockwell's tiny hand move to cover Tamt's thick wrist, for a moment, and give it a little squeeze. Tamt, instead of drawing away, simply covered the little human hand with her large Jao one, gently squeezing in return.

It was a bit unsettling to watch. Aille himself—Yaut even more so—would have found that physical intimacy annoying, even repellent. But association proceeded down complex channels, even among Jao. Tamt, it had long been obvious, suffered from an emotional state which was uncommon among Jao.

Humans had a name for it, though. She had been "lonely."

Yaut spoke again. "That does leave the possibility of an attack upon you by humans."

Aille did not bother to glance at Kralik. He was sure of the response before it even came.

"The Pacific Division would be honored to provide the Sub-commandant with whatever he requires in the way of a bodyguard," the general said, almost snapping the words. "Up to and including my best battalion, if he needs it, assigned permanently to the duty."

Aille drew up the figures from memory. "A battalion would be excessive, General Kralik. I should think a company would be quite sufficient. Perhaps the same company that came with us on the whale hunt?"

"Yes, sir." He pulled out his communicator. "They're on this same shuttle, I think. I'll give Captain Walters the order immediately."

As Kralik spoke quietly into the comm, Caitlin opened her blue-gray eyes and regarded Aille with *puzzled-gratitude*. "What will I be required to do, as part of your service?"

"Provide advice on human behavior and psychology," Aille said, "as well as interpreting where needed. You speak fluent Jao with almost no accent and move better than any human I have yet met. Your assistance will be quite valuable. Perhaps you can even train the rest of my human staff to move properly."

"I'll do my best."

There was more she could do, Aille thought, as he examined the landscape passing below. Insanity was rare among the Jao. But Aille was now convinced that the Governor was indeed insane. Or, least, not sane.

And it was for the reason that Yaut thought, he reflected, though it was more subtle than Yaut realized. It was not because Oppuk had "gone native," in the sense that the veteran Wrot had done. That was healthy, even if Wrot had done it in a typically coarse and uncultured Wathnak manner. It was because Oppuk had done the opposite. He had "gone native" not to associate, but to dissociate. He had adopted only those human attributes that were discordant and disruptive, ignoring all else. No, more—*repelling* all else.

Some deep, compulsive, festering anger and resentment was at work here, which Aille did not understand. But, for whatever reason, the Governor had twisted the necessary association between victor and vanquished into something grotesque. Something . . .

Yes, Yaut was right. Something *human*.

He turned to Caitlin. "There are some terms I have encountered, studying your history. They puzzled me, and I would ask you to explain them."

"Yes?"

"The first term is: 'tyrant.' The other is 'despot.'"

Tully watched Aille and the Stockwell girl from a seat further down. For some reason, the Subcommandant seemed especially interested in the President's daughter, though he wasn't sure why.

As far as he knew, Jao did not perceive any degree of sexual attractiveness in humans. Whatever other outrages they had committed upon the human population, there had been no instances of rape. Or, indeed, of any kind of sexual interaction. The reason was not simply physical. Jao sexual organs were similar enough to human for intercourse to be possible.

But by all accounts, they mated only with their own kind—and infrequently at that. It wasn't simply that Jao didn't consort sexually with humans. They didn't seem to consort sexually with each other, either, even though their sexes did everything together including toiletry and bathing. There were no Jao young on this planet. In fact, no human had ever reported even seeing one. Jao kept their families, or whatever passed for families among them, strictly off-world. As a result, humans knew less about the personal lives of their conquerors than they knew about the mating habits of jellyfish.

The hard rectangle of the locator's controls bit into his hip through his back pocket, still in his possession though Yaut had clearly not forgotten about it. He only needed one look at the fraghta's enigmatic black eyes to know that. He was still testing Tully, and the price of failing would most likely be death.

Tully had faced death many times since his childhood and the Jao invasion. But he sensed another, higher price lurking behind that more obvious consequence—loss of honor. If he took the opportunity to run, he might make it, but he would lose what the Jao called *vithrik*.

There was no reason he should care what Yaut or any other Jao thought of him, no reason why he should do anything but devote his energies to escape, which was after all the primary duty of all prisoners. He had learned that along with the alphabet and counting numbers back in the rebel camps, had eaten it for breakfast in the frosty gray dawns, then mouthed it as a prayer at night.

Yaut had beaten him, exhibited not the least sense of patience or good will, required things of him that he could not even begin to understand, yet refused to explain, calling it only "*wrem-fa,*" body-learning. He did not owe him or the Subcommandant a damned thing, and yet—

He pulled the black box out and sat with the hard cool shape in his hands, staring. Finally he put it back in his pocket.

Governor Oppuk was on the rampage. That much was clear. The Pluthrak Subcommandant had . . . done something back there in Oregon. In human terms, he'd "pulled a fast one" on Oppuk. And now, Tully suspected, Aille intended to oppose the Governor still further. Things were tense and bound to get only worse. Maybe the Resistance could find a way to use this to their advantage. And, if so, no one was in a better position than Tully to observe it. Analyze it, even.

He would wait. His "third way" still seemed . . .

Acceptable. Even honorable, to human and Jao alike.

God help me, I'm starting to understand these bastards.

Caitlin leaned back in her seat, closing her eyes and trying to ignore the pain of her broken arm. She needed to think.

Partly, she needed to think about the feel of the furry Jao hand still cupped over her own. In twenty-four years of life, most of it spent in close proximity to the aliens, this was the first time she'd ever felt anything remotely close to affection for one of them.

"Affection" was the right word, too, and Caitlin was too honest to lie to herself about it. For someone like Aille, she could feel respect—even admiration. But whatever her relationship with Tamt was, or was going to be, there would be genuine warmth to it. On her part, for sure, and she thought it would be reciprocated by Tamt. In whatever way, at least, Jao could feel what humans would consider personal warmth.

If for no other reason, in Tamt's case, than simple loneliness. Tamt was not an outcast in her own society, no. But she was one of such low status that she had enjoyed little in the way of respect from her own kind, much less intimacy. Caitlin realized now that her perceptions of the Jao had been heavily skewed, all her life, by the fact that she'd only been in contact with Jao from the stratosphere of their alien society, or their close hangers-on. But how did that same society look—feel, if you would—when you were one of the members at the bottom of the pyramid?

And it *was* a pyramid. The Jao could delude themselves all they wanted about their egalitarian ways, and deride humans for their obsessions with the petty perks and protocols of prestige—such as having doors opened, and salutes. But, in another way, the Jao were far more status-ridden than humans ever were. In modern times, at least.

It was interesting—and worth pursuing. The glimpses Caitlin had gotten of that old fellow Wrot were just as intriguing. Another Jao, it seemed, who had . . . not turned his back on his own, no. He was obviously pleased now that he was part of Aille's service. But, clearly enough, Wrot had a very different attitude toward humans than Caitlin would have thought any Jao did, until very recently.

Perhaps her father's long-squelched hopes were not just daydreams, after all. Perhaps "association" was not simply a Jao euphemism for the relationship between a drover and his oxen.

Her own motivations, when it came to Tamt, were clear enough. A lot of it was pure and simple gratitude, combined with savage glee. Banle had oppressed Caitlin all her life, since she was four years old, had been a constant and never-ending looming shadow. A ghoul, she'd sometimes seemed, and always a troll.

To finally see that troll twisted into a pretzel, by someone stronger than she was . . .

Ha!

Caitlin smiled. *That* was a memory she'd treasure all her life, for a certainty. The shrieks of human doctors and nurses, scattering everywhere while two great Jao slammed each other back and forth in the clinic. Caitlin herself, despite her injuries, had been the only one who *hadn't* looked for shelter.

She wouldn't have missed that, for all the world! The first shock—and despair—at discovering that the hated Banle had not only survived after all but had come to take her back into the darkness. Then, to her surprise, seeing Tamt bristle and growl with indignation and fury—which Banle had returned immediately, and in kind.

That had been foolish. Tamt was not only bigger and stronger than Banle, but Yaut had been training her in the Jao methods of hand-to-hand fighting. No doubt Banle, being Narvo herself, had received equal training. But that had been long ago, before she'd spent twenty years overseeing a human girl who didn't begin to match her strength. In the here and now, in the savagely physical battle that had erupted between the two, she'd been overmatched.

Caitlin had watched avidly, without a thought for her own safety, despite being in the position of a human caught in a room when two walruses went at each other. Okay, small walruses, granted. But the Jao method of hand fighting was a lot like sumo wrestling—combined with a use of their big teeth, which would have had any human referees frantically blowing whistles. By the time Tamt finally left Banle lying on the floor hammered into a pulp, they'd just about wrecked that room in the clinic.

Caitlin's own cot had been included in the wreckage. She'd had to scramble hastily aside, at the end, broken arm or no, when the battle finally brought the two Jao her way.

She hadn't minded. Tamt had put the cot to good use, pounding Banle's head against it until the cot was in splinters—twisted metal, rather—and Banle was unconscious.

She sighed happily, even with the pain. Yes, that was a memory to cherish.

But, there was more. Caitlin had been very lonely too, and she knew she'd enjoy Tamt's company, once she managed to overcome the Jao female's odd combination of shy reticence and social awkwardness.

Thoughts of loneliness, however, brought up another subject. One which Caitlin could no longer avoid thinking about.

She opened her eyes, just to slits, in order to peek.

Yup. Ed Kralik was looking at her. As usual, with that still face and those gray eyes that revealed as little as possible. But Caitlin wasn't fooled. That was not the look of a major general, that was the look of a man—and one who'd apparently decided that the fact he was almost twice her age just didn't matter.

Which, it didn't. Rather the opposite, actually, from Caitlin's point of view. Her world would chew up any man she knew her own age. Kralik, on the other hand . . .

Yeah, maybe. And isn't it nice, for the first time in my life, to allow that word into my lexicon? Such a nice word.

Maybe.

CHAPTER
29

Oppuk knew he should get back to his palace in Oklahoma City as fast as possible, but he was still too furious to travel. If he had boarded his personal transport and been cooped up with only a few attendants, he most likely would have slaughtered them all to satisfy his wrath and then been forced to find replacements.

He had already sent a message back to the primary Narvo kochan-house on Pratus, requesting experienced servitors to be dispatched to him from the home world. They . . . might, or might not be. Replacements for staff killed by rebels might possibly be provided, even though he had been out of favor now for many cycles. But replacements for those killed out of pique most certainly would not.

Instead, he stalked down to the unsatisfactory local sea with its audacious golden sand and swam the rest of the day, submerging beneath the tossing waves until his brain reeled from lack of oxygen, his vision went gray, and he was forced gasping back up into the damp air.

How dare that Pluthrak upstart! He should have taken the pieces of that broken bau and rammed them through the jinau officer's brain! If Oppuk wished to kill one of these filthy humans, then he would! Terra was overpopulated anyway. It did no harm to thin the herd.

He swam back to the beach and stalked out dripping in the cool air. His service hovered with an air of *respectful-attention*, watching from a prudent distance to see what he desired.

One of his new staff approached, ears properly *deferential*, but shoulders outright *alarmed*. Marb, perhaps, or was it Ullwa? Oppuk turned his back, refusing to have such an unharmonious combination inflicted upon him.

"Governor?"

It was Marb, then. Though their *vai camiti* were similar, he could distinguish the pair's voices. "I hear you," he said, in no mood for inanities.

"We have received news from the observation station in orbit," Marb said. "Dreadful news!"

Oppuk turned and regarded the servant with half-lidded *cool-indifference*. "Compose yourself," he said. "If you wish to serve at this level, you must remember above all else to move well."

Marb closed her eyes, exhaled, then dropped into a sketchy version of *concerned-haste*. "The framepoint in this solar system is showing activity," she said. Her ears betraying *fear*, despite all efforts to control herself. "The advance signature is not Jao!"

Oppuk froze. His mind raced, but his thoughts refused to come together and make sense.

The Ekhat, here?

"It is too soon," he said finally. He felt his body all adrift, every line gone to meaningless, babbling angles. "This lazy, primitive world is not ready."

"What do you wish us to do?" Marb's eyes were filled with the bright striations of terror.

"Alert my staff," Oppuk said, "and ready my transport back to the palace."

The situation was hopeless, of course. But once the initial shock was over, Oppuk began to feel better.

Much better, in fact. If nothing else, he would probably soon be rid of this vile planet, since the Ekhat would most likely destroy it. And, in the doing, he could see many possibilities for encompassing the destruction of the young Pluthrak in the pyre.

So the Ekhat had come, Aille thought, as he and Kaul studied the holo tank display above a vast black control grid. Everyone had known they would eventually sweep through this portion of the galaxy, and possibly even this system. But the Naukra Krith Ludh, who coordinated the efforts of all kochan, had hoped to have more time. Any possibility of help was far away and most of the

Jao fleets were committed elsewhere. Terra would have to defend itself as best it could.

"Have they attacked?" he said, his body at *ready-willingness*.

"No." The Dano Commandant looked ill, his angles confused, his nap patchy and ill-favored. "The signs indicate only one ship approaching the framepoint. The signal being broadcast in advance of its arrival is of the Interdict faction. It seems they wish to parley."

"That is—unexpected," Aille said, his mind whirling with possibilities.

Yaut stepped forward. "There is precedent, and when parley is requested, Interdict always follows through. There has never been deception on this account."

"You will go, and represent us at the parley," Kaul said. "The Governor has expressly commanded. You yourself, young Pluthrak."

Dano looked aside. His whiskers sagged against his muzzle as though they had died. "Take whatever ship you deem appropriate. I have several available in orbit. Find out what they want and then report back."

Another maneuver by the Narvo, Aille realized. Negotiation with the Interdict was always a chancy business. No doubt Oppuk hoped that Aille would perish in the attempt.

So be it. Where there was peril, there was also opportunity. The Narvo continued to blunder, responding to Pluthrak's widening advance-by-oscillation by taking petty countermeasures. He glanced at Yaut and saw that his fraghta obviously shared Aille's own attitude.

"I have already put the shipyards on full alert and notified all bases on the other continents," Aille said, throwing his halfcape back. Eagerness to prove himself prickled through his veins and it was difficult to maintain a neutral *wishing-to-be-of-service* stance. "Refitting has been suspended and all available weapons and vessels, converted or not, will be deployed. If we have to fight, we will use whatever is at hand."

"Terran tech will be useless!" Kaul punched a button on the console, then gazed bleakly at a simulation based on the predicted emergence point. A tiny point of orange light blossomed near the sun and grew. "These are not crechelings to be impressed with the rattling of spears! These are the Ekhat, who made us as casually as a child makes a figure out of mud and who dispose of entire star systems as we dispose of worn-out harness. They will do as they wish."

"Unless we stop them," Aille said. "It has been done."

"With Jao ships and Jao armaments, not half-witted primitives wielding sticks and stones!" The Commandant's form slouched into *bitter-acceptance*. "You are young and but newly arrived. Do not fool yourself that, because you took a few humans into your service, you now know the full measure of these creatures. If you had been here longer, you would understand that they cannot agree upon anything, even to save themselves. They would rather see their world perish than seek strength through association with the Jao."

The humans in the room stiffened a bit. Aille realized Kaul was unaware that they understood enough Jao to follow the conversation.

"I realize I have been here only a short time," he said carefully, "but I have found humans to be inventive, as well as clever and determined. They are not Jao, and do not reason as Jao, but if we can persuade them now to turn their strength outward against our mutual enemies, rather than inward against competing factions and ourselves, we may yet prevail."

"Pah!" Kaul turned his back. "Tell it to the Ekhat. They are insane enough they might even believe you. I weary of prattle."

Aille motioned to his service and they led him out through the Commandant's command center. Yaut took the lead, letting Wrot and Tamt share the honor of second. "We will take my courier ship," Aille said as they walked, his mind racing ahead with plans.

"Then there will not be room for all of us," Yaut pointed out. They had reached the entryway, and the fraghta passed through. "Still, I agree, it is the best ship for the purpose. Whom do you wish to take?"

"You, of course." Aille stepped out into the glaring yellow sunlight streaming out of the west. "And General Kralik, Tully, and Caitlin Stockwell."

Aguilera stiffened and his face reddened. "Why not me, Subcommandant?"

"You are injured," Aille said, "and your specialty is the refit of ground assault vehicles. I want you to stay here in the refit facility and make sure preparation and deployment are proceeding as ordered. You have my authority to make whatever changes are needed. Speak to Nath. She will provide you with the necessary assistance."

Tamt's ears waggled with *shamed-distress*. "I am Caitlin Stockwell's bodyguard," she said. "She will be in great danger facing our most deadly enemies. Should you not take me?"

"If one bodyguard, however excellent, could stand between one human and the Ekhat, we would not need armies and fleets here," Aille said. "I wish you and Wrot to go instead with Aguilera and help Nath to swell his prestige. There are some here who will be distressed that a human has been given such authority."

Kralik cleared his throat. His hands were clasped behind his back and his carriage stiff. "Miss Stockwell is injured, sir."

"But not badly," Aille said. "I want Tully and Caitlin to see for themselves what we face. They both have important contacts here on Terra. So, if they see and believe, then it will be easier for those others as well. Most on this world will be required to fight without seeing. It is necessary someone they trust sees first for them."

"I don't understand," Tully said. "Caitlin is important because of her father, but I'm nobody."

"Of the many things you are," Aille said, "that is not one of them. I think it is more important for you to go than anyone else. You are a part—whatever the details, which I have never asked—of what humans on this world call the 'Resistance.' Indeed, you have been demonstrating its philosophy and arguments for my education every day since I first encountered you."

"Does *vithrik* not demand that you see for yourself?" Yaut demanded, his ears and whiskers stiff with *impugned-honor*. "If you believe we Jao are distorting the truth about the threat imposed by the Ekhat, here is your chance to test it."

"I do want to know the truth," Tully said. "We all do."

Aille turned to Yaut. "Summon Caitlin Stockwell. We leave as soon as the ship is ready."

The blood thrummed in his ears. Few of his kind had ever stood whisker to whisker with an Ekhat and lived to tell about it. They were notoriously unpredictable and given to actions that made no sense to ordinary sentient beings. He had much to do before leaving, files to review, protocol to absorb, preparations back here on Terra to direct.

An entire world to save. In the end, it was for this that Pluthrak had shaped him, not quarrels with the Narvo.

*   *   *

Tully preceded Aille and Yaut out of the command center and onto what humans would have called a "parking lot," as inappropriate as the term was here. Jao construction was all irregular curves, like everything of Jao origin, and lacked even a level surface to walk on. When Tully looked at the "pavement" closely, he could see slim flickers of green and blue deep inside, like fish darting in the black depths of some alien ocean.

The two Jao, bent over the fraghta's comboard, stopped at the edge to wait for the groundcars and ignored him. They seemed to be reviewing downloaded files from their database on the Ekhat, making last minute comparisons and notes.

He still couldn't get over it—the Ekhat were actually coming. It seemed these reputedly monstrous alien aggressors were not just a fiction, used by the Jao to compel obedience, much like a human parent invoked the bogeyman to send fractious children to bed. But there was no way this could be a pretense.Sweat rolled down his temples and pooled between his shoulders as the two Jao consulted. The late afternoon heat was intense, but, as always, it didn't affect them. If their concern was an act, he thought, it was a damn good one, and in all his time masquerading as a jinau, he had never known Jao to be any kind of actors, good or bad. What they felt was always written all over them, if one knew how to read their body language.

He certainly wasn't as accomplished as Caitlin Stockwell, but he could interpret well enough now to get the gist of what was going on. Aille, Yaut, Wrot, and Tamt were definitely worried. Before she'd been dispatched back to Aille's rooms to fetch Caitlin, the curve of Tamt's spine had even suggested fear. But then, Tamt seemed a simple soul, who saw things in bright, unalloyed colors and reacted accordingly.

Caitlin and Professor Kinsey emerged from the command center, Tamt leading the way. The Stockwell girl was dressed very simply in a white shirt and jeans and carried her own small travel bag slung over one shoulder.

"I don't like this!" Kinsey said, his normally mild face tight with disapproval. "She's already been injured, and now you propose to take her out in space on a small ship to meet with—those—violent creatures?"

Aille turned and his eyes flickered with pinpricks of green. "Those 'creatures,' as you put it, Professor Kinsey, are the enemy of human and Jao alike, not to mention innumerable other species. They 'cleanse' entire planetary systems, whenever it suits their fancy, and it often does."

"But why should they bother us?" Kinsey blinked behind his glasses. "Earth has never attacked them. We've never even traveled beyond our own solar system!"

"They do not have a reason for cleansing the Jao have ever been able to understand," Aille said, "so I doubt humans will be able to understand what they want either. At any rate, if they parley, then at least for that short time they will not be exterminating this world. We will do as they request and it behooves your species to have representatives present."

"Then take me!" Kinsey gripped Caitlin's shoulders and gazed over her blond hair at Aille. "I will witness for her."

Shaking her head, she put her bag down, then reached up and covered his hand with hers. "No, it's all right," she said quietly as though soothing a distraught child. "I want to go—to be of use, as a Jao would say. It's my duty."

Kinsey pulled her around and made her meet his worried gaze. "You're only a student. You have no duty other than to return home safely to your family and get on with your life!"

"On the contrary," she said with a half-smile, "I'm a member of the Subcommandant's personal service now, and it is my duty to serve him."

Startled, Kinsey stared at Aille. "When did this happen?"

"Last-sun," Yaut said, "after the whale hunt."

"And lucky it did," Caitlin said. "Otherwise I'd be dead—or, at best, still be attached to Governor Narvo's household as a mere servant, being readied to perform for his guests like a trained dog. Until he decided the right day had come to kill me."

Kralik stepped forward. "I'll look after her, Professor. I promise." He picked up her bag.

"I'll be back soon," she said, still in that soothing tone of voice, "—and with tons of data! In the meantime, if my presence serves the Subcommandant in any way, I am glad to help."

"I'll watch after her, too," Tully said, almost despite himself. "We all will."

"I don't suppose it's occurred to any of you macho men that maybe, just maybe, I can take care of myself!" Caitlin glared at Tully so fiercely that he stepped back.

Dr. Kinsey threw up his hands. "I'll notify President Stockwell then. There's nothing more I can do."

"I'm a grown woman." Caitlin took his hand awkwardly with her left and squeezed. "I have to make my own decisions. Sub-commandant Aille is on a crucial mission and it's important for us to support him. Tell my father that. I'll contact him as soon as I get back."

If you get back, Tully could see written on Kinsey's face, but the professor only crossed his arms as two cars pulled up. The man's dark eyes were bleak. Tamt, standing next to him, looked even more upset.

Tully piled into the first vehicle after Kralik and Caitlin. Aille and Yaut took the second.

The windows were rolled down and the air was already blistering hot. Tully leaned his head and let the tepid breeze stream over his face. He closed his eyes and could almost feel a dark, malign presence out there in space, hovering over Earth like a blow about to fall.

The Ekhat. He was beginning to believe in them already—and he did not like the sensation, not at all.

CHAPTER
30

Ed Kralik did not seek out luxury. In fact, extravagance made him uncomfortable because the money spent on frills could have been employed elsewhere to make things safer or more efficient. After boarding the Subcommandant's sleek courier ship, he realized, though, he had subconsciously been expecting luxury at some level.

Instead, it was a tight little vessel without a right angle anywhere, and, though it had no wasted space, was much larger inside than he had visualized. That was due mostly to the difference in human and Jao proportions. With those shoulders and massive bones, they simply required more room to move around. So, what was probably Spartan for Jao spelled a certain measure of comfort for his kind.

Only two seats were evident when they first boarded and he had a momentary flash of riding all the way to this momentous parley seated on the floor, legs crossed like a kindergartner. Others proved available to be folded out from the bulkheads, however, and soon they were all seated and harnessed in.

Aille would be their pilot, a fact Kralik found interesting. Most human officers would have preferred someone else to pilot so they could concentrate on tactical matters. Aille, however, went through his prelift-off check as though he had done this all his life.

Caitlin took the seat next to Kralik and sat with her eyes closed. Dark smudges underlay them like bruises. "He was so upset," she murmured.

He leaned closer. "Your father?"

"No." She sighed. "Dr. Kinsey. I didn't dare call my father before we left. He would have just made it harder."

"The Subcommandant isn't afraid."

"No, but I'm not sure Jao experience fear in the same way we do."

She opened her eyes and he found himself caught up in their blue-gray depths. She had gold striations in the irises. He'd never looked close enough to notice before.

From deep underneath their feet, a whine began and built rapidly into a thrumming roar. The ship lifted without preamble, as different from the lumbering suborbital shuttle as a racehorse was from a steer.

Aille concentrated on piloting and left his service to fend for themselves. From time to time he was vaguely aware of conversations in English, movement around the cabin, the preparation of food. He had eaten just yesterday, so did not partake. Fortunately, whoever had stocked the ship had seen to the needs of the Terrans aboard, else they would have been forced to subsist upon provender more appropriate to Jao. He had observed at the Governor's reception that most humans did not care for traditional Jao delicacies.

He could feel the cabin humming with their suppressed nerves. Even the Stockwell female, injured as she was, got up and moved about, seeking to burn off unused energy. He glanced over at them, but made no comment until finally Yaut suggested the humans view some of the ship's files on the Ekhat.

"Aren't they restricted?" Kralik asked, settling on the arm of a seat.

Yaut blinked. "Why would they be restricted?"

After that, the three humans crowded around the screen Yaut pulled down and peppered Caitlin Stockwell with questions and demands for translation. She bent her dark-gold head over the information and refined her answers until they were satisfied, or as nearly as they could be, considering this was the Ekhat they were studying.

Finally, Tully came and stood beside Aille's command chair. "I do not understand."

"Which aspect?" Aille's fingers flew over the controls, dampening, adjusting.

"Their actions do not make sense."

"Not to a human," Aille said.

"Do they make sense to you?"

"No. Though there are entire kochanata devoted to the study and interpretation of Ekhat research and lore. I was not assigned to any of them as flow indicated Ekhat were not expected in this location for quite some time to come."

"How much longer is it going to take to get there?" Tully asked.

"You mean in terms of Terran units, do you not?" Aille turned back to the control board.

"Yes."

"Jao do not chop time up into small divisions and then count them," Aille said. The readouts were soothing, red and amber and black, weaving back and forth, telling him where he was and how far yet he had to go. His eyes followed the lines almost without effort. "There is a flow to travel, just as there is to construction and study and interaction and every other activity in life. We will be there when our journey is complete, when flow has taken us to where and when we need to go."

Tully's hands clenched in what Aille read as frustration. "'Flow' means nothing to humans. You know that."

"We will speak more on this later," Aille said. "If we survive what is to come, I may familiarize myself with these divisions you are so fond of. For now, I have more important things to consider."

Tully's eyes glittered, green and challenging. There was strength there, if only Aille could learn to tap and direct it. Terrans did not give up easily. That could be of great use in what was to come.

"Rest while you can," he said, letting the readouts wash over him. "We have to travel beyond the innermost planet of your system. As humans gauge these matters, I think it will not be 'soon.'"

Caitlin slept finally, curled up in her oversized seat, head pillowed on Kralik's shoulder, the thrum of the engines and the murmur of human and Jao conversation lulling her until she drifted off.

Sometime later, she woke with a start, cheek pressed to the arm support, and looked up to see everyone crowded in behind Aille, staring up at a large oval viewscreen that had not been activated before. The picture displayed the yellow-orange maelstrom of the sun, swollen to fill the entire display. Her broken right arm twinged as she tried to pull herself back into a sitting position. Her cheek peeled away from the hard armrest, leaving an indentation in her flesh.

"Subcommandant?" Her voice was dry and cracked. How long had she been asleep?

"There," Yaut said, pointing upward. "It will emerge in that sector."

Lines appeared over the display, bracketing an area in the center. Jao numbers flickered to one side, changing rapidly.

She put a hand to her muzzy head, trying to wake up. "Is it the Ekhat ship?"

"They haven't arrived yet," Kralik said without turning around, "but the readings from the gate—they call it a 'framepoint'—indicate it will come through soon."

Slowly, a ball of flaming yellow-white plasma erupted from the surface of the sun, expanding toward them with measured grandness. "God Almighty!" Tully exclaimed.

"Is that a solar flare?" Caitlin levered herself awkwardly onto her feet and went to join them.

"No." Aille's experienced hands flew over the controls. His forehead wrinkled. "That is the Ekhat ship."

"But—" She felt her jaw hanging slack, her ears ringing with shock. "—it's *inside* the sun."

"The framepoint must be formed beneath the surface," Aille said, "in what your scientists call the 'photosphere.'"

Kralik turned around and took her good arm to position her in front of him where she could see more clearly. "But that's not possible," she said lamely. "Inside the sun—they'd just burn up, wouldn't they?"

"The forcefields protect the ship," Aille explained. "For a time, at least. But, no matter what the risk, the framepoint must be created under those precise conditions. Triangulating a point locus in open space does not work. It has been tried many times, and always failed."

The fiery ball grew larger and they could see white-hot gases roiling around its shape.

"Nothing could live through that," Tully said. His head was bowed, but his eyes were riveted on the screen and his fingers gripped the back of Yaut's seat so hard, they were bloodless.

"If that were true," Yaut said, "then the Jao would never have come to this system."

"You use the same mechanics in star travel?" Caitlin said, with a sudden sense of how truly alien the Jao were. Every Jao presently on Earth must have traveled in just this same fashion. Thinking of being down there, inside the sun, surrounded by the hellish fires of creation themselves—the floor seemed to drop out from beneath her feet. She felt giddy and afraid.

"Not exactly the same, but derived from the same technology," Aille said. "The Frame Network was developed originally by the Ekhat. It was later modified by another one of their subject races, the Lleix, and then eventually adopted by the Jao."

Humans had always understood the Jao must have some form of faster-than-light travel, but their conquerors had never explained its exact nature. Whenever humans had asked, the Jao had put them off in much the same fashion as an English colonialist in Africa or India would have dismissed a native bearer's questions regarding the laws of thermodynamics.

"Where are these Lleix now?" Caitlin asked, thinking that here perhaps was the first hint of a future ally, someone they could possibly seek out and apply to for help in ridding themselves of their conquerors.

Aille's ears waggled with concentration. His hands hovered above the controls, changing settings, compensating here, altering balances there. "They were exterminated."

The white-hot ball grew bigger, then its outer layers seemed to slowly explode. Streamers of flaming gases sheared away and for just a second, a dark shape was apparent within the hellglow, angular and unbalanced. Hideous.

"These—Ekhat killed them?" she said as the burning plasma closed again around the alien vessel.

Aille turned, looking up at her from the pilot's seat. His eyes scintillated green and his posture was strangely unreadable. "No," he said, "the Jao did, at Ekhat direction."

"Oh." The blood drained from her face. Kralik's hands tightened on her shoulders as she swayed.

"At one point during the attack, a faction of the Lleix contacted the Jao," Aille said, "and made certain proposals, offering to help if we wished to break free of the Ekhat."

"You must have accepted," Kralik said, "or things wouldn't be as they are today."

"Not right away," Yaut said. "But the Lleix did initiate the idea of separation, which filtered slowly through our culture as we examined it for usefulness. The Jao are not impulsive like humans. By the time flow had brought us to a decision, and then action, the Lleix were extinct."

The ship in the viewscreen shed more fiery plasma, in measured bursts that resembled preconquest fireworks displays Caitlin had seen on old vids; and then again, each time becoming more clearly recognizable as a vessel, though one configured in a truly alien style. The Ekhat ship resembled two tetrahedrons oriented in opposition to one another, with an immense and lumpy almost-pyramid close to what would have been its center. A multitude of connecting girders or beams gave the whole ensemble a strangely delicate aspect.

Caitlin could only begin to guess at the amount of heat being dissipated. She shuddered to think how it would vaporize living flesh.

Finally, with a last stupendous burst of flames that winked out like dying embers against the blackness of space, the alien ship took up a new position, well inside the orbit of tiny, barren Mercury. Aille studied the readouts, his hands busy as his own ship edged closer and the Ekhat ship grew in size until it occupied the entire viewscreen.

At length, he stood, his body taut with *determined-readiness*. "They have activated a beacon," he said. "We must dock and listen to what they have to say."

Tully stared, cold fear in the pit of his stomach, unable to look away. "How big is that thing?"

Yaut flicked an ear, considering, then stood and straightened his shoulder harness. "In your terms . . . about two miles in its greatest dimension."

Tully's nerves crawled. "Are all of their ships this big?" he asked, as Yaut and Aille shed their side arms.

"Yes," Yaut said. "None are smaller, and some are larger."

"It looks incredibly fragile," Caitlin said, "like it's made out of Tinker Toys. I guess it was never meant to actually land on a planet."

Following the Jao's lead, Kralik unbuckled his holster and laid it aside. "If they can't even land, why do they want Earth?"

"Most likely, they do not," Aille said.

"Then what exactly do they want?" asked Tully.

"Nothing we will be able to understand clearly," Yaut said. "This faction, the Interdict, believes contact with other species is polluting."

"Then why are they seeking parley?" Caitlin asked.

"I do not know what is behind this request," Aille said. "And I doubt any of us will, even after it is concluded. Despite their antipathy toward lower life-forms, the Interdict is prone to such requests, so it is reasonable to conclude they extract something of use to them during the experience, though Jao rarely do. Still, there is always the hope one may come away with useful information of some sort. And, in the meantime, while they are parleying, they never attack."

The ship lurched sideways to their present orientation, unbalancing Yaut. The Jao stumbled against Tully and knocked him into the wall. A moment later, Tully squeezed out from under him, scowling slightly. Being "stumbled against" by a Jao was a bit like being stumbled against by a small, furry tank.

"Be warned: there may be more sudden moves. I have surrendered control of this vessel to their systems," Aille said. "That is a requirement in this situation."

Caitlin Stockwell returned to her oversized seat, buckled herself in, and then stared at her clenched hands. In jeans and a white shirt, short hair combed back with her fingers, she looked even younger than her twenty-four years.

The view in the screen changed inexorably until the lumpy pyramidal structure was all they could see. A door in its most proximate side didn't so much open as fade, providing access to an immense docking bay.

Their ship, minute in comparison, drifted into the aperture, which was much larger than Tully had first thought. An aircraft carrier could have sailed through that hole, he realized numbly.

Inside, lights flared in measured red and blue bursts, so bright he blinked in pain. His arm came up to shield his eyes before the viewscreen dampened the intensity. Ghost images danced on his retinas wherever he looked. He blinked hard, trying to clear his vision. "Is that normal?"

"I have studied fifty-two accounts of similar situations involving the Interdict," Aille said. "This effect has never been noted, but every account contains unique elements."

"You mean they never act the same way twice," Tully said, "so that business about them not attacking while we're here, or not killing us on sight, doesn't hold water."

Aille keyed the ship's lock to cycle open. "They are unpredictable, if that is what you mean."

"Will we be able to breathe?" Kralik asked. Tully detected a trace of nervousness in the general's normally stoic military bearing.

"Most likely," Aille said, "although I examined several accounts where the Ekhat either forgot to provide a breathable atmosphere, or deemed it unnecessary."

Caitlin got to her feet and shivered. "What did the envoys do?"

"They died," Aille said.

Yaut nodded him curtly into the front. Tully realized with a start that, following Jao protocol, the three humans would have to go through that damn hatch first. He closed his eyes and reached for composure. No matter what it took, he wasn't going to look weak in front of the Jao.

"Like this," a soft voice whispered in his ear. He looked sideways to see Caitlin Stockwell canting her head just so, shifting her weight to a back leg that was straight while her front was bent, her unbroken arm curved with the fingers extended at precise angles. "*Calm-assurance*," she said, then turned to Kralik on her other side. "Try it. You'll look better, even if you don't really feel it."

Tully exhaled and tried to emulate her stance, head, arms, legs positioned as she demonstrated. The wild beating of his heart eased, but the sickening thrill of adrenaline still rocketed through his body.

Instead of opening, the outer lock simply disappeared in a little yellow flash. The interior of the little ship was flooded with blue so intense, Tully could taste it as a raw bitterness. The air, though breathable, was suffocatingly hot and reeked of oils and tortured bearings.

"Now," Yaut said, "we exit."

There was sound too, like a whole chorus of machines grinding metal against metal. Tully stepped into the open hatch and looked out. Suspended globules of red light played throughout the cavernous space while in the distance dim shapes flitted here and there. He swallowed, trying to orient himself.

"Go!" Yaut said. "Firsts are critical. We must not show fear."

CHAPTER
31

Tully stepped through, Caitlin following, Kralik at her side. The overheated air was so torrid, it was like walking into a wall of heat. By his estimate, the temperature was at least 120 degrees Fahrenheit, maybe higher.

The three emerged at the top of the courier ship's extended ramp and were engulfed in a stinking miasma. *Skunk marinated in rotten eggs*, Tully thought. His eyes watered until he could hardly see. At least this ship had artificial gravity, though it was much less than Earth standard. His foot seemed to float back down to the ramp each time he picked it up so that he felt like he was moving in slow motion and on the constant edge of losing his balance. "Where do I go?" he asked without turning around.

Two of the shapes in the distance oriented on the Jao ship and moved toward it. "Stop at the bottom of the ramp," Aille said from behind. "There is no need to go farther. They will probably come and speak to us, though there is the possibility they will not."

"And if they don't?" asked Kralik.

"Then protocol suggests we wait," Aille said. "Communication has still been known to occur when flow was slower than expected, though sometimes it does not happen at all. There has been conjecture in those instances that the envoy was unable to properly judge the flow of that particular moment."

On Tully's other side, Caitlin was performing *calm-assurance* again. It was an alien ritual, but . . . Tully shrugged, and did his best to copy her. Curve the fingers, he told himself, distribute weight between the front and back feet, arch the neck.

The creatures continued to approach and he began to appreciate how very large they were and how truly immense this landing bay was, too. If an aircraft carrier could have fit through the aperture, a destroyer escort on either side would fit in this central chamber. It must have taken up a good portion of the entire ship. Floating spheres hovered overhead, flashing brighter and more intense with every passing moment. Tully's head was reeling.

Calm-assurance. He concentrated on the stance, holding to it, letting his eyes unfocus, choosing not to see, or at least, not to lose himself in, the visual fireworks. Sweat drenched his blue jinau uniform, plastering the fabric to his back.

"Are those the Ekhat?" Caitlin asked, her voice almost lost in the escalating noise.

"Yes," Aille said.

"But there's only two," she said. "On such a large ship, I thought there would be more."

"No doubt there are," Aille said, "but these are the only two they have chosen to debase through contact with us. Perhaps they would sacrifice only one, except their minds function in pairs. It has never been possible to speak to only one Ekhat, as you would a Jao or human."

"The Interdict seemed to regard all other species as 'unclean,' as nearly as I could tell from the records," Kralik said, "though I admit my knowledge of Jao script is only so-so."

"Very perceptive," Yaut said. "'Unclean' would be a reasonable translation, or perhaps 'tainting.'"

"How long has it been since the Jao escaped Ekhat enslavement?" Tully asked.

The two Jao shifted uneasily, but did not answer.

Caitlin sighed. Sweat was pouring down her face. Grime was rapidly accumulating on what had once been an expensive frilly white shirt, and she did not look like anyone's cherished daughter. "Jao do not perceive time in the same way we do," she said. "They were enslaved until the flow of that particular situation was complete and no longer, as nearly as I understand it, and I admit that I really don't. I doubt any human ever can."

The bursts of light from the hovering globes intensified into a strobelike effect. Inside the pulsating flashes, two immense creatures loomed, their bodies striding toward them on many legs, all of which appeared too fragile to hold their weight. Tully blinked hard, trying to focus.

"I think I count six legs," Kralik shouted over the noise, which was growing louder, "but it's hard to tell with all these special effects."

"Six is common for Ekhat," Aille said, "although many variations on the type have been observed. They are not really a species. More in the way of what your human biologists would call a 'genus,' or even a 'family.'"

The two aliens stopped about a hundred feet away. They had segmented torsos somewhat rectangular in shape. Tully could now make out a row of lidless white eyes circling the immense heads, spaced about a hand's breadth apart. They seemed to shimmer red and blue, which might just be a reflection of the light show. A fringe of what looked to be moss covered their pates and necks. One pair of limbs positioned on the sides of the torso evidently doubled as arms. "Is this display supposed to impress us?" he asked.

"Ekhat do not concern themselves with other species' opinions," Yaut said. "They simply *are* impressive. They do not need to make us believe so."

Caitlin pressed a hand to her head, abandoning any pretense at *calm-acceptance*. Her cheeks had gone fiery red and the breath rasped in her throat. "It's so hot! I think I'm going to pass out."

Kralik took her good arm. "Why don't you go back into the ship?"

"*No!*" Aille's voice was much louder than Tully had ever heard it, even in battle. "She must stay. We must all stay. To do anything else would be exceedingly dangerous."

Tully glanced over his shoulder. Whatever stance the Subcommandant was executing, it sure as hell wasn't Caitlin's *calm-acceptance*. Probably something more like *about-to-shit-a-brick*, he told himself.

The Ekhat began speaking, both of them at once. The sounds were similar but not identical, as though the creatures were singing an atonal song with separate melody lines and verses. If he had thought the grinding metal noise bad, this was even worse. The cacophonous sound of the clicking and warbling voices felt as if they were being carved into his writhing brain. He had to restrain himself from clasping his hands over his ears.

"We notice you," a mechanical voice said from behind him in Jao, "infesting this framepoint."

Tully realized that Aille held a compact device against his chest, probably a mechanical translator.

"We occupy the third planet, not the framepoint," Aille answered, also in his own language, "but the Interdict has never concerned itself with planets. Do you intend to permeate this system?"

The device screeched out a thunderous translation. Caitlin bit her lip and shuddered.

"This infested coldness!" The closest Ekhat wheeled away as the mechanical translator repeated its words. It resembled a tall, elongated spider on those thin, segmented legs, now striding in a intricate pattern around its fellow. "Unspokenness! Unsaiding!"

It was oddly compelling, Tully thought. Each movement was precise and controlled, yet utterly spontaneous, as though its kind were somehow born dancing. The Jao with their formalized stances looked positively wooden in comparison. But Tully now realized that they'd acquired their obsession with postures from their one-time masters.

The bizarre light show was getting to him, more and more. He concentrated on *calm-assurance*, the back leg straight, weight distributed just so, fingers curved.

The two Ekhat prowled closer, their legs twitching. Their hides looked soft and pale, the unwholesome color of whey. They spoke again in that odd dual mode that was not unison. A second later the translator bleated, "Interstitial brilliance surfacing."

"What?" Tully leaned forward, straining to make some sense out of its words, but Yaut jerked him back into place by the shoulder.

The foremost Ekhat stopped, its body pulsating in time with the lights. "Complete Harmony condition of contemplating."

Aille's ears swiveled. "We have not detected any sign of the Complete Harmony in this solar region."

Tully looked at Kralik. "Is that another faction of Ekhat?" he asked in a low voice.

"A competing faction." Kralik shook his head. "There's at least four, if I understood the records correctly."

"Tonal motif unmodulated for this key," the other Ekhat said.

The throb of an organ badly out of tune underlay its voice, before the translator rendered the words into Jao. "Improvisation recommended."

"Jao motif?" Aille said.

"Full dynamics approach this red place," the first Ekhat said. "New notes in a condition of blue. Unharvesting. Heeding take."

"You spoke of the Complete Harmony," Aille said, returning to one of the few bits of sense Tully had been able to make out. "Is it their motif?"

"True Harmony unharvesting," the Ekhat said, turning its head so that the circle of immense eyes glowered down at the small group on the ramp. "Complete Harmony unharvesting. Condition of unharvesting all."

Tully watched the two creatures grow ever more agitated, circling one another as though they were binary suns caught in the wells of one another's gravity. "What does 'unharvesting' mean?"

"I am familiar with the term 'harvest,'" Aille said. His eyes flickered. "It refers to sweeping through a solar system and selecting those species that can make themselves of use. The Interdict, who find all lower lifeforms repulsive, do not harvest at all. Neither does the Melody. But both the Complete Harmony and True Harmony carry out such operations from time to time, depending upon their mood."

"Then 'unharvesting' indicates the opposite?" Caitlin said. "They're not coming?"

"Far more likely, it means we can expect what some call a 'weeding,'" Aille said. "Extermination of all life in this system."

"It sounds like they're trying to warn you, then," Caitlin said. "If the Complete Harmony is coming, maybe the Interdict wishes to become our ally."

Aille turned the translator off. "The term 'ally' is meaningless, applied to them. Interdict does not concern itself with the fate of lower lifeforms, any more than a human on your world would take an interest in the affairs of carrion flies. All Ekhat are xenophobic, but the Interdict is perhaps more so than any other faction. Their horror of interstellar travel is linked by some scholars to the fact that it exposes Ekhat to pollution by lower species. That they lower themselves to intervene here means only that they are using us in some way to thwart another faction."

The taller of the two Ekhat fingered the moss on its head with what seemed a nervous motion and Aille switched the translator back on. "Chord completion!" the creature cried and turned toward its partner. "Condition of minimizing!"

"Watch," Aille said grimly. "What comes next is one of the few common elements in all Interdict parleys."

The two Ekhat orbited one another in increasingly tighter circles. Their arms were extended as though they would embrace in another second, their movements becoming less graceful, more stilted. Tully suddenly became even more apprehensive. Humans did not belong here, he told himself. In fact, nothing sane belonged here.

Abruptly, the taller alien leaped upon the other and tore one of its legs off. Thick white fluid spurted as the injured Ekhat threw back its head and screamed, a terrifying, shrill cry that vibrated into Tully's marrow. Then it tackled the first, crashing with it onto the floor, where the two fought like a pair of tyrannosaurs out of Earth's past, rending gobbets of flesh and casting them aside, bellowing in pain and rage.

Caitlin backed against Kralik and closed her eyes, but Aille and Yaut only watched, their postures identical. "You knew!" Tully said. "You knew this would happen!"

"This is inevitable," Yaut said stolidly. "Members of the Interdict faction consider themselves irreversibly tainted by any contact with lower lifeforms. After communicating with us, they would never be allowed to rejoin their own kind and taint them as well. This is a form of sterilization."

"It's horrible!" Caitlin said. Her face was flushed with the terrible heat, but beneath it, she was as pale as a new moon.

"They are Ekhat," Aille said. "It is their way."

"Then let's leave," Caitlin said. "They aren't going to tell us anything more and I can't bear just standing here while they tear each other to bits."

"It is required that we watch," Yaut said.

The fraghta's gaze was level, his arms positioned carefully. Tully knew he had seen that stance before. Resignation, he wondered, or perhaps aversion?

"It has been well documented that attempting to leave before the matter is concluded," Aille added, "will trigger them to suspend their attack on one another and effect our deaths first."

The carnage slowed as the two aliens weakened, but still they fought on in a pool of viscous white fluid, seemingly determined to rend each other limb from limb.

"How—" Caitlin gave a muffled sob, then tried again. "How could they have enslaved the Jao, if they can't stand even to talk to you?"

"The Complete Harmony advanced the Jao to the point of usefulness, not the Interdict," Aille said.

The taller of the two Ekhat crashed to the bloodied deck like a felled sequoia and lay twitching, the white of its eyes slowly discoloring to yellow. The other, staggering on only three legs now, continued to disembowel its companion until its strength failed. It then collapsed onto the corpse, where it tore weakly at its own flesh before finally subsiding into unconsciousness or death.

The light flashes had slowed. Aille's whiskers shifted and he looked around. "We can leave. Indeed, we must."

Kralik, his arm around Caitlin's shoulders, strode back up the small ship's ramp.

Tully hurried to keep up with them. "I never really believed in the existence of the Ekhat," he said in a low voice as they stepped through the missing hatch. "I thought it was all just Jao propaganda."

Caitlin turned reddened eyes to him. "The Jao almost never lie. Whether that's a cultural trait or something biologically hard-wired in their brains, I couldn't tell you, but they don't. They can and do exaggerate readily—sometimes even wildly—or refrain from mentioning, but they rarely invent from whole cloth. They're just not easily imaginative, the way we are. That's why they find our fascination with novels and movies so peculiar—even distasteful. To them, fiction is a form of lying." She raked perspiration-soaked hair out of her face and shuddered. "They definitely weren't exaggerating about this."

Aille and Yaut climbed in behind them.

"How are we going to leave?" Kralik said. "They've damaged the ship. We don't have a hatch left."

"I can generate a field to reinforce the inner hatch," Aille said. "It will draw our power down very low, but it will probably hold until we reach Terra."

Caitlin hugged her broken arm across her chest. "Do you have spacesuits, in case it doesn't?"

"We have suits for Jao, none for humans," Yaut said. "This vessel was never intended to transport your species."

So the three of them, Caitlin, Kralik, and himself, might not make it back. Angrily, Tully dropped into one of the seats. Just because the Ekhat were too damned impatient to wait until they'd opened the fricking door.

Insanity was one thing, but that plain pissed him off!

After Aille piloted the small ship safely away from the Ekhat vessel, Caitlin found a flavored drink in the ship's stores and offered it around, one-handed. Aille and Yaut waved the carafe away, preferring to analyze recordings of what had just transpired. She could tell by their twitchiness that what they really wanted was a good long swim. Banle had often displayed a similar mussed discontent during long formal occasions and always made her way to the nearest pool afterward.

Humans, though, liked to have something to do with their hands, when they were under stress, so she wasn't surprised when Kralik and Tully drained their cups and asked for more.

Caitlin served them, then retreated to her own seat, her head reeling, suddenly cold with an intensity that indicated shock. That terrible ship with its deranged crew—she could still taste the miasma that passed for their atmosphere, feel that excruciating racket jangling through her bones. Jao had been warning humanity about the Ekhat for over twenty years, but no one had ever really believed them. And, unfortunately, with their lack of imagination and creative expression, they had never been able to fully communicate the depth of the Ekhat's strangeness.

She herself had only thought she understood how alien another species could be before today. Compared to the Ekhat, the Jao were almost human and their rule positively benevolent. The universe was clearly a much more dangerous place than humans had ever credited. She had to get back and warn her father.

"'Unharvesting.'" Kralik looked up from the work station where he was searching the ship's archives. His face was as grimy as hers surely must be, his jinau uniform stained with dark circles of sweat. "So far I can't find any references, but I don't like the sound of it."

"It may not mean an attack," Caitlin said, glad to have something to focus on. Her broken arm throbbed and she needed a bath herself. The Ekhat ship had been sweltering and her clammy shirt clung to her body. Her hair would probably carry that stink for days. "The Subcommandant wasn't sure. It could mean something so totally off the wall, we'll never be able to make any sense of it."

Tully had wedged himself in the back of the cabin, as far from the two Jao as he could get, and had the look of a caged animal. His eyes kept returning to the missing hatch. The forcefield Aille had rigged glimmered green and was all that stood between them and naked vacuum. Some of the brighter stars were visible beyond. "All they had to do was wait five more seconds," he muttered, "and we would have opened the fricking door!"

"Get over it." Kralik punched up another file. "They're aliens. *Really* aliens. They not only don't understand doors or humans— or Jao, for that matter—they don't want to." He hesitated, then scrolled down through the data on the display. "Okay, here it is. I found a reference to 'unharvesting.'"

Yaut crossed the cabin, ears lowered, and bent over Kralik. His whiskers stiffened. "Yes, it is as we thought. Unharvesting indicates extermination. The Complete Harmony must be planning to come through this system and sterilize it." He straightened, the line of his shoulders indicating *worried-contemplation*. "The Subcommandant has already communicated that probability to the Governor."

"Then they'll be ready," Caitlin said. "We'll be able to defend ourselves."

"Harvesting is a ground operation," Yaut said, "which we could defend against using the troops and materiel currently stationed on Terra. Unharvesting, or 'weeding' as it is sometimes known, is an assault on a planetary scale. The Complete Harmony will attack by discharging plasma in Terra's atmosphere. Under those circumstances, tanks, artillery, and foot soldiers will be useless."

"Then we'll have to stop them out here," Kralik said, "as soon as they emerge from the framepoint. We can't let them get close enough to Earth to attack."

Caitlin tried to think. "But Earth has very little in the way of a space fleet, just a few old shuttles, and I've been under the impression that most of the Jao ships from the initial conquest have been assigned elsewhere."

"They have," Aille said, "and long since." His ears were canted very low. "The Ekhat press on many other fronts."

She read *cautious-indecision* in his posture. Not at all reassuring.

"What about the submarines being refitted at Pascagoula?" Tully said from the far wall.

"Didn't you see the size of that Ekhat ship?" Kralik said. "They would be too little, too late. The Jao need to bring back their heavy hitters."

"We have no available ships large enough to be effective in that sort of warfare," Aille said. "The vessels the Complete Harmony will bring will be as large as the one you just saw. Possibly larger."

And that one had been huge, Caitlin thought.

"Earth still has missiles," Tully said. "I think. Unless you Jao destroyed them all."

"They won't be any use." Kralik shook his head grimly. "I understand now why the Jao have never spent any time developing missile weapons. You saw when that ship came through the framepoint. They wrap burning solar plasma around their hulls! Anything you shoot at them will be like tossing a match at the sun. A missile would be vaporized before it got anywhere near the actual hull. And what's the point of setting off a thermonuclear device in what's already a thermonuclear holocaust? As far as I can tell, you'd just be adding more energy to the plasma ball and making it worse."

"Lasers are equally ineffective," Aille said. "In the Jao experience, there is only one effective tactic against Ekhat ships using solar plasma weaponry. It is necessary to wait until the plasma ball has been discharged, when the ship will be vulnerable to lasers."

"But what will happen to Earth if they release that much plasma in our atmosphere?" Caitlin asked.

"Temperatures in the exposed areas will rise rapidly," Yaut said. "Combustible materials such as vegetal matter and building materials will burn. And there will be a rolling blast wave similar to that produced by some of your most powerful weapons."

"You mean a hydrogen bomb?" Kralik stood and put an arm around Caitlin, who realized she was trembling. "This will be as destructive as a thermonuclear blast?"

"Similar, though not the same," Aille said. "In some ways, worse. The amount of energy contained in one of those plasma balls greatly exceeds that of any nuclear weapon. At least, any that either Jao or humans have ever built. However, it is almost pure energy, with little of the contaminating radiation typically produced by nuclear weapons. Many of your species would survive the initial attack, therefore, especially if they have taken shelter below ground. Ultimately, though, if the Complete Harmony makes enough runs through the system, all of your kind would perish. So would all other forms of life on Terra. Enough of those fireballs will strip the atmosphere from a planet."

"How many would die—the first time?" Caitlin heard herself ask, though she could have sworn she was too dazed to talk.

"Perhaps a twentieth or even a tenth of your population, if the Ekhat fleet is as large as usual." Yaut said. "Even a single plasma fireball in the atmosphere can wreak havoc across much of a continent. It is difficult to predict. There are many variables and every world is different."

Caitlin's mind tried to wrap itself around the figures. *A twentieth—at best. Dear God, that'd be something like three hundred million people. More fatalities in a few hours than all the wars in history put together, including the Jao conquest.*

Her palms were sweating. "And you've seen this before? It isn't just conjecture on your part?"

"It is unfortunately quite common," Yaut said. "The Ekhat criterion for 'usefulness' eludes us, so we cannot accurately predict where such 'weeding' will take place."

And Oppuk had known this would come, she thought. *He's had years to arm Earth against just this possibility and hasn't done so, because he's been mired in his self-absorbed anger. Deep down, he's probably been hoping for this all along.*

"We have to do something," Kralik said. "We can't just sit on our hands and wait for them to annihilate us!"

"What can be done, will," Aille said. "I have relayed what little we learned and Governor Oppuk is forming a strategy now. We will join him at the palace."

"How long?" Tully rose and looked from Aille to Yaut. "How long do we have before these murdering bastards attack our world?"

Yaut closed his eyes as though measuring something inside his head. "When the flow is complete."

"I goddam knew you were going to say that!" He sank back against the wall and crossed his arms.

"The flow here feels swift," Aille said. "I fear it will not be long, as humans measure time. A few solar cycles, at best."

CHAPTER
32

Oppuk swam. His advisors hovered nearby, discussing the current crisis, concocting foolish plans that would not work, but still he swam. The water was cool, the salts balanced just so, the scent wrapping him round with the memories of better days, when his future still held promise and he was not tethered to a world doomed by its own savagery.

This marvelous pool would not exist, once the Complete Harmony reduced this world to slag, so he might as well enjoy this small bit of luxury while he could. Nothing in the realm of possibility would save Terra and its inhabitants.

He had not foreseen this, though perhaps he should have. Flow eluded him more often than not, these days, and he found it difficult to judge the pace of events. But Terra was a worthless world, its dominant species treacherous and fractious. How could the Complete Harmony not have perceived that? Of course they would weed, rather than harvest. The Jao should have done the same, twenty years earlier.

Vithrik demanded that he defend this dismal outpost to the best of his ability, though, so he would. At least, if he survived, Narvo would be forced to give him another posting. Somewhere with better seas, he hoped, where he might have a chance to be of use; unlike here, where he had fought this endless holding action against human defiance and truculence.

At length, he emerged from the pool, water sluicing off his head and whiskers. His advisors, along with a few human officials and the members of his service, stared at him like stricken crechelings, waiting for a responsible adult to make sense out of unmitigated disaster.

"Governor." A jinau officer stepped forward. Major General Wilbourn, Kralik's counterpart in command of the Atlantic Division. "What are your orders?"

A trembling human servitor knelt before him, face averted, holding up his ceremonial bau. Oppuk accepted it, then examined the carvings for nicks and discolorations. "We will withdraw Jao ground forces into shielded enclaves. I had a number of them prepared after the conclusion of the conquest."

The general's face was peculiarly colorless. "I see. And your jinau troops?"

"There is no room," Oppuk said. "They will have to take their chances with the rest of the population."

"What about our dependents?" The jinau swallowed with what appeared to be difficulty. "I was hoping we could at least shelter them."

Oppuk let himself fall into the canted lines of *bored-exasperation.* "Can they fly spacecraft? Fight the Jao in vacuum?"

"Well, no, but—"

"Then what is the point of shielding them? We cannot waste limited facilities on those who cannot make themselves of use."

The general's eyes seemed much more white-rimmed than usual. "Governor, please! We're talking about our families, our children!"

Oppuk seized him by the throat so that the human dangled from one hand, choking, arms and legs thrashing. "I weary of you creatures. You are not worthy of serving the Jao." He motioned to Ullwa. "Take this beast outside and put it down."

Ullwa moved forward without so much as the flick of a whisker and accepted the writhing human, her own fist closing around the throat in imitation of Oppuk. The creature was able to emit only a single hoarse squawk before its air was once again cut off.

Oppuk's ears flattened with *disgusted-impatience.* "Any others wish to instruct me on my duties?"

The remaining human officials shuffled their feet and gave one another fleeting glances, most prudently not raising their eyes to his; which were, he was certain, fiery green with displeasure. The

Jao watched him with carefully dampened eyes, each and every one *waiting-to-be-of-use*.

"Then," he said, accepting his shoulder harness from a cringing female human servant and speaking only to the Jao present, "go and organize the preparation of our flotilla, small as it is. We will remove ourselves to behind Terra's moon and wait until after the attack, when the Complete Harmony's ships have made themselves vulnerable. Though we cannot stop them, we can exact a high price for their targeting of this system."

The servitor edged back and forth, fastening his buckles, tugging strips of harness into place. "I will board my own vessel," Oppuk said, "and remain there until the situation is resolved."

The humans parted as he stalked out, their silence following him down the corridor as he headed for his personal ground transport. His nap was still damp and he regretted that the rapid flow of the situation denied him the opportunity to go back and swim one more time. Really, it had been a most exceptional pool.

Outside, he saw Ullwa dragging Wilbourn's body toward the disposal unit. By the angle of the jinau general's head, Ullwa had put him down by the simple expedient of snapping his neck.

Oppuk approved. It would have been absurd to give the human the dignified ending a Jao received when the offer of life was accepted. For a moment, Oppuk fingered the ceremonial dagger attached to his harness, imagining the distasteful task of cleaning human ichor from the blade.

His ears flattened with harsh amusement. Fitting, really, that the humans even had an expression for this situation as well.

Shooting's too good for him.

Aille was relieved to touch down in Oklahoma City. There was so much to be done, he hardly knew where to start.

Rafe Aguilera and Willard Belk, who had flown in from Pascagoula along with Tamt, Wrot and Nath, met the ship out on the tarmac. Yaut had squirted a datastream back to Aguilera and Nath at the refit facility for evaluation. Caitlin, Tully, and Kralik fell into their accustomed places before him as naturally as breathing.

Despite the unusual composition of the group—much more variegated than normal in terms of kochan, as well as of mixed species—they were a fine start on assembling a useful service. But they were too few to do what needed to be done. Some of his kochan-parents had kept services of over a hundred.

If only the flow of the situation were less demanding. *Desperation* tried to insinuate itself into the line of his shoulders and he had to concentrate to amend it to *aggressive-concern*.

As always at this location, the sunlight was blazing down and the sky was a hard blue bowl devoid of clouds. Aille narrowed his eyes against the unwelcome glare.

"What happened to the hatch?" Aguilera, pale, but walking unassisted, gazed over Aille's shoulder as the cooling metal popped.

"The Ekhat," Tully said. "They liked the damn thing so much, they kept it for a souvenir."

Tamt stepped forward, her big-boned body full of *eagerness-to-serve*, which no longer seemed forced. "Governor Oppuk has ordered the Jao flotilla into hiding. He will attack the Ekhat ships after they penetrate the atmosphere, as is normal procedure in this situation. Shall I have your courier ship repaired and refueled, or would you prefer to observe the operation from one of the shielded enclaves down here on the planet?"

Aille's mind whirled. The Narvo was just abandoning this world to an inevitable destruction, not even trying to make the available defenses work? "I will consider both options," he said, attempting to make sense of the situation.

"Sir?" Aguilera held out a folder stuffed with papers. "We've been studying the intel you sent back and have some ideas to discuss with you, a few things that have never been tried before."

"Oppuk will only do what has been done in the past," Yaut said quietly. "It is his strength, to follow procedure as closely as possible. Then no one can say he turned away from *vithrik*. He will be protected in a fortress of custom, from which you can only pry him by widening outward yet again. It is always so, with advance-by-oscillation."

Never, since leaving Pluthrak's comfortable, mist-swathed kochan-house on Marit An, had Aille felt so young, so utterly out of his depth. It was as though unsuspected deep water had closed over his head and he no longer knew in which direction the surface lay.

Wrot flattened his battered ears. His stance was enigmatic, not wholly one thing or the other, though Aille thought he glimpsed an element of *exasperation*.

"What has been done in the past has never worked!" The old combat veteran's whiskers quivered. "I have had enough of Narvo's famous strength. Here, at least, that strength is false. Rigidity masquerading as rigor. Look elsewhere, Pluthrak. Humans excel at *ollnat*, thinking up things-that-might-be. They see beyond the limitations of what-has-always-worked to what-could-work. It is their genius—often also their weakness—but their ability to innovate is the single biggest cause of our long struggle to control this world. Which will never end until we associate with it. Properly!"

There must be a course of action here that satisfied the *vithrik* of all, human and Jao alike. "Does the Governor have orders for me?"

"Not specific ones," Tamt said. Her posture faded into *abashed-regret.* "He has not mentioned you by name, since your report arrived. However, he has ordered the fleet prepared and Jao ground forces sequestered in prepared shelters on the surface. As one of his officers, you are included in that command."

"I must speak with him, after I study Aguilera and Nath's proposals."

"You cannot," Wrot said. His tattered ear gave him a comical aspect Aille had not noticed before. "Oppuk krinnu ava Narvo has already boarded his personal transport and left to join his flotilla, which he's apparently positioning behind this planet's moon."

"Then I will speak to his service," Aille said, though the news left him even more off balance. "They can set up a vid conference."

"I will arrange it," Tamt said. "As soon as possible."

Caitlin shook her head and walked toward the groundcars suddenly. Aille was surprised, as he had given her none of the subtle body clues indicating his readiness for such an action. Ah, well, perhaps Yaut had. Or perhaps she simply misread the situation. She was human, after all, and young. Though she was the most accomplished of her species when it came to bodyspeech, she could hardly be expected to be as proficient as a Jao.

He had Aguilera and Nath ride in the back with him while Yaut took the front, and the others squeezed into the second vehicle. It was undignified, true, but time was short. "Now," he said to Aguilera as the car began to move, "explain your new ideas on how to fight the Ekhat."

Aguilera shuffled through his folder, then held up a picture of the Ekhat vessel, generated during the previous encounter. "Nath and I have studied the specs on this ship in the Jao records. It's surprisingly flimsy, for all its fire power."

Aille leaned his head back against the cushioned seat and closed his eyes, trying to picture all he had learned back in the Pluthrak kochanata. "Yes." Weariness pulled at him like an outgoing tide. It had been overlong since his last dormancy period.

"What about ramming them?"

Aille's eyes opened. "Ramming? With what?"

"Another ship, sir." Aguilera was sitting bolt-upright, his body rigid with clearly recognizable anticipation.

Yaut turned around from the front seat. "Narvo would never waste one of his ships on such an unproven action."

"Not Narvo's ships, sir." Aguilera straightened the edges of the papers in the file. "Ours."

"Are you speaking of Pluthrak?" Aille waggled an ear in desultory *consideration*. "I brought only one ship with me, upon my assignment to this world, and it is hardly suitable for ramming."

Aguilera's eyes were strangely bright for a human. Aille could almost see the thought patterns dancing across them. "No, the ships in Pascagoula, the ones we've been refitting!"

"The submersibles?" Yaut sat back, his snout wrinkled in unalloyed *bafflement*.

"They're as big as any of our Jao spacecraft, and much more massive," Nath pointed out. "They were built to resist tons of pressure from without. Even if they didn't survive the ramming, I am certain they would inflict a great deal of damage."

Aille thought of the ships cradled like children-yet-to-be-born in their berths back in the refit facility. They were indeed heavily armored and of amazingly stout construction.

"And I bet the Ekhat wouldn't be expecting that kind of attack either," Aguilera added. "From what I can tell, neither you nor the Ekhat ever fight inside the sun, because your lasers won't work there. Fancy missiles wouldn't either. But it takes them time to form that plasma shell around their ships, according to the reports. You could bring in a whole squadron of refitted submarines and attack from a number of angles. If your people provide us with their opinion on where the most vulnerable areas lie, we might even be able to take them out before they make a run at Earth."

Aille turned the concept over in his mind, trying to view it as his instructors back in the kochanata would have, or even the fabled tacticians and strategists of the Ebezon Harriers. Would they perceive this as opportunity, a chance to make one's self of use, or dereliction of duty and the purest folly?

"The idea has merits," he said at length. "We will examine it further."

When Aille and his service arrived at the Governor's palace, a blustery wind was blowing out of the direction called "west," scattering twigs and dust and debris, and whistling around the overhang's supports. He stepped out of the groundcar into the blaring sun. There was change in that wind, a subtle lessening of the intense heat of this region, and the promise that *hai tau*, life-in-motion, flow, was making itself known even here in this alien landscape. Balances were altering, that wind said, priorities shifting. It was up to him to decipher how and where.

Aille bounded up the steps, hoping at least a rudimentary staff had been left in place to attend to urgent matters. But the building seemed to be deserted. Several groundcars had been left in the drive, abandoned, while the massive native-style wooden doors stood open.

Apparently, as Tamt had reported, Oppuk had posted both staff and service to his flagship, while dispersing the rest to safe areas and dismissing the unneeded human servants. Across the entire planet, the remaining occupying forces must also have received orders to either flee the surface or conceal themselves in bunkers constructed and supplied against just this possibility.

Aille entered the puzzling gray stone chamber just beyond the doors and closed his eyes, assessing the situation. The artificial temperature controls had been turned off. Within, the heat had already built to an oppressive level, even to Jao senses.

Flow was still fast, events and discoveries occurring at an ever accelerating rate. He could feel the need to act decisively rising like a restless tide in his blood.

He tightened his timesense to slow his perception somewhat. "We need to locate the command center," he told Yaut.

The fraghta's body was stiff with *worried-doubt*. "Think this through before you act. Your orders are clear. Narvo holds *oudh* here. Pluthrak has no official status beyond your assigned rank.

If you disregard Oppuk's orders, he will petition the Naukra to have you declared *kroudh*."

Outlawed. Aille's whiskers straightened. Individuals were pronounced *kroudh* from time to time for outlandish behavior and refusal to honor association, but he had never actually known anyone so designated.

"I hear you," he told Yaut, though he knew the possibility would make no difference. He would do what he had to do as the current flow played out. He knew where his own *vithrik* lay, no matter how someone else might view it. He could do no less than make himself of the fullest use in this situation—and that was not to hide, lying in wait while the Ekhat laid waste to this world, when there were viable alternatives available.

Yaut flicked an ear, willing for the moment to wait and see what might be shaped from this difficult dilemma. He motioned Aille's service into the empty building, then followed.

Silently, the four humans and two Jao threaded through the massive residence. They lost their way in the labyrinth of halls more than once and had to double back. The power was still on and Terra's garish sunlight flooded through the many skylights and windows as they searched, but the emptiness was eerie.

When they finally stumbled upon the command center, Aille was startled to find a tattered-looking human male slumped in the central chair. The man was staring blankly at gleaming real-time tactical displays that had been left running.

"Dr. Kinsey!" Caitlin hurried over to him. "What are you doing here?"

Kinsey's flushed face turned slowly, as though he were a device tracking a faint signal from some other galaxy. His eyes narrowed. "Caitlin?"

She took his hand awkwardly in her left one, her blue-gray gaze probing. "Did Oppuk strand you here?"

"No." He shook his head. The age-grooves in his face were much more pronounced than Aille had ever seen them. "I was told to leave, just like everyone else," he said, passing his free hand over facial skin rough with that peculiar hairy stubble human males were prone to exhibit. "They ordered all the humans in residence back to their homes to wait for instructions. I guess when one of the jinau generals objected—not even that, just pleaded—Oppuk had him killed. But—" He broke off and stared at the display over the strategy table. "I was hoping you might come here, so I decided to stay. I was worried about you. And if I understand the situation properly, it doesn't seem to matter where anyone is, when the Ekhat come. Unless you're in a specially designed underground shelter, you're dead anyway."

Yaut took the human by the arm and levered him onto his feet, then had to support his weight as the man swayed in his grasp. "We must contact the ranking Jao officer left on the planet's surface," he said over his shoulder to Aille. "I will use Oppuk's database to ascertain who that might be."

"Come over here, Dr. Kinsey," Caitlin said, taking the man's arm from the fraghta. "Everything's going to be all right."

"No, it's not," Kinsey said wearily. His lips twisted into a half-smile, half-grimace. "I'm absentminded, Caitlin, I'll admit. But that's not the same thing as absence of mind. So it turns out the Ekhat are not just some myth to frighten recalcitrant children, they're actually coming—and from what I can gather, they're going roast the Earth to cinders."

"Maybe," Tully said. "Maybe not. Rafe has some ideas about stopping them, and the Subcommandant's at least willing to listen." He helped Caitlin ease the exhausted professor onto another seat by the curved wall, where he'd be out of the way.

"Ah," Yaut said, skimming through the records. "Here it is. Commandant Kaul has left also, along with, of course, the Subcommandant in charge of the flotilla. The ranking Jao officer left on the planet's surface, aside from yourself, is Pleniary-Superior Hami krinnu Nullu vau Dree. She has been assigned to a bunker in the moiety called 'England.' I will transmit a command for her to report to you here, along with her staff and service."

"Good," Aille said. "Check the logs and see who else remaining on the surface might be of use." His skin itched almost unbearably and he had to resist the urge to disrobe and scratch. "Until then, I am in desperate need of a swim."

Caitlin looked up from Kinsey's side. "Governor Oppuk certainly had enough pools in this monstrosity, if he didn't punch holes in the bottoms before he left."

Aille's whiskers drooped in *baffled-misunderstanding*. "Why would he destroy something useful in that fashion?"

"Because he wouldn't want anyone else to enjoy it!" Caitlin said.

Aille reflected that if her ears had proper range of movement, they probably would have been pinned in blatant *disgust*.

Yaut looked up from the holo display, his fingers tented. "I wish to do more checking on assignments," he said. "I will join you later."

"I'll stay too," Aguilera said, "if that's all right."

Aille nodded before he realized what he was doing, then wondered at how easily he was picking up human bodyspeech.

Caitlin took up the lead, with Tully on her heels. "I may know where the biggest pool is," she said, "the one in that huge reception hall. I think I spotted the entrance several halls back."

Aille let her precede him. Tamt stalked through the dimness at Caitlin's side as naturally as though they had grown up swimming the same pools. Tully followed the two of them, along with Belk and Wrot. A small service, Aille thought, but one of surprising quality. Perhaps even great quality. If he survived the coming time, he might recruit more, but this was a most excellent start.

CHAPTER
33

Tully paced the length of the pool room while Aille plowed through the water. Waves lapped against the rocky sides of the pool and the ceiling crawled with reflected light. Despite its origins, and the stifling heat, this was a peaceful room. Had the situation been different, Tully might have been tempted to swim too.

Instead, it galled him to be hanging around, ineffectual, while somewhere out there in space a fiery doom approached. He needed to be doing something, anything!

What were the rebels up to, now that Jao forces were withdrawing, he wondered. Did they have any idea of the danger Earth faced? Would they believe it, even if they were told? He was sure he would not, if he had not stood on that Ekhat ship himself and seen those creatures reduce one another to spare parts rather than bear the shame of having been exposed to aliens.

A Jao entered the vast echoing room, an unfamiliar male. Caitlin looked up from where she sat on the floor, arms resting on her knees, then rose and went to meet him. She had disappeared long enough to bathe and change into clean clothes, and now looked composed again, even elegant, in only a simple pair of jeans and a blue University of New Chicago T-shirt. How did she manage that? he asked himself.

Aille, who was knifing through the waves with the energy and speed of a dolphin, had not yet noticed the new arrival, so Caitlin greeted the Jao with a graceful flutter of her hands, which Tully knew must signify something about the status of both speakers to a Jao. "Vaish," she said, which he thought meant something like "I see you." "I am a member of the Subcommandant's personal service. May I assist you?"

The Jao seemed familiar. Tully looked closer at the sketchy facial markings and realized he did recognize this particular one after all. It was Pleniary-Adjunct Mrat krinnu nao Krumat, a mid-level officer from the Pascagoula base. One of the better ones, from a human perspective.

With a splash, Aille climbed out of the pool, then shook the water from his nap, showering the three of them. Tully surreptitiously dabbed at his wet face with the back of one hand, though Caitlin appeared not to even notice the water dripping down hers and soaking into the neck of her T-shirt.

"Vaist, Mrat krinnu nao Krumat," Aille said. "Your haste is appreciated. The flow of this situation is very swift and we have a great deal to accomplish." He cocked his head. "Did you bring the experts from the refit facility I requested?"

"I did." The Krumat's eyes managed a dull flicker before going flat-black again. "They wait outside, ready to be of assistance. Supervisor Nath is here also."

"Aguilera has an interesting theory. He thinks we can use refitted Terran submersibles to attack the Ekhat as they emerge from the framepoint."

The pleniary-adjunct's shoulders slumped. "Why should anyone think those primitive constructions might succeed where a fully armed Jao ship could not?"

Still dripping, Aille slipped into his harness, and Tully found himself reaching automatically to adjust a twisted strap. He was getting too damned good at playing this role.

"Humans excel at visualizing *ollnat*, things-that-never-were," he said, "as we do not. Listen to his ideas and then give me the benefit of your experience."

"I strive to be of use, Subcommandant," Mrat said, "as do we all."

Aille convened his experts in the vast reception hall, letting them swim when they arrived so they would be refreshed and ready to work. The walls soon echoed with their voices as they settled down to debate his radical proposals.

Pleniary Hami krinnu Nullu vau Dree, an older, stalwart female missing most of one ear, arrived from England. She brought with her an experienced staff, one of whom was actually a wiry older human male by the name of Monroe. He had been with her for some time, it seemed, though Hami had kept him largely out of sight.

The most useful addition, though, had been Chul krinnu ava Monat, the Terniary-Adjunct from Pascagoula who had been developing plans for using the human submersibles once refit was completed. He and Aguilera, along with Mrat and Nath and Kralik, retreated off to the side to study diagrams and figures, arguing stress ratios with gestures and in a patois neither wholly Jao nor English.

Once done with his initial discussion with Hami, Aille turned his attention back to his informal panel of experts.

Terniary-Adjunct Chul looked up from a small rotating light-display as he approached. "We think we can damage or even destroy an Ekhat ship while it is still within the photosphere, before it has been able to form the plasma shell. We cannot use lasers or normal missiles inside the sun, of course. But using human-style kinetic energy weapons—the crude and simple projectile ones, not missiles—it may be possible to attack effectively."

His whiskers waggled. "Very difficult, of course. The pilots would have to bring the attacking ships insanely close. Still, if that fails, we could probably destroy the Ekhat by ramming them with the refitted submersibles. The human ships are very massive. Of course, the kinetic energies involved would be so great as to destroy any of our ships also, you understand, no matter how robustly designed. That's almost certain."

Aille pondered the notion. "How would we retrofit the submersibles with such kinetic weapons in the time available?"

Chul gestured at Aguilera. "He has a proposal."

The human stepped forward. "I thought about it some more. We could use the boomers, the big submarines. Just weld tanks onto the former missile hatches and use them as improvised turrets. They'd still be inside the forcefields and we could feed them a cool air supply as well as communications." His face made one of those peculiar human grimaces. "I doubt if it would stand up for very long. Those forcefields of yours aren't really designed to stay inside a sun, just to protect you long enough for the passage through the framepoint. For sure, there'd be some leakage. It could very well be a suicide mission for the people manning the tanks."

Kralik nodded soberly and locked his hands behind his back, assuming a square stance that seemed to mimic *focused-attention* to Aille.

"None of us are eager to die," the jinau general said. "But the alternative is to let these damned Ekhat rain fire down on our whole world and cook us to ashes for reasons that nobody will ever understand. We can either die down here, cowering, or die out there fighting. There's not much difference in the end except if we're successful. Then our deaths would mean something."

"Will enough human jinau volunteer?" Aille asked. "Not many Jao can fit into those submarines, beyond the pilots. None, in the tanks you propose to attach to them. And if you simply order the soldiers aboard, they are likely to be too afraid to fight effectively. That would be true even for Jao, on such a mission."

Kralik stiffened his shoulders in some posture Aille could not quite read. "Yes, they will. I'll lead them onto the ships myself, and I'll be in one of the turrets. I started off as a tanker, so why not end that way? I'm willing to bet—no, I'll guarantee—that there'll be more than enough volunteers to fully man every one of those boats. Twice over, in fact."

Wrot assumed the posture of *gratified-respect*. An instant later, Nath and Hami and Chul mirrored it. After hesitating, and with some awkwardness, Mrat did the same.

Aille studied the postures, then exchanged glances with Yaut. His fraghta's own posture was a rarely used one, that of *truth-finally-accepted*.

Yes, thought Aille. It was indeed so. The posture of *gratified-respect* was reserved by Jao for the recognition of *expected* honor. Respect, of course, that one in their midst had satisfied *vithrik,* but no surprise that they had done so. They could do no other, after all.

He had never seen a Jao on this planet extend that posture to a human. No one, guided by Narvo, expected honor from humans. Those postures, so quickly and easily taken, signified that, like he himself, Wrot and Chul and Nath—even Mrat—had come to recognize how badly the Jao had blundered here, misled by Narvo.

Such a waste. Aille was quite sure that, in their own quiet and uncertain way, Wrot and Nath and Hami and Chul had come to that realization before he'd even arrived on the planet—long before, in the case of Wrot, and probably Hami. No doubt there were many other Jao across the planet who had done likewise. But with Narvo's ferocious rule, and no clear counterposition by one of sufficient status, they had kept their opinions to themselves.

That, too, was a gross dereliction of Narvo's duty. Oppuk had not only failed to complete the conquest with association, he had also disrupted association within the Jao themselves. Gone native, in the worst possible way, killing the messengers.

So be it. The lines of association with Pluthrak in this room were strong and powerful—with the Jao as much as the humans. And now, finally, Aille understood his proper course of action. All of it, from beginning to completion. It was clear and transparent, a more limpid flow than he had ever experienced.

The dance continued. It was time for the next swing. Outward, ever outward. He had always known, after all, that advance-by-oscillation was dangerous. What he had never realized was that it could also be exhilarating.

"It sounds like a promising strategy," Aille said, "but if we follow this course of action, we will be disobeying Governor Oppuk's explicit orders. It is not right that others, only following my lead, should accept that risk. So I will take the responsibility entirely upon myself."

Yaut stiffened, understanding suddenly what Aille intended, then relaxed almost at once. It was most gratifying to see that quick support from his fraghta.

"He will send word to the Naukra and demand that you be declared *kroudh*," Hami said.

"He will not need to. I will declare myself *kroudh*. And will demand that he—or Dano, if he refuses—transmit my posture to the Naukra. And the Bond."

All the Jao present except Yaut slipped into *stunned-disbelief*.

Wrot was the first to recover, his ears quivering with *delight*, then Hami. Hami was more solemn than Wrot, of course.

"It is a shrewd move," she said, "very shrewd. That will relieve anyone who follows you from responsibility, but—with your status and prestige—they will surely do so nonetheless. Narvo has made itself too many enemies here. Most kochan are quietly incensed at the dissociation. Even Dano, I suspect, is unhappy. Subtle as a Pluthrak, indeed."

She now bestowed upon Aille the posture of *gratified-respect.* "You will probably not survive, of course, when the Naukra convenes. But neither will Oppuk, most likely—and, if nothing else, you will have stripped him of his honor. Narvo will be greatly shaken. Shaken loose from Terra, for a certainty."

Aille waved a hand in dismissal, deliberately using a human gesture. "That is for later flow. I will probably not survive until then, anyway. I will pilot one of the submersibles myself, leaving you here in command of the ground forces."

He turned to Caitlin. "Explain to me what would most increase association, in these circumstances."

He wasn't sure she would understand, but she did. After glancing at Kralik, she said: "The human custom is to reserve shelter for the children. Then the females and old ones. It is less important now, for the females, since our customs have been changing in that regard for some time. But the children are essential. Even if only some of them, as a symbol. And they will need to be accompanied by their mothers, or, if they are motherless, some other related adult."

He nodded, again deliberately using a human gesture, and issued rapid orders.

To Nath and Chul and Aguilera: "Begin refitting the submarines."

To Mrat: "You are now in command at Pascagoula. See to it that Nath and Chul and Aguilera are obeyed instantly and fully. Put down immediately any who object, be they Jao or human."

To Hami: "Order the Jao soldiers out of the shelters, all but those needed to maintain the equipment. Tell them to return to their regular military compounds. Put down any who resist."

To Caitlin: "Instruct your father to organize the transfer of human children to the shelters, however many is possible. He can do that on his own authority directly, in this continent. Tell him to establish liaison with the other regional districts so that the human authorities there can begin doing likewise."

To Kralik: "Since most of the Pacific Division will not be needed on the submersibles, have your subordinates organize your division to provide the needed security for the shelters. Jinau troops would be much better for that than Jao regulars. There will probably be some chaos."

"Yes, sir. But we'll also need to get volunteers with submarine and tank experience. There's no time to train anyone from scratch. I'm not sure I'll have enough experienced men in my division alone."

Aille considered. He had a point. "Very well. I will place you in overall command of all jinau forces in North America. Among the three divisions, there should be enough experienced soldiers, yes?"

Kralik nodded, and began to turn away.

"One moment, General. You will need a promotion. What is the next rank up, in human parlance, from 'major general'?"

"'Lieutenant General,' sir."

Aille stared at him. "You will forgive me, Kralik, if I still often find human customs purely bizarre. In what possible sense does a 'lieutenant' outrank—? Ah, perhaps you can explain to me later. 'Lieutenant General' it is."

Now, Aille turned to Tully.

"I suspect the Resistance forces around the globe are going to take advantage of this crisis. You had best resolve it quickly, or things are going to get out of hand."

Tully's chin was very high, the light in his eyes unreadable. "What about this?" He held up his wrist with the black locator band. "I can't 'resolve' anything on my own. I'd need to get to the Rockies—quick—and talk to . . . His name's Rob Wiley."

"You have held your own *vithrik* for some time now," Aille said as Yaut approached. "How does it feel?"

Electricity crackled between the three of them, as though they were all linked in some unlikely fashion. Though the flow of the situation had been swift up to that moment, suddenly it was slow and deliberate. Tully poised on the brink, clearly caught between one impulse and the other, undecided.

Yaut flipped Tully's wrist over and applied the deactivator disk. The black band released into a long coiling strip and clattered to the floor. Tully stared down at it and rubbed the white flesh that had lain hidden beneath it with his other hand.

"You are a member of my service," said Aille, "trusted above all others. We have need of you in this moment and you have the opportunity to be of use as no other among your kind can."

Tully looked from Yaut to Aille, his face tight, his eyes narrowed. He was breathing at a much more rapid rate than usual. "Okay," he said finally, "I'll do what I can." He kicked the black band into the pool as though it were a living thing capable of attack. "But a radio call won't do it. I have to see Wiley in person. He'd never believe I wasn't being coerced, otherwise. The Rockies are a long way off. How do I get there?"

Aille and Yaut stared at each other. Bizarre customs, indeed.

"You are a member of Pluthrak's service," growled Yaut. "Requisition what you need. Command whomever you must. How is this difficult?"

Perhaps the most bizarre thing was the way Tully laughed, all the way out.

CHAPTER
34

Being shut up on the ship put a dangerous edge on Oppuk's temper. He was accustomed to having the resources of his palace at hand, the many luxuries acquired down through his interminable assignment on this tawdry world. Of course, he availed himself of the tiny pool on his vessel, but it was inadequate, to say the least. The salinity and mineral mixture were badly skewed from his personal preferences and he had no expert aboard, indeed, none even within the system, who could satisfactorily adjust it to mirror his home seas back on Pratus.

Nostrils flaring, he shook the execrable water out of his nap. "This slop is not fit to soak a corpse!"

The only member of his service present, Ullwa, bowed her graceful head. "Shall you require my life, Governor?"

He considered accepting her offer, but then decided against it. "Surely even an idiot like you realizes that would leave me with an even less adequate service and still would not improve the water!"

Ullwa bowed her head in *perception-of-truth*. She had a lovely vai camiti, four dark-brown parallel stripes across the muzzle that merged on her cheeks, and she knew how to position herself so that it showed to the best advantage. He had elevated her for that reason and no other, because she was appealing to look upon.

"The Governor is wise," she murmured respectfully, but she kept her eyes tactfully averted and unreadable.

"Have the Subcommandant rendezvous with us, once he refuels his ship and leaves Terra. He and his ship can join us in the battle, when it is joined. It will be excellent practice for one so newly emerged."

"Yes, Governor. I will send the order immediately." The last words came over her shoulder, as she left the room. Hurried out, more precisely, which only increased Oppuk's ire.

He threw himself down onto a luxurious pile of dehabia, all worked with the red patterns of Narvo. His ears danced back and forth between *anger* and *expectation*.

In point of fact, the Pluthrak's vessel was not designed for use against Ekhat warships. But Aille could hardly refuse, and was quite likely to be destroyed in the battle. That would be excellent. Oppuk's craving for the Pluthrak's death was now almost as great as his craving to see Terra destroyed.

Oppuk spent some time enjoying various reveries concerning the Pluthrak's possible end. Battle in space against Ekhat was always dangerous, even in warcraft designed for the purpose. It was true that, for reasons the Jao did not understand, the Ekhat never varied from the odd design of their spacecraft, despite its fragility. Still, the huge vessels wielded immensely powerful lasers. A single hit from such would split the Pluthrak's needle of a ship like a red-hot ax, spilling the survivors into an almost-sure lingering death, cast alone and adrift in space.

He was well into a reverie concerning Aille krinnu ava Pluthrak's last struggling gasps for air in an exhausted lifesuit when Ullwa's return forced him to break it off.

Ullwa withdrew slightly, as soon as his eyes fell on her; just a fraction of an *az*, but Oppuk caught the motion. "What is the problem now?" he demanded, half-angry, half-exasperated.

His servitor's ears waggled with indecision. "I just finished speaking with the Subcommandant. He states that he intends to remain on the planet's surface to organize an assault on the Complete Harmony's ships when they emerge from the frame-point."

"I have not authorized that!" Oppuk jerked onto his feet, scattering his dehabia. Several slid into the tiny pool and began to sink. "We have no ships with enough firepower to be effective in that situation! Any attempt to stop the Ekhat at that stage will just result in an even greater loss of ships and personnel than we are already facing. He is to follow standard procedure to the best of our limited resources!"

The female's whiskers quivered and he thought he detected something quite unexpected in the line of her shoulders. "I reminded the Subcommandant of your orders, and very forcefully. But the Pluthrak declines to obey at this time." She forced her body into *shocked-disapproval*, but it did not hang well on her. Her lines kept slipping and he was certain something else, far less appropriate, lay beneath it. "The Subcommandant says he must follow his own *vithrik* in this matter."

"His own *vithrik*?" Oppuk leaped upon the hapless Ullwa and crushed her to the wet deck with his weight, hands anchored in her luxurious nap. "*Vithrik* is *vithrik*!" he cried into her face. "It does not vary from one individual to the next! I will have him declared *kroudh* for this!"

She writhed within his grasp, ears flattened, then visibly forced herself to be still, surrendering to his authority. Her nap was soft beneath his hands, her scent pleasantly fresh. He ran a finger across her cheek, tracing that oddly compelling pattern.

His own eyes must be blazing with unmitigated fury, but she did not look aside.

"Aille krinnu ava Pluthrak has declared himself *kroudh*, Governor. He asked me to relay that new status to the Naukra. Which I did."

Oppuk stared down at her, his mind dumb. *Declared* himself *kroudh*.

Dimly, in that long-unused part of his mind that had once glided easily and surely through the tactics of kochan rivalry, he realized what a disaster had just befallen him. Whatever happened, Oppuk would be shamed irrevocably. Shamed, and dishonored. Even if Aille died, Oppuk's own life was sure to be demanded by Pluthrak—and, most likely, Narvo would accede to the demand. At the very least, he would be declared *kroudh* himself. He faced ruin and destruction now, not simply exasperation and bitterness.

Advance-by-oscillation. Why did I not see it before this moment? I have been a fool!

He was still staring at Ullwa. She, for her part, was straining every muscle to remain quietly and safely neutral. But then her body and mind betrayed her and he realized *profound-admiration* had crept into her limbs. A posture which was certainly not being bestowed upon *him.*

It was too much to bear. With an incoherent cry, his massive muscles surged, snapping her neck as easily as if she had been human. Then he lurched back onto his feet. The ship's engines thrummed through the hull as he gazed down at the lifeless body.

Aille would follow "his own *vithrik*," would he? As if there could ever be two equally proper courses of action in a situation, rather than one best!

He shoved aside—drove under—that decrepit ancient part of his mind that nattered at him about tactics. It was all nonsense. The Naukra Krith Ludh would never condone such disrespect.

Surely not. Long ago, Narvo had been granted *oudh* status here, first among all kochan on Terra. By refusing to follow orders, Aille had placed Pluthrak firmly in the wrong. Oppuk could demand a price for this insubordination, not the least of which would be Aille krinnu ava Pluthrak's life. He would see Pluthrak itself shamed in the bargain.

He was breathing more easily now, relaxing again. Still, that annoying part of his mind chattered at him, but he ignored it completely.

All that assumed, of course, that the crecheling survived the Ekhat attack on the planet. Oppuk thought it extremely unlikely, but rather hoped the fool did. It would be so much more entertaining to accept his life before an assembly of high-status Jao than to hear he had perished and his ashes were mingled with whatever was left of this lost world.

But, either way, Terra would be no more, Aille krinnu ava Pluthrak would be dead, and Pluthrak's precious *vithrik* would be forsworn—all outcomes very pleasant to anticipate.

His satisfaction ebbed a bit, as his eyes fell on the corpse of Ullwa again. Now he had no servitors left who were even half-competent.

Though, now that he thought about it, Ullwa had not been a servitor. She had been a member of his personal service. The only one left, in fact.

Odd, that he should have forgotten that.

Caitlin, unlike the others, had not left immediately to carry out Aille's orders. "I need to be able to pass along more general guidelines to my father," she said after Tully had gone. "Organizing the children to be taken into the shelters is clear enough. But there's much more that will need to be done. The Jao administrative officials are now either in orbit with Oppuk or in the shelters. Even the ones in the shelters, by the time they get back to their posts, will be too few to handle everything."

Aille's head was cocked in some posture she couldn't quite read. *Careful-consideration*, perhaps, or *subdued-disapproval*? It seemed years since she'd had enough sleep and she felt utterly adrift.

"You are correct," he said finally, ears changing mood too rapidly for her to read. "Contact your parent in my name and communicate our proposed plan of action." He hesitated, his body all *deliberation*. "Tell him to assume command of the continent—and have him tell the other human regional authorities to do the same, on their continents and areas. That includes command over whatever jinau forces are stationed there. He and the other regional authorities can report to Hami, who will be serving as my assistant—and then, after I leave with the warships, as my representative on the entire planet. I do not have time to take direct command myself and the human authorities will be more useful and adept at close supervision in any event."

Surprised, she spread her arms in *willingness-to-be-of-use*, struggling to hide her reaction. The jinau were a large, highly trained and well equipped army, a third of them stationed in North America. A force more than enough to change the balance of power on this world. Oppuk would never have turned authority over them to human officials. What did Aille mean by this?

She left the echoing reception room with its vast pool, Tamt at her side, then dropped by the Subcommandant's quarters to check on Dr. Kinsey. He was sitting in a chair, staring down at his hands. Someone had found him clean clothes in the abandoned servants' quarters, though they were too big. Both the twill pants legs and cotton sleeves had been rolled up. The man's eyes, though bloodshot, didn't seem as exhausted as they had earlier.

"Why don't you come with me?" she said, taking his arm. "I'm going to the communications center to contact my father."

"Certainly," he said, rising. "I'm tired, but I'm sick of just sitting around with nothing to do except wonder what it feels like to be a piece of frying bacon. How are you feeling?"

She grinned wryly. "I feel great, believe it or not. Exhausted, sure, but . . . Like I'm really alive, for the first time in my life. I'm a trusted member of the Subcommandant's personal service instead of a combination flunkey and hostage—and now I'm working to avert the greatest danger this world has ever faced. Best of all, I don't have Banle breathing down my neck anymore. Instead I've got a Jao bodyguard"—she glanced at Tamt, and bestowed on her a smile that was not wry at all—"who's a friend of mine as well as a real bodyguard, and no one's treating me like some stupid china doll to be stuck on a shelf in the corner so she won't break. For once in my life, I'm actually getting to do something important!"

She tugged him toward the door. "And you are too, so get moving. Except for me—and then, only in some ways—you know more about the Jao than anybody. My father will want your advice."

They found several Jao in the palace's communications center, apparently assigned to this duty out of the retinue brought from Pascagoula by Terniary-Adjunct Chul. The two technicians, both female, gazed at Caitlin as though a pet monkey had escaped its cage and demanded to use the telephone. But they established a connection to her father in St. Louis without comment.

She settled in a chair as Ben Stockwell's image formed on the Jao hologrid. Her father was still a vital man, though in his early sixties, silver-haired and tan, and right now looking as worried as she'd ever seen him. His hands twitched when he saw her, and he leaned toward the sensor relay, as though he could reach through it. "Caitlin! It's been days since we've heard from you, and . . . everything's in chaos. Most of the Jao packed up and left, leaving no orders." He looked closer. "What happened to your arm and face? My God, are you all right?"

A lump closed her throat and she hugged her broken arm against her chest. "I'm fine, Dad." Her eyes drank him in and she realized with a rush how much she missed her parents. She'd been too busy to even think about such things in the past few days. "But, like you said, there's a lot of problems on this end. This isn't a personal call. I'm to pass on an official message. How much do you know about the current crisis?"

His mouth thinned. "Damn little. Supposedly we're in danger of an imminent attack by these mysterious Ekhat. Governor Oppuk has ordered all Jao troops either off the planet or into reinforced bunkers. No humans have been offered similar protection, as far as I can find out. If this is a ruse, it's a damned thorough one!"

"It's all true," she said and resisted the urge to lean closer herself. "I—" She broke off, the horror of those two Ekhat savaging one another rising up strong in her memory, then rubbed her eyes. "I've been on one of the Ekhat ships with the Subcommandant. I've—seen them—seen things that make clear to me that the Jao are telling the truth, and they have been all along. The Ekhat are truly beyond understanding. In fact, I see now why the Jao were never able to explain adequately about them. I hardly know where to begin myself. The one thing I can say for sure is that the Ekhat are very frightening."

"You went with the Subcommandant?" Ben Stockwell glanced over her shoulder at the professor. "Why?"

Kinsey raised weary eyes to the image. "She's part of the Pluthrak's personal service now, Mr. Stockwell. In fact, that's how he kept her from being murdered by Oppuk. After Oppuk broke her arm and ordered one of the soldiers to shoot her."

"His service?" Her father half-rose to his feet. "But . . . Jao don't take humans into their personal service. For God's sake, that's the equivalent of being part of their most trusted immediate staff."

Then, seeing the expressions on Caitlin and Kinsey's faces, he fell back into his chair. "I will be damned. So Pluthrak really does live up to the legends."

"There's more, Dad, lots more."

For the next few minutes, Caitlin gave her father a summary of everything that was happening, along with passing on to him Aille's orders.

When she was done, her father's face was very tense.

"In a moment, we'll talk about the political situation. But first . . . Caitlin, do you have any real understanding of what your new position involves?"

She hesitated, then shook her head. "Not really."

"I didn't think so. All you've ever seen is Oppuk's version of 'personal service,' which—by Jao standards, mind you—is a travesty. His so-called service wasn't much different from simple household servants. But that is not the normal pattern."

Kinsey nodded. "No, it isn't. That much is clear to me from my studies, though I still don't quite have a feel for what the Jao ideal really is."

Ben Stockwell ran fingers through his air. "I probably have a better sense, Professor—in practice, if not in terms of book learning. I've been around enough Jao from other great kochan to get the flavor of it. The Dano Kaul is an arrogant bastard—but he never treats his service the way Oppuk does. Certainly not his fraghta, Jutre."

He paused, obviously searching for words. "In human terms, I think the closest equivalent would be the personal staff that our former U.S. Presidents used to assemble around them. Not the Cabinet, mind you, but their own immediate advisors. White House chiefs of staff, that sort of thing."

Caitlin choked down a laugh. Now she understood why Aille and Yaut had been so puzzled by Tully's question. It would have been like a White House chief of staff asking how he was going to pay for the cab fare to carry out the President's instructions.

"I didn't know that," she said. "I knew it was a fairly prestigious position, but—"

"*Fairly* prestigious?" Her father barked a laugh. "Being added to the personal service of a leader from one of the great kochan is like . . . Well, my earlier analogy only goes so far. It's much more what we would call an aristocratic thing. For a Jao, like going from a lowly knight—or a yeoman—to a sudden earldom."

His face was tense again. "But there's one thing you need to understand, Caitlin. In at least one respect, being added to personal service is completely unlike the old White House staffs. It's permanent, not temporary, from all I can tell. You don't quit a great kochan leader's personal service when you're ready to move on to something else. It's . . . not allowed."

"Oh." Caitlin felt a little light-headed. "Well, I can live with that. Aille krinnu ava Pluthrak is . . . impressive. God knows, he's nothing at all like Oppuk." She shook herself. "Besides, we have more important things to worry about right now."

"Caitlin," he said in a strangled voice, "this Subcommandant won't always be stationed on Earth. He's important. If he—and we—survive what's coming at us, at some point, he'll be reassigned and his service will go with him. You might never walk on Earth again!"

He was seeing her dead brothers when he looked at her, she realized, reliving all the long ago loss and heartache, about to be repeated. The Jao had plundered this world, in the process taking almost everything and everyone he loved. He didn't want to lose her too.

"You may be right," she said, "but none of that will mean anything if we don't figure out what to do about the Ekhat first. Forget whatever situation I've gotten myself into and concentrate on that for now. We'll worry about the rest later, once we make it through the next few days."

He nodded and she could tell he was biting back words. And tears, she thought. "All right." After a moment, his eyes moved to Kinsey.

"You're probably the human race's expert on the Jao, Professor, as least as far as their history goes. What's your assessment of the situation? I'm not talking about the problem with the Ekhat. That's a military problem which will either be handled or it won't. I'm talking about the overall political situation. I have a feeling we're sitting on a powderkeg here."

Kinsey sat up straighter and made vaguely groping motions with his hands in midair. Again, Caitlin had to stifle a laugh. Kinsey was unconsciously trying to adopt his favorite professorial stance when explaining something to his students while seated—clasp his hands before him on the desk. The problem was, he had no desk.

After a moment, realizing what he was doing, Kinsey sighed and lowered his hands into his lap. He did clasp them, though.

"Powderkeg is right. In essence, Mr. President, what you're looking at is vaguely analogous to the Indian Mutiny of 1857—except, in this instance, the rebellious natives and their sepoy troops are being organized and led by the equivalent of an English duke. For all practical purposes, except for the flotilla under Oppuk's command on the moon, Aille krinnu ava Pluthrak has seized control of Terra—its military forces as well as its civilian administration. And he proposes to turn over all effective control to the natives, subject to the final approval of him or his appointed staff." He glanced at Caitlin. "Which includes humans as well as Jao."

Ben Stockwell sucked in a breath. "Jesus. Correct me if I'm wrong, Professor, but didn't the Indian Mutiny turn out really bad for the mutineers?"

"Yes and no. In the immediate sense, yes. The British crushed the rebellion, and did so ruthlessly. But it was the Mutiny that finally alerted the British Empire to the British East India Company's misrule of the subcontinent. Shortly thereafter and as a direct result, the East India Company was given the heave-ho and the British Empire started administering India directly. Less than a century later, India got its independence."

Stockwell stared at him. "I see."

Kinsey shook his head. "I don't think you do, Mr. President, not fully. I used that analogy just to focus our thinking, but the analogy only goes so far. There's a least one difference, and it's a big one—two differences, actually. The first is that this 'mutiny' is being led by a very prestigious Jao, not by the 'natives.' That will make quite a difference in the way the Jao look at it."

"What's the second difference?"

Kinsey gave him a solemn look. "The second difference is that—so far—there's been no equivalent of the Black Hole of Calcutta. Where, if you don't recall the history, the Indian rebels murdered a large number of Englishmen in India. Actually, that happened in many places, but the Black Hole of Calcutta was the single most notorious episode. Especially after the British seized on the incident and exaggerated the fatalities for propaganda purposes."

Stockwell sucked in another breath. "I see your point."

"I certainly hope you do, Mr. President. Aille krinnu ava Pluthrak has declared himself *kroudh*. That term is usually translated as 'outlaw.' But the connotations, in this situation, are actually quite different. The term 'outlaw,' for us, is associated with ruffians. For the Jao as well, to a degree, when *kroudh* status is *imposed* upon a Jao. But for a scion of a great kochan to do this, to declare *himself* a *kroudh*—to take what is, from a Jao viewpoint, such an extreme measure—is equivalent to Martin Luther nailing his theses on the door of the Church. It's almost never been done, in the history of the Jao. Only four times, that I know of. And every time it has happened, the *kroudh's* memory in Jao history resonates with our concept of 'noble martyr,' not Jesse James or Billy the Kid. Well . . . 'noble martyr' would be western civilization's take on it. The Japanese might think of it more along the lines of 'true samurai' or 'exemplar of the Bushido code.' In a number of ways, Jao culture is more akin to Japanese than to ours."

"What happened to them?"

"In three of the cases, the Naukra ruled against the *kroudh*—although, in two of those, they still implemented what the *kroudh* had demanded. But all three of them offered up their life, when the Naukra convened, and the offer was accepted. They died."

Stockwell took another deep breath. "The fourth case?"

"That's the most famous of the cases. Another Pluthrak, as it happens, a female by the name of Fouri. In her case, the Naukra ruled in her favor, and her demands were accepted."

"And what happened to her? Did she die, too?"

"No." Kinsey gazed at him solemnly. "But her *kroudh* status was not lifted. Pluthrak attempted to get it revoked, but the Naukra refused. Apparently at Narvo and Dano's insistence."

Caitlin felt her face grow pale. "Oh, Lord."

Her father gave her a sharp glance. "I don't think I quite understand."

"No, you don't, Dad. For a Jao, being a *kroudh* means . . . oh, what would be a human equivalent? Like being an Amish, shunned— except there's no outside world to go to. As if all humans were Amish. You will have no social interaction beyond what Jao consider casual ones. Most of all, you will never have the hope of returning to your kochan in order to join a marriage group. You will be lonely and celibate the rest of your life."

"Celibate, at least." Kinsey unclasped his hands and waved one of them. "Fouri krinnu ava Pluthrak was not lonely. Her entire service chose to declare themselves *kroudh* also, after the Naukra's refusal to lift her status, and spent the rest of their lives in her company. From what I can tell, although there's some misgivings about Fouri's behavior, there's none at all about her service. They are revered in Jao memory—the Great Service, they're usually called—much like the Japanese revere the so-called forty-seven loyal ronin."

"Why celibate, then? I would think that among her service . . ."

Kinsey shook his head. "The thing that's still the most mysterious about the Jao—to us, anyway—is their sexual habits. They obviously don't mate the way humans do, but the difference is deeper than simply a cultural one. That's clear to me. I have no idea exactly how it works, biologically, but the Jao simply don't get sexually aroused except in the context of a marriage-group, and marriage-groups are ultimately what the kochan *do*. It's not something that can be jury-rigged, so to speak. No kochan—or taif, at least—and there's no marriage-group. Don't ask me how it works, because I don't know. Somehow or other—the way their pheromones operate, who knows?—they just don't get sexually active except in a proper social context. Extramarital fornication and adultery are simply unknown among the Jao."

Stockwell gave Caitlin another sharp glance. "And what happened to the service of the other three? The ones who died?"

Kinsey's lips quirked. "Relax, Mr. President. The Jao do not have the custom of burying retainers with the dead emperor—nor the equivalent of *suttee,* where the widow is expected to hurl herself onto her husband's funeral pyre." He shrugged. "As near as I can determine, in fact, most of the services became highly prized individuals after the death of their patrons. The Jao place tremendous stock on loyalty, which they'd certainly demonstrated. In not one of the four instances, did any member of the personal services abandon their patron."

The relief in Ben Stockwell's slumping shoulders was obvious. Caitlin's too, truth be told.

"Enough of that," she said, a bit sharply. "If Dr. Kinsey's right—and everything I can sense tells me he is—your course is obvious. Uh, Dad."

Stockwell managed a grin of sorts. "Don't teach your grandmother—or your wily old father—how to suck eggs, youngster. Yeah, I'd say it was blindingly obvious. First, make sure there's no Black Hole of Calcutta. Second, do everything possible to insure that whenever the dust finally settles—assuming we survive the Ekhat—that Terra is a nice and peaceful and very well-run little planet. So that when the Naukra scrutinize us, Narvo can't claim that Pluthrak opened Pandora's box."

"Exactly," said Kinsey. "What we want is an Indian Mutiny that's really more along the lines of well-organized nonviolent resistance. Call it a sit-in on a planetary scale."

Stockwell winced. "Somehow, I can't imagine the Jao being all that patient with nonviolent protestors."

"Protestors, no. Not if they were led by humans. But led by Pluthrak . . . That's a different story, Mr. President. As long as we keep the peace, they're not going to use Bull Connor tactics—or the equivalent of the massacre at Amritsar—any more than humans would have turned fire hoses on . . . on . . . Hell, I don't know. Eleanor Roosevelt, maybe."

This time, Caitlin couldn't stifle the laugh. "Eleanor Roosevelt! God, don't let Aille hear that analogy."

Kinsey smiled. Stockwell did too, though more thinly.

"I've never met him," Caitlin's father said. "But he seems like a great man."

Caitlin shook her head. "Man, no. Not even close. Great, yes."

She rose. "I'll let the two of you figure out the details. I need to get back." She paused a moment. "I am proud to be in his service, Father. Very proud. And if the Naukra rules against him—assuming any of us are still alive—I will remain in his service, if he wants me. *Kroudh* or not."

On her way back to Aille's command center, Caitlin pondered all the implications of her last statement.

Sure, why not. What the hell, it's not as if I'd have to stay celibate. Speaking of which, it's time I settled that. And since my damned cloistered life has left me with all the aplomb and sophistication of a turtle when it comes to sex, I'd better just tackle it straight up. At least I'll look like a simple fool instead of a fumbling idiot.

She decided that "flow" didn't require her immediate return to Aille's presence. Instead, calling up her exhaustion-fuzzy memory, she took a different corridor, looking for the chamber that had been turned into an impromptu military headquarters. She managed to find it fairly soon, even though she'd been muttering to herself the whole way and only dimly aware of the turns she was taking.

"Great, just great. I may be the only twenty-four-year-old virgin in America, outside of religious orders. I can't believe I'm doing this."

When she got to the chamber, she stuck her head in the entrance. Kralik was there, to her relief, discussing something with Hami.

"Ed, could I talk to you a moment?" She blurted it out immediately, only realizing then how nervous she was. Still more nervous, she fluttered her hands. "I mean, I don't want to interrupt you—"

He studied her for a moment, with a quizzical expression, then glanced at Hami. The Jao pleniary-superior assumed a posture which Caitlin thought was *relaxed-patience*. She wasn't sure. It wasn't a posture she'd seen any Narvo adopt often. If ever.

"There is time," Hami said. "Not much, but some."

A moment later, Kralik had her by the shoulder and gently eased her out of the chamber.

"Okay, Caitlin. What's up?"

*   *   *

She never remembered exactly what she babbled for the next few minutes. If she babbled at all. Kralik claimed afterward he had to pry it out of her, like a clam, but she thought his memory was suspect.

She'd never be able to prove it, though, because when she was finally done Kralik's smile was both cheerful and relaxed. Very cheerful, and even more relaxed—and it was the second of the two that she cherished the most.

"I'd be delighted, Caitlin Stockwell. Deeply honored, too. Yes, I understand you might be in Pluthrak service the rest of your life. I already knew that, actually. I find that I don't care, since this all assumes that we're both alive a few days from now, and if we are . . ."

He shrugged. "Who cares? After all, I'm in his service too—and, as it happens, I've seen the movie about the forty-seven loyal ronin. It was a good movie. I liked it."

It was a very masculine smile, too. At the moment, that didn't mean much to her. Not under the immediate circumstances, between exhaustion and a broken arm and an impending battle. But she knew it would—a lot—if they had a future.

"Do you have a preference in engagement rings?" he asked softly. His hand came up and caressed her cheek.

She swallowed, covering his hand with her own. "Nothing fancy, Ed." Her voice sounded squeaky, even to her. "Just . . ."

She couldn't say the last words. In a few days, Ed Kralik was going to be in a tank turret in the middle of the sun, fighting the galaxy's most insanely murderous species. Even if she survived, he probably wouldn't.

Just something to remember you by, if nothing else.

CHAPTER
35

Aille received a priority communication from Pluthrak that night. He had already surrendered to dormancy, but came fully aware when Yaut's shadowy form appeared beside his pile of dehabia. He brushed at his ears, shook out his whiskers, and stood. The situation's flow was even more urgent than it had felt earlier. He had fully expected contact from his kochan, though not so soon.

He followed the fraghta through the corridors of the palace, wondering if Tully would be successful in swaying the Resistance. Caitlin remained back in the quarters he'd appropriated, along with Willard Belk and Dr. Kinsey, all three utterly dormant at the moment with that peculiar unresponsiveness that made their species so vulnerable to nighttime attack.

The temporary signal staff, two female techs provided by Terniary-Adjunct Chul, awaited him uneasily. They did not turn around when he entered, but the lines of their shoulders betrayed misgiving. One glanced up from the familiar sinuous Pluthrak sigil in the holo tank, then assumed *neutrality*, struggling to express no further opinion of what Aille's progenitors most likely had to say about his latest actions. It was a difficult stance to achieve under the circumstances, he was certain.

The older tech was out of Binnat, by her *vai camiti*, and no doubt familiar with this world and its complicated politics, both Jao and Terran. Light from the main image tank flickered across

370

her snout. "Subcommandant," she said, her ears precisely neither up, nor down, "shall we clear the facility?"

"That would be appropriate," he told her. "I will notify you once your presence is again required."

Ears back, she left, drawing the remaining tech with her. Yaut stood gazing up at the waiting tank. "You risk much by this course of action. Do you want me to compose a return message and plead on your behalf? I can verify the extreme speed at which decisions have been forced upon you."

Aille considered. But, despite the risks, he sensed the existence of possibility here, where there had been none before—a chance to be of use in a truly meaningful, even unique way. "No."

Yaut released the message from the buffer and stood back, his ears *doubtful*.

The sigil exploded into a shower of golden light, then solidified into venerated Meku himself, kochanau over all Pluthrak. His noble face with its impressive *vai camiti* gazed into the image tank as though he could see Aille. But this was a recorded message, transmitted through the framepoint via drone during the last solar cycle.

"Offspring," he said, "Narvo has lodged a complaint with the Naukra Krith Ludh—that you refuse appropriate orders and are now conducting independent and unsupported action instead. They are demanding that you be declared *kroudh*. And now we are given to understand—also by the Naukra—that you had earlier sent a message on your own behalf declaring yourself *kroudh*."

Meku had adopted a stance of *admonishing-caution*, modified with a thread of *interest*. "We have investigated the situation, as best we can from a distance, and feel that, though your stance may be correct, we cannot at present support insult at this level against Narvo. If you wish to persist, we will not contest the registration of your *kroudh* status, thus freeing you to do what you feel necessary." His eyes took up an odd glint . . . anticipation, perhaps?

"We did not send you to Terra to be cautious," he said, "but neither should you spend yourself unwisely. Some choices, however intriguing, can never be amended. Their final cost may be more than you wish to bear."

Admonishing-caution was now replaced, in that smooth and silky manner that was always Meku's style, with *assessment-of-opportunity*. "Be aware, also, that the Bond of Ebezon is already moving, without waiting for the Naukra to deliberate. A Harrier task force is on its way to Terra. Quite a large one, we believe. We are not certain, but we suspect the Bond has been seeking for some time to intervene in the Terran situation. If so, the possibilities are vast. Consult closely with your fraghta, of course, but also follow your own sense of things. This flow seems . . . very powerful."

The transmission ended. The tank dissolved into random flashes of golden light that darted like insects before flickering out.

"The choice lies before you, then," Yaut said, his body curiously in flux, now *bereaved*, now *proud*, now *aggravated*, as though the fraghta were too overwhelmed to know what precisely he felt. "The prudent path would be to accede to Oppuk, follow his orders and conduct the remainder of this operation as custom dictates. If you do so, I am almost certain the Naukra would remove your *kroudh* status. It seems clear enough—the Bond already intervening!—that many are unhappy with Narvo's conduct here."

Aille turned to him, skin once again prickling with anticipation. "I do not think—not really—that is what Meku wants. You heard him yourself: The possibilities are vast. Not only in terms of finally forcing association on Narvo, but, what may be even more important, in terms of the war with the Ekhat. What if we can stop them, using these new tactics? Think of the gain! To be able to save worlds, instead of simply revenging them."

"Duty—caution, at least—dictates that I advise you differently," Yaut said, slowly. "But in the end, you are ava, root kochan, while I am only vau, subsidiary. It is not bred in me to abandon you, if you decide to go on."

"Send a message back," Aille said, "and route it to Oppuk as well. I accept *kroudh* status. What I do from this point forward no longer reflects on Pluthrak." He gazed at the empty tank. "I act for myself alone."

"And for this world," Yaut said, "though I doubt they will understand the honor you do them this day."

In that, at least, Yaut proved to be wrong.

Perhaps. It was hard to say. The manner in which Terrans expressed their appreciation of honor was most peculiar to the Jao way of looking at things.

After the signal techs returned, they suggested that Aille might want to see something else. Quickly, the two techs changed the settings for the holo tank to relay the images that were being transmitted on the human communications web. What Terrans called "television."

Aille and Yaut stared at the images. Gigantic masses of humans thronging in many cities—on no planet but Terra could such immense mobs be assembled—and engaging in the most bizarre rituals.

The Binnat tech explained. "President Stockwell sent out instructions and counsel some time ago to all human authorities and communications centers. The human comm web ever since has been spending all its time reporting on the current situation. Shortly thereafter, these assemblies began taking place."

"If you can call something like this an 'assembly,'" snorted the other tech. "I am reminded more of the swarms of fish on my home planet during spawning season."

"Summon Kinsey," Aille commanded. "I want him to explain this to me. I think it is time I added him to my service anyway."

Yaut hesitated, his posture suggested *apprehensive-doubt.* "He will be very difficult to train properly. From what I have seen of him, I think he is oblivious to *wrem-fa.*"

"I will not use him for official occasions, then. Still, he is shrewd in his own manner."

Yaut did not argue the matter further. Shortly thereafter, he returned, more-or-less herding a rumpled-looking Kinsey into the room ahead of him. The human scholar still had the look of semi-dormancy in his eyes. But he became alert quickly, once he observed the events being shown in the holo tank.

His first words were meaningless to Aille. "Jesus H. Christ." Thereafter, his speech became more coherent, although he continued to pepper his words with that same peculiar phrase. Aille was only able to grasp a portion of what he was saying, in any event.

"—called 'demonstrations,' sir—also 'rallies'—and they're an ancient human custom—"

Here came some meaningless words involving the complicated history of something called "bill of rights" and "petition in redress of grievances."

"—though this isn't that kind of rally, sir, but what you'd call a 'demonstration in support'—that's obvious not only from the banners and placards but the nature of the speeches—"

Yaut was starting to look as if he were about to apply vigorous *wrem-fa,* whether or not the human scholar would respond to it. He was not, in some respects, the most patient of fraghta. Aille decided to forestall him.

"Scholar Kinsey! Most of your words are sheer gibberish to me. Simply explain one thing: *what is the import of all this?*"

"Oh." Kinsey rubbed his face with his hand, a peculiar gesture Aille has noted before on several humans. Tentatively, he thought it was the approximate human equivalent of *singleminded-concentration.* "Well, sir, the gist of it is that it looks as if the human race—most of them anyway—has adopted you as their new hero. And Pluthrak as its—the word we'd probably use is 'champion' or 'party of preference,' terms which have no direct Jao analogue so far as I know."

He pointed at one of the images in the holo tank. It was that of a young human male with a strange mask on his face, covering his eyes except for slits. "But it's mostly in support of you, personally. Humans like to personify abstractions."

Aille thought back to his first time on Terra, when Aguilera had tried to explain to him why humans would give gender to weapons. "Yes, I have seen that. But how does that young human's unusual head-covering—I see many others with the same—"

Understanding came to him, in a flash. He'd seen humans with those grotesque attempts to paint *vai camiti* on their faces, at the reception Oppuk had given him shortly after he arrived. For a moment, anger began to suffuse him—Yaut too, judging from the angle of his ears.

He restrained the anger, remembering Wrot. And softly repeated the old bauta's words aloud, as much for Yaut's benefit as his own. "Crude and coarse Wathnak may be, young Pluthrak, but I was taught even as a crecheling that to begin by assuming disrespect is a grave offense against association."

Yaut's whiskers quivered, but then his posture also reflected his ebbing indignation. "Yes. Here too, it seems."

Aille studied the images in the holo tank, giving particular attention to the human script on the multitude of banners and placards being carried in the demonstrations and rallies. Most of them were variations on the themes of "We Want Pluthrak"—that was clear enough—but there were also a number of inscriptions urging a long life upon Aille.

Bizarre, those were. A being lived as long as he or she did. Pure mysticism to think otherwise. What was important was to live with honor, and die well.

Still, he understood that the sentiment involved was favorable, however superstitiously worded. What disturbed him, however, were the large number of inscriptions which proffered great insult to Narvo. Some of them, he was quite sure, were outright curses.

"That must cease," he stated firmly. To one of the Jao techs: "I need to speak with Stockwell. The father, not the member of my service."

The techs were efficient. Very shortly, the image of the human administrator floated in the holo tanks. After Aille explained what he wanted, Stockwell's expression seemed dubious.

"I'll do what I can, sir, but I really don't control these demonstrations and rallies and marches. What you're seeing is pretty much a spontaneous outburst—all over the world, not just here in North America—in which twenty years of anger is erupting. Fortunately, most of it seems to have channeled into support for Pluthrak, and yourself. But the hatred for Oppuk, and all things Narvo, is by now bred into the bone on this planet."

The last expression was murky, although Aille understood the gist of it. Nor was he surprised. But still he pressed onward.

"It is essential to avoid insult to Narvo in this situation. I cannot emphasize—"

To his surprise, Yaut interrupted him. "Leave it be, youngster. You can no more prevent this than you can control this planet's orbital cycle. And, besides, you are worrying too much."

Aille stared at him, confused. It was normally a fraghta's duty, after all, to be the guardian of custom and propriety.

Yaut's whiskers bristled, his ears upraised and his stance proclaiming *ferocity*. "The Bond will arrive here before the Naukra. The Harriers are less concerned with propriety than the old kochanau. Much less. So let them see the hatred and rejection Narvo has created—and the alternative you have provided for association. It will do no harm, be sure of it."

A bit uncertainly, Aille deferred to Yaut's judgement. In any event, other and more pressing issues immediately came to the fore.

First, Tully sent a message. *Wiley is willing to come to negotiate in person, if you will provide him a guarantee of safe conduct.*

Again, Aille had to settle Yaut's outrage at the implied insult. Aille had studied more of human history than his fraghta, and understood that humans did not necessarily follow long-established Jao principles of honor in this matter. Not surprising, really. A species that could come up with the expression "killing the messenger" would hardly have the Jao automatic respect for envoys and negotiators.

But, no sooner did Aille assure Tully—and through him, Wiley—that his safety would be assured, than it was necessary to change the arrangements. As soon as Aille instructed Kralik to make the arrangements for the parley with Wiley, Kralik informed him that a new development had just occurred.

"We've got a problem, sir. Might be a major one. The Resistance in Texas has launched an uprising in Dallas and Fort Worth. I can't determine yet how much popular support they're getting from the citizens of the area, but they've got a number of combatants and seem to have seized at least part of both cities. My recommendation is . . . ah, perhaps a bit bold."

Aille's ears pitched forward in *forthright-invitation*. "Yes?"

"I think we need to smash this, immediately and as hard as possible. In other to do that, however, I'd have to order the entire Central Division into northern Texas—which would mean pulling the Second and Third Brigades out of Colorado and Utah. That would leave Wiley and his people unrestrained—and over half the shelters are located in that area of the continent. In the Rocky Mountains, I mean."

Aille saw immediately the logical end point of Kralik's proposal. So did Yaut.

"I agree," said the fraghta. "We may as well discover immediately if this Wiley human can behave honorably."

Aille nodded, a part of his mind interested to see how automatic that human gesture had become. "Do as you see fit, General Kralik. As a member of my service, you can speak with my authority."

After Kralik ended the holo transmission, he stared for a moment at the empty tank. "I'll say this for the Jao," he mused. "Pluthrak, anyway. They sure don't waste a lot of money on red tape."

He smiled crookedly and ordered the tech—a human one, this

time, since it required human technology—to transmit a message back to Tully.

> *Change of plans. Resistance in Texas has launched a major assault in Dallas-Fort Worth. I intend to crush it, using the entire Central Division. With the authority vested in me by Aille krinnu ava Pluthrak, I am reinstating Colonel Rob Wiley back into military service, with the brevet rank of major general. He is now in command of the new Mountain Division, which consists of whatever forces he has. I will expect General Wiley to maintain order in the area and see to the safe and speedy transfer of as many children as possible into the Jao shelters in the Rockies.*
>
> *Don't screw this up, Rob.*
> *Tell him, Tully. Tell him.*
> *Ed Kralik, Lt. General*

In sultry Pascagoula, Rafe Aguilera found himself pacing the rows of the black submarines long after midnight. The immense building rang with the sounds of last-minute work. His shoulder still ached from the bullet he'd taken in Salem, however small caliber, but the base doctor said it was healing nicely. He stared up at the massive cradles, while the refit went on at a feverish pace that made the previous rate look like loafing.

Spotlights glared as another disemboweled tank was lowered onto a boomer by a massive overhead crane. The tank's drive engines had been removed and heavy-duty air-conditioning units hurriedly installed in the space left open.

In essence, what had been a tank was now a turret with a beefed-up environmental control system which—they hoped—would be enough to keep the crew alive during the coming battle. The forcefields would protect against the sun's heat and radiation, but only up to a point. What that point might be, no one knew—but the tanks, being the most exposed, would be the first to give way.

As soon as the hooktenders pronounced the tank settled into place, the welders swarmed over it and began to work. Meanwhile working from within the submarine hulls, other technicians began installing the environmental and communication conduits and links.

Aguilera waved at one of the foremen, Scott Cupton, up on

scaffolding. "Hey, Scott, come down! I want to go over these specs with you."

Cupton waved back, dragged a forearm over his sweaty face, then began clambering down the ladder attached to the scaffolding.

Rafe Aguilera laughed. He was going to make this work, going to be "of use," as the Jao liked to put it—and it was such a rush, that, for just a second, he thought he finally understood how their furry brains worked. Sort of.

Early the next morning, before daylight had fully asserted itself, Aille wrapped up the final details of their pieced-together defense in Oppuk's command center in Oklahoma City, then piloted his courier ship back to Pascagoula. Yaut, Caitlin Stockwell, Wrot, and Willard Belk accompanied him.

Aille could feel the moment drawing near when they must take what assets they had gathered and launch for the system's frame-point. Events raced like the swift center current of an ever deepening river, a sure sign they must go soon.

He thought Oppuk must feel it too. All Jao must be aware how close the moment was. He wondered who among them were more nervous, humans stumbling through this timeblind, or the Jao, who new only too well how short time was.

It was midmorning, as humans liked to term it, when his courier ṿ set down again on the tarmac at Pascagoula. He sat at the ·ds longer than necessary, relishing the feeling of the controls ː own hands. The sensation of his senses extended through- ẹ ship as though its hull were an extension of his own body. ṇes he regretted that the needs of Pluthrak determined he ˙ of more use as a military officer rather than a pilot. He ẹ been satisfied to be no more.

dcar pulled up even before the five of them had time ˙he ramp. Aguilera jumped out, his face flushed with "Subcommandant!" he cried. "Come to the refit floor. see this!"

ʼrot hastily stepped before Aille, as did Belk. Yaut's the unseemly exuberance of Aguilera's greeting, ˙t to notice.

vehicle, which was, as always, meant for lesser ˙s. Yaut squeezed in after him, but Caitlin balked. "There's not enough room for all of us, and this isn't my area of expertise anyway. With your permission, I'll catch up later."

"Nor is it mine," Belk said, his shoulders expressing *polite-reticence* quite well, for a human. "I will follow you to the refit facility."

Aguilera was strangely agitated, glancing from one to the other, his brown eyes dancing. Even Aille could decipher that much of his emotional state, though nothing more precise. The dark-haired human didn't even seem aware he had provided insufficient transport for Aille's party.

Caitlin, he was sure, wanted to take advantage of the opportunity to visit Kralik, who had come down here the night before. Belk, as always, was simply being practical.

"Yes, that seems sensible," Aille said.

Aguilera threw himself back into the front seat and motioned to the driver, a human female. "Take us to the refit floor and don't spare the ponies!"

Aille was still puzzling over exactly what "ponies" were and why he hadn't seen any up until now, when they pulled up before the huge, hangerlike building.

"Okay," Aguilera said, leaping out to open Aille's door before he could do it himself. "I wanted you to see this, now that we've gotten a number of them installed. I know it looks absolutely crazy, but I really think it will work."

Nath and Chul met them at the entrance, and they wound their way through the cradles holding the oblong, dull-black ships. The pace of work had heightened to what he might term a "frenzy." Lights gleamed, cables and power conduits snaked across the floor and up through the scaffolding. Humans scrambled over the great hulls, intent on different tasks, calling to one another. As they neared the first ship, Aille studied the tank being welded onto the back of the hull.

"What do you think?" Aguilera asked eagerly.

In truth, Aille did not know what to think. His ears waggled with *baffled-indecision*. It was one thing to hear a proposal this radical and quite another to see it brought into reality. He realized now he had not really understood Aguilera's idea, when the human had first described it. The ship looked so—misshapen, even ludicrous.

Chul sensed his unease. "It will work, I think, Subcommandant. There is no way to know until it is put to the test, of course, but if we can get close enough to the Ekhat ships, those tank guns should be able to do a lot of damage."

"Even in a star's photosphere," Aille murmured. It was not so much a question, or a protest, as a simple expression of wonder.

"It should work," Aguilera said forcefully. "We'll be armed with DU sabot rounds. Each one is fifteen kilos' worth of uranium driven by liquid propellant. The penetrators will be traveling more than a mile a second. We'll lose the outer layers in the heat, but enough should be left to punch holes in the Ekhat ships and wreak havoc inside. If nothing else, I'm thinking the sabot rounds should damage the Ekhat ships enough to let the sun's own heat do the rest. Those forcefields are essentially the same as yours—that's what Nath and Chul tell me—and they won't work all that well once the structural integrity of the hulls starts to weaken."

Later in the solar cycle, Aille convened a panel of Jao engineers recalled from bunkers to inspect the vessels. They looked askance at the Terran experts attending, but listened to Aguilera's ideas.

Most were skeptical, but agreed the tolerances and stress ratios were within the realm of achievability. It was estimated they had enough time available to outfit fourteen submarines, as well as the human crews needed to staff them. Pilots, though, were another matter. Humans had no real experience in flying spacecraft, even in ideal conditions much less the conditions that would exist within the sun's photosphere. So, although most of the crews would consist of humans, the pilots would need to be Jao.

Oppuk had taken the most experienced ones with him to lie in wait for the Ekhat. Thus far, Chul had only been able to find eight pilots skilled enough for the task—nine, counting Aille himself. Wrot suggested they recruit retired combat veterans who had made their homes on Terra, then volunteered to track them down.

"It must be soon," Aille told him. "Flow accelerates with every twitch of my skin. Do you feel it? They will come through in a few solar cycles, no more."

Sober-agreement stiffened Wrot's lines, then the old soldier disappeared into the base's comm center to reach out to all his old contacts.

*   *   *

Between the work of assembling the crews for the submarines and the sudden crisis in Texas, Kralik had gotten hardly any sleep for longer than he could remember.

Caitlin found him in the comm center, just having finished a discussion with Major General Abbott, the commander of the Central Division. She touched his cheek with fingers like silk. "My God. You look half-dead."

"We'll all be dead if we're not ready before they open that framepoint," he said, but his own hand reached up to take hers. Her fingers were long and slim.

"You're off duty, mister," she said, "as of now."

With that, she dragged him back to his quarters where she fed him a ham sandwich, then closed the curtains and told him to lie down.

"I don't have time," he said wearily. "None of us do."

"You're not Jao," she said, "so you can't get by with a few hours of halfhearted dormancy like they do. You have to get some real sleep if you want to be any use when you launch."

She stifled his protests with a hand over his mouth and more-or-less forced him onto the cot. Then, after positioning a pillow behind his buzzing head, she stretched out beside him, pulling his arms around her.

She felt wonderful in his arms, her skin fragrant with scented soap, her hair like satin against his cheek. He closed his eyes, feeling as though he were sinking into a thick black fog. "Just a few minutes then," he murmured.

"Forget about that. You'll sleep as much as you need." She nestled against him. Her neck, her cheek, her throat, all were cool fire, and he recognized the scent she wore, juniper, like the high forests of New Mexico he'd roamed in his youth. "Forget everything, but here and now."

He tried to summon a suave leer. Clark Gable style.

"If that's supposed to be a leer," she chuckled, "you *really* need to get some sleep. I've had squirrels ogle me more lustily than that."

"S'just my nat'ral gentlemanliness. Your broken arm, y'know. I wouldn't feel right . . ."

He fell asleep in mid-sentence. Caitlin didn't get to sleep herself for two hours. The spartan cot put their bodies in very close proximity, and, even clothed—even with a splinted arm—she quickly found herself becoming very frustrated.

It was a nice feeling, in a way. Or, at least, it would be—if Ed was still alive in a few days, to deal with it.

PART VI:
Inferno

"You will not intervene?"

The Preceptor's response was an elegant tripartite stance, *assured-negation* coupled with *understanding-of-risk.* "No, Tura. The Pluthrak is already surpassing my hopes. Let us see by how far."

"If he fails . . ." Tura's own stance was *aghast-anticipation.* "Hundreds of millions of humans may die, before we could arrive."

"Yes. All beings die. What matters is that they die well, making themselves of use."

CHAPTER
36

No other intelligent species would ever really understand the Ekhat. That was something the Ekhat knew themselves; and, in the knowing, found further proof of their own destiny. Further indication, rather—the Ekhat, recognizing none of the limits of formal logic, did not recognize the concept of "proof." The universe was in constant flux and opposition. A thing which could only be understood as the unfolding dance of the Ekhat with their surroundings, whose only sureness was the music of reality and the eschatology of the dance itself: the completion of the Ekha, when the very notions of "Ekhat" and "Universe" could no longer be distinguished.

Human scholars, had any such been able to penetrate the murk surrounding all things Ekhat, might have said they were psychopathic dialecticians run amok. Jao scholars would have understood them better, perhaps. The greatest of them might even have come to see the reflection of their creators' mentality in the very bones of Jao cultural patterns. Even human ones, as fragmented and discordant as those were. There was a sense in which the Jao, as they emerged into sentience under Ekhat control, had translated the peculiar Ekhat mentality into social concepts and behavior. Shaping them—twisting them, the Ekhat would have thought—into a form suitable for the creation of an intelligent polity. "To be of use," stripped of its messianic endpoint and the sheer horror of its methods.

But all those terms were human or Jao, and the Ekhat would have recognized none of them. There was much about the Ekhat that was still mysterious even to themselves, much less any alien species they encountered. Even such basic things as where and how they evolved. That they *had* evolved, no Ekhat doubted. "Evolution" was one of the few concepts that the Ekhat shared—overlapped, it might be better to say—with Jao and humans. But on which of many possible home planets, and in what original form, no Ekhat remembered any longer and True Harmony only claimed to approximate.

None of it mattered, really, not even to True Harmony. However and wherever they had come into existence, all Ekhat agreed on their destiny. The division was simply over the means to that end. The universe would eventually be Ekhat. Not "controlled" by Ekhat—they were not imperialists in the sense that humans or even Jao would understand the term—but would literally *be* Ekhat. The subject and object of reality no longer distinguishable in a new synthesis.

The Ekhat understood that the eschatology was unfortunate from the viewpoint of augment species. But they cared not at all, any more than Beethoven cared that the paper upon which he penned his music was the remains of a tree's carcass, or that the fuel that lit his endeavors was made possible by the death of animals. What did that count, against the *Ninth Symphony* or the *Hammerklavier*?

Nothing. All was subordinate to the music with which the Ekhat were creating a true universe. Rather, the music which *was* the true universe.

Rendered very approximately, those were the stray thoughts of the Point as it entered the choreochamber. Seeing the Counterpoint entering from the opposite gate, it set the idle thoughts aside. The view on the huge screen dominating the far wall of the chamber made clear that emergence was near. Time to begin the dance. Concentration and care was needed, lest the sacredness of the moment and the greater moments to follow be marred and rendered ugly.

Point begins, always, so the Point spoke the first words. They would have startled a human, had any been present; and misled them into assuming a concordance of mind.

Let there be light!

As if on cue, the screen brightened. The solar photosphere was emerging through the frame point. A sunspot swam into view, and the Counterpoint's voice rang through the chamber.

Light against darkness! Darkness from the light!

Without opposition, all was meaningless. The Point took its first dancing steps toward the center, gleeful with renewed assurance.

It passed the ranks of the Huilek, assembled on the great floor of the chamber, looming over them like a spidery brontosaurus. To a human, the Huilek would have borne some resemblance to erect four-foot-tall chipmunks, except their fur would have seemed sparse and more like cilia than actual fur. The little creatures who maintained much of the ship's functions were trembling with fear and religious ecstasy. The Dance of the Gods was beginning, and those who survived would penetrate further into the state of grace. Those who did not would have found the state of grace.

It was early yet, but since the initial chord had been so powerful, the Point decided to add punctuation to the melody. It was confident the Counterpoint would follow its lead. Ekhat musical creation was characterized by much in the way of improvisation. A human jazz composer, had any been watching, would have understood he was seeing a jam session. Of course, he would also have thought it was a jam session being played by homicidal maniacs, and would be desperately looking for an elephant gun— but, again, all those concepts were alien to Ekhat, and beneath their notice.

The Point reached out and plucked one of the Huilek. Holding the creature up in two great forehands, it took a few more prancing steps toward the screen. As the sunspot swelled, like some ghastly flower, the Point opened the Huilek to match. Blood and intestines flew everywhere.

All levels of creation the same!

To the Point's pleasure, but not surprise, the Counterpoint immediately echoed. In dance as well as music, plucking its own Huilek from the ranks assembled on that side of the choreochamber, and shredding the creature.

Life out of death, death out of life, so Ekha unfolds!

Point and Counterpoint reached out again, this time plucking a Huilek in each forehand. The four little beings were crushed like grapes, adding their juice to the moment. Ekhat did not recognize the distinctions between "music" and "dance" and "painting." All art was one, and one with reality.

The well-conditioned Huilek began their own ululation. The chant was designed, insofar as the limits of the creatures permitted, to augment the blessedness of the moment. A human might have called it another voice added to the madrigal; assuming, of course, the human could have kept its composure. Ekhat aesthetic notions were radically different from those of humans; even stoic Jao would have been unsettled by the blood and grue now splattered all over the chamber.

But the Huilek did not waver. Not for the first time, the Point was pleased by the creatures. True, the Huilek lacked the sure capability of the Jao and the cleverness of the now-completed Lleix. But, on balance, they were a more suitable leitmotif species. Less fractious; less likely to inject unwanted discordance into the tune.

The Point began the first circuit of the dance. Moving in a slow and stately manner, now, to provide pleasing contrast to the sharp opening chords. Surely, the Counterpoint matched its steps.

The lengthened moment allowed the Point to muse again. It found itself wondering whether the new species soon to be completed might have made a suitable leitmotif. It was difficult to estimate, even had the Ekhat possessed more information than the simple name "Human." Of all the aspects of reality, intelligence—even the limited intelligence of leitmotif species—was the most unpredictable. The Point's thought was not one of complaint. That same unpredictability, of course, accounted for the strength of its chord.

The *discordance* also, True Harmony argued. But the Point had shifted to Complete Harmony in large part because it found True Harmony too limited. Discordance had its place also.

That remembrance, for a moment, brought something very like amusement to the Point. Leitmotif species, it knew, tended to think the Ekhat were "divided" into something they called "factions." They even introduced the bizarre notion of "politics" to the equation.

All nonsense. The superstitions of semi-sentients. All Ekhat were one, united in the unfolding Ekha. Even the Interdict was needed, to add the necessary Limit. But One was meaningless without Many; Unity, empty without Opposition. Thus True and Complete Harmonies maintained their dance, creating the Ekha in the only way creation could occur, with Melody adding its own still further Opposition.

The idle thought bloomed into the music, giving the impetus to sudden action. Daring, true, but the Point thought it would make for a tasty atonalism. Complete Harmony was always more daring than True, even when, for the purposes of the moment, it took True Harmony's methods for its own.

They had come to complete a species without even gauging it for leitmotif, after all. An abrupt and atonal chord should be given its place in the opening melody, even during stately moments of the dance. The Point, passing another rank of Huilek, smeared several of them across the floor with a hindleg. Across the chamber, Counterpoint immediately matched.

The Huilek ululation yammered response. There was something a bit hysterical in the sound, which pleased the Point. Even the dull-minded Huilek could sense that this was to be a great dance.

"The first one's coming through," came the voice in Kralik's earphones. It was obvious from the tone that Aguilera was doing his best to stay calm, but was having a hard time of it.

So was Kralik, for that matter. Flying through a sun is not, all things considered, the best way to relax. Even leaving out of the equation the fact that a battle was looming that would likely kill all of them.

Kralik studied the screen in front of the tank commander's seat, trying to block everything out of his mind except the image of an Ekhat warship emerging from the frame point. It was . . .

Difficult. The Jao technology that enabled a ship to exist at all inside a star's surface—for a time, at least—also shielded it from the radiation and magnetism. But it couldn't turn the actual visual imagery translated onto the screens into anything less frightening than it was. Nor, although the same Jao technology provided the ship with its own gravity field and thus protected everyone from being crushed by the sun's gravity and the g-forces produced by their travel through the photosphere, could it eliminate the visual effects of that travel upon the human stomach. The former submarine was, in effect, swooping through a solar roller coaster. Rising and falling and veering this way and that depending upon the turbulence of the granular cells and the pilot's skill at using them.

Aille himself was piloting Kralik's vessel, and the young Jao leader was proving once again what a superb pilot he was. But not even a pilot as good as Aille could prevent the ship from being cast about like a woodchip in a maelstrom.

And "maelstrom" was what the ship was traveling through. The photosphere was the outermost layer of the sun except for the chromosphere, and was dominated by granular cells. Ever since Aille's fleet of converted submarines had penetrated the photosphere, the ships had been swept into the vertical circulation of those cells. Normally, spacecraft emerging from a framepoint within a solar photosphere left as rapidly as possible in order to escape those granular cell currents. But there had been no way for Aille's fleet to do so, given that they were trying to lay an ambush for the arriving Ekhat.

Most of them had survived. The Jao and human technicians, working together, had calculated that the converted submarines could withstand the stress of the granular cells. And, indeed, they had. But two of the submarines had gotten trapped at the bottom of the circuit, swept down into the supergranular cells that formed the sun's convection zone. They were gone, and certainly destroyed by now. Jao technology was not magic, after all. Those supergranular cells would carry the ships all the way down to the radiation zone, over a hundred thousand miles below. Nothing material could possibly survive that passage, no matter how well shielded.

Still, twelve ships had survived. And now the Ekhat were coming through. Whether Aille's fleet could survive the encounter with the Ekhat remained to be seen, of course. But at this point, Kralik found the prospect of a battle something of a relief.

He squinted into the screen, trying to spot the emerging enemy warship. He was unable to do so, which was not surprising. The image on his screen was produced by the same computer that provided Aille and Aguilera's view, but the screen itself was of human design and neither as large nor as sophisticated as the holo tank in the submarine's command deck.

"Coming through," Aguilera's voice half-whispered in the ear phones. "Taking shape now. God, that's a big mother."

Kralik could see it now—a faint, still vague outline against the flaring turbulence, visible mainly because it was made of straight lines and nothing else in the sun was. A moment later, he spotted two other outlines taking shape, then another, then two more, then two more again. Then . . .

Nothing. Eight ships, in all, which was what the Jao had guessed would be the most likely size of the Ekhat invasion fleet.

The first of the Ekhat ships was now a solid image in the screen, no longer fuzzy.

"Big mother," indeed. There was no way to gauge size through direct visual examination, since the sun provided nothing in the way of recognizable scaling objects. The swirling granular cells that filled most of the screen could have been mere meters across, for all Kralik could tell, instead of the hundreds of miles they actually were. But the computer provided a scale for him, and . . .

Big mother. At its greatest lateral dimension—call it "wingspan" except the term was silly applied to such a weird-looking contraption—the Ekhat ship was almost three miles across. Granted, most of the ship was empty space contained within the spidery latticework of the peculiarly shaped craft. But even the central pyramid where the Ekhat were located was half a mile wide. The submarine swooping toward it was like a minnow attacking a whale.

Kralik shook his head, dispelling the image forcefully. It wasn't *that* bad. Say, a catfish attacking a shark. Except this catfish had very sharp teeth, and this shark had very thin skin.

He didn't find the new image all that comforting. Fortunately, his gunner was a man with either less of an imagination or just more in the way of sheer grit.

"We'll chew 'em right up, General. You watch."

Kralik was a little amused at the man's tone of voice. Awkward, it was, as you'd expect from an enlisted man suddenly finding himself with a lieutenant general as his tank commander. On one level, of course, there was something absurd about Kralik's insistence upon personally fighting from one of the improvised turrets. But . . .

Why not?

If they didn't succeed in destroying the Ekhat here—most of their ships, at least—everything else became a moot point. Kralik had decided that his willingness to personally fight in the engagement, in the most dangerous position, would have a good effect upon morale.

Which, it had. Civilian morale, to his surprise, perhaps even more than military. For the first time since the conquest, the human race had living heroes again. And not just human ones. Kralik had watched the relayed images of the rallies and demonstrations himself, and quickly understood what Aille had not. With few exceptions, and those only among diehard members of the Resistance, the human race had taken Aille krinnu ava Pluthrak for their own with all the fervor that Scot highlanders had once embraced Bonnie Prince Charlie.

In the turret, he grimaced, remembering the battle of Culloden and the harrowing of the glens thereafter. That was perhaps not the most auspicious analogy he could have come up with.

The enthusiasm for all things Pluthrak extended to the members of Aille's personal service, human even more than Jao. Ben Stockwell was a canny politician, and he'd seen to it that all the stops were pulled out in the propaganda being broadcast throughout the human communication network. That official network was still very extensive, even twenty years after the conquest. The Jao on Terra had always been too few to simply suppress human activities and institutions. Much like the English in Africa and India, they'd had to use those existing institutions as the instruments of their imperial control.

Now, the institutions were slipping the leash, although Stockwell was being careful to maintain the formalities of Jao rule. Given Aille's immense personal popularity with humans, that had been easy enough. Even the pirate TV and radio stations that seemed to be springing up all over like mushrooms— on the internet, like wildly infectious bacteria—spoke at least respectfully of Pluthrak.

It was dangerous to do otherwise, in fact, and not because of the Jao. The Resistance in Texas had discovered that, after they began their uprising in Dallas-Fort Worth. Before General Abbott and his troops had even entered the metropolitan area, a full scale civil war was raging. Most of the inhabitants of Dallas-Fort Worth were hostile to the Resistance, because of its past behavior in the area, and given Aille as a rallying point around which to organize, they'd quickly taken up arms against them. "Arms," in fact, not just as a literary expression. The ever-practical Jao had never bothered with the hopeless task of trying to disarm the human population of its hand weapons.

Kralik had finally been able to speak to Rob Wiley, by then. Through a full comm link, not simply a telephone connection.

"Hammer 'em, Ed," had been Wiley's terse advice. "Frankly, the best favor you could do the Resistance is getting rid of Kenny George and his thugs in Texas."

Kralik had considered the advice, for a moment, as he studied Wiley. The colonel—major general, now—looked not too different than he had the last time Kralik had seen him, after the surrender following New Orleans. Older, of course, but the fact was that Wiley resembled his twenty-year-earlier self a lot more closely than Kralik did.

"I knew they were bad," he commented mildly.

Wiley snorted. "Bad? The Resistance—as you damn well know— is about as politically homogenous as a bouillabaisse. All the fascists gravitated to Kenny George in north Texas. KKK, Posse Comitatus, white citizens' councils, so-called 'militias' and 'survivalists'— you name it, George has got 'em. You sure as hell won't find anybody of my color in that crowd. Nor any of Hispanic or Oriental descent."

Wiley was a black man. It was a mark of his capabilities that he'd quickly risen to be the central leader of the Resistance in the Rocky Mountains, an area whose population was predominantly white.

Not too surprising, perhaps, given the general prominence of black people in the Resistance in most parts of the former United States. Oppuk had never made the attempt to understand his human subjects, so he'd never thought to use long historical grievances to pry America's black population away from its former political allegiances. He'd simply left the black population to suffer even worse than ever—after slaughtering a disproportionate number in Chicago and New Orleans.

"Okay, Rob," he'd said, smiling grimly. "Hammer 'em, it is. I don't imagine Orrie Abbott will have a problem with that." Like Wiley, Major General Orville Abbott was black.

Hammer them, he had, and Abbott had been none too concerned about human legal customs. He was, after all, a jinau officer—and he followed Jao practices when suppressing rebellions. In broad outlines, at least. The Jao never bothered with curlicues like "hanging them from lampposts."

The so-called "Dallas Uprising" had been over before Aille and his little fleet even lifted from Terra. Kenny George had decorated a lamppost himself.

*   *   *

The submarine was now racing toward the first Ekhat warship. Aille was taking advantage of a sudden swirl in the currents to bring them alongside as quickly as possible.

As quickly as possible, and as closely as possible—a task made all the more difficult because their target was the central pyramid, which required threading a trajectory through the outer lattice. Kralik hissed before he could restrain himself. For a moment, he thought that Aille had decided to ram the Ekhat, even though they'd all agreed that ramming was a tactic of last resort. Given the speeds involved, ramming was almost sure to destroy the submarine that tried it despite the flimsy construction of the huge Ekhat ships. And even if the submarine itself survived, the tanks that had been welded onto its back to serve as makeshift gun turrets would surely be stripped off. And the men inside it with them, including a certain Lieutenant General Ed Kralik, the laws of physics being no respecter of ranks and titles.

"Here we go!" Aguilera exclaimed—as if Kralik needed to be told. The huge flank of the Ekhat ship loomed like a cliff. Aille's superb piloting was going to bring them into point-blank range.

"Just say the word, sir," murmured the gunner.

Kralik's turret was the lead one. The submarine, a former boomer, had had eight tanks welded onto its back, each one above a former missile hatch. Four on each side, providing the submarine with the equivalent of a broadside, assuming the pilot was skilled enough to bring them into proper position.

Aille was skilled enough. "Light 'em up," commanded Kralik.

The tank's 140mm cannon erupted. The depleted-uranium penetrator blazed across the mile distance in less than a second. It looked like a tracer round, not because it was designed to be but simply because the surrounding ambient temperature—six thousand degrees Kelvin, once the penetrator shed the sabot and left the shield around the submarine—stripped away the outer layers of the projectile.

But not much of it, not with a muzzle velocity of over two thousand meters a second and less than a mile to travel. Just enough to allow Kralik and the gunner to follow the trajectory and see the fifteen-kilo penetrator strike the hull of the Ekhat warship. They managed to get off four shots before the submarine's own trajectory carried them past the Ekhat central pyramid and Kralik called off the firing.

The computer immediately confirmed what had been Kralik's own estimate. The four turrets able to bring their guns into line had hit the Ekhat warship with fifteen out of sixteen rounds. Kralik's own turret had fired the only miss, and that simply because it was the first in line. Kralik's last shot had been fired after the submarine carried too far past the enemy. The penetrator sailed off into solar oblivion, adding its own miniscule trace of heavy elements to the untold jillions of tons already there.

"Didn't look like much," muttered the gunner, half-complaining.

Half, but only half. Like Kralik, the gunner was an experienced tanker. The Ekhat ship was so gigantic that neither one of them had expected the pyrotechnics that always resulted when a DU penetrator hit another tank. But they knew full well that fifteen sabot rounds would have turned the inside of that ship into a charnel house. That much of it, at least, that the rounds could penetrate.

From the outside, it didn't look like much. Fifteen holes, mere inches in diameter, stitched across a vast surface. But once those projectiles penetrated the thin shell of the Ekhat ship, each of them would turn into an explosion of uranium fire. A bloom of sheer heat which would ignite almost anything it touched.

When it hit a tank squarely, a DU penetrator essentially incinerated everything inside. That wouldn't happen here, with the much greater volume of the Ekhat ship to absorb the blow. Neither Kralik nor Aguilera really knew exactly what would happen under these circumstances. But what they suspected, was that the explosions would send molten and half-molten droplets of metal and other substances scattering through the Ekhat ships. If they were all designed like the Interdict ship—and the Jao records seemed to indicate as much—that huge central chamber would become an abattoir. A good portion of it, at least.

His previous fear was gone, now, replaced by cold fury and something that was almost battle lust. Kralik didn't expect to survive, and for the first time in his life understood something of what the ancient berserks must have felt.

"Damn, that Jao bastard's good!" exclaimed the gunner.

Indeed so. Somehow, Aille had converted another careening granular swoop into a flank attack on a second Ekhat warship. Bringing the submarine even closer than before, less than half a mile away at its nearest approach.

Unfortunately, the passage was also even faster, so neither Kralik nor any of the other turrets were able to get off more than two shots. And, again, Kralik's last shot sailed off as the submarine carried past the target.

CHAPTER
37

The discordance was extreme, true, with whole ranks of Huilek swept aside in mid-ululation. Still, the blazing fireflowers brought ecstasy to the Point and Counterpoint, causing them to shift into their own frenzied syncopation.

Short-lived, though, much too short-lived. Another series of percussive fireflowers removed the Counterpoint's legs; then, another series ruptured the Counterpoint altogether and turned its remains into a blazing pyre.

For a moment, the Point tried to maintain the dance alone. But the Critic intervened.

End the dance. We are under attack. The leitmotif creatures must resume their normal posts.

The Point was confused, even more than it was outraged. Attack was impossible within a sun. But then, observing more ranks of Huilek destroyed by another percussive round, the Point was forced to shed that function-mode. The Melodist emerged and began shouting commands.

To your posts! To your posts!

Many of the Huilek had already broken ranks, fleeing toward the far gate of the choreochamber. The Melodist crushed several in the way of reprimand before giving up the enterprise. Futile in the face of such discordance. Best to begin a new melody altogether. It began striding toward the gate.

Two strides only.

The tanks that contained the aromatic compounds necessary for the olfactory component of the dance were located in sections of the outer hull. Several of the tanks had been damaged and now one of them burst open entirely, spilling its complex organic substances into the choreochamber. Exposed to the intense heat, the chemical compounds ignited in a flash explosion that sent the huge body of the Melodist flying across the choreochamber, shredding its limbs along the way and carbonizing its integument. When the Melodist landed atop a crowd of fleeing Huilek, crushing them in the process, it was already half-dead. Its last thoughts, blurred and confused, were simply wonder at the meaning of the extreme dissonance.

In the control chamber of the craft, the Critic stared at the image being relayed from the choreochamber into the holo tank before the Conductor. The Conductor voiced the Critic's own thoughts.

The work is not finished and cannot be. Many Huilek have been completed before their time. Without a Melodist, the remainder will be useless. The craft cannot be operated without its leitmotif components.

The Critic understood the thoughts, but still groped at their meaning. Everything had unfolded too quickly, too unexpectedly.

The Conductor, naturally more decisive, provided meaning also.

My function-mode ends.

That much, the Critic could comprehend. With a quick strike of its forelimb, using the genetically-modified forehand-blade specific to its own function-mode, the Critic completed the Conductor.

The Lead, after gazing at the corpse of the Conductor, lowered itself to expose the thoracic joint.

The craft will be swept down, to premature completion. There is no way to prevent it, with neither Conductor nor Melodist nor sufficient leitmotif components. My function-mode ends.

The Critic completed the Lead. Then, in quick succession, as they each reported the end of their own function-modes, the three remaining Ekhat in the control chamber.

Of course, it completed the eight leitmotif components also present. The Critic was forced to seal the gates to prevent the augment species from escaping. The squeals of the little Huilek added further disharmony to an already dismaying performance.

When it was alone, the Critic changed the view to display the craft's exterior. Already, it saw, the craft was plunging down one of the granular currents. Soon, with no Lead to guide the way, it would be swept into one of the supergranular cells; and, soon thereafter, would be completed long before it reached the radiation zone.

That was a pity. The Critic would have found solace, even ecstasy, in the music of death-in-creation. But there would be nothing, beyond the increasing discordance of a craft being shattered by crude convection.

The Critic completed itself. Not without difficulty; being forced to strike four times, very awkwardly, until the forehand-blade found the thoracic ganglion.

"Until this moment, I did not really believe," Yaut said softly, almost whispering. "That ship is out of control. Thrown out of control, by your guns. It is doomed. Truly, I did not believe it could be done, until now."

Aguilera glanced at him, startled by the fraghta's tone of voice. Yaut's mood usually ranged from unflappable to caustic. This was the first time Rafe had ever seen him shaken by anything.

He and Yaut were standing in the center of the sub's control room, just behind Aille in the pilot's seat. By the time he looked back at the holo tank, the Ekhat ship had vanished into the solar fog. Fighting a battle in the sun's photosphere was like a dog fight in heavy overcast, except these clouds were fiery bright. An ambient temperature of six thousand degrees—and more turbulent than any storm cells in Earth's atmosphere. Were it not for the force-fields, the submarine would have been ripped apart by the shear stresses even before it melted and vaporized. What made the experience even more disconcerting was that the sub's artificial gravity field kept those in it from feeling any of the vessel's sudden and sharp movements. There was a complete disconnect between someone's tactile perceptions and sense of balance and what they could see in the holo tank.

Aguilera winced. He had suddenly realized that one of the dangers they faced, which he simply hadn't thought about, was the very real possibility of two submarines colliding with each other. There was no way to maintain electronic communication in the photosphere. For all that Jao comm technology was more highly

advanced than human, it still depended on electromagnetic signals. Here, trying to send or receive such signals would be like
trying to talk in the middle of a waterfall.

About the only thing they could still do was detect other ships
by their faint magnetic disturbances, until they drew close enough
for visual spotting. But those magnetic signals were fuzzy. Just
enough to give the sub pilots a sense of where another ship was
located—which they then tried to zero in on as best as possible.
Given that the solar turbulence made "steering" here more akin
to white water rafting than what Aguilera normally thought of as
piloting . . .

It was a grim thought. Two or more submarines, targeting the
same Ekhat ship, might easily be thrown into each other by sudden shifts in the currents.

But, since there was nothing Aguilera could do about it, he
pushed the worries aside. He had other concerns, anyway, and more
predictable ones.

"What's the turret environmental status?" he asked the human
tech monitoring those readings. Kenny Wong, that was.

"Pretty good," he replied, "except for Turret Six. Their environment's degrading faster than the others, and by a big margin. I
think there's a leak somewhere. A material leak, I mean." Wong
glanced at the screens in front of a woman seated next to him,
which monitored the forcefields. "Jeri's the expert, but those readings look okay to me."

Jeri Swanson grunted sourly. "Okay to you, maybe. To me they
look like my mother's wedding gown when they hauled it out of
the trunk for me to wear the first time I got married. Can we say
'tattered and moth-eaten'?"

She glanced up at Aguilera. Seeing the look of alarm on his face,
she grunted again, even more sourly. "What? You were expecting
something else? We're in a fricking *sun,* Rafe." Jeri went back to
studying her monitors. "Relax. We're still a ways off from a field
collapse."

Aguilera swallowed. He'd been so busy and preoccupied getting
the tanks converted to turrets that he had only a dim awareness
of other aspects of what faced them. "Will you have any warning, if the fields are about to fail?"

Grunting was Swanson's stock in trade. "Some. Few seconds.
Enough to tell you to bend over and kiss your ass goodbye. Stop

pestering me, Rafe. There's nothing you or me or anyone can do about it, so why waste time worrying? It'll happen or it won't."

"What the hell happened to military protocol, anyway?" grumbled Aguilera.

"Excuse me? As I recall, you're technically still a civilian—and were never anything more than a sergeant when you were in the service. Whereas I happen to enjoy the exalted rank of major."

That acerbic response seemed to mollify Swanson, a bit. "Okay, sure, a staff weenie. Still a major. *Relax,* Rafe. I might mention that I did wind up wearing that stupid dress. It worked, well enough. Way better than the bum I married, that's for sure."

Aguilera decided to let the matter go. Swanson was right—there really wasn't anything anyone could do about the forcefields. They would withstand the stress, hopefully long enough to enable them to complete their mission, or they wouldn't. And he didn't want to get anywhere near the subject of Swanson's marital habits. The woman was in her mid-thirties and had been divorced four times. All bums, to hear her tell it. She seemed to have a built-in radar for detecting them, which, unfortunately, never sent off any signals until after the weddings.

So, he turned back to the other problem. "How long can they survive in Turret Six, the way their environment's degrading?"

"Hard to tell, exactly. Partly it depends on them, of course. We need to ride herd on those cowboys, Rafe. They'll try to stick it out as long as they can, but if they push it too far they'll start passing out from heat prostration before they can get themselves out."

Aguilera nodded. "Give me two minutes warning, as best you can figure it." It would take the crew in Turret Six about a minute to evacuate. That would give Rafe another minute to try to convince them to do it. He'd need it, too, with that crew. The tank commander in Six *was* a cowboy. He'd grown up on a ranch in Wyoming.

"And now again," Yaut said softly.

Aguilera brought his eyes back to the holo tank. Sure enough, another Ekhat ship was starting to take shape in the solar fog. No—two of them, close together. The second Ekhat vessel had been partially obscured because it was behind the first one.

Aille, as before, would try to bring them alongside rapidly and then slow their own sub's velocity as much as possible to allow the tank crews to fire off multiple rounds. The piloting skill involved was phenomenal, but Aguilera had already seen Aille do it. Maybe he could again.

He spoke softly into his throat mike. "General Kralik, we're coming up on another ship. It'll be on your side again."

"Roger. Any estimate on time and—Jesus Christ!"

Aguilera echoed Kralik's startled outburst. In his case, with a low *Mary, Mother of God.* Another sub had suddenly loomed in the holo tank—close enough that Kralik had seen it in his own more limited turret screen—and Aille had barely managed to avoid a collision.

Aguilera watched, paralyzed, as the other sub veered out of control. The pilot of that sub had also maneuvered sharply to evade the collision, but apparently didn't have Aille's consummate skill. The sub was now yawing, speeding toward the first Ekhat ship.

It all happened in seconds. The other sub's pilot managed to realign his vessel, but not in time to avoid colliding with the Ekhat ship. It was a glancing blow, yes, scraping the sub against one of the Ekhat ship's fragile-looking exterior lattice-beams. But, as fragile as the thing looked, it still massed more than the sub. All the turrets on one side were stripped away—those men dead in an instant—and a great tearing wound inflicted on the hull of the vessel.

Whether there was more extensive structural damage or not, Aguilera couldn't determine. But it made no difference. With that big a hole torn in the sub, it was doomed. In the cold vacuum of space, the crew might have been able to rig a forcefield to maintain the internal environment—much as Aille had done when the Interdict stripped away the airlock on his small vessel. But there would be no way to shield that large an opening, not with the heat and pressure inside the photosphere. Long before the sub could claw its way out of the sun, everyone aboard would be asphyxiated or cooked alive.

Aguilera couldn't think of a worse way to die. Apparently, the sub's pilot had reached the same conclusion. He might not have been as good a pilot as Aille, but he was damn good—and with all a Jao's stoicism in the face of death. A moment later, the pilot had the wounded sub straight on a course toward the second Ekhat vessel.

He's going to ram.

"Interesting," said Aille. "We will see if it works. Watch, fraghta—you too, Aguilera. I will be too busy."

Too busy, indeed. Aille was now trying to bring his own sub to as much of a dead halt as possible, in order to give his gunners maximum time on target. In their first encounter, Aguilera had been fascinated to watch the young Pluthrak's skill. But now, he was almost oblivious to it, his eyes riveted on the sub speeding toward its collision with the other Ekhat ship.

The collision came just seconds later. It was a perfect ram, too, the sub impacting bow-on against the side of the central pyramid. It was a former boomer, almost six hundred feet long and weighing in the vicinity of twenty thousand tons. Aguilera could only estimate the velocity. It wasn't high, by aerospace standards, since maneuvering inside the sun's photosphere was more akin to traveling in a fluid than empty space or even an atmosphere. Probably less than two hundred miles an hour, at a guess.

But it hardly mattered. The sub punched through the relatively thin hull of the Ekhat pyramid almost as easily as an awl penetrates thin leather. For a moment, Aguilera expected to see it punching out the other side.

But that was impossible, of course. At the last, the forcefields would probably have kept the crew from being killed by the sudden deceleration caused by the impact—most of them anyway, although certainly not the men in the surviving turrets. Still, the energies involved would have been enough to bring the sub to a stop somewhere inside that great central chamber.

Aguilera could envision it in his mind, from the nightmare scene Tully had described to him when he'd visited the Interdict ship. The dying submarine, nestled inside the huge enemy ship as if it had been swallowed.

But the relationship between predator and prey was reversed here. If the crew *had* survived, especially the men in the missile rooms . . .

They hadn't converted all the missile launchers to position tanks as jury-rigged gun turrets. They'd decided to leave four intact, just in case this very eventuality came to pass.

Rafe began softly reciting the Lord's Prayer. Yaut glanced at him, curiously, but said nothing.

Suddenly, a great bursting flare erupted from the wound in the side of the Ekhat ship caused by the sub's ramming. Within a second, the opening was torn wider still.

"That seems too mild for a nuclear explosion," said Yaut, his ears and whiskers indicating obvious puzzlement even to Aguilera's unpracticed eye.

"It's not one," Rafe replied. "That's the effects of the rocket fuel we're seeing. They must have fired at least one of the missiles. Those are three-stage rockets with graphite-epoxy hulls, loaded with propellant. The missiles probably would have impacted something even before the rockets ignited, just from the force of the compressed air launch. That would have been enough to rupture or shatter the hulls and spill burning fuel everywhere—and judging from the stink when I was aboard one, those ships are full of flammable compounds."

He added, sadly, "They did all they could, and that ship's probably dead anyway even if the warhead doesn't go off. Those warheads don't get armed immediately. They're on timed fuses for safety. If the fuses survived the impact, though—"

A sudden thought came to him. Even in the middle of the sun's photosphere, a thermonuclear explosion was nothing you wanted to be anywhere near. He started to turn toward Aille, to warn him, but saw that the young Pluthrak had already adjusted course. With another dazzling display of pilotry, he was positioning his sub to leave the one Ekhat ship as a shield against the other—and, Aguilera could now see, was going to be bringing them almost to a dead halt in the process. A slow walk, anyway.

Just as the rammed Ekhat ship had almost disappeared from view behind the first ship, the granular cells were roiled still further—not much, of course. But the blaze of light was nothing to sneer at, not even here. The fuses had survived—one of them, at least—and several hundred kilotons was enough to completely destroy even an Ekhat behemoth.

"Deliver us from evil," Rafe whispered. "Amen."

Standing at his side, Yaut's look of puzzlement vanished, replaced by a posture which Aguilera recognized. *Gratified-respect*, the same posture he had bestowed upon Kralik, when Kralik had predicted there would be more than enough volunteers for the ships. Honoring the courage of the men and Jao who had just destroyed an Ekhat vessel at the cost of their own lives—but not surprised that they had done so.

Aille was now bringing them alongside the surviving Ekhat ship. The enemy vessel had been set slowly spinning by the collision that had doomed the sub. So, Aille was staying perhaps half a mile outside the sweep of those outer lattice-beams, lest one of them smash into his sub. Instead of threading his way through the lattice as he'd done before, to bring them into point blank range, this engagement would have to take place at a considerably greater distance. On the other hand, he'd almost brought the sub to a standstill relative to the enemy—and, spinning the way it was, the guns would be able to riddle it on every side.

"It's all yours, General," Rafe said into the throat mike. "Tear that bastard apart for us, would you please?"

Kralik and his gunners did, even though the heat in the turrets was now so intense that they'd stripped to the waist and were trying to see and work through pouring sweat. The environmental conditions in the turrets were now so bad that they'd have to be evacuated after this engagement. Fortunately, Turret Six was on the opposite side and thus out of action, so Aguilera was able to persuade the crew to abandon it before they died. It took him exactly fifty-eight seconds to do so.

But, sweat aside, it was a turkey shoot. Even at three mile range, the DU penetrators didn't ablate enough to lose any significant impact. The turrets' auto-loaders were working at full speed now, since there was no need to track the target, slamming the rounds into the chamber and igniting the liquid propellant. Ten rounds a minute, from each of four turrets, and Aille was able to keep them on target for almost two minutes.

Rafe estimated that something over sixty rounds had hit the Ekhat ship, before the already collision-damaged enemy vessel simply began coming apart. The heat and shock of the DU penetrators was igniting everything flammable aboard it, and he was sure the intensifying heat was spreading on its own throughout the vessel. A chain reaction of explosions, in temperature ranges where almost anything would burn.

Suddenly, in at least a dozen places, the central pyramid ruptured. As it did, the outer lattice began separating and disintegrating. It was like watching a gigantic and grotesque flower slowly unfolding—until the structural damage finally caused the ship's forcefields to collapse. Thereafter, the photosphere's own heat and pressure and turbulence completed the destruction within seconds.

"And that's that," Rafe murmured. More forcefully, into the throat mike: "Ed, you've done all you can. Get yourself and all your men out of those turrets. Now."

Kralik didn't argue the point. Courage was meaningless, under these circumstances. The turret crews were willing enough to die fighting, but the environmental conditions were now so bad that they'd simply die pointlessly if they stayed much longer. As it was, Aguilera was sure that at least half of them would need immediate medical attention.

For that matter, the sub's own environment was now starting to degrade badly. Aguilera hadn't noticed before, he'd been so engrossed in watching the enemy's destruction, but he himself was drenched in sweat and having a hard time breathing.

Jeri Swanson was her usual charming self. "Hey, Rafe, if we're going to parboil can I start peeling yams to go with the long pig? Too bad we don't have any pineapple."

I'd 've divorced her in two weeks, myself. But he kept the thought to himself, turning instead to address the back of Aille's head. Even the two Jao in the control center seemed to be wilting a little.

"Ah, sir, if I might recommend—"

"No need," interrupted Aille. "I am taking us out of the photosphere. We have done what we can."

Done plenty, Rafe thought, with considerable pride and satisfaction. *Two dead 'uns, and . . . we'll call it one assist. No, two— we riddled that second ship some too, even if we don't know what happened to it afterward. If the rest of the subs did as well as we did, this Ekhat task force is toast.*

The others hadn't done as well, they discovered once they emerged far enough from the chromosphere to regain communication. Several of the subs, in fact, had never managed to get close enough to the Ekhat to fire off a single shot.

Aguilera was not really surprised. Now that he had experienced it, he understood the kind of superlative skill it took to maneuver a converted submarine in those hellish conditions. Only Aille and one other pilot had really been good enough—one of the old retirees that Wrot had dug up, by the name of Udra krinnu Ptok vau Binnat. Between the two of them, they'd accounted for four of the six Ekhat ships destroyed.

Six destroyed—out of eight. In the holo tank, Aguilera could see the two surviving Ekhat ships hurtling toward Terra like comets.

Damn. I was hoping we could get them all.

Still . . . He leaned closer, peering at one of the images in the tank.

"There is something wrong with one of those ships," Yaut stated firmly. "Look. The plasma ball is fluctuating and uneven."

The fraghta had put into words Aguilera's own half-formed thoughts. "We must have damaged it some. Do you think?"

Some part of him was amused to see Yaut shrug. Yet another piece of crude human body language which the fraghta had unconsciously acquired.

At least, he thought it was unconscious. But, maybe not. Rafe now understood enough about the role of a fraghta to realize that anyone who occupied that position for one of the great kochan would be expert at many things. One of them being what the Jao called "association." Was this part of it?

Suddenly, the fluctuating plasma ball in the holo tank began unraveling completely. It reminded Aguilera, a bit, of the sight of the Interdict ship shedding its plasma. But this was a much bigger ball, and it was obviously not being shed in a controlled manner.

This time, it was Aille who verbalized his thoughts. "Yes, they must have been badly damaged in the battle. But still, with typical Ekhat mania, attempted to carry out their mission. Now they are losing control—and their own plasma ball will destroy them for it."

Within seconds, it was obvious that he was right. The Ekhat had tried to control a literal piece of a star—and now the star took its revenge. There was more than enough energy in that plasma ball to rip the Ekhat ship to pieces as it came apart.

One left, then. There was no way to stop it until it had unleashed its plasma ball in the Earth's atmosphere. After that, it would be up to Oppuk and his flotilla to destroy the Ekhat ship before it could return to the sun to gather up another.

Would he do so? Rafe wondered. Or would the Governor's now obvious hatred for Terra lead him to simply stand aside and let the Ekhat ship return again and again?

There would be little the subs could do to stop it. Only eight of the subs had survived, and they'd all suffered so much damage that to attempt another return would be sure destruction to no purpose. And, outside the sun, they would be no match even for a single Ekhat warship. Not with the huge lasers that ship would carry. In the photosphere, the advantage had been all with the subs. But in the vacuum of open space, it would be suicidal for them to attack the gigantic enemy ship. Only specially designed warships could manage that feat—and, even for them, it was risky.

He must have muttered his thoughts aloud, because Yaut spoke in response.

"Oppuk will not fail. True, he is not sane. But he is a not-sane Jao. He will retain enough *vithrik*. And, did he not, his own crews would demand his life."

He was probably right, Rafe suspected. He'd listened, a couple of times, to Dr. Kinsey's ruminations about the parallels between the Jao and the ancient Romans—as well as the ancient Mongols. And while Aguilera was not sure how closely those parallels held, of one thing he was quite certain. The Jao could be brutal, but they were not brutes. If they had the vices of conquerors, they also had the virtues. They would no more tolerate cowardice in the face of the enemy from one of their own that would any ancient Roman centurion or Mongol cavalryman.

He felt a moment of sheer camaraderie toward Yaut, then. Fortunately, he remembered in time to restrain himself from clapping the fraghta on the back. He'd also chatted with Tully once, and, like Tully, Rafe had seen a number of Toshirô Mifune movies.

The intelligent man does *not* take personal liberties with Yojimbo. Even in a good mood, on a good day.

Zzzt. Plop goes the offending hand.

CHAPTER
38

When Kralik emerged from the converted submarine after it landed at Pascagoula, the fierce afternoon light made him squint. The heat, on the other hand, even for Mississippi in late summer, didn't seem bad at all. The air was not nearly as hot as that within the sub and felt almost cool against his face. The stench of scorched hull washed over him, combined with the miasma of unwashed bodies and sweat that the sub's air scrubbers had not been able to suppress.

Blue-green ocean glittered just a quarter of a mile away, but closer in, a restless tide of humans and Jao waited at the edge of the tarmac. A few hopeful souls held up signs of welcome, but most were silent, radiating dread.

Then he spotted Caitlin, lovely and straight, watching as he forced his rubbery legs to climb down the portable staircase the base workers had brought onto the tarmac. Numb with fatigue, he had to cling to the handrails.

A murmur went up from the crowd as the rest of the dazed crew appeared one by one behind him, their faces tight with strain. There wasn't a man or woman among them, he thought, who wasn't running on pure nerve at this point.

Overhead, the golden light streamed down with only a hint of the same devil's fire that fueled this entire solar system. He realized it would take some time before he could stand out in the sun without remembering those hellish currents.

"Ed!" Caitlin dashed forward, bursting through a temporary cordon erected to keep onlookers back.

A jinau soldier caught her around the waist, but Kralik waved him off. "It's okay," he called. "The lady's with me. My fiancée, in fact."

His voice was hoarse with weariness, but the last sentence picked up his spirits immensely. Kralik had led a lonely life, the past two decades. There had been girlfriends here and there—two of them fairly serious—but the peculiarities of his position as a top jinau officer had always seemed to get in the way of any really serious romance. Though Caitlin was much younger than he was, with her that wouldn't be a problem. She understood the Jao and the realities of dealing with them up close even better than he did.

What was even more important—for once, he cast aside his normal caution—was that he'd come to adore the woman. It didn't hurt anything, of course, that she was so damn good-looking.

She threw herself into his arms and pressed her lips to his, kissing him hard before she drew back. It was an inexperienced kiss, but you certainly couldn't fault her enthusiasm.

"They said almost half the subs were lost." Her voice cracked. "And they didn't have a survivors' list. I guess—" She straightened. "I guess that sort of thing isn't a priority with the Jao."

He drank in her face. Her blue-gray eyes were wet and darkly luminous, the pupils only pinpoints in the bright light. "How bad is it? I know one of the Ekhat ships got past us. Did—"

"Governor Oppuk's forces destroyed it, but not before the Ekhat unleashed its plasma ball over south China." She turned her head and looked back over her shoulder, as though the devastation were visible, even from here. "The loss of life—it was pretty bad, Ed. Even with everybody taking what shelter they could, that's a densely populated area. Whole forests are gone, entire ecosystems obliterated, God only knows how many people dead. At least a million, probably a lot more. The Chinese are being as close-mouthed as they usually are."

His jaw tightened and he could feel a knot behind his eyes. "Damnation."

"No," she said and turned her gaze to the scorched subs. Other men and women were finding those who'd come to meet them, conducting reunions, but, off to the side, many stood silent, their loved ones lost forever in the burning fires of the sun. Her fingers tightened on his arm. "After seeing what's left of the affected areas, everybody knows this world is lucky to be here at all. If their entire force had gotten through—"

He nodded, then buried his face in her clean-smelling hair and held her close. "Well, it's over."

Caitlin shook her head, still pressed against his shoulder. "No, it isn't, Ed. It may get worse. The comm center is now reporting that Oppuk is preparing bolides." She leaned back and stared at him, hollow-eyed. "They think he's going to start bombarding the planet, in the name of crushing a rebellion. It'll be Chicago and New Orleans—and Everest—a hundred times over."

A groundcar pulled up, with a military driver. As always, rank had its privileges, even in the midst of disaster. Kralik started to open the door for Caitlin, but she did for herself before he could reach it. He smiled ruefully, half at himself and half at the situation in general. Leave it to Ed Kralik to fall in love with a woman who had Jao habits; sometimes, even, Jao attitudes.

He climbed in after her. He was so weary, the black tarmac seemed to shimmer before his eyes like a heat image. He ached to stretch out in some cool, darkened room with Caitlin in his arms, as he had the night before the submarine fleet had lifted off, but such indulgence was out of the question. Since Oppuk's fury was undimmed, the real battle was most likely just beginning.

He rested his head back against the seat as the groundcar lurched forward, then gained speed. The base slipped past with its strange conglomeration of poured black crystal Jao buildings mingled with stiff-looking human structures.

"'The woods are lovely, dark and deep,'" he murmured, quoting an old Robert Frost poem. "'But I have promises to keep.'"

Caitlin nestled in the hollow of his shoulder and sighed. Her fingers stroked his cheek, scraping across stubble. "'And miles to go before I sleep,'" she said, finishing the lines for him. "'Miles to go before I sleep.'"

"I need to shave," he said, apologetically.

"No, don't." She chuckled softly into his ear. "Your beard looks like it'd be all gray. It'll make you look like a distinguished cradle robber, so I can tell everybody I was bowled over by your suave mature charm."

Kralik thought about it. "Nobody will believe that for an instant," he predicted. "I drink beer, just for starters."

" 'Course not," she murmured happily. "They'll think I'm an airhead for saying it, but that'll still keep them from nattering at me. Nobody gives unwanted advice to a blond airhead. What's the point, since she's obviously got the brains of a carrot anyway?"

Aille had thought, upon returning to Terra, that flow would ease. But it was swifter than ever, rushing with such urgency that he had to tighten his timesense and slow perception by several degrees in order to be able to think.

It was Oppuk, he realized. The Governor's flotilla had suffered losses fighting the one surviving Ekhat ship, but enough ships had survived for Oppuk to order them to begin outfitting bolides for planetary bombardment. Hami had told him that when she tried to speak to the Governor he simply broke off the comm signal.

Down here on Terra, humans were going about the remediation of the environmental damage in an orderly, methodical manner. Ben Stockwell had taken responsibility, as ordered, reaching out to other political moieties, though the affected areas were not contiguous with his own. Since it was obvious that a native would understand both what was needed and available much more thoroughly than a Jao, Aille allowed Stockwell's efforts to proceed unimpeded. He was well aware, though, that Oppuk was furious with that also— and would present it as further evidence before the Naukra that Aille was leading a rebellion. Not simply *kroudh,* but a traitor.

Nath had appropriated the Commandant's quarters on the Pascagoula base for Aille's use. Kaul krinnu ava Dano had vacated them to command a ship in the battle above Terra. Although he was numbered among the survivors, Kaul had not yet returned and it was unclear if he would return at all. Dano's stance in Oppuk's preparations for a planetary bombardment was still unknown. Indeed, no one even seemed to know his whereabouts.

Nath thus felt that until the Commandant returned, he had no use for these quarters with their intricate command systems. But Aille did. Finding no fault with her logic, he took possession, appreciative of her typical forethought and practicality. Nath's splendid *vai camiti,* he had long since realized, was no illusion. Had the female come from a more prestigious clan, she would have advanced much farther in rank by now.

He sat now in the dimness, considering his possible options.

They were few, and none good. Aille now held the allegiance of all the Jao forces on the planet itself—as well as the jinau, of course. But the only spacecraft he had at his disposal, other than his own small ship, were the converted submarines. Those, he dismissed with hardly any thought. The submersibles had done splendidly against the Ekhat fighting under the special conditions which obtained in the solar photosphere, but they would be hopelessly overmatched in an open space battle with Oppuk's flotilla. They were not mounted with lasers, and the human missiles could not be used against Jao electronic countermeasures. Not, at least, without a great deal of time spent in upgrading them—time which did not exist. Oppuk would be ready to begin his bombardment within a few solar cycles.

"Subcommandant?" a Terran voice said.

He looked up to find Caitlin Stockwell waiting. He was a bit surprised to see that Kralik was not with her, but then realized that the jinau general would be asleep. Humans did not recover as easily as Jao from exhaustion. Kralik would have tried, he was sure, but he was just as sure that Caitlin would have forced him to get some rest.

Her posture, he noted, was a finely executed *patient-concern*. Aside from the ears, no Pluthrak adult could have done better. She really was quite remarkable. "Yes?"

"There is a new development." Now, her posture wavered, as if she were both hopeful and apprehensive at the same time. "A number of ships have arrived in the solar system—a great number—and they say they are from the Bond of Ebezon. They are ordering Governor Oppuk to refrain from using the bolides. Indeed, they have ordered him to dismantle them."

Aille rose. "The Bond? *Already here?* But that is not possible." He gazed at the wall, confused. "They would have only received word of the situation here very recently. In that short time, they could have dispatched at most a single vessel."

Then came sudden clarity, and for a moment his posture slipped involuntarily into childish *astonishment*.

"They have been planning for this," he half-whispered, "and for a long time. Their strategists are famously patient."

"What does it mean, Subcommandant?" Caitlin asked nervously.

"How numerous is the Bond fleet? And what class of vessels?"

"Hami says at least sixty ships. And they seem to be very big ones. Hami calls them 'harriers.'"

The Bond of Ebezon's soldiers were named after that class of ships. The very largest, and the mightiest, ever built by Jao. Not even Narvo could match them, in size if not in number.

Sixty of them!

Aille composed himself. "It will mean whatever the Bond of Ebezon decrees that it means. Of that you may be certain. And there will be no bolide bombardment of this planet."

The young woman's fear was just under the surface, covered by a patina of self-discipline—and now, hope as well.

"Are you sure?"

Yaut entered that moment. "Sixty-three harriers. You understand what this means? The Bond's strategists must have been planning this stroke for a very long time. Pity Narvo!"

The fraghta gave Aille a penetrating look, leaving unsaid what was now equally obvious. The Bond's strategists and the Pluthrak *kochanau* must have been working together in secret.

Thus, Aille, in his innocence and youthful vigor, sent to Terra. *Namth camiti,* used as a scalpel to cut open a festering wound and expose the corrupted flesh to the light. With, needless to say, the scalpel never being told what it was supposed to do.

Clever, that. A self-aware scalpel would not cut cleanly, or deeply enough. Aille had cut to the bone.

Yaut turned to Caitlin. "Is he sure of what?"

"That Oppuk won't . . . won't be able to destroy the Earth?"

It was Yaut's turn—just for an instant—to lapse into *astonishment*. The embarrassment that caused him leant extra force to his growled words.

"Of course he won't! How could he? The Bond has decreed otherwise."

She still didn't really understand, Aille saw. More gently than Yaut, he said: "Caitlin, believe it true. This is why the Bond exists. No Jao will defy them. Even should Oppuk's unsanity drive him to, his soldiers would refuse to obey."

She sagged weakly against the wall behind her. Then, to his surprise, began that peculiar form of human laughter known as *giggling*.

"I guess that means I'll have to start looking for a wedding dress, after all. And Tamt! She'll have conniptions when I tell her about being a 'maid of honor.'"

Yaut stared at her. "Sometimes I still think humans are all insane."

Oppuk bristled with pure *fury*, every line, every angle, crossed and recrossed until no one could look at him and not feel the extent of his anger. All of his subordinates and servitors wisely stayed as far away from him as possible.

They were all Jao. He had killed the last of his human servitors a short time earlier, displeased at the condition of the salts in the miserable little pool provided for him aboard the ship.

As he floated in the pool, he savored the moments to come as much as he detested the pool itself.

If the Pluthrak had just followed orders, Terra would be a smoking ruin now! No, not even that. Smoke required oxygen, and the Ekhat would have stripped the planet of its atmosphere. Not worth even a manned outpost, much less the extensive commitment of troops and ships required to hold it. Best of all, Oppuk would be on his way to some new posting and the frustrations of dealing with this benighted species would be a fading memory.

So be it. If Stockwell survived the coming bombardment, Oppuk would have him put down as soon as he reestablished control over the planet. If she survived as well, he would force Stockwell's daughter to observe the execution of her father. Humans were quite sentimental about both progeny and parents. He'd seen that over and over again in his long assignment here. They could make an amazing amount of fuss over the most insignificant and unpromising of their clan members. She was sure to provide more diversion than he'd had in quite some time.

In fact, he thought he would have all of the surviving regional human governors executed in the coming days, just to drive home his point. As well as all of the top jinau officers, of course.

Oppuk heaved out of the water and shook himself dry before accepting harness and trousers from a cowed member of his service who scuttled back out of reach, radiating *abject-fear*.

Over on the far wall, the main doorfield crackled and faded to golden sparks. Four figures entered, the top officers of his command vessel.

"You wish?" He spoke curtly, not looking at them, irritated at the disturbance.

"The Bond of Ebezon has arrived in the solar system, Governor. A great fleet. The Harriers have ordered us to dismantle the bolides."

Oppuk struggled desperately to retain his composure, to show nothing of his shock.

He failed, rather miserably. His posture one of pure *desperation,* he lunged through the door toward the control center. Wisely, the four officers quickly stepped aside. He would have trampled them under, otherwise.

The black-garbed figure of the Harrier in the holo tank was frighteningly enigmatic. He was a short Jao, originally from one of the Dano affiliated clans, judging from his *vai camiti*, perhaps even Dano itself. But that no longer meant anything, of course.

Oppuk had had little contact with the Bond in his life, but he knew their reputation. The Bond of Ebezon arbitrated between kochan, when kochan could not do so for themselves. Its members were drawn from all kochan, choosing Bond status voluntarily and then forswearing all ties to their birth-kochan, so that they were well and truly *naukrat*, or neutral. Most astonishing of all was the manner in which they disciplined themselves in both mind and body so their bodies were *naukrat* as well and betrayed nothing of their innermost thoughts.

"You have been instructed to disarm the bolides," the Harrier said. "We expect you to do so at once."

Oppuk had wondered, even been skeptical. But now, seeing the Harrier commander's posture, he believed. The Harrier's body was almost frighteningly without affect, now not even composed for formal neutrality. Oppuk found it something like conversing with a granite post.

"You do not understand these creatures!" Oppuk exploded. "They are in rebellion, and must be crushed! I will not waste more Jao lives trying to fight them on the planet."

"You could not do so in any event," the Harrier responded, still in that disturbing posture-which-was-not-a-posture. "All Jao ground troops in this system have given their allegiance to Aille krinnu ava Pluthrak. So your protestation of concern for Jao lives is a falsehood, since what you really propose is to destroy the Jao troops as well."

The Harrier's head swiveled, as if he were looking at someone out of the holo tank's image. "Have the flotilla technicians assembling the frameworks evacuated the bolides?"

Oppuk heard a female voice reply: "Yes, Preceptor."

Preceptor. Oppuk suddenly realized he was talking with one of the Bond's five top commanders. A member of its legendary Strategy Circle. That long-unused part of his mind that had once understood how to maneuver in kochan rivalry was crying out shrill warnings.

This was all planned, he realized dumbly. *Plotted and schemed for, beginning long ago. I have been herded like a beast into a pen.*

"Strip the bolides from the Narvo, Pleniary-Superior," the Preceptor commanded. "Cast them where they will be harmless."

A moment later, the female voice said: "It is done. There is a giant gas planet not far from the asteroid belt where the bolides were being assembled. They will be consumed there with no danger."

Oppuk's eyes moved to the bolide control panel on his own ship, and saw that it was so. The bolide frameworks were nothing more than simple structures embedded in their rocky surface, designed to augment a ship's magnetic control impulses. The bolides were selected for the purpose in the first place, of course, because of their high ferrous content. With the vastly greater power available to their huge ships, the Harriers had simply stripped control of the bolides from Oppuk's own flotilla. Much as an adult easily removes something from a crecheling's hand.

All the more easily, because the technician sitting at the panel had made no attempt whatever to stop them. Indeed, she was sitting back in her chair, her hands resting on her knees.

Oppuk's fury finally had a target it could strike at. He took a stride toward her, raising his hand for a blow.

"*Stop him.*" The Preceptor did not raise his voice, but the two words rang with command. "The Bond strips Oppuk krinnu ava Narvo of all *oudh.* Any who obey him henceforth will be subject to Harrier punishment."

That was, for all practical purposes, synonymous with being put down. Harrier discipline was more stringent than any kochan's, even Narvo or Dano.

Still, Oppuk managed to strike the tech a first blow. The female's head was jarred by the impact, but she did not flinch otherwise. Indeed, the look in her eyes was simply one of contempt.

A moment later, Oppuk was brought down; overwhelmed, despite his massive build, by every Jao in the control room.

The Bond Preceptor watched carefully, noting the excessive force with which Oppuk's former subordinates were subduing him. It was closer to a beating than a simple restraint. Great and long-suppressed hatred was welling up here, obviously.

When it was over, he turned away from the holo tank and looked at Kaul krinnu ava Dano, whose fraghta Jutre was standing next to him in the Harrier ship's control center. The Commandant had come immediately to meet the Bond fleet as soon as it emerged from the framepoint, badly stressing his ship's engines. In a frantic hurry, obviously, to put as much distance as possible between Dano and Narvo.

"As I told you," Kaul growled. "A maddened lurret. He is unsane."

The Preceptor was not impressed, though he let none of his contempt for the Dano show in his posture. Kaul had obviously known as much, and for a long time—yet had chosen to remain neutral; even, until very recently, supporting the Narvo. More concerned, as always, with the petty interests of his kochan than the needs of the war against Ekhat.

The Preceptor had been Dano himself, once. He had left his kochan, more than anything, because in the end he could no longer tolerate stupidity and shortsightedness.

Thankfully, having established his neutrality and not-so-innocence, Kaul and his fraghta left the control center. The Preceptor turned back to the holo tank and reset the controls, bringing up an image of the planet they were nearing.

His Pleniary-Superior came to stand beside him. "It seems a beautiful world, at least from this distance," she commented. "I can see no signs of the environmental degradation the Narvo reports tell of constantly."

The last sentence has been spoken in a neutral tone of voice, as befitted one who had risen so high in the Bond's ranks. But the Preceptor knew her quite well, and did not mistake the sarcasm.

"Be careful, Tura," he said softly. "The great danger which faces us now—the second greatest, I should say—is that we too will allow long-festering anger and resentment at Narvo arrogance to erupt out of control. Narvo must be humbled, yes—at long last—but not humiliated. The courage and strength and determination of that kochan has, many times, been the shelter of the Jao—and many other intelligent species. It will be again, if we do not crush its spirit."

In private, the Harriers made no attempt to maintain the strict posture control they exhibited before kochan members. Tura flicked an ear.

"I understand. And the greatest danger?"

He pointed at the blue-and-white image in the holo tank. "There, where the Jao have already failed once. Faced with the first real test of association in our history—I leave aside the matter of the Lleix, when we were too immature to be held responsible—we failed. Completely and disastrously."

"Narvo," she murmured. "The worst choice possible, to have been given *oudh* over that planet. Even Dano would have been better."

The Preceptor's whiskers flattened. "That is the easy answer, but it is inadequate. Narvo was given *oudh* because the Naukra so ruled. All Jao are thus, in the end, responsible for their conduct. None questioned the wisdom of the decision, after all, on its own terms. I was there, when the decision was made. The kochan maneuvers concerned only matters of petty status."

"Even Pluthrak?"

He considered his answer. "Yes, even Pluthrak—and still even now, truth be told. Pluthrak is more subtle, yes, but even Pluthrak only sees the needs of the Jao. Which they confuse with the needs *for* the Jao, which is not the same thing at all."

He adjusted the controls again, now bringing up the image of the galactic disk. "Consider its immensity, Tura. We forget, most often, that even the Ekhat have only spread across a portion of one spiral arm. What lies beyond? What dangers and challenges will we face, after the Ekhat are finally exterminated?"

Tura pondered the image, for a moment, then assumed *rueful-amusement.* "It is hard for me to imagine a time when we will no longer be fighting the Ekhat," she admitted. Softly, she recited one of the first precepts learned by all newly-joined Harriers: "Ends are not means. So do not let your means determine your ends."

"Yes. And this one too: 'Bad mistakes are always simple ones.'"

He gestured toward the image of the planet. "Conquest is a means to an end, nothing more. Yet always the great danger that faces a conqueror is the simplest—that they will forget their purpose and come to see it as conquest itself."

Again, he adjusted the controls; taking a bit longer, this time, since he was bringing up stored recordings rather than shifting images.

The face of a young Pluthrak appeared in the holo tank.

"What a marvelous *vai camiti*," Tura said admiringly. "The quintessence of Pluthrak."

The Preceptor grunted. "More, I think. This one may be—at long last!—the transcendence of Pluthrak. I have long found that Pluthrak subtlety can be as exasperating as Narvo force or Dano crudity. Less abrasive, true enough, but still every bit as exasperating. Even more exasperating, at times."

A slight subtlety in Tura's posture indicated some reservations. That did not surprise the Preceptor. Tura had come from one of Pluthrak's many affiliated kochan. Jithra, as it happened, perhaps the closest. She was still relatively new in the Bond, and old kochan ties were hard to overcome completely.

He was not concerned. Over time, Tura would shed those last residues. Patience was one of the Preceptor's most outstanding qualities—the main reason, in fact, that he had been the one selected by the Strategy Circle to oversee their plans for Terra.

Twenty years ago, that had been, to use the native term. A long time, even by the standards of the Strategy Circle.

And now, finally—hopefully—coming to fruition.

He studied the image in the holo tank. "Transcendence," he repeated. "That is what we need. And, perhaps, what we have found. A *namth camiti* sent to do one thing, who learned to do another. I did not really hope for that. Courage, one can expect from the young. Wisdom, rarely."

"Another thing?"

"A conqueror, Tura, who learned to do what conquerors forget. How to *listen*."

PART VII:
Firsts

CHAPTER
39

Aille monitored the holo displays as the skies above Terra filled with ships over the coming period, at least half of them the massively built harriers favored by the Bond of Ebezon. Those Aille had expected, along with the round Narvo and elongated Pluthrak ships, but also present were the designs of Dano and Nimmat, Kanu, Hij, and Jak. Others, too. Every root clan had sent at least one ship, as had their affiliated kochan and even a number of taifs.

The ships themselves were equally diverse. They ranged from dreadnoughts too immense to land on the surface of any planet to tiny personal couriers. There were troop transports as well, most of them Dano; and even one colossal mobile repair dock summoned all the way from the nearest Dree world.

Sixteen solar cycles had passed since the Bond had arrived and removed Narvo from *oudh* over Terra. Thereafter, the Bond had not intervened at all, apparently desiring to wait until the Jao kochan could send their representatives to Earth and assemble the Naukra.

Some of the other Jao from the lesser kochan had come, as it happened, primarily because they wished to learn how the Ekhat had been defeated. But, most came to see how, and if, Pluthrak and Narvo would resolve this thorny matter between them.

The long-festering tension between the two most powerful kochan seemed at a breaking point. A certain amount of kochan rivalry was healthy in the long-range scheme of things, motivating every kochan to always do its best, to sacrifice for the greater good and allocate resources to the struggle against the Ekhat, when keeping to their own worlds might have served them better individually. What had grown between Narvo and Pluthrak, however, was not productive. As long as a polite veneer had glossed over the antagonism, other kochan could pretend the problem was not acute. But now, the Terran Crisis, as it had come to be known, had ripped that veneer away and exposed the situation for the lurking danger it really was.

Either new association would be forged, or . . .

The alternative was dire, for all Jao. More than anything else, the other kochan had come to do what they could to contain divisive tendencies and encourage association.

As he waited for the Naukra to finally assemble, Aille continued to work in the command center at the Pascagoula refit facility. For the most part, he let Stockwell and other humans continue to organize and manage the natives' affairs, so that he could concentrate on repairing and further modifying the submarines. Other Jao could be as preoccupied as they wished with kochan affairs, but Aille's foremost concern remained the Ekhat. It was impossible to know how the aliens would react to the disappearance and presumed destruction of one of their task forces. But it was by no means precluded that they might simply send another, and soon.

Aille intended to be ready for them—and he did not intend, this time, to lose almost half of his own forces in another battle. The key, immediately, was pilot training more than anything else, which was the reason that Aille was pressing so hard to get at least some of the subs back in operating condition.

Truth was sometimes bitter, but truth was truth—and Hami had spoken it harshly at the battle evaluation meeting that had taken place soon after. The human crews of the subs had done better than the Jao pilots, Aille and one other aside. Much better. Most of the subs had played little effective part in the battle, because of the inadequacies of the pilots. And four out of six of the destroyed subs had not been lost in direct action against the enemy. Their pilots had simply not been skilled or experienced enough to keep their vessels from being swept down into destruction in the supergranular cells.

Aille and *two* other pilots aside, actually. In retrospect, it was clear that the pilot of the sub that had rammed the one Ekhat ship had possessed great skill. She would be sorely missed, in future battles.

Her name, Aille discovered later, had been Llo krinnu Gava . . . vau Narvo.

He was not surprised, really, although the humans seemed to have been astonished. Oppuk's monstrous behavior had its roots in long-standing Narvo customs, true, but roots were not leaves and branches. Over the years, as his unsanity grew, he had become more of a caricature of Narvo than its exemplar.

If the humans had been astonished when they discovered Llo's kochan affiliation, they had, in turn, astonished the Jao with their response. Aille as much as any.

Ben Stockwell, working with his fellow regional governors around the globe, had cobbled together an organization they called the "United Nations" to serve as an overall coordinating body for their work. Apparently it was some sort of council that had once existed, before the Jao conquest, which they intended to resurrect— although, Stockwell had privately told Aille, he intended to see to it that it had "more teeth" than its predecessor. Specifically, he proposed to place all jinau troops under the authority of the UN rather than the regional administrative entities.

Aille had found the expression peculiar, coming from a species whose dentition was so pitiful compared to Jao, much less a true predator. The Jao expression for the same thing was logical: "more mass." But, by now, he had grown accustomed to the fractured human way of looking at things.

Aille had not objected. It would make the situation easier for him, after all, to have a single body to oversee instead of the existing welter of regional districts. And, beneath the surface, he had seen the lines of association growing between humans, interwoven with Jao. It was a potentially dangerous situation, to be sure, since a single authoritative human governing body would enhance their abilities in the event of an outright rebellion. But Aille had faced the truth squarely: no matter what, if the Jao could not find proper association with the humans, a reconquest of the planet would be needed. And it would be much more difficult than the initial one, which had been very difficult to begin with.

For all practical purposes, Jao control over Terra now depended almost entirely on Aille's own prestige and popularity with the human masses. Should that be lost, for whatever reason, Aille had no doubt at all that the jinau forces under Kralik would no longer be controllable—just as he had no doubt at all that, in his private negotiations with Wiley and other leaders of the Resistance who had come to St. Louis, Kralik had given as well as taken. The humans had been very circumspect about it—circumspect enough that Aille had chosen to ignore the matter—but the traces picked up by Jao orbital monitors were clear enough: Kralik was quietly seeing to the storage of weaponry in secure and hidden redoubts in the mountains.

And not just the mountains of this continent, either. Kralik had also been negotiating a peaceful settlement with Resistance leaders from China, as well, where the Resistance had been as strong as it had been in North America. The volume of seagoing traffic on this planet was enormous, far too great to be monitored directly by the Jao themselves. Aille was certain that the North Americans were secretly transferring weapons to the Chinese, and other moieties they considered potentially militant allies in the event of a new outbreak of war.

The situation was potentially explosive. It was for that reason, even though he personally found the custom strange, that Aille had immediately approved of the UN's first official action: the adoption of what humans called "the highest medal for valor" and the awarding of the individual variant to Llo krinnu Gava vau Narvo. The group variant had been awarded to the entire crew of the ramming submarine.

After much squabbling—humans seemed incapable of deciding upon any course of action without squabbling first—they decided to call the first variant the "Star of Terra" and the other the "Solar Unit Citation." The Star of Terra was then presented, with much fanfare in the human public communication system—what they called, with equal illogic, "the media"—to the Narvo Association Hall in Oklahoma City.

The Narvo representatives who accepted the little metallic symbol were even more puzzled by the custom than Aille himself. Humans seemed to find it a great honor to be recognized "posthumously," as they put it, whereas Jao could see no point beyond pure superstition in presenting what amounted to a bau carving to an individual who no longer existed—and, in Llo's case, had never possessed a bau to begin with. She had been a pilot, not a commander.

But, like Aille, they had chosen to accept the honor without demurral. Even Narvo, as Wrot had commented at the time, was capable of learning a lesson. And Wrot had taken the occasion to mention to Aille another of those human sayings of which the old bauta was so fond: *The prospect of being hanged concentrates the mind wonderfully.*

Aille had appreciated the sentiment, even if, applied directly to Jao, it was rather meaningless. Indeed, Wrot had to explain the term "hanging" to him. With their much stronger vertebrae, shorter necks and massive neck muscles, suspending a Jao in such a manner in a strong enough gravity field would eventually asphyxiate him, but it would certainly not break his neck. Thus it had never been a Jao method of execution.

Indeed, from a Jao point of view it would be a form of torture, and the Jao despised torture. Not for its cruelty, but for its implied weakness, of the torturer even more than the tortured. Torture, when all was said and done, was a form of wheedling. Conquerors commanded, they did not wheedle.

But even Narvo, confused as they might have been, were able to see immediately how well Stockwell had gauged the mentality of his own species. The media coverage of the presentation ceremony had been very extensive—"blanket coverage," as humans put it, which was a far more sensible term than "media" itself. Once the identity of the heroic pilot became widely known as a result, the anti-Narvo demonstrations began fading rapidly, both in frequency and size.

Dr.Kinsey had proven very valuable in that regard, as well, somewhat to Aille's surprise. Despite Aille's own misgivings—Yaut's had been worse—Aille had agreed to let Kinsey appear on what humans called "talk shows." Another odd custom, that, in which a population assembled before a multitude of separate comm devices observed a small group of supposed experts discourse upon a given subject. Humans had a related custom, even more peculiar, called "the speaking circuit."

From a Jao point of view, it was all rather grotesque—as if kochan elders were so indiscreet as to hold their private discussions in a public place. But humans seemed to take it for granted, and it was notable that Kinsey quickly became an immensely popular guest on these shows, as well as being flooded with invitations to speak.

That was Oppuk's damage, again, being repaired as best as possible. Unsanely, the former Governor had chosen to keep as much as possible about the Jao mysterious to their human subjects. Now, Kinsey was rectifying the damage, and since the information came from a man who was both the humans' own recognized expert on the subject, as well as a member of Aille's personal service, his words were taken for truth. "Good coin," as Wrot put it.

(Then he had to explain to Aille and Yaut what "money" meant. They were able to follow that, well enough. But understanding collapsed entirely when Wrot moved on and tried to explain something called "counterfeiting.")

Not all of what Kinsey said was accurate, in truth. But, whether from an unusual degree of percipience or simply from his enthusiasm on the subject, Kinsey peppered his accounts of Jao history with many tales of Narvo and its resolute struggle against the Ekhat. Difficult not to, of course, given Narvo's centrality in that long war. And that, too, had the salutary effect of diminishing the anti-Narvo sentiment among the human population. However much they hated Narvo, they had only to see the imagery of the devastation in south China—which Stockwell also made sure was constantly portrayed in the media—to understand that the Ekhat were far worse than even Oppuk.

And, more and more, they were coming to distinguish between Oppuk and Narvo. Skillfully—far more skillfully than any Jao could have done—Stockwell was maneuvering human sentiment, isolating Oppuk from the Jao as such and focusing twenty years of hatred and bitterness on his figure alone. Within a few days, Aille noted, Oppuk's name was used less often than what had become his new unofficial human titles: "the Evil Governor," or, sometimes, "the egomaniacal Satrap."

Still, it was a tense situation, and, as he worked, Aille found himself wondering often whether the devastation in south China would soon be repeated everywhere on the planet's surface. If not by Ekhat plasma balls, by Jao bolides. No matter how politely and discreetly it was being done, Terra was essentially a planet in rebellion. And the Jao, like any conqueror, were not prone to dealing with rebellions gently.

*   *   *

Nath entered Aille's office in the command center. Even with her superb posture control, Aille immediately detected traces of unease.

"Subcommandant, one from Pluthrak itself wishes to speak with you."

The initial Pluthrak representatives who had arrived on Terra had paid short visits to Aille. But they had been lesser figures, often simply from affiliated kochan, and had had little to say beyond polite expressions. Aille had thought his own kochan-parents would communicate again soon. Flow in that regard had been feeling almost complete for several solar cycles now. But he had lost himself in all the thousand everyday details of the ongoing refit and pushed the matter to the back of his mind. He straightened and glanced aside at Yaut, who was, as usual these days, doggedly noncommittal. That was Yaut's own way of disguising worry and uncertainty.

"Have them put the message through in here."

Her ears wavered, her whiskers went limp. Very unusual, for Nath. "I have not made myself understood. The kochanau himself waits just outside."

Aille could not process the words. "The kochanau? Outside?" he echoed blankly. "Here?"

"Yes." Nath's body was now rigid. "When he made himself known to me, I wished to admit him at once, but he insisted I relay his request."

"Then—bring him in," Aille said lamely. He could not wrap his mind around the idea of Meku, kochanau of Pluthrak itself, asking permission of him to do anything.

Aguilera motioned to the other Terrans present. "With your permission, Subcommandant, we will withdraw."

"I—yes," Aille managed. "That would be best, but—"

He looked again at the diagrams they had laid before him, his attention drawn back to the tantalizing melding of Jao and Terran tech. It was the plans, still tentative, for a new type of warship specifically designed to fight Ekhat inside solar photospheres. "I wish to see the changes we discussed implemented as soon as possible. Contact me when they are ready."

Aguilera nodded and Aille thought there was a hint of *respectful-concern* in the human's shoulders. The native's brown eyes narrowed.

"Will you be all right, sir? I don't pretend to understand all that's going on here, but we will gladly speak on your behalf, if you think it would do any good."

The doorfield faded and Aille saw, not Meku, as he had expected, but Dau krinnu ava Pluthrak. Dau was a highly venerated and very old Jao who had been kochanau two generations before. Aille had only seen Dau once in his short life, when the elder had been between postings and had returned to Marit An. But the impression of wisdom, of having encountered Pluthrak's greatest living treasure, had been lasting.

"Vaist," he said, rising to his feet and performing *grateful-welcome* in its most classical mode. "I had not expected to see one so illustrious on this world."

"I have assumed Meku's responsibilities for now. He felt inadequate to cope with the intricacies of this—" Dau was old, but still vital, his body stringy with age, but not weak. His snout wrinkled as though he scented something peculiar. "This—complex situation. As far as you are concerned, it is but barely begun, but the roots of conflict with Narvo go back through the generations."

His gaze flicked over the Terrans, his eyes a tranquil black. "So it is true. You do surround yourself with natives."

"Yes." Aille read a trace of *perception-of-error* in Dau's stance and for an instant, he was a callow, impulsive youth back on Marit An again, observed by Dau as he was being taught to spar through *wrem-fa*, body learning, the most ancient of their ways, in which nothing was ever explained and conscious thought bypassed altogether. He had been baffled then, when his elders refused to clarify what was expected, and went on trouncing him until on some subconscious level he finally divined the proper response and thereby absorbed the lessons they wished to impart.

He pushed aside the memory. *Wrem-fa* was a matter of life's experience, even more than a crecheling's training. When it came to humans, it was a simple fact that Aille's *wrem-fa* now greatly exceeded that of any Jao except Wrot and a few others like him. It was certainly much superior to Dau's, however wise and venerable the kochanau might be in other regards.

Aguilera ducked his head and led the other Terrans out of the office. After they had gone, Dau regarded him steadily with *expectation* in the lay of his ears. He intended Aille to do or say something, but he was not going to indicate what. It was to be *wrem-fa* all over again, apparently. Despite his respect for the kochanau, Aille found that a bit irritating.

"I am *kroudh* now," Aille said brusquely, almost challengingly. "What I do no longer reflects upon Pluthrak."

"Not officially." The enigmatic black eyes swept the office, alighting finally upon Yaut. "But you will always be Pluthrak by birth. That cannot be altered."

"If I die, my origin will no longer be an issue." Aille turned back to the image tank and called up a cross-section of one of his space-going submersibles. The oblong black shape hung over his immense desk, rotating slowly, alien and fascinating. "Oppuk has demanded my life repeatedly, since he was removed and placed in captivity by the Bond. I have thus far refused to surrender it, of course, since he no longer possesses *oudh*. That will change though, if the Naukra assigns alternate leadership to this world. They may, after all, decide to return *oudh* to Narvo—and Narvo may then choose Oppuk as Governor again."

Caught off-guard, Dau's eyes flashed green. "That is hardly likely. And you will not surrender your life to *that* oaf, no matter what!"

Aille pitched his ears at an ironic angle. The elder had spoken in unaccustomed haste. Neither Dau, nor Pluthrak, had the authority to command him any longer, and they both knew it. That was in the nature of *kroudh*.

"Before I came here, I viewed his so-called 'palace'! Where, apparently, he insists on spending his captivity while the Naukra assembles." Dau snorted in disapproval. "Disgraceful! The monstrosity is surrounded by useless vegetation that can be neither eaten, nor made into any useful product. The building itself, though it appears Jao without, is riddled inside with windows, tiny enclosures, straight lines, and corners. It is positively hideous."

His ears flattened. "And the state of disrepair on this world! We detected entire regions where the infrastructure has been left in ruins from our initial conquest. No wonder the natives are in a constant state of revolt! Their most basic needs have been ignored. Even animals have to be properly husbanded, or they produce nothing of value. That truth is widely known. Even to Narvo. Even to Dano!"

"And these are very far from animals," Yaut said abruptly. The fraghta's whiskers twitched and he turned away, appearing to study the approach to the refit facility through a single small, darkened window. "They are clever sentients, often shrewd. Sometimes, I even think, wise. True, they are lacking in many respects, compared to Jao, but they are highly advanced in others. More advanced than we are, in fact."

Dau's whiskers quivered with amusement. "You too, fraghta? You are referring to their famous *ollnat*, I suppose. They are obsessed with it, I am told."

"A different form of *ollnat*," Aille said. "Not the fanciful vagaries of a Jao mind, when it knows not what to do, but innovation of high quality, which thwarted not only Oppuk, but defeated the Ekhat."

"A fluke," Dau said. "The Ekhat will be prepared for such crude tactics the next time. It would not work again." But his posture as he said it conveyed subtleties. He was asking a question as much as making a statement.

"It would certainly be more difficult," Aille said. He leaned over his console and pulled up the image of the new design for a sunship; then, set the holoimage to rotating. "But my advisors are already developing something else, equally innovative. We will succeed—if the Naukra rules wisely, this time."

"Your human advisors."

"Human and Jao," Aille said. "My personal service consists of both." He gestured at the image above his desk. "This design, for instance, was initiated by humans, but since then is being drastically modified in light of the experience of such veterans as Chul and Hami."

Aille found himself performing the difficult tripartite *unashamed-steadfast-resolution*. "You should trust in my training, in all you have given me. What I have done is best for us all, Pluthrak, Terran, and Narvo alike."

"I hope you are right," Dau said, and his aspect shifted to an unguarded moment of *weary-fondness*. "We all do. But you have removed yourself from our protection, and we cannot intervene directly on your behalf."

"I do not wish you to intervene," Aille said, on the edge of offense. "My actions should be judged by the Naukra on their own merits."

"That is fortunate," Dau said, "for I suspect that is all you will receive—and not even that, should Narvo hold sway at the council.

Though, it seems, the Bond will be playing a much greater role than usual. Very difficult to tell, how that will affect the outcome."

The old kochanau's whiskers quivered with amusement again. "'Subtle as a Pluthrak,' they say. Ha! They only say that, who have never encountered a Bond Preceptor."

To Aille's surprise—astonishment, even—Dau then bestowed upon him the posture of *gratified-respect*. "You have met our hopes, young one. Perhaps even exceeded them. I am not certain of your wisdom, in all of these matters, and I much fear the doing of it will require your life. But never doubt Pluthrak's pride, *kroudh* or not. Narvo will never recover from this, and can finally be brought into proper association."

Dau straightened. "And now, I need some dormancy. Alas, I am old and no longer as resilient as I once was."

Nath, respectfully, immediately moved toward the door. "I will lead you to a suitable chamber, kochanau. It has a very good pool, if a small one."

After the kochanau was gone, Aille stared at Yaut. The fraghta's uncertainty was all gone now, clearly enough. His posture was even tripartite, very rare for Yaut. *Gratification* combined with *relaxed-certainty.*

Aille looked away, bringing his eyes back to the rotating image of the new sunship-in-design.

Yaut did not understand, he realized. Not surprising, of course. Until that moment, Aille had never really understood either.

It is all so stupid. *In the end, is this all of Pluthrak's vaunted "subtlety"? Another maneuver against Narvo? With half a galactic arm infested with Ekhat?*

It is so—so—

Another of Wrot's little adopted sayings came to him:

Like children, in a sandbox.

CHAPTER
40

Though it had once been his refuge, Oppuk now found the palace in Oklahoma City oppressive. Since recovering from the minor injuries suffered when his subordinates had seized him at the Bond's orders, he had spent most of time there. Swimming in the pools of what his human servitors had called "The Great Hall."

Back when he'd had human servitors. He had none any longer, and would not have tolerated any even if the Bond gave permission.

Which, they certainly wouldn't. The only servitors they now allowed him were a handful of Bond members, who obeyed Oppuk's orders but showed him little else in the way of respect. Very junior members, all of them, to make the insult worse.

One of them, Bori, was fortunately somewhat skilled. She was now adjusting the salinity of his favorite pool in response to his complaints, adding off-world salts, imported especially from Pratus, testing, then adding more. Already, the scent had improved to the point of being soothing again.

It was infuriating just being back on this world. At the very least, he needed his comforts fully restored. Even though Bori had not finished, Oppuk slipped back into the pool and settled on the rock-covered bottom, letting the cool simulated waves rock him as he tried to think.

It was difficult, because his anger continued to roil, as it had for what now seemed a near-eternity. Finally, giving up the effort, he surfaced and gazed about the vast room. Light blazed down from the holes in the ceiling, dividing the floor into a series of golden squares. Bori crouched silently by the far wall, polishing Oppuk's harness, the very essence of neutral readiness. Tactful enough, to be sure, but hardly the exhibition of respect Oppuk deserved.

His fists clenched, as though he wished to strike someone, anyone, in fact. He glanced around the cavernous room, but there no human servitors or Jao menials conveniently to hand. There were none left, in the palace, besides Oppuk himself and the Bond servitors. Not even in his current rage was Oppuk unsane enough to visit violence upon a Bond member. They were "servitors" in name only.

The female rose and departed, unseemly haste implicit in all her lines. Another subtle insult.

Oppuk floated on his back, watching reflected light waver across the ceiling. He had constructed this residence to impress the locals, incorporating elements of human design in order to make it grand in their eyes. Perhaps that had been a mistake, giving them an exaggerated concept of their own importance. He decided to have the building razed in the near future, once the flow of the moment had completed itself, and then have a new Jao quantum crystal palace poured.

Elsewhere, on one of the coasts. Perhaps he would have Oklahoma City destroyed by a bolide, to remove the vile memories.

As soon as *oudh* was returned to him, he would start.

Oppuk was not relieved when a Narvo elder presented himself at the palace, the next day, ending at last the dreary solitude of his palace-become-prison. How predictable. After endless orbital cycles of disregard and silence, this sordid mess had finally commanded their unwilling notice.

The doorfield faded, revealing an older male. Oppuk had known this one but slightly in his youth and now did not even recall his name, though he did seem to remember they had never regarded one another with favor.

"Long have you have shamed us," the male said. "Will it never stop?" Even at his age, he had that muscular vigor Narvo always prized, classic ears, a plush brown nap. As befit his station, his harness was very fine, the trousers the green of the finest cloth, the cut supremely flattering.

The elder had not offered his name, which meant this was not to be discourse between equals.

"I have shamed no one," Oppuk said angrily, his ears pinned back. "I have made myself of use, taming this vile world, as I was bid."

He lurched out of the pool, feeling desiccated the moment he left the water. "It is not my fault these creatures are so intractable. I have never shirked this noisome duty to which you bound me all those cycles ago."

The elder's eyes flashed a fierce, unforgiving green. "Is that what Shia krinnu ava Narvo would say?"

His old fraghta. Oppuk fought not to flinch. "Shia chose to leave, I did not send her away."

"You were kept here, safely out of the way—we thought!— precisely because she did leave." The male's whiskers twitched with distaste. "After such reckless behavior on your part, ignoring your own fraghta to the point of driving her off, we would have been fools to trust you with a more civilized assignment!"

Oppuk tried to protest, but could not. The old harridan had been irritating beyond belief and he had most certainly desired her departure.

"I am rightful governor here," Oppuk said, trying to shift the discussion to ground he felt he could properly defend. "Will Narvo back my authority, or will you permit this barely emerged Pluthrak upstart to go on discrediting me?"

"We will do what we can," the male said, "but your neglect of duty is obvious for all to see. If you do not take adequate care of the natives put in your charge, then it is only right they should be given over to the authority of someone else."

He gazed around the empty room. "What were you thinking, when you constructed this muddle for your principal residence? How could a true Jao ever be comfortable in such surroundings?"

He did not wait for an answer. "Come," the elder said. "We have received permission from the Bond to remove you from their custody. You are to come to our command ship. Make haste. All the kochan representatives have now arrived. The Naukra will be assembling very soon."

Though this was exactly what he had been waiting for, Oppuk was alarmed by his kinsman's stance. Whatever awaited him on the Narvo ship up in orbit, he dreaded to learn its name.

*   *   *

The name, he discovered, was Nikau krinnu ava Narvo, and his
foreboding was not mistaken. One of his pool-parents, she had
been, and it was a particularly unpleasant surprise to see her. As
aged as she was, Oppuk had been certain she was long since
deceased.

Her first words were as unpleasant as he remembered her.

"You fool!" She regarded him with angry angles and a jumble
of displeased lines.

"Have I not already been abused enough?" Oppuk's posture was
one of crude and undisguised *outraged-anger*. "First, you maroon
me on that dreadful, primitive world, and then, when I defend it
against Pluthrak and Ekhat both, you join Pluthrak in accusing
me of incompetence!"

Her eyes went a preternatural green, so bright, they might have
been lit from inside. He had seen them so during her infamous
furies, only twice in his long ago youth. "Do not assume that
posture with *me,* crecheling!"

Startled, he stepped back. Even now, the old female possessed
the power to intimidate him.

"What more can you do to me?" he said, ears lowered. "Do you
wish me to offer the Pluthrak my life?"

With a visible effort, she restrained her fury. "You will stand
before the Naukra and tell of your most earnest efforts to subdue this recalcitrant world," Nikau said. Darkly: "I do not care in
the least whether they believe you, providing you shame Narvo
no further." Her posture was one of *threatened-imminent regret.*

He gazed at the new harness and fresh pale-green trousers laid
out on a bench for him to don. "The natives are demented, that
is all which can be said of them. I have done the best anyone
could. This young Pluthrak is much smitten with these creatures.
They flatter him with lies, and, because he is foolish, he listens.
Leave him in place an orbital cycle or two and they will fight
him as hard as they ever fought me. Almost, I would like to see
it."

"Then that is what you must say." Nikau picked up the trousers and threw them at his feet. "I will speak the truth, arrogant
crecheling. So long as our honor is not further sullied, I will be
perfectly willing—delighted—to see another kochan given *oudh* over
this planet. These wretched Terrans have drained Narvo's resources

enough. Let some other kochan have the misery of dealing with them."

He began to remove his clothing. "Even Pluthrak?" he demanded, with as much visible outrage as he dared.

Her posture shifted to *sour-regret*. "No, not them, much as it would be pleasurable to see them founder in this swamp. But that would be too great an insult. As it is, Narvo's status has slipped greatly with respect to theirs, thanks to your misconduct."

A cold shiver ran through his body, and, for a moment, he wished he had perished in the Ekhat attack. He could see now that he would be blamed for this crisis by everyone, even his own, despite the true cause being Aille's treachery.

Fury came, to drive away the moment's despair, though he kept it from his posture. His only crime was having failed to make the natives fear him enough, while Aille krinnu ava Pluthrak wished Terrans to believe that he was their fraghta. In that, Oppuk knew, the youth was doomed to failure. Terrans respected no one and nothing, not even each other.

He finished donning the trousers, his self-confidence returning with the anger, then shrugged into the stiff new harness. He had nothing for which to make excuses. He had done only what he had been sent here to do, and had done it well, until the Pluthrak had arrived. He would make the Naukra see that. Narvo should still be *oudh* here. They would listen. Would even, he found himself certain, chasten the Bond for their hasty actions.

"Fool," he heard Nikau repeat. But the word did not really register. The female was old, her fury nothing more than a decrepit spasm. He was as sure of that as he was of anything.

Aille went out to the landing field early in the next solar cycle, when the Bond representatives descended to Pascagoula. Once their diplomatic ships committed themselves to landing, a bevy of smaller ships also converged on the same spot with that unerring timing that baffled humans so.

Aguilera, Tully, and Kralik stood before Aille, now automatically giving him status without being directed. The sun beat down, bright and brash. A breeze gusted inland from the sea, bearing the steamy fragrance of brine-soaked seaweed.

"How do they know?" Kralik said, without looking back over his shoulder at Aille. "I have worked with Jao now for years and still

I have no idea how your kind manages to know when it's time to do anything without clocks." He gestured at the expanse of tarmac beside the ocean, now bristling with ships. "It's amazing. They're like a flock of birds or a school of fish, all turning at the same instant without hesitation. There must be hundreds of Jao here and every one of them arrived within a half hour of each other."

Aille experienced a brief dissonance at the thought of always having to depend upon mechanical devices, which must be calibrated and maintained, in order to know when to act. His fingers traced the carvings on his bau. "They came when flow completed itself."

"But how do they know?"

"They felt it," Aille said, "as you feel hunger or weariness or joy." He could see by their expressions his explanation was inadequate, but he knew no other way to explain.

A contingent of Jao separated from the crowd already congregated on the landing field and drifted toward Aille. The elder Dau krinnu ava Pluthrak waited over to one side, silent, his posture unreadable. Aille willed calm into his own limbs, the lay of his ears, the droop of his whiskers. He had been unorthodox, yes, but had done nothing wrong. *Vithrik* had bade him save this world from the Ekhat, using the resources at hand, and that he had done. Just as the same *vithrik,* once the nature of Oppuk's misrule had become clear, bade him remove Oppuk from control over the planet. No matter what it cost now, he did not see how he could possibly have acted otherwise.

Nine Jao, all robed and well fed, their naps sleek with frequent swimming, stopped and gazed past his human service, regarding Aille with serenely black eyes. They were Bond Harriers, severed at some point in their lives from their birth-kochan for various reasons, and subsequently sworn to the military arm of the Naukra Krith Ludh. They owed allegiance to the Jao as a whole and to no kochan in particular. They even changed their names upon joining the Bond.

From Aille, the eyes of the Harriers moved to his human personal service. They spent most of their time studying the bau which Kralik, at Aille's insistence, held in his hand. The carvings on that bau were no longer simple. Not with Kralik's deeds at Salem and Sol recorded on it. Aguilera and Tully shifted uneasily under their scrutiny, but Kralik remained still and calm.

"Aille krinnu ava Pluthrak," the foremost said, "you are summoned before the Naukra to explain your actions." He was very short, for a Jao, wide of frame, short of ear. His *vai camiti* was intriguing, hinting at a Dano origin with its strong diagonal striping. A similar diagonal stripe on his robe indicated that he was a Bond Preceptor, one of the members of their Strategy Circle.

"We propose to judge the matter here, since too many kochan have come to be fitted easily into a ship or edifice," the Harrier said. "Do you have any objection?"

"No," Aille said. "This world remains on the edge of rebellion. I cannot afford to leave the surface now. My absence would most likely encourage one or more of the insurgent factions to act."

The Preceptor's eyes remained black and his posture elegantly neutral. He seemed to consider as the waves rolled in and the wind picked up. Avians flew in formation overhead, a curious double line joined at one end. "Your husbandry does you credit," he said at length. "It is obvious these primitives have been neglected under the deposed Governor."

"They are not primitives of any kind," Aille countered immediately, maintaining perfect *calm-assurance*. "That was the beginning of our error here, which I suspect was made out of anger because of their effectiveness in resisting the conquest."

The Preceptor did not seem offended. Indeed, his posture shifted slightly, inviting Aille to continue.

"Although their thought patterns do not closely mirror our own," Aille said, "they are highly intelligent. Highly civilized, also. More so than we are, I have come to suspect, in many regards. It is just a different kind of intelligence, a different shape to civilization. Disregard of that has led us into these difficulties in which we are now mired. We must adjust our views on this species if they are ever to be of use against the Ekhat. Form association with them in a different manner than we have with any other conquered species."

"You have been here but a short time," the Preceptor said. His body was almost frighteningly without affect, now not even composed for formal neutrality. Aille found it rather disconcerting— which, he suspected, was the point. "Do you really think you know these creatures better than your elders, such as Oppuk krinnu ava Narvo, who has dealt with them since the initial conquest? And even if they are all that you say, are they worth forsaking your kochan and its ties forever?"

It was a formal question, a *sant jin*. Aille closed his eyes and considered, as his pool-parents had long ago taught him. A formally phrased question required a well thought-out answer. Could he truly know the natives of this small green-and-blue world better than the elders who conquered it and held it for so long?

He thought of Caitlin, clever and Jao-like in her graceful postures and speech; Tully, who, despite his defiance, had demonstrated the unfailing courage and sense of duty of a Jao, over and over again; Kralik, who never faltered when the opportunity came to be of use; and Aguilera, who held to the truth even when he knew he would be punished. Were they not each one as worthy as Jao?

"Yes," he said at last, opening his eyes, knowing by the sense of peace running through him that his own must be as serenely black at this moment as the Preceptors. "I have lived with them in my quarters, watched as they strung startling new ideas together one after the other like jewels on a chain, fought at their side, and watched them die. They are unique and often difficult, but the same could be said of any promising crecheling."

The Preceptor regarded him without any visible reaction. Did he believe Aille, or did he just consider him enormously mistaken? His interrogator's whiskers twitched and then were still. "Oppuk krinnu ava Narvo is elsewhere," he said. "I shall have him brought here, at which time we will resume."

He turned and walked away, the other eight Harriers falling in behind him.

Aguilera watched, his big hands knotted behind him. "How long will it take for the Governor to arrive?" he said. "This mess has barely even started and already it's driving me crazy."

Aille knew in his bones exactly how long it would take Oppuk to be conveyed to the wind and sand and heat of this shore. He felt it, inside, like the length of a cord precisely measured, knowing as well how long he had to work before he must come back and meet his obligations. What he did not know, and most likely never would, was how to explain it to his human staff.

"He will be here when it is time," he said at last, as a small white avian skimmed overhead.

Then he turned to Kralik. "Summon Caitlin from St. Louis. She must be present."

The jinau officer stared at him. Normally impeccable in his conduct, Kralik suddenly spoke bluntly: "Why?"

Kralik and Stockwell were now bonded in preparation for marriage, Aille knew, which explained his unusual behavior. So, he explained, rather than simply commanding.

"Nothing changes now, General, on one level. This is still, whatever else, a matter between Pluthrak and Narvo. I have succeeded so far with advance-by-oscillation and I intend to continue. Nothing enrages Oppuk so much as Caitlin, because she stands as the clearest proof that his claims are false. That unsane fury, I think, will finally bring him down."

Kralik nodded, slowly, understanding the logic. Still, he was reluctant.

"It might be dangerous for her," he pointed out.

This called for a human gesture. Aille shook his head, firmly.

"No, General Kralik. It *will* be dangerous for her."

CHAPTER
41

Caitlin, Tamt and Dr. Kinsey arrived at the Pascagoula base late that afternoon. She had been working with her father in St. Louis for the past week, but then Kralik had sent for her. He said little, as was his way, but his silences communicated almost as much as words. He had not sent for her from a personal desire to see her again, as much as he might feel that also. Ed was worried, clearly enough, and Caitlin thought he had good reason.

She wasn't certain, because it was always difficult, if not impossible, to be certain about the Jao. But she suspected the assembly of the Naukra was about to begin. They had all been waiting for that, the past two weeks, with as much anxiety and fear as hope.

It was still hard to believe that only a few months had passed since the first rumors of a new high-ranking Jao assigned to Earth had filtered through to the university. So much had happened since then, and even more had changed.

Her father was hopeful. As long as Aille retained power, Earth could prosper again. It would not be the same, but she had read enough of her planet's history to know not everything that had passed away had been good. No one except fanatics would miss the political chaos of pre-conquest Earth, with its seemingly endless wars and conflicts. And with the ongoing efforts to repair the devastation in south China still at the center of the world's attention, every human was mindful of the overwhelming lesson of the Ekhat attack: find a way to live with the Jao, even under the Jao, or the human species would simply perish altogether. Left to their own resources, there was no way the human race could fend off the genocidal aliens.

As her helicopter came in for a landing, Caitlin could see her supposition confirmed. Almost the entire landing field of the huge military base was covered with Jao ships, all glittering in the last rays of the setting sun. Apparently, they had decided to convene the Naukra here rather than in Oklahoma City or St. Louis. That made sense—even reassured her, a bit—because it suggested that Jao of a more sane outlook and temperament than Oppuk were now in control. They would want the close proximity of the ocean.

The ships were of an amazing variety of shapes and colors, which surprised her. Somehow, she'd thought Jao designs would be more standardized.

Dr. Kinsey took her good arm, still mindful of her cast, and steadied her as they half-ran out from under the whirling blades. Tamt led the way, bent almost double. The Jao bodyguard was wary of human transport in general, and helicopters in particular. The first time she'd ridden one, Tamt had grumbled sourly afterward that with Jao transport you never had to worry about your head being cut off by the drive system.

Caitlin smiled at Kinsey as they straightened, doing her best not to grin outright at Tamt. "I won't break," she said, "at least not again. You don't have to worry about me so much."

"I don't think I can stop worrying about you, so long as Oppuk is anywhere nearby." He glanced around at the bustle of troops, both human and Jao. "I've heard the monster will be here in person. What if he—?"

"He won't lose his temper in front of all those prestigious kochan elders," she said. "He wouldn't dare." Her lips quirked in a little smile, as she looked him up and down. "Besides, Doctor Kinsey, be realistic."

He matched the smile. "Well, okay. I admit I can't see any way an elderly human—and a portly academic in the bargain—could protect you physically from that massive bastard. Even by Jao standards, Oppuk is an ogre."

Tamt's ears were now flat with *displeasure*. In truth, even Caitlin's impressive bodyguard would be overmatched by Oppuk in a physical confrontation—but Tamt, obviously, did not like to think so.

"I appreciate the sentiment," Caitlin replied, "but I really think you're worrying too much. Oppuk's temper tantrums are actually not normal for a Jao. He could get away with them so long as he was Governor, surrounded by flunkies. But if he tries it here, in front of the Jao's most powerful representatives, they'll give him short shrift. I hope he does lose his temper, actually. That would only hurt him—and help us."

It was still hot at this latitude, even though autumn had technically begun. Caitlin peeled off her jacket, then carried it over her good arm. Thunder rumbled in the distance, far out in the Gulf. She could see storm clouds forming into the classic anvil shape.

Old-fashioned combustion engine and converted maglev vehicles drifted back and forth on this side of the landing field, all filled with jinau soldiers. Jao were visible between the ships. Her overall impression was of barely restrained chaos.

She craned her head, checking faces. Kralik must be here somewhere.

A converted Humvee came up, and a snub-nosed blonde leaned out. "Ride, lady?" She grinned and Caitlin recognized Lieutenant Hawkins of the company Kralik had assigned to be Aille's personal bodyguard.

"I'm looking for General Kralik," Caitlin said. "Do you know where he is?"

"Matter of fact, the boss sent me to fetch you, as soon as your helicopter landed. Along with his apologies that he couldn't meet you in person."

Hawkins, clearly, had now been exposed up-close to the Jao for long enough to have picked up some Jao habits. Instead of getting out and opening the door for Caitlin and Dr. Kinsey, she simply reached across and clicked open the passenger door. "Hop in."

Caitlin, dressed in a dark-green suit and low heels she'd hoped were suitable for an official Jao gathering, hiked up her skirt and tried to climb in, with Kinsey making fumbling efforts to assist her. She was still a bit awkward, with her arm in a cast. But, luckily for her, Tamt had picked up some human habits. The Jao more or less elbowed Kinsey aside, picked up Caitlin and plunked her in the seat as an adult might do for a child.

The big Jao female and Kinsey then climbed into the back, and

Hawkins immediately set the vehicle speeding off in the direction of the Jao base.

Just the other side of an invisible dividing line, Jao were literally swarming, all armed with energy weapons.

Well, that wasn't surprising. All those years with Banle as her warden had left Caitlin no illusions as to how most Jao regarded humans. Dangerous and unpredictable creatures, the Jao equivalent of "wild Injuns."

She hadn't seen Banle since Tamt had beaten her up in the clinic. She'd heard, later, that Banle had been on one of the ships in Oppuk's flotilla that had been destroyed in the battle with the surviving Ekhat warship. The news had left Caitlin feeling nothing but tremendous relief. Banle could never torment her again. It was almost like coming of age.

The vehicle swerved again, then came to an abrupt halt. It seemed the human lieutenant had also picked up Jao driving habits. Hawkins jerked her chin toward a tent set up on a stretch of sand bordering the tarmac. "In there."

Caitlin was surprised, since she'd been expecting to be brought to Aille's command center, the imposing Jao edifice that Kaul had formerly used. But she assumed she'd find out the reason for this odd arrangement from Ed himself.

"Thanks." Caitlin opened the door and stepped down, much more easily and gracefully than she'd gotten in. Tamt and Kinsey jumped out behind her, Tamt obviously relishing the softer light of late afternoon and Kinsey looking hot, windblown, and rumpled. Of course, Kinsey almost always looked rumpled, at any time.

Two jinau were standing guard at the entrance. One of them held the flap open for her as she approached.

Inside, the light was dim, even though a panel on the far side had been tied up to admit fresh air. Kralik was standing with his back to her along with a group of men and women studying an electronic display of data on a portable screen.

He looked good, she thought, solid, dependable, reassuring. Handsome, too, at least so far as she was concerned. She had to force her hands to remain at her sides.

Kralik turned, as though he could feel her there. "Caitlin!"

She flushed at the warmth in his voice, remembering that night they'd spent together before the Battle of the Framepoint, how reassuring his arms had felt, the length of his body pressed against hers—

Inhaling deeply, she thrust the image out of her mind. No time for that now. No time for anything but the problem at hand. "General Kralik," she said, deciding the situation called for formality even though their engagement was open knowledge. "You sent for me, so I came. Can Dr. Kinsey and I be of assistance?"

"Yes." He almost reached for her too, then stopped and took Dr. Kinsey's hand instead, then hers, shaking them firmly. "Good of you to come, both of you. The Naukra is apparently convening a hearing—or however Jao think of it—tomorrow morning, we think, to examine the Subcommandant's actions here on Earth and decide what response to make. Narvo has lodged formal charges against him."

The wind blew a strand of hair in her face and she brushed it back. "Is Oppuk here?"

"He's on his way, apparently, and will be present in person at the hearing." Ed hesitated, then said softly: "Aille insisted that you come, Caitlin. But I warn you, he also thinks it will be dangerous for you."

"I figured that out myself, Ed. Whatever else he is, Aille is also a great schemer. He plans to wave me in front of Oppuk like a red flag before a bull." She appreciated the concern in his voice— even more, that in his stance—but simply shrugged. Then, smiled wryly. "It'll probably work, too. Although I'll admit I'd rather be of use some way other than a punching bag. But—whatever works, as they say."

Kralik pulled up a camp stool for her and gestured for the older man and Tamt to sit in other ones nearby. "You'll have to forgive these arrangements. So many Jao have piled into the command center over the past two days that we scruffy humans found it easier to set up shop here. And it's a lot less unsettling, to be honest, given that most of the newly arrived Jao seem none too fond of us and some of them seem almost trigger-happy."

He was half-lying, she suddenly realized, after spotting Tully in a corner of the tent. Tully gave her a friendly nod of recognition but then immediately resumed his conversation with the man he was standing beside. An older man, about Kinsey's age as well as Kinsey's approximate skin color, but looking far more physically fit than the professor. Caitlin had never seen a photograph of the man, but she was quite certain this was the legendary Rob Wiley, once a lieutenant colonel in the U.S. Army, and, in the many years since the conquest, the military leader of the Resistance in the Rockies.

Ed, she knew, had wanted privacy, not simply breathing room. She gave him an uncertain look.

Kralik's gray eyes hardened and he seemed to stand taller, straighter, as though granite suddenly pervaded his being. He glanced at Tamt, for an instant, then apparently decided her loyalties were clear enough.

"Don't ask for the details, Caitlin. Colonel Wiley—General Wiley now, officially—is willing to try it our way. But if that doesn't work, I told him we'd do it his way. If the Naukra restores Oppuk, we'll have no choice."

Tamt grunted. "Any fool understands that much. Even the Narvo veterans have informed their kochan elders they will no longer serve on Terra if the situation is not resolved properly. They specified the removal of Oppuk."

She grunted again, adding a whisker-waggle of amusement. "Their kochan elders were outraged at the effrontery—and they were already outraged by the new insignia in the kochan hall."

All the humans stared at her.

"It is true," she insisted. "I was told by one of the Sant, who was present. She said the veterans had made it a point, before the elders arrived, to have the Star of Terra prominently displayed on one of the walls of the association hall."

The Jao bodyguard, though still seated on her stool, bestowed upon them a quite good *reproof-of-crechelings*. The mildest version, Caitlin recognized, the one reserved for humorous chiding rather than more serious forms of reproof.

"Do you really think your preparations have gone unnoticed, General?" Tamt demanded. She glanced at Riley and Tully. "From the officers, perhaps. Not from the soldiers."

Kralik sighed. "Well . . . I'd hoped. Rob told me it wouldn't work, not with so many Jao troops still stationed near the mountain shelters."

Tamt now did a respectable version of a human shrug. "You all worry too much. The Naukra will perhaps not act wisely. But they are not outright fools. Whatever else, Narvo will not have *oudh* returned to them here. Certainly not Oppuk! And the attitude of the veterans—all of them, you can be sure, with even Narvo taking that posture—has made clear enough that whatever kochan takes Narvo's place it will either have to rule lightly, or it will need to bring in entirely new soldiers to rule at all. And soldiers with no experience dealing with humans will suffer massive casualties."

This time, her whisker-waggling was almost flamboyant. "Ha! As every veteran has taken great pleasure in informing the newly arrived troop contingents. Wrot even says they are acting almost like humans. Something called 'Grimm's Fairy Tales,' which were used to frighten crechelings into proper attitudes."

Caitlin burst out laughing. So, a moment later, did Kinsey.

Even Kralik managed a grin. A rueful grin, to be sure. "I guess we've got a reputation," he muttered. "Gawd, to think my life would come to this—reduced to being a troll in a fairy tale."

"Nothing wrong with that," Caitlin said firmly. "Anything that will lead the Naukra to avoid mistakes is fine with me."

A young aide came up and handed Kralik two steaming cups of coffee. The aroma of fresh-ground beans filled the air as he passed one cup to Kinsey, then offered the other to Caitlin, who shook her head. With the state of her nerves, caffeine was the last thing she needed.

Uncertainly, the aide looked at Tamt. He'd had little close contact with Jao, apparently. She wrinkled her snout, indicating that whatever human attitudes she'd picked up, Tamt still retained the normal Jao distaste for coffee. Any kind of caffeine-containing substance, in fact.

"I need nothing," she stated. The aide hurried off.

"What is the Naukra, exactly?" Kralik asked. "I tend to think of it as roughly equivalent to what we'd call a 'congress,' but I don't think that's really right."

"No, it isn't," Kinsey replied. "Close, as they say, but no cigar. For starters, it does not meet on any regular schedule. It's more akin to the medieval assemblies, in that sense, than a modern congress or parliament. It meets whenever it's summoned, to deal with specific issues, the way the old English Parliament only met when the king called for it. Except the Jao have no equivalent of a king, of course. Any great kochan—or the Bond of Ebezon— can summon a Naukra. Secondly, it's not elected by anyone you could characterize as a 'constituency.' The Jao who form the Naukra, when it convenes, are those representatives whom each kochan—

taifs too, I think—select to speak for them. Thirdly, decisions of the Naukra once it convenes aren't made by a vote, as would happen with a congress or parliament. Apparently, they just keep talking until a consensus emerges."

"And what if it doesn't? They can't *always* agree."

Kinsey took a thoughtful sip of coffee. "Well . . . that brings up still another difference, which is the peculiar role of the Bond in Jao politics. Apparently, if the Naukra can't reach a consensus, the Bond just goes ahead and imposes whatever decision it chooses."

Kralik frowned. "I though the Bond was under the authority of the Naukra."

Kinsey smiled. "Not exactly. You're thinking too much like a human, General. A modern human, I should say. I suspect our medieval ancestors would have understood the Jao better, in many ways."

He paused for a moment, choosing his words. "Probably the nearest human analogue to the Bond of Ebezon—in western history, anyway—are the old militant monastic orders. The Templars, Hospitalers, Teutonic Knights, that sort. They were also, technically, under the authority of the Church. But as any medieval pope could have told you—with considerable exasperation, heh—the militant orders often did pretty much as they chose. Hard to keep them from doing so, of course, since they were often as militarily powerful as any king or prince."

Kinsey finished his coffee and studied the bottom of the cup. "But don't read more than there is, General, in these little analogies of mine. There's something else about the Bond . . . I can't tell what it is, because it's very elusive in the historical records I've seen. There are some ways in which, obedience aside, they remind me more of the Jesuits than any militant monastic order. For one thing, insofar as the Jao ever seem to think very much about their basic attitudes—call it their 'secular theology,' if you will—it's the Bond that does the thinking."

"Of course," Tamt interjected. "That is their use, other than to keep the kochan rivalries within proper bounds. What kochan will think about the Jao as a whole?"

Caitlin stared at Tamt. Her bodyguard—and now friend—was normally so shy and self-effacing that Caitlin had a tendency to think of her as many Jao did: crude and coarse still, in many ways, despite Yaut's training—what humans would call "unlettered." Nor for the first time, though more forcefully than ever, Caitlin reminded herself not to underestimate the female. There was a good mind at work beneath that unprepossessing figure.

Kinsey was continuing. "Basically what will happen here, General, is that the Naukra has been summoned—by Narvo and Pluthrak both, it seems—to rule upon Aille's conduct and status and determine which kochan will be given *oudh* over Terra. The two issues are related, but separate. In the case of Aille, his life may be demanded and given; or, it may not—but he still remains outlawed. *Kroudh*, as they call it, which is in many ways a fate worse than death for a Jao. That decision may, or may not, correlate with whatever decision the Naukra makes regarding Terra's status. It is quite conceivable that Aille's life will be demanded and given— and then *oudh* turned over to Pluthrak. Indeed, so far as I can tell—I don't say this with any pleasure, believe me—that is the most likely variant. It would seem to satisfy the honor of both great kochan, at least."

Kralik's gray eyes were probing. "Is there any chance they would let Oppuk resume control?"

"The Naukra wouldn't decide anyway which *individual* is made Governor. That decision is entirely within the purview of whatever kochan is given *oudh* on Terra. All the Naukra decides is which kochan that is to be."

"That's what I was afraid of," Kralik muttered. "They could hand *oudh* back over to Narvo—and then Narvo would be within its rights to reappoint Oppuk."

Kinsey shook his head, firmly. "Not a chance. You don't really understand how this works, with Jao. To begin with, whatever their other faults, the Jao are far less prone than humans to what we'd call 'political back-stabbing.' A deal's a deal, in their eyes. It would be understood by everyone that, even if Narvo were to be returned to *oudh* status—which is highly unlikely, by the way, and I don't think even Narvo wants that—it would only be done to avoid humiliating them further. For Narvo to then turn around and reinstate Oppuk would be, under the circumstances, a grotesque insult to Pluthrak and, to almost the same extent, every other Jao kochan. Even worse, it would be a direct slap in the face to the Bond of Ebezon, which has made its attitude toward Oppuk very clear—and, so far as I can tell, that is something that *no* kochan, no matter how powerful, has ever been willing to do. The Bond can be ... what's the word?"

"Direct," grunted Tamt. Her ears flattened, at the same time as her whiskers twitched. The combination was the Jao equivalent of grim humor, emphasis on *grim.* "Other words come to mind. 'Forceful,' perhaps, or 'short-tempered.' But perhaps one of Wrot's little human sayings fits best of all, if I understand properly the nature of the beast referred to: 'as grouchy as a grizzly bear with a sore tooth.'"

This time, even Kralik joined in the laughter. "Okay," he said. "I guess we don't have to worry about that. Still ..."

His eyes moved toward the wall of the tent beyond which lay Aille's command center. "I would miss him dearly, I surely would. I never thought the day would come, when I'd ever say that about a Jao."

Caitlin felt her own eyes start to water. She too, now that the reality was curling over them like a great wave, understood how desperately she would miss the young Pluthrak, if he died.

And he would die, of that she was certain, if his life was demanded and he decided meeting the demand was the best way for him to be "of use." However close he had become to humans, in that respect he was still Jao.

"*All* Jao," she whispered.

Tamt was watching her, as she so often did, studying the woman she guarded as if to understand her. Now, she spoke softly, and Caitlin realized how thoroughly Tamt had come to know her.

"Yes," she said, interpreting the two words correctly. "Even those who oppose him now understand that much. He is a *kroudh* of legend. The greatest of all Jao, because they will hold us all to *vithrik.*"

There was a flurry of movement out on the tarmac and Caitlin rose to watch. As though they had but one mind between them, Jao were streaming toward the center of the landing field.

"I would say flow has completed itself," Kralik said. "It must be time for the Subcommandant's hearing. I thought they'd wait till the morning."

"I see," she said, but she really didn't see at all. No human ever would. That she was sure of.

CHAPTER
42

Now. The moment was now. Flow strengthened, summoning Aille across the base to the landing field with its flock of ships. It was strange to be surrounded by so many different kochan, he thought, as he walked out to the meeting stage. During the entirety of his youth on Marit An, he had only known individuals born of Pluthrak and its associated submoieties. On all sides, eyes, bright-green with curiosity, tracked him like targeting mechanisms, and whispers closed behind him like a wake. Flow surged and he felt how matters rushed to their conclusion. He tightened his perception, giving him time to consider each placement of his foot, each flick of a whisker. So much scrutiny required his carriage to be flawless.

A number of minor kochan had been represented, along with Narvo and its subsidiaries, throughout the expeditionary forces on Terra. But the Bond pulled members from all of the kochan. Aille wished he could sit down and speak with the elders who had come to tease apart the tangles in this dilemma, especially the Preceptor. Their accumulated wisdom must be great indeed.

Dau krinnu ava Pluthrak and Yaut preceded him across the field, allowing him status, for perhaps the last time. They really should not. Having become *kroudh*, he was not entitled to their regard, but they would not yield to his arguments and so he let them have their way.

Occupying the central-most portion of the landing field in a loose ring, the Bond of Ebezon ships were of a black alloy imbued with a rainbow hue that shimmered in the fading sunlight. Their members, the Harriers, were harnessed in gleaming black, which complemented their enigmatic eyes. Their bodies were beautifully neutral, neither curious, distracted, angry nor accusing.

Bond forces, under the loose direction of the Naukra Krith Ludh, outnumbered those of any single kochan except Narvo, Pluthrak and perhaps Dano. They possessed enough firepower to enforce whatever decisions would be made here on Terra. No kochan ever opposed their rulings once they had been formulated, much less rulings formulated in full Naukra assembly. It was shameful enough not to be able to forge association and solve one's own difficulties. How much worse then would it be to have compromise forced upon your kochan?

He'd heard creche tales of kochan so shamed by their failure to form association that their entire adult population had laid down their lives in order to end discord and allow the rest of the Jao to preserve alliance. Such incidents had been very rare, even in ancient times, and did not happen since the Naukra Krith Ludh had been formed. But the possibility was always there. Above all, Jao could never forget that the Ekhat, who had long ago made them for their own complicated reasons, now unmade them at every opportunity. Division among the kochan only allowed that grim ambition to be more easily achieved. The Jao had to fight together or die, and if they lost, the rest of sentient life in the universe would eventually die along with them.

Oppuk waited in the clearing, where the temporary tribunal had brought in black rocks of pleasing harmonics and placed them strategically to properly structure thought. They had been shaped by wind and wave and were curved so perfectly, there was not an edge anywhere on their gleaming ebony surfaces.

Within that boundary, he knew flow would be rich and smooth. Marit An had possessed such a circle. He had been allowed to experience it a few times, before achieving emergence and being assigned to Terra. He halted beyond the first outcropping and studied the configuration, trying to judge its influence before he submitted himself to it.

Dau and Yaut entered without looking back, then stood heartward, waiting, their ears already quieting, their eyes lulled.

They had arrived at the best portion of the local solar cycle, as the star's light subsided to a mellowness that did not overwhelm Jao eyes as the fullness of the day did. The Bond had gauged the flow well in convening the Naukra at this particular moment.

Off to the side, the green-gray ocean rolled toward the shore, its energies agitated by a storm cell hanging low and black on the horizon. The rising surf was white-capped, the air alive with spray. It would be difficult to put its potent invitation out of his mind and concentrate on the matters at hand.

He took a step toward the gleaming black rocks, which were as tall as his head, and felt the subtle pressure already building within. Flow at its finest. He already felt more at peace with what had to be accomplished.

Pluthrak, of course, was hoping to validate his actions here on Terra. This would allow Aille to take up his Pluthrak affiliation again, securing both his career and future, as well as bringing honor to his progenitors. Pluthrak was too subtle to seek outright *oudh* status over Terra, for that would be too humiliating for Narvo. They wished, instead, to use the crisis to finally force Narvo into proper association. The beginning of it, at least.

Narvo sought just the opposite, to prove Aille had been selfish and motivated only by kochan politics, that he had cared nothing for the welfare of his kind, but had only sought to make of himself a hero and Oppuk a fool, that it had been both a personal disagreement between the two of them of the basest sort and a move to increase the fortunes of Pluthrak. They would be willing, he was certain, to cede *oudh* status on Terra—but only at the price of Pluthrak suffering an equal humiliation. Which, of course, could only be Aille's punishment. If they had their way, he would be cut off from the solace of Pluthrak forever, shorn of any opportunity to enter a marriage-group and continue his career. Most likely, he would have to give up his life.

Neither outcome would be good for the Jao. The Pluthrak solution, in the long run, no more than the Narvo. They were still thinking in the old ways, Pluthrak no less than the others, as if traditional kochan relations encompassed all of a universe's wisdom. Aille had once thought so himself, but did no longer.

What he still failed to comprehend was whether the Bond understood. What was needed was not simply to develop association between the two most powerful of the Jao kochan, but to begin transforming association itself. Or the Jao, in the end, would come to resemble the Ekhat who had created them.

But how could he, barely emerged, bring the Jao to that realization? Aille was still looking for the answer, although he felt it, shimmering just beneath conscious recognition.

"Aille, formerly krinnu ava Pluthrak, now *kroudh*," a low voice summoned him from within the sleek circle.

He entered, feeling the carefully tuned energies shear around his body. Oppuk glowered as Aille took his place in the center, but his whiskers tingled, his ears flexed, even his blood sang as the flow of this configuration swept around him. It was as though the essence of water itself were here and he swam in a deep, cool sea which invigorated every cell in his body. Positive energy was building here. The Bond designers had done well.

He let it flow through him, sluice his worries and apprehensions away until he felt thoroughly purified. Without conscious intention, *calm-acceptance* now softened his angles and cleared the emotional sparkles of green from his eyes. He knew they must be as quiet as those of any Harrier present.

Oppuk looked out of place, his body clearly in the throes of *angry-resentment*. A number of Narvo elders flanked him, their *vai camiti* similar to his, but more balanced.

"It is forbidden," said the Preceptor who had called him inside the circle, "for one kochan to challenge another, once *oudh* status has been bestowed, Yet you seized control of this world against the lawful Governor, Oppuk krinnu ava Narvo." The black eyes, still as the depths of space, turned to him. "How will you defend your choices?"

"With my life," Aille said.

Yaut felt a surge of pride. It was quite proper to offer one's life to alleviate unintended damage, but he knew many here had not expected one so young to be willing. Therein lay the quality of Pluthrak, that even its most youthful scions understood the nature of *vithrik* and were willing to do what was right, no matter the cost.

The Preceptor regarded Aille and flow seemed to stand still. His entire body was devoid of extraneous expression, so that he seemed composed of tranquility itself. "So be it," he said at last, and Yaut felt how measured that response was, how carefully considered. "We will hear of those days, of your actions and of Oppuk's." He turned to the Narvo who stood on the other side of the vast circle. "Oppuk krinnu ava Narvo, are you also willing to surrender your life, if you are found at fault?"

Crude *outrage* suffused Oppuk's every line. "I have done nothing which should require my life! For over twenty orbital cycles, I have been stranded on this barbaric outpost, surrounded by incompetents and savages, and yet I have done all that was asked of me, even repelling the Ekhat when they did finally come. Where is the loss of *vithrik* in that?"

The Preceptor gazed at him. Again flow eased, so that even the wind, threading through the black rocks, seemed to stand still and an eternity passed between one breath and the next.

"He will." A female Narvo elder stepped forward and her eyes flashed. Her nap was pale-russet and her *vai camiti* stood out as though painted on with a bold hand. "*Vithrik* is the same for all, Pluthrak or Narvo. Oppuk will do whatever is deemed appropriate by the Naukra."

She had spoken for him, as though he were not even emerged. A current shivered through the watching crowd and all present felt Oppuk's hot shame.

Only the Harriers did not react, their bodies much more devoid of expression than a Terran's. With the natives, Yaut thought, one always knew they were thinking something, just not what. The Harriers, though, with their training, seemed to suppress all opinion.

"Summon those who witnessed the events in question, then."

Narvo, who had brought the complaint against Aille, would go first. Yaut thought Oppuk would be the primary witness, though he would have been wise to choose another. Kaul krinnu ava Dano, Commandant of all military forces in Terra's solar system, would have been ideal. But Dano had chosen to remain neutral, it seemed. Yaut did not see Kaul anywhere.

Apparently, he had gauged correctly. Oppuk stepped forward.

His posture was overbearing, an awkward combination of *contempt* mingled with *disdain*, too similar to perform well in tandem. "From the start, this Pluthrak would not listen to more experienced officers," he said. "He was counseled not to trust Terrans, that jinau soldiers were savage and unpredictable, requiring a firm hand. His response was to draft Terrans into his personal service at the earliest opportunity!"

Ears dipped as the crowd took this in, but the Harriers seemed unaffected.

"Then," Oppuk continued, "when Terrans went whining to him about having to scrap their outmoded tech, he conducted field tests to assuage their pride and argued they had a point!" He glowered at Aille. "He actually believes their addiction to *ollnat* is a strength!"

"But it did work, did it not?" The Preceptor seemed stillness itself, as though nothing exterior touched him.

"They lost half their ships!" Oppuk exploded, as though the words were being torn out of him. "And it will never work again. Next time, the Ekhat will expect their primitive tactics and be ready!"

"It is possible, of course, that the Ekhat ships sent a message back before being destroyed, regarding what they had encountered." The Preceptor turned black eyes to Aille. "What then?"

Aille found his lines gone to *careful-consideration*. "No single tactic, however effective, has to work forever. And I have found that human inventiveness coupled with Jao practicality is a very effective combination. We will devise something. Indeed, we have already begun working on it."

Oppuk turned to the assembled crowd of Naukra representatives. "Do you hear that? The crecheling is besotted with these creatures! He never stirs without one of them in attendance! He has at least twenty in his service by now!"

"Actually," Yaut said, "he has but four."

"Four out of how many?" Oppuk demanded, glaring at Aille. "How many Jao has he taken into his service?"

"Several," Aille said. He began to name them, but Oppuk interrupted.

"Perhaps Pluthrak has nothing to learn from other Jao!" Oppuk strode into the center and faced Aille. "Perhaps Pluthrak is more comfortable surrounded by worthless lifeforms!"

This was the long-standing aggression between Narvo and Pluthrak at its most blatant. Yaut could see how the naked demonstration pained the Narvo elder at Oppuk's back. It was shockingly bad manners, on display for all to see.

If only he could have instructed Aille how to handle a situation like this—he'd hoped to have more time, and he should have. Flow had not seemed so rapid, when they had first arrived on Terra.

Aille was still, his body magnificently loose and neutral. His eyes were so perfectly black that even Yaut, who knew him to possess superb control, was amazed.

To Yaut's surprise, another Jao suddenly spoke, stepping forward from behind another Naukra representative. "I have a question for Oppuk krinnu ava Narvo," he stated forcefully. "How many Jao does *he* have in his personal service? And if there are none—none left—what happened to them?"

To Yaut's even greater surprise, he saw that the Jao who had spoken was Wrot. The old bauta had left Pascagoula several solar cycles earlier, excusing himself from Aille's service temporarily in order to attend to what he called, vaguely, "my kochan's affairs."

Wrot bestowed a quick bow at Aille. "I am one of the young Pluthrak's personal service, as it happens. But I am speaking for my kochan here. I have been selected as their representative at the Naukra."

He turned back to Oppuk, and any pretense of politeness vanished. Blunt as always, to the point of coarseness, the old Hemm's posture was *angry-contempt.*

"Answer the question, Oppuk!" he commanded. *"Where is your service?"*

Oppuk seemed frozen, for a moment. When he spoke, his words came awkwardly. "My . . . fraghta left long ago. Too old and weary to serve any longer, she said."

Yaut saw the Narvo elders standing behind Oppuk shift their stance, uneasily. Clearly enough, Oppuk was not telling the truth— not all of it, at least.

Wrot was unrelenting. "I am not concerned about 'long ago.' You had a Jao in your personal service very recently. Ullwa is her name. Or rather—*was* her name."

The bowlegged old bauta advanced upon the much larger Oppuk, his ears flat, his whole body now shrieking *furious-determination.*

"Answer the question, you Narvo whelp! You—who boast of your Jao-ness. *Where is Ullwa?*"

Oppuk, involuntarily, stepped back a pace. "She—she is dead."

The stance of the Narvo elders now shifted again. Their unease was no longer disguised at all. Indeed, the eyes of the old female who led them—Nikau was her name—were shining green with suspicion.

Nikau now stepped forward. "Dead? How?"

Oppuk glanced back at her, then looked away. His stance shifted, exuding what he obviously meant to be *firm-determination* but was much closer to childish *petulant-stubbornness.* "She was hopelessly incompetent at her duties. I put her down."

A vast sigh swept through the Naukra assembly. Nikau, on the other hand, seemed frozen in place.

Wrot spoke again, quickly. "So. Now everyone knows. This is the truth of Oppuk's self-named 'firm rule.' He is a beast, nothing more—and treats his own Jao service as brutally as he has the humans placed under his charge."

The bauta pivoted, gracefully for his age, and pointed toward Aille's service. "Now I will show you, in contrast, how well Aille krinnu ava Pluthrak has trained his human service. Caitlin Stockwell, step forth."

Yaut glanced at Aille, wondering. But some subtlety in the youngster's stance made clear that he had not planned this with Wrot ahead of time. Aille, clearly enough, was as surprised as Yaut by Wrot's intervention.

Brilliant intervention, as it happened. The old bauta had skewered Oppuk—and now, Yaut was sure, would skewer him again.

Hopefully, Stockwell would survive.

Caitlin lowered her head and slipped off the blue fabric sling that supported her broken arm.

"Wait a minute," Kralik said urgently. "You're not anywhere near healed yet."

"I need both arms for this," she said, cradling her elbow with her good hand.

"I'm going with you," Kralik said.

"She must enter the circle alone," Yaut said, "if she is to speak."

Caitlin stepped forward, then stopped and pulled off the heeled shoes and dropped them. Behind her, she heard Ed's low chuckle, full of humor despite the strain of the moment.

She forced a smile from her own face, since the Jao new to Terra would misunderstand the expression. It wasn't easy. Like Ed, for reasons impossible to explain, pitching those shoes seemed like a transition; the end of one order, the beginning of something else entirely new.

*   *   *

The wind sang through Aille's whiskers as he waited. The air was rich with brine and spray, and *hai tau*, life-in-motion. Avians wheeled overhead, soaring low enough for him to pick out the elongated shape of their heads and the whiteness of their body coverings. This world was fascinating. He wanted to go back to the sea and follow another whale, perhaps even swim with it this time.

But duty lay elsewhere. Flow, which had been almost stagnant a moment before, suddenly surged. As he had gauged himself— obviously, Wrot had reached the same conclusion—Caitlin's appearance would prove decisive.

Caitlin strode past him into the center of the black stones. Her body expressed *request-for-attention*, the form so well executed, no well brought up Jao could have done any better. Even her broken arm was held properly, though, at that angle, she must be feeling considerable discomfort.

The Bond Preceptor shifted his notice so subtly that even Aille could not have said when Caitlin became his focus, instead of him. "You wish to speak?"

She was still concentrating on her next posture, no doubt. Aille felt himself straining to perceive it, his own ears at *intrigued-inquiry*. What did she mean to do here?

"Vaish," she said, using the greeting's proper form, signifying 'I see you,' rather than vaist, 'You see me,' a subtle distinction most humans did not grasp. "I am told my testimony might be of use here."

"Your designation?" the Harrier asked, seeking her function, rather than her name.

"I am a member of the Subcommandant's personal service," she said, correctly divining his intent.

A ripple ran through the onlookers. Testimony had already been presented as to how he had taken natives into his service. But Aille knew that most of them were astonished at the ease and grace of her postures.

"What would you say?"

"What I wish, if that is permitted."

The Preceptor's response came instantly, easily. "That is a given, when one steps into the Naukra circle. How could it be otherwise?"

She nodded; then, as if realizing the momentary error, shifted into *accepted-understanding*. The flow of the movement was so smooth, so sure, that the two gestures—one human, one Jao—seemed to form a new whole. Aille was certain that he was not the only Jao present who suddenly glimpsed a new language emerging.

"Humans, of course, cannot perceive all the considerations, but it seems appropriate that we be allowed to present our viewpoint. The conflict developed on our world, and it is our world which will bear the consequences, should an ineffective solution be adopted."

Aille watched her move, the slow sweep of her arms toward *earnest-conviction*, the tilt of her head adding *desire-to-be-of-service*. A tripartite stance? His whiskers stiffened. Would one so young and inexperienced really be so ambitious?

The Preceptor stared too, along with the rest of the crowd, some of whom forgot themselves so far as to climb up on the rocks and watch. Her forehead furrowed as she concentrated, wisely going slowly, edging toward completion. To compensate for the extra finger, she held two-as-one on each hand, as Aille had once suggested back in the Governor's palace during that fateful reception. Her immobile ears contributed nothing to the stance, of course, and her lack of whiskers was jarring, but the rest of her—

Aille sucked in his breath in admiration. She was magnificent. He had been right to employ her in his service—and Oppuk's bigotry was now obvious to all.

"There are two solutions contemplated here," she said, trembling with the effort of holding the unusually complicated posture. "Though they are not equal to the Jao, neither will much vary the Terran condition."

The Preceptor watched, his gaze black and steady, not giving away the least of what he thought of this amazing display.

"There must be another path," she said, "a third alternative, which would not only satisfy human honor but best enable humans to be of use in the war against the Ekhat." Her stance altered seamlessly to *profound-respect*. "I wish to suggest that third way."

CHAPTER
43

"No!"

Oppuk found himself lunging at the brazen creature before he had even known he was in motion. Of all the insults heaped upon him, this was the one impossible to bear.

"This is an animal, a savage!"

Oppuk struck her down with a single slapping blow. Unfortunately, she jerked her head back at the last instant, so only his fingers made contact with her cheek. Had he struck her full-handed, as powerful as he was, he would have broken her neck.

As he'd intended. No matter. Fury was still surging through him. He would make good the lack.

The Stockwell female stumbled back and fell, then stared up at him; dazed, but her hands still forming the curves of *profound-respect*. In that moment, she represented all of Terra to him, a world of barbarians who would not yield to his rightful authority, yet fawned upon the first Pluthrak who flattered them. He threw himself on her.

She tried to fend him off, though it was impossible to do so, as pathetically weak as she was. Oppuk gripped both her fragile wrists in one hand and raised the other for a killing blow. He should have put her down the first time he saw her parody that guard's postures! He—

Iron fingers jerked him off the struggling female and cast him aside as though his weight meant nothing. His head rocked with a blow, then another and another—and then sheer agony paralyzed him. The same iron fingers had dislocated his ankle; then, the other; and then, so quickly it all seemed as one moment of torture, both of his wrists.

Stunned and crippled, Oppuk sprawled on the sand. Still, he struggled to rise—until iron fingers seized his shoulders and iron landed on his back, low down where it was most vulnerable even on a Jao, and ruptured his spine.

Yaut was already moving the instant Oppuk began his strike at Caitlin. Moving, in the way that only a great kochan fraghta can move, at a moment of clan outrage. To all those who watched, he seemed more like a predator than a Jao.

But Yaut krinnu Jithra vau Pluthrak was far more dangerous than any predator. With its power and vast associations, Pluthrak could select and shape the finest fraghta. Deadly as well as shrewd— and Jithra was a kochan famous for its savage fighting skills.

Large and powerful as he was, Oppuk had no chance at all. Nor would he, even had he been facing Yaut's charge directly. What followed would simply have taken a bit longer. Not much.

"Holy shit," hissed Tully. Even his glee at seeing Oppuk brought down was an undertone. Mostly, he was just shaken, finally seeing Yaut's full fury unleashed.

Yojimbo, for sure.

Oppuk's great Jao bones were crushed and mangled in the fraghta's hands like so many chicken wings. Each grip perfectly placed, the maximum possible leverage applied—each blow, the same. Then, a sudden and utterly vicious kneedrop to the lower spine, done while Yaut positioned Oppuk's shoulders to prevent any cushioning of the impact. Tully could *hear* the vertebra give way.

And I thought he gave me *a hard time!*

It all took but seconds. Yaut ended by seizing Oppuk's heavy nape and, one-handed, heaving the broken body back onto its knees.

Then, slapping the back of Oppuk's head to lower it and expose the neck vertebrae, Yaut half-crouched and drew a dagger from his harness.

Staring green-eyed with fury at the Narvo representatives, the fraghta bellowed: *"I demand his life!"*

His posture meant something too, Tully was sure, but he didn't know what. He'd never seen that posture on any Jao before.

Specifically, that is, Tully didn't know what it meant. The general idea was clear enough.

Readiness-to-dismember, let's call it. Or, how about: *give-me-any-shit-and-you're-all-dead-meat?*

Nikau krinnu ava Narvo did not think to argue. Oppuk's transgression of custom was so extreme that his life was forfeit the moment the first blow landed. No, the moment the blow was even launched.

Human or not, the female was in Pluthrak's service, not Narvo's—and the fact that the Pluthrak in question was now *kroudh* was simply irrelevant, under the circumstances.

Bad enough, that Oppuk had admitted to killing a member of his own service. But that deed, however barbarous, was a matter for Narvo to settle privately. Never—*never*—did the great kochan attack the service of another. They did not do so, for that matter, with the service of a minor kochan. Even a taif. That was the open road to civil war, which the Naukra existed to prevent—and the Bond would prevent even quicker. Had the Pluthrak fraghta not demanded Oppuk's life, the Bond Preceptor would have done so.

In truth, Nikau was relieved. Oppuk's unsanity—outright *madness*—was so obvious to all that Narvo itself could now escape with comparatively little damage from this hideous affair. They could be faulted for selecting Oppuk in the first place, and for leaving him in place, to be sure. But . . .

That could be explained away, over time. Eventually, it would be forgotten, as a clean wound leaves behind nothing worse than a scar. And, for the immediate purpose, Oppuk would serve splendidly as the focus of all outrage. At long last, the wretched creature would be of use.

Besides, Nikau thought there might be a small victory to gain here.

"Take his life," the Narvo elder stated, firmly, her own eyes green with fury. "Narvo casts him out."

Yaut grunted and began to position the dagger for the killing thrust.

"Not you!"

He looked up, puzzled. The old Narvo female was pointing toward Aille's service.

"Not you, fraghta. Since the insult was delivered upon a human, let a human in the *kroudh's* service take Oppuk's life. Narvo insists."

Yaut had to force himself to restrain his anger. The Narvo's ploy was obvious—and petty. She would try to gain what little satisfaction Narvo could from the situation by having a human bungle the business. Driving a blade through heavy Jao vertebra in a proper killing stroke would be difficult. A human would most likely hack away, dissolving the ritual of the moment into crude butchery.

Petty . . . and stupid.

Now, Yaut had to restrain himself from showing any humor. The Narvo elder might not be unsane, but she shared Oppuk's bigotry. There was at least one human in Aille's service, Yaut was sure, who would serve the purpose admirably.

Not Caitlin herself or Kinsey, of course. Neither of them was strong enough. Nor Kralik. He was a soldier, in the end, not a warrior. And, besides, his personal ties with Caitlin would probably make him too angry to do the deed properly.

The choice was obvious. And Yaut found himself wondering, for a moment, if in some strange way Aille had sensed it, that very first day on Terra. Green eyes which had been willing to challenge Jao, as if they were Jao themselves.

"Tully!" he called out.

Tully came forward, moving in that easy, slender-but-strong manner which Yaut now knew humans would call "pantherish."

"May I be of use, fraghta?" he asked. He even managed—would wonders never cease?—to assume a reasonable rendition of *readiness-to-serve.*

"Take this creature's life." Yaut flipped the dagger, now holding it by the blade and extending the hilt toward Tully.

"My pleasure," Tully growled, taking the dagger and another step to bring him over Oppuk.

"It must be done well," Yaut murmured. "One blow, quick and clean, killing him instantly." He placed a finger over the exposed joint where the blade needed to penetrate.

Oppuk shuddered slightly at the touch. The former Governor was strong enough that he might still be conscious. Yaut hoped he was. Let the beast know that a human was about to put him down.

Tully eyed the target, nodded. Then, to Yaut's surprise, shifted his grip on the dagger to bring the blade below his palm instead of above it.

Yaut felt an instant's concern. That was the overhand grip of a novice blade-fighter.

But his worries were moot. Tully knew what he was doing. In a motion more swift than any Jao could have managed, Tully reared his body high and then coiled down like a striking serpent, driving the blade hilt-deep into Oppuk's neck.

The massive body jerked, once, and Yaut let it fall. Oppuk was dead before he finished sprawling ungainly on the sand.

Yaut stared at the blade. Then, reached out his hand and gave the hilt a tentative little jiggle.

As he suspected. He would need both hands—and all the muscles in his back—to draw the blade out. Even then, he'd have to pry it back and forth before easing enough of the pressure of the neck bones. Yaut was not sure he could have driven it in as deeply himself.

He did so, not disguising the effort it took. And then, done, let his hard green gaze sweep over the assembled Naukra.

They seemed shaken, as well they might be—all except the veteran soldiers who, here and there, were among the selected representatives. Those simply looked satisfied.

As well they might. In Tully's murderous, lightning-quick deathstroke, the Naukra had finally gotten a glimpse of the frightening truth that had lurked on Terra for twenty of its orbital cycles. Which the veteran soldiers understood, and so few of their superiors ever had. Yaut knew that, to the Naukra representatives new to the planet, as once to him, humans looked silly at first glance. Almost like misshapen crechelings, with their ridiculously little ears and their too-widely-spaced eyes, and their flat faces.

They would seem so, no longer. They would think of Tully now, when they thought of humans. And understand better, hopefully, what they truly faced.

"It was well done, Tully," he said softly. "Very well. You are a credit to yourself and your service."

Tully grinned, thinly, somehow managing to combine that human expression with a *grateful-to-be-of-service* stance that was . . .

Truly pitiful.

Yaut sighed. Tully's training, he now realized, would never be complete. But he also thought that was perhaps the secret to the creature, his way of being of use—which Aille had recognized, however dimly, from the very beginning.

Kralik was the first human at her side. He straightened Caitlin's neck with careful hands, probing the bruised flesh for damage, trying to tell if she was concussed or if vertebrae had been damaged by the blow—or if she just had a badly bruised cheek.

Her voice was a harsh rattle. "M'okay, Ed. So—important! Must make them listen!"

"No, it's all right." He cradled her in his arms, rocking her gently. "Oppuk can't hurt you anymore. It's all right, sweetheart. He's dead. The stinking bastard is fucking *dead*."

The short Preceptor dressed in the Bond's black harness and trousers came up and gazed down at her with cryptic black eyes. His manner was calm, as though nothing untoward had occurred here. "Do you still wish to speak?"

"Yes. I do. Help me up, Ed."

Caitlin rose to her feet, Kralik assisting. She was shaken and bruised and a trickle of red ran from the corner of her mouth. She dabbed at it with the back of one hand. Oppuk's blow had been stunningly powerful, even though only the heavy fingers had struck her.

"There is a third way, I think." Her voice was fainter than she wanted, so she did her best to speak more loudly. "One that I believe would create new association and honor all concerned. Human as well as Jao—and avoid insult to any kochan."

Silence fell over the assemblage as she straightened, desperately trying to push aside the dazed feeling. She was still too fuzzy-headed to be able to develop any elaborate logical preface, she realized. That would have been hard, in any event, since she was more-or-less thinking on her feet to begin with.

Best to just come to the point.

She closed her eyes, swayed, then forced them open again. "I ask you not to grant *oudh* status on this world to either Narvo or Pluthrak."

She turned first to Narvo, and managed a reasonable rendition of *honorable-recognition*. "Narvo because, through no fault of its own, that kochan has come to be indelibly associated among humans—at least for the moment—with Oppuk's unsane rule. They would simply be faced with suppressing endless rebellions on Terra, which would be of no use to anyone."

The elderly female who led the Narvo delegation stared back at her; for a Jao, wide-eyed. Then, almost but not quite managing to conceal her surprise, returned the posture with the same.

Caitlin's head was starting to clear, thankfully. She'd spoken those words from sheer instinct, but they'd been the right ones. Even though, judging by the angry tension in his stance, Ed thought she was letting the Narvo bastards off the hook.

Which she was, of course. That *had* to done, if anything else was to happen. Whether the Narvo deserved to be suspended on a meathook or not was a trivial issue. Narvo kochan was simply too powerful, too necessary to the Jao—and humans, for that matter—in the life-and-death struggle against the Ekhat to be openly humiliated. It was going to be difficult enough for Caitlin to persuade the Naukra to implement the proposal she was about to advance. Impossible, if Narvo was openly opposed.

Besides, Caitlin's words—the Narvo elder's almost immediate acceptance made this quite clear—had, ironically, now made Narvo something of a human . . .

Not "ally," certainly. But, if nothing else, they'd be the last, in the future, to criticize Aille for taking humans into his service.

Caitlin had to choke down an hysterical little laugh. *Since it was a human member of his service who salvaged their precious honor from near-disaster.*

She turned, moving more easily, and bestowed the same posture of *honorable-recognition* upon Dau krinnu ava Pluthrak.

"Nor do I think Pluthrak should be given *oudh* here, though that would certainly meet the approval of most humans. In the short time since he had been here, Subcommandant Aille has done as much to repair the Jao reputation as Governor Oppuk did to damage it in twenty years."

There was a little stir in the Naukra, at that. Caitlin wasn't surprised. The Jao were not accustomed to caring, one way or the other, what might or might not be "popular" with their conquered species. Conquerors were conquerors, subjects were subjects, and there's an end to it.

But, although she'd been too dazed to see much of it, Caitlin had only to glance at Oppuk's corpse and his human executioner, still standing beside it, to know that even the most crusty-minded Jao in the assembly understood now that humans had to be dealt with . . .

Gingerly.

Leaving Tully aside, by now I'm sure they've all heard the story of the Narvo veterans' defiance of their own elders. Probably heard the same from their own veterans, for that matter, if they've been listening at all since they got here.

"What is the problem, then?" asked the Preceptor. "Pluthrak would seem the obvious choice."

"Too obvious, that is the problem. As popular as the choice might be, for humans, too many Jao kochan would be suspicious that this crisis was created by Pluthrak in the first place in order to displace Narvo here."

There was another stir in the crowd, and not a little one. Caitlin had just stated, aloud, what many of them suspected to be the truth.

That was not surprising either, of course—since it *was* the truth. Close enough, anyway. Caitlin was sure of that much. She was also sure that Aille had been an innocent party to the affair—the "dupe," insofar as that word could possibly be applied to his very-effective self. And she was pretty sure, though not positive, that Pluthrak's ambitions had actually been more subtle. Not so much focused on gaining *oudh* over Terra, in itself, but forcing Narvo to make concessions elsewhere. That was the subtle and indirect way that Pluthrak operated, she'd come to understand.

But, from the viewpoint of the Naukra crowd, the distinction hardly mattered. It was just as essential, for Caitlin's purpose, to remove Pluthrak from becoming, in a different way than Narvo, another obstacle to proper association.

Fortunately, the Pluthrak elder representing his kochan at the Naukra was quick-thinking and as subtle as Pluthrak's reputation. Without even the moment's hesitation of Narvo, he was returning her posture of *honorable-recognition.*

"It is true, what she says." Dau krinnu ava Pluthrak's posture then shifted to something Caitlin didn't quite recognize, but tentatively categorized as the Jao equivalent of *butter-wouldn't-melt-in-my-mouth.* "Thought to be true, rather, since there is actually no truth in it. But suspicion is a reality in its own terms, and must be dealt with correctly. I agree that to give *oudh* over Terra to Pluthrak would create—or reinforce—existing tensions which are already unfortunate."

The collective posture of the crowd visibly eased. This was, suddenly and unexpectedly, going quite well. The worst immediate danger, a sharp and open clash between Narvo and Pluthrak, had now been averted. Caitlin could practically see them all rubbing their hands, like so many human horse-traders about to get down to serious dickering.

And that needs to be headed off at the pass, before it even gets started. Brace yourself, girl. Here comes the hardest part. Well . . . the second-to-hardest.

As if on cue, the Preceptor spoke again. As always, his stance impossible to read.

"You wish to suggest another kochan altogether then? Perhaps Jak or Hij or Dano?"

"No, not another kochan. I think the Naukra should grant status to Terra as a taif. Two taifs, rather, one human and one Jao—and both affiliated directly to the Bond of Ebezon."

Finish it. The hardest part. Sorry, boss, but sometimes the road forward requires a stab in the back.

She forced herself to turn and gaze directly at Aille, standing not far away. "And I think you should not remove Aille's status as *kroudh.* His affiliation with Pluthrak must be severed forever. Not to punish him, but to free him. So that he can be adopted, if he and they so choose, by the new Jao taif to be formed on Terra. That alone would give the new taifs the stature they need, among Jao and humans both, while dishonoring no one."

CHAPTER
44

Wrot immediately stepped forward. "It is a superb proposal. Hemm supports it completely. So will all of Wathnak, I am sure." He reached up and stroked the bauta on his cheek. "Indeed, I will give up my bauta and seek adoption into this new taif myself."

He gave Aille a benign gaze. "This one is so impulsive he will need sage elders to advise him. Of course, he will have to release me from his service first. Unseemly, otherwise. How could anyone possibly be sure I was selecting his mates for their valuable qualities instead of"—he waggled ears and whiskers simultaneously, conveying a comically-exaggerated version of *suspected-impropriety*—"those petty matters of comeliness which matter so much to callow youngsters."

Most of the Naukra's members were elders themselves, familiar, as Aille was not, with the secretive workings of kochan-parents. Wrot's amusement was shared, for a moment, by many of them.

Aille himself had been too surprised by Caitlin's proposal to think clearly, much less appreciate the humor involved in Wrot's jest. He was still trying to grapple with the idea of being severed forever from Pluthrak, even though that outcome had been at least half-expected. He was in no position to start thinking about the needs of a newly formed taif. Any taif, much less one as peculiar as this would be.

Him? At his young age? Already a kochan-parent?
Absurd.

He pushed that personal matter aside, to concentrate on the proposal as a whole. It was . . .

Intriguing. That much, for a certainty. Aille could immediately see a multitude of problems, but he could also see an even greater multitude of possibilities.

His intrigue, Nikau immediately made clear, was not shared by the Narvo elder. Her posture, in fact, bordered on *indignant-disbelief.*

"It is a ridiculous idea!" she exclaimed. Then, catching herself, shifted quickly to a stance of *skeptical-consideration.*

"A new Jao taif . . . perhaps." She gave Aille a glance. Then, a much longer and considering look at Dau krinnu ava Pluthrak.

"Narvo would not object to that," she said abruptly, "as a way to avoid unnecessary humiliation of Pluthrak as well as Narvo. Whereas we would object—strongly—were Pluthrak to demand the removal of its scion's *kroudh* status and his return to Pluthrak. Narvo alone will not pay the price for resolving this crisis." Her eyes began to move toward Oppuk's corpse, but shied away. For a moment, even her fierce figure held a hint of grief. "The one we lost here was once *namth camiti,* whatever he became. Let Pluthrak balance that loss with one of its own."

Aille had already seen that advantage himself. So, obviously, had Dau—and Yaut, for that matter, judging from his stance. To restore Aille to Pluthrak at this point would be to place all blame upon Narvo. On Oppuk, at least. But even cast out and his life given, Oppuk still reflected on his kochan of origin. Whereas retaining *kroudh* status for Aille would satisfy Narvo that his personal rebellion was being adequately punished. No self-stated *kroudh* in Jao history had ever had that status removed by the Naukra, after all, for precisely that reason. It would have been too great an insult to the kochan who had been his or her opponents.

On the other hand, if a new and low-status taif chose to adopt him . . .

Who would care? Officially, at least, such would be beneath the notice of a great kochan. Taifs, after all, were often given to impulsive actions and behavior. Such foolishness reflected on no one, not even the kochan which had agreed to take them into affiliation. It was the very function of taif status, after all, to allow a kochan-in-formation the time to learn from its mistakes. Much as crechelings were not held to the same standards as adults.

Nikau continued, more forcefully. "But the idea of a human taif is simply ridiculous. Taif—kochan—these are Jao things. They would fit humans as well as—as—"

Unwillingly, her eyes were drawn to Oppuk's corpse.

"Did you not yourself," Wrot demanded, following her own obvious thoughts, "demand that a human take Oppuk's life? And was there any ground for complaint, after, at the manner in which he did so?"

"It was barbarous, the way he struck," she protested.

Wrot shrugged. "As barbarous as this human gesture? This awkward heaving of the shoulders which is their way of expressing *acceptance-of-reality*?"

Actually, Aille knew—Wrot knew even better—a human shrug could express a multitude of things. Their body language was crude as well as unformalized, as poorly shaped as any crecheling's. But this was not the time to dwell on that.

Nor did Wrot do so. "What does it matter, truly? If the strike was barbarous, it was also effective. Was it not? As quick—no, quicker!—and, in its own way, as effective as any Jao's."

He pointed at Tully. "Learn to *think,* all of you. Unless we leave Terra altogether—which no one now proposes, not even humans— we will have to learn to—to—"

He broke off, groping for the words. Then, barked a laugh. "Ha! Human postures are pathetic, I admit, for all but a few like Caitlin Stockwell. But their sayings contain endless wisdom. Here is one, which they apply to marriage—the males to the females, and in reverse: 'you can't live with them, and you can't live without them.'"

All the Jao in the crowd, for a moment, looked almost what humans would call "cross-eyed," trying to follow the jagged logic. But there was something . . .

Wrot barked another laugh. "Yes, intriguing, is it not? So hard to make sense of it, but there's always *something . . .*"

His posture, though reflecting more than a trace of amusement, settled into *benign-acceptance.* In the blunt Wathnak version, to be sure. But, given the moment, Aille thought that bluntness was perhaps appropriate.

"Learn to live with it," the old bauta stated. "Caitlin Stockwell's proposal is indeed peculiar—even barbarous, if you will—but it will *work.* And nothing else will, of that I can assure you."

Now, Wrot pointed to Kralik. "That human is the commander of the Terran jinau. I assure you—and if you don't want to accept my words alone, ask any veteran of Terran service—you do *not* want him in rebellion. In his own way, and a much larger way, he will be as frightening as Tully."

He stepped back, almost but not quite merging into the crowd. "I have spoken enough. As humans say, 'you can lead a horse to water—a horse being a useful but dumb beast—but you can't make him drink.' So with a Naukra."

The statement verged on insult, but not even the Narvo representatives seemed inclined to take it so. They, perhaps, less than any.

Suddenly, decisively, Nikau krinnu vau Narvo spoke again. "Narvo removes itself from this discussion. We have stated our reservations, but we will not object if the Bond chooses to accept."

A Hij representative stepped forward. "Yet that is what concerns me the most. Never in our history has the Bond been affiliated with any kochan. Is it wise to change that?" He glanced, somewhat apologetically, at the Harriers. "The dangers are obvious."

"Obvious, indeed," echoed the Preceptor immediately. "Yet I have studied human history myself, and believe that the subtleties of the human female's proposal are being misunderstood." He turned to Caitlin. "Correct me if I am mistaken, but I believe your proposal is really for the Bond to assume what you would call 'protectorate status' over these new taifs. As opposed to what you would call 'colonial status.'"

She nodded, wide-eyed. Caitlin was obviously even more surprised than Aille at the Preceptor's knowledge of the details of human history.

The Preceptor turned back to address the Naukra. "The distinction, in human custom, is clear. The Bond's status would be temporary, not permanent. Once the kochan was formed—judged so, by the Naukra—the Bond's status would end. There would be no continuing affiliation, which might lead the Bond to become overly strong and develop particular interests unsuited to its function."

The Hij representative's posture slipped into *puzzlement.* "How can an affiliation *not* be permanent? I can see that, to be sure, with the human taif, since no bloodline connection is possible. But with the Jao taif being proposed—*ah.*"

In the corner of his eye, Aille saw Yaut struggling not to adopt the same posture Aille was struggling not to adopt. *Incredulity-at-blatant-stupidity* was a most impolite stance to take at any gathering, much less that of the Naukra.

The Hij, clearly enough, had just realized what was obvious. And the Preceptor, though neither his stance nor his tone indicated anything beyond neutrality, put it into words.

"The Bond is not a kochan. We do not breed. Therefore the normal bloodline ties which would develop between a taif and its kochan are impossible."

His next words were spoken even more decisively than Nikau's.

"Only the Bond can make this decision. We will, of course, consult with kochan representatives." His eyes went quickly from Dau to Nikau and back again. "I will specifically want Pluthrak and Narvo involved in the negotiations."

Nikau began to stiffen, but the Preceptor's gaze upon her was now hard, not neutral. "I understand that Narvo has removed itself from *this* discussion. But there are other matters which will need to be discussed."

"Such as?" she demanded, half-angrily.

"Let us begin with the fact that this planet has suffered immense damage—and then neglect." Tactfully, he did not name names. "If the Bond is to assume this burden, it will *expect* the greatest of the kochan to assist in the necessary reconstruction. Our own resources are primarily devoted to the war against the Ekhat."

The same could be said of Narvo's, of course—or Pluthrak's, or the resources of any of the great kochan. But, with only a moment's hesitation, Nikau indicated her assent. With the barest possible posture, true, but assent nonetheless. She might not like it—did not like it—but she realized she could not evade the matter. Narvo had escaped open humiliation, but they would still pay a price for their neglect in overseeing Oppuk. Still, a price in resources could be paid, easily enough, by a kochan as great as Narvo, since there was no insult implied to the kochan's honor.

Dau krinnu vau Pluthrak had already assumed the posture of *agreement-assent.* The Preceptor glanced at him, then his eyes moved over the assembled Naukra.

"It is settled, then. Unless there is open opposition, I propose this Naukra has ended."

He waited, politely, to see if any opposition would emerge. None did, of course. With the Bond taking such a firm stance, and with both Narvo and Pluthrak assenting, no kochan would be foolish enough to object.

Besides, Aille thought, for the most part they were all simply relieved. They might think privately that the proposal was preposterous. But it was no longer any of their concern, after all—let the Bond deal with the human maniacs. The matter which had *truly* concerned them, and caused every Jao kochan and most taifs to send representatives to this Naukra, was now settled.

Narvo and Pluthrak were no longer on the verge of open conflict. Indeed, the first possibility of association seemed even to have emerged. The Human Problem remained, to be sure. But that was the Bond's problem, henceforth. The Terran Crisis was over.

Suddenly, the sense of completed flow was overwhelming. Moving as if with a single will, the Naukra dispersed, each kochan moving toward its own ships.

"That is *still* purely creepy to me," Aille heard Tully mutter. "How do they do that, anyway?"

But Tully's savage grin was back also. "Not that I wouldn't mind it if humans could learn the trick. After watching Rob Wiley's headaches trying to get a damn Resistance meeting to end. Or start on time."

Kralik bent low over Caitlin's white face and smoothed a stray golden tendril back. She was lying on a cot, now, back in the tent, after having gotten some medical attention.

He desperately wanted to kiss her but was afraid of hurting her face. The bruise was spreading.

"It's a pain, isn't it?" Caitlin asked softly, chuckling. "Maybe the Jao will finally stop beating on me long enough that we can—you know, Ed. Get *laid*, dammit."

Kralik smiled. He'd been thinking exactly the same thing. When Caitlin had first proposed to him—okay, suggested that he propose to her—he'd agreed instantly because of his general attraction to the woman. But, once the situation settled into his mind, the more profane aspects of their new relationship had surged to the fore. To his loins, to be precise. Caitlin was gorgeous on top of everything else, even with her arm in a cast and her face bruised.

It had been . . . frustrating, to say the least. And still was.

But there was no point dwelling on the problem. It would be

happily resolved, and soon, once Caitlin healed enough. Caitlin might be inexperienced, and therefore a little nervous about sex, but she'd made perfectly clear she was not reluctant. Quite the opposite, in fact.

"Something to look forward to," he murmured, kissing her forehead. "But now that the dust seems to be settling, sweetheart, how about explaining this little bombshell you just dropped on everybody. What the hell *is* a taif, anyway? Exactly, I mean. In general, I understand it's something like a junior kochan."

Dr. Kinsey's voice interjected. "A probationary kochan, would be more accurate. Or, better yet, a trainee-kochan."

Kralik hadn't seen him coming. The professor waved his hands apologetically. "I don't mean to intrude though, if this is a private moment."

Caitlin smiled up at him. "Private moment? In a tent jammed full of soldiers? Please, Doctor Kinsey. I'm not a prude, but—still!"

Kinsey chuckled. So did Kralik. She nodded toward a nearby stool, and raised her voice. "Have a seat. And I imagine everyone here would like to hear what you have say."

Kinsey perched himself on a stool and waited until the people in the tent had gathered around.

"The origin of the institution of taif goes all the way back, in Jao history. It's something of a necessity, if you think about it. There are still isolated groups of Jao slaves to this day, in Ekhat captivity. There were far more, in the time after the Jao rebellion began. So, from the start, the Jao were faced with the problem of what to do with newly freed slaves. In some cases, so far as I can determine—especially when the number of freed slaves was small—they were simply adopted into whatever kochan freed them. But marriage-groups are deeply innate in the Jao, and were so even among slaves. Personally, I suspect the Ekhat bred that into them, in order to keep their numbers under control."

By now, he'd adopted his favorite professorial stance in the absence of a proper desk—hands clasped in his lap, when not gesturing with them right and left.

"You can see the difficulty. Breaking up a Jao marriage-group is even more traumatic for them than divorce is for us. So, the taif was created to resolve the problem."

He paused, looking professorially alarmed. "You all understand, of course, that I'm simplifying grossly. No doubt the taif-institution was never 'created,' in the sense that one creates a machine. Rather, it would have evolved—"

"Cut to the chase, Professor," Tully grumbled. "We're not scholars. We'll all forgive you any lapses into imprecision. Personally, I'd appreciate them. I'm a simple-minded grunt."

Kinsey looked a bit startled, but recovered quickly. "Well, then. So long as it's understood—" He hurried on, since Tully was starting to glare.

"The point being that Caitlin's proposal fits us rather neatly into an already existing Jao custom. The only unusual aspect of it, in fact—other than the obvious one of applying the institution to a species other than Jao—is her proposal to have the Bond serve as the overseeing kochan. The 'trainer kochan,' if you will."

Tully rolled his eyes. "Oh, great. *Wrem-fa* on a planetary scale." But he didn't really seem aggrieved.

"It's the best possible solution," Kinsey insisted, "if the Bond agrees. For humans, certainly. We'll have roughly—very roughly—a status equivalent to one of the old United Nations trusteeships or protectorates. Except, with the Bond, I don't think we'll have to worry that the supposedly benign colonial power is really using its protectorate status to maintain what amounts to permanent colonial rule. Maybe, we'll see. But as problems go, that one's in the future and nothing like the problem of being under direct Narvo rule—or the direct rule of any kochan. The Bond, of course, would oversee us, and would effectively control matters of defense and 'foreign relations.' But they'd leave our own internal affairs to us. The truth is, since 'defense' and 'foreign affairs' now refers to the Ekhat war, we're in no worse shape than we were before the conquest when we didn't know about any of that anyway. Except—ha!—give the Jao this much, they got rid of all those damn endlessly bickering nation-states. I, for one, won't miss that at all."

His clasped hands were now waving back and forth. "The best part, though, is Caitlin's proposal of a *double* taif, because that will . . ."

Kinsey's voice trailed off, his eyes now riveted on something in the direction of the tent's entrance.

Kralik swiveled his head and saw that Aille had entered the tent, with Yaut and Wrot preceding him. When he looked back down at Caitlin, he saw that her face was paler than ever.

"He's going to beat me to a pulp," she predicted. "Sorry, Ed.

You'll be horny a while longer. If Yaut starts in on me, at least a year."

But there was no anger in Aille's posture, as he gazed down at her. Caitlin couldn't quite tell what there was, since Aille's body was flowing from one posture to the next, never settling on any. As though he, too, hardly knew what to think.

"A fascinating idea," he said. "Why did you not propose it to me before?"

"I—" Caitlin blinked. "I only thought of it myself as we walked out to the circle." She smiled wanly. "There only seemed two alternatives. The Bond would find either for Narvo or Pluthrak, neither of which I thought would be good. But I was remembering that my father says there is always a third way, if you look hard enough."

Tully grunted, smiling strangely.

"Will the Bond agree?" Kralik asked.

"They already have," announced Wrot. "No sooner than the Naukra were safely back on their ships, all except Narvo and Pluthrak, whom the Preceptor had instructed to remain behind. I think the Narvo was most aggrieved."

His ears waggled sheer glee. "And Dau krinnu ava Pluthrak even more so. Ha! Enjoyable, that was. To see a subtle Pluthrak elder realized he'd been out-maneuvered by someone. Of course," he added, in an ameliorating tone, "it *was* the Bond's Strategy Circle."

Aille's own posture flickered, for a moment, into an odd combination of *chagrin* and . . . yes, *amusement* also.

"It is true, I suspect," Aille admitted. "I think now this entire affair, from the very beginning, was—was—"

" 'Engineered,' would be the human term," Wrot advanced, not perhaps helpfully. "Or better still, 'orchestrated.' "

"That is not helpful," growled Yaut. "Wisely has it been said— by Jao!—that old bautas are often a curse."

Caitlin frowned. "Surely the Bond didn't . . . I mean, they certainly have never had any contact with *me*."

Yaut shrugged, the gesture coming to him now as easily and smoothly as it would to a human. "Their strategists do not think in human terms, Caitlin. When you think of 'strategy,' your thoughts are like those of you who play that silly game I have seen. Called 'chess,' I believe. Angular, if you will, this move leading to that. Such is not the Bond's way. They think like Jao, in terms of flow. Create a situation and let it unfold."

He gave Wrot a none-too-friendly sidelong look. "So. Whether he is right or not, I do not know. What I do know is that dealing with this old one will be difficult, in the years ahead. He is too smug."

Wrot looked smug. "Especially since I am, so far, the eldest of the new elders of the new taif. Though I won't be, if that Binnat makes up her mind. Ha! Binnat has always been prone to indecisiveness. But she is also very shrewd, that one. She would make an excellent elder."

"You've *already* decided upon elders?"

Yaut and Wrot stared at her, as if she were a cretin. "Of course," Yaut snorted. "How is this difficult? Who else would there be, beyond me and Wrot and Hami? And, as he says, the one Binnat, if she agrees."

He glanced at Aille. "The others—this one especially—are obviously too young and impulsive and immature. Though, I admit, the breeding stock looks splendid."

Caitlin shook her head, trying to catch up. "That's not what I meant. How many Jao have agreed to leave their existing kochan and join the new taif? I would have thought . . . that would take a long time, for a Jao to decide. It can't have been more than two hours since the Naukra dispersed."

The answer was obvious, even before they spoke. All of Aille's personal service, of course. And . . .

"How many?" she whispered, already knowing she had become part of a new legend.

"Hundreds, girl," Yaut said softly, "here at Pascagoula alone. Thousands—tens of thousands—once the news spreads across the planet. Aille's name will draw them like a magnet. He has become almost as popular among Jao here as among humans. And why not? Has he not rescued them from what seemed an eternity of endless confrontation with humans?"

For a moment, Yaut looked uncomfortable. "Besides . . . There are many veterans on Terra who like it here, if the conflicts would cease. It is a stimulating world, whatever else. And—being honest—it is not always easy, for those who are of low-status in low-status kochan. With a new taif, their lives will be more open, their possibilities for association greatly expanded."

Wrot's snout wrinkled. "That—coming from a Pluthrak fraghta! I could tell you tales . . . But, it is not needed."

He drew himself up into a flamboyantly self-righteous posture: "I will not be the first to dredge up ancient grievances! Not Wrot! Once Wrot krinnu Hemm vau Wathnak—and now, Wrot krinnu Aille vau Terra."

He was looking smug again. "We already chose the name. Me and Yaut and Hami—even consulted with the dilly-dallying Binnat—as the new elders. Took no time at all. Jao do not squabble like humans. The name was obvious, once we settled with the Preceptor that it would be unseemly to name the Bond as the root clan."

Krinnu Aille . . .

Living in a legend, indeed. Caitlin knew that the names of Jao clans derived from that of their most illustrious founding member. Sometimes male, sometimes female—but, always, not one of the elders but one of the founding *parents*.

She realized, suddenly, why Aille's posture—normally so controlled and elegant—was wavering all over the place. And could not stop herself from bursting into laughter.

Whatever else he was, however impressive in so many ways, Aille shared one characteristic in common with Caitlin herself. He was a virgin, too—and, unlike her, knew almost nothing about sex, even intellectually.

Just to make things worse, clearly enough the new taif elders were not about to waste any time. *A bride—okay, groom, what's the difference when you're that naïve?—on the eve of his wedding!*

Wrot confirmed her guess. Smugly.

"We will begin pouring the new kochan-house tomorrow. On the Oregon coast. With a big mating pool, of course. This will be a vigorous taif, ha! We will gain kochan status in no time!"

He and Yaut both bestowed looks of firm resolve upon Aille.

"And this one will make himself of use," Yaut stated.

EPILOGUE

The Lovers

"Are you okay?" Kralik asked, leaning over Caitlin and stroking her hair.

She burst into laughter. "Is that a trick question? For Chrissake, Ed, *of course* I'm okay. Women have been doing this for millions of years, y'know. Getting rid of virginity is our most ancient and hallowed custom. Besides, it's been two weeks since Oppuk thumped on me. Those bruises are all gone, and you sure didn't inflict any new ones. Casanova couldn't have been slicker."

He smiled and glanced at her arm. The cast covering it was the only thing she was wearing. The feel of her nude body pressed against his was still exciting, even now, after their passion was spent.

"I was just a little worried . . ."

She nuzzled him, pressing lips against his throat. "If you keep this up, I'll have you committed to a rest home. I swear, if I discover I'm marrying a fretful codger . . ."

He met her lips with his own, and they spent some time in a long, lingering kiss. When it was over, Kralik's smile was the relaxed and assured one she treasured the most.

"Fine, fine, forget I asked. Speaking of which, how's it coming?"

Caitlin frowned. "Well, most of the preparations for the wedding are set." She snorted. "And don't bother telling me—again—that your side of it is all ready to go. Smug frickin' generals with their ready-made staffs, and what's there to do anyway except get a ring and a tux and a best man? Rafe did agree, I assume?"

Kralik nodded. Caitlin's frown deepened. "I'm the one with all the grief. The worst of it's Tamt. I think I'm going to have to ask the whole damn Jao taif to help me hold her down while we get her fitted for a maid-of-honor's dress. She is *not* going to wear that damn warrior's harness!"

"Good luck," grunted Kralik. "I predict they'll refuse."

"That's what I'm afraid of," Caitlin said gloomily. But not too gloomily. Kralik's hands were starting to wander again.

"You decrepit old lecher," she said happily.

The Rebels

Awkwardly, Willard Belk advanced into the human-designed room connected to Aille's command center at Pascagoula which his human service and aides used as a lounge. Tully, Rob Wiley and Rafe Aguilera were sitting around a coffee table littered with newspapers. A fair number of the newspapers had coffee-stain rings decorating their already-garish multi-colored pages.

Tully cocked an eyebrow at him. Willard shuffled his feet a bit.

"I just came to say I'm sorry I helped them put that locator on you, Tully. While back."

"Don't worry about it, Will. Ancient history. The name's Gabe, by the way."

Belk nodded and glanced at the table. "I see you already saw them. D'you think—I mean . . ."

Aguilera chuckled. "Do we think the Jao will go on a rampage? No, Will, we don't." He gave Wiley and Tully a sly look. "Even these Lost Cause fanatics aren't worried about it. The Jao on the base are buying even more of these rags than the humans are—and getting those of them who can read English to translate, while they all sit around and gossip about it."

Wiley pointed a stubby finger at one of the tabloids. *The Terra Tattler,* that one. "Mind you, Yaut did have a fit when he saw the headlines. But I think he was mainly just pissed because they seem to have got it right."

"From what we can tell anyway," added Tully, grinning. "Nobody will know for sure, except the taif elders, until Aille finally emerges from the kochan-house with whoever-it-is."

The former rebels and collaborators, now allies, studied the headlines.

"Me, I hope they are right," pronounced Aguilera. "She is one fine lady."

Aille's Mystery Bride Revealed!
Exclusive to the Tattler!
Photos and Story Inside!

The Mates

Aille advanced toward the entrance to the mating pool, forcing his posture to remain steady despite the new and unsettling emotions rippling through him. Until this moment, he had steadfastly refused to speculate. But now, it was impossible not to begin thinking about his hopes.

Sternly, he told himself to set those hopes aside. His first-mate would be whomever the elders selected, for those reasons which seemed valid to them. Aille's personal preferences were irrelevant. Such was the Jao way with marriage, and Aille did not disagree. Whatever else about humans he had come to admire, he still found their notions of "romance" sheer superstition. Marriage was far too important a matter to be left to the vagaries of emotion.

Still . . .

He would have other wives, selected over time by the taif's elders, as his first-mate would have other husbands. But always, by custom, the first-mates would remain the center of the marriage-group. Whichever female waited for him in the pool, she would be, for the rest of his life, the most central person in his existence.

And he *did* have hopes, as foolish as that might be.

So, when he entered the pool chamber and saw that splendid *vai camiti*—he saw nothing else, for a moment—relief swept through him so strongly that he was not able, completely, to keep it from his posture.

"I hoped," she said throatily, deep-voiced, reading the posture instantly. "I hoped you would want it to be me."

The rest of her came into focus, as much as he could see. Nath was in the pool already, standing waist deep, her lustrous russet nap already sleek with water.

"I did," he said. "Though I should not have."

Nath's laughter was as throaty as her voice. "I cannot say I regret that I was never creched in Pluthrak, or any great kochan. As aggravating as it often was, being of minor clan status, at least I was spared that silly high-clan frippery."

She spread her arms, running her fingers sensuously through the water, stirring up the salt-scents a trace more. The same scents which were already causing Aille to feel warm and full of life and—
—and—

"It is called *desire*," Nath said, her little laugh seeming a bit choked. "I am so full of it I could burst. Come to me, husband."

The Prince

Nervously, Jonathan Kinsey was ushered into the new command center the Bond of Ebezon had poured for itself on Terra. On the Oregon coast also, as it happened, not very far from where the new Jao taif's kochan-house was nearing completion.

Kinsey was still a bit amazed at how rapidly the Jao could erect very large edifices. Yaut had given him a tour of the new kochan-house only yesterday—those portions of it which were not restricted exclusively to the use of the taif's members, at least. They had only begun pouring it two weeks earlier, but the edifice was almost finished even though it was even larger than Oppuk's palace had been.

Though much more tastefully designed, even to Kinsey's eyes. Unlike Oppuk, the taif had kept the design almost entirely Jao throughout, instead of the former Governor's mishmash. Of the two concessions to human design the elders had made, one had been more-or-less wrung out of them by the adamant demands of too many veterans. That was the addition, off to one side, of a Jao version of an auditorium, where those veterans who had developed the taste could enjoy the performances of human musicians. That was the only part of the kochan-house which was still not quite ready.

The other concession had been made willingly. That was the addition of human insignia and art work to the traditional Jao wall decorations. Indeed, one human insignia occupied honored space in the central public room of the kochan-house:

The Star of Terra, awarded by the United Nations, posthumously, to Llo krinnu Gava vau Narvo. Every member of Gava kochan resident on Terra had chosen to join the new taif, and they had insisted that Llo's medal would go with them.

Narvo had not argued the point. Indeed, Kinsey thought they had been relieved to get the bizarre and unwanted human "honor" off their hands. In general, Narvo was arguing nothing, these days. If anything, they seemed to take an almost malicious glee in out-doing Pluthrak when it came to offering resources to help in the Earth's reconstruction.

The Bond had begun pouring its own headquarters less than a week ago, after most of the Harrier fleet departed, leaving the Preceptor and his chosen pleniary-superior behind. She was named Tura, Kinsey knew. He still did not know the name of the Preceptor. Even in those few days, the structure was already complete. True, it was not as large as the kochan-house. The Bond favored austerity in all things, including their own quarters. But it was still impressive.

Kinsey did not know why he had been summoned. But, as soon as he was ushered into the Preceptor's private quarters, at least one minor mystery was resolved.

"I am called Ronz," were the Preceptor's first words, spoken in English, as soon as the aide who had led Kinsey there passed back through the doorfield. He gestured toward a nearby divan, designed in the low Jao manner. "Please, Doctor Kinsey, have a seat. I apologize that I have not yet been able to acquire human furniture. But I think you will find that reasonably comfortable."

Kinsey could not have cared less about physical comfort. Despite his nervousness, he was too fascinated by the Jao's demeanor. First, the easy grace with which the Preceptor moved. Here, in private, there was not a trace of that un-Jao-like neutrality of posture which Bond members exhibited in public. Instead, the Preceptor was exuding a certain kind of restrained graciousness. A polite host, welcoming his guest.

Even more fascinating, was his command of English. Grammatically correct, fluent—even the usual heavy Jao accent was barely noticeable.

That seemed as safe a place to start as any. As soon as he sat down, Kinsey said: "Your English is excellent, sir—uh, if you'll forgive me saying so."

"Why should I forgive a compliment?" The Preceptor lowered himself to a seat nearby. "It *should* be excellent. I have spent twenty of your years mastering the language. Along with several others."

Kinsey stared at him. *Twenty years?* When most Jao, even resident on Earth, barely managed to learn a passable pidgin?

The Preceptor's whiskers twitched. "Why are you so surprised, Doctor Kinsey? By the way, is that the correct title?"

"Uh—yes, sir. Well . . . To be honest, although it's become the custom, I personally think it's a bit silly. To me, at least, sir, a 'doctor' is a medical specialist. A purely academic scholar like myself should more properly be called just 'professor.'" His nervousness led him to attempt a witticism. "There's an old joke, sir, about someone at an academic conference having a heart attack and his wife calling for a doctor. And then the paramedics having to fight their way through the mob to do the poor fellow any good."

The moment he finished, he felt like an idiot. What would a Jao new to Earth understand about that joke?

But, fortunately, the Preceptor didn't seem annoyed. "Very well, then. 'Professor', it shall be." Again, his whiskers waggled. "And you needn't feel it necessary, by the way, to keep peppering your speech with 'sir' every other sentence. I assure you I am not easily insulted. Certainly not by acts of omission."

Peppering your speech. For Christ's sake, he even knows colloquial expressions.

Kinsey drew a deep breath and decided—caution be damned—to take the plunge.

"Well, I think one rumor is confirmed. You *did* plan for this, didn't you?"

Not to his surprise, the Preceptor even managed a fair approximation of a human shrug. "Yes and no, Professor Kinsey. Yes, in the sense that, twenty years ago, once we studied the reports of the Terran conquest, the Bond realized that we had both a crisis and an opportunity on our hands. That was obvious, even reading the very—ah, what's the correct English term? Yes—the very *slanted* reports. If I'm not mistaken, I think you would also call it the 'Narvo spin.'"

The Jao leaned back in his chair, spreading his hands on the very humanlike armrests. "No, however, not in the sense that we foresaw exactly what would happen. Nor, even, exactly how to proceed to a proper solution. We certainly never foresaw the final developments, which were shaped and driven entirely by Aille and his service. What was obvious to us, from the beginning, was simply the problem itself—and, more important still, the great opportunity."

"Which was? The 'great opportunity,' I mean."

The Preceptor gazed at Kinsey solemnly and calmly, for a few seconds, before replying with a question.

"Tell me, Professor Kinsey—as a student of human history—what do we Jao remind you of? From your own past, I mean."

Kinsey hesitated. Ronz lifted a hand. "Please, Professor, speak freely. I am not trying to trap you into anything."

"Well . . . The Romans, more than anything, I think. Sometimes, the Mongols. Other times—some of your customs here, not so much your way of ruling—the Japanese of the Shogunate Era."

"Good analogies, I agree, within the limits of any analogy. I think there is something to be learned, as well, from the experience of the British Raj." His ears lifted. "I am certain there must have been times, during the recent crisis, when you could not help but think of the Sepoy Mutiny. And its very unfortunate immediate aftermath."

Kinsey almost choked. "Uh—well, yes. In fact, I remember telling President Stockwell how essential it was to avoid any Black Hole of Calcutta."

"Essential indeed, Professor. The Narvo would have responded far more savagely than the British. Though, to be sure, they would not have thought of such grotesque twists as blowing humans out of cannons. Or wrapping their corpses in the skin of—what is that beast? Swine, I believe?"

Mutely, Kinsey nodded.

"You do, I trust, agree with me that there are at least some aspects in which Jao share few of your human vices. Whatever vices we may have of our own."

"More than a few, being honest. There's no equivalent in your history, so far as I can determine, of such things as the Nazis or the Khmer Rouge or the Taliban. Jao just don't seem to descend to the level of sheer mania of which humans are capable. Well, except for Oppuk."

"Yes, Oppuk. A great pity. He was once a very impressive *namth camiti*, as difficult as you may find that to believe. That was our most unpleasant decision, we of the Bond, and one taken only with great reluctance."

Kinsey grew still. Still as a mouse. Absentminded professor or not, he was a student of human history. Just so, he was quite sure, did a man feel when Caesare Borgia was about to draw him into confidence.

"Oh, shit," he couldn't help but murmur.

Under his breath, he thought, forgetting the preternatural Jao sense of hearing.

"Not a bad expression. 'Shit,' indeed. But great dangers—just as great opportunities—sometimes require hard decisions to be made. Decisions which, as you say, are malodorous in the extreme."

The Preceptor leaned back still further, as though to distance himself as much as possible from a bad smell. "It was my decision, in the end, and I made it. Reluctantly, but I could see no other way to bring the Terran situation to a speedy enough conclusion. So, yes, I ordered Oppuk driven mad."

It seemed fitting, somehow, that he followed that with another human shrug. "It was not difficult, given Oppuk's natural temperament and his increasing frustration—and his increasingly obsessive use of pools. A matter, merely, of properly tampering with the salts. Easy enough, especially as Oppuk's unsanity grew, since he paid little attention to the doings of his servitors."

"Rough on the servitors, I would think," Kinsey commented, "given Oppuk's temper."

"Rough, indeed. Three of our agents were badly beaten by him. And the last, slain."

"Ullwa," Kinsey whispered. "That's how Wrot knew to challenge Oppuk over her whereabouts. *You* told him."

"Did more than tell him. We showed him. As I will now show you. By the end, we had surveillance devices on him everywhere, his ship as well as his palace. Nothing he did was a secret from us."

The Preceptor picked up a small device lying on a table next to him. Kinsey had noticed it, when he sat down, but thought nothing of the matter. A Jao control device of some sort, which they always had lying about.

A holographic image appeared to one side. "Watch, Professor Kinsey," the Preceptor commanded. "I will want your opinion afterward."

Ullwa's murder was brutal and horrible to watch; but, thankfully, over soon enough. And by the time it was, many things had fallen into place for Kinsey.

Oppuk had almost seemed to be raping Ullwa, as impossible as that crime was for a Jao, not just killing her. And Kinsey remembered, now, what Caitlin had told him after Oppuk was finally dead. Of the one frightening instance where he had made her posture before him, almost like a human despot might force a slave girl to dance. And the other time, even more disturbing, when he had summoned her and subjected her to bizarre questioning—which even Banle, afterward, had clearly been shaken by.

"That's the secret to your breeding, isn't it? The right chemical combination in your pools. You drove Oppuk mad by constantly stimulating him sexually—when he had no outlet for the stimulation. Probably didn't even realize what it was in the first place."

"Did not realize it at all. One of the characteristics—a particularly stupid one—of the great kochan is that they insist on surrounding all matters involving sex with great mystery. Never explaining anything to their offspring, until and unless one of them is summoned to become a pool-parent." Ronz lowered the control device back to the table. "The lesser, more provincial kochan, are not so obsessive about the matter. But Oppuk . . . I come myself, Professor, from one of the great kochan. I can assure you that Oppuk never had the slightest idea why his moods had become so turbulent and unstable."

He gave Kinsey a level stare, disconcerting in its complete neutrality. "You are doing very well, Professor. Matching my hopes. Tell me what else strikes you about this matter."

"Well . . . it seems like—if you'll forgive me for saying so—a positively grotesque way for an intelligent species to have to breed. Having to dope yourselves, I mean, in effect. Uh, 'to dope' means—"

"I know what it means, Professor. It is quite an accurate characterization. And does it strike you as plausible that such a characteristic would *evolve* in an intelligent species? Or any animal species, for that matter."

Kinsey thought about it, for a moment.

"No, not to that extent. Certainly not in an animal with a highly developed nervous system. It's true that all animal species, so far as I know, require a chemical component for their sexual activity.

But not anything that intricate and artificial. It's counter-evolutionary, actually."

He took a deep breath. "The Ekhat designed you that way, didn't they? Manipulated your genetic structure."

"Yes. And embedded it so deeply in the Jao genome that it has— so far, at least—proven impossible for the Bond's genetic technicians to find any way to circumvent. Oh, yes, Doctor Kinsey—we have certainly tried. For well over three of your centuries, now, once we finally realized the truth."

The Preceptor's whiskers and ears moved, in what Kinsey thought was a subtle, Harrier-like way of indicating *amused-chagrin.* "The Bond must not *procreate,* Professor, lest we lose our use and purpose by developing what would amount to kochan ties and attitudes. Which we most surely would, if we began producing crechelings of our own instead of relying upon the kochan to provide us with recruits. But we have no superstitious prohibition against engaging in sexual activity for its own pleasure. As did—I am sure this analogy has come to you also, by now—the militant monastic orders of your own history."

He emitted a little sigh, and, for the first time, Kinsey realized how old the Preceptor was. Still very fit-looking, but genuinely aged. "In truth, Professor, given the often severe emotional strains upon Bond members, it would be a blessing for us if we could. But, sadly, we can't—because there is no way, so far as we have been able to discover thus far, for a Jao to do what humans do routinely: separate copulation from procreation."

Kinsey didn't know what to say. To extend his commiseration would be . . . presumptuous at the very least.

"But all this is preface, Professor. Tell me, now, what is the point of everything I have unveiled to you. And why I summoned you here, and took you into such close confidence."

Without even thinking about the propriety or lack thereof, Kinsey rose to his feet and began pacing slowly. As he always did, whether at home on in a lecture hall, when trying to bring some problem into clear focus.

It didn't take him long. Perhaps a minute.

"It's obvious, isn't it? What *else* did the Ekhat breed into you? What other limitations—far less obvious ones—did they make sure you would always possess?"

The Preceptor lowered his head. "Indeed. That is the true concern of the Bond of Ebezon, and always our greatest fear." He waved his hand, casually. "Our other work is also important, to be sure. But this may, when the flow arrives, prove to be our downfall. To point to something obvious: Why are Jao generally so unimaginative? There is nothing mystical about '*ollnat*,' after all. It is not as if humans possess magic powers. There seems no obvious reason—especially given our much greater experience—that *we* should not have developed the idea of using simple kinetic weapons to stop an Ekhat extermination before it even started."

"It could just be a cultural trait," Kinsey pointed out. "Societies structured along clan lines are usually very conservative. That's been the human pattern, at least."

"To be sure. But perhaps it is genetic—and how do we tell which it is? Given that we are in the midst of a great war for our very survival and do not have the luxury of leisurely research. The time will come, be sure of this—our strength grows against Ekhat—when even the Ekhat, in their unsanity, will realize they must unite against us. What then, Professor? What hidden Achilles' Heel will they strike at? Which they know about, because they implanted it in us, and we do not?"

He leaned forward, his posture intent. "And—put yourself in my position, for a moment—what would be the best possible preventive countermeasure?"

That, too, was now obvious. "Find another species. One that you *know* is completely out of Ekhat control. But also—this must be much rarer in the galaxy than simple intelligence—one which is culturally and technologically on more or less your own level. A constant challenge to you—a partner, if you will, instead of another subject. Even a quarrelsome partner—one which you cannot, in the end, control either."

"Yes. That was the great opportunity which Terra presented us. Finally—after centuries of conquering nothing but primitives. Who, because of their own low level of cultural development, simply became Jao clones. Augmenting our strength, perhaps, but doing nothing to offset our possible weaknesses."

"But you couldn't take advantage of the opportunity, could you? Not with your kochan setup. There was no way, from the beginning, for the Bond to take control of Terra."

"No way at all. The kochan would have united against us, for encroaching on their customary privileges. So, for twenty years, we maneuvered to gain what we have now accomplished. Using, in the end, not-so-subtle-as-they-think Pluthrak for the killing blade. Ruthless, indeed, even cruel. For we also destroyed the life—worse yet, the honorable memory—of a Jao who once deserved the name of *namth camiti*."

Kinsey rubbed his face. "No way to rehabilitate Oppuk's name now, of course." Sighing heavily, he looked at the door.

"'Dead men tell no tales,' as we humans say. Will *I* walk out of here alive?"

"That is up to you, Professor Kinsey. Think of me, if you will—of the Bond, rather—as a Roman emperor who needs Greek philosophers he can trust. Or a Mongol khan, if you prefer, who needs loyal Chinese mandarins. Human philosophers and mandarins of all kinds, to slowly transform his Jao empire into one which cannot simply conquer, but *rule*. For how long? Who can say? So long as our rule is needed, to exterminate the Ekhat. After that . . ."

Again, that almost-human shrug. "Let what happens, happen. The Jao will survive as a species, surely. And if the Jao empire of that distant future is as much human as it is Jao, as the Roman Empire became as much Greek as it remained Latin, I find myself not caring in the least."

Still, Kinsey hesitated. Not from general considerations, but from a very specific one.

The Preceptor's next words eliminated his anxiety on that score, however:

"I would not expect from you, nor require of you, anything that might conflict with your service to Aille. I can assure you, Professor, that the Bond thinks most highly of that youngster and will certainly not be working against him. Quite the opposite."

So much for that. Kinsey was relieved; and, with the relief, came the beginning of interest—no, fascination, even enthusiasm. It was a grand vista, after all, the thought of helping to shape a new and hybrid stellar empire that would, over time, blend the best of Jao and human cultures.

Even if, to be sure, Kinsey's new boss would be a rather scary individual.

On the other hand, Kinsey told himself firmly, *there are worse things in the universe—lots worse—than loyally serving a Machiavellian prince. Especially a very capable one.*

What the hell. It was even true.

"Done," he said. Then, a bit startled by his boldness, began to stammer. "Uh . . . you understand, Preceptor, I'm an elderly man—and none too vigorous even in my youth! I—ah—"

The Preceptor barked a laugh. "Please, Doctor Kinsey! Rest assured that if I require—ah, I think the crude human phrase is 'wet work'—I have many vigorous young Jao to draw upon. And soon enough, I am sure, equal numbers of vigorous humans. No, what I will require from you is simply sage advice. A mandarin's work."

He rose from his seat. "I have found that the elderly are often my best agents. If for no other reason than their creaking bones, they have to *think*."

He stooped and picked up the control device again, fingering it for a moment. "In fact, it is now time to introduce you to one who will be your closest colleague. My most long-standing agent on Terra—from the beginning, in fact, twenty years ago—and always my very best."

The doorfield shimmered and the figure of a Jao began to appear in it.

"Even if," the Preceptor added, his voice sounding a bit sour, "he rarely acts his age."

Wrot came sauntering through the doorfield, carrying a glass in his hand.

"Splendid, my dear professor! I'm so delighted to see we'll be working together again—even more closely than before!"

He extended the glass. "Here. I brought you one of your human alcoholic concoctions. Nasty stuff, but I knew you'd want it. Need it desperately, in fact. Preceptor Ronz can be unsettling. It's what you call a 'martini.'"

Kinsey took the glass, shuddering. Not at the contents—he was partial to martinis—but at the words he knew were surely coming.

"Shaken, of course," said Wrot, his whiskers waggling gleefully, "not stirred."

GLOSSARY OF JAO TERMS

Ata: suffix indicating a group formed for instructional purposes.

Az: Jao measurement, slightly longer than a yard.

Azet: Jao measurement, about three fourths of a mile.

Bau: A short carved baton, usually but not always made of wood, issued by a kochan to those of its members it considers fit for high command. The bau serves as an emblem of military achievement, with carvings added to match the bau-holder accomplishments.

Bauta: An individual who has retired from service honorably and has chosen to relinquish his automatic kochan ties.

Bodyspeech: Postures, used to communicate emotions.

Dehabia: Traditional soft thick blankets used for lounging.

Early-light: The period between dawn and early morning

Formal movement: Codified postures, taught to young Jao.

Fraghta: An older and experienced batman/valet/advisor/bodyguard assigned to young Jao of high kochan status.

Framepoint: A stargate, the means for interstellar transit.

Hai tau: Life-in-motion.

Heartward: Right.

Jinau: Sepoy troops recruited from conquered species.

Kochan: Jao clan. The term is used also to refer to "root clans" or "great kochan."

Kochanata: Instructional group taught in the kochan.

Kochanau: The leader of the clan, at any given time, chosen by the elders. The office is neither hereditary nor permanent, although some kochanau retain it for long periods of time.

Kroudh: Outlawed, officially severed from one's clan.

Last-sun: Yesterday.

Late-dark: Midnight or after.

Late-light: Afternoon.

Lurret: A large herbivore found on Hadiru, a Dano world. Specifically, an old rogue male, notorious for its belligerence and unstable temperament.

Mirrat: Small finned swimmers on Jithra's homeworld.

Natal compound: Where one was born.

Namth camiti: To be of highest ranking in an emergent generation, sometimes referred as "of the clearest water." Loosely equivalent, in human terms, to graduating first in the class from a military academy.

Next-sun: Tomorrow.

Ollnat: Conceiving of things-that-never-were, or what-might-be, lies, imagination, creativity, etc. It is a quality mostly lacking in Jao, except in a frivolous manner.

Oudh: In charge, having official authority in a situation.

Sant jin: A formal question requiring a formal answer.

Smoothface: An insult, implying no incised bars of rank or experience. Roughly equivalent to such humans expressions as "wet behind the ears" or "green-horn."

Tak: Woody substance burned for its aromatic scent.

Taif: A kochan-in-formation, affiliated to and under the protection and guidance of a kochan.

Timeblind: Having no innate sense of time as the Jao do.

Timesense: Innate ability to judge the passage of time and sense when something will happen.

Vai camiti: The characteristic facial pattern by which one may often recognize a Jao's kochan; faint vai camiti are considered undesirable, a mark of homeliness.

Vaim: Traditional Jao greeting between two who are approximately equal in status. Can also be used as a compliment by a higher status Jao to a lower. The literal translation is "We see each other."

Vaish: Traditional Jao greeting of inferior to superior. The literal translation is "I see you."

Vaist: Traditional Jao greeting of superior to inferior. The literal translation is "You see me."

Vithrik: Duty, what one owes to others, the necessity of making one's self of use.

What-is: Reality.

What-might-be: Something imagined.

Windward: Left.

Wrem-fa: A technique of instruction through body-learning in which nothing is explained, laid down in the brain too deep for conscious understanding. Also, in a broader sense, used to refer to life experience.

APPENDIX A:
THE EKHAT

The Ekhat are an ancient species which began spreading though the galaxy millions of years ago, an expansion which reached its peak before the onset of what human geologists call the Pleistocene Age on Earth. That final period of expansion is called by the Ekhat themselves, depending on which of the factions is speaking, either the *Melodious Epoch*, the *Discordance*, or by a phrase which is difficult to translate but might loosely be called the *Absent Orchestration of Right Harmony*.

Three of the four major Ekhat factions, whatever their other differences—the Melody and both factions of the Harmony—agree that this period was what humans would call a "golden age," although the Harmony is sharply critical of some of its features. A fourth faction, the Interdict, considers it to have been an unmitigated disaster. The golden age ended in a disaster usually known as the Collapse. (See below for details.)

The era which preceded this golden age is unclear. Even the location of their original home planet is no longer known to the Ekhat. They spread slowly throughout the galactic arm by use of sub-light-speed vessels, and in the course of that expansion began to differentiate into a number of subspecies, some of which became distinct species, unable to crossbreed with other Ekhat lines.

The Ekhat today are a genus, not a species, and some human scholars even think it would be more accurate to characterize them as a family. They are widespread throughout the galactic arm, but are not very numerous on any particular planet. That is partly because they are a slow-breeding species, and partly because they are still recovering from the devastations of the Collapse.

The golden age began when Ekhat scientists discovered the principles behind

500

the Frame Network, a method used to circumvent the lightspeed barrier. By then, they were already widely dispersed and the Frame Network enabled them to reunite their disparate branches into a single entity. Whether that entity was purely cultural and economic, or involved political unification is a matter of sharp debate. This is, in fact, one of the main issues in dispute among the factions of the Ekhat in the modern era.

It is unclear how long this golden age lasted. The lack of clarity is primarily with the beginnings of the era. There is much greater agreement about its end: approximately two million years ago, the entire Frame Network disintegrated in what is usually known as the Collapse (although the Interdict faction calls it the Rectification or the Purging).

The collapse of the Network was quite clearly accompanied by (and probably caused by) a massive civil war which erupted among the Ekhat and quickly engulfed their entire region of galactic space. By the end, Ekhat civilization was in ruins and most Ekhat had perished. There was an enormous amount of collateral damage, including the extinction of many other intelligent species.

Slowly and painfully, in the time which followed, three different Ekhat centers were able to rebuild themselves and begin to reconstruct the Network. Two of them did so for the purpose of restoring the Ekhat to their former position (although one of them proposes doing so along radically different lines) and another wishes to prevent it.

The factions can be roughly depicted in the following manner:

THE MELODY

The Melody can be considered the "orthodox" faction. It believes the "golden age" was truly golden, an era during which the different strains of the Ekhat were working together toward the ultimate goal of merging and becoming a species which would be "divine" in its nature.

The Ekhat notion of "divinity" is difficult for humans to grasp, and can sometimes be more clearly expressed in quasi-musical rather than religious terminology. Each branch of the Ekhat contributes to the slowly emerging "supreme work of art" which is the "destiny" of the Ekhat. No faction of the Ekhat seems to have anything close to the human notion of "God." The closest parallel in human philosophy is probably Hegel's notion of God-in-self-creation, except that the Ekhat see themselves, not some outside deity, as what Hegel would call the Subject.

The Melody advocates a pluralistic approach to Ekhat advancement. They are insistent that no single branch of the Ekhat is superior to any other, and that the "emergence of divinity" (or "unfolding of the perfect melody") will require the input of all Ekhat. In this sense, they are supremely tolerant of all the distinctions and differences within the genus.

But, while they tolerate differences, they do not tolerate exclusion or isolation. Since, according to them, the talents of all Ekhat will be needed for "divine emergence," no Ekhat can withhold themselves from the developing "Melody." In this, they are a bit like the old Roman or Mongol emperors: you can believe whatever you want, but you must submit to Melody rule and you must subscribe (formally, at least) to the Melodic creed. In short, they are uncompromising "imperialists."

On the other hand, the Melody is utterly hostile—genocidal, in fact—toward any intelligent species which cannot trace its lineage back to the Ekhat. All non-Ekhat species are an obstacle to the Ekhat's "divine emergence," considered by them to be static or noise impeding the "perfect melody." The Melody envisions a universe in which the transformed Ekhat are all that remains.

Scholars suspect the Melody's eventual goal is to exterminate all non-Ekhat life of any kind. The Melody believes the Ekhat were well on their way toward "divine emergence" when the sudden and unexpected treason of a faction which they call (translating roughly) the *Cowardly Retreat* or the *Deaf Lesion* launched a vicious campaign of sabotage which brought down the Network and collapsed Ekhat civilization across the galactic arm.

Human scholars believe that the *Cowardly Retreat* is essentially identical with the faction known in the modern era as the Interdict. What can be determined of current Melodic policy seems to substantiate that belief—the Melody is utterly hostile to the Interdict and will slaughter them on sight.

THE HARMONY

The Harmony arose after the collapse of the Network and can be considered the "revisionist" wing of the Ekhat. They believe the civil war which produced the great collapse was due to the anarchic and disorderly nature of Ekhat civilization which led up to it, an era they do not consider to be a "golden age" so much as a "bronze age." (Keep in mind that these are very rough human approximations of mental concepts which, in the case of the Ekhat, are difficult for other intelligent species to analyze.)

In the view of the Harmony, all Ekhat are not equal. Basing themselves on what they believe is a true genetic picture of Ekhat evolution, the Harmony ranks different branches of the Ekhat genus (or family) on different levels. All Ekhat have a place in the new "Harmony," but, to use a human analogy, some get to be first violinists and others belong in the back beating on kettle drums.

The Harmony ranks different Ekhat branches according to how closely they fit

the original Ekhat stock. The closer, the better; the farther apart, the more inferior. Not surprisingly, they consider the Ekhat branch which inhabited the planet
where the Harmony first began spreading as the "true Ekhat." In fact, they seem
to believe that theirs is the home planet of the Ekhat (which no one else does and
the claim is apparently very threadbare).

The Harmony advocates a genetically determined hierarchy, in which all Ekhat
will have a place, but in which (for most of them) that place will be subordinate.

To complicate things further, the Harmony is split by an internal division of its
own. The *True Harmony* believes the rankings of the Ekhat species are permanent and fixed. The *Complete Harmony* believes all Ekhat, no matter how lowly
their genetic status at the moment, can eventually be uplifted into "complete Ekhat-
dom."

This division, whose ideology is murky from the outside, does have a major
impact on the external policies of the different wings of the Harmony. The True
Harmony shares the basic attitude of the Melody toward non-Ekhat intelligent
species: they are destined for extermination. The Complete Harmony, on the other
hand, believes that non-Ekhat species have a place in the universe. The process of
uplifting all Ekhat will require replacing the "sub-Ekhat" strains with other intelligent species to, in essence, do the scut work. The flip side of "improving" all
Ekhat is to subjugate and enslave all non-Ekhat.

It was this wing of the Harmony which uplifted the Jao into full sentience.

THE INTERDICT

Of all the Ekhat factions, the Interdict is probably the hardest to understand.
The closest equivalent in human terms would be something like "fundamentalist,
Luddite reactionary fanatics."

The core belief of the Interdict is that the Network was always an abomination.
Some human scholars think that the origins of the creed were scientific—i.e.,
that some Ekhat scientists became convinced the Network was placing a strain on
the fabric of spacetime which threatened the universe itself (or at least the portion of the galaxy where it had spread).

Whatever their scientific origins might have been, the Interdict, as it developed
during the long years after the Collapse, became something far more in the nature
of a mystical cult. From what can be gleaned from their extremely murky writings,
the Interdict seems to believe the speed-of-light barrier is "divine" in nature and
any attempt to circumvent it is "unholy."

It seems most likely that the Melody's charge against the Interdict is correct: it
was they, or at least their ideological predecessors, who launched the civil war

which destroyed the Network. In fact, that seems to have been the purpose of the war in the first place.

What is definitely established in the historical record is that it was the Interdict which freed the Jao. Not, of course, because of any concern over the Jao themselves, but simply to strike a blow at the Complete Harmony. It was they, as well, who provided the Jao with the initial technology to obtain control of a portion of the Network and begin to create their own stellar empire.

The fact that they did so—and still, in an off-and-on and unpredictable way, maintain a certain quasi-"alliance" with the Jao—underscores the bizarre nature of the Interdict creed. The Jao, after all, are also maintaining and even extending the Network. Yet the Interdict seems not to object.

One theory is that whatever scientific underpinnings originally lay beneath Interdict ideology have long since been lost. What has come to replace the notion that the Network itself threatens the universe is a more mystical notion that the Network is "unclean." The danger is spiritual, in other words, not physical.

One contradiction this situation presents is that in order to destroy the Network, the Interdict must use it themselves. Indeed, in many areas of the galaxy, it is they who are rebuilding the old framepoints and extending new ones. Apparently, Interdict adherents go through some sort of purification rite which allows them to do so. As always, the precise tenets of the Ekhat creed are at least murky if not quite unfathomable to non-Ekhat.

APPENDIX B:
INTERSTELLAR TRAVEL

The method of supra-light travel used by all intelligent species is usually called, by the Jao, the "Frame Network." The method involves warping spacetime using extremely powerful generators positioned in at least three widely spaced locations in the stellar neighborhood. (Three will work, but is risky; four is better; five is ideal; more than five is redundant.) These "framepoints" must be at least three light years apart, but are not effective if the distance between any two extends much more than eleven light years.

Existing frame points allow ships to cross the stellar distances between them in what is effectively an instantaneous transition. There is theoretical debate over whether the transition is "really" instantaneous. But from the subjective standpoint of any human or other intelligent species, the travel is instantaneous. The dispute is whether or not it actually requires a few nanoseconds.

In essence, two framepoints working together are creating what can be called an artificial wormhole. New territory, where there does not exist a framepoint, can be reached in one of two ways. One way is to use sub-light exploratory ships. Once arrived at a suitable location for a new framepoint, the ship (or multiship expedition) can begin to create the new framepoint, which can then begin to participate in extending the entire Frame Network.

Of course, this method of extending the Frame is very slow. The other method is to use existing FP generators to create what is called a "Point Locus."

Triangulating (more often: quadri-angulating or quint-angulating) their power, these framepoint generators can create a temporary Point Locus at a distance. For a certain period of time, ships can travel to the Point Locus from any one of the FP generators which created it.

This is the normal method used for invasion fleets, since it is impossible to invade a framepoint held by an enemy. (They just "turn off" their end of the Network and the invaders vanish, no one knows exactly where.) Invaders from the outside can triangulate on an enemy solar system, create a point locus which is independent of the enemy's side of the Network, and send an invasion fleet that way.

The expense and risk involved is considerable, however. Point loci tend to be unstable over any extended period of time, so the window of opportunity for an invasion is limited. To use an historical analogy, each invasion is like a major amphibious assault during World War II. If a large enough beachhead is not secured quickly, the invasion will face disaster by being stranded and overrun. Moreover, because of the impossibility of matching loci in open space, the point locus must always be created within the photosphere of a star. In essence, the star itself serves the participating frame generators as a common target. But that obviously presents its own set of dangers.

How unstable and temporary a point locus proves to be, varies according to a wide range of factors. These include: the number of FP generators used, distance, and a multitude of more subtle factors involving a lot of specific features of the galactic neighborhood—dust cloud densities, nearby novas or neutron stars, etc. Creating a point locus is as much as art as a science, as well as being extremely expensive, and is never something to be undertaken lightly.